MORE PRAISE FOR ISAAC BASHEVIS SINGER
AND *SHADOWS ON THE HUDSON*

"One of Singer's most revealing novels. Under its rough surface, the author was playing with powerful material, dealing, albeit in lurid colors, with many of his key preoccupations and concerns . . . an ambivalence toward organized religion, a concern for the place of Jews in the modern era, the centrality of both sex and spirituality to the human condition." —*Los Angeles Times*

"Rarely does a posthumous publication add much to a writer's stature, but *Shadows on the Hudson* is Singer at his best. Lovers of Singer will feel that they have received a great and unexpected gift....In its size, scope, and its moral intensity, it ranks among his most important works." —*The New Republic*

"It is not an exaggeration to say that Singer shared many of Tolstoy's descriptive powers, along with Dostoyevsky's psychological insights." —*New York Post*

"A passionate, perfectly crafted work. Nowhere is Singer's anguished power, that chastening bleakness of his vision, stronger or more penetrating." —*New York Observer*

"This addictive melodrama reflects the thoughtfulness and dark humor of the late Nobel Prize winner's work....As with Dickens, Trollope or Dostoyevsky, contemporary readers will find themselves resisting Singer's eventful plot in order to parcel this book out as a series of treats it once was."
—*Publishers Weekly*

"*Shadows on the Hudson* has an unself-conscious energy and honesty that gives it, even after forty years, a shocking power....Singer is very good at evoking the palimpsest imprint of his characters' layered lives in a way that gives them...modernist complexity. He is also good at making their highly personal adventures seem the outgrowth of historical and metaphysical circumstances."
—Jonathan Rosen, *Slate*

"*Shadows on the Hudson* is the best of Singer's posthumous volumes."
—*Baltimore Sun*

"Marriages and affairs fall apart; age and death take their toll; the wisdom of the scripture and kabbalah and the precepts of the great philosophers and avatars of modern science are passionately debated in extended conversations that seethe with drama. This is a soap opera raised to the level of genius, in a consistently absorbing novel whose amazing breadth and verisimilitude suggest a contemporary Tolstoy. And Singer concludes it triumphantly, in a series of summaries of his several protagonists' fates."
—*Kirkus Reviews*

"A major addition to the Singer ouvre....The book's claim on the status of masterpiece stems from its largeness, the depth and complexity of its exorbitantly vivid, intelligent characters and from Singer's Dostoyevskian skill at weaving into a seamless tapestry various disorderly responses to the savagery of life. Despite many passages of caustic humor, this novel is Singer speaking in an unfamiliar raw and brutal voice, the grandfatherly Yiddish writer stripped of the kindly, gentle tone and the flights of supernatural fantasy that we mostly know him by."

—*New York Times*

Isaac Bashevis Singer began to write fiction while working for a Yiddish-language newspaper in Warsaw. In 1935 he emigrated to America and found work at the *Jewish Daily Forward* in New York, which serialized many of his novels in Yiddish before they appeared in English translation. The author of more than a dozen novels, short story collections, and children's books, Singer received the Nobel Prize in Literature in 1978. He died in 1991.

Books by Isaac Bashevis Singer

NOVELS

The Manor [I. The Manor II. The Estate]
The Family Moskat • The Magician of Lublin
Satan in Goray • The Slave • Enemies, A Love Story
Shosha • The Penitent • The King of the Fields
Scum • The Certificate • Meshugah
Shadows on the Hudson

STORIES

Gimpel the Fool • A Friend of Kafka • Short Friday
The Séance • The Spinoza of Market Street • Passions
A Crown of Feathers • Old Love • The Image
The Death of Methuselah

MEMOIRS

In My Father's Court • Love and Exile

FOR CHILDREN

A Day of Pleasure • The Fools of Chelm
Mazel and Shlimazel or The Milk of a Lioness
When Shlemiel Went to Warsaw
A Tale of Three Wishes • Elijah the Slave
Joseph and Koza or The Sacrifice to the Vistula
Alone in the Wild Forest • The Wicked City
Naftali the Storyteller and His Horse, Sus
Why Noah Chose the Dove • The Power of Light
The Golem • The Topsy-Turvy Emperor of China

COLLECTIONS

The Collected Stories • Stories for Children
An Isaac Bashevis Singer Reader

Isaac Bashevis Singer

Shadows on the Hudson

Translated by Joseph Sherman

A PLUME BOOK

PLUME
Published by the Penguin Group
Penguin Putnam Inc., 375 Hudson Street, New York, New York 10014, U.S.A.
Penguin Books Ltd, 27 Wrights Lane, London W8 5TZ, England
Penguin Books Australia Ltd, Ringwood, Victoria, Australia
Penguin Books Canada Ltd, 10 Alcorn Avenue, Toronto, Ontario, Canada M4V 3B2
Penguin Books (N.Z.) Ltd, 182–190 Wairau Road, Auckland 10, New Zealand

Penguin Books Ltd, Registered Offices: Harmondsworth, Middlesex, England

Published by Plume, an imprint of Dutton NAL, a member of Penguin Putnam Inc.
This is an authorized reprint of a hardcover edition published by Farrar, Straus and Giroux, Inc.
For information address Farrar, Straus and Giroux, Inc., 19 Union Square West, New York, New York 10003.

First Plume Printing, January, 1999
10 9 8 7 6 5

 REGISTERED TRADEMARK—MARCA REGISTRADA

The Library of Congress has catalogued the hardcover edition as follows:
Singer, Isaac Bashevis
    [Shotns baym Hodson, English]
    Shadows on the Hudson / Isaac Bashevis Singer : translated by
Joseph Sherman. — 1st ed.
        p.   cm.
    ISBN 0-374-26186-5 (cloth : alk, paper) (hc)
    ISBN 0-452-28003-6 (pbk)
    I. Jews—New York (State)—New York—Fiction. I. Sherman,
Joseph, II. Title.
PJ5129.S49S4713   1998   97–18677
839'.133—DC21

Original hardcover design by Jonathan D. Lippincott
Printed in the United States of America

PUBLISHER'S NOTE
This is a work of fiction. Names, characters, places, and incidents either are the product of the author's
imagination or are used fictitiously, and any resemblance to actual persons, living or dead, events, or
locales is entirely coincidental.

BOOKS ARE AVAILABLE AT QUANTITY DISCOUNTS WHEN USED TO PROMOTE PRODUCTS OR SERVICES. FOR
INFORMATION PLEASE WRITE TO PREMIUM MARKETING DIVISION, PENGUIN PUTNAM INC., 375 HUDSON STREET,
NEW YORK, NEW YORK 10014.

Publisher's Note

The events related in *Shadows on the Hudson* are set in the immediate post–World War II period, at the start of the Cold War era. The story takes place between December 1947 and November 1949, principally in New York, before the state of Israel came into being. The book concludes with a short epilogue in the form of a letter written in 1949. Isaac Bashevis Singer published his original version in Yiddish in *The Forward*, where it appeared in serial form twice weekly between January 1957 and January 1958. The translation was rendered by Professor Joseph Sherman of the University of the Witwatersrand, and the editing was done by Jane Bobko and Robert Giroux.

Part One

1

That evening the guests gathered in Boris Makaver's apartment on the Upper West Side. The apartment building into which Boris had just moved reminded him of Warsaw. Built around an enormous courtyard, it faced Broadway on one side and West End Avenue on the other. The *cabinet de travail*—or study, as his daughter Anna called it—had a window overlooking the courtyard, and whenever Boris glanced out he could almost imagine he was back in Warsaw. Always quiet at its center, the courtyard enclosed a small garden surrounded by a picket fence. During the day the sun crept slowly up the wall opposite. Children ran around on the asphalt in play, smoke rose from the chimney, sparrows fluttered and chirped. All that seemed to be missing was a huckster carrying a sack of secondhand goods or a fortune-teller with a parrot and a barrel organ. Whenever Boris gazed into the courtyard and listened to its silence, the bustle of America evaporated and he thought European thoughts—leisurely, meandering, full of youthful longing. He had only to go into the *salon*—the living room—to hear the din of Broadway reverberating even here on the fourteenth floor. Standing there watching the noisy automobiles, buses, and trucks and catching the subway's roar from under the iron gratings, he was reminded of all his business affairs and thought of telephoning his broker and arranging to meet his accountant. The day had suddenly become too short and he felt the need to take out his fountain pen and scribble in his notebook. On such an occasion Boris thought of the biblical verse "The Lord was not in the earthquake.''* When it was snowing outside, however, Broadway became cozily familiar. Since it was winter, the windows were fastened tightly, protected with shutters and covered with drapes.

This was such a night. Boris had invited his daughter Anna and his son-in-law Stanislaw Luria to dinner, as well as his nephew Herman Makaver, who had been spared Hitler's Holocaust. Herman had left Poland to fight for the Loyalists in Spain, then made his way to Algiers and from there, with Boris's help, to America. The other guests were Professor Shrage, Hertz Dovid Grein, Dr. Solomon Margolin—a friend from Boris's student days at the yeshiva in Ger—and Dr. Zadok Halperin and his sister Frieda Tamar.

Before eating, Boris put on a yarmulke and, after inviting the others to do the same, washed his hands while reciting the prescribed blessing. This ritual was also scrupulously observed by Frieda Tamar, who was the widow of a German rabbi and a learned woman who had published a book in English about the role of women in Judaism. The remaining guests, however, behaved like unbelievers. Boris was a widower and the meal had been prepared by his female relative Reytze, who had kept house for him since his wife's death twenty-three years before. She had accompanied Boris on all his wanderings—from Warsaw to Berlin and, after Hitler took power, from Paris to Casablanca, Havana, and finally New York.

After dinner they all went into the living room. Boris had furnished his new apartment like the old ones in Warsaw and Berlin—with heavy mahogany furniture, ornate chandeliers with dangling crystal prisms, and plush- and velvet-upholstered sofas and chairs draped with lace antimacassars and fringed covers. In America he had steadily acquired many volumes of rabbinical learning and all sorts of antique Hanukkah lamps, clocks with Hebrew dials, Passover seder platters, Sabbath candlesticks, and the breastplates, crowns, and fescues that beautify Torah scrolls. He had even set up a little prayerhouse in one room: it contained two copper candelabra, a Holy Ark, a lectern, and a wall plaque with a verse from the Psalms to encourage reflection and meditation. Though as a young man he had changed his name from Borukh to Boris, out of business expediency, he had never abandoned his Jewishness. After the Hitler slaughter Boris resumed strict religious observance. Wrapped in a prayer shawl and phylacteries, he recited the morning service every weekday and no longer

---

* Elijah heard the Lord not in the strong wind nor the earthquake, but ''in a still small voice'' (1 Kings 19:9–13).

neglected the afternoon and evening prayers. In Williamsburg he had sought out a Hasidic rebbe to whose father Reb Menachem Makaver—his own father—had once traveled. And he still recalled a page or two of the Gemara.

Now in the living room Boris quoted another rebbe's rhyming aphorism: " 'Since the Gentiles kill us all the same, / Let us keep our Jewish name.' Even though they murder us as individuals, why should we choose to die as a nation? Let us at least remain Jews and not assimilate."

Dr. Margolin grimaced. "The way you see things, Borukh, if one doesn't follow every petty decree by every two-bit rebbe, one is automatically an assimilationist. Believe me, if Moses were to rise from the dead and take a good look at those primitive Williamsburg loudmouths in their black coats, always waving their arms about, he would curse them. Remember, Moses was a prince of Egypt, not a *shmegege* with sidelocks. According to Freud, he was as Egyptian as they come."

"Quiet, Shloymele, quiet! Freud was a filthy German. All we know about our Teacher Moses is what's written in the Torah."

"Moses had two wives—one was the daughter of a Midianite priest and the other was black. Here in New York he'd have to live with her in Harlem."

"Blasphemer! Keep your wit to yourself! What do we know of the past? Every generation has its own customs."

"They've talked you into believing that every Jew is a stoop-shouldered snuff taker, and the picture is stuck in your head. For you, the only Jews are Polish Hasidim in primitive Russian capotes snatching scraps of food from the tables of nitpicking rebbes. What about the Jews of Spain? Of Italy? Wasn't Manoello Giudeo a Jew? And Rabbi Moshe Chaim Luzzatto? And Joseph Solomon of Candia? And Rabbi Leone da Modena? If you'd learned a bit of history, you wouldn't be so close-minded."

"History, mystery, chicory! What does it prove? I know one thing, Shloymele: our fathers were Jews, we've become half-Jews, and our children are . . . well, I'd better not say anything. If young Jewish men can join the GPU and shoot people on the other side of the world, then we ought to tear our garments in mourning and sit shivah—not for seven days but for a whole lifetime."

"So sit shivah. Your father's and your grandfather's Jewishness no longer exists and it'll never exist again. It was a brief episode in Jewish history."

"It still exists, and it'll continue to exist!" shouted Boris Makaver.

"Only yesterday I bought a holy book printed by yeshiva students in Shanghai. We were starving, and we printed holy books. We fled from Hitler and Stalin, and we published the commentaries of Rashba. And where? In China! I swear to you, Shloymele, a thousand years after we've forgotten all you intellectuals, we'll still be studying the Gemara."

"Well, if you swear, there's nothing more to be said."

The same controversy, the same argument, was repeated with every conceivable variation each time they met, but neither Boris nor his guests tired of these debates. The winter evening had just begun. Of the seven men present, five were without women. Margolin had married a German girl in Berlin twenty years before. In 1938 she had left him to live with a Nazi, taking their small daughter, Mitzi, with her. Professor Shrage's wife had perished in the Warsaw Ghetto. Herman had never married. Hertz Grein did have a family, but he was the type of man who never took his wife with him when he went visiting. He was sitting on a chaise longue chatting with Boris Makaver's daughter Anna, Stanislaw Luria's wife.

He murmured confidentially to her, "They're starting the Jewish Question again."

"I've heard the same talk since I was a girl this high," Anna answered, indicating with a gesture how little she had been then. On one of her fingers an enormous diamond ring flashed in the lamplight with all the colors of the rainbow.

2

Stanislaw Luria, Anna's husband, was trying to win over his host's nephew Herman. While Herman remained a staunch Communist, Luria was bitterly opposed. His only grievance against America was its failure to drop the atomic bomb on Moscow instead of Hiroshima. Luria and Herman had one thing in common, however: they both spoke eloquent Polish. Luria had trained as a lawyer in Warsaw, and Herman had studied in the jurisprudence faculty before going off to defend Madrid.

Now Luria reasoned: "*Proszę pana,* I know exactly what you think. I know more Marxism than all the Marxists put together. To my regret, I too made a fool of myself for a while. There was a time I even believed in Lenin. Ah, in one's youth one makes mistakes. When a young man doesn't make mistakes, there's something wrong with him. But one thing I hope you'll grant me: that without Uncle Sam's help, without lend-lease, your Comrade Stalin would never have marched into Berlin. This, I expect even the most ardent Stalinist will concede . . ."

Luria spoke as if he was begging Herman to see reason. Luria, past fifty, was short and broad-shouldered, and had an enormous head, no neck to speak of, a disheveled shock of brown hair streaked with gray, and a face that was either bloated or swollen by self-importance. His thick eyebrows overhung yellow eyes set in blue pouches flaked with crud. His nose had unusually large nostrils. There was something brutish and wild about him, yet he seemed sluggish, half-asleep. His narrow forehead was deeply clo-ven—whether with a wrinkle or a scar it was difficult to say.

Herman was barely thirty-three, but he looked older. He was short like his uncle but not so homely. He had a square head with hair cropped short in military fashion—in Spain he had been promoted to the rank of either captain or major—and cold, steel-gray eyes behind a pince-nez. Herman spoke slowly and with the deliberation of a diplomat watching every word.

His voice beat woodenly. "No one can know what would have happened without lend-lease. That is an academic question. One thing is beyond doubt: America delayed opening a second front until the Soviet Union was on the verge of decisive victory."

"Are you suggesting that the invasion of France was superfluous?" Luria demanded.

"By that time the fascists had already been smashed."

"If we let Stalin write world history, he would more than likely record that the Allies fought on Hitler's side," Luria retorted acidly.

"Until Stalingrad, the Allies always hoped for a Soviet defeat."

Luria raised his eyebrows. His yellow eyes kindled with fury. His right hand—broad, heavy, with swollen veins and fingernails resembling claws—twitched as though about to strike a blow. But it never left his knee. Instead, he countered ponderously: "Oh God, look at the might of false-hood! How incredibly vast and powerful it is! Like a bottomless pit."

Boris was not a scholar, not a learned man, but he loved both Torah and knowledge. Although he had been successful in business, he regretted more than once that he had not become a rabbi, a scholar, or simply a hack writer. Short, stocky, with hands and feet too big for his small frame, large black eyes, a crooked nose, and thick lips, he wore a goatee and spoke in a booming voice. He persisted in speaking Warsaw Yiddish, having never learned either German or English properly. While he could make out a page of the Gemara, when he had occasion to write in Hebrew, it was riddled with errors. Boris had one aptitude—for trade. He smelled out business. When he arrived in New York from Havana, he understood not a single word of English, but after only four weeks of wandering about the city, he knew exactly where to make money. Of course it was hardly a great feat to get rich in those years. Washington was spending billions. He had become a partner in a factory that manufactured leather goods. Here in America he knew businessmen with whom he had dealt while he was still in Berlin, so he easily obtained credit, established connections, made contacts. Boris used to observe that in business, as in all other matters, there were many crooked ways but only one straight road. One had simply to tread the path of probity. But books, holy and secular, were something else. They comprised a sea in which one could swim one's whole life and never reach any island of understanding. Many times he had heard how rabbis, professors, and scholars abused each other as ignoramuses and blockheads. However deeply a man might have studied, there was always another to sneer at him.

Boris loved listening to the way these intellectuals talked, wrangled, mocked, and even slandered one another privately. Zadok Halperin, for example, was one of the people Boris had supported in Berlin. Halperin was something of a celebrity. He had obtained a degree in philosophy in Switzerland, and for a time had been a lecturer at the University of Bern. Halperin's German works on Kant, Solomon Maimon, and Hermann Cohen were cited in philosophy textbooks. His Hebrew monographs were studied at the University of Jerusalem. His proficiency in Talmud and other sacred studies knew no limits. When challenged, he could recite any passage by heart. But he had never succeeded in making a living from this enormous knowledge. Now he sat in an armchair in Boris's living room: short, stout, with a protruding belly, a head of white hair, and a pair of thick whiskers that made him look like Nietzsche. Half-laughing eyes full of boyish mischief peeked out from under his bushy eyebrows. The more generously Boris helped him, the more captiously Halperin behaved toward his benefactor. Having remained a Maskil, Halperin despised religion. Now, as always, the discussion revolved around Jewishness, and Halperin remarked, in his clumsy Germanized Yiddish, "What do you want, my dear Herr Makaver? One cannot turn back the clock of history. Just because Hitler was a maniac, a psychopath, must the world return to the Middle Ages?

Foolishness! There is only one source of knowledge and that is experience—the good old sense experience of Locke and Hume. Everything else is useless. I go even further than Hume: for me the only valid determinant is empirical mathematics. If there were no straight line, if everything had humps, then we would need another geometry—"

"Now we have another geometry," Margolin interrupted. "Have you never heard of Lobachevsky and Riemann?"

"I know, I know. But I maintain that Euclid's geometry will exist forever and the others' will remain nothing more than games. Call me a heretic, but I don't care for Einstein's theory, either."

"One needs to understand before one can dislike," Margolin retorted.

"True indeed, and that's why I don't like it. Whatever one cannot understand is a priori rubbish. I knew Einstein, I knew him. I had many discussions with him in Berlin. He is, pardon me, an impractical man."

"An impractical man to whom we owe the atomic bomb."

"Without Einstein there would still have been an atomic bomb."

"Well, well. They're starting already!" Boris intervened. "Always arguing about apples and oranges. Einstein is a genius, and you're both geniuses as well. Why lock horns? Because Rockefeller is a millionaire, there can't be another millionaire tomorrow? There's enough money here for both. And it's the same with knowledge . . . Reytze, bring in the tea! Doctor, try this strudel. I'm not much of an expert on Einstein, but I can tell you without fear of contradiction that this strudel is delicious. Reytze baked it. You can't put in your mouth the strudel they bake here in America."

"Yes indeed, strudel is a weighty matter," said Halperin with a smile, revealing a mouthful of blackened teeth patched with bits of gold. He had been provided with a fork, but he preferred to eat with his hands. His fingers were short, covered with tufts of hair, and the nails had been bitten down. Besides eating a great deal, he could spend the whole day smoking cigars. Boris used to say that Halperin didn't smoke cigars, he swallowed them. He perpetually scattered heaps of ash around him from his tobacco-stained fingertips. Reytze followed after him with an ashtray and an unblinking eye to prevent him from burning holes in the furniture. His black suit, which he wore in every season of the year and on all occasions, was irreparably stained. Clumps of hair bristled in his ears and nostrils. Even in America he insisted on wearing European-style stiff collars, broad ties, and detachable shirt cuffs. Since he refused even to try on any other kind of shoe, friends had to rummage through the whole of New York to find him rubber-soled ankle boots. A watch with three lids was stuck into his vest pocket. Margolin used to say that spiritually and physically Halperin was still living in the nineteenth century.

Of all the men present, Dr. Margolin was the tallest. Carrying himself erect, as he always did, he stood over six feet. He had a long, severe face and the cold gray eyes of a Prussian Junker, and he always dressed according to the latest fashion—his head shaved and his fingernails manicured. In Germany he even wore a monocle. Rumor had it that he had grown rich from performing illegal abortions. It was difficult to believe that forty years earlier Margolin had been a student at the yeshiva in Ger. He spoke Russian like a Muscovite, German like a Berliner, and English with an Oxford accent. All his life he had been a devotee of the athletic pastimes of the upper classes, so as a matter of course he had come to treat an aristocratic clientele in Berlin. In New York he belonged to all sorts of Gentile clubs. Despite this, however, both in Berlin and in New York he had remained on intimate terms with Boris Makaver. He came to all his dinner parties, he was his family physician, and on those rare occasions when Dr. Halperin's memory failed him when reciting passages from the Gemara, it was Solomon Margolin who prompted him and who caught his Latin errors.

Boris used to tease him: "That's not a head you've got—it's a musical instrument. Oh, Shloymele, if you hadn't surrendered to all this foolishness, you'd've surpassed our Sages in brilliance."

Now he said only, "Do as I say, Shloymele, take a piece of strudel. It can't possibly harm you. All this nonsense about calories isn't worth a kopeck."

Dr. Margolin stared at him coldly. "I don't want your paunch."

3

On a cane-backed chair sat Professor Shrage, a small man with a white beard and a wrinkled face, white hair scattered over his head like swamp grass, and bloodshot blue eyes topped by unruly white eyebrows. David Shrage, who had also studied in Switzerland, was descended from Warsaw Hasidim, learned and wealthy people. Ten years older than Dr. Halperin, he belonged to an earlier generation and, while still a student of the scientist Chaim Zelig Slonimski, had been among the first Hasidic youths in Poland to study abroad. Shrage was a mathematician, and for a time had even been a lecturer in mathematics at Warsaw University. For the past twenty years, the professor had devoted himself to psychic research, to which he applied his mathematical knowledge. In Poland for a time he had been closely associated with the famous Madame Kluski. Professor Shrage had come to America on the eve of the Second World War, but his wife, Edzhe, had died at the hands of the Nazis. To this day he continued to mourn for her and never ceased trying to contact her spirit in the world beyond. The professor seldom took part in the discussions at Boris Makaver's. He was both hard-of-hearing and so soft-spoken that people barely understood what he said. He was neither able nor willing to outshout Dr. Halperin. And in any case, what use was it to argue with a fanatic caught in the most vicious of nets, conviction of the supremacy of human reason? The professor wore an expression of scarcely concealed pain. He could not bear this high-flown talk or the stench of cigars, and he never touched the refreshments which had been laid out for him. He came here only because Boris supported him.

On the chair opposite him was Frieda Tamar, Dr. Halperin's younger sister. A woman in her late thirties, with a fair complexion and dark eyes, she wore her hair combed into an old-fashioned bun and a black dress with sleeves to her wrists and a high collar that hid her throat. Frieda was Zadok's half sister. Their father, the rabbi of Grawicz, had remarried in his old age and his second wife had been a woman of illustrious descent. Studying in Germany, Frieda had met and married Dr. Tamar, a Reform rabbi from Magdeburg. The rabbi had died in Auschwitz, but Frieda survived and obtained a visa to America. She prayed three times a day. Since she wrote articles for religious journals, she was often to be found in the Public Library on Forty-second Street absorbed in one or another book of rabbinical learning. Frieda was as quiet as Halperin was noisy. She loved her older brother, but she seldom agreed with what he said. As soon as he began speaking, Frieda would shake her head vigorously in disapproval. People said that Boris was preparing to marry Frieda. He had made her a formal proposal some time before, but Frieda hesitated. Now, as she sat bent forward, her hands on her purse, her dress tucked around her ankles, wearing no lipstick, there was a stillness about her that reminded Boris of the hallowed women of long ago he had read about in holy books. From time to time she waved away the puffs of smoke that her brother blew into her face.

Boris murmured to her, "Frieda my dear, if you wish, I'll open a window. Your brother smokes like a chimney."

And Frieda answered, "No, thank you. Whom does the smoke harm? There's no danger."

For a moment her brow furrowed, and Boris understood what she was thinking: the smoke in Auschwitz had been much worse.

4

Solomon Margolin rarely wore his monocle in America, but now he sat in Boris Makaver's living room with one eye focused and staring ahead, exactly as if a monocle were jammed against it. He seemed to be turning a single thought over and over in his brain.

Margolin mused that Boris was truly a genius at obtaining credit, at buying up houses dirt cheap, at building prosperous undertakings from absolutely nothing, but was utterly incapable of seeing what was going on under his very nose in his own house. His beloved daughter, Anna, his only child, for whose sake Boris had ruined his life, was not satisfied with making two mistakes. She was now preparing to make a third, and this would be the most serious of all.

Anna's first mistake had been marrying the Galician comedian Yasha Kotik. Kotik had been a celebrated actor in Berlin, but his chief talent lay in mocking Eastern European Jews. He mimicked their bad German, even though he himself hardly used the language any better. Beset by scandals, the marriage lasted barely a year, but Anna was shattered by the experience. She developed a serious depressive illness. Margolin had treated her during that time and had been privy to all her secrets.

Years later, fleeing from Hitler, Anna did another wildly foolish thing: she fell in love with Stanislaw Luria, a widower twenty years older than herself, who had lost a wife and two children. He was both violent and sickly and was, moreover, a chronic failure and a liar. Although his family had been wiped out by Hitler, Luria had managed to save himself, but years passed during which he earned nothing. Apart from speaking florid Polish and boasting of his sexual prowess with a wide variety of women, he was useless. In Warsaw he had never been licensed to practice law, but to the end remained merely an applicant: it was his wife who had a job somewhere. Here in New York he was a millstone around Boris's neck, and Margolin had bluntly advised Anna to rid herself of this parasite before he drove her into a madhouse. Even before throwing over Luria, however, she was planning a third folly. Right here, in her father's salon, she was openly making advances to Hertz Grein, a man with a wife and grown children. Everyone except Boris saw plainly what was going on. She fluttered about and danced attendance on Grein. First she sat close to him on the chaise longue and whispered some secret in his ear; next she showed him some photograph; and finally she positioned herself directly opposite him, making eyes and smiling with the brazenness of those who have totally abandoned themselves to passion. From time to time Luria fixed his yellow eyes on her. Frieda bit her lips. Even old Shrage smiled into his white beard. Margolin had often urged Boris to stop inviting Grein, to recognize that Anna was behaving recklessly, but Boris made light of it: "You're imagining things, Shloymele. What you come up with! He means nothing to her."

And each time he invited Grein again.

Boris and Margolin had both known Hertz Dovid Grein back in Warsaw. When they were young men, Grein was only five or six years old, but a prodigy. He could calculate in a moment the date on which any Jewish festival had occurred a hundred years before. In seconds he could perform arithmetical operations that would take experienced accountants hours or days. At the age of seven he had played chess in the Commercial Union against twenty-four veteran Warsaw chess players, winning seventeen games and drawing four. Both the Polish and the Yiddish newspapers had written articles about him and published his photograph. Professor Samuel Dikstein, the noted assimilationist, had paid a visit to the wunderkind's father, a poor religious scribe living on Smocza Street. But this had been almost forty years ago. About that time, Solomon Margolin went to study in Germany. And Borukh Makaver—he did not yet call himself Boris—married the daughter of a wealthy Warsaw family, grew rich, lost his wife, and, at the end of 1924, left Warsaw and moved to Germany. Anna was then eleven years old.

When he got to Germany, Boris learned that Dawidek (or Hercuś, as the Polish newspapers used to call him) had abandoned the Gemara in favor of secular studies in a Yiddish-Polish high school, and had then enrolled at Warsaw University. He had grown into a handsome youth, and while the Makavers still lived in Warsaw, he had been a frequent guest in their home. For a time he had even helped Anna with her schoolwork. He had volunteered for service in the Polish-Bolshevik War of 1920, and had risen to the rank of noncommissioned officer. Later he had fallen in love with a poor girl from a small village, had gone off with her to Vienna, and from Vienna to America. He had promised to write, but many years passed and no one heard from him. Hitler had to take power before Boris Makaver and Hertz Dovid Grein were to meet again.

Even here in New York they had not come across each other until four years after Boris's arrival in America. From the way Boris had described his encounter with Grein, Margolin saw straightaway that it would lead to an imbroglio. Anna had not forgotten her former tutor. In Berlin, after her breakup with Yasha Kotik, she used to speak of Grein during Margolin's attempts to cure her with psychoanalysis. She kept Grein's photograph stuck in an album which he had inscribed with the kind of affectionate verse adults write to children. However ridiculously, throughout the terror-filled flight from Berlin to Paris, from Paris to Africa, from Africa to Cuba, and from Cuba to New York, Anna had treasured that album and carried it with her. Now her "first love" had turned up again. By this time Hertz Grein was forty-six years old, with a son about to receive an engineering degree and a college-age daughter. For years here in New York he had been a teacher in a Hebrew elementary school and painfully short of money. Later he had become a consultant in an investment firm on Wall Street. But he still looked boyishly young: tall, slim, with a head of golden hair that covered the beginnings of a bald patch, a high forehead, a cleft chin. His nose had a Jewish hook, but then had second thoughts and straightened itself out. His lips were thin, and his blue eyes revealed a curious mixture of bashfulness, sharpness, and something else that was difficult to define. Margolin used to say that he looked like a yeshiva boy from Scandinavia. Grein had studied philosophy both in Warsaw and in Vienna and had tried living in Palestine. Here in America he had learned enough English to publish an occasional article in a chess journal, and even to write a detailed study of a distinguished Polish-Jewish scholar murdered by the Nazis. He devoted his leisure time to mathematics, and in conversation with Margolin showed such proficiency in the new physics that he might easily have become a professor in the field. But Hertz Grein was apparently disappointed in himself. He spoke like a pessimist and a doubter. Having lost his entire family in Poland, he had ceased to believe in humanity and its moral prescriptions. By mere chance he had bought into a mutual fund and made money selling stocks. His wife had opened an antiques shop on Third Avenue and she, too, was prospering. By this time he lived in a large apartment on Central Park West and drove an automobile. Margolin had heard that he kept a mistress.

Now Margolin contemplated the way Anna was fussing over him. With scientific detachment Margolin noticed that Anna had recently started looking younger, as if Grein's early acquaintance with her had brought back her childhood. She blushed before him, and teased him like a little girl. First she smiled and then she was sad; now she waved her hand at him, now she stuck out her tongue. She seemed to have forgotten that she had a husband and was among guests. Margolin appraised her with an experienced eye. Anna had inherited Boris's build but some force within her had either corrected or disguised her father's physical shortcomings. She was a little taller than he, with a high bosom, a narrow waist, and small hands and feet, even though her calves were broad. Her eyes were her father's— black and sparkling, with eyebrows which nearly met, but her nose was almost straight. Full-lipped, her mouth was puckered up like that of a child preparing to plant a kiss. Her hair was as black and glossy as velvet, but unlike many dark people, she had a fair complexion. There was something strongly Polish-Jewish in her appearance. She reminded Solomon Margolin of Warsaw's suburban boulevards and its Saxon Gardens.

5

Not long before a painter named Jacob Anfang had finished Anna's portrait. Boris had commissioned it only because Anfang, a Polish-Jewish refugee from Germany, was in desperate financial straits. Anna now led Grein into the room in which the picture hung—her own room, where she spent the night when she had occasion to sleep over at her father's. Here she kept a number of books as well as clothes that were too good to be thrown away although she no longer wore them. Since Grein hesitated to go with her, afraid of distressing either her father or her husband, she seized him by his sleeve and pulled him after her down the corridor. She opened the door and switched on the light in a young girl's room with a narrow bed, a set of shelves full of books, a few photographs on the walls, an empty flower pot. On a round table stood an alarm clock. The portrait in its carved frame was out of place here, but Boris had lately grown so strict in his religious observance that he refused to keep any pictures near him for fear of transgressing the commandment against graven images. Moreover, Jacob Anfang had painted Anna in décolleté. Grein looked at the picture for a long while before murmuring, "Yes, it's a very successful portrait."

"Papa says it's not a good likeness."

"The painter has captured your character."

Anna's eyes lit up at Grein's words, and even more because he had addressed her informally.

"And what is my character? It seems to me that generally speaking I have no character."

"He's understood that essentially you're still a girl—an ardent and half-frightened high-school student."

"Is that a virtue? It's true that I'm frightened, because a phantom's pursuing me. But my youth's over. Often I feel old and broken."

"Your face doesn't show it."

Anna was standing sideways, allowing Grein to compare the copy with the original. She was bashful, but not in the way adults are bashful. She seemed to have lain down to sleep as a young girl and mysteriously woken up a mature woman. Meeting Grein after a separation of twenty-three years had brought both hope and bewilderment into her life. Layers of time had been inverted and confused by a harrow that plowed up and turned over the earth of ages and epochs. Before and after had vanished. Everything had become a jumble, a bizarre dream from which one kept snapping awake. First she addressed him informally, then formally; now she spoke to him in Polish, now in German. Sometimes it seemed to her that he was a relative—an uncle, or even an older brother. He brought back Warsaw for her, the time when she still had a mother. Being with him made her young again, vivacious, the only child of long ago. Again and again Grein looked first at her and then at the portrait, and Anna stood like a submissive schoolgirl, as if he still exercised his former power over her—when he used to conduct grown-up conversations with her seriously ill mother, bring her books and flowers, and send her, the child, out of the room when they wanted to discuss something private.

Grein raised his eyebrows. "Well, he has talent, but what is talent?"

"Yes, what is it? I can't even draw a duck."

"God gives each person his own gift."

"Are you going to start talking about God, too?" Anna cried out. "Oh, I can't bear to hear about God. After what happened in Europe, I don't dare even to mention the word God—because if God really does exist and allowed it all, it's even worse than if He did not exist.''

"Either way it's bad."

"Look—it's snowing outside!"

With childlike excitement, Anna ran to the window. Grein followed. She pulled up the lower sash and they stood exposed to the chilly air. The courtyard was white. The branches of the tree in the little garden were white. Only the sky above the roof was luminous in the glare of New York, half red, half violet, without a single star, as if a cosmic conflagration were in progress. The snowflakes fell evenly, slowly, full of wintry calm. The heat of the radiator spread into the cold outside. Anna stood so close to Grein that her shoulder pressed against his arm. Both looked out for a while in silence, stunned, as if they had been born in a tropical country and were seeing a snowfall for the first time. Grein was seized by nostalgia, a hankering he had never felt before that combined Hanukkah, Christmas-tide, Warsaw. He wanted to embrace Anna, but he restrained himself. He stretched out his hand and a snowflake settled on it. Filled with boyish exhilaration, he left his palm on the windowsill for a while, as though to cool the heat within him.

"Winter still comes," he murmured.

"Yes. Very often I'm amazed there's a world here at all."

They could not stay long. Stanislaw Luria was quite capable of bursting in and making a scene. But neither could they tear themselves away from each other and from the crystalline landscape. When Grein had first arrived in New York, the snow used to fall so heavily that however much one shoveled it up or swept it away, one seemed never to be free of it. In Brownsville, where he had been a Talmud Torah teacher, huge mounds of snow that reminded him of Poland lay all about. He would have to wear high overshoes or even snow boots. In the last few years, however, snow had become a rarity in New York. Now he glanced upward to see where it was coming from. The flakes appeared to originate in the fiery redness and fell in thick spangles which fleetingly revealed their hexagonal shape, the eternal pattern of snow. Some force or other fused Grein's thoughts with Anna's, and he knew that she was experiencing exactly what he was: the same tingling, the same desire. A form of electric current that could not be insulated, that often reached him when he was in his own home, in his own bed, ran through the silk sleeve of her dress and the woolen sleeve of his jacket. For a moment they were captives of this strange pulse that came from within and without, and that eluded them like the half-conscious beginning of a dream.

Suddenly Anna moved away, seeming to take fright. "Come."

She shut the window and he wiped his hands on his handkerchief. Once again they stopped in front of the portrait.

"Do you really think it's good?"

"Yes, outstanding. But I prefer to be with the original."

Anna paused a moment. "You know that's impossible."

"All you have to do is say yes."

Anna bit her lower lip. She made a movement as if swallowing. "Suppose I said yes—what would happen then? Oh, it's absurd."

"There's still love in the world."

"Yes, but there's something that's stronger than love."

"What's that?"

"Laziness. The fear of moving from a fixed place."

"One only needs to start."

"Where would you take me?"

"To a hotel."

"And after that?"

"To Tasmania."

"Why on earth to Tasmania? Really, you're ridiculous. Since I was a child, I've dreamed about love. When I saw the way my father lived, I promised myself never to follow his example. But I made two grievous mistakes, and those are enough for one life."

"All you need to do is pack a bag and leave."

"Oh, everything's so easy for you. You talk like an adventurer, but I suspect you're tied body and soul to your family. I warn you: be careful. I'm gullible by nature—I'm capable of doing exactly as you say."

"That would be the happiest day of my life."

"Come. We can't stay here so long. You're not serious, but I can't stop thinking about you. I even dream about you."

"You're already as good as mine."

Anna seemed scalded by his words. Agitated, she gave him a half-questioning, half-reproachful look, as if to say, If you don't mean it, why are you torturing me? He wanted to put his arms around her, but at that moment Reytze opened the door.

"Anna, your papa is looking for you."

"What does he want? Never mind, I'm coming."

"*Panie* Grein, come to the kitchen. I want to show you the new refrigerator."

Reytze had found a pretext to prevent the two of them returning together. Reytze knew every secret. After all, she had brought Anna up.

6

After Reytze had shown him the refrigerator, Grein went back to the living room. He stopped in the hallway to look at an antique mirror which hung there. Ever since his wife, Leah, had opened her shop on Third Avenue, he had become something of an expert on valuable old objects. The frame was a tangle of flowers, leaves, and adders, while the glass had a bluish sheen like the water in a well. He saw his reflection as if at a great depth.

Why am I so happy? he asked himself. Nothing will come of it. She won't leave her husband, nor I Leah. Well, and what about Esther? I won't wreck any families. There is a God in heaven. I've only recently vowed to observe the commandments.

Despite these thoughts, he remained in a state of inebriation. For his first ten years in America everything had gone steadily downhill for him, but in the second decade he had risen steadily upward. He lived in a large apartment, had money in the bank, wore good clothes. The stocks of the mutual fund which he had bought into and had recommended to his clients had risen many points overnight. Only today, without the slightest effort, he had made more than three hundred dollars. There had been a time when to earn such a sum he had been compelled to grind away in the classroom for two full months.

But she loves me—there's not the slightest doubt, he mused. How did she put it? "I'm capable of doing exactly as you say."

He went into the living room and heard Professor Shrage stammering: "What is empirical? It all depends on what one asks Nature. As long as we didn't ask why the lid on a pot jumps when the water boils, Nature didn't answer us and there was no theory of kinetics. People today have stopped asking the essential things, so why should we give them an answer?"

Dr. Halperin took the cigar out of his mouth. "And when we did ask, did we get an answer? During the Middle Ages people were preoccupied with the so-called occult matters. What did they find out? How many demons could stand on the head of a pin?"

"The literature of the Middle Ages is full of facts proving that there are higher powers . . . spiritual powers. Dybbuks and poltergeists showed themselves every day, both among Jews and among Gentiles."

"Excuse me, Professor, you're mistaking folklore for science."

"What is science? As soon as something can be repeated by pressing a button it becomes scientific. Not all things can be duplicated in a laboratory. The Red Sea can't be parted every Monday and Thursday."

"And who says it was parted even once? What evidence proves it? The fact that it's written in the Pentateuch? On my life, Professor, you're really oversimplifying. All religions have scores of miracles. In every village old women sit on doorsteps and tell stories about spirits and hobgoblins—"

"Spirits and hobgoblins do exist."

"Where are they? In the attic?"

"Perhaps they are here."

"Where? Under the sofa?"

"Can you see protons? Can you see cosmic rays? Perhaps they, too, are under the sofa."

"What a comparison! Nonsense! All nonsense!" Zadok Halperin began snorting and blustering vehemently. " 'A judge has nothing but what his eyes can see,' " he quoted from the Talmud. "You can keep on telling me there's a marketplace in heaven, but as long as I can't buy a bundle of wood or a bag of potatoes there, it's nothing but empty talk. In my time, people made fools of themselves with planchettes and crystal-gazing hags. Those I knew were all charlatans. Conan Doyle was an idiot. Lombroso, pardon me, went senile in his old age. Oliver Lodge was a good physicist but an incredible simpleton. William James just had a screw loose. The Anglo-Saxons have a weakness for this sort of imbecility. They're afraid of death, poor fools."

Boris, too, removed the cigar from between his lips. "Shloymele, why are you quiet?"

Margolin stared straight ahead. "What should I say? It's not my line. But, Dr. Halperin, you speak as if no mystery can withstand scrutiny. Telepathy is a proven fact."

"Not for me, not for me it isn't."

"You know why? Because you don't have any love affairs. Love is built entirely on telepathy. People who love each other are in telepathic contact."

"True, true!" Anna interjected, throwing Grein a sidelong glance.

Dr. Halperin knocked a heap of ash off his cigar, and it fell on his knee. "Well, well, you're young and know better. I haven't had a love affair for a long time"—here he broke into a fit of coughing—"a very, very long time. But as the Talmud asks, 'What has farming to do with revelation?' Any two fools in love think alike. The way starving people all think about the same thing. About bread. Humankind's greatest possession is still logic. I've read the spiritualists' accounts. They tell you that the deaf hear what the dumb say to the blind. Cows fly over rooftops and lay brass eggs. All sworn to by unreliable witnesses. But here stands a television set; I have only to turn a knob and you'll see more than all the spiritualists put together."

Boris tugged at his beard. "What can you see on television? Vanity and stupidity."

"And what do spirits say at séances? They talk the same rubbish as the mediums. They prognosticate. Why don't they tell us about the world beyond instead? When someone travels to Tibet, he writes a book about his adventures. But summon up corpses that've spent three hundred years in the hereafter, and they start prattling about how we need peace on earth. We know that without their advice"—another fit of coughing—"Let them give us real information instead. What've they been doing for the past three hundred years? Eating blintzes?"

"Zadok, don't forget that calling up the dead is recorded in Scripture," Frieda called out. "Saul went to a woman who had a familiar spirit and she summoned up the ghost of Samuel."

"I don't forget, I don't forget. It only shows that it's an ancient superstition. Ecclesiastes says something different: 'The dead know not anything.' "

"Do you know how the Gemara interprets that verse?"

"I know how everyone interprets everything, but I trust only my own eyes and scholars who can back up what they say with facts. It's a new fashion, religion. Right-wing religion and left-wing religion. What is Communism? Also a religion. Not so, *Panie* Herman?"

With great deliberation, Herman removed his pince-nez from his nose. "As far as I am aware, Lenin was a scientist not a prophet."

"What kind of science did he found? Based on what? Sociology is not a science."

"This is the first time I've heard so."

Conversation momentarily ceased, and all thought their own thoughts. Professor Shrage ruminated: Could it be that Edzhe's spirit was here listening to all this chitchat? How comical Halperin's certainties must sound to a spirit! Spirits were probably not permitted to make themselves known. It would deprive people of freedom of choice . . . Boris glanced at Frieda and asked himself: Should I speak to her tonight? How? Should I invite her into another room? She might find that offensive. Who could know how women might react? But truly, she was sensible. What she had said about Saul and the woman with the familiar spirit had been full of conviction . . . Zadok Halperin stared at a small piece of strudel: Should I eat it? What harm can it do me? With it or without it my arteries will stay clogged. I'll never lose that twenty pounds anyway. Thin people also die. All these statistics are for the birds. Halperin hastily snatched up the piece of strudel and popped it into his mouth. A crumb got trapped in his mustache, and he deftly pulled it in with his tongue. The idea occurred to him: Would this be the end of it all? To stuff himself with strudel and die? What an empty ambition . . . In his mind Luria confronted Anna: Don't think you're fooling me! I saw everything. You took him to see the portrait so you could arrange a rendezvous with him. You common whore! I'll live to have my revenge on you. You're no better than the Nazis. He snatched up his cigarette and violently stubbed it out on the rim of the ashtray, scattering a shower of sparks.

Grein had positioned himself at a window. Having tucked up the drapes, he stared down at Broadway. The traffic lights changed from green to red. Dozens of automobiles were piled up in each direction. From where he stood they appeared very small and he could feel their harnessed power, the impatience of the engines. Yes, she loves me! This is genuine love. But Anna is not Esther. For Anna I would have to give up everything. And Luria? It would kill him. To add to my good deeds, I'd have to murder a man. Then how long could it last? Fifteen years from now I'll be an old man. Here people die like flies. Grein glanced upward. Above the apartment building, in a break between two clouds, a light gleamed. Was it a planet? A star? What was it doing there in the heavens? Was it an intelligence? Did it really look down on the earth? Or was it only a chunk of matter? But what did matter count when everything was energy? The formula $e=mc^2$ had turned all previous conceptions upside down. Everything vibrated and emitted rays, even a clump of mud.

Anna made a movement toward her husband, as if she wished to say something to him. But when she glanced at him and caught the malevolence in his yellow eyes, she stopped herself. Why was Grein looking outside? What was he searching for there? she asked herself. Oh, it isn't easy for him either. I must put an end to this escapade before it's too late. Her thoughts wandered to her husband: Luria'll never divorce me. He's an implacable enemy. And what'll my father say? He'll have one of his attacks of high blood pressure.

Anna heard her cousin Herman say, "After all, it's a fact that capital tends to concentrate in a few hands. Even the farmland in America is falling under the control of the big companies. Marx could not foresee every detail, but the capitalist system is growing more degenerate all the time. It keeps needing to be inoculated, so to speak. Is it really sound economic practice for the federal government to buy grain, butter, and eggs from farmers? And do you call it healthy that Washington has to pay farmers billions of dollars not to cultivate the soil? If capitalism is so good, why must Washington keep bribing the governments of Europe to maintain the capitalist system through political terror? Why do you have to bribe people to do something if it's so obviously in their own interest?"

Luria suddenly sprang out of his chair. He pointed his thick, tobacco-stained index finger and half spoke, half shouted in a hollow bass that seemed to come from the grave.

"Do you know why they have to be bribed? Because the people of Europe want to commit mass suicide! They're like those little creatures—I've forgotten what they're called—that gather in the millions and migrate for miles until they all drown themselves in the sea—in Scandinavia, I think. They're like those fish that deliberately beach themselves and die. The other day I saw a man standing high up on a roof shouting that he was going to throw himself off. People stopped and begged him not to do it. The police promised him money, a job, whatever he wanted, as long as he went back inside. But he didn't want to listen. He had got it into his head that he'd had enough of the world. His picture was in the newspaper. I think he was a Puerto Rican or a Cuban."

"If they'd given him a job sooner, they wouldn't've had to promise him one later," said Herman. "He'd probably been unemployed for a long time."

"People like him are usually lazy," Margolin interjected.

"Doctor, you wouldn't work hard either if they paid you eighteen dollars for a week's labor and then deducted taxes."

"When I was a student in Germany, I earned less than the worst-paid

Puerto Rican or black here. I used to eat bread dipped in pickled-herring brine, and not enough of it at that."

"But you had a clear goal."

"Who stops them from also having a clear goal?"

"Your beloved capitalist system."

"You blame everything on capitalism, even the weather outside. I hear that the streets of Russia are swarming with drunkards and prostitutes. If the masses spent on education a tenth of what they spend on liquor and lewdness, the world would be a paradise. You quote pamphlets, I speak from experience. Twelve-year-old girls get pregnant. On Saturdays men collect their wages and drink them all away, down to the last penny. It's become the custom to blame all our sins on our leaders. But I assure you, the masses are no less corrupt than their leaders—they're perhaps even more corrupt."

"So what, in your opinion, should we do with the masses? Burn them in Treblinka?"

"Neither burn them in Treblinka nor send them to slave-labor camps in Siberia. Criminals and lunatics must be sterilized. If not, our civilization will end the way Rome's did. Wherever the intelligentsia practices birth control while the rabble multiplies without restraint, a catastrophe must follow. It's as inevitable as the moon eclipsing the sun."

"Pardon me, Doctor, but I hear Hitler talking."

"I knew you'd say that. Me a Hitlerite? Hitler murdered my family and took everything from me. Hitler and Stalin had a common purpose—to exterminate human individuality. According to you and your pamphlets, a class war is being waged in the world. But for me there's only one perpetual war—the war of the genes."

"That's barely disguised racial theory."

Frieda Tamar half rose from her chair. She made a slight motion with her hand. At the same time she darkened with the blush peculiar to middle-aged people who are naturally shy. The blood rushed from her throat to her jaw and stopped there, as if halted by a self-control more powerful than any emotion.

"May I say something?"

Margolin nodded. "Certainly, madame. You've been very patient all this time, listening to our banter."

"I want to say that the class war, or what you call the war of the genes, is not in our hands . . . It depends on evolution. How has humankind developed until now? It doesn't lie in our feeble power . . . When humankind sets itself such immense goals, it must inevitably fail. As if we wanted to drain the ocean . . . If we accept that God directs the world—and it's the simple truth that He does—why should humankind want to control it? That was the sin of the generation that built the Tower of Babel . . . Understood symbolically—"

"Bravo, Frieda, congratulations!" Boris shouted, clapping his large hands. "You've taken the words right out of my mouth! I was just about to say the same—"

"Don't interrupt, Borukh," said Margolin reprovingly.

Frieda bowed her head. "No, that's all I wanted to say."

"What, madame, ought we to do?" Margolin asked in a quiet, courteous voice. He leaned toward her and raised an eyebrow, like an adult listening to a child. Frieda's face, too, flushed. In a fraction of a second the blush reached her hairline, leaving the part strangely white. She moved her lips but no words came out.

Her brother Zadok answered for her: "We ought to recite the psalms! My sister has one remedy for all afflictions—from toothache to anti-Semitism."

And Halperin let out a braying laugh, flicking the ash of his cigar into a glass half full of lemon tea.

The moment Boris Makaver's fusee clock chimed twelve, everyone rose to leave. As he did on each occasion, Boris reproached his guests for leaving so early. Just when the conversation was getting going, he complained, everyone began fussing with overcoats, galoshes, and umbrellas. He professed himself astonished and uncomprehending. Why did they all need so much sleep? He himself found a short nap more than sufficient. Many times he had sat up through the night poring over sacred books or pondering life's complexities. His pleas notwithstanding, everyone had an excuse. Dr. Halperin wrote up his work at night. Frieda had to rise early to attend morning prayers at the Sha'arei Tzedek synagogue before teaching a class of Orthodox girls. Dr. Margolin swam for half an hour in an indoor pool and then heaved chunks of iron about and clambered up and down rope ladders, all to strengthen muscles which were already as hard as steel. Hertz Grein had a wife and children at home. Herman worked as a proofreader in a printing shop. Professor Shrage had no say over his life. Mrs. Clark, the crazy dentist who was his landlady, ordered him about like an errand boy. Anna wanted to stay late, but her bellicose husband, Luria, was eager to get home. But why this haste all of a sudden? What would he be late for? Boris asked himself. After all, instead of a good day's work, all Luria did was boast of the many wonders he had performed in Warsaw. Boris recognized long ago that he had made a terrible error: he should never have permitted this marriage. But when one is fleeing for one's life and has no idea what trouble the next day will bring, how can one properly weigh a marriage's suitability? Anna's first husband, that comedian Kotik, had been a lunatic, a rogue, a jack-of-all-trades, to whom the words of our Sages could be literally applied: he bore no resemblance to a human being. It had been a miracle that Anna had escaped his clutches. If he were still alive somewhere, let him die a violent death. And if he were no longer in this world, let him be miserably punished in the next. Well, what was the saying? Out of the frying pan and into the fire. Luria would never amount to anything. He would leech off Boris for the rest of his life.

"Good night, Mr. Makaver."

"Don't be in such a hurry, *Panie* Grein, and please don't call me 'Mister.' What kind of a 'Mister' am I?" Boris replied courteously, with old-fashioned formality.

"How should I address you? As Reb Borukh?"

"Why not? Call me Borukh. If your father and my father could see what has become of us, they wouldn't believe their eyes. Yet in the world beyond, they needn't concern themselves any longer with us below. Do you still look into the sacred books, Reb Hertz Dovid?"

"I have a bookcase full of them."

"Indeed? I can still remember when they wrote about you in the newspapers. The Warsaw wunderkind! How long ago was that? You're still a young man. You don't look more than forty."

"Forty-six."

"The years run by. Wait, Khanele"—Boris turned to Anna—"wait. Grein will take you home in his car. You're going in the same direction, aren't you? So, he'll stray a little from the straight and narrow. Right, Reb Hertz?"

"With the greatest of pleasure."

"And what do you find in the sacred books, *Panie* Grein?"

"Helpful things. But where is one to find faith, if everything they say is true?"

"But how can it be otherwise? Does the world function arbitrarily?"

"No. But who knows what forces are at work? There is certainly a plan, but we don't know what that plan is. I suspect that the author of *The Sanctification of Levi* himself didn't know."

"And Einstein does?"

"Einstein admits that he doesn't."

"Who does know, then?"

"God, perhaps."

"Then you believe in God?"

"In my own way."

"What is your way? Oh, my children, it seems such a pity to me. The Gentiles don't need faith. What is faith to them when they start one war after another? But Jews need faith. Look what is going on in Israel: young Jewish men have become terrorists. They blow up hotels. Jewish boys are members of the GPU in Russia. Here in America we've raised a generation of ignoramuses. Of course I want my Khanele to have children. I have no son to say Kaddish for me—let me at least have grandchildren. But what kind of Jews are American children? They haven't the faintest idea what it means to be a Jew."

"Papa, you have nothing to worry about. I won't have any children."

"Why not? You're not so old yet. Your husband hasn't reached a hundred."

"I often feel two hundred," Stanislaw Luria remarked.

"Foolishness. What do you say, *Panie* Grein? What will happen to the world?"

"I don't know, *Panie* Makaver. Only yesterday in the museum I saw a fifty-million-year-old skeleton. It's written there in black and white. The creature resembled an elephant, so it seems that the Master of the Universe has been experimenting with the elephant for a long time. He could experiment with human beings for just as long."

"Are you suggesting that the Master of the Universe is playing games?"

"Sometimes it seems so."

"That's nonsense, really. Well, don't drive too fast. I have only this one daughter. Stay in one piece yourself. Is your wife still running her antiques shop?"

"She's become a success overnight."

"Well, I might look in on her. I'm very fond of beautiful things myself. Are you still on Wall Street?"

"Don't speak so loudly. Your nephew might hear."

"Herman? No, he's left already. I don't think Wall Street is an abomination. Deals must be made. When King Solomon praised the Virtuous Woman, he said, 'She is like the merchant's ships, and delivereth girdles unto the merchant.' The world cannot survive without commerce. All the wicked of the earth start out trying to abolish buying and selling, the Bolsheviks and the Nazis alike, may their memory be erased. Our Father Abraham was also a merchant. Stocks are going up, eh?"

"Yes. They rose again today. Especially those of the mutual fund I recommend."

"Well, as some rise, others fall," Boris remarked, quoting from the Talmud. "You were a Hebrew teacher, after all. How did you discover this mutual fund? The pessimists are predicting a new crash, like the one in 1929. But I don't believe it. Roosevelt saved both America and the world. Here in America things started going downhill first. Because America loves business, they don't persecute Jews here. *Panie* Grein, we ought to get together sometime and have a chat. I feel close to you—very close—as if you were my own son—"

Boris Makaver broke off abruptly. He hardly understood why he had said these words. Grein blushed, and his eyes turned a more intense blue. Anna, too, blushed. She lowered her eyelashes and murmured something. Stanislaw Luria grimaced as though there were a sour taste in his mouth. He seemed to choke on his words: "That man has luck! Love from all sides . . . But it's getting late. We must go. Even love affairs can't be carried on all night—not at our age."

2

All three went down in the elevator. Anna was wearing a blue overcoat with a gray fur collar. Her hat resembled a skullcap dotted with silver. There was something boyish about her face that reminded Grein vaguely of the youths in the Hasidic study houses of Warsaw. He recalled Schopenhauer's opinion that a woman is half child. Luria, a brown plush fedora on his head, was enveloped in a fur coat he had dragged with him through France, Africa, and Cuba. He was no taller than Anna. His broad shoulders slumped, and his feet were thrust into extraordinarily large overshoes.

Anna remarked to him, "You're muffled up in fur like a bear."

"I am a bear," he answered irritably.

The snow had transformed Broadway. In the center of the sidewalk it had been trampled underfoot, but it lay piled up in soft heaps at the curbsides and on top of cars. A few flakes were still falling, and the air had a freshness unusual in New York. A long-forgotten solemnity enveloped the closed shops, the side streets where the snow had not been disturbed at all, and the few passersby who stepped quietly in the wintry hush. It seemed as if the snow had wiped away all sorrows, had brought down with it a measure of supernal tranquillity. The streetlamps gave off the bright, cozy light of European boulevards. The sky glowed red like the Arctic midnight sun, as though by some cosmic reversal day were preparing to break. Grein breathed the purified air in deeply, as if it were an invigorating drink. The sound of sleighbells seemed to jingle in his ears. At the same time he imagined that the breeze off the Hudson bore the scent of summer, as though the borderline between the antipodal seasons lay just across the river in the hills of New Jersey. Grein wore his light overcoat unbuttoned, yet he felt warm. This is love, love, he said to himself. My luck never seems to run out. But how will it end? How will it end? I don't want to build my happiness on someone else's misfortune.

Grein's car was parked on a side street. The three of them walked toward it with the silent preoccupation of those who are enmeshed in love. Although Grein had owned a car for many years, each trip was an adventure. Every time he drove he feared a catastrophe. He opened the rear door so that husband and wife could sit in back together, but Anna said, ''I'll sit next to you.''

''All three of us can sit up front,'' Grein answered with a tremor in his voice.

Boris Makaver's admission that he loved him like a son, and Anna's openly expressed wish to sit beside him inebriated him, making his movements unsteady. He seated himself behind the wheel and Anna snuggled up close to him, as she had once before when she was a little girl and rode with him in a droshky. Once again there traveled through his coat and hers a sensation no scientist has named, which inflames the heart and marrow with wantonness and a desire that cannot be withstood. But he had to concentrate on driving. He lacked the facility of those who learn to drive in their youth. Grein lived on Central Park West, but Stanislaw Luria's apartment was on Lexington Avenue. As it was impossible to turn the car around in the narrow side street, he swept out onto Riverside Drive.

Going downhill, the car veered from side to side, as if it felt Grein's agitation. Grein had lived in America for twenty years, yet he retained a greenhorn's wonder and a tourist's curiosity. Everything amazed him: the Hudson lapping against piers resembling fiery pillars, the industrial skyline of New Jersey, its factories illuminated through the night and alive with mysterious bustle, neon signs, radio towers—he found it difficult to grasp how, from these skeletons of iron or steel, waves whose nature no one fully comprehended were diffused, bounced off the highest strata of an atmosphere no one knew anything about, and transmitted foolish songs, cheap gossip, and empty advertisements. Soon Grein was driving through Central Park, made bright by the snow, as if remnants of day had been imprisoned here at night. The trees seemed covered in blossoms. The traffic lights changed from green to red and the car stopped next to a muddied bridle path. Grein could smell the horse dung. He inhaled deeply: the odor reminded him of Warsaw, of his childhood, of a journey by ox wagon to some distant relative in a small village. He was filled with longing. If only he and Anna could live on a farm and go horseback riding! Or run away to Canada and be pulled in a sleigh! God in heaven, how many opportunities for enjoyment lay hidden among fields, woods, lakes, and country houses. But some power always made sure that he was without the right partner.

As though reading his thoughts, Anna asked, "Do you ride?"

"If the horse is good, like a king."

"*Proszę pana*, the best horse can stumble," Luria interjected, his words seemingly charged with warning and hidden significance.

"Yes, nothing is certain in this world," Grein replied, himself not knowing where his tongue would lead him. "Horses stumble, hopes are dashed, years run by. A whole generation was destroyed before our eyes." Oddly, his words were the opposite of his feelings, as though he were trying to hide his self-assurance. Anna moved closer to him. He felt her knee through their coats.

"Don't be so pessimistic. There's happiness somewhere."

"Try reaching out a hand to grab it and all the forces in heaven and earth will cry out, No! It often seems to me that every human institution has one purpose: to prevent us from enjoying ourselves too much. People fear good fortune more than death."

"What are they afraid of?"

"That the evil spirits will exercise their malignant powers."

"Oh, you're just talking wildly. One never knows when you're being serious and when you're joking," said Anna, blending reproof with tenderness. "No one believes in spirits anymore, not in good ones or in bad ones."

"Perhaps not in good ones, but definitely in bad ones. Only one nation in the world is not afraid of evil spirits, and that's America. Uncle Sam's a hopeless rationalist, which itself defies understanding."

"Wait, the evil spirits have not spoken their last word," said Luria ponderously and hoarsely.

"Yes, that's true. Here's Lexington Avenue."

"I'd love to drive like this all night," Anna remarked in a wayward, hopeful tone.

Luria half coughed, half growled. "Well, if *Pan* Grein is willing and you are ready, you can." He weighted his words as though to give them a double meaning. "I'd better get to sleep. I'm too old for such diversions."

"*Pan* Grein has a wife and children to get home to."

Without speaking, Grein drove up to the apartment building. He got out and Anna deliberately stretched out a small hand in a thin black glove for help to emerge on his side. Luria got out on the other side, and for a moment the car formed a barrier between him and them. In the middle of the street he tried to light a cigarette. The wind blew out the match and he struck another. He lingered, leaving them to themselves, but neither said anything. They simply stood side by side in silence, like people who have long sought and finally found each other. After a while Luria headed for the sidewalk, taking a route behind the car longer than was necessary; his face wore the heavy expression of a man who swallows an offense and knows something others do not. He walked with his feet spread wide and the ungainliness of someone who no longer needs to please. A single spark glowed at the end of his cigarette.

"Well, thanks for the lift. Perhaps you would like to come up?" The invitation was uttered boldly, from deep within his chest, as though he had suddenly overcome all human weaknesses. "We'll make coffee. What's the tragedy if one misses a night's sleep? As it is, I can't sleep."

"What do you do all night?"

"I think."

"What do you think about?"

"About tortured women, burned children. I don't mean the morality of it—I'm not that naïve. But the psychology interests me: what goes through people's minds when they shove a child into an oven? Some thoughts must occur to them; they must even find some justification. But what passes through their minds? Afterwards, what do they tell their wives, fiancées, parents? How does a man come home to his wife and children and say, Today I burned fifty infants? And what does his wife answer? What does such a person think about when he finally lays his head on his pillow? I simply want to know how the mind works in such fiends."

"You're starting with the horrors again! Why should anyone want to come up to our apartment when you speak about such things?" complained

Anna. "Everyone knows what happened in Europe—you don't have to keep throwing salt on the wound."

"What? I won't speak about it. *Pan* Grein asked me, so I told him . . . Yes, come up. I assure you the invitation is sincere. It's not so late yet. And even if it were—would it matter? From the philosophical point of view, there's no such thing as early or late—"

"Yes, do come up," Anna interrupted her husband. "It's impossible to sleep on such a glorious night. Even if I were to lie down, I wouldn't shut an eye."

She shot Grein a half-pleading, half-beckoning glance that seemed to say, You don't have to be afraid of him. He knows all our secrets—he knows and he consents.

For a few moments Grein hesitated and tried to decline, but Luria took him by the sleeve and drew him along. Grein stepped into the entrance hall. With its dark walls, bronze lamps, and two urns on a mahogany table, the foyer reminded him of a funeral parlor. A late-night abstractedness lay over the room, the silence of a public place abruptly emptied after a day of tumult and bustle and now left to itself. Grein was convinced that this visit was a mistake, but he could not help himself. He and Anna had fallen into a state where one cedes the initiative and events start happening of their own accord.

For more than a year he and Anna had conducted one of those aimless flirtations which involve no obligations, promise nothing, and which Scripture sums up in the phrase "Cast your bread upon the waters." He made no effort to meet her. He seldom telephoned her. In her father's home he spoke to her without considering what he said. He turned their contact on and off like a switch. He still thought of their relationship as one between teacher and pupil. With no need to search for words, he was able to chatter on with her about whatever occurred to him and could always be certain that she would read meaning into his every utterance. Dr. Margolin was right: love was built on telepathy. His and Anna's love affair was carried on in the mind. He thought of her and in return received signals that she was thinking of him. Every time he met her, their secret grew and the gulf between them narrowed. She stared into his eyes with open desire and pleading. She used words that gave her away. Playfulness changed to irritation, to sharp exchanges. Luria, who had long pretended not to notice, dropped hints. Because of Grein, husband and wife had started quarreling. Alone in their bedroom, they traded the ugly accusations that always pass between couples in such cases. Now Grein was nonchalantly going to pay them a visit in the middle of the night. In the elevator, Grein took off his hat although Luria kept his on. Luria took a key from his back pocket, his yellow eyes gleaming with the satisfaction of someone acting to spite himself. Anna wore an expression of boyish seriousness mixed with truculence, as though she were displeased at the treat Luria was giving her and suspicious that he might be laying a trap. All three were silent with the speechlessness that comes of doing something against one's will, as though at this late hour the powers that determine human action had made known what they normally keep hidden.

Luria opened the door of the apartment and switched on the light in the hallway. Anna led Grein into the living room. How different this living room was from Boris Makaver's salon. Here everything was bright and modern. The beige carpet spread from wall to wall. The walls themselves were brightly papered. Built-in bookshelves held volumes with colorful covers. The chairs, the sofa, the coffee table—everything had been chosen for the comfort of guests who smoked, drank, and did not remain long in the chairs assigned to them. On the walls hung various paintings and drawings that Luria had bought in Havana and New York—a jumble of symbolism, expressionism, and every other modern trend—the most striking of which was a representation of an androgyne. Even the lamps here were designed not solely to light the room but also for the sake of effect, as if the dwelling were a stage and husband and wife the actors. Luria busied himself with something in the hall. Anna went into the kitchen to make coffee. In the middle of the night every object was alive with its own thoughts, its vital essence exposed as if intruders had stumbled upon it in the midst of furtive activity. Grein threw back his head and shut his eyes. Master of the Universe, why am I dragging myself around in the dead of night? What do I want with this couple? Why do I force myself into the lives of strangers? He suddenly remembered Luria's words about children thrust into an oven. They had not been meant only literally. It was happening figuratively to his own wife and children. A shudder ran through him. Can I really want to steal the wife of such a man? Have I sunk so low?

Luria came in. "Well, make yourself comfortable. The coffee will be here soon. My father-in-law thinks sleep is unnecessary, and I'm beginning to agree with him. It's good, but it's too good. Why should people be able to escape for seven or eight hours? If they must suffer, let them suffer the full twenty-four hours of the day."

"Speaking for myself, I suffer more asleep than awake. I have hideous dreams," said Grein.

"You too? As soon as I close my eyes, I'm in a bunker. Nazis are trying to bury me. I wake up screaming and my wife has to calm me down. Is it any wonder? What do you dream about?"

"I'm always in a crisis, a dilemma. The Maker of Dreams is like a great writer. He never lacks a plot. Every night he comes up with something new, but the main theme is always the same—I'm caught in a quandary."

"It must be something in your subconscious mind."

"I don't have to delve into my subconscious. Modern man's whole life is one long predicament."

"Why only modern man's? I don't believe it's anything new. There were Nazis three thousand years ago and six thousand years ago. They just had different names, that's all. There were Bolsheviks then, too. Who was Genghis Khan? My father-in-law is always trying to talk me into believing that human beings today are split personalities, whereas the people of the past were whole. But what does 'whole' mean? How can a person ever be whole?"

"Whole in the sense that he could make a decision and act on it. Today man can do everything but make up his mind."

"What do you mean by that? You're speaking in riddles."

"I'll give you an example. Our fathers and grandfathers knew that it was forbidden to lust after another man's wife, so they didn't lust. If they did, they smothered the desire in themselves, never admitted it, never let their bodies get the best of them, and lust gradually wore off. Modern man can be given every demonstration that he's forbidden to do something, and he'll still do it. I know this from my own life," Grein said, astounded at his own words. He felt distinctly uncomfortable—as though he had not merely given an example of the modern lack of wholeness but had articulated exactly the personal quandary that manifested itself in his dreams. There was more: he had attributed to a dream the reality that kept him awake when he should have been sleeping. His conscious and subconscious minds had merged. Luria regarded him somberly from beneath his bushy eyebrows.

"Well, that's a very fine example. But it's simply because our parents had faith and we do not."

"Faith alone does not enable a person to make up his mind."

"What else does one need?"

"Organization. Just as patriotism is not enough to win a world war, so faith is not enough to win the war with oneself. One needs strategies, tactics, all the generalship of war. Our fathers and grandfathers did not fight alone. They had an army. They had fortresses, trenches, commanders and subordinate officers. They had uniforms.''

''If you mean their fur hats, their sidelocks, their study houses, then I absolutely cannot agree with you.''

Anna came in carrying a glass percolator. ''Gentlemen, coffee is served.''

3

E ach took coffee and a cookie. Anna also brought them fruit. Pulling up a chair opposite the men, she sat and crossed her legs, and Grein glanced at her broad calf in the nylon stocking and at her knee barely covered by the hem of her dress. She was evidently aware that he found her legs attractive, because she had pulled her skirt up more than was necessary for the position in which she sat; and she was apparently no longer embarrassed in her husband's presence but emboldened with the self-confidence of a woman whom men admire. Grein knew perfectly well that the pleasure he might receive from this woman's body would never be as strong as his lust for it. Many times he had tried to analyze sexual pleasure, but he had never been able to discover how long fulfillment lasted. Everything stopped with lust. In no other area was Schopenhauer's formula of will and boredom as convincingly demonstrated as it was in physical lust, where the forces of biology had not even bothered to conceal their deception. Nevertheless, Grein could not take his eyes off Anna's leg, which seemed to have hypnotized him. After a while, Anna pulled down the hem of her dress, but only an inch or so, like a cunning merchant. She turned a questioning look on her husband as though to ask, Why is he so entranced? Has he never seen a woman's leg before? Luria stared into his cup and drank like someone who is cold and warms himself with every sip. A smile skulked on his lips, as if to say, You cannot know what I know. He drank to the dregs and replaced his cup on the coffee table.

''I wasn't aware that your friend Grein is so religious,'' he remarked to Anna.

"Religious?" retorted Anna scornfully.

"I'm not religious, I simply acknowledge a fact," Grein replied. "I said that in religion, as in war, organization is necessary. One cannot subdue the instincts without effort. To do that, one has to have a plan of attack, because the enemy is fully mobilized. Hitler couldn't be beaten without an army, without a strategy, without a whole military machine."

"Why does one have to subdue the instincts?" Anna demanded, partly of her husband and partly of Grein.

"He cited the example of a man who wants to steal another man's wife," Luria disclosed, as though giving away a secret. "What exactly is organization? If a man wants to seduce and a woman wants to be seduced, they go ahead. Quite simple."

Luria took out a pack of cigarettes, and lighting up, he offered them around. Grein declined, but after some hesitation Anna took one. The conversation was suspended, although Grein felt he owed it to himself to respond. In this intellectual conflict, Anna was on her husband's side. Luria had as good as exposed him for a fool.

"I said that in order for someone to conquer a passion—let's say a passion for another man's wife—at the moment of crisis it's not enough simply to make a decision to curb oneself. Such discipline is available only to those who have prepared themselves for it since childhood, who curb themselves day and night the way our grandfathers did, who almost never looked at a woman, prayed three times a day, studied the Torah, devoted themselves to observing the commandments. I was trying to argue that because they had a military machine to fight Satan, they were able to score victories as a result. Modern people are part of Satan's military organization. What else are worldly books, theaters, art exhibitions and all the paraphernalia we call modern culture? We can't conquer Satan as long as we're on his side."

"In other words, you're preaching that we should grow beards and sidelocks and spend the whole day poring over the Gemara!" Luria raised his voice.

"I'm not preaching. If I were preaching I should practice what I preach," Grein answered. "I'm simply saying that the two things are connected. It's the same as saying that if we want to brew coffee, there must be coffee and a stove in the house. In short, even to keep the Ten Commandments requires a large and complex organization."

Anna put down her cup. "Isn't the Church just such an organization?"

"Yes."

"Then how is it that the Christian nations wage wars and break the Ten Commandments wherever one turns?"

"That's proof that their organization doesn't work."

"And whose organization does work? The Jewish one?"

"The fact is that for two thousand years Jews have followed both the tenets of Judaism and all that Jesus preached—that we should turn the other cheek. For two thousand years we've been both Jews and Christians. I mean observant Jews, not Jews like us—"

Luria raised his eyebrows. "Our forebears couldn't wage any wars because they had no territory."

"Yes, but they could easily have converted and become part of the other nations. To this day, Jews are the only people who have been hounded from their home for two thousand years, yet they haven't lost their identity, their religion, their language. Just try driving the Germans out of Germany to the far corners of the earth and see how long they remain Germans—"

"You're confusing religion with nationality."

"Among Jews they were always one and the same."

Anna folded her arms. "These are academic questions. I'm not religious and I don't want to belong to a religious organization. We shouldn't steal or murder—the police take care of that—or should—and that's enough for me. I can't serve a God without proof that He exists and wants us to serve Him. As far as I can see, you hold the same view. If you didn't, you wouldn't be sitting here with us."

"Yes, that's true. But only partly."

"Why partly? For two thousand years they've slaughtered and burned Jews, and they're slaughtering and burning them even now. I can't think of a single instance in which God has taken their side."

"In other words, if you want to steal someone else's wife, steal her and don't think too much about it," Luria interjected. There was a derisive glint in his yellow eyes. Grein had a preternatural feeling that husband and wife had brought him up here deliberately to deceive him. With his own words he had driven himself into a corner. He grew agitated and ill at ease. I must leave immediately, he decided. He raised his wrist to look at his watch, but the glass was foggy or smudged. Well, I've destroyed everything, he mused. I've smashed everything with a single blow. He had an impulse to get up, but he remained seated. I didn't say what I wanted to say, he brooded. Everything came out wrong. He felt ashamed—not the outward shame of youth when one blushes and loses one's tongue, but a deep inner humiliation. He had to say something to rehabilitate himself, but he knew beforehand that he would only make things worse, as if within him sat a trickster, a mutineer who did the opposite of what he ordered. He started searching his memory for a joke with which to lighten the tone of the conversation.

Anna rose. "I'll make some more coffee."

"What do you say to my wife? She speaks forthrightly. She speaks to her father in the same way. She spares no one, least of all me. But it's an unvarying rule that the stronger a person is, the greater are his weaknesses. Such a principle of compensation operates universally. Perhaps you will persuade yourself."

"How will I persuade myself?" Grein answered, shocked at his own question.

"Ah, one can never know. Before the war I believed that there were laws in life and that human conduct was subject to a little order. As you know, I was a lawyer and I was guided by a code of statutes—the *Shulhan Arukh*, if you like, of my profession. But after September 1939 I became aware that there was absolutely no madness that people could not perpetrate. Now I no longer know what I might do tomorrow. A close friend of mine, practically a confidant, became a Kapo under Hitler and helped to send members of his own family to Majdanek. Another acquaintance did the same thing in Russia. I read somewhere about a son who shoved his own father into the ovens."

"Under political terror one is capable of anything. The Talmud tells us that if Hananiah, Mishael, and Azariah had been tortured, they'd have worshipped idols. It was they Nebuchadnezzar threw into the fiery furnace."

"What? I know. There was a time I used to peruse the Bible myself. Terror takes all forms, but the worst form is compassion. When you love someone and feel compassion for him as well, you can be driven to do the most brutal things. Not long ago the newspapers reported that a man shot his wife because she had cancer. To ease her suffering, he became a murderer and went to prison."

Anna came in with the coffee. "Well, what conclusion have the two of you reached?"

"Your friend Grein is a moralist. He's even quoted the Bible to me," said Luria with a glint in his eye.

"He's not such a saint."

"I was saying that by using terror one can force any person to do the worst, even saints."

"What? There are no saints. You're still clinging to outmoded notions. If you see someone ready to sacrifice himself for you, you ought to know that he gets the greatest pleasure from it. Try to stop him from sacrificing himself, and he'll stick a knife in you——"

"If you mean me, Anna," Luria put in, "you're making a great mistake."

"I don't mean you."

"Well, I'll go," Grein said loudly.

"Drink your coffee, drink your coffee," Luria called out. "You'll get home late no matter what, and your wife's thought every bad thought she can about you already."

"Don't go, stay awhile longer," Anna added. "There's not much left of the night."

"Yes, stay. I'm in a frame of mind that permits me to speak frankly. My wife loves your company and I love my wife. From this it must follow that I, too, love your company. Or perhaps that's not a valid syllogism?"

Anna turned red and immediately afterward went white. "Are you drunk?"

"Late at night I get drunk automatically."

Grein got up. "Well, good night. I'm fond of your company, too. Goodnight, Madame Luria. Thank you for the coffee."

"Don't run. I've made more coffee especially for you, and you can't just leave it. And please, I beg you, don't call me Madame Luria. I've grown accustomed to my husband, but I'll never get used to his name."

"It's an eminent name. You know, of course, from whom he is descended?"

"My wife prefers the name Kotik," Luria threw in contemptuously.

Grein looked at him. Though Luria's yellow eyes laughed, his mouth was angry. For the first time Grein noticed that two deep grooves stretched from the sides of Luria's nose down to his broad chin and that his chin, like his forehead, had a cleft resembling a scar. Anna rolled her eyes up impatiently.

"Kotik is a disgusting name, but it's perfect for a comedian. That name drew vast audiences in Berlin. Whatever else one might claim about Yasha Kotik, he had a great deal of talent. The name Luria says absolutely nothing."

"Well, you'll have to quarrel without me. Good night."

"Wait, Hertz, we're not quarreling," Anna said. "What's there for me to fight with him about? He speaks day and night about his first wife. One can't be jealous of a dead woman, and I wouldn't be jealous even if she were still alive and came back tomorrow. I'd give up my place to her with the greatest of pleasure. That's the bitter truth.''

"I speak about my first wife because Hitler reduced her and our children to a heap of ash. That has nothing to do with love and sex in the accepted sense. You speak day and night about that pervert Kotik, and about our friend Grein. That's something else altogether. You could at least choose one of the two.''

Grein walked to the door.

"Wait, Hertz, wait. My husband enjoys playing to an audience and you can't rob him of the pleasure. He should've been an actor. He's no lawyer, anyway. In Warsaw he was never admitted to the bar—all those years he was merely an applicant. Here in America he can do only one thing— boast. Wait a second, I'm coming with you—'' Anna suddenly altered her tone.

God, how like my fantasy this is, Grein thought. I seem to have acted out this scene in a dream. I must have some sort of precognition. I could swear that only last night I dreamed all this.

But now, when he was fully awake, all the embarrassment, the pain, the regret were absent. Grein noticed his own pale face in a mirror. An aberrant spirit had seized him. He was completely detached, as though through some kind of bedevilment all emotions had seeped out of him. He was too tired to feel shame. It occurred to him that those who commit violence and savagery must feel this way. He said, ''I beg you, Anna, spare me this . . .''

But he did not finish his sentence.

"Spare you what? I'm going to my father, not to you. I'm not so desperate yet. It's difficult to get a taxi at this hour.''

"Don't stop her, Grein. One should never refuse a lady. Take her wherever she wants to go. After all, she said she wanted to drive around with you all night,'' Luria added sardonically. He stood in the middle of the room with his legs spread wide, holding a coffee cup by its handle. He smiled half sarcastically, half aggressively. Grein suddenly noticed that his shock of brown hair was gray at the roots. Evidently he dyed it. The suspicion crept over Grein that this whole scene had been contrived between husband and wife. Was it possible that Luria wanted to be rid of her? Or was he one of those men who were willing to share a woman? Well, it's all the same to me. I won't back away from anything, said something inside Grein. He was filled with a mix of courage and fear, as if he were party to a poltergeist's mischief or an actor on the stage. The feeling that he had already been through all this before never left him. What did the French call it? *Déjà vu.* Anna came up to him, her eyes burning with anger and the passion of someone in the heat of an argument.

"I want to get my coat." And she stormed out into the hall.

"Well, here you have an example of how two souls struggle in one cage," Luria remarked, in the tone of a professor or a psychiatrist describing a clinical case study. Suddenly he grew serious, and the blue pouches under his eyes seemed to lengthen and swell. His glance expressed the disappointment and bewilderment of someone who has toiled wearily to achieve something that has finally come to naught.

"Truly, I want no part in all this," Grein began. "I swear to you, I . . ."

"You want no part, eh? She lives more with her father than with me. She knows I'm dependent on her and she exacts her revenge. Take her wherever she wants. I mean what I say literally. Before you, you see a dead person. Dead in all respects except that the heart still beats to no end or purpose. They burned me together with the others . . ." And Luria gestured into the distance with his index finger.

Anna appeared in coat and hat. "Well, come."

"Wait, Anna, wait. We can't end the evening this way!"

"What do you want? Many evenings end this way with us. Unless you'd prefer to stay here and keep him company? I'll get a taxi. Or else I'll walk."

Anna opened her purse and snatched out her gloves. She removed her wallet and scrutinized a bill with furrowed brow, evidently prepared to pay for a taxi if Grein should refuse to give her a lift. Suddenly she dashed to the door with the startling haste of someone who is compelled to commit an act that no power can prevent.

4

Grein stood with Anna waiting for the elevator. Had anyone ever found himself in such a predicament before? he wondered. Or was this event occurring for the first time in human history? Here he was, in the middle of the night with a married woman for whom he had not stopped lusting for over a year, and on the other side of the door her husband was lurking in silence. His detachment had passed and Grein had been seized by something like dread, the fearfulness of someone upon whom the higher powers were bestowing gift upon gift. How oddly everything had turned out this evening: with what lightness of touch the director of the human drama had twisted the action to make the impossible possible! What was Luria thinking back there? Grein had the feeling he was standing breathing heavily at the door. He broke into a cold sweat. Perhaps at the last moment Luria would rush out at him with a knife or even with a revolver. As though out of spite, the elevator did not come. The operator had probably fallen asleep. Perhaps we should take the stairs, Grein was about to suggest to Anna when he heard the hum of the elevator.

Anna instructed him: "Go down a floor. I don't want him to see us together."

Grein blundered about looking for the door that led to the stairwell, which seemed to have disappeared. Anna pointed it out. He pushed at it and overturned a trash can someone had put out on the landing. He hurried to the floor below so he would have enough time to press the button before the elevator went past. But the elevator remained stuck above. Grein could hear the call bell ringing inside it. How strange that the elevator had been delayed up there. Had Anna forgotten something? Had Luria regretted his actions at the last moment and called her back? If so, the elevator would surely not have stood still. Grein listened attentively, holding his breath. Perhaps he should walk all the way down and wait in the lobby or even in the street. Something like delirium possessed him. What shall I do? I'm getting ensnared more tightly. No good ever comes of such things. Well, let her stay up there. I don't want to get involved in such dishonorable conduct! Then he heard the door of the elevator clang shut. But how odd——the elevator did not stop but instead skipped his floor. Grein gave yet another ring, short and sharp. He had made up his mind to use the stairs and was already pushing at the stairwell door when he became aware that the elevator was returning. Was he drunk? The door opened and Grein recognized Anna. She stared at him quizzically, the way one does at anyone who impedes the progress of a public conveyance. He got in and the operator started apologizing to him.

"Excuse me, sir, just an oversight, sir."

"It's all right, it's all right," Grein assured him.

But the operator was obviously accustomed to making small talk. Even after they had reached the ground floor he did not immediately open the door but instead detained the passengers until he had had his say.

"Sir, I was supposed to go home at midnight but the man who was due to relieve me didn't show up. Got drunk or something, who knows? People are so irresponsible. I've been on my feet for twelve hours straight. It'll be a fine thing if the guy who's supposed to take over at six o'clock doesn't show either. Then I'll have to work his shift, too."

"Oh, I'm very sorry."

Grein took a half-dollar out of his pocket and gave it to him. The operator made a gesture as though to refuse it, but grabbed it almost immediately.

"I appreciate that, sir. Thank you very much. I really appreciate it!"

And he opened the door. Grein let Anna exit before him. For the first time it occurred to him that they were acting out a foolish comedy. Earlier in the evening the very same elevator man had brought him up with Anna and Luria. He must have recognized him, because people in that job are usually sharp-eyed. Instead of making things better, Grein was making them worse. But that was the case with every wrongdoing. Grein had caught up with Anna and was opening the front door for her when he heard whistling. It was the supposedly exhausted elevator man, suddenly reinvigorated. There was something gleeful and impudent in the shrill sound that seemed to say, I can see through all your tricks. You're going about it very clumsily.

Grein went out with Anna and they walked for a while in silence, moving apart as though each was afraid of the same thing: that the elevator man, peering through the glass door, would see them together. They strolled to the corner of the block. Outside, a frost had settled and a chill snowy wind blew from the East River. The street was deserted, and the snow on the sidewalk as thin and dusty as powder. Only now did Grein realize that they had passed the car. He had been driving for years, but he kept forgetting about the car and often speculated on the Freudian significance of this forgetfulness. Was he subconsciously afraid of it?

He said to Anna, "Wait here. I'll bring the car."

He turned back. What if disaster were to strike and we were both murdered? he mused. Wouldn't it be ridiculous? What satisfaction that would bring Luria! Perhaps that's the whole purpose of this little play.

Perhaps it's one minute till the final curtain. Well, come what may, we must act it out to the end.

Getting into the car, he had a premonition that he would have difficulty with the engine, but it started smoothly. He glanced at the glass door of the apartment house. No, the elevator operator wasn't looking out. At the corner Anna got in quickly and immediately slid close to him. There was something mechanical in all these movements, almost as if they were two gangsters on their way to commit a long-planned crime together. He knew that he ought to ask her which direction to take, because if he was driving her to her father's he would have to turn the car around, but he wanted to get away from here as quickly as possible. Luria might still rush out and stop them. The traffic light happened to be green and Grein drove some distance before he came to a red light. It even occurred to him to go through the light, because the road was empty. Something in him seemed to say, If you're transgressing, then you ought to break every law. He grew lighthearted and self-confident. He was possessed of the unholy joy of someone who has enlisted the help of the powers of darkness. Having seized his prey, he now ran with it like a fox with a goose. He was reminded of what Deuteronomy says about pillage: "When thou goest forth to war against thine enemies . . . and hast taken them captive." Yes, the beautiful woman enslaved there had also been someone else's wife, and that wasn't all: they had murdered not only her husband but her parents as well . . . They had given her a month in which to mourn them. His thoughts tumbled rapidly over each other without control, ranging widely through associations as disjointed as the chimeras and babbling of a dream. He breathed in deeply and stopped at a red light.

"Well, Anna . . ."

"Where are you going?" she asked in a muffled voice that was at once intimate and gruff.

"I don't know. In the middle of the night I lose all sense of direction."

"You're going uptown."

"Yes."

"Do you want to go to Harlem? Turn around."

"I thought you wanted to drive with me all night."

Anna was silent, as though thinking something over. Meanwhile, the light changed to green and he drove on. It had occurred to him more than once that a man driving a car spoke to a woman passenger in the same way that observant Jews once used to speak to all females—sideways, his face turned in another direction. That was how his father, Reb Jacob the Scribe, used to address women who came to him to have their mezuzahs checked.

He drove along a cross street to Fifth Avenue, and headed downtown. Stopping at a red light once more, he said to Anna, "What do we do now?"

Anna sat bowed and shrunken. It was good that it was dark and she did not have to look him in the eyes. The words barely passed her lips.

"Whatever you want."

"Our plan is to go first to a hotel and then to Tasmania."

"Yes."

So that means . . . Something spoke in him. He had scored a victory, perhaps the greatest victory in his life, but where was the joy, the celebration? Even passion seemed momentarily to have drained away. Everything had been reduced to one limited objective: to find a hotel in the middle of the night where a couple could arrive without luggage. On the dark avenue there were no such hotels. He had to drive past Central Park and west once again. Or perhaps he would find something on Third Avenue. No, it was too dirty there. He drove into the park. In the pre-dawn silence the park rose like a crystal palace, absorbed in its own beauty, illuminated with an extraterrestrial light. The lake shimmered like a copper mirror. The wind that blew in through the window carried with it intimations of an icy spring. The car emerged on Central Park West, almost opposite his home. Soon he found himself on Broadway. He said to Anna, "Now it's a pleasure to drive. I wish New York were always like this."

Anna did not reply.

He started slowly down Broadway, looking to see whether there was perhaps a hotel. Anna, also looking, turned her head. A car overtook him and he saw it was a police car. Are they going to arrest me? What would happen if the police stopped us? Where would I say we were going? But the police car soon disappeared. Grein spotted a hotel and stopped. He got out and held the door for Anna. A conscious silence had developed between them, a state in which words were superfluous and actions sufficed; they communicated like dumb animals, making themselves understood in the way prehistoric people—Neanderthal man or the primitives before him—had perhaps interacted with each other. Grein opened the door for Anna, and together they entered the lobby of a third-class hotel. Behind the desk sat an old man with a rectangular face, a long nose, bags under his eyes, thick lips. His eyes stared with the gelid weariness of one who did not sleep nights; his entire being exuded somnolence. His cranium was lumpy and furrowed, reminding Grein of freshly baked kugel. Something infinitely sorrowful and world-weary dulled his gaze, as though he were not a hotel clerk but an ascetic who sat here, cut off from all human vanities and, however much he might be surrounded by manifestations of karma, had long ago entered deeply into nirvana.

Grein asked, "Can I get a double room with a bath here?"

The clerk never moved. "Nine dollars."

"Can I leave the car here?"

"Your risk."

"Where's the room?"

"Pay in advance."

Grein took out a ten-dollar bill. The clerk slowly stretched out a hand as rigid as a robot's, and Grein said, "It's all yours."

"Thanks."

He passed Grein a book in which to sign his name, gave him a key, and pointed to the automatic elevator. Only now did Grein look at Anna, who had been standing behind him all the while as silent as one who ought to be ashamed but has abandoned all modesty. Her face expressed only stubbornness and a determination to accomplish what she had long desired. He walked with her to the elevator and they waited for it to come down; they went up in silence as though the state of intimacy they had achieved had now mysteriously separated and estranged them. They were like partners in an unlawful and dishonorable act which they were compelled to perform and from which they could not retreat. Perhaps this was the way murderers behaved on the way to dispose of their victims. The elevator stopped and Grein let Anna off first. It was dark in the corridor. Next to the wall lay a heap of sheets and towels. Grein examined the doors, but the room number was not to be found. He hurried back and forth while Anna stood waiting with the patience of someone who is prepared to let come what may.

"Where the devil is the room? Where is the room, damn it?" muttered Grein.

While Grein searched, a dread that had been lying in wait all the time overcame him: would the tension make him impotent? Knowing that this was more than possible, he felt it was already happening. An inner enemy, a power that derided and subverted from within, was preparing to betray him, to deny him his victory, to expose him to shame and ridicule. Grein tried to steel himself to defy this subversive force he himself could not identify: was his enemy his rational self or the moral qualms of his better nature? I must keep calm! he cautioned himself. I cannot lose control! But his movements already showed every sign of nervousness. Rushing back and forth, he grew agitated and angry. Had the clerk fooled him? Or had they come to the wrong floor? Suddenly he saw the room number at the same time Anna did. Opening the door and switching on the light, he found himself in a typical third-class-hotel room, with green walls, a wide bed in the center, a worn carpet, a greasy armchair. The bathroom was small and dirty, with a crumpled shower curtain and a tiled floor with pieces missing. Half to Anna, half to no one, he said, "Well, this is it."

"I haven't even got a toothbrush," she answered. "Just a second."

Still wearing her coat and hat, she went into the bathroom and shut the door. It was cold in the room. As Grein went over to the radiator and turned the heat up, he noticed a telephone. Perhaps I should call home? he wondered. I didn't tell Leah not to expect me back. But to wake her at four o'clock in the morning—if she was sleeping—made no sense. Perhaps the clerk would listen in. Such people were adept at blackmail. Grein suddenly remembered Luria. Had he deliberately arranged this? Or had he subconsciously wanted to bring Grein and Anna together? Was there some deep-laid scheme in all this? Well, I took the lure and I'll never be able to wriggle free again. What an imbroglio I've got myself into. Something in Grein laughed. How easy it had been for him to become ensnared! How utterly childish everyone is who seems to be an adult! He started rummaging in his pockets, searching for a candy or a piece of chewing gum that would take the place of a toothbrush and make his breath sweeter. But he found nothing. Having no other choice, he lit a cigarette. He stood in the middle of the room, inhaled the smoke deeply, and took stock of himself. He was preparing to do something against his interests, against all his convictions and principles. Like a criminal, he was preparing to commit a wrong in full awareness of the law and knowing in advance the consequences of his action both in this world and perhaps in the next. Nothing here has happened by chance; it was all premeditated, he said to himself. What does the Gemara call it? Sin out of lust for forbidden pleasure . . . and only today I was mouthing words about religion and religious discipline. Absurdly, he was overcome by something resembling piety. He felt a strong urge to appeal to the higher powers, to pray. But he dared not turn to God at the very moment he was breaking one of God's holiest laws. He felt that his lips were unclean. In such a condition one could not pray. One could only hope that God the Merciful would of His own accord show some compassion.

5

Boris Makaver fell asleep around one o'clock. In the middle of the night he started awake. On his night table stood a clock with a luminous dial. Glancing at it, he saw that it was half-past five. Well, he'd slept for four hours! He woke with a heaviness in his stomach and a tightness in his head. I had some kind of dream, but about what? he wondered. He could remember nothing of his dream, but it had left him with a sense of oppression and disquiet. Dear God, in dreams one lives another kind of life, he said to himself. He recalled what he had heard from Dr. Halperin, that according to one philosopher, the only reality was to be found in dreams. Possible. But in everyday life if one buys an apartment house, one owns a block of apartments and receives rent, while the apartments in dreams produce nothing tangible. Although one could argue the reverse: in dreams one can imagine that one is getting rent.

Boris got out of bed and went into the bathroom. With a dipper he performed the ritual of washing his hands, prescribed by Jewish Law, pouring water three times on his right hand and three on his left. Then he went into the room that held the Holy Ark and the lectern, the room he called his "little prayerhouse." Switching on the lights, he began to walk back and forth, praying in motion. This, he knew, was permitted before the morning star had risen. The chief prayers, to be recited only when standing still, were the repetition of "Hear, O Israel" and the Eighteen Benedictions. He recited the opening meditation of the morning service in Hebrew, translating the words to himself as he went along: "How goodly are thy tents, O Jacob, thy dwelling-places, O Israel. By Thy abundant grace I enter Thy house, and worship before Thy holy shrine . . ."

As Boris prayed, his brow furrowed. Where were they, all the saints, the holy ones, the pure who had died for the Sanctification of the Holy Name? Where were they, the six million whom the Nazis—may their names be erased—had burned, gassed, hanged, tortured? Where the mur-

derers were was clear: they sat in bars in Germany, drinking beer and
boasting of their atrocities. Germany was being rebuilt. America was sending billions. The world was filled with compassion for the suffering German
people. Even a few Jewish journalists bewailed the fate of Germany and
found all sorts of excuses for the Germans. Pah! There was no lack of
scum among today's Jews! For a few dollars, or to justify the Party line
at every turn, they would whitewash anything. But what about the victims?
They are here, here! Boris cried out within himself. They are all in Paradise. They have been found worthy to be a light which those of us trapped
in the darkness of the body cannot conceive. But if we assume for a moment, God forbid, that it isn't so, then there is no Judge and no Judgment,
then everything is arbitrary and Hitler, may his name perish, was right:
force is the only law. Then it's normal to play with the skulls of small
children and to order a father to dig a grave for himself and his family.
Then it would appear that the Creator Himself is, perish the thought, a
Nazi.

Boris shook himself out of these disturbing thoughts. With a groan, he
struck his forehead. How can we go on living when we know that among
the human species there are such bloodthirsty killers? After all, they shame
the image of God! Only by a hairsbreadth had he himself and Khanele, his
little Anna, escaped being trapped there among the most wicked of the
earth. Miracles had been performed for him, miracles! But why was it
fated that he should have been protected while devout Jewish children had
endured such suffering that by comparison death was a mercy? This was
solely because he, Boris Makaver, was too absorbed in the things of this
world to have been deemed worthy to die for the Sanctification of the
Holy Name. There had been no willingness to admit him to the company
of pure souls. He was a materialist, a maker of money, a glutton and a
drunkard—for that, he had been given an American visa and been sent to
the United States to get rich. Gorge yourself till you choke! A sacred
barrier divides you, ignorant boor, from God's beloved children, whom
He Himself—if it were possible to conceive Him so—has seated around
the Throne of Glory and to whom He now teaches the secrets of the
Torah.

An infinite sorrow overwhelmed him, an agonized cry of mourning tore
his insides. He wanted to howl out at the Master of the Universe as if to
a corporeal being: Dear God, for the sake of heaven, how long will you
be silent? How long, O Lord, how long will the wicked triumph? How
long will the darkness of Egypt endure?

Boris switched off the lights. Let it be dark! Why fool oneself with electric light? What kind of light is this that shines on whores, on murderers, on Nazis? He remained standing in the blackness. How odd it was: by day he was absorbed in commercial dealings like any businessman, but at night he was overcome by self-condemnation, an enormous remorse, a grief that harrowed his heart like physical pain. What am I doing? What am I doing? To what end are we all so feverishly buying and selling? I should sit on a low stool and mourn, not for seven days but forever. I should rend my garments and keen until my death, taking a piece of bread with water once a day and sleeping fitfully on a hard bench. What do those holy souls think when they look down from heaven and see Jews consumed by their businesses, as though there were nothing else, as if the greatest devastation in Jewish history had never taken place? Surely they are ashamed; perhaps they even curse this stiff-necked and perverse nation, this deformed and iniquitous people, these sons and brothers who do not even observe the customs of mourning. And who could be certain that those who had escaped might not at some future time be punished for their frozen hearts and meet, God forbid, miserable ends? Those in the World to Come would not remain silent.

In the impenetrable darkness, Boris found a chair, turned it over, as on Tisha b'Av, and sat down on it. He began to list in his mind the members of his own family who had been exterminated in Poland: his brother Dovid Meyer, his two sisters, their children, grandchildren, sons-in-law, daughters-in-law. Later in Russia those other bitter enemies of Israel, the Bolsheviks, had shot his brother Mordechai. Without restraint or compunction, they had shot, hanged, poisoned, burned—and he alone, the survivor, had escaped to bring the tidings to Job. But who was Job? What was he? Instead of rending his garments, binding up his loins in sackcloth, scattering ash on his head, and taking a potsherd to scrape his wounds, this Job merely puts up another office building in New York and decorates a salon. Woe to that Job who is a fool and does not even know that he is a Job! To such a Job, God would assuredly not speak out of the whirlwind.

Suddenly Boris heard the telephone ringing in his *cabinet*. Who could be calling now in the middle of the night? he asked himself. It must be a mistake. But the ringing did not stop. One could never be sure. Perhaps something terrible had happened. He rose and stumbled through the dark, bumping into a table, a chair, as he made his way to his study. There it was lighter, for the drapes had not been drawn. The sky above the rooftops was the color of copper; the night glowed as if with a self-generated light. Boris answered the telephone.

"Hello!"

"It's me," said Stanislaw Luria.

"What's happened?"

"Excuse me for telephoning. I'm deeply worried and very uneasy. Is Anna with you?"

"Anna? No. What's the matter?"

"Didn't she come to spend the night at your place?" Luria asked.

"No. Wait. I'll look. Perhaps she came and I didn't hear. Hold on."

Boris went straight to Anna's room. Yet he knew beforehand that she was not there, because he always slept lightly. The slightest rustle woke him. His feet dragged heavily. He opened the door to Anna's room and switched on the light. The harsh glare hurt his eyes. The bed was still made up.

"What kind of trouble is this?" he said aloud.

On the way back to his *cabinet* he bumped into furniture and hurt his knee. With great reluctance he picked up the receiver.

"She's not here. What's happened?"

"She left with Grein. She said he would drive her over to you, but I knew he was taking her to a hotel."

Boris Makaver's throat burned. "You're talking nonsense!"

"It's not nonsense. They're having an affair. She told me right out she loves him."

"How? After all, he has a wife and grown children."

"I'm not lying to you."

Boris was silent for a long time. He was clutching the receiver so tightly that he could feel a sharp pain in his wrist.

"Did he come up to your apartment?"

"Anna asked him up for coffee. Then she left with him."

"Perhaps, God forbid, something's happened to the car."

"Nothing's happened. They've gone to a hotel somewhere."

Again Boris paused a long time. Everything inside him grew heavy and quiet.

"Well, what can I do?" he answered. "I thought I had a daughter, but I haven't got even that."

"I warned you."

"When? . . . I thought you were—what's the expression?—green with envy. She denied everything vigorously. It never even entered my head. Well, I've earned it . . .''

And Boris returned to his little prayerhouse. He walked with a quiet step, feeling his way before him like a blind man. An inner darkness enveloped him, an emptiness he had never experienced before. It occurred to him that perhaps this was the way Jews had felt on their way to the gas chambers.

6

Grein fell asleep and woke with a start. He had dreamed something, but he could not recall what. God in heaven, he could not even remember who he was! Something in his brain had stopped functioning. He was alert to his own oblivion. This feeling, though it lasted only a few seconds, was staggering and bizarre. He was someone, but he did not know who. He was somewhere, but he did not know where. For a while everything was incomprehensible, as though he had emerged from a stupor. He stretched out a hand and touched a woman's back. In a moment he remembered who he was: Grein. But otherwise he had a case of amnesia. Who was this woman? And where was he? Was he at home? Was this Esther? In the dark it was impossible to know. He was forced to lie still for a few seconds until the blankness passed. Then he remembered his dream. He had been a guest somewhere, and with a spade or shovel he had been scraping away at his host's floor. How idiotic! But this had not been the whole dream. There had been someone else in it and something else had happened, something wild, disjointed, senseless, something that now, in full wakefulness, could no longer be recalled or blamed for having happened, because it could still not be fitted into his memory.

Suddenly his head cleared. It was Anna! He had come with her to this hotel, somewhere on Broadway. Before he had remembered nothing; now every detail returned. God in heaven, he had achieved what he most desired, what only yesterday had been an impossible fantasy. But was it only yesterday? Was it morning already? Some things still remained muddled in his mind. He was uncertain even about the date. But what was the difference? He had begun existence anew, as it were: satiated, filled with fear and with joy. No, he had not failed. Anna had reawakened in him a long-forgotten sexual prowess, restored his virility, and given him a vigor that was new, new . . .

He made a movement to wake her, but Anna resisted sleepily. She was too tired. He was tired himself, but with the kind of fatigue that rejects sleep. The hotel room was cold, and it occurred to him that a coat was lying on the blanket—probably his own. He stretched out a hand, groping for something to lean on, a chair or a wall, but he flailed in a void. Where was the door? Where was the window? he wondered. He felt like a child who wakes and does not know whether he is lying lengthwise or crosswise in his bed. The pillow rested against nothing. Well, I don't dare wake her, he decided. He lay quietly, thinking back to the beginning of that night. How had all this happened? he mused. I went to dinner at Boris Makaver's. Then I left with them and went up to drink coffee. They quarreled. But what actually took place? What did they actually say? Why did she leave? Grein was missing vital links in the chain of cause and effect. It happened, and that was all. Some force, or a combination of forces, had brought him here, and here he was, together with her. But what was Stanislaw Luria doing now? Did he imagine she was at her father's? Perhaps Luria had telephoned Boris Makaver in the middle of the night. Well, it's a fine mess, something in Grein observed. This is probably how a killer feels after the murder, the thought ran through him. Murdered and *basta*! One can't bring the victim back to life. One can only hide.

Grein probed his feelings for remorse, but he was a criminal with no regrets. He was merely astonished at the tangled web he had woven so ineptly, and he was a little afraid of the consequences. Boris Makaver would go berserk.

Stanislaw Luria would raise all hell. With Esther, well, things were bad as it was. Leah . . . at the name Leah Grein's ruminations lurched to a halt. That name fenced in, as it were, the free run of his thoughts. He had wronged Leah for years, but this was the first time he had not spent the night at home without offering an excuse. Leah would swallow any number of stories and lies, but never the naked truth. This was the straw that would break the camel's back. This would finally destroy his home. And what about Jack? and Anita? and the business? But what did all that matter compared with Anna? Leaning toward her, he started kissing her with childlike eagerness and the heedlessness of those for whom day and night have been turned upside down.

Anna resisted awhile, clutching at the last moments of sleep. Then she suddenly asked in a wide-awake voice: "What's the time?"

"I don't know. I only know that I'm happy and I love you."

Anna sat bolt upright with startling abruptness. The mattress springs twanged dully under her. She embraced him like a little girl, just as she had done long ago in Warsaw when he brought her a gift and she would leap up to him in delight. Everything had begun anew.

The darkness steadily lifted. A glimmer of light penetrated it, causing what physicists would call a chain reaction. One white circle begat another, speckling the blackness until Grein knew that, outside, the dawn had come. The papered walls in the room grew gray. Grein could already see the door, the window, part of the armchair. He withdrew from Anna, turning his back to her. She did the same. Bodies, like batteries, need to be re-charged. But everything remained: the love, the lust, the fear of the new day. Jerking up the blanket, he covered his face as the ordinary worshipper does in a synagogue when the priestly caste offers the congregation the ritual blessing on the High Holy Days. He did not want to watch the sun rise, the day break. He shut his eyes tightly, warming himself in his own body heat. He was awake, but his interrupted dream tried to pick up the dropped stitches, its knitting needles clicking rapidly and quietly. What was sleeping slept; what was awake paid attention. Who said that one can't be asleep and awake at the same time? Where is it written that one can't be happy and unhappy simultaneously? Leah is Leah and Esther is Esther and the children are the children. Oh, how cold the air is! Don't they provide any heat? Although the window did not overlook the street, even from here one could catch the sounds of New York awakening. A truck revved its motor, gasping repeatedly like a mortally wounded monster hovering between life and death . . . *khakh-khakh, khakh-khakh.* A car ground its gears. Were there birds here in New York? Yes, there were. One let out a cry: a single flat squawk, signaling that it was day in the bird family. Yes, I love her, Grein murmured to himself. The whole thing is inevitable . . . it's fated, destined. Once again he found himself in that other apartment and—how comical!—once again he was scraping away at his friend's floor. Now he knew who the friend was, and he wanted to laugh at his own dream and his own foolishness. What does his floor matter to me? And how can one smooth it without a plane? Truly, it was ridiculous.

His consciousness became even more blurred as the dream world took over, leaving behind only one point, one sensible drop in a stream of absurdity. The floor was rough. It had to be smoothed. But why him, Grein? Was this his trade? Had he given up Wall Street? Anna tossed about on the bed, dragging some of the blanket off him. He gasped at the early-morning cold. He couldn't possibly permit this, because while love is love, cold is cold. Grein grabbed back the blanket and pulled it over him. For a while they struggled for possession of it, two birds with one worm. Finally they came to a compromise: a bit for you and a bit for me. Unwittingly she gave him a shove with her foot. He laughed inwardly: the Battle of the Blanket. Suddenly Anna turned around to face him, and nestling close to him, she clasped him around the ribs as if to say: If we must freeze, let's freeze together. She panted against him with renewed ardor, a revived intimacy; she was his, his.

3

When Professor Shrage left Boris Makaver's that night, he did not have far to go—merely to cross Broadway and walk in the direction of Central Park. Mrs. Clark, with whom he was a boarder, lived in an apartment between Columbus Avenue and Central Park West. But he found the route difficult to remember. Although he had lived in New York since 1939, he had not fully oriented himself. As a rule, instead of walking east, he went west. He could never tell what was uptown from what was downtown. The Warsaw émigrés made fun of him: a professor of mathematics who couldn't make head or tail of street numbers. He himself believed that his blundering about New York could be explained only in Freudian terms: it was rooted in his subconscious and must have a symbolic meaning. Moreover, Professor Shrage's eyes took in less and less. There was nothing physically wrong with his sight, yet his ability to see was continually diminished. Even by day he saw as if through a mist. Black spots floated before him. At night his vision virtually vanished altogether.

Three times the traffic lights changed before he found the courage to cross the road. The rows of automobiles on either side growled at him, snarling and hissing as if competing to run him over. Fearfully he discerned an enemy in every motorcar; the drivers behind their wheels were merely waiting for the signal to hurl themselves forward. Some cars would not stand still, boiling and rumbling with the malignity of bridled beasts. Professor Shrage shuffled along, tapping his cane like a blind man. He held his breath so as not to inhale the stench of gasoline and oil. These were not people hurrying to get home but the wicked inhabitants of Sodom, who venomously propelled their machines at full speed, whirling themselves around in the Sling of Gehenna. They had no choice, it would seem, for on the eve of every holiday the newspapers confidently foretold how many would be killed and how many maimed; yet despite this they hurtled along insensately, whipped into a frenzy of speed like multitudes of demons. Many of them called themselves Jews, sending money to Palestine and wearing skullcaps above their clean-shaven mugs.

Professor Shrage edged his way across one lane and stopped to rest for a while at the divider. How odd: in Warsaw it had never once occurred to him that he was small, but here in New York giants strode about, true sons of Anak, described in Numbers, in whose sight the spies sent by Moses were as grasshoppers. The pounding and rasping never stopped, even late at night. The professor walked along on sidewalk grates lit from below, covering cavities where subway trains rattled incessantly. Over the rooftops an airplane thundered past, flashing a string of lights and roaring ferociously. Young men yelled, young women giggled. Above the cinemas, blazing lights shone on posters of monsters, harlots, cutthroats. This was their entertainment. Set back from the street was an Automat; people were shoving violently against its sides, pouring out all kinds of liquors, like those who knew the secrets of the Cabala and could tap wine from walls. Directly across the way was a funeral parlor displaying a garish illuminated sign as if it were a store with something to sell. So this was America.

The professor leaned on his stick. Was it any wonder that the human species had grown blind to higher matters? How could spirits exist in the midst of such a bacchanalia? Souls, too, needed the proper ambience. What, for example, did one who had passed on think of such a charnel house? Well, I have only one request of the higher powers: let me not die here in this chaos of lost souls. It would be better to fall into the sea.

Professor Shrage had a key to the outer door of the apartment building, but every time he had to use it he was compelled to grope about for a long while before he found the keyhole. The slot seemed to vanish, and however much he fumbled he could never find the opening. Inanimate things played hide-and-seek with him, flustering and bamboozling him. Did imps really exist, then? Everything was alive. Every object was possessed by a spirit: a key, a doorknob, a pen, a coin. How often didn't his slippers disappear? Ten times he would search for them under the bed and they wouldn't be there. By the eleventh time, they stood plainly before him as if nothing had happened. Apparently every single object could hide itself, could see while remaining itself unseen. What were rays of light after all? Vibrations in the ether, or however one wanted to describe them. These days, both hypotheses were accepted, Newton's corpuscular theory and Huygens's wave theory. But how could both possibly be true? The whole matter of light was pure spirituality . . . The professor eventually found the keyhole and unlocked the door. The stairs were pitch-dark. Somewhere there was a light switch, but the professor had to start his endless fumbling all over again. Wherever had it got to? It used to be here on the left, but now the wall was smooth. What have they got against me, all these contraptions? They're obviously hostile to me. For every force there is an equal opposing force. I don't like them, so they don't like me. Never mind, I'll climb up in the dark.

Clutching the banister tightly, the professor slowly mounted the stairs. Although he could not bear New York's neon signs, he also had a great dread of the dark. He was conscious of all the specters astir here in the blackness, lying in wait, fully prepared to harm and terrify those in blank despondency. How could the wicked ever have gained power if behind each of them there had not stood a fiend? Around every Hitler, around every Nazi, around every Bolshevik clustered innumerable evil spirits which infused him with brutality. According to the Cabala, the Evil Spirit strives forever upward, trying to reach even the Sphere of Emanations . . . The professor became aware of a humming, a buzzing as if countless termites were consuming the dwelling, undermining its foundations. Who could know? Perhaps even at this moment the central support on which the whole building rested was crumbling away and would collapse this very night.

At the door, the professor took out another key, which opened the apartment, but Mrs. Clark, it turned out, was not yet asleep and she opened the door herself. She stood on the threshold in a long dressing gown, slippers with pom-poms, her face smeared with night cream and her dyed hair caught up in a net. Short and stout, she had a deeply wrinkled forehead and cheeks. Above her snub nose were set a pair of small black eyes, crafty and oily. She had already taken out her false teeth, so that a void lay behind her thick lips.

Henrietta Clark was the widow of a Boston aristocrat, but she herself had been born somewhere in Galicia or Bukovina. Her father had been a ritual slaughterer. For many years her late husband had devoted himself to psychic research, and it had been he, Edwin Clark, that Professor Shrage had come to visit in 1939. Clark had sent him the necessary affidavit. But during the weeks that the professor's ship was sailing toward America, Clark died. He had children by a former marriage and left no will. Henrietta inherited very little of the estate, but she was by profession a dentist, having studied in New York before her marriage. She had moved back to New York, opened a practice there, and acquired a wealthy clientele. In her spare time, she practiced automatic writing and automatic painting with the help of her control, "Madgie," and organized séances. She published letters in journals for psychic research and in all manner of occult publications. It was she who had taken care of Professor Shrage during the terrifying years of Hitler's Holocaust, when his wife and family had all perished at the hands of the Nazis.

Henrietta spoke to the professor sometimes in English, sometimes in German, and occasionally in broken Yiddish. Now she remarked, "My goodness, I was already beginning to worry that you'd got lost."

"Got lost? No."

"How are the Warsaw folk over there? Still talking in circles?"

"Yes, always."

"Come in. Take off your coat. I have a message for you."

Something trembled inside Professor Shrage. "Where from?"

"From automatic writing. I also have Edzhe's picture."

"Well . . ."

The professor took off his coat. He was overcome by both curiosity and disgust. She's playing with my life, he thought. He accompanied her into the middle room, the *atelier*, as she called it. She switched on a solitary lamp in the big room, all four walls of which were covered with Henrietta's paintings. From the gloom there emerged hazy figures with veiled faces dragging amorphous trains like the tails of comets. Devils with horns and scales stretched out long black fingers with sharp-pointed nails. Angels spread out golden wings. Here, too, were pictures relating to theosophy: the faces of unseen tumescences, wheels that symbolized different kinds of consciousness, as well as the Third Eye, the Silver Rope, the Springs of Achievement, and the Races of Atlantis. On an old desk, crowded with papers, journals, paintbrushes and paints, lay an open notebook in which were a dozen or so lines of tiny mirror writing. Henrietta gave it to him.

"Go to the mirror and read the letter."

"You know I find it difficult."

"Well, I'll read it to you:

My dearest David, in a month's time it will be thirty years since we joined our souls together in a bond which can never be sundered. The Nazi murderers burned my body in a lime pit, but my soul is with my nearest and dearest, with my parents and yours, with my sisters and brothers and yours. The children are also with me. They have grown up and have received a very high level of education here. They are extremely handsome and enormously proud of their father, whom they love very very much. We are all here together, one happy crowd, and we often discuss your situation. Be strong, don't lose hope. You still have much to accomplish in the Vale of Tears. The Masters look upon you with love and wait for you to reveal the truth to those who remain sunk in darkness.

"Is that all?"

"Here's the picture."

From somewhere under the clutter, Mrs. Clark produced a sheet of stiff paper bearing a watercolor painting of a legless figure supposed to represent Professor Shrage's wife, Edzhe, with an aureole around her head and wings on her back, surrounded by red-and-green stripes and multicolored spangles. The professor brought the paper close to his eyes. This was not Edzhe, though it bore a vague resemblance to her. Mrs. Clark had Edzhe's photograph. He peered at the painting, breathing heavily through his nose as if he were sleeping while wide-awake. This was all lies, falsehood, and deception, he thought, but it did not necessarily follow that Edzhe was not here. Did the North Pole cease to exist because Frederick Cook had fraudulently claimed to have discovered it? Not at all—the desire to deceive proved that a truth lay behind the deception. Idols themselves bear witness to the existence of God.

Putting down the paper, he went to his room.

I'm tired, tired. Who knows? Perhaps my last night has finally come, the thought flitted through his mind. Professor Shrage removed one of his shoes and rested. Then he took off the other shoe. Somewhere he had a hanger on which to replace his suit. If I die, let them at least not bury me in creased clothes. The hanger should have been behind the door, but he couldn't find it. Well, it's playing hide-and-seek again. The professor placed his garments on a chair. The room had electricity, but he could not bear the bright light. Should I go blind, let me be used to doing things in the dark. Lying down on his bed, he covered himself with the blanket. A verse from Job occurred to him: "I should have slept; then had I been at rest." Everything was in the Bible.

He heard footsteps. Mrs. Clark opened the door slightly.

"Are you asleep?"

"No, I'm just lying down."

"Have you hung up your suit?"

"The hanger has disappeared."

"How silly! I've told you a thousand times to hang up your suit. To-morrow you'll walk around looking like a beggar."

"It's draped on the chair."

"Well, I'll hang it up. My blessed Edwin also used to misplace things. But he was as tidy a creature as Nature can make."

The professor made no reply. He heard Mrs. Clark sitting down in the armchair, on the very suit she was urging him to take care of.

"Professor, what's the matter with you?"

"Nothing, nothing."

"I give you a message and you don't say a word. Are you angry with me?"

"Why should I be angry? You saved my life. You've done me countless kindnesses. I'll never be able to repay you."

"To judge from the way you behave, a person might think I've done you nothing but harm."

"No, my dear, only good. But one needs strength for everything, even for gratitude."

"You know all the answers, but you lack the will to be healthy. After Edwin's death, the doctors gave me up for dead as well. All my vital organs had virtually stopped functioning. They recommended I have an operation for gallstones, but they couldn't guarantee that my heart would hold out. I made up my mind that I must get well. I simply had to build up everything from scratch again."

"Well, you were younger."

"You lack faith, Professor, that's what you lack. Why do I do all this for you? People say all sorts of nasty things about us. But you know the truth. I want to help you, professor, because the world needs people like you. We are witnesses to the birth of a new civilization. We need learned people who know the law of cause and effect. The law of karma is no longer sufficient. For the first time the Ashram of Shambhala is descending directly, not through the hierarchy of the Masters . . ."

"Yes, yes."

"Professor, I know what you want, and you'll soon have it."

"What do I want? I don't know myself."

"Edzhe will show herself to you in her body. You will speak to her and embrace her . . . just as if she were alive."

The professor seemed to freeze.

"When? Is this possible?"

"Yes, it is possible. And it'll happen sooner than you think."

4

By dawn there was a fresh fall of snow and early morning was frosty and sunny. The inhospitable hotel room was filled with sunlight that gave an early-morning glow to the rumpled bedclothes, the threadbare carpet and the wrinkled wallpaper. It shone on Anna's face, in her eyes, on every silver dot on her velvet hat. She sat in an armchair fully dressed, in her coat and snow boots. Grein, also in coat and hat, was half sitting, half leaning on the bed. He said to Anna, "Yes, we must do it. Nothing decrees that we should be unhappy our whole lives. We can be happy together. Now I have no doubt at all."

After a pause, Anna said, "You are my husband and I am your wife. You're the person closest to me in the whole world. You and Papa."

She paused again, and then added, "I'm certain Luria telephoned him. At this moment, Papa is probably cursing me with the deadliest of curses. But he'll make peace. Only yesterday he said he loved you like his own son. Papa doesn't speak such words casually. He regards someone who doesn't know a little Talmud as only half a person. Another thing: in your own way, you're religious, while Luria is always boasting about his atheism."

"What we've done isn't very religious."

"No, but we'll get married. You can't hold anyone by force. Papa is rich, richer than you can imagine, and everything he has is ours. We can be happy together for many years."

Grein got up. Anna also rose, and they embraced and kissed long and passionately. Her mouth open, she bit into him with the voraciousness of an animal that cannot sate itself however much it devours. Their weariness evaporated and they stood against each other with the self-absorption of those who are consumed by lust. Clasping her close, Grein was astonished at himself. Sexual arousal always amazed him, coming as it did both from within a man and from outside him. It sapped his strength completely; through it, he felt, a person became one with *das Ding an sich*, with the very essence of being that lay behind the shell of illusions.

To reach Grein, Anna had to stand on tiptoe. He bent down toward her. For a while he seemed to forget about the dirty room, the sleepless night, the sin he had committed against her husband, her father, his family, Esther. The body did things of its own accord, in its own manner. They had possessed each other all night, yet now they desired each other afresh. Anna tore herself away from him, and her lips seemed as crimson and lacerated as a wound. She reminded Grein of a lioness in the zoo that briefly lifts her bloody mouth from the chunk of raw meat thrown to her. The look she gave him was charged with the intensity of love.

"We can't stay here!"

To Grein it seemed that her words had a hidden meaning, as if she had really meant to say: We must leave this Garden of Eden on our own, before they drive us out. He paused awhile, to still the seething desire within him. They gazed at each other with the anguish and sorrow of two creatures who had become totally dependent upon each other.

"What do you want to do?" he asked.

"You won't believe it, but I'm hungry—terribly hungry."

"Everything's terrible for you. Come, we'll eat soon."

"What will you give me? Ah, I could eat you up alive!"

"Many spiders do that."

"Come, we'll get coffee. Then I'll have to go, either to him or to Papa. Wherever I go, I'll walk into an uproar."

"We can drive off somewhere together . . ."

"I can't be without clothes, without underwear. I need my things. You can't just run away either."

"No."

"I'll go home. Let him say what he has to say. I won't deny anything. I'm not afraid of anyone. That's the truth."

"How will I contact you?"

"Call me on the telephone."

"And what if he answers? I can't face that."

"Speak to him plainly: say you love me and I love you. He can't keep me by force. I don't have to coach you what to say to your wife. You'd better know one thing: there aren't any half measures with me. If I want someone, I want him totally and completely."

Grein took Anna by the arm and they went out. He had nothing to take with him except the key. He glanced behind him: soon they would change the bed linen, rinse out the bath, and no sign would remain of the extraordinary night they had spent here, except for those vestiges or chemical reactions in the mind that people call memory. In the corridor a bulb glowed dully in the daylight. The pile of sheets and towels lay in the same place as the night before. A black chambermaid, carrying a bucket and a mop, passed them. On her way, she threw a glance at Grein and Anna that seemed to echo the words of Ecclesiastes: "All things are full of labor . . . There is no remembrance of former things; neither shall there be any remembrance of things that are to come."

A door opened and another couple came out. The man carried a blue satchel with red-and-white stripes. Both couples walked toward the elevator. The other man was apparently a South American. He looked Latin, with pitch-black hair, a close-clipped mustache, sideburns, and brightly colored clothes that spoke temptingly of summer and tropical climates. His companion was short, with a high bosom and spreading hips. The lineaments of her face pointed to Indian descent.

The elevator arrived, and while it ejected a woman carrying a huge bundle of laundry, the two men dickered briefly over who should enter first. At the desk where the old man had sat the night before, there now stood a young man with curly hair. This one, the early bird, was as lively and exuberant as the night clerk had been gelid and stiff. He appraised the couples with an experienced eye, pursing his lips as if about to whistle. His sparkling eyes seemed to say: I understand, I understand . . . I overlook, I overlook.

Grein put down the key without a word. Before he opened the outside door, he looked rapidly around to both right and left. They might easily run into one of his or Anna's acquaintances here. The hotel was situated not very far from Boris Makaver's apartment building. A passage from Proverbs suddenly flashed through Grein's mind: "Such is the way of the adulterous woman: she eateth, and wipeth her mouth, and saith, I have done no wickedness." He was somehow embarrassed by this verse. It had come unbidden, of its own accord, for no apparent reason, like the verses from Scripture one finds on one's lips when one is startled from sleep. Grein recognized the car. It was held fast and partially covered over by a thick pile of snow, like the relic of an already half-buried civilization.

2

While the car was eager to go, one wheel preferred to stay put. It spun rapidly on its axle. Anna was already seated inside. A group of children gathered around. Grein returned to the hotel for a shovel. It was very odd to stand here, fifteen blocks from Boris Makaver's apartment, three blocks from Central Park West, shoveling snow. He didn't have sunglasses with him and the glare dazzled his eyes. Though frost crackled all about him, he broke into a sweat. At the beginning he worked vigorously, but the shovel soon told the real truth: he was a middle-aged man.

How the snow had altered Broadway! Whole mountains had fallen, ice-blue, sparkling as if with gems. Icicles still hung from ledges and eaves. Snowplows were clearing the snow, heaping it up in piles that front-end loaders dumped into trucks. The sun was already high in the sky, luminous with white light, its center fine gold; smoke ascended to it from the white roofs, as if the buildings were altars on which sacrifices were being offered in its name. The air pulsed and tingled. The passing automobiles no longer roared but blared as though with trumpets. In the distance, the Hudson shimmered, half-frozen, half-flowing, polished like a mirror, full of gold, full of fire.

Over the elevated New Jersey shore, an afterglow steeped the sky in the indigo of twilight. A factory studded with windows refracted the light across the river: glassy, translucent, pure, it glimmered in the haze like a fugitive image on a photograph.

From the hotel someone brought out a small wooden block to put under the wheel. The car lurched forward and moved away. Grein did not know which foot was which; he no longer knew which was the accelerator and which the brake. Anna snuggled close to him as she had done the night before. Her knee touched his. I only hope my bliss doesn't end up killing her, he cautioned himself. Although he intended to drive uptown, in the direction of Columbia University, he ended up going downtown. As he drove past Boris Makaver's apartment building, the traffic light changed to red, and Grein glanced into the courtyard with the emotions of a criminal returning to the scene of his crime. The little garden was piled high with mounds of snow; the fence posts wore snowcaps. Lumps of snow hung from the tree like white fruits. At any moment Boris or Reytze might come out. A boyish irresponsibility possessed Grein: God had abandoned the world. It was once more the domain of idols and idol worship.

The car passed Lincoln Square and continued to roll down Broadway. Although this was no longer Broadway but a thoroughfare in the most ancient of pagan cities: Rome, Athens, or even Carthage. Here the idols had their worshippers and priests. Their effigies stared down from snow-covered billboards—raging murderers, naked whores. In front of a theater, young women jostled and shoved. They were waiting to see an idol. In a window, a man clad in white garments and wearing a tall white hat roasted meat over glowing coals. In another window gigantic lobsters twitched atop blocks of ice. Cacophonous music—screams of lust and the shrieks of the tortured—blared from an open door. Tiny figures swarmed all over a building, painting a huge female image, each of its legs four stories high. Hirelings stood in doorways urging passersby to enter. The air stank of smoke and slag, of booze and burning.

Grein tried to park the car but there was practically no place open. He was about to take a vacant spot when a blond, red-faced fellow with hair like a hog's bristles hooted loudly and swore at him. Grein drove into a parking garage. Anna took his arm. "Today our honeymoon starts."

They started walking, looking for a restaurant. Grein opened one door and shut it again. Finally they entered an establishment that combined a restaurant and a bar. The ceiling was dotted with light fixtures that scarcely alleviated the gloom. A solitary drinker was seated at the counter, swaying over an empty glass. The tables were set but no one was sitting at them. The mirrors reflected one another. A long-forgotten melancholy overcame Grein, the feeling of someone who has reached the end of the road. He murmured to Anna, "At least we won't meet your father here."

They settled themselves in a booth and ordered the kind of dishes consumed by people who, having scorned the normal progress of day and night, have lost their bearings. They asked for orange juice and cognac, omelettes and chicken. The waiter, intuiting their fatigue, began bustling about. He switched on a table lamp that diffused shadows rather than light. In the silence of those who have no more strength, Grein and Anna ate and drank.

The empty room started to fill up. The men who came in were tall, thickset, muscular, faithful sentinels of Baal and Ashtaroth. They brought with them the kine of Bashan described by Amos, fat and sinful women, hennaed, painted, with nails the color of blood. In huddles, they groped, drank, smoked, guffawed. Grein poured liquor for Anna and himself. She clinked her glass against his. Then she lit a cigarette and the smoke swathed her face like a veil. He heard her say, "If I can't be happy with you, then no happiness exists."

"Yes, we'll be happy," he echoed her.

Grein leaned his head against the wall, noting how the fumes of alcohol rose from his stomach to his brain. Everything suddenly became indistinct, wavered, lacked coherence. Was he really prepared to leave Leah? Did he really love Anna that much? Was he willing to start a new family with her, have other children by her? How had all this happened? How does one rush into such things? In truth, he didn't have enough strength even to be amazed. His whole life had been one long improvisation. He had wanted to study natural science, but instead he had enrolled in the philosophy faculty. He had made up his mind to remain a bachelor, but he'd married the first girl who kissed him. He had dreamed of the academic life, but he had emigrated to America and had become a broker on Wall Street. Now, without the slightest compunction, he had grabbed the wife of Stanislaw Luria and the daughter of Boris Makaver. He would be cursed for what he had done, and bring others grief. He had noted in his diary that whoever violated the Ten Commandments set himself on the road to physical and spiritual ruin, and still he had broken them.

"What are you thinking, dearest?"

"Oh, nothing."

"You're thinking something, my darling. Believe me, it's not easy for me either. It's more difficult than you imagine."

The waiter brought the check. Grein tipped him a dollar, rose, and helped Anna put on her coat. His legs were unsteady under him, and the walls of the restaurant swayed as though he were on board a ship. He paid and went outside with Anna. The sun had gone. The snow had been trodden underfoot. The sky was overcast. A gray wintry day, cold and oppressive, enveloped New York and its overpowering thumping, grating, clatter, and haste. Anna took Grein's arm and for a while they walked in silence.

"I still have a thousand things to do today!" she said. "I must go home at once."

"I'll drive you there."

"No, I'll take a taxi. Call me at seven o'clock. I'll be waiting by the telephone."

"Yes, my darling."

"Remember: I don't want any favors from you. If you consider this just another affair, don't drag me into any of your filth."

"You're talking nonsense," he answered. "This is the happiest day of my life."

She looked at him sideways, appraising him, evaluating his words. Her glanced seemed to ask: If he's lying, what's the point of it?

She waved for a taxi but none stopped. She clung to Grein's arm with unusual firmness. He noticed how short she was. Even in shoes and snow boots she barely came up to his shoulder. They stood side by side, simultaneously close and far apart, with the chagrin of those whom fate has betrayed. A taxi pulled over, and Anna tore herself away from him.

"Seven o'clock!"

And she blew him a kiss.

The taxi rolled away. For a while Grein followed her with his eyes. Then he headed back to the parking garage for his car. Although he was in a hurry he walked slowly, with the abstractedness of someone doing something against his will, against all logic, propelled by an alien hand, driven by a hidden force.

3

He drove his car to the apartment building on Central Park West. There was even a place to park. How short the days were in winter! He got out and stood for a while. Twilight was already closing in. He should have gone to the bank, but now it was too late. He had also intended to call his office, but now he was too tired. He was cold, his nose was stuffy, and his skull was tight. Every part of him longed to lie down, to rest, to sleep. Am I getting sick? he wondered. The elderly doorman was shoveling snow away. In the lobby sat the umbrella stand usually put out on rainy days. Grein waited at the elevator in the silence and humility that come from deep anxiety. Was Leah at home? Did the children know what he had done? It wasn't the first time he hadn't slept in his bed, but this

time he had no excuse. He hadn't even called Leah. Was he really prepared
to leave her? Could he deliberately destroy a life, bring shame on those
who were faithful to him? Could he twist injustice into justice, wrong into
right?

The elevator man prattled on about the weather. The radio was fore-
casting snow, winds, frosts. Even this early the Gentile was half-drunk.
Grein unlocked his front door. It was dark in the entryway. On the commode lay the mail and Grein glanced through it in the half-gloom—*The
Wall Street Journal*, the Dow Jones Index, a newsletter from the synagogue
in which he worshipped on the High Holy Days, a solicitation from some
charitable institution. Well, who would write to me? Grein mutely greeted
this meager correspondence. He paused and listened attentively; no, Leah
was not at home. Jack definitely not. Anita was probably in her room, but
one didn't hear the slightest sound from her at the best of times. The
apartment smelled of overheating and stale cooking odors; it was heavy
with the stillness of a dwelling that houses only adults. Passing the kitchen,
Grein went into the dinette. On the table lay a left-wing weekly. Jack had
evidently spent the night and eaten his breakfast here. How odd, a single
fly was still alive in the room, in the middle of winter. It hugged the lip
of the sugar bowl, lost in the abstraction of a being that has outlived its
time and should be dead. The kitchen window faced south, and from it
one could see the buildings of Central Park South, the skyscrapers of
Rockefeller Center, and the Empire State Building. The twilight mist deepened. Here and there a window was already lit up, and the sharp electric
light sent a glow through the haze. A solitary airplane flew overhead,
shrieking like some monstrous bird. The Central Park reservoir was framed
in snow like a silver mirror. In the evening dusk, New York appeared still,
white, a city without people, a forgotten settlement locked in ice on the
shores of the Arctic Ocean. Even the rows of automobiles winding along
the roads in Central Park had a mechanical emptiness about them, like toys
that had been wound up and now moved automatically. The window was
open a crack and cold air blew in.

Grein looked out, staring blankly in front of him, wordlessly ruminating.
To wreck homes? To destroy people? Had he been sent into the world
only for this? He felt chilly and shut the window. For a while he wandered
about in the corridor. He wanted to switch on the lights, but didn't. He
felt a sudden urge to speak to one of the members of his household, as if
to prove to himself that he still belonged here, that he was still head of
his family.

He knocked on Anita's door, but there was no response. He pushed at the door and it opened. The room was filled with an early-morning disorder, as if Anita had only just awakened from sleep. The bed was rumpled; clothes, books, and magazines were scattered over the desk, the chairs, the floor. Anita stood in the middle of it all in creased pajamas and shabby slippers, tall, angular, flat-chested, her auburn hair (like her grandmother's) disheveled, her narrow face covered in freckles. Each time Grein saw her he was astonished. Anita resembled neither him nor her mother. Every time he had exactly the same feeling: that her limbs were wasting away like those of someone in a coma. Her cheeks were sunken, her nose sharp, her chin pointed, her forehead high. Her green eyes stared at him with the fear of an animal disturbed in its burrow.

"Oh, Father!"

"Why didn't you answer when I knocked?"

"I did."

"Why is there such a mess in here?"

Anita was silent.

"Where's your mother?"

"At the shop. As usual."

Father and daughter had been at loggerheads for some time now. After Anita had dropped out of college, Grein steered clear of her. To tell the truth, Grein was no happier with Jack. The young man was a radical leftist, virtually a Communist. He chased girls. He came and went as if the house were a hotel. But at least he had made something of himself. He was almost licensed as an engineer. He had been offered a job. Anita had not studied, had not looked for any employment, had no female friends. She was everything at once: egotistical, melancholic, insolent, rebellious. But what did she want? Whom was she fighting? She spent days on end alone, read trashy novels, wrote bad poetry that editors returned to her. She locked herself up in the house as if in a jail. Leah maintained that their daughter was psychologically disturbed and that they ought to send her to a psychiatrist, but Grein had no faith in psychiatrists and Anita didn't want to be helped. At nineteen, the young woman had no way out.

"What happened with your job?" Grein asked, for the sake of saying something.

Anita tensed. "Nothing came of it."

"Why not?"

"They didn't want to pay decently."

Grein frowned. Why should they pay her high wages? What were her qualifications? Where did today's generation get the idea that they should be given everything they asked for? He had a sudden urge to quarrel with her, but he controlled himself. Now wasn't the time to start a new war.

"Aren't you going out?"

"Not today."

"When, then?"

"When it's warm."

Anita always spoke this way, with the result that all attempts at conversation with her soon petered out. Her remarks were terse, abrupt, to the point. After a moment Grein shut the door. Does she know I didn't spend the night at home? No, probably not.

In this household, people went their separate ways. Anita apparently had only one desire—to be left alone. She dropped hints with mystical overtones. She gave Grein to understand, for example, that he, her father, had consumed her just portion of life in this world. He had taken too much for himself and had left nothing for her. Jack behaved like a complete stranger. Since Leah had opened her antiques shop and become a businesswoman, she spent the whole day either there or at auctions. Along with objets d'art, she dealt in furs which rich women sold after only a few years' wear. The times when Leah had depended totally on her husband and had fought to be with him were long past. He had pushed her aside for so many years that she had developed her own interests. Leah, too, set herself against him, with the passive opposition of one who loves but is not loved in return.

Although no one here followed a routine, a kind of order had been established. The cleaning woman had a key to the apartment. Leah left her pay in a drawer, and the woman helped herself to food from the refrigerator. Once a week Leah telephoned a supermarket and ordered food supplies. The elevator man opened the door for the delivery boy and put all the perishables—the butter, cheese, milk, and meat—in the refrigerator. Each week Leah stocked up for only one meal—breakfast. Grein, Jack, and Leah herself all ate lunch and supper in restaurants. Anita virtually fasted all day, getting by on an egg, a glass of milk, a banana. There had been a time when the whole family had gone to a restaurant together on Sundays, but in the last few years Jack and Anita had wriggled out of even these weekly meals.

No, Grein really did not understand America. He complained at every opportunity that American minds functioned according to categories different from those that operated in Europe, that people born here were the biological antitheses of Europeans. Nonetheless, Americanness had entered his bones.

4

G rein went into the bedroom and only now realized how exhausted he was. He had to lie down immediately. He did not even remove the taffeta bedspread or take off his jacket and shoes. Neither asleep nor awake, he lay and listened to his weariness.

His marriage to Leah had been rocky for a long time. He had always kept someone else, apart from her. In the last few years, solely on account of his infidelities, Leah had become frigid and thrown herself into her antiques business with excessive zeal. Of course, she was no longer young. Grein suspected that she was actually older than he was. In the village where she was born, the town records had been burned during the First World War, and Leah had a birth certificate made out on the testimony of eyewitnesses. Grein could never discover her exact age. She never celebrated a birthday, could not endure ceremonies of any kind focused on her person. She remained a modest woman of the old-fashioned type.

Their family life survived on tolerance. More than once, Grein had reflected that Leah's tolerance was inherited from the matriarch Leah, Laban's daughter, who had given her husband, Jacob, a concubine to lie with, and who, with her son Reuben's mandrakes, had hired Jacob from her sister Rachel. Leah retained the meekness of generations of wives made wise by the suffering of generations of great-grandmothers who knew that a man was but a man, and that if a woman wanted to live with him, she had to be capable of patience, devotion, and humility.

During their first years in America, her neighbors and friends from the old country would berate Leah, deride the greenhorn wife who worked hard, struggled to bring up her children with hardly a piece of bread in the house, yet allowed her husband, the lowly Talmud Torah teacher, to go off gallivanting with other women. They made it clear to her that in America one could take a husband to court, get alimony out of him, and even have him thrown in jail. They showed her reports in the Yiddish newspapers describing how cunning young wives cheated on their husbands and squeezed money out of them with the blessing of the American courts. But these ill-intentioned provocations had no influence on Leah. She loved Grein deeply. She could never forget that he had been a student of philosophy in Warsaw and she a small-town girl; that he was tall and blond and she short and dark. To this day she had never understood what he saw in her nor why he had married her with such alacrity. She knew about his peccadilloes, but she had accepted his wandering eye as she might have accepted a physical deformity. She forgave him everything. Leah maintained that when she got up each day and found him lying in the other bed, that was reward enough for her. Often in the mornings she would go up to his bed, kiss him, smooth his blankets, and murmur, "Sleep well, my dearest, sleep well."

Grein had given Leah a solemn promise, which he held sacred, that whatever happened he would never divorce her. Leah was his ideal of what a wife should be. She was like his mother and grandmother, who were the pattern for the image of the virtuous woman he took with him from his father's house. Deep inside he detested wanton women and held them in contempt. He was one of those men who, out of the house, throw off every restraint, but at home long for chasteness. He was even jealous if Leah kissed a male relative at a family celebration. This double standard had been pointed out to him countless times, but he cited support for his conduct from the highest authority—the Bible. Had not Abraham, Isaac, Moses, David, and Solomon all kept concubines? Grein regarded modern talk about the emancipation of women as the idle chatter of spiritual eunuchs. He had repeatedly argued that flattering women and pampering the backward would inevitably destroy contemporary civilization. The first victims would be those waited on so attentively. He identified in such service the idol worship of modern times.

But last night he had also made a promise to Anna: because of him, she had broken with her husband and perhaps also with her father. Though Grein was exhausted, he could not fall asleep. Every time he started dozing off, he twitched awake again. How had all this happened? Why did I say all those things to her? he asked himself. Something like amnesia seemed to have come over him. Some details he remembered, others had vanished from his memory, leaving a blank. He was cold, and he shivered. What was all that blather about religious organization? What absurd example did I give? What imp filled my mouth with exactly those words on exactly that night? One thing is certain—I know what is right, and I do what is wrong. How does the Gemara put it? "Though he knows his Master, yet he desires to rebel against Him." Well, I'm drunk, he said to himself. I've lost interest in everything but this. I've abandoned God even though I loathe the world. And in any case, what can the world offer? Only a quart of whiskey and a whore.

Grein lay still, preoccupied with his hangover. He wanted to sleep and to think at the same time. Stabbing pains zigzagged along his spine. His knee ached. Boyish daydreams floated up at him. A sense of utter futility sighed within him—a moan of the kind that schoolboys hear when they press shells to their ears to catch the surge of the sea. Well, I'm killing myself! In every sense. I'll lose everything: my health, my family, my livelihood. What had Luria said? Certain creatures were instinctively driven to suicide.

Night fell. The bedroom filled with shadows. Through the window a violet sky peered in, illuminated by a solitary star. Grein lay there spent, like someone in the grip of a fever. An idea occurred to him, but he did not know what. His eyes were open but he was already dreaming. Something in him was speaking a broken mixture of Yiddish, Polish, English, Hebrew. He was simultaneously in New York and in Warsaw. Through some trick of the conscious mind, Anna was both herself and Esther. Grein was carrying on a lengthy argument with someone, an argument filled with disjointed remarks, indistinct images, idiotic examples. He woke briefly and laughed at his deformed visions, but they soon returned with the secret power of hallucination and madness.

Anna had the taxi drive to her apartment on Lexington Avenue. She did not ring the bell but opened the door with her key. Braced for the storm, she was ready to answer Stanislaw Luria's rage. On the threshold, a fearful thought ran through her—perhaps he had hanged himself. She was prepared even for that. As she did normally, she strode boldly down the hallway. If something has happened, I must call the police immediately. She entered the living room and saw him. In a dressing gown and slippers, unshaven, he sat in an easy chair, his hands resting on its arms. The stubble of his beard was white, as if in one night old age had overtaken him. His eyebrows seemed to have grown bushier, and in the sockets below them, the dark pupils of his eyes were fixed in a blank gaze of utter despair. Bluer and more swollen than ever, the pouches under his eyes had new double folds. Anna stood for a while at the door. He looks like an embalmed corpse, something inside her reacted. A living dummy. She simultaneously despised and pitied him. She wanted to have it out with him, not so much to hurt him as to get past the initial expression of outrage.

She gave a little cough and smiled coldly. "It's me, Anna."

Luria did not respond.

"Are you dead or paralyzed?"

Luria remained silent.

"If you're dead, I'll call a funeral parlor, but if you're alive I just want you to know that I've merely come to collect my things."

Luria made not the slightest movement and Anna was left at a loss. Perhaps he's been struck dumb. She'd been prepared for him to curse her, to revile her, even to beat her, but he had apparently taken a vow not to utter a word. A fleshy male leg, thickly overgrown with hair, protruded from under the hem of his robe. Beneath the hair, the skin was as pallid as that of a cadaver. After a few moments Anna noticed that he was breathing. His paunch slowly rose and fell like a bellows. Well, come what may, I've suffered enough because of him, Anna decided. She went into the bedroom. On the way she bumped into an end table and knocked off an ashtray. I've had nothing but trouble from him! Anna justified herself to some unseen person. Not a husband, not a provider, not even a friend. He's still living with his first wife in Warsaw.

She shut and bolted the door and immediately began undressing. She hadn't shut an eye all night. She simply had to sleep for a few hours, she could hardly stand on her feet.

She crept under the bedclothes, under the sheet, burying her face in the pillows, and curled up like an animal.

5

Grein fell asleep and dreamed that it was an early summer night and he was somewhere in a small village in Eastern Europe. He found himself in the courtyard of a synagogue. Inside the house of worship, people were at prayer, ritually counting the days between Passover and Pentecost, but he had been left outside. An enormous moon was shining, covered with unnatural shadows and strange hollows. Was he imagining it, or could he see the dark side of the moon? Had Creation come to an end? A billy goat appeared opposite him, its twisted horns angled aggressively in his direction. Grein wanted to escape, but there was nowhere to go. Should I climb into the water barrel? I might drown. He wanted to enter the prayerhouse, to join the congregation, but he suddenly became aware that he was naked. Where are my clothes? Why am I wandering about naked in a synagogue courtyard? I must have been robbed! I can't complain either, for does "Thou shalt not steal" supersede "Thou shalt not commit adultery"? Jewish law even permits that I be punished by death. To those such as I God will not set a sign, as he did for Cain, to prevent any who might find me from slaying me.

The goat caught him up on its horns and ran with him. Where was the bridle? Surely there was a bridle . . . Suddenly there was light and Grein opened his eyes. It was now evening, and in the doorway of the lit bedroom he saw Leah: short and stout, her hair piled high on top of her head, with a small nose, a high bosom, and slightly crooked eyes; she looked vaguely Japanese. She stood contemplating him with the tender smile of a mother whose child has sinned grievously. Leah had not yet taken off her coat, a clear sign that she had just come in from the street. Her thin upper lip was curled back to reveal her fine, small teeth. These teeth were Leah's jewels. They were whole and white, without a single dental filling. To this day, Leah could crack plum pits with them. Even though she had grown as round as a barrel, the sweet ingenuousness of girlhood still illuminated her face. Grein heard her ask, "Well, have you slept it off?"

"What time is it?"

"What time do you have to call her?" Leah retorted shrewdly.

He glanced at the alarm clock that stood on the night table. Yes, he was supposed to telephone Anna now. Leah's face immediately grew serious.

"Hertz, I must speak with you."

"What's wrong?"

"Hertz, at six o'clock this morning someone called Stanislaw Luria telephoned here. You know who he is."

Grein did not answer. There was a bitter taste in his mouth.

"Hertz, this is the end."

"Well, if it's the end, it's the end."

"However you got into this, the whole thing makes no sense," Leah said quietly and easily, as if it were a matter of small importance. She turned around, opened the door of the closet, and hung up her coat. She smoothed out a dress which had slipped from its hanger.

"What do you want to do?" he asked.

Leah turned sideways. "I don't know. But we can't live together any longer. An hour after Luria, Boris Makaver called. He shouted so loudly I nearly lost my hearing. I was ashamed for the children."

Grein paused. "Well, I'll move out."

"I'm not forcing you out. It's your choice. But you must find some solution."

And Leah half entered the closet. There she puttered mechanically, rehanging all her clothes, straightening out the hangers. She trembled with the emotion of one who is ashamed to show her face. Grein got up and went to his study to telephone. His legs seemed suddenly to have gone limp. He switched on the light and shut the door. Well, it's better this way, he thought. I'll spare myself the endless talk. He almost fell into the chair behind the desk. He hesitated awhile before dialing Anna's number. His sleep had left him feeling not rested but even more worn out than before. It took him longer than usual to dial the number and Luria answered the telephone. Grein heard the heavy, angry shout of someone who has been interrupted in the middle of a violent quarrel.

"Hello!"

Grein wanted to reply, but no words came out. He wanted to put down the receiver, but he didn't do that either. He listened to the charged silence at the other end of the line. The stillness lasted a long time. Then Luria began choking and snorting like an antique clock before it strikes.

"*Panie* Grein, I know it's you," he said in Polish. "I'll call my wife in a moment. She's in the bathroom, taking a bath. But before that, I beg you to hear me out."

Grein did not reply.

"Hello? Don't hang up. If you don't want to talk with me, then that's that. But you might at least listen to what I have to say."

"Yes, I'm listening," Grein managed to stammer hoarsely. Only then was he aware that his mouth and throat were dry.

"*Panie* Grein, to begin with, I must tell you that I have nothing against you personally. Absolutely nothing. As I see it, it was she who swore fidelity to me under the bridal canopy, not you. Perhaps it's not the custom among Jews actually to swear fidelity, but then, as you know, I'm not very knowledgeable about Jewish Law. In Polish a marriage is called a *ślub*, and *ślub* also means 'vow.' However, I don't want to get involved in the philological side of the question. Whether there was actually a vow or not, she became my wife, and no one forced her to do so. Certainly I'm older than she is, and I had lost everything, but you mustn't think that I threw myself at her. To begin with, that's not in my nature. In my own way, I'm an aristocrat—as the saying goes, I'm poor in everything but honor. Second, after I had lost my entire family, the people dearest to me in the whole world, I was in no frame of mind to begin life all over again. Please believe that I'm not lying to you. In my present situation, it would serve no purpose to lie. The truth is that she fell in love with me—to this day I don't know why—and *she* ran after *me*. I don't say this to humiliate her, God forbid, but because it's a fact, and her father knows it. She went so far as to use her father as a go-between, as though he were a matchmaker. She pinned me into a corner, one might say, because men are by nature more diffident than women. In us there's a thoroughly foolish and impractical gallantry. Women don't have it. Women acknowledge nothing beyond their own wants and needs. But I don't mean to deliver an anti-feminist lecture, *Panie* Grein. I'm simply anxious that you shouldn't have the wrong idea and believe that I led her on, or anything like that. She knew everything about me, about my age and about my state of crisis, both physical and psychological. I'm a broken man, *Panie* Grein, and when a man is broken, he's sick and he's not normal. God alone knows, it would have been better for me to have stayed in Africa or even in Havana, where an educated European might have adjusted more easily. I want to tell you something else, *Panie* Grein, and I don't do it out of revenge or to spoil her good fortune, because I've thrown in my hand, and what took place last night has destroyed whatever was left. I've already forgotten what I want to say. It would be far better if we could meet and speak face-to-face—man-to-man as they say. You needn't be afraid of me. You can be quite sure that I won't come armed with a revolver or a knife.'' Luria laughed mirthlessly. ''At least I'm that much of a Jew. I find any act of physical violence alien and repugnant. I could tell you a lot more, but she'll be coming out of the bathroom at any minute and she'll interrupt us. What I really want you to know concerns a certain affair she had before she set her sights on me, in the same place, actually—in Casablanca. I don't want to tell tales about her, but since you're planning to join your life to hers and to wreck your home—I spoke with your dear wife earlier today—or perhaps it was yesterday. I've lost all sense of time. But would it perhaps be possible for us to meet? When? Where? Here she comes. Will you telephone me? One moment, here's my wife—I beg you, I implore you, please call me! Well—''

Luria fell silent. Grein heard a brief scuffle and some jangling. Anna had evidently tried to wrench the receiver out of his hand.

6

Grein had been expecting Anna to get on the phone, but it appeared that either someone had hung up or the connection had been cut, since all he heard was the steady hum of the dial tone. After some hesitation he redialed, but this time the line was busy. Grein couldn't understand it. Who could be using the phone over there? He waited a few minutes but it was still busy. He had an uncanny feeling that the line would now be busy indefinitely; in fact, he knew it with a certainty that defied logical explanation. And so it was. He waited for five minutes, ten minutes, but he could not get through. He went over to the bookcase and examined the spines of the volumes. There they all stood: Plato's *Dialogues*, Aristotle's *Nicomachean Ethics*, Spinoza's *Ethics*, selected works of Locke, Hume, Kant, Hegel, Schopenhauer, Nietzsche. Each one of them had something to teach, but what help were they in his present predicament? He was afraid. Could the receiver be dangling on its cord and Luria be preventing her from speaking? Or had Luria become violent? Or had Anna been overwhelmed at the last moment by regrets? Grein remembered what Luria had told him—that she had had an affair in Casablanca.

"She's a firebrand, no question—a firebrand," he murmured.

Luria's revelation struck him two ways. Grein both applauded and reproached Anna for the affair. He was ashamed of his emotional ambivalence. There had been a time when such a disclosure would immediately have sickened him, but now his judgment had gone haywire. She simultaneously attracted and repulsed him. At least I won't be bored with her, he rationalized. Marry her? I'll simply have to juggle things in such a way that Leah doesn't divorce me. I must have a home to go back to. He tried calling again, but the line was still busy. He took down Spinoza's *Ethics* and read a few lines about controlling the emotions. Why did God give us emotions if we have to keep controlling them? Above all, what was the biological significance of this love late in life? Ah yes, last night Anna had prattled on about a child. She wants to have a child by me! Perhaps that is behind everything. Perhaps in the highest sphere, the image of our son or daughter is already formed and we have no choice but to give physical realization to a spiritual predetermination.

Going into the kitchen, he came upon Leah sitting at the table eating bread and pickled fish. She stopped chewing.

"If you want, I'll make supper for you."

"No, thank you."

"Sit down for a minute. Surely I've earned the right to have you speak a few words to me?"

"I won't disturb you while you're eating."

"How important is my eating? Hertz, I want to ask you something."

"Well, ask."

"Hertz, what's the matter with you? Why are you doing all this? You're not a young man any longer. God knows I've forgiven you everything, and I'm quite prepared to forgive you again. But now you want to wreck everything."

"I can't force you into any divorce. If you don't want a divorce, then you'll remain my wife."

"What's the sense in remaining your wife under such circumstances? This isn't just another of your furtive affairs. This is a major scandal. The husband calls, the father calls. The husband threatened to have you deported."

"Is that what he said?"

"I'm not lying."

"Well . . ."

"So what is it? Are you so much in love with her?"

"I know only one thing: I'm bored. Bored to death. There are days when from sheer boredom I want to put a bullet in my head."

"Even with all your love affairs?"

"I don't have any love affairs."

"So what happened to that Esther?"

Grein did not reply.

"Why should you be so bored? You have a family, children, a beautiful home. Thank God we have a good income, and even some money put away. Have you forgotten how hard you struggled in the Talmud Torah in Brownsville?"

"I've forgotten nothing."

"After all, you always used to say that when you were free of financial worries you would write a book."

"I haven't got anything to write about. What do I know that others don't? I went into a field that was bankrupt from the start—philosophy has been dead for two hundred years. It was almost born a corpse. The riddle grows greater, not smaller, and there's absolutely no way to solve it. It's all hopeless."

"And Boris Makaver's daughter will clear it up for you?"

"At least with her I can forget myself."

Leah pushed aside the plate of fish. "What can I do? I can't entertain you. Why did you marry me if I was so provincial?"

"I don't regret it, Leah. I loved you then, and I still love you now. You're the mother of my children. But you must set me free."

"How much more free? There isn't a man in New York freer than you are. You do what you want and you go where you please. Believe me, I'm not so stupid. I see and I know everything. You don't even bother to hide things from me. But there must be a limit."

"The limit is that whatever I might say or whatever I might do, we remain man and wife. No power on earth can force you to give me a divorce. I'm getting older, not younger. If we remain man and wife, sooner or later we'll be together again."

"When? I can see through all your schemes, Hertz. You don't want to marry her, so that's why you want me to remain your wife. You want to fool us both—both her and me."

"If it's a question of fooling, then everyone—"

"You're fooling no one but yourself."

He didn't answer, and Leah drew the plate toward her once more. For a while Grein regarded the head of the fish. Strange: that fish had once been alive, had probably suffered, too. If souls lived on eternally, as Professor Shrage believed, then that fish would get its share of immortality. Grein gazed at Leah, observing her every movement. He felt like a child sitting and contemplating his mother. How long was it since he had been a schoolboy? His father used to sit in the glow of a naphtha lamp writing on sheets of parchment with a goose quill. His mother, may she rest in peace, peeled potatoes, scraped carrots, kneaded dough for dumplings. It was so quiet in their garret that one could hear the scratch of the pen on the parchment. Now his parents were both dust, Warsaw had gone up in flames, all its Jews were ash. He was all that remained, Hertz Dovid the survivor, and he smothered his sorrow in sexual fantasies, wanton talk, debauched desires. What should he do? Recite the evening prayers? Once again praise the mercy of God and the favor He shows to his people Israel?

The telephone rang. It's Anna! something in Grein exclaimed. He sprang up, overturning the chair and banging his knee. He very nearly tripped over the carpet in the corridor. It was dark in his study and it took him a while before he found the light switch. He was trembling as he lifted the receiver, only to hear a man's voice asking for Anita. This was the first time a man had ever called Anita. Had things reached this stage? Do they want my daughter already? He went to her room, but it was pitch-black in there and he returned to tell the caller that she was not at home.

"Would you like to leave a message?" he asked.

"No, thank you."

And the unknown caller hung up. Grein held on to the receiver for a while longer before replacing it. He liked neither the voice nor the manner of the caller, who sounded like a middle-aged man of overbearing personality. Something in Grein both smiled and shuddered. Well, it was unavoidable—it was measure for measure. Sitting down, he stared at the telephone as though trying to discover merely by looking at the appliance whether Anna was still talking or whether the line was now free. No, it was busy. I'd better wait a bit. I'll count to a hundred. He started counting, but in the mid-twenties he broke off. I must be patient, patient. Jerking open a drawer, he found one of his manuscripts, some of the countless notes he had once made in preparation for a book on the Cabala. He read:

In what way does God's completeness accord with His need for the service of humankind? There is only one answer; service to God can have but one meaning. However limitless God's power might be, there are certain repairs to the torn fabric of Creation which only human beings possessed of the gift of free will can make over the course of time. While the future belongs to God solely through might, not through labor, God needs humankind to assist Him in bringing the cosmic drama to a beneficent end.

So what does this have to do with my life now? He lifted the receiver and started calling Anna all over again, but the line continued to be busy. Now he had the weird suspicion that some hostile power was keeping the telephone in use, a force that wanted to obliterate him, to destroy all his joys, to drive away all who were closest to him—the Enemy that continually sabotaged him, sometimes from within, sometimes from without.

7

I must have patience, Grein told himself. Otherwise I'll really go mad. He sat down in an armchair, leaned back, tried to compose himself both inwardly and outwardly. If the telephone was busy, he would be busy as well. Let things take their own course. I'll imagine that I'm a fakir and this is a tree. I've sworn to sit here until the end of my life. What would happen if I were really to sit in this chair forever? At least it wouldn't rain on me. I'd even be able to earn a living—the telephone's nearby. Grein shut his eyes. Since childhood he had toyed with ideas of this kind. He had always wanted to hide away somewhere: in an attic, in a cellar, in a cave, on an island. Over the last few years he had fantasized about living on a yacht moored near a deserted reef somewhere in the Pacific. There had been a time when he wanted to have Esther on board this yacht with him, but now he wanted Anna. Oh, how tedious I find the winter! I'd rather be in a place where the weather is always mild, warm. I'd lie in a hammock stretched between two fig trees and read a book that explains the essence of things, clears up the riddles of existence, instead of advancing some empty theory of knowledge that elucidates nothing.

The telephone shrilled and Grein leaped up. He knew with deep inner conviction that this time it was Anna. Rushing forward, he snatched up the receiver. For a moment he lost his breath.

"Hello!"

There was no immediate reply, and Grein started shouting, "Hello! Hello! Hello!"

He recognized Anna's voice. "Is that you, Hertz?"

"Yes, me."

And he could not utter a word more.

"Can I speak to you?"

"Yes, speak freely."

"Are you alone?"

"Yes, alone."

"I want to tell you that I love you and I'll always love you," Anna blurted out rapidly, in the breathless voice of someone who has much to say and little time in which to say it. "I can't meet you tonight, but I'm yours, yours . . . Tomorrow I'll come to you and I'll never leave you . . ."

The words tumbled over each other as if someone was trying to interrupt her or drag her away from the telephone.

"Why did you break off earlier?"

Anna was silent for a moment.

"Hertz dearest, you can't imagine what's going on here . . . Papa's arrived . . . I've no idea when I'll be free again tonight . . ."

"Well—"

"But I want you to know one thing—neither Papa nor any other power on earth can stop me."

"Your telephone's been busy the whole time."

"What? I know. Papa was speaking with the rebbe. They're driving me mad . . . I'll meet you tomorrow morning at nine o'clock. Where? Let's say at Grand Central. Perhaps we can leave New York for a few days."

"I can do anything."

"Wait for me at nine o'clock. If I don't come, then you'll know I'm dead."

"Don't talk nonsense."

"This intimidation has to stop. I love you—no one else. I have to go now. Nine o'clock."

And she hung up.

Grein tried to get in a last word, but all he could hear was a low hum. He held the receiver to his ear for a while and then replaced it. What was going on over there? What did Boris Makaver want with the rebbe? Grein stood at his desk and stared at the wall. Isn't it odd? I've never really noticed the wallpaper pattern before. It's got yellow-and-brown stripes. Anything to make people happy. It occurred to Grein that adults were treated in the same way as children: they were given all sorts of playthings, but never what they really wanted. Everything was permitted—wallpaper, rugs, lamps, paintings—everything, except the woman one desires. He glanced at the clock. It seemed a terribly long time before nine tomorrow morning. What should he do until then? He had only just woken up. Read? Read what? Go to a movie? The very thought disgusted him. He remembered Esther. He must call her. He should have called her yesterday. He couldn't just run away from her like a thief. But what should he say to her? He went to the door and shut it. Heading back to his desk, he stopped at the bookcase and glanced once again at the spines of books both sacred and secular. Everything was mixed up: a Gemara with commentaries next to a German-English dictionary, a copy of *The Sanctification of Levi* next to a collection of mathematical formulas by a Professor Birklen. What could Rabbi Levi Yitskhok of Berdichev have to say about his predicament? he wondered. He opened *The Sanctification of Levi* in the middle and read:

"Lo, in the beginning is Thought, and thereafter comes Love, and later, when Love has performed its task, it leaves behind it both sign and cipher, and this sign is called Form . . ." Grein frowned. What kind of love was meant here? Not his love for Anna, certainly. Those Jews of Rabbi Levi's time knew of only one love—the love of God. Why should someone love Anna when he could love her Creator? Why love a fleck of foam when beneath it swells a mighty sea? But when one is only a fleck of foam oneself, it is difficult to carry on a love affair with an entire ocean—that was the whole problem. Insignificance can only love that which is itself insignificant.

He went over to the desk and dialed Esther's number.

"Esther, what are you doing tonight?"

Esther did not respond immediately. "I thought you'd forgotten I'm alive," she said finally.

"I forget nothing."

"You were supposed to call yesterday."

"I couldn't."

"Are there no telephones in Manhattan?"

Grein made no reply.

"Well, what do you want to do? Do you want to come over?"

"Yes."

"Well, come over. I hope you haven't eaten supper yet."

"Yes. No. I'll be there in an hour."

And he put down the receiver.

He walked out, not knowing where he was going or why. Stopping at the built-in closet, he started searching for a small bag that could be carried easily. He knew how this would end: if he went to Esther, he wouldn't come home tonight. But if he intended to go off with Anna, he had to take a few things with him. He rummaged among the suitcases, but they were all too big. Opening the smallest, he found it full of various papers and other things that had been mislaid without his having missed them. He pulled out a necktie that had once been one of his favorites; there was a faded shirt whose collar was crushed and crumpled. He rapidly glanced over the papers. How on earth could I have forgotten about all this? He was astonished at himself. Emptying the bag, he packed a few freshly laundered shirts, handkerchiefs, socks, a sweater. His actions were all vague, uncertain, as though he were rehearsing a role he was going to play only later. Am I really leaving home? Is this how I'm going to destroy my Leah? And what's the sense of this visit to Esther? This is completely crazy.

Nevertheless, he took with him everything he would need on a long trip: his checkbook, his bankbook, his citizenship papers, the key to the safe in which he kept his stocks and bonds. He went into the kitchen. Leah had finished eating and was washing up at the sink. He hovered in the doorway.

"Leah, I'm leaving."

Leah turned her head. Mute and stunned, she regarded him sadly. "Where are you going? Will you come back?"

"Yes, Leah, don't be a fool."

"I am a fool. What shall I say if people phone for you?"

"Say I'm on vacation."

"For how long? Well, the ruin is of your own making."

And Leah turned back to the dishes in the sink. He picked up the bag and went out, shutting the front door quietly. Well, at least she's not making a scene, he said to himself. He felt a surge of love and gratitude toward Leah. Now there's a woman! something inside him exclaimed. I'll never divorce her! This is my home, my haven. He rang for the elevator, feeling like someone drunk or drugged. No, he was more like a sleepwalker or someone in a hypnotic trance. Behind all his sober calculations lurked something irrational, disordered, involuntary, and above all improvised. He was going to Esther now only because a long winter's night stretched ahead of him and he didn't know what to do with it.

Outside, freezing cold had set in. A raw wind blew. Should I take the car? He suddenly felt too sluggish to drive. Moreover, Anna's choosing to meet him at Grand Central indicated that she wanted to travel by train. As he pulled up his collar and hurried to the subway, it occurred to him that in such a mood a murderer goes to kill his victim, or a suicide to destroy himself.

8

Grein did things and was astonished at what he did, almost as if he were a being divided into two, with one half watching the other. In the subway he dropped a dime into the slot and pushed against the turnstile. The lights released a billion, a trillion quanta of energy that struck Grein's retina, traveled up the optic nerve, and set off a reaction in every particle of gray matter we call the brain. The enormous headlines of the late-edition newspapers bearing tomorrow's date screamed about a bride who had been shot on her wedding day. She graced the front page wearing a wedding dress, a veil, a chaplet of flowers. Next to hers was a photograph of the stunned culprit. His bulging eyes seemed to be asking, What on earth has made me a murderer? What kind of role is this? God alone knows that I am innocent.

Grein descended the stairs and immediately boarded the Brighton train. How old and familiar everything was to him: the dirty green walls, the red-checkered floors, the litter of papers, the peanut shells, the dilapidated horsehair seats, the naked lightbulbs, the advertisements for socks, brassieres, chocolate, funeral parlors. The passengers read the freshly printed newspapers and, all as one, chewed gum. Grein had been caught up in a system where everything was predetermined. He knew everything by rote. At Fifty-third Street the car would be crowded by women who had been bargain hunting in the department stores that stayed open late that night. At Union Square there would be a new crush. After Canal Street, the train would emerge aboveground for a while and the night-darkened windows would be filled with the murky river on which tugboats chugged, pulling coal, rocks, or freight cars. In the distance, factories, poolrooms, garages would rush past. Wasn't the whole of life a trip exactly like this one? Wasn't Anna just another subway station on an undeviating journey through time?

For a while Grein studied a black man. His whole being expressed the inescapability of heredity: the black skin, the broad nose with its wide nostrils designed to inhale the humid air of the tropics, the scalp with its woolly tufts like bushes in a stony wilderness. His body sat here, but his spirit roamed in the African jungle. He stared back at Grein with the instinctive astonishment with which his forebears had probably regarded the American slave traders. Soon Grein began to scrutinize a young white woman who was chewing and reading. Her skirt had crept up above her knees. Though he had had his fill of flesh and lovemaking, Grein repeatedly ogled those knees in nylon stockings which the young woman thrust forward with impudent nonchalance. He savored the thought that she would be different than the other women he had enjoyed until now.

What's the matter with me? Will I be like this until I die? he asked himself. Is this the sole purpose of my life?

Someone got up from a recessed seat, and Grein hurried to take his place. He had to consider his situation. What should he tell Esther? How should he settle things with Anna? Would she agree to become merely his mistress and lead more or less Esther's existence? There was a great difference between Anna and Esther. Esther was by nature a bohemian. She had distanced herself from her relatives, settling in Brooklyn as though on an island. Anna had a father, a husband, a circle. Serious family rifts were caused by people like her. Grein sat in his little booth and ruminated. The bench under him grew warm—the car was heated—and Grein imagined that he was back sitting by the stove in the old study house. How long was it since he had been a yeshiva student? The years darted by like a dream. Was he positive that he was in love with Anna? Did anyone know precisely where lust stopped and love began? Wasn't the whole notion a vulgar fabrication, a concoction of all sorts of fancies, a hash of every kind of delusion?

Once again the train emerged from underground and ran above Brooklyn back yards: tiny houses, small stony gardens, and streetlamps that merely deepened the night gloom. All kinds of ethnic groups lived and raised children here: Jews, Italians, Poles, and Irish; black people and yellow people. In these dwellings, cultures flickered and died out. Here children grew up without any heritage, like Jack, like Anita. Their spiritual fathers were stock Hollywood characters, their literature trashy novels and the tabloid press. How long could all this last? Sometime in the future, wouldn't the ice caps at the poles melt and raise the surface of the ocean by several hundreds of feet? Then wouldn't the entire Atlantic shoreline be washed away? Everything was built on sand, shifting strata, temporary foundations. Somewhere in the depths of Asia new barbarians were already on the march, voracious tribes poised to devour and ravage all before them.

But what shall I do? What does God want me to do—me, Hertz Dovid, the son of Reb Jacob Moshe the Scribe? My children, Jack and Anita, are already lost. Grein had not taught them Jewishness, nor did they want to learn. They would soon leave home and be entirely beyond his influence. With Leah, there was nothing to talk about except trivial domestic details. Leah had become absorbed in her shop, in auctions, in sniffing out bargains. He was surrounded by banality, acquisitiveness, and ennui. He believed in God, but belief was not enough. He lacked the fundamentals: the structured ritual, the ordered environment, the iron discipline of his grandfathers and great-grandfathers. Though Grein could not live with God, he had no idea how one lived without Him.

A Brooklyn avenue appeared alongside the train, brightly lit, with neon signs, banks, department stores displaying mannequins in their windows, streams of automobiles. After a moment, everything went black again, and the train soon stopped in Sheepshead Bay. As Grein got off, the wind struck him and shoved him about. His hat flew off his head and he caught it in mid-flight. Since he could not arrive at Esther's carrying the overnight bag, he hid it in a rental locker. He could have walked to Esther's, but it was far too cold, so he took a taxi. The house in which Esther lived stood close to the sea. Grein got out and paid the driver. In the half-darkness the sea moaned its eternal moan, went its eternal way. Crowned with foam, the waves beat against the breakwater, yielded and withdrew with the patient strength over which time has no power, with the self-confidence of those for whom victory is assured.

Spray spurted up into the air and Grein wiped the salt water from his face. Somewhere far away, at the edge of the horizon, a light flashed. From Far Rockaway the beam of a lighthouse cut through the darkness. An isolated star flickered in the sky and Grein gazed at it intently. Unlike him and his concerns, the star was eternal. What joy that the heavens existed and one could at least glimpse their lights! Without them, human beings would sink entirely into insignificance.

He was uncertain why he had come to Esther, and equally unsure what to talk about with her. Should he tell her the truth? Should he tell her that he had come to break off with her? Was he really ready to put an end to this relationship? He had disrupted her life. She would long ago have had another husband were it not for him. He had grown accustomed to her, both mentally and physically. Recently their relationship had reached a crisis: bitterness had crept in, the reproaches and wrangling of a couple who can live neither apart nor together. But it was one thing to quarrel, to make up, and then to fall out again, and another to break up for good. That was death. How does one break off? How does one make an end? Only God has such power.

He stood and breathed in the cold, salty air. He knew every house in this neighborhood, every tree, every bush. Now that Anna was in her own home on Lexington Avenue and he was skulking at Esther's door, Esther had once again become Esther and Anna had receded into the background of memory. He glanced up at the top story and recognized Esther's silhouette in the lighted window behind the venetian blinds. She had probably heard the taxi drive up and was waiting for him with the blessed faith of the deceived.

Grein did not ring but unlocked the door with his own key and entered. He saw her immediately: she stood looking at him with a blend of resentment and curiosity—Esther, the cultured daughter of an eminent rabbinical family, the granddaughter of deeply learned men, a world-class beauty who had once carried off all the honors at balls, the former daughter-in-law of a wealthy family, a woman who painted, wrote poems, and had even distinguished herself on the stage. Esther was now forty-three years old, but she was still a very beautiful woman. To this day she continued to braid her silken hair. She had the face of a rabbinical aristocrat, pale, with a classical nose, huge gray eyes which shaded off into green, and a throat whose womanly fullness had not diminished its whiteness. Though she was now somewhat too buxom, her waist had remained narrow. This evening her hair—subtly dyed—was wound around her head in two plaits, and a pair of valuable old-fashioned earrings, inherited from her grandmother, dangled from her ears. A refinement and gentility rarely encountered these days radiated from her rounded brow, from her sparkling eyes, and from the finely shaped mouth about which, even before words issued from it, played the wit of a woman of taste and breeding. Grein was prepared for her to start bickering with him straightaway, because he should have telephoned and did not, but Esther was apparently in a cheerful mood.

"Here he is, the great Casanova! Well, little boy, come closer. Don't hide by the door. Mommy won't spank you!"

She went to meet him and embraced him, seeming to hang on him for a while. She kissed him eagerly and at length, as if there had never been any squabble between them. Esther was wearing a kitchen apron over a silk dress, a combination in which she imitated her grandmother Esther Hadas, of whom it was said that she kept the Sabbath stew warm by wrapping it in a fur and tying it up with a silk kerchief. Esther smelled of the kitchen and orange marmalade. Reaching out her thumb and index finger, she plucked a hair off Grein's lapel with feminine dexterity.

"What's this? A dark one."

"Are you starting already? Throw it away!"

"Let's see, first, let's see. I'm like Sherlock Holmes. You can't keep all the clues from me."

Esther carefully held the hair up to the lamplight. Grein instinctively pulled back.

"Throw it away now!"

"Wait, wait. Black as a crow. What's this? A new one, eh?"

Grein made no reply.

"Well, what's the point of looking? When I woke up today and saw the snow, I decided I would cook my mother's groats for you. I went shopping for dried mushrooms. You can't get them in Brighton, and there's

only one shop here that stocks them. You were supposed to phone yesterday.''

''Yes, I know.''

''Of course you know. Who should know if not you? I expected to hear
from you the whole day. When I saw it was getting dark and you still
hadn't called, I started to worry. Suddenly at seven o'clock, maybe even
later, I hear from you. What's the sense of it? You ruined my whole day.''

''How are you?''

''How am I? Don't change the subject. I know everything. I know it all
as clearly as if I'd been there myself. When you can't even spare the time
to call, it's bad. But take off your coat and sit down at the table. You look
pale. Didn't you sleep last night? With my constitution, I'm ensured that
as soon as I shut my eyes, I'll be plagued by dreams. I've scarcely dozed
off than I'm already with my father. I can't understand it. I loved my
mother, too, may she rest in peace. How could I not love her? But I
seldom dream about her. I'm almost always with my father, and it always
seems to be on a festival day, because he's wearing his fur hat and his satin
capote. He takes me by the hand and speaks to me about Torah and all
sorts of other things. I never remember what he says, but the tone of those
conversations lingers with me. I try to remember, but I doze off again and
then he's with me once more. To tell you the truth, Hertz, I'm beginning
to think that this might have some meaning. Perhaps my own time has
come.''

''Don't talk nonsense.''

''Would you like to wash your hands? Give me your coat. It's not
nonsense. In my family people die young. How old was my sister Rosa?
And my brother Jonathan? I ask only one thing of you, Hertz my darling—
you must have me cremated. I don't want to lie in an American cemetery.
It's better to be ash.''

''What's the matter with you, Esther? Stop this tirade.''

''Sit down. Start with the grapefruit. For whom should I make out a
will? My children? At my age my mother already had grandchildren, and
all I do is carry on idiotic love affairs. In any case, you don't need me.''

''Truly, Esther, if you don't stop all this nonsense, I'm leaving.''

''Well, let it go. For the time being, I'm still alive, I'm still alive. I
long for you all the time. When I lie awake at night, I always think I would
lack for nothing if you were lying next to me. But I gave up on that ages
ago. Then I try to read, but there's nothing worth reading. Once, a book
was something worthwhile, but today's writers are as dead as wood. What

they write has absolutely no appeal. The essentials are missing—the soul. Hertz, I want to tell you something."

"What?"

"I want to tell you that you'll never get a wife like me. You'll long for me, but it'll be too late."

"Why are you talking like this?"

"Because I talk. I'm my grandfather's child—there's a breath of the Divine Spirit on me, too. You'll look for me, Hertz, but you won't find me. We stem from the same roots, and you can't cut yourself off from your roots. The telephone's ringing!"

Esther made a dash for the phone, which was located in the bedroom. Grein put down his spoon and sat quietly, stunned by all Esther had said. No, I can't tell her, he decided—not tonight. It'd be better to write a letter. He got up and went over to the window that overlooked a garden with three snow-covered trees. A bit farther on was another house in which two windows were dimly lit. There people were evidently watching television. Shadowy figures were sitting in chairs, engrossed in their viewing.

I must make a decision now, one way or the other, Grein told himself. She'll find out no matter what. That friend of hers, that Liuba, hears all the gossip. Who knows? Perhaps she's phoning with the news at this very moment. If so, what should I do? Deny it? Oh, I almost wish I'd never come here!

He heard Esther returning.

"Why are you standing by the window? What's there to see? Sit down at the table. Liuba called."

Grein's throat immediately went dry. He turned toward Esther. "What did she have to say?"

"What? Oh, her usual chatter. She wanted to have a long gossip, but I told her I had to give you supper. Eat up your grapefruit. You're not a rebbe, you don't need to leave any leftovers on your plate. What do you think of the snow? It's a nuisance, but I love it. It reminds me of the old country, of my childhood, of all the best things. In our family, not only the boys but the girls as well were given Hanukkah money. I can't begin to describe what went on in our home during Hanukkah. There's not another celebration like it in the whole world. What's happened to people? Where's the joy these days?"

"All spent."

"Why, my darling? Why? I sometimes look through Graetz's *History of the Jews*. There you find only one thing—persecution. But the world has forgotten the way Jews used to rejoice. I have a theory that if Jews hadn't been such joyful people, the world wouldn't have hated them so much. Every enmity is built on envy.''

"If that's true, then the world ought to love the Jews of today without reservation.''

"Even today's Jews are happier than the Gentiles. Some trace of joy has remained. Hertz, I want to ask you something. And I want a straight answer.''

"What?''

"Who is she? What happened? I'm too old for you to fool me.''

"Truly, Esther, I don't know what you mean.''

"What? Well, I'll find out in the end. Once, we had an agreement that whatever happened, you'd tell me the truth.''

"I've got nothing to tell.''

"If that's true, then my instinct's deceiving me. I've made soup with rice. You love rice, don't you?''

"Yes.''

"I'll cook you my mother's groats some other time.''

9

After the meal, Esther poured out two glasses of liqueur, one for Grein and one for herself. She also smoked a cigarette. Once, she neither drank nor smoked, but during the last few years she had taken to smoking thirty cigarettes a day, and she kept a shelfful of spirits, wines, liqueurs. She had originally vowed never to drink alone, but she'd broken that vow long ago.

Now Esther sat next to Grein on the sofa with her legs crossed and a cigarette in her mouth, blowing smoke rings. Suddenly she demanded of Grein, "Tell me a story!''

Grein smiled. "Another story?''

"Yes, tell me something. I've become like a child. I can't go to sleep without a story.''

"What shall I tell you?''

"Something with bite to it. I'd like to feel its teeth! Since God hasn't created anything good, we'll have to get pleasure from the bad. Who knows? Perhaps the bad is the good. In a magazine the other day I read about a father who used to strip his children naked and beat them every night. You won't believe it, Hertz, but it aroused me.''

"You're a sadist.''

"I'm everything—a sadist, a masochist. If you were to offer me a million to lay a violent hand on a child, I wouldn't take it. For me a child is holy. But the human mind is a freakish mechanism. What stimulates today's human beings? Only what's bad. In the movies they shoot people. On the radio they massacre them. In novels they commit unbelievable wickedness. So one gets used to it. But all the same I detest it. I detest it. Tell me something spicy.''

"Later.''

"Later never comes. What would you have done if you'd unlocked the door and found me lying dead? It could happen, after all. It could just as easily happen as not.''

"I'd've been very upset.''

"What'll you do on the night when I'm lying in a funeral parlor? Who will you be with? With your wife or with the other one?''

"Esther, you're talking nonsense again.''

"It's not nonsense. People drop like flies every day. Each morning when I get up I feel my breasts to check that there's no lump there. My mother died of breast cancer, and I'll go the same way. I know that as surely as I know that it's night outside.''

"How can you know that? You've become a hypochondriac.''

"I know, I know. When one sits alone and does nothing but think day after day, one inevitably thinks about death. One half of my family died naturally. The other half was murdered by the Nazis. Whenever one thinks at all, one comes face-to-face with the dead. It often seems to me that I've died as well and I'm simply wandering about in the World of Illusion.''

"Really, Esther, you're falling into a depression.''

"What's depression? The truth is depressing. At least you move about— you go here, you go there. It's difficult for me to get out. I've grown afraid of the streets. I don't even like the sea any longer. Why has it been hurling itself backward and forward for millions of years? How long will it go on restlessly flinging itself about? I'm aware that I'm thinking the same thoughts over and over again, and I'm ashamed of myself.''

"What are you thinking, Esther? What?''

"Ah, nothing. Wild imaginings. I picture us on our way to some island together. They've exiled us or something. I hate the cold. Once, I used to love winter, but I can't stand it anymore. Heat is better. I'd really like to read, but today's writers are afraid to tell the truth. Why are they so afraid of the truth?''

"The truth is horrifying.''

"Aren't lies just as horrifying? I know exactly how you operate. After you've sweet-talked me, you go off to someone else, and either you repeat it all word for word or you vary it here and there. You do it because you're bored: but we would be more bored together than we are apart. I'm asking you for the last time—who is she?''

"I beg you, Esther, leave me in peace.''

"Well, no is no. But I'll find out anyway. What's the news with Boris Makaver?''

"The same as usual. He's religious and he makes money.''

"What? That's being smart—he gets both this world and the World to Come. What's happening with his daughter? Are you having an affair with her?''

"Why especially with her?''

"Why not? You knew her when she was a child. She's unhappy with her husband. In her eyes you're a great hero. And you, you're too lazy to look elsewhere. You're one of those men who follow the line of least resistance. I ought to be angry with you, Hertz. I ought to be your worst enemy, because you've ruined me. You've done me more harm than any other person in the world. But one can't hate you. You're just a big, helpless child. You trample on people the way children step on toads or worms. You've got a sharp mind, you were once a prodigy, but I get the feeling that you use only one side of your brain. Just as one can still see with only one eye, so one can still think with only half a brain. For my part, I'm afraid of just one thing—age. I don't mean eighty. For me, even fifty is old. I'd like to live another five years, but they must be good years. The telephone's ringing again!''

Esther left the living room. Stretching out on the sofa, Grein reached for Esther's glass and drank down the last of the liqueur. He also finished smoking Esther's cigarette. Then he shut his eyes and lay still, thinking about nothing.

Well, everything will sort itself out with all of them, he said to himself. Time makes things happen. The physicists will yet discover that time is a force like gravity.

He suddenly laughed. The same scene was repeated each time he came here: Esther got more and more depressed, they went to bed together sunk in pessimistic gloom. But as soon as the lights were out, their spirits revived like those of beings that can live only in the dark. Then the kissing started, the fondling, the wanton talk and the arousal—an intense ardor akin to madness. Then even talk about death served as fuel for the fire. But today he had made a choice. He had sentenced to death a great love or a great lust.

This time Esther spoke for a very long time. Grein could not hear anything of the conversation, since most of the talking was done by the person on the other end of the line. Esther merely let out an occasional exclamation or made an odd comment, sighed or added a few words. Though she had repeatedly bemoaned her loneliness, in New York she still had her confidantes, her friends from the old country, even distant relatives. She was always being sought out by dozens of men and women who were in some way connected to her on her father's side, on her mother's side, through all kinds of relationships by marriage. She gave and received gifts. She was invited to family celebrations. No, she was far from being as cut off from everything and everyone as she tried to pretend before it was time for bed. At bottom, she was far more sociable than he was. This love affair, however, had certainly driven her into a dead end.

She's right, of course, Grein considered. I do think only with one part of my mind—in a single dimension, one might say. The plans I make never extend more than a day ahead.

It occurred to him to switch off the lamp, first because Esther was quite capable of chattering away for an hour and he could take a nap in the meantime, and second because the light was completely unnecessary. He got up and switched it off. Immediately the room became cozier. He was aware of the hissing of the radiator, of the wash of the sea. White and red, light and dark, the snow outside was reflected in the window. Once more Grein lay back on the sofa, half awake, half dozing in the unmoving silence of a creature whose yoke has been removed.

Grein must have fallen asleep, because when Esther came back he started up. For a while he could not remember where he was.

He heard Esther's voice: "Why have you switched off the lamp? Have you been sleeping?"

"I was taking a nap."

"Well, it's the best thing you could do. In my mother's Yiddish Bible it was written that the sleep of the wicked is good for them and good for the world.''

Grein was suddenly fully alert. ''Have I now become one of the wicked as well?''

''Yes, dearest, one of the wicked. Respectable scoundrels don't do such things.''

Even in the darkness, Grein was aware that he had turned pale.

''What's happened?''

''What should happen? Now I know everything. All your little doings. What did you think? That no one would find out? That you could snatch only the one single night in secret? Liuba called again. They're talking about you in town. The whole of New York—the whole of our circle, that is—is abuzz with you. Well. So.''

And Esther fell silent. Grein couldn't see where she was, whether she was still standing by the door or had sat down in a chair. He was overcome by the speechless stillness that follows the climax of every crisis. After a while he saw Esther's silhouette, rigid in the doorway like a sheaf of shadows, a spectral figure perhaps of the kind that spiritualists and mediums call up. He glanced at her with a blend of curiosity and dread. That blur was Esther: a knot of accusations, contempt, perhaps even hatred. He made a movement as if to sit up, but his head seemed weighed down on the sofa cushion, almost as if he were suffering from paralysis of the nerves.

''Well, why are you silent?'' she asked.

''What can I say?''

''Have you abandoned your family?''

''Yes.''

''Well, congratulations. For years you've pleaded that you can't leave Leah. You'd made a vow to her or something. But now you're allowed to. Who released you from your vow? Her father?''

''It's got nothing to do with her father.''

''Well, you're even more despicable than I thought.''

''Shall I leave?'' he asked after a while.

''Yes, go! Get out! . . . Wait a second, I'll be back in a moment.''

He heard Esther go into the bathroom and bang the door. He listened attentively. As long as she didn't harm herself! Gushing and gasping sounds reached him, almost as if Esther were gargling in there. Then all was quiet. He lay mute, tense, empty, in a state of expectancy that, waiting for

nothing, nevertheless occupies the flow of time. As his eyes grew accustomed to the darkness, he steadily recognized the contours of the secre-
taire, the floor lamp, the picture frames. He knew everything here. Most
of these objects had been his gifts. What was she doing in there? Why was
she delaying so long? he wondered. He wanted to stand up, to knock on
the door of the bathroom, to call out to Esther, but he felt as if his feet
had been amputated. The short nap he had taken while Esther was on the
telephone had apparently sapped his last strength. He could barely keep
his eyes open. Now would be a convenient time to die, the thought ran
through him. The door of the bathroom opened and Esther turned to face
him.

"Hertz, you've hit me over the head with an ax."

Grein seemed to shrivel up. "I beg you, Esther, wait awhile."

"What should I wait for? Well, I'll wash up."

And she went into the kitchen.

How odd women are! he thought. Is this a time for her to wash the
dishes? But that was exactly what she was doing. She clattered the plates,
letting the water pour from the faucet. Grein closed his eyes. Let it be
quiet, quiet. Let her go on washing the pots in this way for seventy years,
like that other Jew in the wonder-tales. As Grein drifted off into a half
sleep again, it occurred to him that however pleasant the dark in the room
was, and however tightly he kept his eyes shut, too much light still penetrated. Or did that glow emanate from somewhere within himself? The
hissing of steam turned to singing. The warmth seemed to enfold him like
a quilt. Something danced before his eyes, trembling, trying to take shape
like a little ball out of primordial chaos, the first molecule from which the
universe was born. A golden halo flared up, a dazzling eyeball, an incan-
descence that was neither imagined nor real but existed somewhere in a
distant dimension. Was this a mirage? Did it have substance or not? I'll
tell Professor Shrage about it, he decided.

His body grew ever more cumbrous and his head pressed down on the
cushion like a stone. His fingers seemed to swell. He had undergone a
similar experience as a boy, when he had fallen ill with typhoid fever and
had lain in the hospital on Pokorna Street. Esther was still washing, splash-
ing, pacing back and forth in one spot like a caged creature. There was
something demented in all this washing. Suddenly she reappeared next to
him. In a voice half broken and half caressing, she asked, "Hertz, are you
sleeping?"

"No, my darling."

"Don't call me darling! Hertz, I want to ask you something, but you must tell me the truth."

"I'm too weak to tell lies."

"Do you love her?"

"I don't know."

"What, then? Purely physical?"

"I no longer know anything."

"May I lie next to you for a while?"

"Yes, lie down."

She lay down carefully beside him. The sofa was too narrow for both of them and its springs groaned. Grein was conscious of her heaviness, the mass that gravity dragged unstoppably to the ground. Someone's bowels rumbled—were they hers or his? How bizarre not to know the difference between oneself and another! He had to flatten himself against the back of the sofa to make more room for her, yet at any moment she might still roll off. As he clasped her around the waist with a protective hand, her bosom, pressing against him, seemed to renew his strength.

"Hertz, do you remember that we once wanted to die together?"

"Yes, I remember."

"I would be ready now."

Grein did not reply immediately. He seemed to be thinking over the meaning of what she had said. "Well, I'm not far from that myself . . ."

"Do you remember how we once turned on the gas and sat in the bathtub together?"

"Yes, yes."

"No, Hertz, you don't have anything to die for."

And Esther pressed herself even more ardently against him. She lay almost on top of him. He wanted to ask her to move away a little, but he said nothing. Every word was an effort for him. Now he had only one desire: to put things off, to wait until later, to leave everything hanging in the air. God in heaven, he had to sleep for a few minutes. He had never been as tired as he was now, struggling with an adamantine weariness that disabled all his limbs. In this condition one could sleep on the sidewalk, in the mud, in the middle of a battlefield.

Besides, Grein knew that he would get no rest tonight. Esther would not let him leave. She would make a vigil of the night, as she did every time there was cause for distress. For a long time they huddled there, somber and comfortless, two beaten creatures who had clawed and bitten each other for so long that both had been left half-dead, without rage, without grievances—two lumps of inertia. They panted heavily but without clamor, calling to mind animals in a slaughterhouse.

Suddenly Esther whispered, "Hertz, this is the end!"

This was the second time tonight he had heard these words, first from Leah, now from Esther. Both women had uttered the phrase with the same inflection. The parallels froze him like a magic spell. Fear choked his voice.

"Well, if it's the end, it's the end."

He gave the same answer as before. He had a sinister premonition that he had sealed his own fate.

"Hertz, what are you doing? You're murdering a great love!"

He did not reply and started to doze. Esther also seemed to drift into sleep. They lay like two robbers in a cave, driven from the sight of God, cast out by decent people. Grein fell asleep, but Esther woke him.

"Hertz, I want to tell you something."

"What?"

"Hertz, until now I haven't done a single thing that's good for me. I've always sacrificed myself for love. For me, love was the holiest thing in the world. My God, when my father, peace be upon him, insisted that I should marry that Piniele, I wept for nights on end. I literally soaked my bed with my tears. When you came into my life, I was ready to go through fire for you. That's not just some hackneyed cliché, Hertz. I would have let my throat be cut for you. To die for love—that was my ideal. But now I've decided I've had enough. In the ghetto there was a pious Jew who recited psalms the whole time. They dragged his entire family to the ovens, but he crouched in a hole somewhere and went on praying and studying from memory. You know the justification: God knows what He's doing. We sinned. In the World to Come we will make atonement. For months he sat in that cellar with some other Jews, all dying of hunger. Then one day he suddenly grabbed his phylacteries and tore them to pieces. He spat on them and he trampled them and he screamed, God, I don't want to serve you any longer! You're worse than Hitler! I don't need you or your World to Come! So he destroyed everything—his fringed ritual undergarment and his prayer books, everything. Then he left his hiding place and gave himself to the Nazis. Liuba, my friend Liuba, described it all to me. I'll do the same, Hertz. I don't want love anymore! I spit on it! If this is love, then prostitution is better. I'll do something bad, Hertz. I'll do something so bad you'll laugh and cry and spit."

"What'll you do?"

"Something unbelievably stupid."

10

The clock showed a quarter past three. Grein shut Esther's door and went down the stairs. This is the end, the end—he repeated Esther's words. During the night, frost had settled. From the sea, a snowy wind blew inland, beating like waves against everything standing. Half-glimmering, the sky hung low. The gelid streetlamps illuminated only their own isolation. Pulling up his coat collar, Grein walked to the El in Brighton. Esther had driven him out. She gave him a last kiss and insisted, "Go, and don't ever come back. From now on, we're enemies. Blood enemies."

He stood on the raised platform and waited for the local train that should have come from Coney Island. But the rails were silent. He walked back and forth to keep himself warm. How quiet and empty everything was below! The shops on the avenue were all tightly shuttered; in the side streets the windows were blind with midnight blackness. Everything slept: the shopkeepers, the customers, even the sea, which seemed to breathe with the heaviness of slumber. A gust of wind lifted a sheet of newspaper, whirling it around and around until it started rolling oddly over the pavement, seemingly buffeted from side to side by demons that had thrown it into some Sling of Gehenna reserved exclusively for paper. For a while it clung to a pillar of the El as if seeking some protection from its tormentor, but it was soon violently ripped away and sent flying once more, pursued by an unseen host. Grein went over to a lamppost to look at his watch. Twenty minutes had passed and there was no sign of a train. Who knows? Perhaps the trains had stopped running in the middle of the night.

The cold bit through his sleeves, his collar, his trouser legs. Stooped from exhaustion, he sought out a corner protected from the wind where a scale stood. For a moment Grein shut his eyes, comparing himself to a weary horse dozing even as it stood in the traces. Well, wherever one lays one's head, that's where one sleeps, he thought, shuddering and pressing his shoulder against the wall. Where should I go now? Perhaps there was a hotel here in the neighborhood. But where?

Suddenly there was a rush and a clatter and the tracks blazed with reflected light. A train pulled in, but going in the opposite direction. It brought passengers from Manhattan or who knew where. Although the train that arrived was not his, it brought some comfort, because if trains were coming *from* Manhattan, then trains were also going *to* Manhattan. In Grein's mind, this was linked with a Cabalistic teaching that the Evil Spirit bears witness to the existence of God. If a left or dark side exists, then a right or light side must exist also. A solitary passenger had alighted and glanced at Grein from across the tracks. His face seemed to say mutely: I've come and you're going . . . that's how life is.

Where is he going? Grein wondered. Has he also got an Esther some-where near here? Perhaps he is going to the same Esther, a goblin whis-pered to him. Perhaps Esther had kept another lover all this time, and when Grein was asleep she would let the other one in.

At that moment the train from Coney Island arrived. Only in the silence of the night could one fully appreciate its deafening roar, the power of its wheels, the glare of its lights. Its doors hissed open with the generosity of powers that do not judge but distribute their gifts with godlike favor. Grein entered with uncommon haste, as if he were afraid that the doors might have regrets and prematurely shut in his face. As a welcome warmth em-braced him, he sought out a seat over a heater. He was alone in the car and this simultaneously frightened him a little and gave him the satisfaction of having everything to himself. It reminded him of his boyhood, when on a Friday night, after the Sabbath meal, he would go into the Hasidic pray-erhouse in their courtyard on Smocza Street, and all the benches, all the tables, all the sacred books, all the candles in the six-branched candelabrum would belong to him alone.

At Sheepshead Bay a drunk got on. He sat down next to Grein and tried to give a political lecture. He prattled on in a way that made Grein suspect that he was preaching Jew-hatred, since he kept on mentioning the name Morgenthau, despite this statesman's having resigned long ago. The vacant eyes that peered slyly at Grein seemed to say: There's no Constitution for a drunk . . . I can do what others dare not.

Only now did Grein notice that the train was not going over the bridge but through the tunnel. Every station brought new passengers—the ma-jority black and wild-eyed, wearing fur coats and caps, deep galoshes, and the grease-stained garments of those who do heavy labor. One looked like a study for a portrait symbolizing the fate of the proletariat. Big, broad, dirty, hairy, with grime under his fingernails and one index finger chopped off, he clutched a tin lunch box. His eyes reflected the submissive silence of those who shoulder a crushing burden without reward and without hope. This train carried only men—not a single woman was present. All were quiet, lost in nocturnal introspection.

At Times Square Grein got off. How mysterious the place looked in the wintry hours before sunrise! The cars merely rustled as they passed by. All the windows in the towering buildings were shut tight. A sliver of sky slowly turned green like a tiny field. The air was cold and pure. A drunk staggered past, seemingly on the lookout for someone to accost. It seemed to Grein that in this unwonted silence everything had again acquired a European dignity: every building, every streetlamp, the signs over the shops, the brightly lit bus. God's breath blew once more over New York. Grein hurried off to a hotel near Eighth Avenue; he had caught a chill and went straight to bed. Not even bothering to remove the bedspread, he laid his head on the pillow, but he did not fall asleep immediately. He could hear murmuring and snuffling from the corridor and from the city, which had already started to rouse itself.

At 7:30 the telephone rang. He had asked them to wake him so he would not be late for his rendezvous with Anna. The room was dark, but a light burned in the window opposite where a young woman busied herself with her toilet. She had not lowered the blind. Utterly without shame she wandered about stark naked, as in the days of the Generation of the Flood. First she displayed the front of her body, then the back. She raised her arms as though about to do gymnastic exercises, clutched her head, and yawned. Then she went over to the window and slowly lowered the blind with the bearing of an actress bringing down the curtain after her own performance. Suddenly Grein started up violently. Last night he had taken the train almost as far as Coney Island and on the way there had hidden his overnight bag in a locker, but on the way back he'd forgotten about it. He hadn't even remembered it when he'd gone to bed. The last twenty-four hours had completely disoriented him. He had rapidly grown accustomed to sleeping in his shirt and paying in advance for hotel rooms.

There was only one solution: to dress quickly, return to Coney Island, recover the suitcase, and get back to Grand Central. If everything went well, none of this would take more than an hour and a half. Only later, sitting in the subway, did Grein realize that his decision had been foolish, impractical, reckless: he could have made the same trip with Anna and saved himself all this tension and rush. He needn't have made it at all—he could easily have abandoned the suitcase entirely and bought himself new pajamas and a shaving kit. By the time he came to his senses, the train was already halfway there. He had done something very stupid, but according to Freud it was motivated by a subconscious wish to postpone his meeting, perhaps even to evade and cancel it completely. It was odd and painfully unpleasant to be traveling back to Brooklyn, Esther's Brooklyn.

A nna opened her eyes. The sun, suspended high above, had woken her. Her window faced east and a fiery orb had risen from the East River, flaring into the bedroom like a searchlight. Stanislaw Luria's unshaven face was suffused with purple, his closed eyelids webbed with shadows, his thick lips puffy. He reminded Anna of a murdered man. It seemed as if his mouth were demanding wordlessly: What exactly have I done? How have I deserved this punishment? The watercolors on the walls, glowing in the dappled sunlight, seemed only now to reveal the meaning the artist had imparted to them. They appeared to be sharing both sunrise and sunset, as if on this early winter morning the two had occurred at the same time. Anna had slept for only three hours, but she awoke rested and clearheaded. She remembered everything: Luria's oath that he would never give her a divorce for all the gold in Fort Knox and her father's expostulations and threats. From this apartment he had telephoned his rebbe in Williamsburg and had given Anna two choices: either she could go off with Grein, in which case he would instantly disinherit and disown her, or she could swear on the Pentateuch and on the bones of her mother that she would have no further dealings with that libertine. Boris had grabbed his checkbook, scribbled his signature on a blank check, and thrust it at her: "Write in however much you want!" He had stormed furiously through the apartment clutching his head and screaming, "You've got two roads: a father, riches, and the World to Come into the bargain, or you can rot on the Bowery! Remember what I say!'' And he had pointed to the left side of his chest, where his heart beat. Anna knew perfectly well that this emotional stress was deadly to him. His blood pressure was dangerously high and he had already suffered one heart attack in Havana.

Yes, she had sworn. Weeping bitterly, she had embraced her father, kissed his hands, and cried out, ''Papa, you're dearer to me than everything in the world!''

''My child, you'll live to thank me. Both in this world and in the next!''

Boris Makaver's deep voice was hoarse with tears. He locked himself in the bathroom, and for a long time Anna could hear him sobbing and coughing. He let the water gush out of the faucets to muffle his anguished groans.

Only at two in the morning did her father say good night and go home. Then Luria's vilification was unleashed in earnest. The upshot of all his abuse and threats was that he would forgive her this time, but from now on he would never permit that Grein to cross his threshold. In his rage he snatched up a shirt and tore it in half. He stamped his feet, screamed like one possessed, smashed ashtrays, glasses, whatever he could lay his hands on. Even worse than his cursing were his attempts to make up. His anger changed to lust and he pursued her through the rooms so that she almost broke a leg fleeing from him. He tried to take her by force, but at the last moment he became impotent. He ranted like a madman and tried to drink iodine. Then he was seized by a pain across his heart and Anna was on the point of calling an ambulance.

The night passed like a horrible dream. But her three hours of sleep seemed to have covered over the wounds. Anna sat up in bed. Luria's clothes were scattered all over the carpet. One of his shoes lay roasting on the hot radiator. Her own things were also strewn all over the place. The bedroom looked like a vacated battlefield. Now that the sun was edging everything in purple, a stream of blood seemed to be dripping from one of Luria's neckties. Anna got up and went quietly into the living room. It was dark there and Anna trod gingerly among shards and splinters of glass. Evidently it had snowed during the night, because Lexington Avenue was blanketed in a whiteness that even the trucks had not yet dirtied. Tinged with electric blue, the snow lay thickly piled on every surface, on every balcony, on every fire escape.

The shops were all shut. Not a single passerby was to be seen. The headlights and sidelights of the trucks still burned, carrying yesterday with them. Anna stood at the window in her low-cut nightdress. Nobody could see her from here, except perhaps God, that God on whose account she had to renounce Grein and remain with Luria.

She had a sudden craving for coffee. Insofar as all her hopes for the future had evaporated, she had to live in the present. Going into the kitchen, she switched on the light and put the percolator on the gas stove. Normally Anna avoided starchy food and seldom ate cake, cookies, or cinnamon loaf, the very things Luria was so fond of nibbling all day. From now on, however, she could eat what she pleased. She took out a cinnamon loaf and cut off a thick slice. Perhaps she should recite the blessing, the thought occurred to her. But what sort of blessing did one make over cinnamon loaf? She could remember only two of the many prescribed by Jewish Law: "Who bringest forth bread from the earth" and "By whose word all things come into being." Well, it was all the same. Was it possible that God listens to every blessing, to every word people speak? Would it really make any difference to God if Luria gave her a piece of paper that people call a divorce, or not? God could hardly be so petty and absorbed in trivial paperwork—it was all a human fabrication. But since her father believed it completely, he would die of grief and she could not make that sacrifice. Nor could she allow the whole of his estate to pass into the hands of strangers. Anna poured out the coffee and added cream. The kitchen window overlooked a courtyard where lights burned in a great many windows. Women in housecoats busied themselves at gas stoves and refrigerators. Men who left early for work were already eating their breakfasts. A woman with a mop washed her linoleum.

I had no idea people got up so early, Anna mused with surprise. Ah, the burdens they bear . . . The bread they eat doesn't come easily. Well, at least I spent one night with him! she consoled herself. Whatever might happen, no one can take that night away from me. It's mine, mine.

Anna sipped the hot coffee slowly, drinking and dozing, dozing and drinking. I'm tired, tired. She thought of returning to the bedroom, but she was revolted by Luria, who was sleeping in there. Her aversion to him had hardened—she could no longer endure the pouches under his eyes, the rasp of his voice. The thought that he could still lust after her was terrifying.

It would be easier if I were at least alone! Oh, if only he would die!

What bliss that would be! Papa loves Grein. He'd be happy to have him for a son-in-law.

Anna shook herself. What's the matter with me? We're forbidden to wish anyone dead. It's not his fault that I can't bear him. God in heaven, I chased him, after all—I was in love with him. Anna recalled this as something that shamed her. Oh, everything's so distorted and devious.

Although it was still dark outside, it was no longer very early. If she was to meet Grein at nine o'clock at Grand Central and tell him what she had to say, she would have to hurry. She would tell him everything, the whole truth. Who knows? Perhaps it would be a relief for him. It wasn't easy to leave a family. Sitting with her hands wrapped tightly around the coffee cup, Anna felt very old, almost as if after yesterday old age had caught up with her. She owned nothing more than this one cup of coffee. She thought back to Warsaw, to her Aunt Sarah Itte, whose kitchen was always crowded with aged Jewish women, to each of whom her aunt would give chicory coffee and a slice of bread. They would gratefully sip the hot drink, dunking the hard crusts and munching with toothless mouths. Now Anna felt she had become one of those crones.

Going into the bathroom, she ran water into the tub, throwing off her nightdress with the elation of an insect discarding its cocoon. She scrutinized her figure in the mirror. No, her body was young. Her hair was so black that it shaded into blue. Her breasts were firm, her hips narrow. Though tired, her eyes were still merry. Anna winked at herself. At least I made a cuckold of him, she gloated over Luria with destructive pleasure. Who knows? This might lead to a divorce. He won't get over it so quickly. Anna was ashamed of her thoughts, but she could not drive away the joy she felt at having given herself to Grein. That night remained with her as a gift, a precious jewel, a souvenir which her memory could turn over as long as she lived. And Gehenna? Let them lay her on the bed of spikes.

She got into the bathtub, started soaping, scrubbing, and sponging herself. The night with Grein had awakened in Anna a strong attraction to her own body. In it Grein had found exotic charms that he had praised lavishly, comparing her to a panther and remarking in wonderment on her capacity to kiss passionately for minutes on end without losing her breath. He had found merits in her that only a man could identify and treasure.

"Ah, I love him! I love him!" Anna exclaimed aloud. "More than ever."

Then suddenly it occurred to her that now, after she had made that sacrifice for Papa, she no longer loved her father. That renunciation had drained her. Now she was quits with him and with everyone.

2

What shall I wear? Anna asked herself. The beaver fur? The blue coat? She was going to tell Grein that everything was over, but she wanted to please him for the last time. Let him at least know that he had lost a beautiful woman. Anna took out the beaver fur and hung diamond earrings in her pierced lobes. She did everything languidly. Having put an end to all haste, she felt the repose in her head, in her heart, even in her guts. A long tension had relaxed, a tautness that had stretched out for nearly two years. The experience was akin to one she had undergone twenty-three years before, after her mother's funeral, when she was eleven years old. An end had finally come to the visits of doctors, the importunities of wonder-working rabbis, the counsels of professors. Everything had suddenly grown silent and void. In such a frame of mind, Anna now thought, one could breathe out one's soul without being ill in the slightest but simply because the pulse no longer had any reason to beat. Yet the opposite could also happen: she could live on for who knew how long, growing wrinkled and shriveled, like one of those skeletons that sit in the foyers of hotels with time frozen around them.

Anna opened a drawer in the bureau, puttered about, transferred something from one purse to another, but had no clear idea of what she was doing. Luria emerged from the bedroom, his hairy chest bare, his belly bulging, his legs too short for his body. He lumbered and snorted like an animal as he approached her. From under his beetling brows his rage flared up.

"Where are you running to?"

"You know where. I explained everything to you yesterday."

"When will you be back?"

Not waiting for an answer, he went into the bathroom and blew his nose furiously. Evidently he was continuing to wreck the place, for a glass bottle lay shattered on the floor.

God, how I hate him! How good to be rid of him! Anna reflected.

Throughout the whole of last night's outburst, Anna indulged a fantasy: Luria and Leah, Grein's wife, die on the same day. She and Grein meet after the funerals. They weep and kiss. He moves into her apartment immediately.

Anna left the apartment. Well, I don't mean it, I don't mean it. Let Luria live in good health, she hastily appeased the unseen powers that eavesdrop on human thoughts. And I've certainly got nothing against Grein's wife.

The elevator, when it arrived, was operated by the same lout as on the night before last. He appraised Anna with a sidelong and speculative glance. It seemed to her that his eyes asked wordlessly: You're still here? Again he puckered up his lips to whistle. Outdoors it was frosty and had turned cloudy. Anna walked downtown along Lexington Avenue. Since she was early, she stopped to look into the antiques shops. How peculiar all these objects displayed in the shop windows were: chess pieces of ivory and ebony, the carved figure of an Indian, a spinning wheel, a pestle and mortar of the kind used to grind matzo into meal, a painting depicting soldiers plundering a Dutch household. Were these Germans? Frenchmen? They would probably very soon start painting pictures showing Nazis murdering Jews, and married couples would hang these up in their bedrooms.

To Anna everything that morning appeared old, faded, oppressive: every passerby, every car, every building. The blooms in the florist's shops were lifeless. The fish put out on ice had bloodstained scales and glassy eyes. Women tramped along in frozen snow boots, men in huge galoshes. Although a policeman gave signals to the motorists, it seemed to Anna that they were ignoring them and that at any moment the officer could be knocked down by a car. From a meat truck outside a butcher's, big-bellied men carted raw sides of beef atop their heads. In the window, among the bloody chunks of meat, hung a whole lamb, its belly slashed open from neck to tail. Well, that could be done to anyone. They might easily have displayed me in the same way. Heaven would not have fallen because of it.

After a while Anna crossed over to Park Avenue. Here there was nothing to arrest the eye. The red and gray buildings rose like enormous jails in which entire human tribes languished in comfort. Not a single tree could be seen growing here, only tiny gardens in which people placed saplings at Christmas time, illuminating them with colored lightbulbs. A poodle, dragged along behind an old woman, suddenly lifted its leg opposite a wall, and urinated a single drop. An elderly gray-haired doorman in a uniform was minding a carriage in which a rosy little girl with the face of an angry piglet lay on a pillow.

Anna entered the station and started looking for Grein. He should have met her amid the hubbub of the main concourse, where the banks were, but he wasn't there. She went into another area where the same din prevailed. Passengers were bustling about carrying suitcases. Lines formed at the cashiers' windows. The information desk was besieged. Through a loudspeaker an announcer called out the names of stations that Anna had never heard of. Although the war was long over, one still saw a great many soldiers and sailors, each with his kit bag and rucksack. Russia and America were now waging a cold war that might turn hot at any moment. Strange, Grein wasn't here either. Had he also had second thoughts? The huge clock with its illuminated dial already showed ten minutes after nine. Anna went off to buy a newspaper and then paced about the waiting room. It reeked of cigars and had the fetid, musty odor that filled taxis, post offices, trains, all places in which many people come and go. A soldier led his young wife by her hand; she was hardly older than a schoolgirl but her jutting belly proclaimed the last months of pregnancy. He was apparently returning to camp, and his young wife gazed up at him with entreaty and a half-submissive, half-mischievous little smile that seemed to be asking: Do you remember? How did this all happen? We've only just met each other, after all. To Anna it seemed that the belly itself demanded to be looked at, admonishing them: You formed me, you filled me, you are my guardians. If you should abandon me, who would take me? The soldier smiled the lost smile of those who have been put under the yoke. Anna felt ill at ease: why are they dragging all these boys away? What do they want with their youth? Why are they inciting them to fight each other? She was ashamed, standing before this young man in her fur and diamond earrings. Who knows? Perhaps because of sybarites like me, the whole world suffers!

It was now twenty past nine, but Grein had still not shown up. Well, he's obviously backed out. It's better this way. Let that be his satisfaction— *he's* given *me* up. Nevertheless, it astonished Anna that so early on he found it unnecessary to explain or to justify himself. Well, I'll just have to swallow this mistake as well.

Anna decided to wait only ten minutes more and not a second longer. She opened her purse and was startled to discover that in it she had put her jewelry, her bankbooks, the key to her safe-deposit box, her citizenship papers. Does this mean I was ready to run off with him? Break my vow? No, I only did it out of habit. I'm always afraid the apartment will be robbed. In any case, Luria might easily tear up and smash everything out of spite—just as he did yesterday, when he ripped up the shirt I bought him for his birthday.

Anna strode from bench to bench, restlessly searching for Grein. Well, she hadn't expected this. This would destroy even the pleasure that the night she had spent with him had brought her. Never mind, I'm quite calm. Anna entered the main concourse once more. Time there passed a little more quickly. The walls were covered with posters, placards, announcements. All these banners and pictures had one theme—love. They showed a newly married couple leaving on their honeymoon. Well, I don't envy them. Truly not. At least I won't have any children. Without sitting down, Anna paged through her newspaper. Normally she only glanced at the headlines, but now she tried to concentrate on the reports. Stalin had given an interview in which he maintained that Communism and capitalism could live together. His image stared down from the front page. To add to all his other virtues, he had now become a peacemaker as well. Now the press had something to make a fuss about. But her Uncle Mordechai would go on rotting somewhere in Russian soil. No one would remember the wrong done to him.

Something inside Anna wept. Grein had no cause to give her such a slap in the face. One doesn't shame even a servant in this way. There was one minute left before half-past nine.

3

She had to go home. Every moment she continued to wait humiliated her. But something held her back. She stood irresolutely in the middle of the concourse. Why am I so impatient? she asked herself. I'm not going away with him, in any event. Isn't this merely pride? No, she simply longed to see him, to have a few words with him. From now on, all ties with him would be broken. How strange that so soon after he had become the person closest to her, he had to become the one most distant. Anna stared in front of her, baffled at the direction everything had taken. There was obviously some mistake here, but where? Could she break the oath she had taken? Could she drive her father to the grave with her passion? Could she reject his help and his estate? She gaped at the huge chandeliers with their myriad lightbulbs. What could they really illuminate? So much outer light, so much inner darkness. What shall I do? Where shall I go? How shall I react? Go home? What'll I do at home? The thought that Luria was there waiting for her made her so nauseous she wanted to vomit. I'll take a trip somewhere. But where? The Catskills? Lakewood? Atlantic City? What'll I do there all alone? I could try to make new friends. But who throws aside someone she adores and goes looking for love where it can probably never be found? And what'll happen if I do get involved with someone else? The same thing all over again: Luria won't give me a divorce and Papa will start screaming that it's a sin. All it means is that I must sit and wait for Papa to die.

Something in Anna laughed. By what right does he demand this sacrifice of me? He himself is bound to get married. The match with Frieda Tamar was as good as settled. That rebbetzin could possibly still have children, and then the inheritance would be divided among them. She might even bear Papa a son. Anna was stunned. How could I not have considered this before? How could I have given him an oath knowing all this? For the first time, Anna started to mistrust her father. He wasn't such a saint as he made out. In his own way he was sly, a wily businessman who could win over a stone. Surely if one wanted to serve God, one was supposed to sacrifice oneself, not someone else.

Suddenly something in Anna made an about-face. There was an upheaval within her, as though her insides had convulsed from sheer rebellion. I repudiate the oath, something shouted within her. I'll do as I please! I spit on everything: on the oath, on the inheritance, on Luria, on all the religious fanaticism! I'll live, I'll live! If not with Grein, then with someone else. I won't let my years be wasted, I won't sacrifice myself for anyone—not for anyone! Papa won't die—he won't die! He's healthier than I am! He'll live to be eighty and fill a house full of children. He's held me by the throat long enough!

An unfamiliar contrariness seized Anna. What did Papa want of her? What right did he have to dictate to her? It was her life, not his. They won't burn him in my Gehenna! Anna no longer stood still but paced rapidly up and down, bumping into travelers and pieces of luggage, charged with vigor and determination. What did they all want? Why had they all ganged up on her? She was a woman of thirty-four—in ten years the best of her life would be over and done with. I'm no one's slave! I'll go where

I want and I'll do what I please! If Grein isn't the one, then it'll be someone else—let him stay with his harridan. In the whole of New York I can surely find someone interested in me—and if no one'll have me freely, I'll buy love! Anna cried out to someone in her thoughts. I'll take a—what do they call it here?—I've forgotten. I'll use Papa's check to buy a lover for myself. I'll use everything. Every opportunity. It makes no difference— I'm not so old and ugly, not by a long shot! I'm still attractive to men. I'll go off with the first one who comes along! I'll stop being so choosy! I've no more time to lose! Enough!

Anna shouted the word "Enough!" aloud. Everyone around her heard and stared. A black porter winked at her.

"Are you looking for someone, miss?"

Anna turned away from him. Shame and self-pity swept over her. They'll drive me insane! she cautioned herself. The clock now showed a quarter to ten.

Well, what do I do now? she asked herself. I'll call him at home. Perhaps he's still at home. If his wife answers, I'll say I want to buy some stocks.

Anna glanced around and spotted the telephone booths, but they were all occupied. A youth with the face of a gangster was talking and gesticulating. His black hair glistened with grease. While he muttered into the receiver he cast an experienced eye over the concourse, as though he suspected that someone was lying in wait for him and was about to ambush him. He wore a diamond ring and a wristwatch with a braided band; the stickpin in his tie sported a horse's head. In the second booth a petite woman intent on being a lady chattered and giggled, a malicious smile frequently lighting up her small painted face. Everything about her was doll-like and artificial: her slim figure, her freshly dyed and newly styled platinum-blond hair, her pointed, blood-red nails. Even her leopard-skin coat looked fake. Anna felt a surge of hatred toward this diminutive person. What was she prattling on about for so long? What could such a frivolous number have to communicate? In another booth someone dropped a great many coins into the slot. He was obviously speaking to someone in another city or sending a cable. All these people looked completely self-assured. Not one of them was in such a quandary as Anna. It seemed to her that they were all part of one clique, determined to jabber on and on for the sole purpose of occupying the booths. But what could they possibly be talking about? Who had the patience to listen to their babbling?

With me it's always either yes or no—I never speak on the telephone for more than a minute or two. Perhaps that's why I make such tragic mistakes. If I had the power, I'd arrest all of them, Anna decided. Let them rot in jail, the scum!

The youth who Anna had decided was a gangster opened the door, but instead of leaving he remained seated. He scrabbled together more coins from his change purse, puckering his thick lips as though to whistle. Anna was struck by his perfectly shaped and well-manicured nails. Suddenly he left the booth. Anna entered immediately to find that his breath remained behind, a blend of cigarette smoke and stale tobacco. She opened her pocketbook and began rummaging for a nickel, but she had everything except a nickel: a dime, a penny, quarters, a half-dollar. I've really got bad luck today! It occurred to Anna to put in a quarter and ask the operator to connect her, but Anna had forgotten Grein's number. She pushed open the door to let in some fresh air and fumbled for her address book. Someone else was now waiting to use the booth, and Anna wryly perceived that this person was probably just as angry with her as she had been earlier with the "gangster." The address book had been mislaid somewhere. The clock now showed exactly ten. No, I won't call! Anna decided. If he can sit at home knowing that I'm waiting for him here, then everything is over in any case.

She left the booth and hurried toward the station exit. A woman passing by called out to her, "Miss, your purse is open!"

"Oh, thank you very much."

At that moment someone laid a hand on her shoulder. Anna turned around. Grein was standing beside her.

4

Grein and Anna emerged from the station and turned left, in the direction of Tudor City. They walked in the silence of those who have too much to say and don't know where to begin. How strange—in just the time Anna had been waiting at the station the weather had cleared a little. The sun was shining. Anna clutched Grein's arm. How on earth could I even have contemplated not going with him? She was astonished at herself. Without him, my life is worth nothing. After a few more paces they stopped.

"May I ask why you were an hour late?"

"Oh, I forgot my overnight bag in a locker and I had to go back for it on the subway. In the middle of the trip there was a breakdown. The train was delayed for twenty minutes."

"I was on the verge of leaving. Didn't you spend the night at home?"

"No."

"Where did you sleep?"

"In a hotel near Times Square."

"Where did you leave your bag?"

"Uptown. What happened yesterday? Why didn't you come to the telephone?"

"What? Oh, Papa came storming over. At the very moment you rang, he walked in. What did Luria say to you? I was in the bathroom. He told tales about me, didn't he?"

"Where are we going? This is the East Side, you know. Let's go back. I need to stop at the bank. He said that you had an affair in Casablanca."

Anna halted. "Did he say that?"

"Yes."

"Well, now I can hate him with my whole heart."

"Let's go to a restaurant somewhere. Have you eaten?"

"Yes. But you certainly haven't. Here's a restaurant. No, it's a cafeteria."

"Do you want to go in here?"

"Why not? It's all the same to me."

They went in. Breakfast time was over and it was still a long while till lunch. The cafeteria was half-empty.

"Let's sit here—at this table," Anna indicated. "What shall I get you?"

"I'll help myself."

"No, from now on I'll serve you."

"Here's some money."

"No, I'll pay. What do you feel like? I'll choose the rest myself."

He sat down at the table, watching Anna buy him orange juice, cereal, milk, coffee, and apricot jam. In this establishment one paid at the counter. Anna's European fur and her diamond earrings were wildly inappropriate here, out of keeping with the tray she was carrying and with the general shabbiness of the place. The women behind the counter stared after her and muttered something. They glanced at Grein as well: it was not the American custom for a man to sit while a woman served him. How is it that she hasn't got an overnight bag? Grein wondered. Perhaps she was afraid to pack. Well, this meal marks a turning point in my life. This is where the second act starts, or perhaps even the third. He got up and took the tray out of Anna's hands. It was heavier than he expected and he very nearly dropped it.

"Be careful!"

"Take off your fur," he replied.

"What? Well, eat."

Anna didn't take off her fur, but sat gazing at him instead. She served him, pouring milk over the cereal, adding cream to the coffee, with an expression that was half-smiling, half-troubled, filled with the bashfulness of those who have suddenly cast aside all restraints and have reached the most familiar level of intimacy. He was also a little embarrassed in front of her, Boris Makaver's little girl, to whom he used to bring sweets and whom he had helped with her lessons. She now smiled in exactly the way she had in those days: childishly, eagerly, even a little foolishly, with that girlish admiration for another that a man can never really comprehend. Grein had long ago decided that idolatry was a female sin: in the Bible it was almost always practiced by foreign women and harlots.

"Shall I put in sugar?" Anna asked, then suddenly grew serious and demanded, "What exactly did Luria say?"

Grein frowned. "I told you."

"What was it? Why don't you ask me if it's true?"

"You tell me whatever you have to say."

"Yes, it's true. But Luria's scum in any case. I didn't believe he could be so despicable. I thought that even with all his faults he was still a gentleman."

"Who was it? How many men have you had in your life?"

"I'll tell you everything. Perhaps this isn't the right place, but what's the difference? When we leave here, I want there to be no more secrets between us. At least, not on my part. I've had three men in my life. Besides you, that is. I loved only one of them—Yasha Kotik, and him for only a short while. I married Luria out of confusion, or perhaps my rotten luck drove me to it. It was madness almost from the start. The moment I stood with him under the wedding canopy, I knew I was heading for disaster. The Greeks have a name for it—for doing something that's absolutely inevitable. Fate? No, not Fate. As always, Papa was to blame, but I was adult enough by then not to have allowed myself to be driven into a corner."

"Who came between Kotik and Luria?"

"What? I want you to know that for five years after Yasha Kotik and I separated, I lived completely alone. He made everything so ugly that for years afterward I couldn't bring myself even to look at anyone else. I'll never be able to describe what he did to me. He was someone who could blacken the sun. I lived with him for barely a year, yet in that time I passed through all seven gates of hell. Many times when Papa starts threatening me with Gehenna, I think I already know all the horrors. There can't possibly be anything new for me. You know, I fell ill and Dr. Margolin literally dragged me out of a psychological abyss. He has many faults, but he's an outstanding doctor. The world doesn't know how remarkable he is, because his greatness is built on practice, not theories. He has a profound understanding of people and immense hypnotic powers. He can diagnose an illness merely by looking at a patient. But in his own way, he's depraved and a bit of a fool. One could write a book about him. He tried to seduce me, but I developed a powerful aversion to him—perhaps because he's such a close friend of Papa's. Neither his hypnosis nor all his Jungian tricks could overcome my resistance to him. He says that because of me he acquired an inferiority complex. The real truth is that to this very day he's still in love with his wife, that German bitch who ran off to live with a Nazi. He also has a daughter who must be seventeen or eighteen by now. I only want to say one thing: for five years, I behaved like an unspotted virgin. I even stopped reading novels. Everything related to love revolted and terrified me. When I wanted to go to the theater, I chose plays that had nothing to do with love. Just then they were performing Romain Rolland's *The Wolves*, and that was tailor-made for me. You'll laugh, but I used to sit and read dictionaries and encyclopedias. I went through Part Two of *Faust*. I even read Clausewitz's works on military strategy, although God knows I always loathed war.''

''What happened to Yasha Kotik?''

''Didn't I tell you? It was thought he had been murdered by the Nazis, but what's the saying? Scum floats to the top. He escaped to Russia and became a big name there. I once went to a movie house where they were showing a Russian film and he was in it. He'd grown a beard, I think. As soon as I saw him, I fled. I've heard that now he's in Poland or somewhere. Papa's convinced he's dead. Papa's not one to bear a grudge, especially against someone who was almost martyred, but whenever he remembers Kotik, he always says, 'May he be the last of his line.' ''

''Have you got a photograph of him?''

''No, I threw everything away. Why aren't you eating the jam?''

"Who was the man in Casablanca?"

"What? I'll tell you. But perhaps we should put it off till another time."

"No, I want to know."

5

"Y ou mustn't think I wanted to hide it from you. I decided immediately to keep no secrets from you. I want to come to you as pure as I would to God, and if my past disturbs you, tell me straight out now. I realize that you're one of those men who gets jealous over a woman's past, even though you're not such a puritan yourself. But I don't intend there to be any lies or misunderstandings between us. Take me just as I am or not at all.

"When the Nazis came to power, we fled to France. I'd never been to Paris before, and I imagined all kinds of wonders. You know the things they write about Paris, of course, and while we lived there I had more *powodzenie*, more success, than anywhere else. The French liked me. And whatever else they are, our Jewish 'Frenchmen' from Warsaw and Bucharest are genuinely cultivated people. But in the end Paris had no real allure for me. Certainly everything was beautiful, and it was probably even more interesting in reality than it had seemed in books, but I wasn't in a romantic frame of mind to appreciate it. When the Vichy shock came and we fled to Africa, though, something in me woke up. Whether it was the climate or the distress and the terrible tension, I don't know. We were continually risking our lives. I can't tell you what kind of gambler Papa is. Either he has no conception of terror or he's such a saint that angels guard him. He managed to save everything, every penny, and how he managed to do it, and how many times he staked his life for it, I'm afraid to think. He's not greedy for money. He gave away huge sums to Dr. Halperin and to Professor Shrage. He can throw thousands around, but when he has a mind to, he'll go through fire for a groschen. You can't begin to imagine what I lived through. I didn't sleep for nights on end. Papa once told me a story out of the Torah: that Jacob crossed some river for the sake of a few small pitchers of oil. Perhaps you know it?"

"Yes, it's in the Gemara."

"Papa said it was in the Bible."

"In the Bible it says that in fleeing from Esau, Jacob crossed the Jordan a second time, and the Gemara tries to explain why he did so."

"Well, at least I remember something. In Casablanca we lived in the same hotel as a family of Jewish refugees from Italy: a husband, a wife, and a son of twenty-one—Cesare."

"So he was your lover?"

"Yes. Can you imagine it? I don't understand myself how it happened. He was a child, and I was a mature woman by comparison. They had fled from Mussolini. The father, Piero, was a manufacturer. The mother, Biancchina, wasn't Jewish—her father'd been a train driver for Mussolini and they'd sent him to Abyssinia. Cesare had studied jurisprudence in Rome, but he was a refined young man, a real mama's boy, and I remember the first thing I said to him, once we had got to know each other, was that he would make a poor lawyer. To compensate for that, he was an outstanding organizer. We spoke French together. I don't know how, but he got hold of a motorcycle and flew around on it like a madman. Where he managed to get gasoline is a mystery to me. It worried his mother to death, because she'd already lost an older son in the war.

"I can't understand how this boy had such an effect on me. Perhaps it was simply sexual hunger; perhaps it was just resignation. In Casablanca I had the feeling that everything was coming to an end, as if at any moment the earth would collide with a comet. As soon as he saw me, he fell in love with me, as only boys of that age can fall in love. He was completely innocent—he'd never had a woman before. He didn't have to tell me that. The whole thing didn't last more than two months, because I soon sobered up. The mother knew what was going on, and I didn't want to have any scandals. She imagined, apparently, that I wanted to marry her son. Papa naturally knew nothing about it. My God, if only Papa knew what his little Anna is capable of. I spoke plainly to Cesare, and I told him it would have to stop, but it wasn't easy. He fell ill with dysentery and had to be taken to a hospital. He also threatened to commit suicide. I have a strange talent: whatever I touch turns to chaos. How I finally got rid of him I can't tell you now. But just then Luria unobtrusively made himself available. As it turned out, I wasn't in my right mind myself. There was no question of love on my part—neither for Luria nor for Cesare, although Cesare was a fine boy—skillful, intelligent, and frighteningly sensitive. I was left with the feeling that I was his mother, even though I was only six years older than he was."

"Where is he now?"

"Why are you so pale? He's in Milan, and he has a wife and two children."

"Do you correspond with him?"

"He sends me a New Year's card. He also remembers my birthday."

"Is that all?"

"That, dearest, is all. God Himself couldn't tell you more. The truth is, I didn't even love Yasha Kotik. You were my true love, from the day you started visiting our house, but you could hardly expect that during the twenty-three years we were separated I should have remained faithful to you. I never imagined we would meet again."

"Come, let's go."

"Is that all you've got to say? I have regrets about my life, but I don't want to hear any reproaches from you."

"You won't hear any reproaches."

"Your expression's changed . . . What do you want to do? What are we embarking on? Remember, Hertz, if you have the slightest doubt, let's not even start. I can't describe what I've been through since we spoke on the telephone yesterday. It's not even twenty-four hours yet, but it seems years have passed. Papa made such an appalling scene that it's a miracle I'm still alive. I thought I'd never live to see you again. I actually came to tell you that we have to part," Anna said suddenly, astonished at her own words.

"Really?"

"Yes, really. They tried to make me submit. But while I was waiting for you during that hour you didn't show up, I realized I can't live without you. You'd better know that I'm breaking the holiest oath I've ever given, and I'll lose everything. If you think I'm an heiress, you're fooling yourself. Papa swore he wouldn't leave me more than a dollar. I have nothing except my jewelry and some money in the bank."

"I don't need your money."

"I've got war bonds worth a few thousand dollars, but they'll only mature years from now. I'm a poor woman, with a past into the bargain. Oh yes, I've forgotten the most important thing—Luria swore that he would never give me a divorce. Last night was a night of oaths. Each of us swore one."

"We can live together without a divorce."

"What? It's convenient for you, but it's a novelty for me. What'll we do? What about your wife?"

"She's not in a hurry to get divorced either."

"In other words, you stay with your wife and have me on the side?"

"I can leave my home, but I can't force her to give me a divorce. You know that well enough yourself."

"I know everything, but how will we manage things? If you think you can go back and forth between me and her, you're making a mistake. I told you plainly: When I want someone, I want him completely. I hope that last night you carefully thought over what you're doing and what your attitude toward me is going to be. There are no big adjustments for you to make. Your children are grown up. Your wife never had you, in any case. But for me this is a fundamental change. I've sacrificed Papa for you. I'm not just talking about his money and all the other advantages. For me this step will bring either total happiness or a death sentence. Perhaps both together."

"If you haven't made up your mind, don't do it."

"I have made up my mind. But you need to make up your mind, too. We're not children. In the first place, you must want to do what you're doing, and not just go ahead recklessly. In the second place, we must have a plan. The road we're choosing is full of pitfalls, and if we don't plan all the details beforehand, we'll hurt ourselves."

"There aren't any pitfalls. We won't starve. I can earn enough for both of us. In our circumstances we can't think of having a child."

"Why not? I want to have a child with you. I want a child more than anything. I'm a normal woman. I have maternal feelings. I haven't had a child up to now because I haven't had the right husband. But that doesn't mean I have to become pregnant immediately. We can wait a few years, and during that time I won't sit idle. I'm Boris Makaver's daughter. Papa never did any business without me. Both in Germany and here, his wealth is just as much mine as his. But I don't want to drag him to court. One can make money in America. You only have to want to. If we have to, I can sell the war bonds and the jewelry. Together they should raise about fifteen thousand dollars. It's not a lot, but we can make a start. What about you? How much have you got?"

"I own twenty-five thousand dollars' worth of stock."

"What? That's not much. But together that makes forty. What about your wife? You'll have to pay for her support."

"I'll make some arrangement with her."

"If Papa thinks he can conduct business without me, he's making a mistake. But we'll see about that later. My goal is that in five years' time we should have a hundred thousand dollars. Perhaps more. Sooner or later we'll both have to get divorced—you as much as me. What's your plan for today?''

''My plan is that we should be happy.''

''You fool, I'm happy already. Happier than I've ever been in my whole life!''

6

Professor Shrage puttered about in his room. The winter twilight had fallen, but the professor did not switch on the lights. He disliked electric light, first because he believed it harmed his eyes, and second because electric light—and light in general—drove away spirits and dulled the sixth sense, the awareness of extra-mundane matters. On his desk he kept a brass candlestick with a wax candle. As far as possible, he avoided using all the mechanical innovations of the last hundred years, since he held the view that technological progress had been made at the expense of humankind's spiritual powers. The professor seldom rode on the subway. He never used the elevator—fortunately Mrs. Clark lived on the second floor. He did not speak on the telephone. When Mrs. Clark was not at home, the telephone could ring all day long and the professor would never lift the receiver. There was a radio in the apartment but the professor never switched it on. What good were all these ridiculous things? How did they benefit human beings? Certainly electromagnetic waves were a great wonder, but the professor believed that it was a sin to use them for trivial purposes. Why harness angels to a wagon when horses could be used instead? That the angels permitted themselves to be harnessed merely showed their magnanimity.

Outside, it was winter, and the steam gurgled in the radiator. At dusk the sky had turned violet. A thin snow was falling that reminded the professor of Warsaw. Yes, where was she now, Edzhe? At all events, her body was no longer here. It had probably been burned to ash by the Nazi murderers. But what of her soul? Where was it sheltered? Did she know that her David was in New York? Did she know that he thought about her every day, every hour, perhaps every minute? Did she observe his comings and goings with regret or with ridicule? Or was she perhaps in such great high places, surrounded by such light, under such sublime protection, that the earth and all its doings no longer concerned her? Everything was possible. One thing the professor knew for certain: all these ''messages'' that he received from Edzhe through Mrs. Clark were lies and falsehood. Edzhe allegedly always said the same thing: that all was well with her up there in the higher spheres, that she took care of young souls when they first rose from the earth. Supposedly she had become some sort of teacher or educator, something that was utterly alien to Edzhe's nature. The signals she gave were ambiguous. In all these years she had never mentioned the safe-deposit box she kept in the Polish Savings Bank. She had never given a single sign that could convince him. Did this mean that Mrs. Clark was simply a liar? But what use were these lies to her? She supported him, not he her. Was she in love with him? If so, why did she not allow herself to be touched? He was often seized by a male desire, a purely physiological need, but she wanted only platonic love. She wanted only to comfort him, to cheer him up, and to show him off to her cronies. Personally she was apparently as cold as ice. She openly expressed a strong aversion to sex.

Well, who could understand them? Woman was a bundle of blind will. She was like matter: inert, impenetrable, ponderous, sinister. This woman did things and didn't know what she did, or why. Her automatic writings were full of him. In her paintings, his image was repeatedly featured. She had so confused David Shrage with her late husband, Edwin Clark, that she no longer knew where one ended and the other began. Professor Shrage would have come to terms long ago with the thought that Mrs. Clark was fooling both him and herself were it not for the fact that over the years he had spent with her, many things had taken place that he could not explain rationally. Several times when he had been sitting with her in the dark, he had been aware of a cold wind, although both the door and the window were shut. The table on which they had laid their hands did in truth rise up. Although it had often made foolish mistakes, it had also given him a number of genuine answers.

But the real wonders, which the professor could never forget, were all connected with Netty, Mrs. Clark's deceased niece. Three times this Netty had materialized for him. She came into being from nothingness. In pitch darkness he had taken her hand, had stroked her hair. He had felt her pulse and tapped her chest. She had also murmured something to him and had brushed his ear with her lips. Then she had glided away from him and had merged into nothingness again. When Mrs. Clark had switched on the light, there was no one in the room. During the entire period of Netty's manifestation, Mrs. Clark herself had been in a trance. Now the professor tugged at his beard: if that had really been Netty, then the whole of science was a charade. Then all values had to be reconsidered. If that had truly been Netty, it meant that at any moment a spirit could become corporeal, not simply assume the shape of a body but acquire a beating heart, flowing blood, warm and vigorous limbs. But how did the spirit produce such a body? Where did it obtain its matter? How did it construct itself in a few fleeting moments? And what became of it later? And there was something else: if all this could be, how could one know for certain, when one met a person in the street, whether he or she was a living human being or a materialized spirit?

It would seem that though the physical body remained behind after an individual had died, so-called astral bodies were similar to physical bodies in every respect. If so, why should Edzhe not materialize for him? And what were the astral bodies doing out there? Did they rotate with the earth on its axis and revolve around the sun? Or did they exist beyond time and place? Or perhaps Mrs. Clark had deceived him yet again. Perhaps she had hidden someone in the house in advance and arranged for her to appear before him. If that was the case, then Mrs. Clark was an outrageous cheat, a vile creature, a worthless being. But every crime had to have a motive, after all. Why should she indulge in such duplicity? As far as he knew, she was a deeply religious woman, kindhearted, ready to sacrifice herself for others. She thought day and night only about the ultimate purpose of the human species, its reason for existing on the earth, and about its role both in this life and in the life to come. How could such a person do things better suited to a criminal? What did she get out of it all? Money? Honor? Fame?

Well, well, it's not good, not good, Professor Shrage mumbled to himself. Everything is created in such a way that we remain perpetually in doubt. Apparently we need such uncertainty for the sake of free will.

The room grew dark. Only a distant light shone in through the window. The professor heard the hissing of steam in the central-heating pipes. The vapor sang a little song, monotonous but bold. The truth is, Professor Shrage thought, there is no fundamental difference between life and so-called death. Everything lives: the stone in the street, the steam in the pipes, the spectacles on my nose. It was simply a question of degree. There was no such thing as death—that was the answer to all questions about the nature of existence. This was the foundation on which every thinking person must build his inferences.

Suddenly the professor heard a ringing at the front door. Who could this be? Henrietta had a key. Could it be a special delivery? The professor hesitated awhile: should he open the door or not? But the doorbell rang again, this time loudly and at length. The professor rose and made his way through the dark and out into the hallway.

"Who's there?" he quavered.

"It's me, Stanislaw Luria."

The professor could not hear the name clearly, but the voice sounded familiar to him. He lifted the latch and opened the door.

2

Professor Shrage had known Stanislaw Luria in Warsaw. Like himself, Luria had been the son of wealthy parents. His father had been a partner in a tannery and the owner of several buildings. Luria moved in the same circles as the professor. He even took some interest in psychic research and had once been seated next to the professor at a table which had raised itself from the floor. Here in New York they had become acquainted again. The professor often met Luria at Boris Makaver's home. As yet the professor knew nothing of what had transpired with Anna. Although he did not regard himself as perceptive, and often failed to see the most obvious things, it occurred to him that Luria had changed since the night before last, when he had spent the evening with him. During the intervening two days he seemed to have grown older and more stooped. No lamp burned in the entrance hall, but the light from the corridor shone in. Before the professor stood a middle-aged man, his clothing disheveled, his face a jaundiced yellow, with bags under his eyes, a furrowed brow, and a head of hair too dark to be its natural color. A pair of dark eyes glowered from under two bushy eyebrows, darting, full of the pain of someone who finds himself in the middle of a tragedy. By some extra sense the professor perceived a mood of desolation, pleading, suffering. He almost lost his bearings. He took a step backward as though to slam the door in the visitor's face.

"*Panie* Luria, is that you?" he stammered. "Well, come in—*proszę bardzo*. Welcome."

"I hope I haven't disturbed you, Professor," said Stanislaw Luria in a resonant bass that seemed to emanate from deep within him and that had an aggressive edge.

"In what way could you disturb me? I'm doing nothing. As Jeremiah says, 'He sitteth alone and keepeth silence.' Come in, come in. It's cold outside, isn't it?"

"Why don't you switch on the light?"

"What? Oh yes, I'll turn it on. I sit lost in thought and I don't even realize that it's dark."

"You mean, Professor, that you're still sitting with the rebbe and enjoying the last meal of the Sabbath?"

"What? Possibly. Well, come in. To tell you the truth, I really don't know how to turn on the light. There ought to be a switch here somewhere, but I don't know where. Perhaps you might know."

"Oh, Professor, you are truly an impractical person," Luria reproved him good-naturedly. "I did telephone, but no one answered. I hear, Professor, that you avoid using the telephone."

"Avoid? I can't cope with it. The callers speak English, and it's difficult for me to make out what they're saying. I learned English from Shakespeare, but here they speak English so fast and it's all slang."

"Well, one can learn to understand anything. When I first arrived here I didn't know a single word of English, and now I read the newspapers easily—that is, except the pages where they write about sports, theater, and horse racing. For those, they use a different language altogether."

In the darkness, by the glow that came from the corridor, Luria took off his galoshes and hung his fur coat with the fox collar on a hanger. Then the professor led his guest to his room. Luria followed with uncertain steps. Once in his own room, the professor found the matches and lit the candle that had dripped down the brass candlestick. As the wick did not catch immediately, the little flame flickered for a while, seeming to hesitate about whether to burn or go out. Luria sat down heavily in an upholstered armchair. He wore a yellow-checked summer suit and a blue-and-white-spotted necktie, with spats over his shoes. His face was unshaven, dark with stubble. The professor noticed that one of his ears had no lobe and remained joined to his cheek.

"So, you can even bring light," Luria half asked, half stated. "You don't want to acknowledge civilization, Professor. You are stuck somewhere in the eighteenth century, and as far as you're concerned, modern things can go to the devil."

"No. Every epoch has its place," the professor seemed to justify himself. "Electric light is simply bad for my eyes. Even at night I wear dark glasses."

"It all comes from pessimism."

"Pessimism? It only has to do with my eyesight. Even as a child, when I used to go out in the snow, my eyes would start watering. I could never go to the *cinéma*"—the professor used the French expression. He was always searching for words, always lacking the right phrase.

"What's there to see at the movie theater? Only gangsters, over and over. In Russian pictures they show endless tractors, and in ours—gangsters. That's because each side shows what it's got the least of. If the Russians were to show all their gangsters and we were to show all our tractors, the movie would never end."

The professor seemed to think about this for a while.

"Yes, but now I'm too old. When I have some free time, I prefer to read or just to rest. In my day, only children used to go to the magic lantern shows. Later when they opened—what're they called here? with Charlie Chaplin and all the rest of them—then adults started going."

"True. But it's all fine and good as long as people have peace and quiet. When a catastrophe happens, however, and the ground disintegrates beneath your feet and you're left suspended in midair with one foot in the real world and the other over an abyss, then all the arts in the world can't console you. Then a man sees that he's been walking the whole time on a narrow plank straddling Gehenna."

"What? Yes, true. In my day—"

"Professor, pardon me for interrupting you." Stanislaw Luria changed his tone. "I haven't come simply to take up your time. I know that you are busy conducting experiments, or thinking about mathematics and other weighty subjects. It's not in my nature to burst in like this, particularly not on someone of your standing. If you don't answer the telephone, it's a sign that you're not interested in the outside world, but preoccupied with your own thoughts—so why bother you with trivialities? I've come,

Professor, about a matter which might interest you from a professional point of view, so to speak. It falls within your field of expertise."

"What? You're welcome in my home," said the professor. "Why not? We're familiar acquaintances."

"Well, and what is familiar? My theory is that everything is alien. I look at my own finger and it's absolutely foreign to me. What do I know of the intricate workings inside it? Or where the fingernail comes from? And what would happen if this finger were suddenly chopped off? In a moment it would no longer be a part of me but an alien object, and it would no longer matter to me if you pricked it, or even if you gave it to a dog to chew. The same goes for all my members. True, there are parts without which I would be unable to live. But even these do not make up the whole human being. What do I know about what goes on in my lungs? How do they understand that they must inhale oxygen? They breathed in oxygen for millions of years before human beings even realized that there was such a thing."

"Yes, certainly. Human intelligence does not reside wholly in the brain," the professor responded.

"Where does it reside, then? There's a theory that every organ has its own intelligence, and that inanimate things do, too. But I'm a skeptic, and I'll remain a skeptic. One can advance a thousand possibilities, but the truth ultimately resides on another plane."

"Yes. Yes. It's self-evident—"

"Professor, I've decided to commit suicide"—Stanislaw Luria raised his voice slightly—"and it's in that connection that I've come to you. I want to help you with your experiments. I should like, as they say, to be your collaborator. Today I've bequeathed my body to the department of anatomy at Columbia University."

3

"What are you saying? What are you saying?" the professor cried out. "God forbid!"

"Professor, the night before last, my wife left me. You know my wife, of course—Boris Makaver's daughter, Anna."

"Yes, yes, of course."

"She went off with Grein—you know Grein, too—the Wall Street broker."

"You don't need to remind me. We were all together only this week."

"I know, Professor, that you're a little absentminded. You're pre-occupied with the higher spheres. But what happens in *this* world is also interesting, very interesting. Grein has grown children. He might soon become a grandfather. In addition, he has a mistress, a certain Esther. Perhaps you know her as well, Professor?"

"Yes, yes. Her first husband's name was Piniele."

"That's her. A little eccentric. Talks a lot. Well, a man like that enters the picture and, as they say, steals the poor man's lamb. I've lost every-thing, Professor, and when one loses everything, one no longer wishes to live. So I've bequeathed my body to Columbia University. They need corpses there. However many cadavers they get, there are always too few. To you, Professor, I should like, if I may put it this way, to give my spirit, assuming that there is such a thing as a spirit. My own theory is that there is no spirit whatever, because in the first place no one has ever seen a spirit. In the second place, where is it, this spirit? The earth spins on its axis and revolves around the sun. A spirit would have to spin around with the earth, and thus be bound by time and space. So it would cease to be spirit."

"Spirits don't exist in time or space."

"But let's say that the earth were to be moved to another galaxy. It's not possible, after all, that the spirit could be left behind somewhere, or that it's on Mars."

"No, but—"

"I know, Professor, I know all the answers you'll try to give me. But what do all these answers prove? Neither you nor I have been to heaven. Everything requires empirical verification, Professor, and that's why I've come to you. I'm leaving this world, and if I retain an identity and memory, I'll do everything possible to communicate with you, to give you a sign. At the end of two weeks, Professor, if you haven't heard from me, it's an indication either that I no longer exist—and what does not exist cannot keep its word, obviously—or that I lack the power or the opportunity to send a signal and need one from you."

"Never mind, don't do anything foolish!" said the professor rapidly. The words seemed to cost him a great effort, and were uttered in a jumble, without a pause between them. He grew red in the face.

"Professor, I want to be perfectly frank with you: I didn't come to ask your advice. There's no question you're a learned man, but when it comes to private affairs, one man cannot teach another anything. Even as we sit here, someone in the world is committing suicide and no one can stop him. I, Professor, have always known that this would be my end. Each of us has his own fate which he cannot evade. I believe that. Before I married Anna, I had been contemplating suicide, because my family had been murdered by the Nazis and to live alone made no sense. But suddenly Anna thrust her way into my life, and a reason for living returned. Even I was amazed. Was it possible that my fate had been reversed? Normally one's fate doesn't change. Now that Anna has left so abruptly and so cruelly, without so much as goodbye, as though our whole life together was nothing but a joke, I've realized that the powers had been giving me false hope. Here in America there are people who have been sentenced to death, but they sit and wait for years in Sing Sing before they are finally given the electric chair.''

''No, no, don't do it! Don't do it!'' As before, the professor spoke rapidly and with difficulty. ''We are forbidden to kill ourselves . . . What intelligence is needed for that? One takes a knife and . . . That is not the solution!''

''I've read Schopenhauer. Only today I looked at his essays again. The world-will, he says, cannot be extinguished. But I have no desire to kill the world-will—merely to put an end to my own troubles. Let me give you an example, Professor. Let's say that at home I have a blaring radio whose continual racket is making me deaf. Let's assume that I can't switch off that radio. Anyone who was in Soviet Russia during the war knows such radios well. There they hang loudspeakers in people's homes to shriek Communist propaganda all day long. One can't even take a nap. All day and all night people are compelled to hear about the greatness of Comrade Stalin and all he is doing to advance socialism. Well, I know of a case in which someone took an ax and smashed the loudspeaker. Although people are sent to Siberia for such an act, this man couldn't stand the lies any longer. He sat in his home starving, half-naked, freezing, but the loudspeaker went on and on about the enormous benefits that Stalin had brought to the Russian people, and how bitter life was for the workers in capitalist America. So this man smashed the loudspeaker and ended it. But what did he end? Not Stalinism and not the Stalinist lies. Millions of other loudspeakers continued to echo over the whole of Russia. But this man wanted to preserve his hearing, his mind. Perhaps he wanted to sleep for an hour. I wasn't there myself.''

"A marvelous example. If only Schopenhauer had heard it! Truly——"

"Professor, I'm a lawyer by profession, not a philosopher. But I always had a fondness for learned books. I understand, I understand. A man can destroy himself, but he can't destroy life. Nevertheless, when a man is in despair, he doesn't want to improve the world, only to stop his own misery."

"Yes, but with the same ax he might have been able to kill a commissar . . . although personally I am opposed to such things."

"And if he were to kill a commissar, what would it matter? For every commissar there are ten thousand candidates waiting to take his place, and each one is perhaps a bigger criminal than the previous one, because he will do anything to beat out the other contenders. That's the lesson of the loudspeaker. My theory is that one can destroy nothing but oneself."

"No, not even oneself!"

"Well, that's what I want to put to the test. If one cannot destroy oneself, what do I stand to lose? It can't possibly be worse for me there than it is here."

"We do not understand the mystery of suffering."

"What mystery can there be? For what purpose did God—if there is a God—need six million Jews to be wiped out in agonizing pain? And why was it necessary to burn children? Perhaps the adults had sinned, or God wanted to put them to the test. But what about the infants whose heads German officers smashed in? What about the children who starved to death? What about the fathers who were forced to dig graves for themselves and their own children while the Nazis stood around and treated it all as a huge joke? What did God need this for? Believe me, Professor, those fathers had passed through hell before they reached the end."

"Yes, I know. It's a mystery, a mystery. But how is God to blame if people choose to be wicked? He gave them free will."

"Infants have no free will."

"Their souls are in a place unknown to us."

"Where are they? I want to know. I also had two children, and they were murdered. If they exist somewhere, I want to see them."

"All of us will see . . . when the time comes . . . if we are worthy."

"I want to see *now*. I have perhaps twenty more years to live. For God that's less than a moment, but for me it's a long time. Too long. And there's nothing to keep me here. I had only one tie to life, and now that she's left, I want to go to my children."

"No, no, don't do it!" The professor's face contorted as though from deep inner pain. "We cannot escape. Would to God we could!"

"We can, Professor. And if we cannot, perhaps I'll live in a better world, among better people. Here, Professor, I find it tedious. I have nothing more to do. I have, so to speak, wrapped up all my business. As Shakespeare says, 'He that dies pays all debts.' "

Thought had turned to speech and speech to action. They had no sooner talked of taking a trip than they were already en route. A desolate landscape drifted past the window—bleached, sallow, misty, lost in a pensiveness as old as Creation. To Grein it seemed the sky itself was astonished: Where do I come from? Who spread me out over the world like a tent? And where does all the rest of it come from—the trees, the rivers, the woods? Everything shared his own amazement, every twig, every windowpane, every cloud of smoke hanging above a chimney. For a short while a bird tried to pursue the train, but it was soon left behind.

Grein breathed in deeply. How wonderful it all was: to sit in a speeding express, to see the sky, and to have seated next to him a person of a different species—a mystery that was called Anna. Riding in the train clarified for him the riddle of time. Time rolled itself up like a small scroll; no, more like the Scroll of the Law, which is swiftly rolled up on the Festival of the Rejoicing of the Law, right after the final two chapters of Deuteronomy are chanted and the reader starts all over again with the first six chapters of Genesis. The prescribed weekly readings from the Torah rush by, the Five Books of Moses are rapidly read through—now here is Leviticus, now here is Numbers. Everything moves, everything is rolled up, and everything remains: every word, every letter, every festival. And in this particular scroll, what was written about him? ''And there was a man, and his name was Grein: and this man abandoned his wife, and his children, and his affairs, and he journeyed into Florida with the wife of his friend: and in his wantonness he thought that there was no God, no law, no punishment, but that all was random chance: and behold, his days on earth were numbered: and those who were farsighted had betimes read his epitaph, and saw his tombstone and the grass that grew on his grave: and in his blindness he thought that his pleasure would endure forever.''

Grein stopped himself. Enough! She is not someone else's wife! How was she Luria's wife? Simply because she had stood with him under a wedding canopy and a rabbi had read a marriage contract? A woman is a wife only to the man she loves. And why did God require a written bill of divorce? Wasn't it sufficient when a woman openly and explicitly left her husband? No one could know what was written in the Divine Book.

He had a justification ready for each one of his actions. Wasn't happiness the only goal of every person, every creature? Did it really make any difference whether one wanted pleasure in this world or in the World to Come? Those who fled from happiness here were seeking it there; even those who killed themselves sought rest. The philosophers had seen that the pursuit of happiness was the central motive of human existence. Grein had his own philosophy: happiness was Godliness. When a human being was happy, all questions ceased, for then the human was united with the divine. So-called inanimate things were always happy, hence they never complained. But life had bestowed another gift which moved people further and further away from happiness—the gift of freedom. Free choice was possible only if both happiness and unhappiness, both truth and lies, both success and failure existed. Freedom went hand in hand with individuality. As long as the human soul was encased in a physical body, it was compelled to be its own boss, to seek its own drop of happiness in the great ocean of bliss. This ongoing though temporary struggle was apparently part of the divine plan. The Cabala explained it best: In order to make Creation possible, the *Ein-Sof* had to withdraw Himself. The world was an island of unhappiness in a sea of happiness. The fate of each person was perpetually to seek that which was the essence of every existence.

Anna dozed or pretended to doze. She had been dragged through more ugly scenes with both her father and her husband. Luria would not allow her to remove her belongings. He had seized her by the throat and tried to strangle her, had snatched up her mink coat and ripped it. Now Anna laid her head back against the padded seat. Her eyes were shut but her lips smiled, as if to say: It was worth it. It was worth it. Now I've got what I wanted. She seemed to be confirming Grein's view that troubles were merely imaginary. The only reality was pleasure. Grein scribbled on a notepad with a pencil. For years now he had been making notes for a book, trying to set out a new kind of hedonistic morality: happiness was *das Ding an sich*. The path to happiness was the path to God. Every planet was an experiment in happiness. God Himself had not exhausted all the potential combinations of happiness. He had to rely on His creatures to develop those powers to the full.

But Grein was utterly at a loss to find the right words to express all he thought. He made his notes in several languages, in signs which he alone could decipher, and in symbols whose meaning only he knew. In addition, he drew all kinds of figures, flowers, apparitions equipped with horns, tails, scales, fins. If everything was divine, as Spinoza believed (and surely it must be so!), then Grein's imaginings, every stroke of his pencil, every impulse of his brain, were all divine as well. For a while he wrote in the Hebrew script employed by Jewish scribes, in the manner of his father, Reb Jacob the Scribe. Then Grein turned the page and started sketching a nude woman. Was this sinful? The whole institution of marriage was a human invention. Actually it was a vestige of slavery. One could not sign a binding contract about a matter that depended entirely on the emotions.

Anna opened her eyes. "What are you doing?"

"Nothing, nothing."

"What are you fiddling with? Show me!"

She gave his drawings a suspicious glance, half-smiling, scientific. What, for instance, would a psychoanalyst have to say about these? Anna wondered. This man is full of complexes. Who can know what goes on in his yeshiva-student mind? And what's he thinking about me? Grein and Anna had taken a sleeping compartment, but now, during the day, they sat in the club car.

Anna took Grein's hand. "So we're on our way at last!"

"Yes, my darling, that's for certain."

"I never believed it would happen."

"I ask God for only one thing—that Luria doesn't do anything foolish."

"Whatever he does isn't your fault. You can't force one person to love another, the same way you can't force someone to go on living."

"I don't want to drive anyone to death."

"He'll live, he'll live. He loves himself too much. I'm more afraid about Papa. But what could I do? I'll tell you this, but don't misunderstand me: I'm ready to give even Papa's life for you."

"That's a shocking thing to say."

"It's absolutely true."

Grein and Anna had made love yesterday, the day before that, every day since she had come to him, yet they continually desired each other anew. Anna's last words had rekindled their lust. She gave him a half-pleading, half-questioning glance, moving closer to him and pressing her knee against his. Apparently the craving for flesh operated according to its own laws. It loved desecrating the holy, defying authority. Its roots were in those dark recesses of the brain from which wickedness sprang. Grein and Anna sat for a while in silence. Grein seemed to be listening to his own hidden feelings. Leah had never uttered such words. She had always been the mother, even before she had children. Esther, on the other hand, had become an increasingly tangled knot of sorrows, grievances, regrets. She talked too much about death nowadays. There was a logical inevitability to his leaving Leah and Esther and taking up with Anna. Possessing everything—youth, strength, imagination—Anna was ready to give full rein to all the five senses. But could he justify what he was doing? Behind his sophistries and equivocations, he knew that he was rebelling against the Creator. What would happen if actions like his became the general rule? Family life and fatherhood would cease. All women would become whores, all men lechers.

2

Immediately after supper Grein and Anna returned to the sleeping car. For the last few nights, neither had slept more than three or four hours. How odd it was to lie down in a speeding train, en route to warm weather in a land of palms and orange trees. At the evening meal Anna had ordered champagne. It was, she argued, the first day of her honeymoon. As she drank, she grew more self-assured, joking with the waiter, chatting across the aisle to a couple at the opposite table, laughing too much. Anna spoke English fluently, but with a German accent. The Americans in the dining car exchanged glances. This refugee from Hitler wore a mink stole around her shoulders, diamond earrings, and a huge diamond ring. It was difficult to believe that millions like her had been burned in the ovens, poisoned in the gas chambers.

Anna clinked her glass against Grein's and called out loudly to the elderly woman opposite: "I've waited twenty years for this day!"

"I beg you, Anna, don't be so loud!" Grein murmured reprovingly.

"What are you afraid of? We're allowed to be happy!"

In the sleeping car they found the journey as good as ever. Early the next morning they would be in Miami. Though it was not late, no more than nine o'clock, the all-day ride, the rich meals, the wine, and the fear of bumping into acquaintances left them weary and wanting to hide, and with renewed desire for each other. They shut the door and were free. Switching off the lights, they fell on each other with a carnality that astonished even themselves. They bit into each other, their mouths clamped together as though powerless to separate, as though struggling mutely to swallow each other, tongues, gums, throats, and all. Anna's jaws were as wide as an animal's and there was a sinewy prowess in the way she kissed. They stood in the dark like two wolves with locked jaws, while outside in the night cotton fields, tobacco plantations, the reflections of houses, the glow of factories rushed by. Unlike the locomotives of earlier times, the diesel engine did not whistle but let out a monster's howl. In the heat of their passion, Grein felt the overweening pride of the human species, of *Homo sapiens*, who had crawled out of the cave and harnessed for himself and his uses all the hidden powers of nature. He and Anna were the ultimate experiment in hedonism, attempting to pack a maximum of experience into a minimum of time.

They did not so much undress as tear the clothes from each other. Grein had only recently read an excerpt from the research of Dr. Kinsey, which was soon to be published in book form, concluding that the male reaches his greatest potency between the ages of fifty and sixty, but what had happened with him and Anna proved that assertion to be wrong. She had awakened a vigor in him that he seemed never to have possessed. How could one take a general measurement of the power that surged from the very depths of the unconscious, from the essence which is no longer appearance but the thing-in-itself? A howl like the shriek of the diesel engine ripped from the couple, a cry of elements united with the universe, its purposes and powers. Anna repeated the same words over and over again: "I love you! I love you! Till death! Till death!" Panting, she rambled on in Polish, as in the old days when he had been her tutor, grunting the violent and wanton words that escape one who is naked physically and spiritually: broken sentences, wild exaggerations, drunken repetitions. The union was not Grein and Anna's but that of a higher power that, through the mystery of spiritual magnetism, had after long yearning become one through them. She and he were simply the go-betweens. "I want to have a child by you!" Anna cried out. Grein put his hand over her mouth so she would not be heard in the corridor, but she tore it away and gasped: "I love you! I love you! I want to have a son with you!"

And she bit his wrist. He fingered the marks left by her teeth.

They fell apart and lay straining for breath. In half-sleep it seemed to Grein that it was Passover night and he had drained the mandatory four cups of wine. Like his father, he had lost himself in an act of worship. These ecstasies did not float out of thin air. They had a root somewhere.

As he dozed, he heard the muffled thud of the wheels and felt the carriage swaying on its springs. The train halted at a station. Apparently they were shunting cars, because the bumpers banged together. While Grein was sleeping through the night, sentries kept watch, checking the axles, giving signals, switching on lamps to shed light. In their own small ways, human beings imitated Divine Providence.

Grein fell asleep and dreamed that someone had died. He didn't know who, but it was someone close to him. For some reason the dead man had to be hidden in a room with closed shutters. Someone was searching for the corpse, but the person was not dead. He was sitting in a chair in the gloomy daylight, yellow, terrified, his melancholy eyes glazed in unearthly stupor, and Grein was giving him a loaf of bread with an egg. He was simultaneously both the deceased and the mourner. But how was this possible? Grein opened his eyes. The train was now racing forward with unusual velocity, as if it were out of control. It seemed to be rushing downhill, falling into an abyss. Anna also started awake.

"What's happened?"

3

Their bodies might be lying alone in a closed sleeping car in an express train, but the spirits of the man and the woman who had earlier possessed them traveled with them. Grein told Anna about Esther, and Anna told him about Yasha Kotik. Anna wanted to know every detail about Esther: was she fair or dark? Slim or fat? What sort of woman was she?

Of what temperament? Grein told her the truth more or less. He lied only about what made him ashamed and exposed his weaknesses. Esther came from a distinguished family. When she was eighteen she had been married off to Piniele, the young son of a rabbinical family, but she had taken a dislike to him virtually under the wedding canopy. After her marriage she started reading worldly books, became an ardent activist in a Zionist movement, acted with an amateur theater company, published poems in Party journals. Piniele returned to his parents and Esther lived for a time in Warsaw, then in Lemberg, then in Cracow. Her father, an affluent and learned man who had rabbinical authority to teach Jewish Law, died suddenly. Her mother lost the family estate, and Esther worked successively as a teacher, a proofreader, and a librarian in a Jewish library. For a while she traveled all over Poland with a theater troupe. Then she went off to Palestine. Oddly, her husband, Piniele, became secularized, and he followed her to Palestine. They could not live together, however, and were divorced in Tel Aviv. Piniele remained in Palestine as an official in an institute of some sort, while Esther emigrated to America. Here she had been a teacher in the same Talmud Torah in which Grein himself worked for a time, and that was where they had met.

Anna listened and wanted to know more. She nestled close to Grein like a child who did not want the story being told to her to end. What did Esther do in Palestine? What did she teach in the Talmud Torah? How did their affair begin? Was it really love? How was Grein attracted? Physically? Spiritually? By her knowledge of Hebrew? Every answer Grein gave Anna prompted new, impassioned questions. It seemed as if Anna knew every answer beforehand and only wanted to force a confession from Grein, because love, like power, requires betrayal. A rivalry always lurks within love, demanding expression. It occurred to Grein that in Russia young Jewish women like Anna donned leather jackets, slung revolvers on their hips, and with single-minded zeal tirelessly searched out real or imagined counter-revolutionaries.

The picture Anna painted of Yasha Kotik was that of a devil. Kotik was a liar, a swindler, a thief, a drunkard, a coward, a drug addict. When he took Anna to Switzerland on their honeymoon, he also secretly brought along a chorus girl, who stayed in the same hotels. When Alfred Kerr gave him a bad review, he attempted to slash his wrists. Now he laughed and now he cried; now he boasted that he was the greatest actor in the world, now he lamented that he did not have a scrap of talent. He sold Anna's jewelry in order to bribe charlatan critics to give him rave notices. At cards he gambled away everything he possessed; his debts mounted up; he sponged off rich and elderly tourists, kept whole boxfuls of pornographic pictures. Onstage he had only one specialty: imitating *Ostjuden*, the Jews of Eastern Europe. He held Jews up to ridicule and contempt at the very time Germany was swarming with Nazis. He even socialized with Nazis and went drinking with them. "My God, he was scum! Scum!" Anna complained. "If I hadn't had the misfortune to live with a monster like that, I would never have believed anyone like him could exist." Curiously, in his own depraved way Kotik was superstitiously observant. On Yom Kippur he crawled into a synagogue. He was the follower of some petty rabbi on Dragoner Strasse to whom he ran for a blessing on the night of every premiere. He carried around with him all sorts of little keys, elephants, exorcised amulets, and even small crosses and crucifixes, all of which supposedly brought him luck.

When Hitler's war broke out, Yasha Kotik fled to Russia, where he immediately became a Communist, cursed the bourgeoisie and the fascists, applauded Comrade Stalin, informed on other actors who had sought refuge in Russia. Because of these denunciations, he became a celebrated actor and film star in the Soviet Union.

About young Cesare there was not much more to tell. He was an adorable youth, ambitious, combining impudence with shyness, thirsty for love, suffering from a mother complex. He never stopped calling Anna *"Madre"* or "Mamma." "But why call back the shadows of the past?" Anna demanded. "Now we love each other and we're together. What's past is over and done with."

But was it really over and done with? All these shadows accompanied them; each played its own role, demanded its own share of immortality. Love was apparently wholly spirit, governed by all the laws of the spirit. What was past was not over, what had died was not dead; words were deeds, thoughts possessed magical power.

Anna kept interrogating Grein until daybreak. Besides Leah and Esther, who were the other women he had known? How old was he when he first slept with a woman? Whom was he living with when he started coming to help her with her lessons? With every question Anna returned to her mother. Did he know that Mama had loved him? She used to ask about him every day. When he took a long time over a lesson, Mama used to beat her medicine spoon on the side of the bed as a signal for Anna to come in. Mama asked repeatedly whether the student had come yet. Why did Grein bring her flowers? Why had he once bought her a bonbonnière?

Grein had long ago forgotten all these details, but Anna recalled everything with photographic precision. Now she made Grein swear to tell her the truth: had he ever kissed Mama?

"Exactly what difference does it make to you?" he asked evasively.

"Oh, my dearest, I want to know. Believe me, it won't make the slightest difference to our love. I'm just curious."

"Yes, I did kiss her once."

Anna was silent for a while.

"Was that all?"

"Nothing more."

"Is that the truth?"

"I swear by all that's holy to me."

"How many times did you kiss her?"

"Several times."

"Why did you kiss her?"

"Oh, just because. She was a beautiful woman. Your papa used to be away for weeks on end. She was lonely and sick."

"Did she kiss you back?"

"Sometimes."

"When was that? When did she start doing that?"

Grein remembered so little that he had to make things up. Anna started shaking and trembling.

"I knew it the whole time," she said in a voice choked with tears.

"How did you know?"

"I just knew. You're disgusting! You're a wild beast!"

And suddenly she enfolded him in her arms and panted, "I love you! I want to love you until my last breath! Until they lay me in the grave!"

"But I'm older than you."

"No. I'll die young, like Mama."

And Anna wept bitterly.

As if the diesel engine had been shocked by the things that were being said in one of the train's compartments, it let out a long wail, a shriek from deep inside its steel bowels. To Grein it seemed as if the engine was shouting: See, God, to what depths your creatures have sunk. Things are past all hope. Woe to the world! It is sinful! Evil! Wicked!

4

Outside, the sun shone. Palm trees rushed past in a summery landscape resembling the Holy Land. The train halted and the passengers flocked out to drink orange juice. Grein never left the window. In the middle of winter it was like Shavuot in Florida and it smelled of the Bible. With scraggly beards, wrapped in rags like holy recluses, the palm trees stood at crooked angles, ready to kneel and bow down before God and His might. When a breeze blew they shook their fronds in all directions, acknowledging the omnipresence of God as if they were celebrating a perpetual Feast of Tabernacles.

How is it possible, with all this beauty so near, I've never come here in my twenty years in America? Grein was astounded at himself. How little initiative one takes! How inadequately words convey reality! How many glories there are around us to which we pay no attention.

The train ended its journey in Miami. Grein and Anna alighted, carrying their winter coats over their arms as freed slaves carry their chains. In a taxi they drove over bridges that looked like huge highways, traversing canals in which palms, villas, oases were reflected. A water-skier clung to the rope behind a motorboat with one hand, while he drank from a bottle of Coca-Cola with the other. Here no one feared evil spirits, Grein mused. Here hedonism was already an established religion.

Having made no reservations, Grein and Anna asked the driver to take them to a small hotel in a quiet part of town. The taxi passed Lincoln Road, turned onto Collins Avenue, and headed uptown. The sea sparkled in the gaps between the immense hotels, pure, green, glassy, and still, like a cosmic neon light. A white ship sailed over it like a piece of stage scenery in an opera. The taxi driver sang as he drove. Nature and humankind had worked together to arrange a carnival here, full of singing, whistling, rare flowers, exotic birds, and Oriental spices. The cars flashed in the sun like toys belonging to the spoiled children of a race of giants. The buildings seemed to have sprung out of the earth like palaces in a fairy tale. A long-forgotten lightness, a careless self-abandon lay over everything and everyone, as if through some magic formula human beings had freed themselves from the age-old curse and returned to the Garden of Eden. Anna could not contain her joy. She seized Grein's hand, pressing it again and again. Here the taxi's horn did not wail but played a melody. Faces laughed: there was no more death, no more weariness, no more sorrow! The perpetual traces had been thrown over. Here one was carried on the waves of eternity. Here they knew the joyful truth.

The hotel to which the taxi drove was located in the forties. An old fig tree—short, thick, knotty, and with heavy roots—stood sentry at the door, and among its branches and the figs which never ripened, an electric light burned in the middle of the day—a theatrical effect created for a nighttime revel and now forgotten. To one side plashed the sea, to the other the Indian River. Grein and Anna were given a second-floor room with a balcony overlooking the patio. Thank God, the place was too small for a swimming pool—this hotel must at one time have been a private mansion. Aging sculptures crumbled away among shrubs and flowers. From a fountain a bird drank water—or perhaps it was the elixir of life? The sky shimmered, blue and transparent. Here it was as quiet as in the court-yard of a philosopher of long ago who had cut himself off from the world and its vanities. Grein could not believe what he was seeing: before his eyes, a cactus bloomed! Between dusty thorns that seemed cast in harsh unyielding stone nestled a fragile flower with soft, delicately shaded petals, evidence of the eternal grace that flows through all Creation.

Anna started to unpack. Grein remained on the balcony. On all sides the huge hotels stared down, but from where he sat Grein could see only their uppermost floors: the solariums, the domes, the water towers. A solitary bird swooped by, performing acrobatics on high. In a window opposite he saw a familiar figure. A woman was undressing and changing, bending over suitcases. How odd—she resembled Anna. Grein gaped. Was this a coincidence? Was he having a vision? Then he laughed: it was Anna herself, reflected in the windowpanes opposite.

Grein stared fixedly in front of him. If there was happiness in this world, then he should be happy now; and if not, there was nothing to look forward to, nothing over which to philosophize. Though his eyes were open, he was looking into himself. He had already forgotten a number of links in the present chain of cause and effect, and what remained were only the essential facts: he had left his wife and children. He had wronged Esther. He had abandoned his livelihood. He had destroyed the happiness of Stanislaw Luria and Boris Makaver. And above all, he had acted against his own deepest convictions. He had surrendered himself wholly to this world with all its idols and illusions.

A woman with badly dyed platinum-blond hair came out onto the patio, her face scarred by acne, wearing a pair of red slacks, her bare shoulders sunburned and covered with freckles. Her feet with their painted toenails were thrust into a pair of shoes with thin high heels. For a moment she stood motionless like some ancient exotic bird, the living fossil of a bygone era; then she raised her head and cast a glance at Grein as though inquiring: What madness brought *you* here?

Anna opened the balcony door.

"I'll need a new swimsuit. My old one is completely faded."

"Yes, yes."

"Aren't you hungry? I'm starving."

Anna did not say so openly, but Grein sensed that she was dissatisfied with the hotel. It was too far from the sea—one had to cross the road to get there. The beach was not private, so there were no cabanas available. Grein preferred to eat here, in the hotel café, but on the way Anna had noticed an expensive restaurant where one had to wait in line for a table. Unlike him, Anna did not propose to sit passively in one place. She had to go shopping. Luria had erupted so violently when she had tried to pack that she had left behind many of the most essential things. Now she had to buy shoes, a brassiere, a pair of slacks, body lotion, a bathing cap. In the hotel lobby several men and women sat watching television. When Grein and Anna passed, they all looked up, scrutinizing the couple inquisitively, searching them, eager to penetrate at a glance the secrets of others and to sit in judgment on their worth. It seemed to Grein that their eyes were asking: Who's this, to begin with? How does *he* come here? And the same eyes rapidly concluded: No, he isn't one of us.

The woman who had earlier appeared on the patio called out to Anna, "How's the weather in New York?"

Resonant with the commonplace and the workaday, this woman's voice lacked any trace of shyness. She was one of those for whom the world was one big sweat bath.

"It's cold."

"Only cold? They've had snow in California. Did you people fly or come by train?"

"By train."

"Who wants to sit for hours on a train these days? I fly! My husband begs me not to, but I tell him, You can always get someone younger and prettier!" She laughed coarsely. "Now he's happy; while I'm here he can do as he likes. I don't begrudge him it, either. Let him also enjoy life.

Right? As long as he pays the bills. Where do you folks live—in Brooklyn or in the Bronx?''

Anna smiled. ''At the moment we don't live anywhere.''

''Honeymooners, eh?''

Grein paled. A fat man in a floral shirt exposing a very hairy chest started cracking jokes. He too introduced himself: he was a dentist from Philadelphia. On the way down, Grein had made up his mind to chat with everyone and not to avoid people as he did year in and year out at every hotel he visited. Once and for all he had to rid himself of empty pride. All the same, he couldn't stand here idly among them, allowing himself to be falsely congratulated, listening to their trite banter. He was overcome by repugnance and was angered by Anna's easy manner. He excused himself and went outside.

5

S everal days had passed—perhaps even a week. To Grein the days had seemed inordinately long at first but then they gathered momentum and rushed by through force of repetition. The mornings were restful. While Anna went off to bathe in the sea, Grein remained in their room. He sat on the balcony reading or scribbling. Since he had become an adult, his fountain pen was his only toy. Although he knew it was bad manners, he even took it out during mealtimes. Every activity of the pen had a unique charm for him, whether it wrote symbols, drew apparitions, or made notes he would never be able to put to any purpose. He had inherited this love of the pen from his father, peace be with him, who would regularly cut goose quills with a penknife and scrape them with a piece of glass, placing them at hand on his table, where they lay with a great many others and assorted rulers and bottles of India ink.

When he was a child, he had insisted that when he grew up he, too, would be a scribe. Later he wanted to be a writer, a scientist, a philosopher. He dreamed of finding a book that would explain all secrets, unerringly reveal the right way. Every time Grein went into a library he searched for just this book. In his daydreams he would imagine that he himself was composing it. But while Grein was fantasizing, others were writing in fact. Books were published in the thousands, the millions. They were read and discarded like old newspapers. They lay on trestle tables on Fourth Avenue and elsewhere and were sold for a nickel each, even for a penny. How could one say anything new in the midst of such mass production? And what value was there in words that never became deeds? Grein's love of books was accompanied by a deepening distaste. In time he grew proud that he hadn't become an author whose words merely added to the mountain of literary refuse.

But the habit of playing with his pen remained. Every time he went into a Woolworth's he bought a pad, a notebook, a writing tablet. He always carried with him several fountain pens and pencils. He even felt the need to keep a diary, like a schoolboy or an old maid. But what did he have to record? Every time he started, he wrote a few lines and then left the book to gather dust. Sooner or later Leah threw it out with the trash. Strangely enough, he had started to forget his Polish. Although he had studied in Germany and Austria, he had never felt comfortable with German. In America he had learned English, but it was still a foreign language to him. His mother tongue was Yiddish, but Grein believed it to be unsuited to the expression of abstract and precise concepts alike. Yiddish had no grammar, no rules of spelling.

Grein knew Hebrew, but only the holy tongue of the sacred books, not the new language they were creating in Palestine. He made his notes sometimes in Polish, sometimes in English, sometimes in biblical Hebrew, and sometimes in all three languages at once. Yes, that was the inevitable consequence of two thousand years of exile. But what sort of Jew would evolve in the Holy Land, even if the British were to get out and it was to become an independent Jewish state? What Jews could he wholeheartedly call brothers? The Stalinists who were blackening Jewish history? The terrorists who planted bombs in hotels? The German refugees who sat in the cafés of Tel Aviv even now preparing to return to Germany? Whenever Grein took spiritual stock of himself, he always arrived at the same conclusion: when one removed the Jew's faith, precious little that was Jewish remained, and even less that bound all these modern Jews together. Even if they themselves did not assimilate, their children did. What kind of generation, for instance, would his Jack and Anita bring up? A Jew without God is a Gentile, even if he speaks Hebrew. And what did worldliness really offer? A few years of struggling on earth, and after death—eternal forgetfulness.

For years Grein had been reaching these same conclusions. But even so he could not become an observant Jew who strictly obeyed all the laws of the *Shulhan Arukh*. To do that, it was not enough simply to believe in God; one had unquestioningly to believe that God directly revealed Himself to man, and that consequently every law, every restriction, every verse of sacred teaching was unalterably true. But could he faithfully honor the countless prohibitions that rabbis and commentators had heaped up generation after generation? Could he honestly attribute to God all manner of human caprices and convictions?

The door opened and Anna came in wearing a short beach robe over her swimsuit, her legs bare and red sandals on her feet. She had on a pair of sunglasses and carried a book, a bottle of suntan lotion, a newspaper, and some magazines. She had already acquired a tan.

"Ah, the sea was wonderful today, dearest—as smooth as a mirror and such a pleasure! I can't understand why you don't want to swim. All the other men come with their wives. Are you embarrassed? You've got a more beautiful body than all of them. Honestly, Hertz, I can't understand you!"

"Get dressed. There's no sense in saying the same thing day after day."

"Tell me once and for all why you avoid the sea. You must have some reason."

"I have none."

Anna gave him a sidelong glance. "Well, I'll take a shower. Then we'll have lunch. I'm starving!"

As Anna went into the bathroom, Grein put on his necktie, his jacket, his hat. He retained his father's modesty and shame at nakedness. Even passing through the lobby with Anna was a torture for him. The men and women all looked at him askance, with hostility. Sitting there half-naked, they smoked, laughed, gawked at the television, prattled on about film stars, horse races, dog races, boxing matches, and the singers in different nightclubs. These people exuded a profaneness that continually pained him. But then what did he expect them to do—study the Mishnah? Read the *Zohar*? What Grein sought did not and could not exist: he wanted the fear of heaven without dogma; religion without revelation; discipline without proscriptions; Torah, prayer, and isolation built on a pure, unadulterated religious experience. But he also knew that what he desired could not be. He was waging a war that was lost before it began. He had to guard against developing a perversion or a spiritual illness.

Anna emerged in the nude. "What did you do all morning? I missed you."

Anna bit her lips. She could have been happy with him, but he kept secrets from her. He wandered about pale, pensive, uncommunicative. Something was bothering him, but what? Did he miss Leah? His children? Couldn't he forget Esther? Perhaps he was sick. Anna would have given her life to help him, but how could she help someone who wouldn't say what was bothering him? You couldn't even send a person like that to a psychoanalyst. Anna went over to him and stood on tiptoe.

"Well, give me a kiss."

6

They didn't take the elevator but walked down the two flights of stairs. Here and there a door stood open while a chambermaid vacuumed the carpet or made up the bed. From behind closed doors floated the sounds of talking, laughter, the crooning of a radio. All the singers, male and female alike, wailed on about love. These tunes all wept with longing, ennui, and sorrow. What can be hurting *them*? Grein wondered. Can they possibly be sharing *my* sufferings? He wanted to caution Anna not to linger in the lobby, but he knew beforehand that she wouldn't listen to him. She always stopped at the front desk, where endless information about excursions, discount tickets for cabarets, and horse racing was posted. Anna always found something to talk about with Mr. Abrams, the proprietor. She helped herself to writing paper, bought picture postcards and postage stamps; she had deposited her jewelry in the safe, and from time to time she exchanged one bauble for another.

This time the lobby was jammed. Grein noticed that a new woman had just arrived. A tiny person wearing a pair of shoes with platform soles and very high heels, she stood in a mink coat among a great pile of elegant valises, her sallow face broad and deeply wrinkled, with a beaklike nose and hazel eyes. Her whole appearance expressed social competence, worldly experience, an eagerness to cause as much commotion as possible and to snatch up bargains wherever she could find them. Anna, rummaging for something in her purse, seemed not to have noticed her. Mr. Abrams, a tall, stout man with a youthful face and a round bald head, called out hoarsely, "Mrs. Grein, we've found your fan!"

Anna was walking toward the desk when she suddenly started back, turning her head and throwing a frightened glance at Grein. Growing pale, she muttered something and tried to give him a sign of sorts. Grein immediately perceived that some disaster had occurred—but what? His first thought was to run back up the stairs, but it was too late for that. The new arrival looked around and recognized Anna, whereupon all the wrinkles in her face beamed with the pleasant surprise of unexpectedly meeting a familiar acquaintance.

"Mrs. Luria!"

Yelling out the name so loudly that the noisy crowd fell silent, she thrust her arms out of her wide mink sleeves as though to embrace Anna. In the midst of his embarrassment, it struck Grein that although her fingernails were blood-red and sharp like those of a predatory beast, her hands, knotted with blue veins, were those of an old woman. Anna took another step backward, assuming an expression of incomprehension, as though the other woman had made a mistake. Realizing the futility of this, however, she coldly and irritably offered a hand to the other woman with a gesture which said plainly: I could have done perfectly well without this encounter.

"This is Mrs. Grein, not Mrs. Luria," Mr. Abrams called out, raising his eyebrows in astonishment.

"What? Mrs. Luria and I are next-door neighbors!" the stranger insisted. She spoke English with an accent and inflection that instantly identified her as Lithuanian. Not taking Anna's hand, she gazed at her in bewilderment instead.

"Mrs. Grein, don't you recognize your neighbor?" Mr. Abrams remarked jokingly.

Apparently it had not occurred to him to suspect anything, but all the women around immediately grasped what was going on. They stared with eyes popping out of their heads, necks craned forward, and mouths agape. Anna regained her composure.

"Mrs. Katz!" she said loudly, so that all could hear. "I've divorced Mr. Luria. Now I'm Mrs. Grein." And she nodded toward Grein.

The pupils of Mrs. Katz's eyes narrowed as she scrutinized Grein from head to toe, displaying a mouthful of dentures. Her face lit up with the sweet delight of a scandal.

"How do you do, Mr. Grein! Can one get divorced so quickly in America?" She changed her tone. Now she spoke half to Anna and half to the lobby at large. "Only a week ago you were still living with your husband, Mrs. Luria. Even in Reno you can't get a divorce with such lightning speed. Or perhaps it's here in Miami that one can divorce and remarry so fast? If so, allow me to congratulate you. I would call a divorce like that an 'express.' ''

One woman started laughing. Another coughed. Someone clicked off the television. A short fat man in a robe with loud sunflowers and wearing a huge pair of sandals—the same man who had introduced himself as the dentist from Philadelphia when Grein and Anna first arrived—wheezed throatily, ''As far as I know, one has to live here for at least six months before one can get a divorce. Perhaps it's even a year. Even in Reno one has to be a resident for six weeks. Things don't move so quickly in America. Perhaps in Russia one could get divorced immediately, but that was long ago. Not today. Over there, people used to be able to go to the local municipal offices, where they stamped a piece of paper and you were divorced. Finished. But as a result of all those instant divorces and marriages, Russia started crawling with—excuse the expression—bastards. This became such a problem that they were forced to change the law. I saw a play about this—or was it a movie?''

The dentist spoke as if he were delivering a lecture, never taking his eyes off Grein, staring at him searchingly and with distaste as though he had long wanted to settle scores with him. All the others leaned forward the better to hear. One woman even pulled her chair closer. Mr. Abrams frowned.

''Ladies and gentlemen, we're all here for only one purpose: to enjoy life, not to interfere in other people's business. Mrs. Grein is our guest, and she's welcome, whatever name she uses. Right, folks? I judge people by their conduct and their intelligence, not by their names.''

''Certainly, certainly,'' interjected Mrs. Katz, her eyes sparkling with sly mockery. ''If I've embarrassed you, Mrs. Luria—I mean Mrs. Grein— I'm terribly sorry. When I looked around and saw my neighbor, I was so pleased. We often have a little chat at the door when she and I are both carrying out the garbage, or when we come back from shopping at the same time. I often meet Mr. Luria in the elevator and he's always friendly. He takes off his hat, not like other refugees who stand in the elevator wearing their hats and blowing cigar smoke straight into the faces of ladies. Well, I'm really very sorry. I always had the feeling that you, Mrs. Luria— I mean Mrs. Grein—were particularly happy with your husband. I always used to think, Here's a truly contented couple, even if Mr. Luria's a good many years older than you, Mrs. . . . er . . . er . . . Grein, and it's such a pity he can't practice law here in America. Well, well! But what's the old saying? No one knows so well where the shoe pinches as he who wears it. Please allow me to congratulate you, Mrs. Luria. Or rather let me say in plain Yiddish: *Mazel tov!*''

''Mrs. Grein, here's your fan!'' Mr. Abrams broke in, raising his voice in irritation. ''Joe found it in the sand, and I recognized it from your description.''

Anna looked at the fan without seeing it for a moment or two.

''Please keep it for me, Mr. Abrams. We're going out to lunch. I'll come for it on the way back.''

''Certainly. Nothing gets lost here. You only have to tell us if something is missing and not keep it a secret.''

''Truly, Mrs. Luria—I mean Mrs. Grein—I wouldn't like there to be any misunderstandings between us,'' Mrs. Katz began all over again. ''Since I've come here and had the good fortune to meet you, Mrs. Luria, I'd like everything to be the way it always was. We're like one big happy family here. This is the fourth year I've come. My husband wants to send me only to the biggest hotels. Money's no object to him, he says. The main thing is that I should feel good and amuse myself for the two or three months I stay here. But Mrs. Luria—I mean Mrs. Grein—I'd rather be among people of my own kind. If I want to go to a nightclub or a show, I take a taxi and I go. Mr. Grein,'' Mrs. Katz called out, ''I must say you've found a real bargain! A nice woman, and a romantic one as well, it seems. Her father's an observant Jew, but a fast one when it comes to business. I've seen him several times—a short man with a beard. He must pray every day, no?''

''Come, Hertz.''

Anna took Grein by the arm.

''Goodbye, Mrs. Luria—I mean Mrs. Grein. You ought to count your-selves lucky you're here. It's freezing in New York, and when it's that cold, even love freezes over, isn't that so?''

The dentist began his sermon all over again, but Grein and Anna pushed their way through the chairs and hurried outside. The laughter of the woman who had tittered earlier followed them—loud, shrill, barbed.

7

In what way are these Jews? In what way are these my kin? Why should it matter to me if they massacre types like these or burn them in ovens? The tragedy is that they destroyed the good ones and left this trash behind. Grein was hot all over. One of his ears seemed to be on fire. He took off his hat. Instead of turning right, they both went left in the mortified haste of people who have been publicly shamed. Anna stopped suddenly.

"Well, if I've survived that, I'm no longer afraid of Gehenna!"

"Strange, I was also thinking of Gehenna," Grein answered, "Maimonides says that Gehenna is shame."

"Does he? Where are we going? Wait a second, I can't walk."

"What's the matter?"

"Hertz, perhaps we can sit down somewhere. I feel dizzy!"

"Shall I get a taxi?"

"Where would we go? I can't possibly sit in a restaurant now!"

"Perhaps we should drive to the park."

"Hertz, I have to throw up!"

Anna looked around fearfully. Her face was covered with beads of sweat. She stood fanning herself with her purse, as if trying to drive away her faintness. Grein attempted to support her and shield her from the passersby.

"I beg you, Anna, control yourself," he muttered, half pleading, half warning.

"Hertz, I don't feel well!"

Anna stood stock-still, struggling inwardly. Blinking her eyes rapidly, she turned first red, then white. She scrabbled in her purse for a handkerchief and spat into it.

"I must go to a toilet somewhere."

"Where? Taxi!"

"Where are you taking me?"

"Wherever you want. Even back to New York."

"Have him go to a cafeteria."

Grein gave the driver directions, and Anna laid her head back on the seat. For a long time she sat ashen-faced, her eyes closed and her mouth half open. It struck Grein that she had suddenly assumed an extraordinary resemblance to her late mother. In one corner of her mouth there appeared something nameless that Grein had not noticed until now—an expression of bitterness blended with humility and an otherworldly forgiveness of the kind one sometimes sees on the faces of the dead. This expression seemed to be saying: I forgive. I forgive. I forgive. I've survived. I've lived it down. She suddenly opened her eyes.

"Hertz, I'll never go back there."

"If you won't, you won't."

"You'll have to go back and pack up our things."

"What about your jewelry?"

"He'll give it to you. If not, I'll just leave it."

The taxi stopped at a cafeteria on Lincoln Road. Walking unsteadily, Anna immediately went to the washroom. Having taken two meal checks, one for himself and one for Anna, Grein found a table for two. The cafeteria was as huge as a railway station, and because it was lunchtime there was just as great a hubbub. Grein sat down and stared in front of him in the stillness that comes after a shock.

Now—now—I truly love her, he murmured to himself. That expression in the corner of her mouth seemed to have disclosed a new Anna to him, the real Anna. A mysterious secret power had given him a glimpse into her soul, as it were, and he had seen the nobility and magnanimity locked in the prison of her body. Her expression had revealed a secret: it had told him that behind the outer façade, behind all passion, all ambition, all foolishness was another, superior being, as yet untried, with a greater knowledge and higher goals. From now on, I'll treat her differently, Grein vowed. I'll give her her due: love, genuine love. I'll give it to other people as well. We're all going to die sometime. In twenty years, the majority of people in this cafeteria will be lying in the graveyard. That old man with the sandwich and the iced coffee, for instance. And that woman with the bowl of yogurt. Why hasn't this occurred to me before now? Why am I wasting my life on folly and triviality? How long will I indulge in what the Cabala calls smallness of mind? After all, I've always wanted to be a human being, not a worm.

Grein sat lost in thought, in the unspeaking silence that comes from penitence and a groping toward the essential purpose of life. And only a moment ago I thought such shocking thoughts! he upbraided himself. I even justified Hitlerism! A shudder passed down his spine and he began to pray. God in heaven, help me! I'm very small! It's difficult for me. Don't let me languish in blindness all my years. But what will happen to Stanislaw Luria? How can I be a decent human being when I do such wrong to another? He found no answer to this question, and his thoughts abruptly stopped. He looked in the direction of the counter. A fat cook wearing an apron and a chef's hat came in from the kitchen carrying a roasting pan of meat. He was like a priest in a pagan temple where the idols were worshipped with feasting. Unlike Hophni and Pinehas, the sons of Eli, this priest did not need to steal meat from the cauldron, Grein reflected. But what about the creatures whose flesh he's carrying in here? A few days ago they were alive. They too have souls. They too are God's children. They were quite possibly made of better material than human beings. Since they were sinless, they were certainly more innocent. But day after day they are ritually sacrificed—angels in the shape of oxen, calves, sheep. I once wanted to become a vegetarian. I wanted everything—and I never got further than wanting.

Suddenly Grein saw someone approaching him, smiling and waving. Grein recognized his face but couldn't remember his name. Who was he? He was a tiny person—in America one never saw such smallness of stature—a miniature of a man, with a sallow face, a wide forehead, a broad bald patch with two shocks of white hair on either side. His glistening black eyes were youthful and full of schoolboy mischievousness. A few blackened teeth peered out of his beaming mouth. He was wearing a floral shirt, rubber sandals, and yellow shorts.

Who is he? There's no doubt that I know him—I know him well! Grein strained his memory.

The other, stopping in front of him, started smacking his lips and rolling his eyes. Grein had long forgotten these Hasidic gestures of joyful recognition.

"The world's like a village, isn't it?"

Grein was silent.

"You obviously don't recognize me!"

He even speaks to me familiarly, Grein noticed, and he replied, "I'm in such a frame of mind that I wouldn't recognize my own father."

"What's the matter with you? Blockhead! I'm Morris Gombiner!"

Even before the other gave his name, at the very moment he uttered the old-fashioned word "blockhead," Grein remembered everything. He rose, and his immediate instinct was to embrace the little man, but the impulse was stillborn. The older man laughed like a yeshiva student, in a thin, reedy voice and with the singsong inflection Grein hadn't heard for decades: a cackling which overflowed into the eyes, spurted out from between the teeth, ran through every wrinkle in his face, and imparted to his features the easy familiarity of the impractical and unworldly. Grein had almost forgotten that such laughter existed. Gombiner's whole mien belonged to the other side of the ocean, to the talmudic debates in yeshiva classes and the traditional gestures that accompanied them, a mien that one forgets in America and is not even aware that one has forgotten.

"When did you come to America?" Grein asked. "As Jacob says to Joseph, 'I had not thought to see thy face.' "

"Of course you thought Hitler made a martyr of me."

"No, I heard that you'd managed to save yourself," Grein lied.

"From whom? I was very nearly a heap of ash, but somehow I managed to pull through. In 1938 I was one of those deported to Zbaszyn on the Polish frontier. Later I was in the Lodz Ghetto. Don't ask, don't ask—I went through all the seven gates of hell."

"Where were you?"

"Where wasn't I? Deep in the pit of Majdanek."

8

B oth were silent for a while.
    "Have you been in America long?" Grein asked.

"Barely a year."

"Where did you come from?"

"Tel Aviv."

"What are you doing in Miami? Come for some sun?"

"My wife has a house here. My second wife, not the first. Fanya is no longer with us. She perished in the Lodz Ghetto."

Again both were silent for a moment.

"Did you know I was in America?" Grein asked.

"Yes. But I live in Detroit, and you're somewhere in New York. I've also been to New York, but only to see a doctor. I had to have an operation, may it never happen to you. Only a few months ago. Well, if it's fated one must live, one lives. Who told you I saved myself?"

"Someone. I don't remember who."

"I come to this cafeteria every day, and not a day passes but I meet someone. Half of New York is here. But I honestly didn't expect to bump into you. I've often thought about you. When you're lying day after day in a death camp waiting for a 'selection' to push you into an oven, you think all kinds of things. I've taken my final leave of you many times. We were once close friends, after all. Suddenly I see you sitting here at a table! Your son must be grown up by now.''

"I have a son and a daughter. My son is just about to get an engineering degree.''

"Is that so! How time flies! Time is also a Hitler. It too destroys everything. How is your wife? I've forgotten her name.''

"Leah.''

"Yes, Leah. Of course. Is she also here?''

"No.''

"Did she stay in New York?''

"Yes.''

"Well, that we've met each other again is a miracle. A thousand miracles, actually. I wanted to get a visa to America, but at the last minute they sent me to Palestine. Nevertheless it was fated that I should be an American—an American woman turned up and we made a match. What can one do? As true as you see me before you, I've worked breaking stones for a highway. But I wasn't strong enough for it. I'm older than you are—a lot older. Why the Nazis let me live is incomprehensible. They enjoyed mocking me because I'm so short. They sent heroes to the ovens, but they let me live. 'Chickenshitter'—that's what they called me. They used to make me sing Sabbath hymns for them, and dance, too. Well, there were never any people like them before. Anyone who didn't see it with his own eyes doesn't know what the human species really is. When it pleased them, they ordered us—excuse me for mentioning it—to take down our pants and do all sorts of shocking things. You haven't changed at all. In America people stay young.''

"I've got some gray hairs.''

"I can't see them. You look upset. Is something wrong?''

"Why are you wearing a shirt with flowers all over it?'' Grein demanded, and immediately regretted his rudeness. Morris Gombiner laughed.

"It's all my wife. She wants to turn me into an American. She'll be here in a minute—she's gone to put money in the parking meter. You have to pay for everything. We drove here from Detroit. What a long way! Well, when was the last time we saw each other? It must be twenty years ago.''

"Yes, twenty years.''

"You promised to write, but you never did. Well, it's like that with all Americans. Now that I'm here myself, I also leave letters unanswered.

Here the Evil Inclination expresses itself in English, and it's always in a hurry. I didn't stay long in Vienna. We went off to Switzerland and Fanya studied there for a while. But she became pregnant, and once you start down that path, you have to stop studying. Later we went to Berlin. To tell you the truth, I can't remember what came first and what came later anymore. Dr. Halperin was publishing an encyclopedia, I recall, and I was supposed to contribute a piece of Hasidism. I hear he's also in New York now.''

''Dr. Halperin? Yes.''

''Does he still live off Boris Makaver?''

Grein's face changed. ''Do you know Boris Makaver as well?''

''Of course. I know them all. But they all left Berlin in good time, and I got deported to Zbaszyn. Is Makaver still a very rich man?''

''Yes, he's got money.''

''Do you still see them?''

Grein kept glancing at the stairs that led to the washroom.

''Morris, I want to tell you something.''

''What?''

''I'm here with Boris Makaver's daughter. Perhaps you remember her—Anna?''

''Yes, I remember. She married some actor, and even then he kept ten other women. What do you mean, you're with her?''

''That's exactly what I mean.''

''Well, I'm not God's policeman. But my wife is—how do you say it?—well, a Jewish wife. I don't find it becoming for her sake.''

''Perhaps it'd be better if we saw each other later. Give me your address.''

''What? I've forgotten the street. Where are you? I'll look you up. I've developed amnesia, may you never know what I suffer. I've written my address down somewhere. Wait, I'll get out my notebook. Ah, I haven't got it with me. I thought I was wearing a jacket. It's so hot here that one goes around in only a shirt. Where are you staying?''

''You'll laugh, but I'm not staying anywhere.''

''What's the matter?''

''We've just left one hotel and we haven't found another one yet.''

''Where are your things?''

''They're still there.''

''Well, they'll probably know where you're moving to.''

''No. I don't want anything more to do with them.''

"So what exactly should we do? Hertz, I can't lose touch with you. I drift about here as if I were in the World of Chaos. I've met quite a few old acquaintances. I even joked about it to my wife: if the Messiah comes, I said, he'll come to this cafeteria in Miami. But you're something else. We were like brothers, after all. You know what? Introduce her as your wife. Who cares? As long as you're living with her, then she is a wife. I heard she'd later married some lawyer."

"Who told you?"

"I can't remember. Someone in Tel Aviv, I think. People meet and talk. I forget things that happened yesterday, but a thousand old foolishnesses remain stuck in my memory. Whatever happens, I won't let you go. This is a great event for me. My wife's on the vulgar side, but in my position you can't be finicky. In the camps I learned very quickly not to be a snob. The wish we express in the Eighteen Benedictions—'May my soul be lowly unto all as the dust'—came literally true for me. Had it not, I'd've been ash long ago. I also taught myself something else, but you won't understand that."

"What was that?"

"Not to think."

Anna came in, but not from the direction in which Grein was looking for her. She was carrying a glass of orange juice. When she saw that Grein was talking to someone, she slowed her pace and even made a tentative motion to go elsewhere. Though she still looked distressed, she had fixed her face and her hair. Grein got up quickly, bumping against the table as he did so.

"Anna, this is an old friend of mine, Morris Gombiner. We know each other from the old days in Vienna. We haven't seen each other for over twenty years."

The glass of orange juice shook in Anna's hand. She threw a half-questioning, half-frightened glance at Grein, standing at the table with the ashen face of someone fighting an illness. Morris Gombiner, his face suffused with childlike good nature mingled with embarrassment, smiled and made a comic little bow. Everything about him immediately became submissive, flustered, abashed. He clicked his heels and offered a diminutive hand to Anna, which she could not take at once because of the glass she held. Morris started stammering to her in German, swallowing the words as he spoke: "Deeply, deeply honored. Delighted to make your acquaintance. Your spouse and I were friends . . . intimate friends. Indeed, truly so. Like brothers. Exactly like brothers. For twenty years now . . . A pleasure. A truly great pleasure. By chance. Quite by chance . . .''

And completely unexpectedly, he suddenly added in English, ''Thank you very much!''

This was apparently the only bit of English he knew.

9

''M orris, you don't have to speak to Anna in German. She knows Yiddish. Anna, put that glass down.''

Anna put down the orange juice and gave Morris Gombiner her hand. He kissed it in the European manner.

''A very very great pleasure.''

''Anna, do sit down. Wait, I'll bring you a chair. Perhaps we should find a bigger table,'' Grein said. ''There's no room for another chair here.''

''Here's a chair!''

And Morris Gombiner pulled one up.

''Have you come from Europe?'' Anna asked.

''No, from Palestine. But I was in Europe before that. Europe is no longer Europe, though. The world has become a jungle full of wild animals.''

''He's a survivor of the camps,'' Grein explained.

''I saw everything. As Jeremiah says, 'I am the man that hath seen affliction.' But what's the use of speaking about it? Today's a day of celebration for me, a great celebration. Your husband and I were close friends. We even lived together for a short time. My wife and I had an apartment in Vienna, and we gave him a room. In the camps I always thought about him: I wonder what's become of Hertz Grein, I used to ask. What does he do in America? What's he thinking? And out of the blue I look around and he's sitting at a table right here. Truly, the world is a village. I wasn't aware that he had such a beautiful wife.'' Morris Gombiner altered his tone. ''In America one never sees faces like yours. Here everything is so commonplace.''

And Morris Gombiner began smiling humbly, showing his blackened teeth.

Anna seemed lost in thought for a while. "Thank you. Thank you very much. You've unfortunately found us in a peculiar situation. But if you're Hertz's friend, then you're mine as well."

"Certainly, madame, certainly. My wife should be coming at any moment. She's gone to put money in the parking meter. If you don't, you can't park. We live in Detroit. My wife has a house here. Your husband told me you've just left a hotel you didn't like. Perhaps you'd like to move in with us. We have a beautiful house in a quiet suburb with a garden and palm trees and every convenience and comfort. But what good is a house when there's no one there to exchange a word with? As the Talmud says, 'Give me either companionship or death.'"

"It's not that bad, surely?"

"One needs a friend. If one has nobody to talk to, how is one to have any pleasure? Where I live, they all speak English, and I don't understand a word they're saying. That's why I come to this cafeteria. One always meets somebody Jewish here. My wife has a car and she's my chauffeur." Morris tittered nervously. "In those unmentionable places I've been, if anyone had told me I'd end up living in America and driving around in an automobile like a lord, I'd've thought him insane. But things are exactly as Heine describes them. First the Jew's a beggar, then he's a prince. That's been the story of the Jew from the very beginning. First he's kneading mortar for Pharaoh, then he's standing at the foot of Mount Sinai, and it's the same in all generations. Here's my wife!"

Morris Gombiner sprang from his chair, and a moment later Grein also rose. Morris ran to meet her, smiling, gesticulating, nodding toward Grein and Anna. Mrs. Gombiner was a stout woman with a huge bosom, a pockmarked face, a narrow brow, and huge flapping jowls that hung down like slabs of dough. She apparently had no neck, for her head sat directly on her shoulders. Her hair, like freshly painted black wire, stood out stiffly in all directions. Clad in fiery red slacks and lavishly ornamented sandals from which crooked toes with flame-colored nails poked their way forward, she was carrying a small box and a huge handbag resembling a basket with a brass lock. A flat nose and a pair of unfriendly, squinting eyes above deep circles completed the face with which she glowered at Grein and Anna. For a while it seemed as though she was unwilling to come over to the table Morris pointed out to her, and was rebuking and abusing him. She shook her head vigorously. After a while she waddled slowly over. Morris gallantly relieved her of the small box.

"Florence, this is my best friend, Hertz Grein. This is Madame Grein."

And Morris Gombiner cast imploring and embarrassed glances at his wife, at Grein, at Anna. He smiled guiltily, and his moist eyes seemed to ask: What can I do? That's the situation. Mrs. Gombiner aggressively sized Anna up with a glance and said in English, "How do you do?"

"Sit down, Florence, sit down. I'll bring another chair!" Morris wheedled her and started fidgeting. Highly agitated, he looked anxiously around on all sides, searching for a chair or a bigger table, making rapid, darting movements like a squirrel. He scuttled forward and tried to snatch up an empty chair, but someone else grabbed it first. Mrs. Gombiner instantly began upbraiding him in English: "What are you running for? Why are you jumping about like a madman? You're not allowed to add extra chairs to this table—you'll block the way for others. This is a cafeteria, not a Hasidic prayerhouse. You're still a greenhorn!"

And she slapped down her bag on the table, almost overturning Anna's glass of orange juice. Anna had barely taken one sip of it.

"Excuse me . . . He's running! Where's he running to? You know each other from Europe?"

"Yes, from Vienna."

"Have you also come from the camps?"

"No. I've been here nearly twenty years."

"Well, let's find a bigger table and we'll sit down together. While I was putting a dime in the meter, I spotted a bargain in a window—a shoe store was having a sale. It's like this every day. I go somewhere for a minute and when I come back he's dug up another one of his greenhorn buddies. But we can sit down together. Have you had lunch yet? I'm on a diet and I have to eat in a cafeteria. If I go to those Jewish restaurants, they push their noodles and their stuffed derma at me and I start putting on weight. I have to eat a light lunch, without any starch. All the tables are occupied."

"Perhaps we can make an exception today and go to Friedman's?" Morris Gombiner suggested timidly.

"No exceptions! *I* gain weight, not you. He can eat up a whole ox, hooves and all, and the next day when I put him on the scale, he's lost a pound. But with me, everything I eat goes straight here, to my hips. Well, there'll be a table soon. They guzzle and go. Who'd you think comes here? The rich folks from the big hotels who pay fifty dollars a day for a room, that's who. They're all on a diet, but the longer they stay, the fatter they get. Why are you wearing a jacket and tie in this heat?" Mrs. Gombiner suddenly turned on Grein. "If you've been in America for twenty years, why do you still go around dressed like that?"

She stood with her back to Anna. Her shoulders were covered with freckles and the peeling skin that comes from too much exposure to the sun. Her arms were extraordinarily thick and seemed to be split down the center, as if they had grown another pair of arms of their own. On one finger she wore a wedding band and an engagement ring with an enormous diamond. The red paint on her fingernails was half worn off.

"Oh, I've always been used to wearing city clothes," said Grein.

"What do you mean, 'used to'? *He* didn't want to dress like a human being either," said Mrs. Gombiner, pointing to her husband. "But I dragged the pants and jacket off him and dressed him like one. If you come to Miami Beach, why go around sweating? It costs plenty in the hotels here. The owners take the guests to the cleaners. I own my own house, but the taxes eat everything up. Here everything's for the millionaires. Here they exploit the workers even worse than they do in New York or Detroit, although Ford, curse him, is the kind of bloodsucker who leaves his workers poor and homeless. I've got a black man working for me, but they don't let him spend the night. Every day he's got to go back to downtown Miami and pay rent, because a black man isn't allowed to stay overnight in Miami Beach. They're scared he'll turn the sea black for them. Oh, here's a table."

10

Morris Gombiner skipped nimbly across to the vacant table and tilted the backs of the chairs against its edges to signify that it was taken. As he did so, he smiled humbly, like a Hasid, and guiltily, like a naughty schoolboy. Mrs. Gombiner, making faces and muttering, waddled slowly across to the new place; it was evident that movement of any kind was an effort for her. Huge earrings resembling bedsprings bounced from the lobes of her ears.

Grein and Anna remained behind at the old table for a while.

"What kind of ill luck is this?" Anna demanded.

"I warned you that Miami wasn't for us. But he's a dear man, really."

"His wife is unbearably vulgar."

"We can't do anything about that. Come, let's go over."

"Everything bad happens to me. I can't be sociable with anyone now, Hertz. My stomach's turning over."

"Well, drink some tea. They have a house—perhaps we can stay with them."

"With those lunatics?"

"Grein, why are you sitting there? Come over!" Morris called out. "We're waiting for you."

Grein helped Anna up, and they went over to the other table.

"My wife isn't feeling very well," Grein explained.

"There's one remedy for all ailments—lemon tea. Whenever I feel out of sorts, I immediately order some lemon tea, and that settles me. All troubles come from the stomach, and from impurities in the blood. Lemon tea cleans up every one. Well, we've got a comfortable table here. Perhaps I can bring you something? Tell me what you want—I like being the waiter—"

"You sit down!" ordered Mrs. Gombiner, flying to the attack. "This is a cafeteria, not a restaurant. There's no waiting on tables here. Here everyone helps themselves. If you're hungry, you go first," Mrs. Gombiner said to Grein. She ignored Anna entirely.

"No, thank you. You go first. We're not hungry."

"Come, then. If I don't eat exactly on time, I get stomach cramps."

"Florence, if you're going now, bring something for me, too—a sandwich or something."

"You come with me!"

So they both went off to the counter. Next to his wife, Morris Gombiner looked even smaller and skinnier. She laid her hand on his shoulder, and it was difficult to tell whether she was leaning on him or pushing him. The trays and the cutlery were placed so high up that Morris could barely reach them, and he was forced to stand on his toes. Anna tried to rouse herself.

"Well, there's a woman who knows her own mind. Hertz, why do you keep referring to me as your wife? What kind of act are you performing for these people? Didn't I have enough in the hotel? I don't want to be called by your wife's name. I haven't fallen that low. I still have my own name."

"What else could I do? Believe me, when I recognized him, my heart sank. I should really have been overjoyed—I had no idea he was still alive—but not now, in the middle of this disaster. We'll eat lunch with them and then it'll be over."

"No, they'll cling to you like leeches. I'm beginning to believe that all Papa's curses are coming true."

"Don't be silly!"

"If only there was somewhere I could lie down! I can hardly sit up. Everything's spinning around me.

"We'll find another hotel soon."

"What kind of hotel? We can't arrive without luggage."

"I'll go back there and pack up."

"What'll I do in the meantime? It's stifling in here. When I saw them, my heart stopped. One trouble after another—what's it called in the Bible? Papa warned me. You won't have any rest, he said. You'll long for death. He's put a curse on me, Hertz. He's put a curse on me!"

"Really, Anna, I never expected you would believe such nonsense."

"Why not? People can put a hex on others. Of all the hotels in Miami Beach, we had to go and choose exactly the one that vulture uses. And now we've run into another pair of the same type. They've both put a curse on me, Papa and Luria. Probably the rebbe as well."

"Truly, Anna, I can't believe my ears."

"I wouldn't have believed it myself if my whole life hadn't been one long chain of disasters. There's such a thing as fate, you know. That Yasha Kotik fell so much in love with me that he nearly died of it, so he claimed. But as soon as we were married he decided to destroy me. I still can't understand how I got out of his clutches alive. Then Luria became my worst enemy as soon as you appeared on the scene. Papa said very ugly things. Only now can I see how ugly they were."

"What did he say?"

"His awful curses and all the rest of it. I've never longed for a bed as much as I do now. I'd like to fall asleep and never wake up again."

"Anna, don't get hysterical. We'll soon have a place to stay and you'll forget all this nonsense."

"They'll find us again. Oh God, here they come!"

Morris Gombiner and his wife approached, carrying two trays laden with meat, pudding, soup, rolls. Grein made a halfhearted motion to rise, but remained seated.

"What shall I bring you, Anna?"

"You know I don't want anything."

"What about some lemon tea?"

"No, Hertz. Just bring me a glass of cold water."

"What kind of lunch is cold water?" Morris put in. "One must eat something. All those theories about calories are nonsense. You have to eat, otherwise you have no strength. The body's insatiable. The soul has to provide it with everything, and the more it gets, the more it wants. It's the story of Chamberlain and Hitler, may no children carry on his name. On the other hand, there's nothing they won't give Stalin——"

"Morris, are you starting again?" demanded Mrs. Gombiner menacingly.

"Well, I'll be quiet. My wife's a Red. You can't say a bad word about Stalin to her."

"I'm not a Red, but you don't have to mimic all the reactionaries. What harm has Stalin done them? He built up a nation of workers, without capitalism and without Fascism. He gave the Jews Birobidzhan. If it hadn't been for Stalin, Hitler would've been in America. In any case, there's no shortage of Nazis here. They're already looking for a new war, the anti-Semites. May they all go up in flames together with Wall Street!"

"Yes, yes, go on repeating everything you hear at your meetings."

"It's the truth, Morris, it's the truth. May Stalin's hands be blessed. For me, Stalin's a holy man, the people's greatest friend. If it wasn't for Stalin, the working classes would have gone to the wall long ago."

And Mrs. Gombiner slammed down an empty tray. It fell with a crash.

"Well well, let's not start with any debates. I've spoken with dozens of people who come from there. It's hell, a living hell."

"You know why it's a hell? Because the Soviet Union lost huge amounts of blood and the fascists, may they all burn, didn't want to open a second front. It was only after the masses had stormed Washington and threatened to lynch the President that he ordered the invasion. But it was all a bluff! On the quiet, they tried to save Hitler so they could wipe out the workers."

"Florence, enough!"

"You shuddup!"

Silence fell. Mrs. Gombiner made a grab for the soup. She slurped, made a face, added salt and pepper. She glanced balefully at the counter. Morris seemed to shrivel up. He sat motionless and ashen, blinking his eyes, biting his lips, and shaking his head vigorously. He picked up a spoon and put it down again. Mrs. Gombiner lumbered off to the counter.

"Well, Grein, go and get something. One must eat, everyone agrees about that. What can one do? I abide by the example of Issachar: 'For he saw a resting-place that it was good, and he bowed his shoulders to bear.'

Does one have any choice, tell me? Madame, I'm truly sorry. How does Heine put it? Oh dear, I've forgotten the words! Oh, yes: '*Herz, mein Herz, sei nicht beklommen/Und ertrage dein Geschick.*' Heart, my heart, be not distressed /And endure thy destined lot.''

11

"**I** don't want to impose on you, madame," coaxed Morris Gombiner, "but our house is paradise. My wife's just told me she'd be prepared to rent out the top-floor apartment cheaply. She's busy the whole day, very busy. She deals in real estate here. She has a partner. She's out all day. What can you lose? To me it's not a question of money, God forbid. What difference does it make to me? All I need is a piece of bread and a place to sleep. But surely we'd all find it much cozier together. You probably also don't know anyone here."

"It's up to you, Anna," Grein insisted.

"I'd really like to stay with you, but I'm a bit afraid of your wife," Anna responded.

"What's there to be afraid of? She goes to leftist meetings and believes that Russia is the holy of holies. She reads their newspapers and all the rest of it. I've told her that she's a bourgeois herself, but you can't talk to fanatics. But what's it to you? You're tenants. She's got no time to sit around, anyway—she does a thousand things. Her business is exclusively in Hollywood—that's the name of the suburb here, not the other Hollywood. You'd have a house, a garden, a palace. You needn't pay for the whole season right away. You can move in for a week and see how things go. And since you're not feeling very well, madame, what's the sense of starting to look all over for hotels and the rest of it?"

Mrs. Gombiner returned, bringing with her a fruit dessert and coffee.

"Well, what've these people decided? I say they should take a look first. Nobody buys a pig in a poke."

"They'd like to move in for a week and see if they like it," Morris Gombiner took it upon himself to reply.

"Why not? I won't charge you anything like a hotel would. Move in, and if you don't like it, move out. I won't cheat you, and for the same money, the hotels'll take you anytime. If you decide to stay, I won't charge you separately for the week. We're all Jewish thieves here, as they say. What's it matter as long as you have your health?''

"How much do you want for the week?''

"As much as the hotels charge for one day—sixty dollars. If you decide to stay the whole season, then you'll pay me four hundred dollars. Come and see what a bargain that is. Where are your things? We'll drive there in the car and get them. The taxis all rob you. This coffee tastes disgusting! Pfui!''

And Mrs. Gombiner spat out a mouthful of coffee into the saucer.

"You'll get better in Russia.''

"In Russia they're building socialism.''

What am I doing? What am I doing? Anna asked herself. I'm crawling into a swamp. But Morris Gombiner was right: she had no strength to go searching for a hotel now. She had a headache and stomach cramps and only one desire: to get into bed and lie down. Although she was wearing sunglasses, the glare in the cafeteria hurt her eyes. She felt totally debilitated, as if the encounter with Mrs. Katz in the hotel had eroded the last vestiges of her youth. Well, how can it be worse with them? I'll shut my door. That Gombiner woman can't force her way in.

Mrs. Gombiner suddenly snatched up the pot of coffee and stormed off to the counter, apparently to fling it in their faces and make a scene. Grein couldn't help laughing.

"Clearly your wife doesn't allow anyone to take advantage of her.''

"What? It's good coffee,'' said Morris in embarrassment. "They'll curse her out into the bargain. Well, I don't know, everyone has their own madness. Why, for instance, are Jews prepared to sacrifice their lives for Communism? They've killed all the Jews over there. Deliberately and in cold blood. It's a thousand times worse than under the Czar. But they're so crazed with ideology that they're blind. What's the saying? You spit in their faces and they think it's raining. As soon as we Jews stop serving an omnipotent God, we have to start serving an all-powerful human despot. But I've ceased to be amazed. If you told me that while they were dragging an innocent person to the gallows, he started singing a song of praise to his hangman, I wouldn't be surprised. You won't believe it, but in the camps there were raging debates. On one side of a wall they were burning human beings, and on the other people intellectualized all kinds of stupidities—if they still had strength left to speak, that is. For the most part,

we had neither time nor strength. The whip never let up. The Nazi wickedness was totally mad. A whole nation was suddenly transformed into
devils.''

"I barely escaped being their victim myself," said Anna, half to herself
and half to Morris.

"What? What they did to women there is terrifying even to think about.
I once saw them herding a crowd of women. They looked exactly like
specters, in rags, with shaven heads. Among them I suddenly recognized
a woman who'd been a famous beauty. Well, I'd better not say anything.''

Mrs. Gombiner returned with a full pot of fresh coffee.

"Such racketeers! Such bums! Such nobodies! Well, I've taught them a
lesson. Here in America, if you're too shy to open your mouth, they'll
tear your guts out. If you want to drink slops, Morris, go right ahead, but
I like a good cup of coffee. For the ten cents you pay them, they can afford
to give decent coffee, not poison. Now at least the coffee'll be better—
that's for sure!''

When they'd finished eating, they all trooped outside to Mrs. Gombiner's new red car parked directly opposite. Mrs. Gombiner got behind the
wheel and her husband sat next to her. Grein and Anna sat in the back.
Mrs. Gombiner drove so fast that it was difficult to understand how she
avoided smashing into other cars. The other drivers yelled and swore at
her, and she swore right back. "Hey, you bum, are you blind?" She never
stopped pounding her horn. For a while the sun still shone, but the winter
twilight fell suddenly. Now all the hotels switched on their floodlights,
illuminating the palm trees and the flowers as if they were stage sets. Here
and there a palm that had fallen victim to the last hurricane was propped
up with planks. Late bathers—women in robes and rubber sandals—were
returning from the beach; early diners—women in mink stoles and fur
collars—were emerging from the hotels. Everything was jumbled together: day and night, summer and winter, deshabille and elegance. The
setting sun inflamed the clouds, throwing a ruddy hue over the sea and
filling windows with purple and fine gold. Somewhere far away on the
horizon a white ship sailed serenely. The air smelled of oranges and gasoline. Materializing out of the dusk, an airplane flew by, roaring and flashing its lights. There was something paradisaical and fantastic about the
evening—a tropical calm, the strange feeling of it being a holiday in the
middle of the week. Grein was filled with a longing for spring. Oh, if we
could only rest! If the powers that harness and harry human beings would
only release their hold for a while so we might enjoy God's gifts, take

stock of ourselves, lift up our beaten spirits! For all sins stem only from not believing in the higher powers, from fearing tomorrow, from wanting to snatch a bit of this world before it's too late.

The car stopped at the hotel where Grein and Anna were staying. Grein got out. "I'll pack up our things in five minutes."

"Take your time, young man," Mrs. Gombiner answered. The pure twilight had evidently put her in a more amiable frame of mind.

Not more than three minutes had passed before Grein returned.

"Anna, Mr. Abrams won't take your jewelry out of the safe. You'll have to go in yourself."

"Did you show him the receipt?"

"I showed him everything."

"Who's in the lobby? All those dreadful women?"

"I didn't really notice."

"Why are you scared to go in, Mrs. Grein?" Mrs. Gombiner intervened. "Since you couldn't get any sleep in this hotel because it's so noisy, you've got every right to move out whenever you want, and he can't charge you for more than the time you stayed. Come, I'll go in with you, Mrs. Grein, and I'll give him such a piece of my mind that his other guests'll also get out as quick as they can."

"I beg you, Mrs. Gombiner, please stay in the car. I don't want any unpleasant scenes!"

"Well, if you're afraid, you're afraid. But in America you don't have to be afraid. This is a free country. Here if a lady speaks to a man, he has to hear her out and say 'Yes, ma'am.' If he gets fresh, you take him to court and the judge sends him to jail. You're all still greenhorns."

"Florence, don't put your nose in other people's business."

"You be quiet!"

Anna hesitated a moment.

"Well, I'll go in. Do me a favor, Mrs. Gombiner, and stay in the car."

"Sure. If people want to let themselves be cheated, it's not my business. Pay that swindler as much as he wants. It's your money, not mine. What fools!"

12

All the lights were ablaze in the hotel lobby. The guests had already dressed for dinner. The television was on. The women were chattering, all with sunburned faces that reminded Grein of freshly baked pastry. They seemed to radiate the scorching heat they had absorbed from sitting the entire day in the beating sun. The bodies which not long before had been lolling about in the sand were now swathed in colorful clothes and glittering jewelry. Mr. Abrams had done everything he could to give his modest hotel a festive air. There were flowers all over the place, and two tubs held small orange trees gilded with tiny fruit. Despite these frills, however, everything remained commonplace. A woman had put a coin in a postage-stamp dispenser, but the stamps wouldn't come out, so she was punching the machine to get her money back. A girl with a large face as red as a tomato was showing a boy some photographs. All the women babbled at once. The conversation revolved around shoes, and each was pointing to her own feet. The men also participated. The dentist from Philadelphia was fighting to say something, but the women outshouted him. What could a man possibly know about women's shoes? The whole time they prattled on, they kept looking in every direction—toward the door, outside, anywhere—almost as if they were secretly awaiting a messenger, an announcement, a piece of good news without which everything would be futile. Mrs. Katz had already acquired a sunburn and had changed into summer clothes. The diamond on her finger refracted the electric light like a blazing prism. Her dress was made of two different pieces of fabric and was half red, half black. She reminded Grein of a figure on a playing card.

When Grein and Anna entered, the buzz persisted for a while, as the guests had evidently not yet grasped the opportunity that had presented itself. But suddenly everyone fell silent, and all that could be heard was the music tinkling from the television. Mrs. Katz leaped up from the sofa.

"Mrs. Luria—I mean Mrs. Grein—wherever did you get to? I've been wanting to see you! Where did you take her, Mr. . . . er . . . er . . . Grein?"

Anna made no reply but walked straight to the desk. "Mr. Abrams, why don't you want to take out my jewelry?"

"Who says I don't want to? But I must have the owner, not a stranger. If you want to move out, Mrs. Grein, that's your privilege, but when I return valuables I have to know who I'm giving them to, and I have to get the correct signature.''

"Be so good as to give us the bill.''

"It's all ready.''

Oddly, Mr. Abrams had not charged for more than the few days the couple had spent here. His eyes filled with regret, and with a determination to behave honorably in the midst of this seething female malevolence. Grein immediately took out his wallet and paid. Mrs. Katz, who had been standing back whispering furtively with the other women, came up.

"Mrs. Luria, don't tell me you're moving out!''

"Yes, we're moving out!'' Anna answered aggressively.

"Why? Don't tell me you're running away because of me! I arrive, I meet a familiar face, I thank God we'll be able to spend some time together, and suddenly you're running away! What's the matter? Aren't we good enough company for you? True, this is a small hotel, a respectable hotel, with no monkey business, for married people, not for sweethearts, but that doesn't mean you have to run away.''

Grein suddenly lost his patience. "Madame, be good enough to leave us alone.''

Mrs. Katz's eyes flared. "Why are you interfering, Mr. Grein? I'm speaking to Mrs. Luria, not to you.''

"All this talk is quite unnecessary.''

"In the meantime you're not my teacher, Mr. Grein, and don't lecture me on manners.''

"Mrs. Katz, I have no desire to talk to you,'' Anna cried out. "Is that clear?''

"Clear, clear—clear as mud! Tomorrow I'll write to my husband and I'll ask him to give Mr. Luria greetings from his faithful wife. If he decides to go to court and get a divorce, all of us here will be witnesses to the way you've behaved. If I'm not mistaken, you're not a citizen of this country yet, and I doubt whether any American judge would grant citizenship to a woman of your sort. My husband isn't a lawyer like Mr. Luria, but I know of a case in which they deported a woman like you straight back to where she came from. She even served a term in prison first, or perhaps it was Ellis Island. There was a report about it in the newspapers.''

"Do what you like, but don't speak to me!'' Anna raised her voice.

"They behave like big shots, these refugees!'' called out the dentist from Philadelphia. "Did they have it better in Germany with Hitler? Uncle

Sam opened his gates for them because they were victims of Fascism, and what did they bring here? They're the worst fascists and anti-Semites themselves. A dentist from Berlin moved into my neighborhood with his family, and they don't even go to pray on Yom Kippur. At Christmas time they put up the biggest tree they can find in the whole of Philadelphia. The Jewish community approached him to support a synagogue center they wanted to build, and what did that swine of a German Jew answer? He preferred not to socialize with the *Ostjuden*, he said, because they have no manners and—that sonofabitch even blamed the Polish Jews for Hitler coming to power in Germany. He said things that Goebbels himself wouldn't've been ashamed of. He made a set of dentures for a woman and—''

In the doorway, Mrs. Gombiner suddenly appeared.

The dentist tried to press on with his account of the woman whose German-made false teeth broke at the very first bite and who almost choked to death on them, but no one was listening to him any longer. Everyone had turned to gaze at the new arrival. Among the smartly attired crowd she looked exceptionally common and badly dressed in her red slacks now rolled up to her knees, her bare feet thrust into her garish sandals, her spiky hair disheveled, and her blouse exposing a slash of bare midriff where it did not meet her slacks. With her ample bosom thrust forward and her enormous backside jutting out behind, Mrs. Gombiner flashed an appraising, angry, threatening glare around the lobby. She breathed in the malice and vengefulness of those who have nothing left but to destroy the happiness of others. To fix her position the more firmly, she supported herself with a hand on the doorpost.

''No wonder people can't wait to get out of here!'' she said in a rasping and strident voice. ''It's as noisy as a Bombay bazaar.''

Mr. Abrams, who had already stretched out an arm to open the safe for Anna's jewelry, grew tense and on guard. Stunned, he stared at the interloper with suspicion and hostility. Anna blanched, fixing a pair of terrified eyes on Mrs. Gombiner. She shook her head in disbelief, as if what she was seeing couldn't possibly be true but must be an hallucination. Grein took a step backward.

''Who are you? What do you want?'' demanded Mr. Abrams.

''Never mind who I am. Considering that your hotel has absolutely nothing to offer—no swimming pool and no entertainment and not even its own beach, so that people who stay here have to crawl across the street to get to the sea and risk being knocked down by cars—why can't you at least see to it that it's a bit quieter in here? People can't wait to escape from you. You can go deaf in this place, it's so noisy. All you do in these hotels is to grab money out of people's pockets and charge high prices. Because of hotels like yours, the best-paying guests escape farther up to the nineties and the motels and God alone knows where else, so that the prices of real estate there have shot up sky-high, and it's become such a racket that a run-down bungalow with no amenities costs six thousand dollars and even more. Ask me, mister, I know what I'm talking about. I'm in the real-estate business myself, not here, but in Hollywood, and I want to tell you that people like you are ruining the trade in Miami Beach, and because of the likes of you—"

Mr. Abrams took his hand from the safe.

"Lady, I don't interfere in your business, so you don't interfere in mine. If I need you, I'll send for you, and make you the manager as well."

"Mrs. Gombiner, please be good enough to go back to the car!" said Grein hollowly.

"I'll go when I want to, not when you tell me, Mr. Grein, and you don't need to be such a snob and a goddamn sucker. These people scoop up a hotel, pay an agent a few hundred dollars, and want to become millionaires in one season. Plenty of sick people come here who need a bit of sun for their health and they spend sixty or seventy dollars a day for a hole that's not worth three dollars. Downtown, nobody'd set foot in a slum like this. If they hadn't greased palms along the way—you know what I mean—a place like this would've been condemned long ago and—"

"Lady, go to the Chamber of Commerce or wherever you want. Leave me in peace!"

"Mrs. Gombiner, I don't understand why you're making a scene!" Anna recovered her speech. "I've got enough trouble without you."

"Ah, they're all a gang of thieves," Mrs. Katz remarked to the dentist.

"Hey, lady, where're you from? Orchard Street?" the dentist called out.

There was laughing and tittering.

"What's the matter with Orchard Street? The fact that poor people live there, ordinary working folk, not crooked gamblers like you?"

"How do you know I'm a gambler?"

"Leave it to me. I take one look at a customer, I know immediately what I'm dealing with. Why do you all come here? Because you've got TB from working all week in the sweatshops and you need some sun if you want to go on living? You come here, gamble away good money on the horses and dogs, and then run to the nightclubs to spend more on cheap whores. And where do you get the money to waste on all this? From exploiting the poor workers from Orchard Street whose bellies are swollen from hunger and—"

"A Communist, are you?"

Anna bent toward Mr. Abrams. "Please, Mr. Abrams, give me my jewelry—I've got to get away from this woman."

"Why did you bring her if you've got to get away from her? Kindly sign here."

Anna picked up the pen, but her hand shook so badly that she could hardly write. Mr. Abrams put the receipt in front of her, but the lines seemed to be moving, falling over one another. Anna scribbled her name across the words printed there. The wall opposite her seemed to be tottering, the floor to be sliding away from under her feet. Spots of flame flashed before her eyes. Bells rang in her ears. God in heaven, this is my death! Anna said to herself. She clutched the desk to stop herself from collapsing. As through a wall, she heard Mrs. Gombiner roundly retort, "I'm not a Communist, but you're all dead scared. You're damned right to shake in your fancy shoes! Your miserable end is closer than you think!"

8

Anna lay in her bedroom on the upper floor. Mrs. Gombiner had already gone to sleep in her apartment below. Grein sat on the veranda. Although it was not yet late, it was as still as if it were midnight. It was difficult to believe that only a few minutes from here, on the other side of the Indian River, lay the huge hotels, the nightclubs, the tumult of Miami Beach. A waning yellow moon hung low in the sky. The stars here were different from those up North, and in their shapes, arrangement, and variety they looked to Grein like the diacritical marks in the Hebrew Bible that tell the reader where to vocalize and how to chant the text. Morris Gombiner had lent Grein a pair of binoculars and he kept them focused on the heavens, moving from one corner to another. In places where the naked eye could see only a solitary, half-blurred, tiny light, the telescopic lenses revealed entire clusters of stars, laughing with golden glee in the infinite heights. Grein tried to identify the constellations. He looked for the Milky Way.

That's what I should have been—an astronomer! he thought. If one loses oneself in the greatness of the divine, one does not see the smallness of the human. It was difficult to believe that every one of these small dots was a sun around which revolved a number of planets just like the earth, planets perhaps also inhabited by intelligent beings. No, our planet earth could not be an exception in the cosmos. Billions or trillions of such earths conceivably existed, each one with its own fauna and flora, with its beauties and blemishes, with its pleasures and troubles. It was strange to sit here on Morris Gombiner's veranda looking into the eternity from which one came and to which one had to return. How foolish were those who thought that man, with his little mind, was the only wisdom in the entire universe, and that everything else was blind, arbitrary, pure physical matter!

Grein put down the binoculars. Here below, everything was silent: the nearby coconut palms, the cactuses, the oleander bush which bloomed in the middle of winter, the ever-changing flowers in the pots which surrounded the house. Warm breezes rustled through the night, carrying messages from the virgin forests of Brazil somewhere along the equator. Warm currents rose from the sea. Behind the house, the garden was thick with oranges, lemons, and other tropical fruit. The air was heavy with spicy smells, with Oriental secrets, with a desire that only warm climates arouse. Everything seemed alive, every blade of grass, every leaf, every pebble. Grein breathed in deeply. That morning he had believed Morris Gombiner was ashes. Now, this evening, he was living in his house. But what of that menacing woman, Mrs. Gombiner? How did *she* fit into the universe? What kind of role did *she* play in the divine drama?

There was the sound of footsteps and Morris Gombiner came out in slippers and a dressing gown.

"Hertz, aren't you asleep yet?"

"Not yet."

"How's Anna?"

"A little better."

"Florence has also gone to bed. What do you think of the house? Not a bad little place, is it? You'll really see it properly only in the morning when the sun's up."

"It's magnificent even now."

"Well, how are you? Without the women, we can talk. You don't know what it means to me that I've met you and you're here. It's no trivial thing! We were close friends, after all. But suddenly you went away—too bad for us. One forgets nothing. There, in Gehenna, every few days I had to prepare myself for a 'selection,' and each time I parted with you all over again. Be well, Grein, I used to say, pardon me if I ever wronged you or spoke a cross word to you. I can't tell you how close we were to death. Death became a familiar presence, a good friend. Many didn't even live to be gassed—they died at forced labor or as they lay on their bunks. One night I was lying talking to someone in the barracks. We weren't allowed to speak—what were we allowed to do? But we didn't even have the strength to speak, because after a day's labor we collapsed at night as though we'd been knocked down. By chance that night the guard relented. So this man lay there and he asked me a question: Morris, what do you think? Will we get out of here alive? And I said to him, Perhaps you will. I'm already dead. I went on talking to him for a while and he didn't answer. I thought he'd fallen asleep. What more do I have to tell you? He died in the middle of our conversation.''

"Of hunger?''

"I don't know. Perhaps scurvy. What didn't we die of? That anyone survived at all was a miracle from heaven. When the Germans saw the Allies were winning and they were finished, they started shooting everyone. They had only one desire: to kill, to kill. They made a game of it. They lined us up in a row and shot down every third person. Others had to dig their own graves. I don't want to distress you, Hertz, but I actually saw Jews digging their own graves. I raised my eyes to the heavens, but they were blue and the sun shone. All was quiet. No angels were weeping. The Master of the Universe was silent. Ai, ai, what do you know about it? What do you know? I didn't expect Jews to forget so quickly.''

"What should they do?''

"Well, I was fated to come out whole. How? Why? For what? You won't believe me, Hertz, but I'm ashamed to this day. When you look around at all this luxury, it becomes shameful to live. Until the moment I set sail for Palestine, I didn't believe I'd live. The Americans had already taken over and were looking after us and all the rest of it, but I still wasn't certain. Arriving in the Holy Land was like coming into Paradise. We had our dignity again. They carried us on their shoulders, and what could we do? We wept. They held banquets for us, they gave speeches in our honor. One day you were lower than a louse or a bedbug, and the next you were being driven around in a bus and other Jews came out to greet you and they looked at you with a love you'd forgotten existed. But it quickly became very difficult. After so much humiliation, honor is hard to endure. It's like a physical pain. Well, nothing lasts forever. The British harassed us. Even after all we'd been through, they still begrudged the Jew a place to lay his head. It's the same to this day. As soon as I recovered, I went to work building new highways, but my strength wasn't up to it. The burning sun was deadly, and the day was as long as our exile, as long and repetitive as the little tune a Yemenite used to sit and sing from dawn to dusk. Who could find the patience for that? For some, perhaps this was already the redemption—but not for me. I went off to a kibbutz then, but it was just as hard there. Most of the other workers were young people.

They laughed, sang, danced, but I drifted through it all like one of the living dead. I'll tell you something, but I know you won't believe me: I started thinking about killing myself. I still don't really know why. It just seemed that I wasn't part of this world any longer, that I was wandering about in a World of Chaos. I was continually drawn back to *them*, to the six million. Then Florence arrived. I don't know what she saw in me. What on earth do we have in common? But since everything in the world is crooked, why should matches between men and women be straight?"

"True."

"We agreed, and it happened, even though it seemed like a travesty to me. All I needed was to get married! Fanya and the children went to the other place—I don't even know when or where. I'd lost everyone, my whole family, yet now they were leading me to the wedding canopy all over again. But I learned to be passive in the camps. That's the only thing I learned there. Are you standing in the mud with the rain pouring down on you? Let it pour. Are they cursing you? Let them curse. Are they beating you? Let them beat. Are they dragging you to the ovens? Let them drag. The worst problem was *thinking*. I learned to block out my thoughts. That's a great skill. At the beginning it's difficult, because the mind is desperate to think, just as the stomach is desperate to digest. But in time I reached a stage where it became hard for me to think. I was like a cow. Even hunger is easier to endure when one doesn't think. Well. Let's talk about something more cheerful. What do you do here in America, Grein?"

"What can I do?"

"Something must have happened to you in all these years."

Grein did not reply. Both seemed to be listening to the silence.

2

"Nothing good is happening with me, Morris."

"What's wrong?"

"You see yourself."

"What've you got against your wife?"

"I've got nothing against her, but it's boring."

"Boring? There are greater sorrows than that."

"This *is* a great sorrow. What's prison but boredom? My wife's become a businesswoman. She spends the whole day in her shop. My children are grown up and leaving home, and in any case I can't talk to them. Here in America there's a gulf separating parents and children, especially among us Jews. Here to be old is a disgrace. Here even the men dye their hair so as not to appear gray."

"Who are they fooling?"

"Themselves. I haven't become observant. Far from it. But it's boring without God. Faith is the only force that keeps people from insanity. Why should it be more boring for us than it was for my father? He had nothing outside his family and the Hasidic prayerhouse. He had no theater, no films, no radios, no newspapers. His library—if you could call it a library—was made up of a few sacred books. But I never heard him complain that he was bored."

"Well, and it's not boring with Anna?"

"For the time being, no. But it won't last long. I know that already."

"So what'll you do then?"

"I don't know."

"How long have you been with her?"

"A week."

"Well well."

"I'm being frank with you, Morris. I never talk to anyone about myself, because what's the point? But I can confide in you. Perhaps because we used to speak freely in Vienna. I have a whole houseful of books, but I have nothing to read. I can't stand literature. I'm at the age when novels don't interest me, even if a second Tolstoy were to come along. Philosophy disgusts me. History always arrives at the same conclusion—that human beings are criminals. God knows, you've learned that for yourself. So there's nothing for me to read. I always believed that the exact sciences— physics, chemistry—were interesting. But they're also boring. Recently I've read everything I could get hold of about the atom, but it's true what they say. Boredom begins in the atom. What can be more terrifying than a piece of matter that never rests? Millions of years pass and the electrons go on revolving around the protons. The old way we conceived the atom, at least it rested. The new atom they've revealed to us throws itself about like a demented thing, twisting and turning without stopping. Perhaps it's the ultimate symbol of man today. Anyway, the most disturbing thing is that I can't believe any of it. Modern science becomes more and more like fiction all the time. Take quantum theory. I don't understand it, and I'm afraid there's nothing to understand. It's the same old formlessness and void, but without a God, without a spirit that moves over the face of the deep. What about you, Morris? Do you have any philosophy?''

"None whatever."

"What, then?"

"Nothing. I don't think."

"The best thing to do. But you need discipline for that. What about your wife? She torments you, doesn't she?"

"Does it matter? All people torment others like wild animals if they can. But it's bearable. She curses me, but then she makes up. Only one thing is really unendurable: when she drags me with her to those leftist meetings. But I've found a remedy."

"What?"

"I block up my ears."

"Literally?"

"Yes. With those little bits of rubber you use on airplanes. I sit and watch them opening and closing their mouths like fish. It's very comical, really."

"What do you do all day?"

"She goes to the office and I cook. Don't laugh. One has to do something, after all. I clean up, I wash the dishes, I take the basket and go shopping. They know me in all the shops by now. In the evenings I often go to the movies with her. She loves gangster films, and I shut my eyes and it doesn't bother me."

"It bothers me. I can't endure the coarseness. In this country, culture is the one thing the masses have appropriated. You need to be in a drugged haze not to go mad with frustration."

"It's not important, as long as they don't push you into the ovens."

"They may not burn you alive, but every time you open the morning newspaper, death laughs in your face. Nowadays you don't have to read ethical treatises to ponder death. You get reminded of it wherever you turn—by the newspapers, in the theater, at the movies, by the insurance agent. At one time I used to go with Leah to visit her friends from the old country and all they could talk about was graves. You won't believe it, but the only shred of Jewishness left here revolves around the cemetery."

"I know. Florence also has friends from the old country. I go to see them every Saturday night. The first time I went, a man gave a whole lecture on coffins, and they went on talking about them till midnight. What's the sense of it?"

"No sense at all."

"There you are!"

"What binds them together? Not a God, not a country, not even a language. Among ourselves we speak a little ungrammatical Yiddish, but our children can't even do that. Many of them are Communists. My own son won't hear a word against Stalin—for him, Stalin's murders are sacrosanct."

"What about your daughter?"

"She's completely depressive."

"Why's that? How old is she?"

"Nineteen."

"Why didn't you give them a Jewish education?"

"They didn't want it, and I didn't believe in it. Children reflect the values of their parents. I was a teacher in a Talmud Torah here, and I've seen firsthand what those values are. Children progress through the grades and learn nothing. The Torah doesn't make a dent, because the Torah isn't in tune with baseball and the filth they hear all night on the radio."

"In that case you ought to be a Zionist."

"What value would my Zionism be? I couldn't go and live there myself, and the children are even less inclined. In any case, how different is the land of Israel? They've also got radios and all the other trash. Young men from Palestine come here and speak Hebrew, but they have the faces of Gentiles. Hebrew Gentiles. Without God there are no Jews."

"Then why don't you go back to the synagogue?"

"You know why yourself. I believe that God is all-knowing, but it's difficult to believe in His goodness. Recently a neighbor of mine died and his family asked me to come to make up a minyan for prayers because they were observing the Seven Days of Mourning. Many American Jews observe those commandments: the Seven Days of Mourning, Kaddish, the annual remembrance of the deceased, everything that has to do with death. So what happened? The young men blundered about like bears, the young women fluttered about like birds, and the whole time they were whispering about baseball because the World Series was being played. Then when the prayers started, they all put on skullcaps. I began reciting the Eighteen Benedictions, but my tongue kept stumbling over the words. Only the other day I read a report about one of those death camps—Majdanek or Treblinka. How can one call a God 'merciful' who allows this? Because in the final analysis this is *His* work. The only answer we're given is that it's free will. But what if that's just a rationalization? And why must animals suffer? Shestov says frankly that God is evil. According to Spinoza, He's even worse than that—He's indifferent.''

''Perhaps He has no power?''

''Then who does have power?''

''I don't know. They also prayed *there*. Even in Majdanek. Not all, but some. Anna is a pleasant woman.''

''I've persuaded her that we'll be happy.''

''Perhaps you will be.''

''How's that possible? Before, I had another woman called Esther, and she let herself be deceived. There's every opportunity for cheating when the victim cooperates. Did you never have a woman through all those years?''

''A woman? No. When one's starving, one becomes a eunuch. In the early days in the ghetto, we all sinned, often in the ugliest way. But afterward our strength left us. There used to be a Jewish cabaret, and all the black marketeers and Kapos used to go there. One had to walk over corpses. On one occasion, a woman went there and was stepping over a dead man when he suddenly grabbed her leg and tore her silk stocking. Evidently he hadn't yet breathed his last. She soon sent him on his way with a mouthful of curses. But I also saw Jews, dying of hunger themselves, giving away their portions of bread to others.''

''Why did they do it?''

''There's good in people as well.''

3

Five weeks had passed. Although Grein warned her that she was doing a very foolish thing, Anna allowed herself to be persuaded differently. She was on the point of buying a house in Miami Beach. It was a fabulous bargain, she argued. Mrs. Gombiner swore up and down that Anna would make a great deal of money. Anna had already traded in her war bonds and sold her jewelry. The house was priced at seventy thousand dollars, but one had to put down only twenty thousand; a mortgage would take care of the rest. Even Grein came to believe it was a bargain. The land alone was worth the money. The main building could be converted into a hotel. But this demanded expenditure and above all work. Oddly, the honeymoon on which Anna had staked so much hope was spent on negotiating, bustling about, asking advice from all sorts of experts. The Jewish instinct for commerce had been aroused in Anna. Almost overnight she became a carbon copy of Boris Makaver. She smoked cigarettes, went back and forth to meetings, continually fiddled with numbers. She talked Grein into becoming a partner, and he was supposed to invest ten thousand dollars in the business. As his stocks were in a safe-deposit box in New York, he would have to go back to sell them. He had to return in any case: Leah had told him over the telephone that Jack was preparing to marry a Gentile girl from Oregon.

As Grein did not have his own car in Florida, Mrs. Gombiner drove him to the airport. The Gombiners sat in the front, Grein and Anna in the back. Anna held Grein's hand and didn't stop chattering the whole way. She'd fallen in love with Florida, she said. Here she would be happy. Let Papa go ahead and disinherit her. She'd show him that she could make money herself, and that she was perhaps even better at it than he. She would never breathe freely in New York, near her father, near Stanislaw Luria, near Leah and her children. Florida was a paradise. At night Anna spoke as if she was drunk or half insane, but by day she was sharp, calculating, demanding. Her main contention was that modern people had a great deal of material needs and there was no reason why they shouldn't give themselves everything they wanted. Wasn't America the richest country in the world? It had everything—raw materials, advanced technology, ample job opportunities. Those who didn't spend money were simply disrupting the national economy.

Anna had worked out a program of action for both of them. She would make a career for herself in real estate. What Mrs. Gombiner could do, she could do as well. She would either convert the house into a hotel or sell it at a substantial profit. Grein could go on being an agent for his mutual fund in Florida, but only temporarily. He had to make an academic career for himself. Why couldn't he become a professor? He had earned a degree in philosophy in Vienna. He knew several languages. He was knowledgeable about mathematics, physics, Judaica, who knew what else? Leah had demanded nothing of him, and when a woman demanded nothing from a man, he lost his drive. *She* would encourage him, Anna insisted—she would establish contacts for him. After all, she herself also had an education. Even in these few short weeks that had passed she had already made the acquaintance of several wives of professors. She even had access to a dean. Once she had put the new house in order, she would throw a party. As she drove the car, Mrs. Gombiner listened in on what Anna was saying. Strange as it was, these two women, who in the beginning had felt only repulsion and disgust for each other, had grown closer. Anna confided totally in the older woman, and Mrs. Gombiner had taken Anna under her wing.

"Hey, you bum, where d'you think you're going?" Florence shouted to the driver of a passing car. To Grein she said over her shoulder, "I should have been as lucky as you, marrying someone the like of your wife! She'll make a decent human being out of you!"

"What do you mean? He's a decent human being right now, thank God!" exclaimed Morris Gombiner.

"You shuddup! In America you have to make something of yourself. You have to be assertive. You could also have been a professor if you weren't such a shlemiel. But you're such a pipsqueak, nobody could ever take you seriously. Here a man must be a man, not a rabbit!"

"The philosopher Kant was no taller than I am."

"That was in Europe, not here."

For Grein, his whole experience in Miami—Mrs. Gombiner's dogmatism, Anna's daydreams, his own departure—seemed a surreal joke. Even the hurricane he had encountered here seemed to be part of a show that Nature regularly staged for tourists. Inside of a moment, bright day turned to black night. Coconuts crashed down. Palm trees lost their crowns. Stems broke. Shrubs and flowers flew through the storm like birds. The branches of trees were splayed like the slats of huge fans and could not be snapped shut again. Wind hammered on rooftops, rain viciously lashed the earth, and balconies groaned as they were ripped from buildings. Electrical wires were torn down and Anna was forced to light a candle. The glimmering little flame seemed to bear witness to what the liturgy proclaimed: that after civilization had spent itself and everything had ended, human beings would be forced to turn back to one small fire.

Now the sun shone again and the skies were mild and blue. The airplanes on the runway looked like cardboard cutouts. Grein signed an insurance form naming Anna his sole beneficiary, and his plane took off. The earth he had trodden for forty-six years now lay below him with its sea, ships, hotels, villas. Rivers snaked along like silver cords. Roads wound like ribbons. Trains seemed to be standing stock-still. Automobiles diminished into tiny dots. Repose hovered over the fields, as if it were the mandatory Sabbatical year. It struck Grein that perhaps, when people died, their souls rose up in exactly this way, leaving the material body below—assuming there was such a thing as the soul, that human identity didn't just dissolve like a fleck of foam.

This was the first time Grein had ever flown, but he was neither astonished nor afraid. What if he were to fall? Then let him fall. He closed his eyes and laid his head back in the corner of his seat. In all the chaos of the physical world, there were nevertheless laws in operation. So that this airplane could fly, gasoline combusted, propellers turned, air supported the wings. And Jack, in turn, behaved exactly as might be expected from a Jew without belief, without Torah: he was reconstructing his identity, mixing the seed of Reb Jacob the Scribe with the seed of idolaters. Well, it was all Grein's fault. He had brought up his children this way. He had set the example and now they followed it.

Grein opened his eyes and found the sun setting amid flaming clouds, tingeing an infinite horizon with a palette of colors and an assortment of shapes never seen below: cyanogen fires, aniline ridges, phosphorescent hands, faces, hair, sheets of parchment. Recently the newspapers were full of reports about flying saucers, and Grein was prepared at any moment to see a gleaming disk, an interplanetary ship gliding into view. The moon had risen early, hanging in the middle of the sky, pencil-thin, peering in through both this window and the one opposite. The earth grew ever darker, shadowy, webbed with night, slowly effaced as though with a cosmic eraser, as if humankind had long since become extinct and the world had returned to the first Sabbath of Creation. The wicked, the powerful, the tribulations, the passions, all had passed from being. Nothing remained but a single tiny airplane suspended between the planets in unmoving somnolence. Since the Angel of Death had now been made redundant—for there was no life left to take—a remnant of existence had consolidated itself up here: men, women, newspapers, a stewardess who distributed sandwiches and smiled like a puppet, and memories of some distant person called Anna who, millions of years before, had been left behind somewhere in Florida. What could possibly have happened to her? Grein reflected idly. Had she gone back to Stanislaw Luria? Had she found someone else in Miami? Had she received the insurance money that Grein had bequeathed her? Whatever might have happened, no trace of any of them now remained. Not even their dust.

Grein glanced out and recognized New York. The windows in the skyscrapers flashed like gemstones. Rows of lights glittered on the bridges, fiery pillars gleamed in the water. The moon had leaped back into view and the few visible stars had scattered as though clearing a path. A city composed of millions of fires stretched out below, its lights expanding, changing, flitting through a luminous haze. Searchlights raked the heights, irradiating other airplanes. New York told a tale of radiance written in a script of lights, its margins illuminated with rivers, lakes, ships. Somewhere amid all this blazing confusion also flickered the little flame that Grein himself had kindled and then abandoned.

4

Grein reached home and within minutes it seemed to him that he had never left. He encountered his entire family—Leah, Jack, Anita, and Jack's Gentile girlfriend into the bargain. Everything was exactly the same: the overheated apartment, the threadbare carpets, the smell of gas in the kitchen. Leah didn't believe in opening windows, and in any case, the windows had jammed. On the commode in the hallway, as always, lay the mail: a pile of letters, magazines, advertisements which would be thrown into the wastepaper basket unread.

In the short time that had passed, Leah had aged: she had gray hairs, deep creases in the corners of her eyes and around her mouth. Her face had acquired the worn and dusty quality of the antiques she sold. Staring at Grein with both hostility and astonishment, she remarked, "You've lost weight."

As always, Anita hid herself in her room. She had taken a job with a law firm and was preparing to move out. Jack, who was sitting with his girl in the living room, came up to his father with a smile that bordered on outright laughter. He was six feet tall, fair-skinned, blue-eyed, rosy-cheeked, with a shock of flaxen hair, a snub nose, and full lips on which his mother's milk still seemed to lie. His entire face and bearing were devoid of a single suggestion that he was descended from Talmud scholars and rabbis. He could just as easily have been a German or a Scandinavian. Even his hearty frankness was not Jewish. Everything about him appeared simple, uncomplicated, robust, in a way that Grein thought alien: his son seemed to be cast in one piece, a human machine that operated with clockwork precision, knowing each second exactly how much it consumed and precisely what it produced. Jack was entertaining a guest, yet he wore no jacket, only an undershirt which exposed a hairy chest and the muscular arms of an athlete. Jack inherited his build from his mother's side, the tenant farmers and dairymen. Despite all the Hebrew lessons Grein had pumped into him, Jack could barely read a few words in the prayer book. He denied that he was a Communist, but he spoke like one and subscribed to Party journals. He gave his father a huge paw.

"Hi, Dad!"

Then he added after a pause, "This is Patricia."

Patricia resembled the young man, a big, good-natured young woman, one of those female giants that came from the West endowed with the inherited strength of generations of Gentile pioneers. When she smiled, Grein was struck by her teeth, which were as sharp and pointed as an animal's. These teeth proved more clearly than any arguments Darwin's theory of evolution. Her water-gray eyes regarded Grein amiably, familiarly, cheerfully. It seemed as if she was asking, Why can't we be friends? Her nose was too short and made her upper lip appear longer than it was. A brash fringe of straw-colored hair hung over her forehead. This Gentile girl evidently knew where Grein had been and what was going on in this house. Jack couldn't keep secrets.

She asked, "Is it pleasant in Florida?"

"Yes, it's hot."

"I'll be there myself in two weeks. My father's driving me there. He'll be coming here from Oregon."

"That's a long trip."

"My father likes to drive."

Well, there it is, there it is, Grein thought. Once you say A, you must go all the way to Z. If you do it yourself, you must let your children do it as well. If one law in the *Shulhan Arukh* can be disregarded, then the whole code of Jewish Law is without value. He excused himself and returned to Leah in the kitchen.

"Is that going to be your daughter-in-law?" he asked.

"Yes—and yours as well." Leah poured water into a pot.

"When does he want to get married?"

"Soon. They're eager to set up on their own."

"Well, you'll be the mother-in-law."

Leah poured the water out of the pot again. "I hope you're not blaming me—"

"I'm not blaming anyone."

"Why did you come?"

He didn't answer, and Leah started filling the pot with water again. He went back into the hall, took up the stack of letters, and went into his study. This was both his home and not his home. He stared at the wallpaper and noticed creases and stains that he had already forgotten. The telephone was strangely silent. Grein felt he was exercising the greatest self-restraint not to make a phone call. The electric light seemed congealed, the walls inspissated. Only the steam in the radiator gurgled with its familiar haunting sough. Grein started reading through the letters. He frowned. It was not long before Leah came in.

"Hertz, I told you over the telephone."

"Don't worry, I'm staying in a hotel."

"Hertz, put away that letter," Leah commanded.

"What do you want?"

"I want to talk to you."

Having glanced up and down the corridor, as if she suspected someone was eavesdropping, Leah shut the door carefully.

"Hertz, you don't look well. Don't think I'm moralizing. I've given you up long ago. Excuse the comparison, but I think of you as a street dog that runs after every bitch he sees. At least one can keep a dog on a leash, but you roam at will. What do you have to say about that Gentile girl?"

"What should I say? I'm not one to talk."

"Yes, what can you say? You're no better—you're a thousand times worse. One day he told me about her and the next day he brought her home. Her father is a wealthy plumber. She wants to be an actress."

"Indeed? Well, there'll be one more woman on the stage."

"Don't you care?"

"What right have I to care?"

"True. You've got no right at all. When we first got married, we wanted to go to Palestine. Our children would at least have been Jews there."

"What would their Jewishness have consisted of? In any case, we're here, not there. Everything's lost now."

"Everything's always lost for you. You might try speaking to him."

"What should I tell him? That he'll lie on a bed of nails in Gehenna? He's no more a Jew than I am."

"Anita's also moving out. Soon I'll be living alone in this apartment."

"You can always take a smaller one."

"What'll I do all alone?"

"What do you want? To marry someone else?"

Leah grimaced as if she had a bitter taste in her mouth. "What? Pfui! Don't talk nonsense. Once is enough. Once was even too much. I just want to ask you plainly—why did you do this? You didn't have to leave your home."

"But you drove me out, after all."

"I drove you out because you were making me the object of scandal and ridicule. Everyone knows that you've gone, and who you've gone with. Even the neighbors are talking about it. Before they never even bothered to greet me. Now they ring the doorbell and come in to console me. *Her* husband has called three times already."

"What does Luria want?"

"I've no idea. He's crazy or something. He wanted to meet me. Perhaps he thinks that because you're sinning with his wife he ought to do the same with your wife. Men always have crazy thoughts. I lie awake in the middle of the night and keep on wondering what harm I've done you. I was a good wife to you. I took better care of you than of myself. You cheated on me during all those years. Why did you have to cast me aside in my old age?"

"You're not so old yet."

"I'm old, Hertz, I'm old. I sit in the shop all day and I can't concentrate on anything. You've gone and chopped off my head. I've got nothing to live for any longer!"

And Leah burst into tears, covering her face with her wrinkled hands, sobbing and shaking like a Jewish woman of the old days. Her shadow on the wall shook in unison with her. Her last words cut Grein to the quick. They were full of prophetic doom. He wanted to go over to her, but he didn't move. He remained sitting abstractedly, perceiving clearly how the sin he had planted had put down roots, spread and sprung up, burgeoned and bloomed with a flower of misery and distress.

5

Grein had expected to stay in New York only a day or two and then fly back to Miami to pay his share of the deposit on the house and its surrounding land. But he delayed. He had received orders through the mail for stock in the mutual fund, as well as invitations to visit old clients who lived outside Manhattan in upstate New York.

Grein regarded this prosperous business of his, like everything else that had befallen him during the years he had been connected with the firm, as a sort of perpetual and self-renewing miracle. He had gone into investment brokering after teaching in Talmud Torahs had driven him into a depression, and at a time when he had been so ignorant about financial affairs that he had no idea of the difference between stocks and bonds, capital shares and securities. The opportunity had arisen as if the powers who watch over each individual, and for whom no trivial detail is unimportant, had decided that the time had come for his rehabilitation. He had been sought out by a certain Mr. Levy, with whom Grein had once been a fellow guest at a Jewish farm that took in summer visitors. This Mr. Levy, who had been a millionaire before the crash of 1929 and who had gone on steadily to rebuild his fortune, had spent weeks searching for Grein in New York without being able to find his address. At that time Grein had been so poor that he could not afford a telephone. Mr. Levy had given up hope of ever finding him again when they met purely by chance on the ferry to Staten Island. Grein had no reason to go to Staten Island: he merely had a few hours free and, wanting some sea air, had made up his mind to sacrifice a nickel and take the trip there and back. Even more bizarre, at the very moment he had decided to board the ferry, they began shutting the entrance. He had no reason to hurry—within a few minutes a second ferry was leaving—but he had made a run for it and had been the last passenger allowed on board. One would have to be willfully blind not to see the hand of Providence in all this. Grein sat down on the first available bench, only to find himself right next to Mr. Levy, who was having his shoes polished by a shoeshine boy.

Levy gave him his hand and said, "I've been looking for you!"

When Levy started to explain that he wanted to recommend Grein as an agent in the brokerage firm in which he was a partner, Grein's immediate response was to insist that he was not suited for it, had absolutely no knowledge of things financial, lacked all power of persuasion and skill in establishing contacts, and that the whole idea was wild, almost absurd. But Levy stubbornly persisted, and from that moment on, a great many other miracles had happened to Grein. People called him on the telephone and gave him business worth thousands of dollars. Gradually he acquired a Christian clientele, one-hundred-percent Americans who lived in towns and on farms outside New York. Grein did no fast talking or exaggerating;

he behaved with moderation and integrity, advising potential buyers of all
the dangers associated with the stock market. He repeated the words of
David Hume: the fact that until now the sun has always risen is no proof
that it will rise again tomorrow. There are no hard and fast rules, no
guarantees. Grein had even assembled a string of facts about firms which
year after year had shown themselves to be as firm as rocks yet which had
suddenly gone bankrupt. Much greater than his desire to do business and
sell stock was his perpetual fear of leading people into error and harming
them. But this very overscrupulousness proved highly successful. He himself prospered as the stocks rose in value. People made money because of
him, and they began to regard him as trustworthy, asking advice and inviting him to family celebrations. Men and women with whom he had
absolutely no spiritual affinity demanded to know why he was so reserved
and did everything possible to draw him into their circle.

During the time Grein had been in Florida, he had neglected his business. However much stocks had risen, a number of his clients had
waited for him, unwilling to buy through anyone else. Now he drove his
car out of the garage and traveled upstate. After weeks of sunshine and
palm trees, it was pleasant once again to inhale the sharp winter air and
good to be alone with himself for a while. He drove his car and thought
his thoughts, trying to take spiritual stock of himself. He had made Leah
unhappy. He had cast Esther aside after an affair of eleven years. Boris
Makaver and Stanislaw Luria cursed his name. But was he any happier
now? He had grown accustomed to his business and had no desire to get
involved with real estate. The landscape of the South was beautiful, but
he had already begun to tire of its semitropical lushness. He had started
longing for bracing chills, overcast skies, bare trees, misty fields. He had
been warned that during the summer the heat in Miami was unendurable. Moreover, he was afraid of Anna's ambitions. He was neither willing nor able to become a professor. In reality he had never wanted an
academic career. He was interested not in the history of philosophy but
rather in those eternal questions to which the innumerable theories
which went under the general heading of philosophy had a direct contemporary application. The thought of standing at a lectern and teaching
students made him shudder.

As he drove, he hummed the little tune that the Hasidim in the Ko-
zienicer study house used to sing at the concluding meal of the Sabbath.
Liturgical melodies suddenly and inexplicably came into his head; he remembered words he thought he had long forgotten. How good it would

be, he told himself, if all those things in which Rabbi Isaac Luria had believed truly existed: angels, seraphim, spheres, worlds. For Jews like that, heaven had been filled with wisdom, grace, compassion, purity. For them, the Jewish soul played the central role: every commandment it observed filled all the worlds with divine joy; every sin it committed diminished those worlds. By contrast, what was the universe as Einstein or Eddington conceived it? A lump of clay packed with blind atoms rushing backward and forward, hurling themselves feverishly about. For all such blindness cared, a new Hitler could arise in every generation. The over-arching conclusion of the whole of modern science was that God had less intelligence than a flea.

In Croton-on-Hudson Grein had a client, a spinster of eighty who forty years earlier had been the mistress of a man who had bequeathed her a house. She had money of her own as well, and only in recent years, in her seventies, had she begun buying mutual-fund stocks. It was strange to hear this old woman vigorously discussing politics, economics, her own plans, drawing up accounts of how much her stocks would be worth in ten or twenty years' time, as if she had entirely forgotten that there was such a thing as death. Holding herself as straight as a ruler, she had the sawteeth of a fish and stared with animal coldness through watery eyes. President Roosevelt was long dead, but this old woman continued to curse and revile him, blaming him for war shortages, inflation, the rise of Communism. Each time he met her, Grein was reminded of Swedenborg's insistence that in the other world foolish souls spend their time in quarreling, fighting, drunkenness, and lust. Who knows? Perhaps they even speculated with stocks there as well. In an odd way, the worldliness of this old spinster was a demonstration of human immortality.

On a dairy farm beyond Poughkeepsie lived Mr. Koerck, a widowed Hollander who had spent twenty years in Sumatra and had emigrated to America with his young daughter during the war. He was now anxious to sell his farm because the place was not protected against nuclear attack and wanted to settle in some small town in the Midwest, where it would give the Russians no advantage to drop an atomic bomb. Meanwhile, until he found the right buyer, Mr. Koerck smoked his pipe, read countless reli-gious journals, and quarreled with his daughter, who went to bars with young men and spent the night with them in motel cabins. Mr. Koerck often asserted that he felt more at home with the Jewish faith than with the Christian, argued that he would be happy if his daughter married a

Jew—not one of those modern Jews who ate pork and disseminated Communist propaganda, but one of those who observed the old traditions. Mr. Koerck spoke less about the stocks he regularly bought according to a carefully calculated plan than about all manner of Jewish laws and customs. He bombarded Grein with questions. Was it true that the Talmud advised Jews to cheat Christians? Were the Hasidim a separate sect? Did Dr. Herzl regard himself as the Messiah? Did the Jews in America have any connection with the Ten Lost Tribes that were to be found in Middle Europe?

Although he could babble nonsense, Mr. Koerck was no fool. His mind, like Grein's, was crammed with disconnected facts and thoughts which, also like Grein's, existed independently of his actions. Grein, too, was everything all at once: a believer and an unbeliever; a voluptuary and an ascetic; bound to his wife and children, in love with Anna, full of longing for Esther; and possessed of an infinite variety of inchoate desires.

He drove past a farm or an isolated house near the road and wondered, What would it be like to spend my last years here? I would never go anywhere, never take any trips. I would study mathematics, the only discipline built entirely on adequate ideas—as Spinoza called them—and live on nothing but potatoes and milk. I'd take refuge here like Noah during the Flood. A few minutes later it occurred to him to stop somewhere and telephone Anna. In Lake George, where he made the call, fresh snow had just fallen, but in Miami it was 80 degrees Fahrenheit. Anna was full of reproaches: why was he dragging himself around to clients in New York State if he was planning to move to Florida? He was holding up all her plans. Because of his delay, the house could be sold out from under her. Moreover, she was bored to death. Mrs. Gombiner never left her in peace for a second, jabbering on so that she was already deaf in one ear. Anna was deeply suspicious. Perhaps he'd made peace with his wife? Perhaps he'd gone back to that Esther? Whatever else he might have done, he was not to make a fool of her. He had to swear by all that was holy to him that at the end of the week he would fly back to Miami and that everything would go forward as they had planned. The operator mercifully interrupted the conversation to indicate that the six minutes were up.

In Lake George, Grein did business with a Mrs. Feuergold, a fortune hunter who was both a widow and a divorcée. Strangely enough, she lived with the daughter of the man she had divorced, a young woman who was bringing up a mentally retarded little girl, her child by a married man, a rich lawyer from New York. Grein knew all the details. Mrs. Feuergold and her stepdaughter had both opened their hearts to him, together and separately. They were united by a shared mixture of love and hate toward Mr. Feuergold, who was in Palm Beach suffering from skin cancer.

How complicated everything was! How much individuality Nature had imparted to every human fate! The wider America with which Grein came into contact was just as complicated as he was himself. He would never understand it properly. America remained for him the one country in the world where people walked with their heads held high, yet he could see that behind all individual differences the eternal human tragedy remained constant. People loved each other and loathed each other, took risks and were afraid. Each of them kept looking for a stable, permanent support upon which to lean, but powers craftier than human beings continually snatched these away, creating a perpetual crisis.

On the way back to New York there was a snowstorm. Grein had neglected to take along the chains for his tires, so his car kept skidding. Its wipers could not clean the snowflakes from the windshield quickly enough and crystals formed on the glass with incredible speed. The side windows were rapidly overgrown with frost trees, small, crooked, spiky, entangled one with another—the image of some kind of pristine forest. The air was thick with whirling flakes of snow driven by gusts of wind. This was no longer New York State but Siberia. Grein knew it was dangerous to travel in such weather, but a power stronger than any logic urged him on. Multitudes of frozen needles falling from unknown heights lay across the length and breadth of his windshield in a sort of heavenly cuneiform. As though swept by gigantic brooms, the snow piled up in heaps. Passing trucks switched on their lights in the middle of the now-darkened day. Like the cries of a bereaved woman, the initially intense howling of the wind shifted slowly to a quiet, steady keening. Driving slowly on with hands stiff from the cold, Grein was possessed by the joy and obstinacy of a schoolboy. The gloomy day reminded him of a solar eclipse, and it seemed to him that he had already experienced all this in a dream or read about it in a tale of enchantment.

6

From the window of the hotel room which overlooked Broadway, one could see the theaters with their glaring electric billboards, the Times Building from which illuminated headlines screamed the news of the day, the hordes of automobiles. Grein had found a resting place right in the center of civilization. He lifted the receiver, asked to be connected to Miami, and less than five minutes later he was chatting with Anna. As he put down the receiver, he said to himself, "Well, it's time for sleep."

He turned back the blanket. The bed was wide and comfortable. He had only to undress and thrust himself under the covers as if into an envelope, but he wasn't sleepy. He wasn't hungry either. He pulled open the drawer of the night table and took out the Bible. Turning to the Book of Hosea, he read how God commanded the prophet to marry harlots, first one and then another. Well, there was no gainsaying God's commands. He could do nothing to avert the decree, that prophet with the red beard. Grein laughed. From what passage in the text could it be inferred that Hosea had a red beard? He lifted the receiver and asked to be connected with Esther. His heart started pounding. What am I doing? This is utter foolishness! She's probably asleep, what's more. And what about Anna? I'm not a human being!

He heard Esther's voice: "Hello?"

"Does Esther Hatelbach live there?" Grein asked.

There was a pregnant silence on the other end of the line. Esther began muttering and stammering: "Hertz, is that you?"

"Yes, me, the king who reigns from India even unto Ethiopia. Because of you, I put Vashti to death, and now you're running around with Haman the Wicked."

"Have you gone mad in that terrible heat? Or is it Purim already?"

"No, Esther, not yet."

"Where are you? I thought I'd never hear from you again." Esther's voice choked with tears.

"Yes, this is my voice. The voice is the voice of Hertz, but the hands are the hands of Esau."

"Why do you keep quoting the Bible? Where are you?"

"In a hotel in the borough of Manhattan, near Times Square."

"Alone?"

"Yes, alone."

"What's the matter? Has that whore left you already?"

"Anna's in Miami. I've come here for a few days."

"Fancy that." And Esther fell silent again.

"How are you?" Grein asked.

"What? I'm all right. I lie barely moving, but I'm still drawing breath. I'd already gone to bed and was looking through the *Telegram* when suddenly the telephone rang. I thought it was Liuba, even though she never calls so late."

"If you're sleepy, go back to bed."

"Sleepy? I don't know what sleepy is any longer. I can't sleep if I don't take pills, and I can't sleep if I do. Nothing helps. What possessed you to call me?"

"We were once acquainted, after all."

"Never mind what once was! Once I was young and beautiful as well! Now I'm old and abandoned."

"Don't denigrate yourself."

"What else am I? Hertz, you must've heard my cry."

"What cry?"

"I called you, Hertz. I called you. You know I've got telepathy. When I need someone, I call to them in my mind and they hear. I've still got a bit of the power I used to have. If I were to tell you what I did in order to get you to call me now, you'd say I was totally crazy."

"What did you do?"

"Recited psalms."

"Well, congratulations!"

"Don't laugh! Don't! I'm in a terrible crisis and I felt I had to speak with you. I called your home, but they always give the same answer: not here. I also wanted to write you at your office. I drafted about ten letters, but I threw them all away. I'm not a writer. No words flow from me through a pen. So I simply asked God—or whatever sits up there in heaven—to tell you to call me."

"Well, He told me. I heard a heavenly voice: Hertz, son of Jacob, call Esther, daughter of Menachem David. I hear, O Lord—"

"Laugh, scoffer, laugh. We're not alone, Hertz. We're surrounded by all kinds of powers—good and bad, small and great. Hertz, I must speak with you!"

"When?"

"Tonight."

7

Grein did the incredible—he got into his car at midnight and drove out to Esther. It's all because of boredom, he rationalized. People even start wars to chase away boredom. I only hope I don't have an accident!

He crossed the Brooklyn Bridge and drove along the waterfront. The docks were crammed with ships. Lights flared through the darkness, dragging trains of mist after them. Smoky vapors hung over chimneys. Cranes and lanterns all kept an unsheltered night vigil because of the crazy whims of humans. On each of these steamers, sailors busying themselves with their tasks cursed in all the languages of the world, homesick for beds in every corner of the earth. Everything stank of oil, dirt, dead fish.

Grein stopped at a red light and glanced to his left. New buildings were going up here, and a huge mechanized hoist pointed a long finger to the glowing heavens. Unfinished apartment blocks stared sightlessly down through their empty windows. The powers of Creation did not themselves yet know how all this would resolve itself; they too had lost themselves at the crossroads of eternity.

Every time Grein took the right road, he was astonished at himself. In the half-darkness he could not accurately identify either the main roads or the side streets. As if blind, he drove into Brighton Beach and out again until he found himself on Esther's block. He got out of the car and breathed in the salty sea air. The waves continued to pound against the half-rotted oak piers with the unflagging vigor of an enemy that never lets up. Knots of darkness moved over the sea, the lighthouses flashing and winking through them, playing hide-and-seek. The Great Bear still stood in the heavens in the same spot where they had abandoned him. A light burned behind the white curtain over Esther's window. In his pocket Grein still had the key to the outer door. Unlocking it, he went up the dark stairs, breathing in a smell which was simultaneously burned into his memory and already half-forgotten. Esther stood in the open doorway, waiting for him like a bride for her groom. She stretched out her arms as if to embrace him, but then immediately withdrew them.

In this apartment he was now both an intimate and a stranger, filled with that sense of the unfamiliarity of familiar things felt by a close relation who has sundered himself from his family. He took off his coat and Esther carefully hung it up in the closet. She looked at him intently, sizing him up with a twinkle in her eye, the suppressed laughter of close friends who are playing the role of fresh acquaintances. Grein noticed a change in Esther. In the intervening weeks she had somehow grown younger. Had she lost weight? Had she changed her hairstyle? She had regained all her former skittish charm, smiling a secretive smile that seemed to say: Somehow one manages without you. As the saying goes, you're not the only fish in the sea. It occurred to Grein that the apartment itself had also been transformed in some way. Had she changed the furniture? Had she bought new decorations? She herself was definitely wearing a new dress. Grein sat down in an armchair and she sat opposite him, crossing her legs and pulling the hem of her skirt a little farther over her knee with ageless female coquettishness.

Then she said, "For someone who's just come from Florida, you're not nearly tanned enough."

"You know I avoid the sun."

"Yes, I know." And she smiled enigmatically, suggesting that her words were loaded with ambiguity.

"Well, what news does a Jewish traitor bring?" she asked.

"You know how things are with a Jewish traitor."

"Yes."

And again she smiled with the expression of one who has developed an immunity to all the venom of life and no longer has compassion even for herself. A flush colored her cheeks with the thrill of hearing the bitter truth about herself and preparing an equally bitter pill for him. They chatted in desultory, broken snatches. She asked him casually about Miami. Was it genuinely hot? Did people really bathe in the winter? What would he like now—tea, coffee, perhaps a little drink? Since he was now a guest it was her duty to offer him some refreshment. She rose and started bustling about, going into the kitchen and staying for a long time. She returned carrying a tray with a bottle of liqueur, a cinnamon loaf, and some cookies, which she lowered carefully onto a little table in front of him as she said, "Well, this is for you."

"I won't drink if you don't."

"I'll also have a drink."

As she filled a glass for him, the bottle trembled in her hand, and she spilled some liqueur on the embroidered cloth.

"*L'chaim!* What shall I wish you? Certainly no evil!" And she clinked her glass against his.

As soon as she had drained it, her expression altered, becoming severe, older, and deadly serious, as if she had only now grasped the full significance of the situation. Blue shadows darkened the hollows under her eyes.

"I must talk with you!" she said.

"What's happened? Has someone proposed to you?"

Esther tensed. "Yes."

"Who is it?"

Esther laughed. "It's not just one, but two!"

"A complete pair?"

Grein wanted to laugh but couldn't. He even felt himself turning red, less from shame than from indignity. Esther emanated the abiding falseness of womankind, coupled to the naked and shameless self-interest that hides itself behind all talk, vows, love affairs.

Why did she ask me to come if she has two suitors chasing her? he wondered. Why all this melodramatic talk about reciting psalms and summoning me telepathically? His ears buzzed; he was overcome by the helplessness of one lured into a trap. The Esther who sat opposite him was no longer a loved one but an enemy who had enticed him out to gloat over him and hold him up to ridicule. Her glance was full of cruelty and pain.

"What do you want? To ask my advice?"

"Yes, your advice."

Nausea overwhelmed him and he wanted to vomit.

"I'm too tired now to give advice."

Esther eyed him askance. "I thought we'd never meet again, but it was you who telephoned me, not me you. What did you imagine? That I would sit and pine away while you were running around with Boris Makaver's daughter? Yes, they still want me, my dear, they still want me. For you, perhaps, I may be an old woman, but for others I'm a young wife. Everything's relative, after all, isn't it? For Methuselah a woman of a hundred was a young girl."

"How old are they? Eighty? Ninety?"

"One is in his late fifties and the other in his early sixties. Don't look so contemptuous. You're no longer a Romeo yourself. Since I can't put any stock in love, I must be practical. I've decided to get married even if it costs me my life. I have to show you that I'm not such a fool as you thought."

"I never thought that."

"Oh yes, you did. You believe I'm fit for nothing except to be an appendage, a fifth wheel on the cart. But two men want me. One is a learned man and the other is very rich. Exactly as in the Hasidic story.''

"I'll tell you straightaway: take the rich one.''

"I shall. The learned one is a Dr. Alswanger—perhaps you've heard of him? He's just arrived from Palestine. He's published twenty books. The papers wrote about him.''

"I didn't notice.''

"He's a widower. An interesting person. A bit of a bore, but crammed with knowledge. Why haven't you heard of him? He socializes with Boris Makaver.''

"I've no idea.''

"Why are you staring at me like that? I'm sinning against you, eh? My conscience is clear. What's good for the gander is equally good for the goose.''

8

"They have one thing in common,'' Esther went on. "Both are short. I like tall men. When I was a child, I used to hold up the braided candle for my father when he was performing the Havdalah ceremony at the close of the Sabbath, and my mother always used to say, 'Hold it high, and you'll get a tall bridegroom.' But it didn't help. Piniele was tiny. Now—my luck—the new bridegrooms are both runts. You're tall, but you didn't want to be my bridegroom. So there you have it.''

"Better than nothing.''

"True. How much longer should I remain alone? That whole business with you wasn't a life. However good it might have been, you always went home to Leah. Well, are you at least happy?''

"Who knows?''

"Who should know, if not you? Why've you left her in Florida and come running back to New York?''

"Business.''

"You're going back?''

"She wants to settle there.''

"I see. What'll you do there—pick oranges?''

"I'll do something.''

"Well, you've always been your own master. As we say of God on

Yom Kippur, 'Who can tell Thee what to do and what to perform?' You would never take me out of New York. All those years you kept promising me a trip, but as soon as push came to shove, you always had an excuse. When it comes to Boris Makaver's daughter, you run there and you fly here and you think as little about your wife as about the neighbor's tomcat. Believe me, Hertz, I ought to be an enemy to you—a blood enemy. But hate isn't in my nature. I don't blame anyone but myself. If I'm a cow, it's because I let you milk me. How could it be otherwise? Cows must be milked—it's written in the Torah. Well, what else? When are you divorcing your wife and marrying her?''

"Leah doesn't want a divorce. Anna's husband also refuses to give her a divorce.''

"Is she really such a treasure? Well, you'll just have to manage without a rabbi's blessing. It's really most convenient for you. As far as I'm concerned, Hertz, I've had enough of free love. I also want to be a wife and prepare a meal for my husband. Enough of fluttering about like a butterfly, especially when that butterfly is over forty years old.''

"Which one will you take? The rich man?''

"It looks like it. I'm more comfortable with Dr. Alswanger. After all, he's a learned man. But one can't eat learning. He's a widower with married children in Palestine. By profession he's a psychoanalyst, but he's religious as well. At one time he was a Hasid of some sort. Who knows? He goes about peddling some outlandish ideas—he wants to build a sanatorium for the healthy, and other odd schemes like that. He lent me one of his books and I'd like you to read it. He's shared all his thoughts with me, but to tell you the truth, I can't make head or tail of them. He wants to combine Freud and the Baal Shem Tov and Karl Marx and make one coherent system out of all of them. His aim is to set up some kind of institution to implement that system in Tel Aviv, but if it doesn't work out there, he wants to try here. You should've heard the way he talked to me—as though I were his equal. He quoted from so many books that my head started spinning. He believes that all people are sick and that everyone's life has to be planned for them.''

"But that's Bolshevism.''

"He's a deeply religious man. He had insights about me that made me shudder. He wears spectacles, but he always looks over the tops of them as if he's looking straight into your soul. He speaks eight languages.''

"A pauper, though?''

"What else? That's the trouble. People like that know everything except how to earn a living. It's not for me, Hertz, it's not for me. I've struggled long enough. The other one, though, is a bit too vulgar. Not exactly a boor, but a crude American businessman. Typical. Alswanger, the doctor, is stout, but this one is, pardon the expression, a fat pig with a huge belly. But in his own way he's also an interesting man. He's—what's the saying?—an original. Oh my God—I ought to have been a grandmother by now, and instead I'm still trying to choose a husband. But what can I do? You make your bed and you have to lie in it.''

"This other one—what's his business? Who is he? What is he?''

"Do you want to know his pedigree? He's a Russian Jew who's been in America for forty-five or fifty years. He's our kind of Jew but Americanized. Speaks mostly English, but if the mood takes him, he can rattle on for hours in Yiddish. By trade he's a furrier, but he hasn't worked for more than thirty-five years. If you want to spend five thousand dollars on a mink coat for Boris Makaver's daughter, you can get it from him. But little by little he's pulling out of the business. He's in your line as well— Wall Street. He even owns stocks in your mutual fund. In addition he owns a house in the country and he drives around in a Cadillac.''

"Well, good.''

"Yes, good. Why've you gone so pale? Is there supposed to be one rule for you and another for me? He's not like you—but then, where's it written that all men should be like you? He has other merits. For him a woman is a human being, not an animal you keep in a cage. He's a modern man, not an old-fashioned bigot like you.''

"What is he? Widowed? Divorced?''

"He's certainly not an old bachelor. He's a grandfather with grandchildren. Does it matter? You and I might've also looked forward to grandchildren by now, if everything had worked out the way I wanted. But he's a lively person—perhaps a bit too lively. He takes walks, he travels, he sightsees. He spends the winter in Florida and the summer in Switzerland or somewhere else in Europe. He made money and now he spends it. His children aren't waiting for what he'll leave them. They're rich themselves.''

"Is he divorced?''

"Yes.''

"So what's stopping you?''

"Nothing, dearest, nothing. If it were up to him, we'd've been married already, but I'm hesitating. Why should I deceive you? I'm not in love with him. But what use is love to me now? He's an understanding man, plain, even a bit coarse, but I've had enough of refinement. A common man can never be as coarse as the refined men I've known. He literally throws money around. Where he gets so much money to waste, I don't know. I'm continually fighting with him about it, but he never stops writing checks. I don't like a man that keeps grabbing his checkbook. But that's how they all are: they make money and spend it on women. If I were to tell you what kind of character he is, you'd laugh.''

''So tell me what kind.''

''Oh, he should be in a novel. He's short, stocky, gray as a dove but with a red face. He's a healthy little Jew. One of my windows got stuck and no one could open it, but he gave it one shove and it jumped. I've never seen anyone eat so much. Whenever he has supper with me, he cleans out the refrigerator. He can eat more in one sitting than you eat in a whole week. Here in America people don't eat so much anymore. I tell him it's not good for him—we still use the formal style of address—and I warn him about calories and dieting, but all he says is 'Rubbish! If the doctors believe in fasting, let them fast themselves. My rule is that everybody's different.' And he goes on stuffing himself to such an extent that I stare and stare and I can't believe my own eyes. A short man, yet he weighs two hundred and twenty or thirty pounds! As if all this weren't enough, he's got a factotum who's another eccentric.''

''What do you mean, a factotum?''

''I don't know how to explain it to you. He employs a sort of all-purpose go-between who waits on him hand and foot as well as keeping an eye on the business. He's everything rolled into one: a friend, an errand boy, a chauffeur. They don't stand on ceremony. The factotum keeps saying to him, 'Moishele, don't be a pig!' and he snatches away his plate of food while he's still eating. They've known each other since childhood. The drudge is a bachelor who never thought of getting married. I think he's an androgyne, because his face is a bit too smooth and he's still got a full head of hair. Here in America he's been a businessman as well as all kinds of other things. He plays the fiddle and knows all the operas inside out. They live together.''

''In that case, you'll get two husbands for the price of one.''

''The other one's definitely an androgyne. He's told me bluntly that he's never had a woman and has no interest whatever in women. He's no spring chicken either—he's in his late sixties, even though he looks young. I've spoken frankly to Morris—that's his name, Morris Plotkin—and I've told him I don't want that servant of his near me. He'll have to take an apartment. On the other hand, if it's good for the business, he should certainly keep him. Plotkin couldn't get a person that loyal and devoted for five hundred dollars a week, and that slave asks for nothing more than room and board. I'm telling you, he's an absolute slave, and if I hadn't seen it with my own eyes I wouldn't have believed it possible. Each of us clings to someone else, but that one—his name's Sam—has stuck to Plotkin like a tapeworm. He's simply a parasite. But what's it to me? He waits on me, too. If I have to go somewhere, he comes to fetch me in the car and drops me off as if he were my chauffeur. My neighbors think that I've become a millionaire. I'm telling you, it's absolutely crazy.''

''Well, I obviously did you a favor when I left.''

''What? Well, you certainly didn't do me any harm. Our relationship had reached a dead end. It's the same in love as in everything else: if you don't go forward, you go backward. What's with you? I hope you'll be as open with me as I've been with you.''

''What do you want to know?''

''Everything.''

''Ask, and I'll answer.''

Esther struck a match and lit a cigarette. ''Do you love her at least?''

''Anna? Yes.''

''Well, that's how it should be. I never did you any harm, but you wanted me to lie around here all alone and die of longing. I know you, Hertz, I know you better than any other woman. During the eleven years I had you, I studied you little by little. I found out everything about you. You don't only want a woman's body—you want her soul as well, her whole existence, her lifeblood. You want to squeeze her empty like a lemon, and even then you don't want to throw her away. You keep a bucket next to you in which you pile up all your squeezed lemons, and from time to time you give one of them another squeeze in case there's a drop of juice still left in her. I'll be perfectly frank with you. Don't think I don't still long for you. I do, so much that I nearly go mad. But I've promised myself that I won't be a slave, and I won't. Another thing: I've also got power, and I know it. You long for me as well, and you'll go on longing for the rest of your life.''

''You talk like a Gypsy fortune-teller.''

''It's the truth, my enemy. It's the pure, merciless truth.''

And a smile appeared in Esther's eyes that Grein had never known until now: crooked, unyielding, avid, full of a grandmotherly sense of the vanity of all worldly things. Her face looked young, but in the corners of her

eyes and mouth lingered an expression one could not define: an old-
womanish wisdom, a shrewd resignation, the sorrow of those who, having
spent their whole lives struggling, finally decide that they must surrender.
She glanced searchingly at Grein, as if she really no longer knew him and
were trying to discover how his mind worked. She puffed at a cigarette
and smoke rings encircled her brow. Suddenly she seemed to shake herself.

"What's the time? It often seems to me that the end has really come."

9

Telephone calls went back and forth between Miami and Grein's New
York hotel. Having had second thoughts about the house he was
supposed to buy in partnership with Anna, Grein now argued that he had
no desire to bury himself in Miami; he didn't want to run a hotel; he
couldn't abandon his business in New York. Anna wept into the telephone.
She had her heart set on staying in Florida. Grein had ruined all her plans.
Mrs. Gombiner also intervened over the telephone and spoke to Grein
sharply and coarsely. But he remained stubborn. He wanted Anna to return
to New York and promised to arrange an apartment for her. Anna, growing
deeply suspicious, sent him long letters by airmail and special delivery,
accusing him of wanting to return to Leah or even to Esther. Grein,
however, denied everything. As a result of her extreme distress, Anna's
periods stopped. Or perhaps she was pregnant.

After lengthy conversations and correspondence, Anna agreed to return
to New York. She lost the five hundred dollars she had given as an advance
to secure the house, as well as other money she had spent for experts to
certify that the house was free of termites and for professional advice about
alterations should they decide to convert it into a hotel. Besides, Anna had
quarreled with Mrs. Gombiner, and in her last letter she admitted that
Grein was right. Mrs. Gombiner had abused her like a fishwife because
someone had suggested that the house was infested with termites and this
was the real reason the sellers wanted to get rid of it. Moreover, Miami
had become as stiflingly hot as in midsummer.

Anna flew out of Miami at noon and should have arrived at the airport
in New York a few minutes after six. Grein went to meet her, but the
plane was delayed. Outside, it was pouring rain. A hurricane that had

swept up from somewhere in Central America and had been expected to
die down in the Atlantic had actually brushed the East Coast with its tail.
There was lightning and thunder in midwinter. Airplanes that should have
arrived in New York landed in distant cities. Passengers who had reservations stood in huddles in the departure lounge, listening attentively to
the weather reports, chatting with the abstraction of those who need to
be somewhere else. Some of them were a little tipsy.

Grein sat on a bench trying to read the afternoon newspaper in the
glaring electric light, but his head was full of turmoil. Leah was ill with
the flu, Jack was preparing to marry the Gentile girl from Oregon, and he
had entered into a bizarre relationship with Esther, a sort of appendix or
epilogue to their former love affair. For her this meant that as long as she
had not yet legally married her Mr. Plotkin, she could do as she pleased,
and Plotkin had apparently gone along with this arrangement. He was so
modern and tolerant that he even wanted to meet Grein. Esther wavered.
She was first cynical, then tragic. She compared what was happening now
between her and Grein to the experience of souls that remained suspended
between heaven and earth, between life and death, in the World of Chaos
or in the World of Illusion.

God in heaven! Grein thought. He had betrayed everyone and everything. He had enmeshed himself in a net of falsehoods whose intricacies
had stunned even him. Esther had started drinking heavily; every time he
went to see her, she smelled of whiskey. She also smoked too much. At
one moment she chattered about taking a honeymoon trip to Europe with
Plotkin, and the next she complained that her end was near. She called
Grein a murderer and a robber, accusing him of having ruined her spiritually and physically, and then she showered him with endearments. As
soon as he entered his hotel room, the telephone rang. Esther had always
been talkative, but now she never paused for breath. She bombarded him
with questions, demanding to know every detail about Anna, asking his
advice. Her moods changed from moment to moment. Perhaps Dr. Alswanger was really a better choice than Morris Plotkin? Perhaps she would
never be able to endure Plotkin's coarse ways? Perhaps she should get rid
of both suitors and withdraw completely from all contact with the world?

Esther never stopped toying with the idea of suicide. What was there
to be afraid of? With a rope or the gas fully turned on, one could put an
end to all complications. Even her hangovers were full of passion. She
desired only to be with Grein, to share with him the last earthly pleasures

before, as she put it, she "fell into the abyss." She salted her talk with a great deal of Hebrew—verses from Scripture or Hasidic sayings which she remembered from the old country. In a perverted way, she even became religious. Was she a sinner? In what did her sin consist? She was not a married woman. Why should she be more virtuous than the Bible's Queen Esther? When all was said and done, Ahasuerus was a Gentile. According to the Gemara, Esther had actually been Mordecai's wife. And what about Jael, the wife of Heber the Kenite? And Abishag the Shunammite? Esther was an educated woman, and she knew what the Gemara taught.

A dark suspicion possessed Grein that Esther was losing her mind. She laughed and cried, bought him gifts he could never use, said things that made no sense. He advised her to see a doctor, but she responded immediately, "You mean a psychiatrist? Too late, dearest, too late. Either I don't need it or it won't help. I'm too far gone. People like me have no possibility of recovery!"

And Esther burst into a peal of laughter which was transmuted into a sob.

In the midst of all this confusion, Grein leased a furnished apartment for himself and Anna from the Brodskys, an elderly couple who had gone to spend a year in Europe. He had a surprise for Anna.

Now he heard the flight from Miami being announced and went out to meet Anna. The rain had stopped, but the airfield was wet and reflected everything like a black mirror. The air was chilly and sharp. Anna, wearing a black suit and a white blouse that emphasized her tan, looked tired, elegant, frightened, and relieved that she had survived the dangerous trip. As they kissed, Grein imagined that the scent of tropical flowers and plants still lingered around her.

Long and brightly lit, their wings outstretched, other airplanes stood on the tarmac, ready to rise into the misty night and fly, like giant birds, over oceans and continents. The illuminated windows emanated an aura of luxury, wantonness, and the determination of human beings to take their fates into their own hands and disregard the good or evil spirits that lurked somewhere above the clouds or in the depths of the earth.

In the car, Anna talked business. What was the sense of starting things and not finishing them? Why had he suddenly taken a dislike to Florida? Why didn't he want to say where he was taking her? What about his plans? The few weeks she'd spent alone in Miami had been a nightmare for her. Mrs. Gombiner was thick-skinned and brutal. Morris was terrified to death of her. He had secretly sent Grein a gift of a necktie. Anna clung to Grein and kissed him, sighing as though suffering from a pain she could not speak of. She lit a cigarette and the flame of the match illuminated her face for a moment before she said, "Ah, you'll never know what I lived through. I began to have doubts about the whole thing. I thought you no longer wanted me."

"I longed for you the whole time," Grein responded, and deep within him he knew this wasn't a lie. Whatever he had done with Esther had no connection with Anna or with his feelings for her. Such behavior probably did not conform to any theory, but where was it written that everything should accord? Did all the other parts of Nature agree with human theories?

The car traveled downtown along Fifth Avenue and stopped at a building on the corner of Washington Square North. Anna was surprised, but she kept silent. The man was mad—he'd squandered his last few dollars, she thought. Grein led her up to the ninth floor, opened the door, and switched on the lights to reveal a small dwelling with two rooms and a kitchen. Anna almost screamed with delight. "This isn't an apartment," she said. "It's a dream!" Everything—the furniture, the carpets, the wallpaper, the bedspreads—was of the best quality and chosen with taste. The Brodskys had sailed on the *Queen Elizabeth* only the day before. Mrs. Brodsky had left the couple a bouquet of roses and a bottle of champagne, together with a note for Anna with instructions about the housekeeping arrangements and her best wishes. The refrigerator was stocked with milk, butter, cheese, sardines, caviar; the grocery cupboard, with tea, coffee, cocoa, all sorts of cereals and preserves. The medicine chest in the bathroom had been filled with soaps and toiletries. It all appeared to be a generous gift, but in fact it was costing Grein $250 a month.

It was strange to go over to the window and look out on Fifth Avenue, the street that symbolized human civilization. To the right was Washington Square Park, to the left a long courtyard. The asphalt was wet and, like a river, reflected windows, streetlamps, the headlights of passing cars whose rubber tires soughed and hummed. An overcast sky lay above the rooftops. Anna raised a sash window and, resting both hands on the sill, leaned out and looked. If worse comes to worst, I can always throw myself out of here, the thought crossed her mind. It was never too late! She immediately pulled back and shut the window.

She started examining the furnishings, opening the clothes closets, the drawers in the dressers, and the writing desk. Everything was empty and ready for use. She went into the kitchen and made coffee. Strange, she had already accustomed herself to the thought that she would start her new life in Florida, but the powers that controlled human destiny had evidently decided otherwise. It occurred to her that she was only a few dozen blocks away from Stanislaw Luria.

Anna was tired, but Grein was itching to go out. He wanted to buy the morning newspaper, for which he would have to walk uptown. What should he do now? He hadn't told Esther he was moving out of the hotel, hadn't mentioned a thing to her about the apartment on Fifth Avenue. He knew that Esther had called the hotel and now probably thought that he had abandoned her without a word. But what could he do? He couldn't tell her that Anna was back here in New York and that he had set up house with her. Now was the time to put an end to this tragicomedy once and for all!

It had started raining again, a sharp slanting drizzle that pricked the face like needles. The street was deserted. Grein strode rapidly on, the wind seeming to push him along. Well, let her marry Morris Plotkin and let there be an end! The burden was growing heavier and heavier. He stopped suddenly in the middle of the sidewalk, his head bowed as though he were bearing a yoke. He took a deep breath of the night air. Should he call Leah? Esther? He was just as afraid of Leah's meek submissiveness as of Esther's maudlin hangovers. Esther's forthrightness was terrifying. She said the most shocking things, loudly proclaiming the most private details. Simultaneously attracted, revolted, and ashamed, he stepped like a drunkard into a bar on Thirty-fourth Street and called Esther from the telephone booth.

She immediately recognized his voice and called out, "Still alive? I was just about to hire someone to say Kaddish for you. Where did you get to? Why did you suddenly up and leave the hotel?"

"I'll tell you everything."

"When? For me everything's over and done with. A corpse is talking to you—a corpse talking from the grave."

"Esther, stop these theatrics!"

"It's the truth, my murderer. I'm dead and buried. I'm a corpse with a telephone!" Esther suddenly started to laugh hysterically and stopped just as abruptly. "Wherever you are, come to me immediately."

10

"I can't come to you now," Grein replied.

"Why not, if I may ask?" Esther demanded after a pause.

"I can't. It's late. Anna's in town."

"What? Indeed. Now I understand. She was supposed to stay in Florida."

"She came back."

"Congratulations! I hope I hear better news sometime! Listen to me: I asked you to come because I wanted to break it off with you. This is our last night and your last chance. Tomorrow everything's over. But if Boris Makaver's daughter is so precious to you, stay with that trollop. Goodbye forever! We'll never see each other again in this world! Perhaps in Gehenna they'll fry us both in the same pan."

"Wait a minute."

"What should I wait for? I've waited long enough. The eleven years I've known you have been one long wait. Perhaps that's why I'm sick. But everything has a limit, my dearest, even love. If you don't even have the courage to come and part with me, I spit on you. I'll tear you out of my heart by the roots. I won't even remember your foul name. A second after everything's ended, you'll be the strangest of strangers to me. All my love will harden into one coil of enmity and poison."

"Truly, Esther, you talk nonsense."

"It's not nonsense! What was between us was a sickness, and now the crisis has come. It's one step from the highest peak to the bottommost depths. Tomorrow I'll call Morris Plotkin and set a wedding date with him. I don't love him, but to spite you I'll learn to love him. I'll give him the best I've got. I'll do for him what no woman ever did for any man before. As for you, don't think I'll let you go. I'll keep you dangling on a string. I'll never let you go until our last day on this earth. You'll long for me so much that you'll yearn for death."

"You cow, I'm longing already."

"You long for me and you run to her. What kind of man are you? Has she cast a spell over you, or what?"

"There's no spell."

"Why do you stay with her?"

"Esther, I can't talk any longer. I have to put in another nickel and I haven't got one on me."

"Where are you? Give me the number and I'll call you back."

Grein gave her the number.

He stood in the telephone booth staring out into the bar. Two men and a woman sat on the high stools. One of these drunks clutched a glass, swaying and dozing. In a sequence of dreamlike movements, the other man tried to lean toward the woman, balancing precariously on his stool, looking as if he was about to fall at any moment. His long body stretched like rubber as he limply extended a hand, but he couldn't reach her. The woman herself was short, stout, with a shock of short curly hair. Her broad face, with its snub nose and thick lips, expressed wantonness and good nature as well as anger, the irrationality of drunkenness that could, without a moment's warning, change from caressing to cursing, from kissing to punching. The skin of her face had taken on a greenish tinge and was somewhat pockmarked; each individual scar exuded drunken frivolity.

What shall I do? What shall I say to her when she calls back? Grein murmured to himself. I must see her again. At least once more! But why doesn't the phone ring? She probably didn't hear the number correctly. This is passion. Genuine passion.

The telephone rang and Grein hastily snatched up the receiver. He seemed to lose his breath.

"Esther?"

"Yes, it's me. Listen, in between I've thought things over. I don't want to give you any ultimatums. If you can't come, you can't. Just know that between us there was a great love"—Esther altered her tone—"but you did everything possible to kill it. Well, thank God it's now in its death agonies. Be well, Hertz, and be sorry. I want you to swear to one thing: don't ever call me again. After you've buried the dead and filled in the grave, you must leave them in peace. Tomorrow I'll be another Esther. You can say Kaddish for the Esther of today."

How is it possible that I find all this prattle so attractive? Grein wondered, as he said, "Wait, Esther, I'll come."

"When? Dawn's already breaking in Pynchon."

"I'll take a taxi, but I must make a phone call first."

"To whom? Hurry up. Tonight's like Hoshanah Rabbah for me—it's an all-night vigil. The heavens will open and I'll make a wish. I'll pray that God obliterates you from my blood."

"Enough, Esther. Wait for me."

"Come quickly. I can't live without you."

Grein opened the door of the telephone booth and wiped the sweat from his brow. He had to get change for a dollar bill, but the barman, propped up half-asleep, his bald pate reflecting the late-night lights, looked in no mood to give it.

Well, I'll have a drink.

Grein went up to the counter and asked for a glass of cognac. The drunks turned fragments of faces toward him. It seemed as if they were saying dumbly, You're fooling nobody. Alcohol isn't your passion. The barman moved lazily, his face expressing what he was thinking. The profit on this is hardly worth the trouble. Grein knocked back his drink, took a sip of seltzer water, got his change, and immediately returned to the telephone booth. He called Anna, who answered immediately.

"Hello?"

"Darling, it's me."

"Why are you calling?"

"Anna, Leah's sick."

"Where are you?"

"With her, at home. It's only flu, but I'm afraid complications have developed. It could become pneumonia. I must get a doctor."

Anna was silent for a while. "Where are your children?"

"Not here."

"Who let you in?"

"Leah got out of bed herself."

"Are you sure you're telling the truth?" Anna demanded after some hesitation.

"You know my number. If you don't believe me, hang up and call me back."

Grein was himself astounded at what he'd just said. What would happen if Anna did exactly that? In one minute she would have exposed his lie. But he had to take the risk. Filled with the excitement of a gambler, he calculated that he was chancing everything now. Anna seemed to be thinking over the implication of his words.

"Well, if she's really so sick, then that's that. I've waited five weeks for this night."

"My darling, we'll spend years together. We'll have everything to ourselves."

"When will you be back?"

"I can't say exactly. But very late."

"What's the matter with her? Is she running a temperature?"

"Yes. And she looks very ill."

"Well, help her. I don't wish her any harm."

"Go to sleep. I love you!"

He opened the telephone booth and made a move to leave, but then shut it again and called home. He hadn't told a complete lie. Leah did have the flu. Moreover, he had said something that was true: nobody was at home. The telephone rang but no one answered. What had been a complete fabrication a moment before had turned into the absolute truth. Grein pressed the receiver to his ear while with his free hand he searched for something in the back pocket of his trousers. Who knows? Perhaps Leah really was dangerously ill. Words often have magical powers. Perhaps she's dead, God forbid. Had there ever before been such a shambles in the world? he wondered. Or was this the first time such an imbroglio had occurred in the history of the cosmos? What were the chances that a situation like this would repeat itself? If the number of atoms is limited, the event had to repeat itself sometime, not just once, in fact, but trillions of times, each with only minor deviations. This is what drove poor Nietzsche mad.

Grein waited awhile, glancing again at the bar. In the congealed light of the lamps the three drunks still sat like dummies. Their mouths neither spoke nor were silent but gabbled like those of children learning their first words. The hands on the wall clock showed fifteen minutes after twelve. The barman yawned widely. No one answered the telephone. Leah was evidently asleep, or simply didn't want to leave her bed. Grein went outside and waited briefly for a taxi, although he doubted whether any taxi would be willing to drive so far so late. The BMT was nearby and Grein went up the stairs. If Anna should phone me at home, I'm lost, he told himself. Overcome by a sudden urge to run, he forced himself to walk slowly. He waited ten minutes for the Brighton express, but it was apparently no longer running so he boarded a local train. What would happen, for instance, if I had to account for all this in a courtroom? How could I explain this kind of psychology? I left Esther and now I'm running back to her. She's exhausted me with her endless verbiage and her hysterical intensity, but I can hardly wait to be with her. Of course I'm behaving irrationally, but as I'm part of Nature, what I'm doing has its place in the cosmos. Since we cannot say that a fly makes mistakes, why should we say that a human being errs? Spinoza is right: there's no room for error in the universe. Why did he make such a fuss about controlling the emotions? It

seems that those who are closest to the truth are the most extreme fatalists—those who play Russian roulette.

In Brighton, Grein took a taxi to Esther's and went up the stairs. Only
now did he realize how overpowering his lust was. He could hardly wait
for her to open the door, and when she did they fell into each other's
arms. For a long time they stood in the doorway, passionately embracing
and kissing like two lovers who, having been separated for a long time,
thought they would never meet again and could hardly contain themselves.
Afterward they walked about with their arms twined around each other,
Esther going backward and Grein pushing her forward as children at play
sometimes do. In this way they went into the bedroom.

Esther's face was radiant with triumph. "My hero!"

"You've put a spell on me."

"Why not? All's fair in love and war. I made a wax model of you and
stuck seven needles into it. As long as the needles remain there, your
heart'll be drawn to me like a magnet, and it'll blaze and melt like wax.
Hocus-pocus, abracadabra, barabas-satanas, kokodover, malkei tzedek."

"Where did you learn all this?"

"Silly fool, I'm an old witch. I whirl around on a hoop, I fly on a
broom. Lucifer and I are old and intimate friends."

"That sounds like the truth."

"It is, silly fool, it is. Witches do exist. I take a soul and bind it up in
my garter. What did you tell Boris Makaver's daughter? Where did you
say you were going in the middle of the night? To visit the Queen of Sheba
in her palace?"

"I told her Leah was sick."

"And did the cow believe it?"

"Leah really is sick."

"What's wrong with her? Well, it's not my fault. I never had anything
against Leah. Quite the contrary. But I hate Boris Makaver's daughter. She
has no right to take a man away from me. She won't get him, either. I'll
make her life a disaster. You're already twitching like a butterfly on a pin.
What'll it be like later?"

"Later everything will be over."

"That's what you think. If I want to end it, then it'll be over—and if
it pleases me, I'll go on having a fling with you."

"And what will Morris Plotkin say?"

"He'll like it or lump it. He'll light my way with a candlestick. Since everything's wicked, I might as well also be a devil among devils. Come, let's drink some brandy—tonight's Belial's birthday!''

"I've already had a glass of cognac tonight."

"So you'll drink some more. Then, my saint, I'm at your disposal."

11

Grein had fallen asleep, and Esther woke him with playful shouting. "Hertz, wake up for midnight study and prayer! The heavens have opened! A comet has fallen and the world's on fire!''

Grein opened his eyes. "What's the time?"

"Late! Too late! It's all over! Hertz, I've got an idea."

"What?"

"Let's get up and run away. Right now!"

"What's the time?" Grein asked again.

"Hertz, I mean it seriously. I can't live without you, and you can't live without me. We're fooling each other to no purpose. We're killing each other with our spite. I can't stand it any longer!''

"But you're going to marry Morris Plotkin, aren't you?"

"I want you, not Morris Plotkin."

Grein was silent for a while, trembling with the agitation of someone who has been startled out of a deep sleep.

"I can't do it, Esther."

"Why not?"

"I've taken her away from her husband."

"Fool, the husband will take her back. It'll be better for both of them. You come with me. Let's take the first train out of the station and ride to the end of the line. Then we'll take a room there and huddle together like two wild animals in a lair.''

"I can't do it, Esther."

"Is that your last word?"

"The very last word."

"Then go! Get out of here this minute, and let me never see or smell you again! Go! I'm throwing you out! March!''

"Wait, I have to get dressed."

"Go! You bastard!"

Grein's clothes were scattered all over the place—his necktie lay on the carpet, his jacket hung on the floor lamp, one shoe had disappeared entirely. With an outstretched hand, Grein fumbled for it under the sofa while Esther started pacing back and forth.

"Get out! Get out! You're my worst enemy! You despicable hyena! I'll blot out your name and memory! When they mention your name, I'll spit. Tomorrow I'll marry Morris Plotkin! For me you're dead! Worse than dead! You're the most evil of all the wicked in the world!"

"Stop your cursing now!"

"Get out of here! You can go barefoot. I'll find Boris Makaver's daughter and I'll tell her the truth. All three of us will cast you out—I, Leah, she. Your own children will spit on you. I'll go to your wife and I'll come to an understanding with her. Then I'll have a little chat with Boris Makaver's daughter. Those who can love passionately can also hate passionately!"

"Esther, be a lady."

"A lady? I'm finished with being a lady. From now on, it's war, and everything's allowed in a war. I told you that earlier."

"You can't frighten me with anything."

"You'll be utterly cast out and cut off!"

Suddenly Esther burst out laughing. "What am I ranting on like this for? Get dressed and go. Good riddance."

"Just wait a minute."

"Take your time. You've made me unhappy, but I'm not your enemy. I won't go either to your wife or to Boris Makaver's daughter. I am my parents' daughter. My father let an estate be taken away from him because he thought it beneath him to fight for it in court. I've still got a bit of pride left. I'm only sorry we didn't have a child. But now it's too late for that as well. Now you'll have children with Boris Makaver's daughter."

"I won't have any more children with anyone."

"The world won't come to a stop because of that. I'm quite calm now. Where do you live with her? In a hotel?"

"Yes, in a hotel."

"Where? In any case, it's all the same to me. What's she got that I lack? And if you love her, why do you come to me? Enough talking. In this world, we shouldn't get attached to any one single thing. My grandmother used to say that. She used to say, 'Tie a bow, not a knot, because you can untie a bow, but you have to cut a knot with a knife.' When you've gone, everything will be easy again. How are you putting on your necktie? Go and look in the mirror."

"I know how to do it without looking."

"Didn't you shave today?"

Grein didn't reply. Esther looked at him tiredly and in bewilderment, and suddenly started speaking without any apparent relevance: "I dreamed about my sister Rosa. As soon as I shut my eyes she was standing there in her white silk wedding dress, wearing her veil and holding a prayer book. I don't understand these dreams. I haven't thought about Rosa for weeks. I remember something else: her husband, Melekh, was standing next to her, and his face was covered in a sort of sheath with spikes. I have no idea how to interpret it: a mask of spikes that fitted his face exactly, without any eyeholes. How would Freud have explained it?"

"Freud couldn't explain all dreams."

"Then who can, exactly? The dead are with us. They're with us all the time. They live with us, but we can't see them. Only when we doze off and let ourselves relax can we see them."

"Why should Melekh wear a mask of spikes in the other world?"

"Who knows? Perhaps they have their own fashions or something."

"It's all in your mind."

"What's in my mind? Where did I get such a fantasy? Oh, my head! I've got some headache pills somewhere. Well, since you must go, go. Don't leave any of your things behind. I don't need any souvenirs."

"Good night, Esther."

"Good night. Go to hell. I hope you're smashed to pieces."

"Is that your last word?"

"Why not? I don't have to leave behind a good impression."

"Forgive me, Esther."

"Demon! Give me a kiss!"

Grein reached Manhattan with the dawn. As he left the subway, clumps of night were breaking up all over the city. Fifth Avenue was deserted, Manhattan itself as quiet as a small village. A fine golden light glowed on the upper stories of the skyscrapers. Grein, too, was quiet, filled with the stillness that sometimes overtakes a person returning from the funeral of someone near and dear. He walked to the apartment slowly, rang weakly, and waited for the night porter to open the door and take him up in the elevator. Everything took place in silence, no word passed between them.

Grein unlocked the door, but the sound did not wake Anna. He went on tiptoe into the living room, where the rising sun shone in like a lamp, and sat down quietly on the sofa. A chapter in his life had ended. He seemed to have grown deaf from lack of sleep and from Esther's raving.

He gently opened the window and breathed in the early-morning air. Suddenly he remembered his mother, who always used to rise with the dawn while he and his father still lay in bed. On rising, his father would perform the ritual washing of the nails, put on his fringed ritual undergarment, his capote, his thick boots. Then he would wash himself again and immediately begin his prayers from the beginning. Then he would sit down to study the Talmud or some other sacred book. Later still, he would resume his copying of a Torah scroll. Every time he had to write the name of God he would stop, murmur something, raise his eyes to heaven. That man did only one thing—he served God. The letters he wrote with India ink on parchment were as old as the Jewish people, rooted in the time when Abraham had smashed his father's idols and discovered that there was only one God. But what did the son of this devout scribe do? He dissipated and laid waste everything that generations of Jews had given up their lives to build. His own grandchildren would now be Gentiles. His soul was tattered, stained, steeped in filth.

Grein picked up a newspaper lying on the floor and leafed through it slowly. On every page was a picture which his father would have regarded as harlotry: half-naked women, seductive legs, torsos in brassieres, hips in girdles. A woman's leg, complete from crotch to heel, was stretched out across the whole of one page, the text arranged around it like the commentary on a page of some obscene and perverted Talmud. In another advertisement, two female legs were lifted high in the air. What would his father, peace be upon him, have said about a newspaper like this? Grein wondered. He would have spat. For him all this would have been an abomination, forbidden even to be touched because of its impurity. But these pictures were published in great and famous newspapers that were read by America's most important citizens. This was their culture, their poetry, their aesthetic. They start every day by reading it. The world as we know it today was in reality one huge underworld.

Grein sat immobile, as though turned to stone. How did I get involved in all this? And Esther? Her father was also a Torah scholar. She is a woman of the most distinguished ancestry. What had happened to Jews? For three thousand years they had resisted idolatry and now suddenly they had be-

come the foremost producers in Hollywood, the major publishers of newspapers, the radical leaders of Communists. In Russia, petty Jewish writers
had continued to denounce one another in the name of the Revolution
until they had all been exterminated. In New York, in Paris, in London,
in Moscow——everywhere Jews had become the preachers of atheism, the
arbiters of fashion, the writers of slander; they took the lead as political
agitators and avidly fed the evil inclination in all people. Now they had
taken on the role of teaching the Gentiles how to enjoy the pleasures of
this world.

He heard footsteps. Anna came in wearing a nightdress and slippers.
She looked confused and half-asleep.

"When did you get back?"

"I didn't mean to wake you."

"Why are you sitting here? You're as white as chalk."

For a while both were silent. Then Anna snapped, "Well, how's your
wife?"

"She's better."

"You weren't with your wife," she retorted flatly.

He wanted to reply but he held his peace. He was too tired to go into
explanations with her. Anyway, what should he do? Swear falsely? She had
probably telephoned Leah. He remembered the words of Esau: "Behold I
am at the point to die, and what profit shall this birthright do to me?"
Anna waited.

"What've you got to say?"

"Nothing."

"Well, I'm going back to bed."

And Anna returned to the bedroom.

Slowly Grein started to undress, with the feeling of one who has only
just realized that he is dangerously ill and does not know when he will
ever dress himself again. He carefully took off his shoes and put shoe trees
in them. He hung up his suit on a hanger. Everything within him was calm
and resigned. He had lost all of them: Leah, Esther, and Anna. How did
the Gemara put it? "If thou hast taken much, thou hast taken nothing."
He went into the bedroom where the night still ruled. Yesterday lingered
here in all the chunks of darkness. Only a solitary streak of gray pierced
the venetian blinds and the curtains. Anna had buried her head in her
pillow, so it was difficult to know if she was sleeping peacefully or thinking
furiously. Grein's bed had been prepared for him. He lay down and covered

himself, listening attentively, wondering what he would do when he was left completely alone.

Well, I always wanted to become a hermit. I'll go away somewhere and no one will know where my bones have ended up. I'll make my last accounting to God.

Part Two

Jacob Anfang had set up his studio in a large attic room with a glass roof-window in Greenwich Village. Either the owner did not provide sufficient heating or the radiator wasn't working, so Jacob Anfang had been forced to turn on an electric heater; although its elements glowed brightly, it did little to warm the room. The furniture consisted of a long table covered with palettes, paints, canvases, pieces of frames, and bottles of linseed oil and an iron bedstead covered with a black blanket. It was a bright early morning and the sun shone in through the glass roof. The walls of the studio were covered with paintings fitted into frames or nailed to strips of molding. The sun played color games with every daub of paint, mixed the hues, gave the atelier a frosty, festive air. Although Purim had already passed, the month of March was still cold.

Anfang stemmed from well-to-do Hasidic parents in Lodz, but he had lived for many years in Germany. It was there, during the Weimar Republic, that he had built his reputation. Initially, he had opposed modern trends in painting and had remained an Impressionist, or simply a naturalist, as others described him. In essays he wrote for German academic journals, he had waged war against Cubism, abstract art, and the whole range of experimental trends that the Modernists embraced. But then Anfang underwent what could be called an inner conversion. Quite suddenly—or so it seemed to him—he became convinced that not only should the artist stop copying nature, he should not use nature to make any statement whatever. The artist had to produce everything from within himself, had to create his own world as God had done. The painter ought to be absolute master over his canvas, with only his fantasies, his caprices, his inner consciousness as his subject. Consequently Anfang started painting fantastic images which gave expression to his sense of self.

For a while this new approach served him well. The art critics praised his work. Museums bought his paintings. He exhibited with all of Germany's leading contemporary artists. The younger artists, who had earlier derided him, now held him up as an example. Articles started appearing about him in the leading art journals in Paris and London. But in the middle of his conversion, Hitler had turned Europe upside down. Anfang abandoned his German mistress, his paintings, his furniture and books, and fled to France, where he obtained a visa to America. Since fleeing the Nazis and coming to America, however, he had had no luck. Anfang believed that art—or at least the kind of art he produced—was not wanted in the United States. No one in America had heard of him. The snobs of the art world pursued only big names. He had no entrée to the galleries, and the reviews of his work that appeared in the newspapers displayed a viciousness unexampled in Anfang's experience. From the time he had boarded the ship to America, he had been thrown into a world of chaos, into a milieu that in his view had abandoned all standards, all criteria. Once in New York, he had found no friends, no café where he could sit in the evenings, no woman. The English language did not lie comfortably on his lips. Even the sky, the sun, the moon seemed to him more commonplace here than in Europe. They lacked the nuances of light and shade he had always known. Day changed to night virtually without a twilight. Everything in America seemed to him flat, mechanical, shallow, almost as if he had fallen into a sphere of only two dimensions. Spirit was missing, the holy presence which infused everything in the Old World, even during that time when people had gone mad and indulged in the most savage atrocities.

But was it really possible that a portion of the world had been robbed of the spirit of God? Was it not perhaps merely his imagination? That urge to create which had possessed him from his earliest childhood had deserted him here in New York. Now he desired only to lie on his bed and doze. As long as the war against Hitler had lasted, he had read a great many newspapers every day. Now he had grown lazy, despondent. He started paintings and forsook them halfway, looking with detestation on his creations. His studio was full of uncompleted work—figures, landscapes, a variety of compositions whose origin and meaning he did not know himself. He was rudely thrust back into the days when he was first starting out, with all their deprivation and pain. He might have died of hunger if Boris Makaver, Solomon Margolin, and other Jews who had known him in Germany had not assisted him by commissioning portraits. The difficulty of earning a living was now only a part of his tragedy, however. During the last few years, he had lost himself spiritually and could not recover.

Now he paced back and forth in his studio, wearing a dressing gown with a woolen muffler wrapped around his throat and his feet thrust into worn slippers. Anfang was now fifty-two years old, of medium height, on the stocky side, his curly black hair already turning gray at the temples, with a round face, big dark eyes, a hooked nose, thin lips, and a receding chin, all features that made his face look owlish. Indeed, he compared himself to a bird growing old in a cage: although he could not fly, the space he occupied was too cramped. There were other victims of Hitler in his circle, but they had all settled down, married again, gone into business, and even grown rich. They lived somewhere uptown, not in the Village, and they did not occupy themselves with painting pictures no one wanted. Immortality? One atomic bomb could destroy a million paintings. In the war that had just ended, countless works of art had been destroyed. And what pleasure did Van Gogh derive from the fact that nowadays every New York stenographer rushed to the Metropolitan Museum to see exhibitions of his paintings? Frieda Tamar was right: without God, one could not breathe.

But what was the value of devising a conception of God for oneself, and writing liturgical poetry celebrating His mercy and goodness, when His creatures burned each other in ovens and played with the skulls of little children? What was accomplished by praying to a Being of whose existence there was absolutely no proof? Where was He, "the One who giveth understanding unto man," when fathers were forced to dig graves for themselves and their children? Where was He, the jealous and vengeful God, now that America and England and Russia were rebuilding Germany? And what was He doing, "He who settest free the captives," for those millions whom Stalin had imprisoned in slave-labor camps? No, even if there was a God, Jacob Anfang would not serve Him. If there was a God, He was probably a cosmic Hitler who for His honor and His greatness was prepared to torture whole generations, entire peoples.

So what was one to do to justify one's existence? Paint two doves preening themselves or sitting next to each other? Anfang demanded of himself. I can't become a charlatan. It's too late. And in any case, there's no will left in me. What use do I have for reputation? For money? I only want one thing—to sleep. Actually, I want to die, but how does one make oneself die? I'm too apathetic to do anything about it. Death will undoubtedly come on its own—I simply have to wait. But on the other hand, it's boring to wait, and while I'm waiting I still have to pay the rent. How ironic!—awaiting death is a privilege one ends up paying for.

Anfang stretched out on his bed and covered himself with his overcoat. He looked up at the pale-blue wintry sky through the glass roof. Something was trembling and vibrating up there. The sky, too, was probably waiting for some kind of cataclysm, the manifestation of some power that would rip space and time apart like a sheet of paper, leaving nothing behind. Less than nothing. Nothing could be squared. Nothing would return to nothingness, to formlessness and void that would lie inert in post-Creation vacancy. How was it written? "When all things have ended, after all Being has ceased, Non-Being will have dominion." No more world, no more God, no more time, no more space. Hush, quiet. Nothing has happened. Everything has been erased without trace. The soap bubble has burst and neither soap nor water remains. Even nirvana no longer exists. Who is dozing, then? I, Jacob Anfang.

He suddenly heard footsteps on the stairs. Someone had come to visit him. He sat up. Who could be calling on him so early? God, perhaps?

2

There was a knock, and as soon as Anfang opened the door, he recognized Frieda Tamar. He had painted her portrait. She stood before him in a long coat with a fur collar, her shoes covered with snow boots, unpowdered, unrouged, without lipstick, wearing a black hat, and embodying in her whole demeanor a lost fragment of nineteenth-century Europe.

Jacob Anfang bowed. "Madame!"

"I'm sure you must be taken aback that I've come without telephoning first."

"Not at all. Why telephone? You were passing and you came up. Just as we used to do in the old days, the good days."

"Ah, it's cold in here. Don't they provide any heat?"

"The landlord is stingy with the coal."

"Pardon? That's very wrong."

"Please be seated, madame. If you have confidence in my observance of the dietary laws, I'll make coffee."

"Pardon? No, I don't need any. I've just had my breakfast. I wasn't just passing. Why should I lie? I live uptown, not here."

"But you have pupils somewhere near here, don't you?"

"That was some time ago. Not now. I've made a special deliberate trip here."

"What? That is truly an honor. Please be seated, madame. May I help you off with your coat?"

"No, thank you. It's cold in here."

"You'll catch a chill when you leave."

"No, I won't. Herr Anfang, at first I wanted to write you a letter, but then I thought it would be far better to speak frankly and directly to you in person. Herr Anfang, ever since you painted my portrait, I've thought a great deal about you. I've also spoken about you with my brother. He and I view the world from quite different perspectives, as you know. You call yourself a freethinker, but in reality, it seems to me, you are a religious man. I firmly believe that every creative person must be religious, because God is the Creator, and when man is creative, he reflects the image of God. The Torah would seem to forbid us to paint pictures, but what is at issue is evidently the intention, not the thing itself. As we learn in the Book of Exodus, the Tabernacle in the Wilderness was decorated with two cherubim of gold, and cherubim are fashioned in the image of birds. Many old sacred books depict faces on their title pages. If the Maharal of Prague really did make a golem, then he was practicing sculpture, but for a higher purpose."

Anfang smiled. "Are you trying to sanctify my trade?"

"It's a very serious question for me."

"Well, today people no longer worship pictures. If only they did—artists would be far better off."

Frieda looked reprovingly at him. "Would you want humanity to return to idol worship?"

"It would make no difference."

Frieda bit her lip. "No, that is false. Herr Anfang, you are a great artist. I'm not an art critic, but every piece of yours that I've seen glows from the walls. You put so much into my own portrait that I am continually astounded. It hangs in my brother's room, and every time I go there, I am overwhelmed anew. How were you able to see so much in so short a time?''

"Ah, the eyes see.''

"Well, it's a gift.''

"Perhaps, perhaps.''

Frieda's face set in stern resolution. "Herr Anfang, it wasn't easy for me to come to you. I thought about it for a long time. You know that I'm shy by nature, but I'm often capable of overcoming my timidity. I'm embarrassed only in front of lesser people. You, however, are a great man, so I feel emboldened in your presence.'' She went pale.

"No, no, you certainly have no need to be embarrassed in front of me.''

"Herr Anfang, a few days ago Boris Makaver made me an offer of marriage. You know my situation and the events that led up to it. My husband was martyred for the Sanctification of the Holy Name. Boris Makaver first proposed to me a year ago, but at that time I gave him the same answer Rabbi Hiyya's widow gave Rabbi Yehuda: 'My husband was holy and you are profane; if I were to marry again, I would be obliged to increase the holiness, not diminish it.' You once studied the Talmud, after all.''

"Yes, I did. But I don't know that particular passage.''

"It's somewhere in the Talmud. Boris Makaver is a fine man, good, honest, a man of great charity. In his own way he is a righteous man. But when I compare him with Dr. Tamar, the distinction the Talmud makes still holds. My late husband was a great personality—a holy man, truly a saint. I've grown away from Polish Jews and their manners. When it comes to so important a thing as marriage, there must be complete empathy— you might call it love; even the Torah speaks of it. When Boris Makaver made me this second proposal, I promised to give him an answer today. Something deeply distressing has befallen him. His daughter, Anna, has left her husband and gone off with Grein. I think you know him—Hertz Grein.''

"Yes, indeed. When did this happen?''

"Oh, not long ago. For the father, this is a tragedy. He is an observant Jew. He's taken it terribly to heart. But sorrows purify one. Now I must say something. I find it very difficult, but I must speak plainly, because otherwise I will procrastinate for years. I must either speak perfectly frankly about this, or remain totally silent. Permit me to close my eyes. It'll be easier for me that way. I implore you not to take offense, and not to ridicule me. On second thought, you can laugh if you wish.

"Briefly, the matter is as follows. When I first met you—at Boris Makaver's, in fact—it struck me immediately how much you resemble my late husband, given the inevitable differences. Later, when we had occasion to talk to each other, I saw that this similarity was not merely physical. For a while I was even convinced that you must be a relative. But that is impossible, for Dr. Tamar was descended entirely from German Jews and you come from Poland. The resemblance was not confined simply to opinions but extended to your whole way of thinking. My husband was a deeply religious man, but he was assailed by doubts. He was always tormented by the eternal questions, painfully tormented, almost as if he knew the terrible end he would have. Later, when you started to paint my portrait—I must tell you that Boris Makaver paid for it, it was entirely his initiative—and we spent time in conversation together, I was even more powerfully impressed by the enormous affinity between you and Dr. Tamar. You blasphemed everything that was holy, but I could not free myself of the conviction that your words actually expressed the suffering of a man of faith. Well, I hope you understand now the thrust of what I am trying to say, but I should like to speak plainly in any case. When I keep my eyes shut, it's somewhat easier for me. When all is said and done, we are neither of us so very young anymore. Before I give Boris Makaver an answer, I should like you to know that, if you feel able to accept, I should be happy, despite all the differences . . . There would be no diminishment of holiness were we to be united. None."

And she fell silent.

Frieda Tamar sat on a chair, Jacob Anfang sat on his bed. He looked at her, at her closed eyes, and his own eyes glowed with an expression simultaneously smiling and sorrowful. She looks like a blind person, he thought, a blind woman in love. Then he said, "Madame, I should like you to know one thing: this is the most beautiful moment of my life. I shall remember it until my last breath."

Frieda did not open her eyes. "You must answer me in plain language!" she said, almost harshly.

"Madame, for me it is too late—both spiritually and physically."

"I see."

"If I had wanted to marry, you would have been the best wife I could ever have hoped for. But I am far from wishing that. I too would like to speak plainly: I am impotent. I have been for several years now."

"I see."

"I know that the causes are spiritual, not organic. But it is a fact nevertheless. I am completely shattered. I have reached a point where I no longer know what to live for. A man in such a situation cannot build a home."

"I see."

"You may open your eyes. Your action showed integrity, beauty, greatness. I repeat: this is the most beautiful moment of my life."

3

Boris Makaver usually recited the morning prayers early. He could not sleep at night, and as soon as day began to break, he donned his prayer shawl and phylacteries. But this morning, for the first time he could remember, he slept long past dawn and woke only at ten o'clock. He had an appointment to meet some businessmen at a restaurant. Although he always rose feeling hungry, Boris normally never ate anything before praying. Now, however, before leaving his home he ruled, as if he were a rabbi, that he was permitted to make an exception and had a glass of tea with an egg cookie.

A particularly big enterprise was in the process of negotiation. The American Navy was selling off ships very cheaply. For some three million dollars one could acquire several dozen cargo ships, each of which would have cost many millions of dollars to build. The businessmen had calculated that even if the ships were sold for scrap, they could yield great profits. Not all the ships needed to be scrapped, however: some were in very good condition and could be repaired and used. At present, the venture had three partners, and Boris was supposed to become the fourth. The snag was that the government demanded to be paid in cash, which would necessitate Boris's investing $750,000 in the project. Having already invested every dollar he owned in commercial enterprises, Boris had no ready cash and actually owed money to the bank. He could of course borrow money against securities, but first he had to establish precisely how much the ships would be worth as scrap. How much would it cost to dismantle some fifty ships? How many of them could be used to transport cargo? And how much profit would they bring? The undertaking was too large and complicated: it demanded engaging all kinds of experts, entering into contracts with all kinds of firms, leasing a shipyard. Boris hesitated about getting involved in so complex a business transaction. On the other hand, this was undoubtedly an opportunity with the potential to make millions. Boris sat down at a table with the other partners, drinking tea, eating egg cookies, and covering pads of paper with figures as he worked out the possible contingencies. He was to give the others his final answer in three days' time.

On the way home Boris took spiritual stock of himself. Today he had neglected the daily recitation of the *Shema* and had postponed his morning study of a page of the Gemara. Why did he need so much money? Why take all these burdens upon himself? He had blotted out all memory that he had a daughter. He was a man in his sixties who suffered from high blood pressure. How long could he go on driving himself? What did he know about ships? Why did he need all these extra worries? If, God forbid, this new enterprise did not succeed, he might be left deeply in debt, having taken the money of strangers. I must be out of my mind, Boris warned himself. Why go looking for trouble? In return for millions? What will I do with those millions? I don't require more than a meal, a bed, and an apartment. What I really need is health and less mental turmoil.

As soon as he got home, Boris went straight into his little prayerhouse. Reytze complained bitterly because he was leaving his meal to get cold, but he appeased her with a pleasant word. In this room with the Holy Ark, the candelabra, the shelves of sacred books, Boris felt at home. This was where he could find solitude, his fortress. He had often thought that he would like to end his days in just such a room as this. A lectern and a seven-branched menorah stood here; on a bookshelf sat an eight-branched Hanukkah lamp. Here he had a scroll and a fescue, a shofar and a white robe, a citron box, all kinds of rare Jewish antiques and valuable ritual objects. Even the smells here were different: it seemed to him that the room exuded the odor of spice boxes and the Garden of Eden. He donned his prayer shawl and sighed. He bound the leather strap of one of the phylacteries around his left arm and was filled with shame before the Master of the Universe. He already earned ten times more than he actually needed. Where did he get this greed for money? What would he do with it all? Take it to the grave with him? He twined the leather strap around his fingers and recited the prescribed meditation, concentrating on the meaning of the words: "I will betroth you to Myself forever; I will betroth you to Myself in righteousness and in justice, in kindness and in mercy. I will betroth you to Myself in faithfulness; and you shall know God."

Now these are valuable teachings! Boris reflected. Every word illuminates the soul. The Master of the Universe is the bridegroom, and the congregation of Israel is the bride, but instead of the bride rejoicing in her bridegroom and seeking to please him, she occupies herself with all kinds of folly and triviality.

He heard someone ringing at the front door. Probably the grocery man or the exterminator, he thought, and went on with his prayers. At that moment Reytze opened the door.

"Herr Makaver, Frau Tamar is here."

Boris gaped in astonishment. "Frieda Tamar?"

"Yes."

He pondered awhile. She was supposed to telephone. She had never come without calling beforehand. Well, she's come to refuse. She wanted to conciliate him. Perhaps she feared her brother might suffer. Boris frowned. Should he receive her wearing his prayer shawl and phylacteries? He reminded himself of the talmudic precept that even if a serpent were to coil itself about his feet, he should not interrupt his devotions. But, strictly speaking, that precept applied only to the Eighteen Benedictions, not to the psalms recited before morning prayers. Those could be interrupted. Well, perhaps it's better this way. I'll feel less ashamed in my prayer shawl and phylacteries.

He asked Reytze to invite Frau Tamar to come in. No is no, he said to himself. If I've been able to manage for so long without a wife, I'll drag on to the end. He touched the phylacteries on both his head and his arm. These were his armaments, his tanks, his battle dress. Boris had heard some gossip to the effect that Frieda Tamar was attracted to Jacob Anfang, the painter. Anfang was a younger man as well. Well, I'll congratulate her. I won't show I'm disappointed, he decided. Everything is foreordained, in any event.

The door opened and Frieda Tamar came in. Seeing him in his prayer shawl and phylacteries, she took a step backward. "Oh, you're praying. Please excuse me."

"I've only just begun. I'm late today. I seem to have delayed my prayers as long as a Kotsker Hasid—I'm still reciting the opening psalms."

"Please finish. I'll wait."

"No, please sit down. Now that you've come, I'd like to hear what you have to say. Otherwise my mind will keep wandering from my worship."

Frieda took a step forward. "I've come to tell you that if you still want me, I'm prepared to become your wife."

Boris could hardly restrain himself from giving a cry of joy. He stretched out his arms as if to embrace her, and his eyes filled with tears. He was ashamed as he stood before her: a creature of flesh and blood who rejoiced more in a woman than in the Master of the Universe. But the prayer shawl and phylacteries reined him in. The leather straps bound him. He was a soldier, God's soldier, at this moment on active service. He took out his handkerchief and wiped his eyes.

"May God make you as happy as you have made me."

"Now you must stop using the formal style of address."

"Yes."

"Finish your prayers, finish your prayers. Prayer is more important. I'll wait in the salon."

"Many thanks."

Frieda went out and Boris glanced at the Holy Ark. Did this mean that heaven still wanted him to live? Did heaven still want to bring him joy in his old age? And only a moment before he had thought his end was near. His eyes again brimmed with tears, and he reminded himself of the verse from Psalms: "Make us glad according to the days wherein Thou hast afflicted us." Who knows? She might perhaps still be able to bear a child. Perhaps he might yet leave a son behind him. Boris Makaver's only desire was to weep, as he was filled with a great love for Frieda Tamar, the scholar, the learned woman who wrote books on religious subjects and, apart from Yiddish, spoke German, French, English, and Hebrew. Well, I am unworthy, unworthy. Master of the Universe, this is all your mercy and grace. He went over to the eastern wall and resumed his prayers where he had broken off: "Let not Thy mercy depart from me, O Lord; May Thy grace and truth protect me forever."

A random thought suddenly flitted through his mind: given the present situation, it was probably worthwhile to buy the ships.

10

As soon as Anna returned to New York, she tried telephoning Stanislaw Luria repeatedly. She had left home having packed hardly anything, so most of her lingerie, clothes, shoes, furs, jewelry, and a great many other things she needed were still in her old apartment. What was the sense of throwing it all away? Besides, Anna hoped that Luria might have reconsidered and would now agree to a divorce. She had made up with Grein, who had given her a sacred promise never to see Esther again. In any case, Esther was planning to marry—or had already married—Morris Plotkin. Anna had convinced herself that Grein truly loved her, and she could not bring herself to break off with him.

But however many times Anna called Luria, no one answered the telephone. Either he'd left town or was simply refusing to answer. Anna began to wonder whether he might be lying ill in bed. Perhaps he had died, God forbid. When a person lived all alone in a great city, without a single friend or relative, anything might happen. After careful consideration, Anna finally decided to go there herself. She had a key to the apartment, to which she was legally entitled since she had signed the lease.

Anna told Grein what she intended to do, and they arranged that if in three hours she had not returned with her things to the apartment on Fifth Avenue, he would call her at Luria's number and then come over immediately if no one answered. Who knew what a madman like Luria might do? He was capable of assaulting her.

Grein was of the opinion that instead of going herself, Anna ought to send a lawyer, but Anna was unwilling to do so. That would certainly infuriate Luria. Though he was a lawyer himself, Luria loathed everything to do with courts, especially American courts, which in his view were governed not by law but by politics, fashion, journalistic opinion, and any number of biases. He never missed an opportunity to point out to Anna how unjust and lopsided the verdicts handed down in American courts were, particularly the fantastic sums that men were compelled to pay in alimony. According to Luria, American courts had always sided with the whore, the exploiting and betraying wife. Here the justice of Sodom prevailed. To send a lawyer to Luria meant starting a war.

Anna called her former home one last time, but again there was no answer. Thus she decided to visit it immediately; she needed no permission to remove her own belongings. If Luria was not at home, so much the better: she would avoid the inevitable unpleasant scene. She took a taxi to Lexington Avenue and got out in front of the once-familiar building. The doorman gave her a questioning glance: Was she still a tenant here? Should he admit her or not? He greeted her uncertainly, stiffly. The elevator man was the same one who had been on duty the night Anna had left with Grein. He did not recognize her at first, but when he did, he again pursed his lips as though to whistle. His eyes seemed to be saying: So? Has the songbird returned to its cage? He stopped the elevator abruptly and rasped, ''Watch your step!''

They're all on his side, Anna thought. She took out her key and tried to open the door but—God in heaven!—the key no longer fitted. Luria had had the lock changed. She rang the bell, but no one responded. This was an unexpected blow. Anna was overpowered by rage and helplessness. What shall I do now? What right has he to lock me out? I pay the rent, not him. Grein is right: I must get a lawyer immediately! I must speak with the superintendent. She tried over and over again to open the door with her key, but the lock steadfastly resisted all her efforts. It too was on Luria's side. How humiliating this was, especially considering that she had been seen by the elevator operator and the doorman. Then, as if to spite her further, Mrs. Katz—the same harridan whom Anna had met in Florida—suddenly opened her own door and carried out a thick Sunday newspaper and several magazines. She greeted Anna, smiled knowingly, seemed on the verge of adding something, but said nothing. Yet again this dreadful woman was a witness to Anna's ignominy: she could no longer enter her own apartment. Did this happen to all women who left their husbands? Or were there malign forces directed solely against her? Anna wondered.

She rang for the elevator, but it was in no hurry to come. Five minutes passed and she still stood there waiting. Were they gossiping about her down below? Eventually the freight elevator arrived, the one that usually carried down the garbage. A black man stuck his head out and asked, "You goin' down, lady?"

"Where's the passenger elevator?"

The black man made no reply, so Anna entered the freight elevator.

This has all been organized! she decided. He's turned all the building staff against me! Yet she felt distinctly ill at ease. None of this was in character for the Luria she knew. The superintendent had an apartment on the ground floor, but he was not at home. There was no one Anna could speak to. Well, he can't keep my things—there are still laws in this country.

Anna went out into the street and started walking. Should she head home? Until today she had felt sorry for Luria, but now she hated him. She had certainly treated him brutally, but she was unprepared for such petty revenge on his part. She was now ashamed that she had ever lived with him and that, for a short time, she had actually been in love with him. Well, one has to swallow many bitter pills in life. No one knows what others have to endure. Anna found herself at a drugstore and went in. She'd drink a cup of coffee. Perhaps in the interim Luria would return to the apartment. She sat down on a high stool at the counter. As happened to her every time she suffered some setback, Anna lost her self-confidence. She got up on the stool like an inexperienced rider mounting a horse and looked around at the others sitting nearby as if to make sure they had not noticed her humiliation and were not laughing at her. The counterman passed several times but managed not to see her. Suddenly he came up. Anna started saying something in English, but he rudely interrupted her in Yiddish: "Whaddaya want?"

Anna did not reply. How dare he speak to her in Yiddish or address her so insolently and informally.

"Howd'ya like America?" the young man demanded.

"Be good enough to bring me a pot of coffee," Anna curtly replied in English.

"You liked Hitler better, eh?"

The surly youth poured her a half pot of coffee and banged down the jug of cream with a clatter, muttering and grumbling as he did so. He was acting like a child.

How is this possible? Anna asked herself. The whole world is at war with me. But how can they know? Is it written all over my forehead? Well, it's one of those days! A serious accident could happen at any moment. I only hope I don't get run over by a car!

Anna put down ten cents and pushed away the coffee, almost falling as she left the high stool. She thought the heel of her left shoe had twisted. The loutish counterman had the effrontery to shout some coarse words after her.

She left the drugstore with no idea of where she was going. Was she walking downtown? Uptown? In all the confusion, she had forgotten the number of her own street. I only hope I don't break a leg! she besought the higher powers. It was as if evil demons, unseen mischief-makers, had fastened themselves to her like leeches and were making every possible effort to destroy her. What was it? Her father's curse? God's punishment? Feeling his way over the sidewalk with a white stick, a cigar box containing chewing gum around his neck, a blind man approached her. I must give alms! I must atone for my sins! Anna started rummaging for some small change, but she had spent her last dime on the coffee she hadn't drunk. Should she give him a dollar? That was too much. And in any case, how did all these good deeds help? The Jews in Europe had also given alms—more than they could afford. Everything depends on luck—that's the bitter truth! Anna passed a movie theater showing a gangster picture. During the day a ticket cost only pennies. Should I go in for an hour? That counterman was worthless trash! She'd have given half her life to see him swinging from a gallows! But what did it matter? He'd be dead in a few decades' time anyway. He'd lie on his deathbed not even remembering his boorish behavior toward her on a day when she had a bad conscience as it was. He'd probably forgotten already.

Anna bought a ticket and went in. God in heaven, how dark it was in here! It was difficult to believe that during broad daylight people chose to sit in such blackness. She was now as blind as that man with the box of chewing gum. And in perpetual darkness like this he had not only to wander all over New York but to try to earn a living as well. Now Anna regretted that she hadn't given him the dollar. After a while her eyes grew accustomed to the dark, and noticing that she was standing next to an empty row, she fell into a seat. She glanced at the screen. A man was running over rooftops and the police were shooting at him. He kept ducking to avoid the bullets. What a situation! Anna reflected. The difficulties people get themselves into! Ask him and he'll tell you that he couldn't avoid it. Fate apparently played a different game with every individual.

Someone fired a shot—the gangster stumbled, fell, and rolled over. Well, he's struggled through his apportioned lot, Anna murmured to herself. No one will hound him any longer. At that moment, a stranger sat down next to her. Anna perceived at once that the man was going to try to strike up an acquaintance with her, using the tricks all lonely and aggressive men do, and sure enough, he soon started brushing her knee with his. Anna was revolted. She rose and moved four seats away, sending an unmistakable signal that he had no chance whatever with her. So now she had made yet another enemy: she could feel his hatred, as if it were a physical presence, cut through the barrier of primeval darkness as his coarse, middle-aged visage registered the frustrated defeat of those whom no one loves.

Perhaps she should move to another row entirely. A man like that might be a maniac. But that would only infuriate him more. For a while Anna concentrated on the film. A woman had now appeared, a vulgar type who spoke in a gravelly voice and smoked a cigarette. She was wearing mourning—apparently she was the gangster's widow. Anna closed her eyes so as not to see what was happening, and only then became aware that she could hear music. Had it been playing the whole time? She sat there, preoccupied with her own anxiety. Would Grein really behave himself from now on? Or would he run back to Esther again after a while? If Papa only knew what she was suffering! Even Grein didn't know. He was so self-absorbed, so caught in his own mad entanglements that he was incapable of empathizing with anyone else's situation. He brushed everything aside with talk, promises, curses, endearments, wandering about in a highly agitated state himself. He came, he went, he dozed, he telephoned, continually maneuvering among her, Leah, Esther, and who knew how many others. He had burdened himself with yokes of his own devising, multiplied his responsibilities in a futile effort to satisfy everyone. He probably had heavy financial obligations as well. He was exactly like the gangster in this movie—racing over the rooftops while bullets flew at him from all sides.

Anna suddenly had an intuitive feeling that Luria had returned home. As she rose to go in search of a telephone, she perceived unexpectedly that it was not at all dark in here. On the contrary, it was almost brightly lit. Now that she could see all the seats, all the people, she couldn't understand why she had earlier felt so blind and helpless. The "maniac" had disappeared. Had he left? Had he gone up into the gallery to smoke? Or was he lying in wait for her somewhere with a knife? The telephone booth was situated in a corridor which led to the restrooms. Going there was taking a risk, since that was exactly the sort of place where such people lurked, but Anna went nevertheless, entered the telephone booth, and called. Yes, Luria was at home. The line was busy.

She called repeatedly but kept getting a busy signal. Evidently Luria was baring his heart to someone, recounting all the wrongs done him. But to whom? As far as she could remember, he had no friends in New York. Had he struck up acquaintanceships in so short a time? Perhaps he had looked up some woman. Anything was possible. A victim could always be found. Anna sat on the seat in the telephone booth. The corridor was deserted. She could hear the muffled speech of the movie's leading characters—a melodramatic exchange between coarse and criminal people who had to fight, hurt each other, behave dementedly, and then fall, in order that a young couple might begin a new life. Everything was foreordained in the projection booth high above, where the technicians operated the machinery. Anna telephoned again, and this time the line was free. In a moment she heard Luria's voice, rough, hoarse, altered—the voice of one who has lost all hope and for whom even coming to the telephone is an ordeal. He didn't say "Hello" but *"Proszę,"* as though he were still in Poland.

2

It was only a few blocks from the movie theater to her former home, but Anna took a taxi. She wanted to get this visit over with as soon as possible. The doorman stared in astonishment: he had seen her enter the building earlier but hadn't seen her leave. The elevator man frowned. Anna rang the bell sharply, but Luria was apparently in no hurry to answer the door. He kept her waiting a long time, and eventually opened the door only a third of the way. Anna barely recognized him. He had stopped dyeing his hair, which was now almost wholly gray. The pouches under his eyes had swollen and assumed a number of hues in which yellow and blue predominated over a variety of puce. Given that he had not been at home earlier, Anna expected to find him dressed, but he was wearing a bathrobe and slippers, as though he had just got out of bed. Unshaven and unkempt, he raised his bushy eyebrows and stared at Anna in despair. He seemed to be hesitating about whether or not to let her in. Then he growled and opened the door.

"Were you asleep or something?" Anna demanded.

"Asleep or something," he repeated after her.

Anna went into the hallway and Luria walked backward in front of her, as if ready at any moment to block her way. The living room was dusty and disordered, strewn with books, magazines, newspapers, even torn bits of paper. A pot stood on the coffee table, and it seemed to Anna that even the pictures on the walls were hanging askew. A musty, greasy odor pervaded everything. Anna grimaced.

"Doesn't the cleaning woman come any longer?"

"What is it you want!" Luria replied brusquely.

"I want to take my things, that's all."

"What things?"

"My clothes, my lingerie. I don't have to remind you that everything here is mine—every stick of furniture, every carpet."

"Do you want to remove everything?"

"For the time being I want only my personal belongings."

"Take them. I don't need your junk. You can take everything, even my bed."

"I don't need your bed."

"Take what you want and get out of here. I never want to see you again."

"Don't chase me out. Until now, I've paid the rent, not you."

"*You've* paid? Your father paid, because he thought that way he'd stop you from becoming a whore. But once a whore, always a whore."

"I beg you, Luria, try not to be crude for the few minutes I have to spend here."

"Crude am I? If I were a man and not a nobody, I'd've torn your hair out by the roots, smashed all your teeth, and flung you out like a heap of trash. That's the way men used to behave. But America castrates men, not physically but spiritually. In time, they'll probably do it physically as well. Here the devil in the form of a woman rules supreme. Here power's in the hands of those who are forbidden to have power. But never mind, they'll soon destroy the country, drown it in cosmetics and filth. What streets are you walking?"

Anna went pale. "I'd better go."

"Why hurry? I won't harm you."

"You're capable of anything."

"I'm capable, all right, but I don't want to dirty my hands!"

Luria abruptly left the living room and returned to the bedroom, slamming the door behind him.

How strange—he's become a man, Anna thought. He'd never spoken like this before. She felt weak and had to sit down for a few minutes. Looking around at the furnishings, she noticed that in the past few weeks everything had become covered with dust, faded, disordered. He had obviously let the sun shine in all day, so the potted plants had withered. She wanted to get up and water them for the last time, but she remained seated. It made no difference. How peculiar to be a stranger in the very apartment she had decorated with so much expense and trouble. Well, this is my final visit here. Grein was right—I should have brought a lawyer. Anna reflected for a while. What things should she take? She needed someone who could help her pack. She got up and opened a closet in the corridor. Her clothing hung there untouched. She owned a huge trunk, but it was somewhere in the basement.

Luria came back. "Well, where are you living? How's it going with your latest lover?"

"What do you want to hear? That he beats me?"

"Whether he beats you or kisses you, it's all the same to me. I'm leaving in any case."

Anna tensed. "Where are you going?"

"To my wife and children."

The blood seemed to drain from Anna's heart. "Have you gone mad?"

"Perhaps. I've had enough of this filth. I should never have abandoned them. I want to talk over some practical matters with you."

"What matters?"

"Your father will disinherit you. He told me himself that he's rewritten his will. He gave you a check, but he stopped payment on it. You'll be left without a penny, and your precious Grein will throw you over and go back to his wife. Certainly you're a whore, but in America there are younger and prettier whores. There's a lot of competition in that trade."

"All you want to do is vilify me."

"I'm not vilifying you. I have some life insurance, and for the time being it's in my name. I could make it over to someone else, but I don't mind if you get the money. Whores need a lot of money. It's an expensive line of work."

"What do you want? I paid the premiums, not you."

"You paid, but the policy's in my name. When I drop dead, I'll be worth ten thousand dollars. If you want, you can arrange things so that I'll be worth twenty or thirty thousand. The whole of America is built on this principle—the women kill the men and get paid for it. Here the victims pay the murderers."

"No one's murdering you. You can live and earn your own bread. You can even borrow against the insurance. I don't care."

"I don't want to borrow and I don't need any bread. I need a whore. I'm in that frame of mind. I can't sleep, and a whore might help me. So if you want to sell yourself, you can do business with me."

Anna jerked back. "I beg you, Luria, stop it!"

"Are you offended? Women like you can't afford to get offended. I know perfectly well that money runs through your fingers. Not every prostitute commands such high prices."

"I beg you, Luria."

"Stop begging me. I've made you a proposal. I'm leaving and I'm deadly serious. Soon I won't need either women or money. I want to see what goes on upstairs—do Hitlers rule there as well, or are even they nonexistent? People have tried to show me the other world, but I remain unconvinced. Really to see the truth, one has to pay with one's head."

"The truth won't run away."

"I'm making you a proposal, so answer me plainly. I want to increase the insurance, so when I die you'll get thirty thousand dollars. All you have to do is to come to me twice a week. Even Madame Pompadour didn't get paid so well."

Anna wept. "What are you asking of me? Sadist!"

"In that case, I promise you, you won't get a single penny." And Luria went back into the bedroom.

Anna took down a suitcase and started packing. She was no longer weeping, but her vision remained blurred. Yes, he would kill himself. He was simply looking for an excuse, she brooded. But what can I do? Unable to decide what to take and what to leave, she threw whatever came to hand into the suitcase, jumbling up and creasing everything, conscious that she was taking frills and leaving necessities behind. Suddenly the telephone shrilled, loudly and hollowly, as if ringing in an empty apartment. Luria was evidently no longer taking calls, since the phone rang and rang. Perhaps it's for me? Anna thought. Not everyone knows I've left him. She went over and picked up the receiver.

"Hello."

There was no answer from the person at the other end of the line. Anna was instantly aware of a loaded and truculent silence.

"Hello!"

Suddenly she heard her father's voice. "Who's that?"

"Papa, it's me."

Anna could say no more. Boris Makaver emitted a choking sound and also fell silent.

"What are you doing there?" he shouted, so loudly that Anna had to snatch the receiver from her ear.

"I came to get my things, Papa."

"Don't call me Papa! I'm not your father and you're not my daughter! I've blotted you out. Blotted you out! May your memory be erased! Don't you dare come near my home, because I've told that man—what's his name?—not to let you in. I wanted to speak to Luria, not to you."

"I'll call him."

"No, I want nothing from you!"

And Boris slammed down the phone.

Stunned, Anna held the receiver in her hand for a while before replacing it too. At the very moment she returned to her suitcase, someone rang the doorbell. Anna could not decide whether to respond or not. No, better not, she decided. Today's been such a bad day that everyone will insult me, even the lazy garbageman. But just like the telephone earlier, the doorbell didn't stop ringing. Luria, it seemed, had decided not to respond to anyone. But then why had he answered when she had called? Anna eventually went to the door.

"Who's there?" she asked, but no one replied.

I won't open it. They'll murder me as well before the day's over! Anna decided, and then immediately did the opposite—she opened the door.

On the other side, she saw someone strangely familiar to her, but she could not identify him. She knew instinctively that this inability was absurd and bizarre, because in front of her was someone she had known for a long time. She experienced something like temporary amnesia. Before her stood a small man, outlandishly dressed in a variety of loud colors. He wore an unbuttoned yellow-checked overcoat over a red-brown suit; a shirt with both red dots and red stripes; and a garish, multicolored silk necktie. The points of his shirt collar, fastened together by a gold clip, encircled a strangely scrawny neck and a wizened gullet with a prominent Adam's apple. As though hypnotized, Anna stared at him in stupefaction. He wore a jaunty hat with a feather pulled forward on his head, over a mass of gray hair that seemed peculiarly at variance with his youthful features and lay atop his skull like a wig. He looked like someone who had just flown in from some remote tropical country. Anna caught a glimpse of his highly polished shoes, covered with white spats of the kind that dandies often wear in the summer. I know him, I know him, Anna kept thinking, but who is he? The visitor squinted at her with the stunned surprise of a close relation who is not immediately embraced. There was something mocking and malevolent in his eyes and in the creases of his nose, as if at any moment he would emit a shriek of cackling laughter.

"But this is absolutely beyond belief," he finally said in German.

And at precisely that moment Anna knew who he was. She turned ashen. It was Yasha Kotik, her first husband.

"My God, what are you doing here?" she gasped.

She did not allow him in but stood on the threshold, holding the door. Now she realized why she had not recognized him: his arrival here was an absurdity, bordering on impossibility. Only now did she perceive the changes which had taken place in him. He seemed to have grown smaller, thinner, older; she noted something alien in his face that she could not identify. He seemed to be laughing with a tragic waggishness, the twisted wryness of a clown who had gone through hell and had somehow crawled out of it. The creases around his mouth had grown deeper, as though modeled in clay. His whole bearing seemed to say: Ai-ai-ai, how distant intimates can become! Look, look at everything time can do! He gave a wintry chuckle.

"Anna!"

3

Anna started speaking to Kotik in German, asking him where he had come from, how long he had been in the country, telling him that he had found her here quite by chance. But he had apparently forgotten German. Now he spoke exactly like the *Ostjuden* he had so often derided on the stage. He tripped over every word. He noticed Anna's astonishment at once and called out in Yiddish, "I've completely forgotten Hitler's language. In Russia I spoke either Russian or Yiddish. I know only three

words of English.'' And he uttered an obscenity. Anna felt distinctly uncomfortable.

''I don't understand why you've come here,'' she said. ''I don't live
here anymore.''

''What? Where exactly do you live?''

''Not here.''

''Have you moved out or something? I've been looking for you for
about two weeks. I called your father, but the old man is never at home
and that Reytze is as deaf as a post. She doesn't understand a word one
says to her. I knew your married name was Luria and I called this number,
but no one answers the telephone here either. I have to go to Hollywood
soon, so I thought I might just try my luck and knock on the door like
Santa Claus. And look—I've nabbed you, ha ha!''

''It's a ridiculous fluke.''

''I'm used to ridiculous flukes. Ten thousand ridiculous flukes must have
happened for me to be standing here at this door.''

Anna paused a moment. ''I can't invite you in. The whole situation is
bizarre. Go and wait for me downstairs. I'll be there soon.''

''You might still flee through the chimney.''

''Why should I flee? I'm not afraid of anyone.''

''You've changed in America.''

''I've grown old.''

''No, not old—different. Where shall I wait?''

''Wait across the street. I have to pack up a few things here. I'm leaving
him, too. That's my destiny.''

''What? Well, I wanted to see you again. I had to have a look at you.
We're old acquaintances, after all.''

And Yasha Kotik made an obscene gesture. It was strangely out of
character with his gray hair.

Suddenly Stanislaw Luria emerged. He peered out of the bedroom, and
a moment later he was standing at the door. He said in Polish, ''Who's
this? What does he want?''

''Ah, here we still speak *po-polski*!'' Yasha Kotik seemed pleased. ''I've
only just arrived from Poland myself. But I have some difficulty speaking
Polish. I confuse it with Russian.''

''What do you want? Who are you looking for?'' demanded Luria in
Yiddish.

''Oh, I'm looking for . . . the past. Your wife was once my wife. I
wanted to ask how she is—that's all. You don't have to get jealous.''

"Are you Yasha Kotik?"

"Who else? Are *you* Yasha Kotik?"

"Why are you standing at the door? Come in. I'm not dressed because I can't sleep at night and I try to sleep during the day. Your wife—she's now more yours than mine—is leaving me. She has a third—or perhaps he's the fifth? Come in, come in. She always spoke of you. She never forgot you."

"Really, Luria, all this talk is unnecessary," said Anna in English.

"What's the difference? Come in. Come here. You see? She's packing. I wasn't fooling you. And where have you come from, if I may ask? Sit down."

"I've come from the whole world. Every country decided to make ashes of Yasha Kotik, and Yasha Kotik decided to live. For what purpose should Yasha Kotik live? To gaze upon Anna—and upon you, too. They've got an eye on Yasha Kotik in the other world as well. They want to settle his hash—but what's the hurry? Hollywood has heard of me, and they want to make me a star. I acted in a film in Russia and they brought it to America. In Russia I sold soap on the black market, and here they wrote reviews about me. I have a cousin here, and she cut them all out and kept them for me. In America, too, Yasha Kotik is a celebrity. Do you smoke?"

"Excuse me, but I must pack my things," interrupted Anna. She stared at both men with shock and embarrassment.

"Well, pack. Sit down over here," said Luria, pointing to a chair. "It's a good thing you're still in one piece. Where in Russia were you?"

"Where wasn't I? I roamed the length and breadth of Stalin's state. I was in jail as well, though not for politics—for dealing on the black market. There everyone is forced to trade on the black market. I traveled around with an acting troupe and they wrote articles about me in *Pravda*. But there was never enough to eat, so as soon as I came to a town, I immediately went off to sell something. On one corner they'd be sticking up posters with my picture on them, and on another I, the famous actor, would stand with a beggar's outstretched hand, trading a piece of soap or an undershirt or whatever else I could scrounge. In Stalin's state, everything is merchandise. I had a woman there and she decided to take up with someone else. She left behind a nightdress, so I immediately went off to sell it. I was standing in the marketplace when she passed by with her new lover boy, so I showed her the nightdress and I egged her on: Go on, Comrade, buy this pretty ball gown, live a little. That's the socialist fatherland for you. I would come to a town with my troupe and there was nowhere to spend the night, so we all lay down on the stage and covered ourselves with the backdrop. I've even slept in the streets during winter. During the war there was a shortage of everything except lice. Lice were the only things the Five-Year Plan produced in abundance.''

Anna bit her lip to stop herself from laughing out loud. ''Really, the things you say.''

''I'm telling you the truth, and the truth is comical. That's why I'm a comedian. What happened between the two of you? Why's she collecting her paraphernalia?''

Luria grimaced. ''She changes her men every few years. It's a sort of principle with her.''

''I beg you both, don't speak about me. If that's what you want to do, I'm leaving. I'll take my things some other time.''

''What did I say? Pack everything you can, otherwise they'll steal it all out of here. I can't be held responsible.''

''Do people steal here as well?'' asked Yasha Kotik. ''Over there they steal everything. Everyone steals, except Comrade Stalin, because he's God and God doesn't need to steal, He can just take what He wants. In Russia I was also a merchant and a bookkeeper. Over there everything has to be written down. But where are we supposed to write if there's no paper? I kept my accounts in a volume of Mayakovsky's poems. He composes short lines, so he leaves wide margins. I had to steal myself now and then, otherwise I'd've died of hunger, so as time went on I tore out pages and threw them away. Then the controller came to look over my accounts, and as bad luck would have it, he knew all Mayakovsky's poems by heart. Hey, Comrade, he says, something doesn't tally here. That's when I decided that in the future I'd do all my bookkeeping in the works of Demyan Bedny.''

''You're lying,'' Anna called out.

''What? Not at all. Why tell lies when over there every single day life presents you with situations no liar could ever dream up? Here, I'll give you an example. Over there I had a friend, a Yiddish writer. In Russia I knew all the Yiddish writers. He had no talent, but that's no disadvantage over there. All you need is to praise Stalin. Once we were talking, and he suddenly said, Ai, this is all so boring for me. I'd give half my life to be able to get away from here. The moment he said it, I thought, Aha, I'll have to go to the NKVD immediately, because if I don't inform against him, he could inform against me. He would report that I heard counter-revolutionary talk and kept quiet about it. You can never tell. Perhaps he was an agent provocateur. I gave him a look as if to say, What did you get out of this? We shook hands, and I went straight to the NKVD. As I got to the door, I saw my friendly little songbird, who had arrived already. He'd gone by another route. We wasted half a day waiting there, and then we informed against each other. Afterward we went home together.''

''Why did they let him go?''

''They maintained he was testing me. As soon as one informs against another, then everything's kosher.''

Stanislaw Luria rubbed his forehead. ''A gem of a country. But if you're going to Hollywood, take my advice and don't tell any of these stories there. The whole of Hollywood is Red. Three-quarters of the writers here are also Red. If you speak a word against Stalin's state here, you'll be totally ostracized.''

''Here as well?''

''Here as well.''

''That's useful to know. I'll just flip the coin. I'll tell them that the workers there never had it so good. It's just as my grandmother used to say: This world lives out the lies they cook up in the World to Come.''

''We'll have to wait and see what's in the World to Come,'' Luria replied.

''I've already been there,'' said Kotik, addressing both Luria and no one in particular. ''During the war I caught typhus and had a temperature of 110. Then my temperature went down to 94, and I was delirious all the time. There weren't enough beds in the hospital, so they laid me down on straw in the corridor. The nurses kept spraying antiseptic over us. They thought I was a goner and were getting ready to drag me off to the morgue, but I suddenly opened my eyes. And what was the first thing I saw? A pair of women's underpants. Those pants revived me. That sight immediately brought me back from that world to this one. Now, why are you making a fool of yourself, Anna? You married a respectable man and have a beautiful apartment in New York—why are you packing your bundle again? In Russia, when people get divorced they still go on living in the same apartment. She takes in another husband, and he takes in another wife, then both wives come home from work at night and bitch over the pots—my pot, your pot, my husband, your husband. I think it's a bad thing—Where are you dragging your bags to now?''

''She's going to a man who deals in stocks on Wall Street,'' Luria answered. ''She's become an American. There's only one love here—love of the dollar.''

Anna was about to answer back when Kotik interrupted her.

"Wall Street? I imagined it to be something quite different from what it is. In Russia they keep on saying that all the world's troubles start there. Even when a woman turns tramp, it's Wall Street that's to blame. And when I get here, what do I see? A narrow little street like the ghetto in Rome, and it certainly doesn't look as if it's chock-full of money from cellar to attic. On the ship coming here, I met a Jewish man from New Rochelle—that's some small town near New York. He started telling me his life story—he's got a son and a daughter. He's quite happy with his son, but he's very unhappy with his daughter. So why aren't you happy with your daughter? Because she married a rabbi. So I say, but then you'll go straight to Paradise and eat the tail of Leviathan forever. So he says, That's fine in Europe, but not in America. Then he tells me he's a Mason. So what's a Mason? I ask. So he says, You don't know what a Mason is? The masons carried the stones to build the Temple in Jerusalem. So I ask him, To what temple are you carrying stones? He says, You're still a complete greenhorn. It's good for business. Here, he says, I've taken out insurance on my wife for fifty thousand dollars, and what do I need it for? She's an old bag. But I need it for business."

Anna shrugged her shoulders. "How does that relate to us?"

"What? I've forgotten. That's what happens to me—my mind wanders. I start speaking about something and halfway through I forget why I started. Oh yes—what's the sense of running from one man to another? Once upon a time I also used to believe that every skirt was different; now I know they're all the same. Now I could be a faithful husband, but no one needs my fidelity."

"You'll find someone in Hollywood," Anna remarked.

"Wait, let me help you close that suitcase. In Hollywood they want to cast me as a Russian, but all I speak is pidgin Russian. I'm being frank now. I've got no taste for Hollywood *grandes dames*. What I need is a wife who'll darn my socks. Tell me, *Panie* Luria, can she darn socks?"

"She not only can't, but she won't. She's become a Hollywood prima donna herself."

"In Russia women have learned to look after themselves. All the time a broad is lying in bed with you, she's checking that you're not deviating from the Party line. In the morning a doll like that gets up, kisses you on the mouth, and then goes straight off to the NKVD to give them a full report about you. If they haven't packed you into the cooler during the course of the day, the same bitch arrives back safe that very night and starts bellyaching: Oh, *golubchik,* I've had such a hard day! You don't know how I've had to run around! My feet hurt! And then she kisses you so tenderly that you turn to jelly. Afterward, in bed, the cunning little vixen starts wheedling, *Golubchik,* what did you think of Comrade Stalin's latest speech? Then you cuddle up close to her and you say, There's never been a speech like that in the whole history of oratory! It was brighter than the sun! Sweeter than honey! More deadly than poison to the capitalists! Correct, absolutely correct down to the smallest detail! Tomorrow, my lovely, you'll be able to rest your little feet. Meanwhile, give me your mouth.''

Anna turned red. ''You haven't changed.''

''Oh, I have, my dear. I'm not at all the same. The reality of Russia has far outstripped Yasha Kotik—very far indeed!''

11

Mrs. Clark stood at her dentist's chair drilling a patient's tooth. The face of the patient—a Russian Orthodox priest—contorted in pain, but the decay had to be stopped. Mrs. Clark had been practicing for years, yet having to drill into someone else's teeth still made her shudder. Until losing her own teeth, she had suffered more than enough herself. She knew personally all about toothache, exposed nerves, maddening pain. But what could one do? Human beings had to suffer. If one escaped small sufferings, one would have to endure great ones. She drilled, then stopped, drilled again, and stopped again. Each time the priest, a large, portly man with long hair, released a sigh like air escaping from a barrel. Mrs. Clark was astonished at herself. Her mother had slaughtered cattle in Bukovina and she, formerly Chaye Sarah, now Henrietta, was drilling into the molar of a priest on Fifty-seventh Street in New York. At least save rather than slaughter, she thought, even though of course one could not in reality slaughter anything, neither man nor beast. The soul—even theosophical books used the word "soul"—soon seeks out another body, another garment. All true, but why did I let myself get involved in this scheme? Am I really doing it only out of the goodness of my heart? Or do I get some other kind of pleasure as well? Was it compassion? Was it love? And wouldn't that young woman at some time or other ruin everything? She might expose me. They could even arrest me. Someone like that could blackmail me whenever she wanted to. At least I have one good intention. I want to save a life. Not one, but two. Am I feeding them lies? As long as people refuse to see the truth, one has to show them its reflection. In the old days, when a child at school didn't want to learn the alphabet, the assistant teacher would surreptitiously throw down a piece of cake, and then they'd all say that an angel had brought it. Could one really call that fraud or deception? Back then, pious Jews believed both in Torah and in angels, but foolish children had to be guided with little pieces of cake.

The priest yelled, and Mrs. Clark called out, "That was the last time! No more! No more!"

It was now a quarter to six. She had no more patients. In the waiting room sat Justina Kohn, who had brought a satchel with her. Into the priest's mouth Mrs. Clark wedged an instrument that sucked up the saliva; she glanced out the window. The pane of glass in the building opposite shone like a precious stone set in concrete. Below, crowds of women clustered in front of the shop windows, wearing almost the same clothes as those on display there. From high above, the mannequins in the windows seemed more alive than those who were gaping at them. The cars looked as small and innocent as toys, and a Fifth Avenue bus threaded its way among them like a big worm among smaller worms. Mrs. Clark opened the door into the waiting room slightly. Justina Kohn gave her a knowing wink. That other woman, Mrs. Kurtz, the dental technician, had been far more subtle and refined. She never winked, never played idle tricks. But Justina Kohn was an actress and spoke beautiful Polish. She also knew Yiddish, having left Warsaw in 1939. She evidently enjoyed the whole business, because there was no Polish theater here in New York and an actress had to act. Now she played the part of an edgy patient to perfection, sitting with her legs crossed, a cigarette in her mouth, a magazine on her knee, tense and expectant, as if she could barely wait for her aching tooth to be attended to. Her face, with its pointy chin and long nose, was heavily made up. She had the round eyes of a bird. Her hair was dyed platinum blond. Her fingernails were sharp, pointed, and blood-red.

The priest prepared to leave. Although the sky was perfectly clear outside, he had an umbrella standing in a corner which he picked up as he put a fur hat on his shaggy head. He gave Mrs. Clark a big, hot hand, and even nodded to Justina Kohn as well. Before he left, he touched both his cheeks, as if to make sure he had all his teeth.

Mrs. Clark smiled. "A genuine Russian—with one hundred percent Russian blood. He stems from somewhere in Siberia."

Justina Kohn winked. "Big as a bear!"

"And he has a wife and children."

"Certainly. They're allowed to have wives. Only Catholic priests have to live in celibacy. All the same, each of them has a housekeeper, and what they do when they put out the lights only Jesus knows."

Mrs. Clark made a gesture of irritation. She disliked hearing evil spoken of anyone, let alone of a religious man, God's servant. According to Mrs. Clark's belief system, all faiths served the same God. The difference lay only in external ceremonies, not in essential realities. Mrs. Clark herself had long outgrown all dogmas. She regarded herself as neither Jewish nor Christian. She accepted all revelation: God had spoken to His beloved servants in all languages, and in all forms. She paused a moment and then said, "We'll have supper together in a restaurant and discuss all the details there. The main thing is not to let them touch the body too much, because that spoils everything. One touch, one breath, is enough. Have you got soft slippers?"

"I've got everything."

"If you haven't, I'll provide them. It's warm in my apartment, so you could be naked, but thin pants will be all right. When you say something, speak softly so they can hear you only indistinctly. A word, a whisper, a caress of the face will suffice. Wash off your rouge and lipstick—there shouldn't be any trace of it. The chief thing is to convey a feeling of love, devotion, warmth. That's all they need. Remember that you'll have to represent two women—Sonia and Edzhe. Sonia was the name of Mrs. Luria, Edzhe the name of Mrs. Shrage. Each has to have a different voice and above all a completely different personality. Also guard against the slightest suggestion of anything sexual. When we free ourselves of our bodies, all our bodily desires cease. In women these desires cease sooner than in men, and that in itself is proof that women are higher on the ladder of spiritual evolution. I myself, for instance, can still love very deeply, but anything physical disgusts me."

"Oh, how I envy you!"

"When you're my age, you'll feel the same way."

"It often seems to me that I'll need a man even in the grave."

And Miss Kohn's birdlike eyes filled with mirth as she gave a sly smile, revealing a mouthful of widely spaced teeth. Mrs. Clark was exceptionally sensitive to teeth and Miss Kohn's did not please her. Few in number, they were broad and too sharp like those of some animal. Her arms were too long for a person of her height, and her waist was extraordinarily narrow. To Mrs. Clark it seemed as if this young woman was supported on bed-springs. She even disapproved of her satchel. The disturbing thought ran through her mind that thieves and shoplifters carried satchels like that. Mrs. Clark was shocked by all these negative thoughts. She knew that if this undertaking was to succeed, those who took part in it had to be motivated by the best intentions. Consequently she prepared herself with love, as it were, speaking half to herself and half to Justina Kohn: "Well, in karma, everything has its purpose—if it did not, what need would there be for karma? Maturation and fruition must take place. None of our deeds is lost; they go into a general treasury, so to speak, and create rose-colored light or stygian shadows in the sphere where they fall, all according to the worth or waste of those deeds. We each make our own contribution, and each of our roles is important."

"What? Yes."

"You need to know these things. They might ask questions. To enter into long discussions with them is impossible. But drop a word here and there. The dominating thought must be that everything is good and full of mercy. That is nothing but the truth. But it takes a long time before we reach it, and whether we stride toward it on the highway or stumble upon it along the byways, the primary concern is that the soul must fulfill its mission."

"Don't worry, Mrs. Clark, I can be Sonia, Edzhe, and six other women as well. I'll be a spook from Spooksville. They'll be one hundred percent convinced that they're talking to their wives in the next world."

"Don't laugh, my dear, don't laugh. We are all spirits. This world is also the next world. When you're my age, you'll understand this."

2

After supper, Henrietta gave Justina the key. Miss Kohn had already visited the apartment and knew all its secrets. It had two entrances and two bathrooms. All Justina had to do was enter quietly through the back door, lock herself in the second bathroom, undress, and wait for the prearranged signal—the cry that Mrs. Clark would let out in the middle of her trance. Henrietta had calculated that from beginning to end the entire presentation—entering, undressing, appearing, dressing, and departing—would not take Justina more than an hour. In payment for her services, Justina had received dental treatment worth at least a hundred dollars, in addition to supper and fare for two taxis, one there and one home. Justina was not scheduled to enter until ten o'clock, and since Macy's happened to be open that night until nine, after supper Miss Kohn went off to Thirty-fourth Street to buy a sweater for herself.

Riding home in a taxi, Mrs. Clark closed her eyes. She had conducted séances of this kind dozens of times, but each gave her fresh cause for fear, especially when a new person was involved. Mentally, she compared herself to a theater director on opening night. Although she had all manner of self-justification, her conscience was never clear. True, she had never derived any material gain from her deceptions. On the contrary, these performances always cost her money, inconvenience, and anxiety. There was always the danger that something would go wrong and she would be exposed to disgrace and derision. Who knows? She might even render herself liable to prosecution. The judges were very severe on mediums although, as God alone knew, they did little enough harm. But Mrs. Clark could not bring herself to give it up.

Her lot in life had been continually to encounter people who were weak, unhappy, lost; all of them had need of help. Just as she knew from personal experience the agony of those whose teeth she drilled, so she understood the sorrows, the doubts, the anguish of people who had lost those closest to them and were seeking some contact, some sign that their dear ones and their love were still alive somewhere. There had been times when she had attempted to call up the spirits in an honest way, through a real trance, but the successes had been few and far between. As she grew older, it became more difficult for her to concentrate, to free herself of all extraneous thoughts, to unite herself with the transcendental powers. But in addition, the older she grew, the more she craved this kind of presentation herself. God in heaven, this was her only pleasure in life! It was her sex, her liquor, her opium. Often she fell into a genuine trance or a state of autohypnosis. Both waking and dreaming, she experienced manifestations: she saw faces, lights, figures. Truth and illusion were so muddled that she herself no longer knew where one began and the other ended. Moreover, she had personally never abandoned hope of making contact with Edwin, her late husband, and with her deceased parents, sisters, brothers. As soon as she shut her eyes, they all appeared to her in visions, alive in body and so vivid and immediate that it seemed as if they had been in hiding the whole time, awaiting the proper moment to reveal themselves.

The taxi stopped at a traffic light and Henrietta Clark emitted a sigh. She was no longer young—she was sixty-five years old—but it was at this age that she had acquired an energy she had never known before. Strength and creativity surged within her. She wanted to do everything at once: to paint, to carve, to write, to play the piano—all automatically, in a trance. She longed to comfort people, to help them, to give them fresh hope, new faith in God, in spirit, in the human role in Creation. She never slept more than four hours a night, often not even that, and her sleep itself was full of divine dramas, crowded with mysteries that one could only sense, not comprehend, and certainly not describe. Journals were sent to her, but they lay unopened; books on the occult arrived at her home, but she had no time to read them. She was invited to all sorts of symposiums by eminent psychic researchers, but she had been unwilling to participate in even a fraction of them.

During the earliest years of Henrietta's close association with Professor Shrage, she had hoped that at last she had acquired a companion, a path-finder, a spiritual father. He was no insignificant person, this David Shrage! His name was mentioned with respect in all the leading journals devoted to psychic research. He had been invited to give lectures at Duke University. He received letters from the British Society for Psychic Research. He corresponded with the great and famous. But all this notwithstanding, he had greatly disappointed her. Instead of growing closer to her, he had withdrawn more and more into himself, had stopped believing in her "messages," and almost openly derided her paintings, her melodies. He was actually her enemy. While she supported him, helped him, even gave him massages to ease his arthritis, he had actually—God forgive him—made physical advances, as if they had both been young. Everything was lost, he had swept their friendship into the gutter. But she could not drive him out and cut off all contact with him. She knew perfectly well that he would perish without her. Here in America he had neither money nor relatives. He was half-blind. To throw out such a person meant sentencing him to death. Besides, it was good to come home at night and find a man waiting for her, not just a being with nose and eyes and ears but a deeply learned man, a profound thinker, one of the greatest contemporary psychic seekers and researchers, whom only later generations would appreciate. Even when a man like him turned sour, fell into intolerance, captiousness, and rebellion, he was still infinitely preferable to the rationalists, the practical-minded, the indifferent, those who did not even wish to consider that beyond the corporeal there exist ethereal, astral worlds of light, a vast spiritual ocean. At the very least, it was never boring with such a person.

The taxi drew up outside her apartment and Henrietta paid the fare, tipping the driver a quarter. Let him have a glass of brandy or whatever he was in the mood for. Getting out was not easy for her. Her body was heavy. She had varicose veins in her legs from standing all day long. But inside her the energy bubbled up, rippled, and overflowed. She went upstairs and unlocked the door. Thank God, the day's work was over. From now until tomorrow morning she could lead her own life.

She switched on the light and hung her coat in the closet. She had ordered food by telephone. Neither she nor the professor ate meat, making their meals instead from cheese, nuts, fruit, vegetables, and all sorts of cereals and crackers from a "health-food store." But why deny it? When the professor was invited to dine with Boris Makaver, he did eat meat. At least neither meat nor fish ever sullied her home, however. Mrs. Clark was firmly convinced that his eating meat was responsible for Professor Shrage's growing ever more frail and depressed. How could one be healthy when one ate meat and absorbed dead protoplasm, the juices and blood of lowly creatures? How could one hope for God's grace when one helped to kill the living and deprived souls of their bodies? Personally Henrietta even believed that one should stop eating cheese, milk, and eggs as well. She regarded herself as no more than a semi-vegetarian, because indirectly she was assisting the ritual slaughterers, the butchers. Perhaps it was for this reason that she was treated so illiberally by the heavenly powers, and was shown so little divine light.

3

Henrietta sat at the kitchen table watching Professor Shrage eat his supper. But for her meal this evening with Justina, she would have returned home hungry, as always. He, on the other hand, was never hungry, never thirsty. She had put out a piece of toast for him, but it still lay there. She had made him a set of dentures, but he kept them in a drawer. He couldn't even finish a glass of tea. He took tiny, intermittent sips and barely got down half a glassful. He kept tugging at his little white beard and sighing.

Mrs. Clark observed, "Tonight you'll see something. I feel it. While I was sitting in the taxi, I could sense Mudgy's presence."

Mudgy was Mrs. Clark's "control," her spirit guide.

The professor raised his eyebrows. "Well."

"I know you don't believe," Henrietta began, speaking half with compassion and half in bitterness, "but Pharaoh also refused to believe, even when Moses transformed his rod into a serpent before Pharaoh's eyes."

"Hmmm."

"I'll tell you one thing: if Edzhe does manifest herself to you, remember that it will be a spirit, not a body. Don't be too demanding. Don't ask too many questions. Every moment a spirit spends in earthly revelation saps my strength. At my age, a very deep trance is extremely stressful. Don't behave immoderately."

The professor shook himself. "In what language should I speak to her?"

"Speak your own language. What language did you speak together?"

"Polish."

"So speak Polish."

The professor doubled over as though he had a sudden cramp in his stomach. Full of misgivings, he cast a sidelong glance at Henrietta. Could a spirit possibly materialize in a manner that enabled it to resume its former body? Was Henrietta really possessed of such powers? Had it truly been ordained that in his old age, sunk in the deepest mire of doubt, he should be vouchsafed a glimmer of faith?

Over the years, Henrietta had procrastinated. She had made promises she had failed to keep, passed on "messages" full of contradictions, painted pictures which bore no resemblance to anybody or anything he knew. Apart from the few occasions on which her niece had manifested herself, Henrietta had never succeeded in summoning up any other forms. She always required that the séance take place in complete darkness. She refused to permit even a red light to burn. The trumpet, the piano that played by itself, the hands that hovered in the air were all legerdemain which had been exposed many times. Professor Shrage had already as good as made his peace with the thought that all mediums were liars. If they succeeded so much as once, the truth was nevertheless lost in falsehood. The professor had debunked even the eminent Kluski, whose soul was now with God. Except for Mrs. Leonora Piper, all of them had been out-and-out cheats, even Paladino, even the Fox sisters, Catherine and Margaret, even the great Haum. The photographs supposedly taken of spirits were almost all cheap forgeries. The so-called ectoplasm consisted of canvas, paper, rubber. Over the last few years the professor had devoted himself exclusively to spontaneous occurrences: dreams that came true, instances of telepathy, clairvoyance, phantoms of the living. He took particular interest in Shackleton's card readings as well as in the miracles of Keysey, the wonder-doctor, and Henry Gross, the "water prophet."

And now suddenly, in the teeth of all her past failures, Henrietta was boasting of having acquired fresh extrasensory powers. She would bring Edzhe to him. She had even promised Stanislaw Luria that she would call up his dead wife, Sonia, who had been burned somewhere in Hitler's lime pits. Luria himself would be arriving very soon.

We'll see, we'll see, something within the professor murmured. Nobody could substitute an impersonator for Edzhe and deceive me. That will be the final test.

Although the professor had hardly eaten anything, he had stomach cramps, was nauseous, and had several times felt a sharp pain across his heart. I hope I don't die now—let me at least survive this night! the professor prayed. From under his eyebrows he glanced furtively at Henrietta. He knew her, he thought, yet she remained a stranger to him. He had never been able to understand her thought processes, her emotions, her intentions. Her refinement was mixed with coarseness, her devotion with egoism. In the middle of a discussion about the highest matters, she suddenly showed intense interest in bargains to be had at the department stores. She owned real estate somewhere, bought stocks on Wall Street, was continually badgering the landlord to paint the walls, to install a new gas stove, to replace the refrigerator. She even hurried off to see mindless shows at the movies and listened to all sorts of frivolous blather on the radio. How could these earthly inclinations possibly coexist harmoniously with extraordinary, supramundane powers? This was one of the countless riddles the professor was unable to solve.

But on the other hand it somehow fitted together. All mediums, all those whom Nature had gifted with sensitivity, were more or less the same. Weren't the great artists also like this? This was typical of human nature, in which greatness kept close company with pettiness. The Cabalists were right when they maintained that this world was a world of evil spirits. Because this was a world of contamination, purity had no value; the whole mission of the human species was to scrabble for pearls in the dirt. We would only have virtue undefiled in the World to Come—soon, if God wills it.

"It's already half-past eight. When was Mr. Luria supposed to come?" Henrietta asked.

Professor Shrage roused himself as though he had been dozing and been startled awake. "He should be here soon."

"Perhaps he's frightened? There are many such people—they very much want the experience, but they have second thoughts at the last moment. They're afraid to look the truth in the face."

"He said he would come."

"Well, if he comes, he comes. Sit next to him and make sure he doesn't do something foolish. Don't let him speak too much, or try to grasp or embrace her. That would be dangerous both for himself and for me—I might die of exhaustion. All of it will derive from my strength alone."

"I'll tell him."

"People simply don't understand that there's a vast difference between flesh and spirit," Mrs. Clark observed with some bitterness. "One cannot embrace a spirit—an astral body is not flesh and blood. It's an immensely difficult undertaking for them to reveal themselves. They get permission only for a minute or two, and that only in the rarest instances. A powerful barrier separates Here from There, and only occasionally does a fissure open in the wall. There are some madmen who try to switch on a lamp or use a flashlight in the middle of a séance. They think they're being clever, but they're actually putting themselves in grave danger, and it's certain death for the medium. So be forewarned, and keep an eye on him as well. You'll both sit on the sofa, and don't let him get up. Hold on to his arm. If he wants to touch her, one hand is enough. If he asks permission to break these rules, give me a signal and I'll stop him in good time."

"You told him all this the last time."

"Yes, but there are some people who never listen. If your Warsaw friend is undisciplined, I categorically refuse to have him in my house."

Just as Mrs. Clark had issued her ultimatum, there was a ring at the front door. It was Stanislaw Luria.

4

Mrs. Clark rose and opened the door, and he stood before her, short, stocky, wearing an old-fashioned European fur coat, his eyes overhung by bushy eyebrows. What a lumbering brute, thought Henrietta. I only hope he doesn't disrupt anything! But she said aloud, "You're a little late, Mr. Luria. But then it's never too late to see the truth."

"It's only ten to nine."

"Come in. Take off your galoshes. Hang your fur coat here, on the hall stand. Perhaps you would like some supper?"

"No, thank you. I've eaten."

"It's not good to imbibe liquor before a séance, but you can take a small drink if you wish."

"No, thank you."

"Professor, here's Mr. Luria. Well, both of you, come with me into the living room."

The professor rose from the kitchen table and went out into the hallway.

"Good evening, good evening!" Professor Shrage extended a diminutive hand, which Luria took in his great paw. Normally Luria's hand was warm, but tonight it was cold and damp.

"Ah, how cold your hand is!"

"There's a frost outside," Luria responded defensively.

The living room had no door but was entered through an archway that led in from the hall. Inside, a single floor lamp glowed. A Ouija board occupied most of a small table. All the walls were covered with Mrs. Clark's paintings. On a variety of pedestals stood sculptures in plaster, clay, and wood—symbolic forms without faces, or at most with mere suggestions of features. The sofa was covered in black velvet but was now rather shabby—the fabric was even torn in places. Until recently, Henrietta had kept a Persian cat that over the years had systematically ruined all the upholstered furniture. A few weeks earlier, this cat had "passed over to the other side," as Henrietta expressed it, and there had already been consoling messages from it. Even the professor imagined that he often heard it miaowing or clawing the sofa or scratching at the door of his room. But was it really possible that the astral body of a cat could perform such feline mischief?

"Both of you sit here," said Mrs. Clark, pointing to the sofa. "During the séance, don't get up, because you'll break my contact that way. A thread of ectoplasm stretches directly from my nostrils to the forms which reveal themselves. But assuming that all goes well, you may question and touch the beloved person. I never guarantee anything to anyone. Everything depends on a thousand circumstances. Remember that light is completely destructive, not only for the success of the undertaking, but also for me and for you. As long as the séance lasts, don't try to light a match or anything else. If you have doubts and want to restrict the movements of my body, I'll sit next to you. If you wish, you may hold my hands and wrap your legs around mine, but do it gently, Mr. Luria, because you have a pair of great big heavy legs and mine are small and weak. All you have to do is make sure that I'm sitting next to you and not playing any of those tricks practiced by fake mediums. Is that understood?''

"Yes," said Luria hoarsely.

"I must warn you against something else. There are people who become terrified and hysterical at a manifestation. That's bad and foolish. Those who have crossed over are in a Sphere of Mercy, and they will do no harm. Of course, there are evil spirits as well, like poltergeists, but even they are prohibited from doing any serious mischief. We certainly need not fear those who in this life were dear and precious to us. They pray and intercede on our behalf. A thick wall separates Here from There, but when they are permitted for a brief while to make contact, there is absolutely no cause for any fear. All the spirits want is love and sympathy—not love of the body, of course, only love of the soul. If you wish to touch your beloved wives, do so, but with dignity, with a gentle caress or a kiss. Why enfold with your rough hands that which has no earthly substance and is composed of otherworldly matter? Have you understood me, Mr. Luria?''

"Yes, yes."

Aha, he's already paralyzed with fear, Mrs. Clark noted mentally. She was expert in situations like these. Sitting tense and trembling, Luria could hardly speak. May he be spared a heart attack! Mrs. Clark quickly besought the higher powers, even as she grew intensely attentive. She had prepared everything in such a way that they would not hear the back door opening; she had oiled the keyhole and the door hinges, and laid double carpets along the route to the second bathroom. She herself was adept at detecting the slightest rustle, since she could not begin the séance until the Polish actress had arrived. One could never be certain—some accident might befall either the taxi or Justina.

Mrs. Clark stole a glance at her wristwatch and said, "Don't be startled if I seem to have fallen into a faint, or even if I seem to have died. I fall into a trance, but my controller makes me sleep deeply before I can be released. There's not the slightest need for alarm. Sometimes I start shouting in my trance, but do not let that disturb you. The most important thing is to ensure that I remain seated next to you and that I do not attempt to stretch out a hand or a foot, as the charlatans always do. I've attended enough séances to be able to distinguish between truth and falsehood. My rule of thumb is that whenever a medium expects to receive money or gifts, one cannot trust her, because those who genuinely want to serve others require no recompense of any kind. Their highest reward comes when they are the humble instruments who awaken in their sisters and brothers new hope, new faith, new joy. Sometimes the telephone rings in the middle of a séance. Leave it. The same applies if anyone comes to the door. A séance is not a game that can be interrupted.''

With startling suddenness, Mrs. Clark rushed over to the floor lamp, switched it off, and immediately started stamping her feet and singing a hymn in a shrill, loud voice like a failed opera soprano. She had heard the back door open. Coming over to the sofa, she gave her orders: "Move apart. I'll sit between you. Hold my hands. If you can, Mr. Luria, assist me with the singing, although it's not absolutely necessary. Here's my hand. Ah, your hand is ice-cold. But never mind, you'll warm it in mine. I repeat, there's absolutely no reason for fear or disquiet. I feel that Mudgy will soon arrive. I'll fall into a trance. Ah, my head is already starting to get heavy. Don't be surprised if my voice changes. God Almighty, help me! Help us! Help us to make contact with those who watch over us with the highest love. Help us, God, to be united for a little while with the holy souls, the holy martyrs who sacrificed their lives for you. Help us, God, accept our prayer. Illuminate us with your light, immerse us in your radiance, in your cosmic consciousness, with your Absolute Being, with the searching spirits of your throne, with the purity of cherubim and ser- aphim, with the luster of Saturn and Latona, Apollo and Artemis, Vulcan and Venus. God of Moses, God of the Prophets, God of Jesus Christ the Redeemer, God of heaven and earth, of Paradise and Purgatory—''

And suddenly Mrs. Clark burst into song:

> An old bent man, worn out and frail,
> Came back from seeking the Holy Grail;
> Little he recked of his earldom's loss,
> No more on his surcoat was blazoned the Cross,
> But deep in his heart the sign he wore,
> The badge of the suffering and the poor.

After the last word, Henrietta Clark snorted noisily and groaned loudly. The trance had begun.

5

Professor Shrage asked the questions and Mrs. Clark, in the person of Mudgy, answered. A masculine voice in another accent spoke from Henrietta's mouth. Stanislaw Luria listened attentively. Mrs. Clark herself spoke like a Bostonian, but Mudgy's inflection and pronunciation were Indian or South American. He spoke in truncated sentences. Luria clutched Mrs. Clark's hand, which was warm, even hot, but his own hand remained ice-cold. The coldness seemed to spread from somewhere deep within him, from a field of inner frozenness.

The professor spoke. In broken English, he asked, "Are any of our dear ones here?"

"I see a woman," said the voice. "Middle-aged—no, younger. A woman of thirty-five or -six. Fair—no, dark. A motherly woman, a little plump, with a rather high bosom. She is telling me her name, but I can't hear it distinctly. Something like Runya, Donya. No, Sonia. Yes, Sonia. She passed over in 1942—no, 1943. She is here together with her children. Two children. One a girl and the other also a girl. Or is it a boy? Yes, a boy. Sonia says she is happy. She has met and been united with her parents and all the other members of her family. The last agonies of the body have been completely erased from memory. Sonia says she longs for her husband, Stanislaw Luria, and watches carefully over him. She and the other souls have witnessed and forgiven everything. But the woman to whom he has at present joined himself is not worthy of him. She will not and cannot be a helpmate to him. She is too egotistical. Sonia says she is not jealous—in the other world there is no envy of any kind. But that woman is not for him. It is good that he has separated from her. At the moment it causes him some distress, but later he will free himself of her malign influence, and then he will see clearly.

"Sonia says the children speak every day about their father. They have grown up and they are studying—not in a school as on earth but tele-pathically: the lessons of the teachers are transmitted directly to the pupils. The medium of communication is thought, and thoughts above all are savored. They are eaten. They are drunk. They serve as garments. Sonia says that life in the Upper World is easier, more comfortable, and more positive. Most important of all, there is no time and it is not wasted on unnecessary activities. Although the sun does not shine, there is perpetual light—a sort of eternal sunset, a purple twilight accompanied by music unheard and unknown on earth, a pure, inviolable harmony.

"Sonia says she will make every effort to reveal herself, but she desires her husband to remain calm. His agitation disturbs her. He must breathe evenly and should not weep. Tears are unnecessary, being merely salt water, a wholly corporeal fluid. In the Upper World, neither laughter nor tears are known—only unalloyed delight has dominion. Sonia says that she and the children are not yet completely settled, since changes occur regularly. Souls of older arrivals are elevated to higher levels and transported to other spheres, while new souls take their places. Nevertheless, a few souls with pedagogical skills are left behind to teach the new arrivals, some of whom are so callow and confused they do not even comprehend that they have crossed over and must be instructed in everything from the beginning. But since all are willing to learn, none remain behind for long. Sonia says that here she has experienced enormous spiritual development, and she often conducts conversations with the children on elevated philosophical and theological subjects.

"Here on high, Sonia says, faith is not sectarian: Jews, Protestants, Catholics, Buddhists, and Muslims all gather joyfully together to discuss common problems. Here Sonia has made the acquaintance of Rabindranath Tagore, and that of several younger philosophers who perished in the Second World War. She reveals that Bertrand Russell continues to make profound errors, and that all his theories are false. Einstein, too, has erred in his calculations, and the atomic bomb has done incalculable harm. In general, Sonia discloses, the process of inner consolidation in the Upper World is relaxing somewhat, as most of the Masters of the Hierarchy withdraw their supervision from the Ashram of Shambhala and orient themselves more toward humanity. At the same time, a vigorous minority of the Masters involve themselves in the Ashram of Sanat Kumara. In other words, activities which until recently were the responsibility of the united Ashrams have now been taken over by a number of Masters."

Suddenly the voice cried out, "She comes! She comes! Sonia reveals herself! Bright spirit!"

Stanislaw Luria let go of Henrietta's hand and tore himself away as though to flee, but Henrietta grabbed his hand back and pressed her shoe on his. For a long while both sat silent in the darkness. Luria moaned and writhed, doubled up like someone suffering agonizing cramps. With his bony hand the professor squeezed Henrietta's wrist so hard that she could barely keep from crying out in pain. Accompanied by a succession of light rustling sounds, quiet footsteps were heard approaching. A white figure materialized, seemingly out of nothing, and stood immobile in one spot, like a coherent pale haze in which the blurs of eye sockets were faintly discernible through the darkness. Henrietta gave two convulsive gasps and the figure came closer, murmuring in Polish: "*Staszku, kochanie moje.* Stash, my dear."

Stanislaw Luria was dead silent.

"*Staszku, to ja, Sonia.* Stash, it is I, Sonia," the figure urged gently.

Luria pressed himself farther back into the sofa, the dull clang of the springs testifying to his agitation.

"*Staszku, nie bój się. To ja, Sonia. Kocham cię. Tęskinę za tobą.* Stash, have no fear. It is I, Sonia. I love you. I long for you."

Luria let out the agonized cry of a mute frenziedly attempting to speak: "*Ty!* You!"

"*Tak, to ja, twoja wieczna żona.* Yes, it is I, your eternal wife."

The figure bent down toward him, caressed him, pressed its lips to his brow. Henrietta had worried needlessly that Stanislaw Luria might seize hold of the apparition, switch on the lights, do something reckless. He sat frozen with terror, merely emitting a breathless snort from time to time, as if he were sleeping while still wide awake. In the darkness, the professor clutched Henrietta's wrist and tried to work out what was happening here. Had she hired some impersonator who spoke Polish? But no one had been heard entering. And to what end would Henrietta engage in such chicanery? He found the strength to stretch out his free hand and tried to touch the manifestation, but it was too far away. He tried to rise, but his knees gave way under him, and Henrietta virtually crushed him into the corner of the sofa. Well, that's that—now I'll never find out the truth! Professor Shrage thought. If I can't do it now, I never will. It's too late. Too late. He did not often sweat, but his hand was now wet with perspiration. He shook violently—and the whole sofa jiggled with the fierce trembling that convulsed him.

Again he summoned his strength and asked, "*Panie* Luria, do you recognize your wife?"

Luria made no reply.

Feeling that he was expending the last of his strength, the professor made another effort: "*Gnädige Frau,* may I ask something?"

The figure made a movement of acquiescence.

"Does the honorable lady perhaps know my wife? Her name is Edzhe— Edzhe Shrage. She was murdered in 1943."

And the professor suddenly began to sob. Henrietta emitted a series of anguished sighs.

"Yes, I know her," the figure responded.

"Where is she?"

"In heaven. With me."

"A sign, a sign!" the professor gasped, himself astounded that he had thought it necessary to demand some proof.

"She will soon be here herself," the ethereal voice answered after a pause.

The figure was starting to glide backward when the soundlessness of its movements was broken by a discordant jar and a dull thump, the unmistakable sound of a human body bumping into a door or a wall. Henrietta began ululating like a somnambulist abruptly startled out of a sleepwalk. She began writhing, wrenching herself away from the two men who held her, shuffling and stamping her feet, emitting a piercing wail, and waking from her trance.

"Where am I? What happened?" she asked.

Stanislaw Luria could not answer. He was overcome by the appalling feeling that something had seized his heart and was squeezing it with all its might. He could not catch his breath and felt as if he were suffocating. The professor's hollow gums chattered.

"Where am I? What happened?" Henrietta repeated.

"Should I turn on the lights?" quavered the professor.

"No! No! God forbid!"

And Henrietta frantically started singing a new hymn at the top of her voice. Between one note and another she listened with the utmost attention. The bang she had heard earlier had been a catastrophe. It was something she had dreaded the whole evening. Who knew what that woman had done to herself? Henrietta was now completely at a loss about how to proceed: end the séance? fall into a trance again? She had made a grave error—she should never have torn herself out of her trance. She should have given that young woman a signal to come in again, this time in the role of Edzhe. But that bang had thrown things offtrack. The best thing would be for Justina to get dressed and leave, Henrietta thought, and deciding to resume her trance immediately, she gurgled and again held forth in Mudgy's masculine voice: "Edzhe cannot come tonight!" she called out.

"Why not?" demanded the professor fearfully.

"They have denied her permission. Not tonight. Not tonight. Another time. Very soon. But Edzhe sends greetings. Very warm greetings. Edzhe will now become better acquainted with Sonia. The tight circle of those assembled here will grow even tighter. Ever closer together. Now Sonia must leave. Leave.''

Henrietta spoke very loudly, both so that the clumsy hireling could hear in the bathroom and to drown out any possible sound that might emanate from there. Overwhelmed by bitterness and resentment, Henrietta wanted to weep. Justina ought never to have banged about so clumsily. She had more than enough time to withdraw slowly and not bump against the door like a thief! She was utterly useless! She was no actress—she was a block of wood! In her despair, Henrietta permitted herself a negative thought. Terrified that someone might turn on the lights, Henrietta began preaching sonorously in Mudgy's voice: "A great wave of inspiration is sweeping down. Divine evolution is commencing a new epoch. The Masters, the Sons of Wisdom, are descending. They will banish the Dragon and suffuse the world with Light. Many among them have wives and children. The Law of Reincarnation is eternal, eternal. Happy are those who serve the Divine. Happy are those who will live perpetually in the cycle of Great Consciousness, in the Holy Logos, in the radiance of Christ the Redeemer!''

For a moment Henrietta fell silent, listening intently. Was that woman still here? Had she gone? An extraordinary wave of fear, mingled with acute shame, broke over Henrietta. That young woman might steal something, God forbid!

No, I haven't any strength left for this, Henrietta decided. I've lived enough for others. I'm tired, tired. Enough, enough! Father in heaven, take me!

And Henrietta collapsed in a fit of weeping.

12

Every Passover Boris prepared a Seder, but this year, since Frieda had become his wife, he was determined to hold a Seder people would remember. Now there was the problem of whom to invite. In the past it was Anna who always asked the Four Questions, and Grein had always been a guest. Now those two had cut themselves off from their roots. Stanislaw Luria had also made it known that he would not attend. Boris had wanted to invite the painter, Jacob Anfang, but Frieda had suggested it was perhaps better not to do so. Only four possible guests remained: Dr. Halperin, now the host's brother-in-law, Professor Shrage, Dr. Margolin, and Boris's nephew Herman. Had Herman not been a Communist, Boris would have allowed him to ask the Four Questions, but as things were, the father of the feast did not propose to have a disciple of Stalin asking him anything.

So that he might have a few more people at his Seder, Boris invited Dr. Alswanger, the controversial scholar from Palestine. Dr. Halperin complained that it was a disgrace to sit at the same table with so pretentious a person. Dr. Margolin had also heard of Alswanger and decried him as a dilettante. But apart from the fact that Boris loved to hear learned people dispute and quarrel among themselves, Dr. Alswanger was completely lost and without friends in New York, and it was out of the question to deny him Jewish hospitality and companionship during a major festival.

Those who read the Yiddish press, as well as those who subscribed to the Hebrew and Anglo-Jewish journals, had heard now and again of Immanuel Alswanger. For a time he had been a professor at the Hebrew University on Mount Scopus, but as the result of some intrigue he had been forced out and had accused the ''Germans'' of taking over the university and discriminating against Polish Jews. He had also written some sort of biblical drama that had been well into rehearsal when there had been a last-minute hitch and the performance had been called off. The Middle East correspondent of an American Yiddish newspaper had published a report about the affair in New York, attributing this debacle to further intrigue, this time on the part of a clique of Hebrew writers. Starting over again, Dr. Alswanger had opened a sanatorium for the broken-spirited in Tel Aviv. He had practiced a bizarre combination of psychoanalysis and Hasidism, attempting to become a sort of modern-day wonder-working rabbi. But this sanatorium came to the same abortive end as all Dr. Alswanger's other undertakings. Some old spinster had publicly accused him of trying to seduce her and cheat her out of her money, Dr. Alswanger had responded by suing her for defamation, and the whole scandal had come to litigation. Although the court found in Dr. Alswanger's favor and awarded him damages, Alswanger's enemies used the opportunity to revile him in speech and in print, denouncing him as a charlatan, a fraud, and a thief. The sanatorium soon had to close and Dr. Alswanger was left deeply in debt. Having vowed to pay off everything he owed and to reopen his sanatorium, he had come to America in pursuit of the means to do so.

But bad luck dogged Alswanger in America, too. He traveled to the New World by ship, but his enemies' malicious postcards arrived ahead of him by airmail. Once in New York, he called a press conference, but no journalists bothered to show up. He paid for advertisements in the newspapers, but they were placed in inconspicuous places, adding insult to injury by abbreviating and misspelling his name. He made the acquaintance of Esther Hatelbach, a most interesting woman, a well-educated former teacher of distinguished family who lived in Brighton Beach. Dr. Alswanger, a widower, fell in love with her almost at their first meeting and there was already talk of their getting married when Esther suddenly announced that she was preparing to marry a certain Morris Plotkin, a wealthy former furrier.

Parting with Alswanger, Esther had told him, ''I'm very sorry, Dr. Alswanger, but I'm tired of spiritual people. With spirit alone, my dear doctor, one cannot pay the rent.''

Alswanger was forced to admit that this was undeniable. He had problems with his own rent. He was staying in a downtown hotel on Broadway which cost only three dollars a day, but when one had nothing, three dollars was a large sum. He was now looking for a furnished room in someone else's home which might cost him less, or perhaps he might get room and board in exchange for giving Hebrew lessons. Other than that, Dr. Alswanger devoted himself wholly to his system of psychoanalysis, carrying about with him letters and newspaper cuttings attesting to his having helped a great many neurotic people in Palestine for whom no other method had worked. His therapy consisted of studying aloud with the sick; they discussed traditional moral legends and tales and selected Hasidic writings, and he instructed them in techniques to build self-discipline and willpower. However, in the first place, as a tourist he was not permitted to take any gainful employment in America. In the second place, who knew of him here? He merely had a bad reputation. That Boris Makaver had generously invited him to his Seder had given Alswanger renewed hope. New possibilities opened up. Perhaps he might meet some rich and influential people there, or even a woman he found attractive. But one couldn't go to a Seder in America empty-handed, without some sort of gift. The welcome invitation demanded unwelcome expense.

Since Dr. Alswanger had a mane of black hair which he wore in the Polish style, his sideburns and mustache had to be trimmed, so he went to a barber for a shave and a haircut. His dinner suit was creased and had to be sent out for pressing after he had removed a spot on his right lapel with an entire bottle of stain remover especially purchased for the purpose. At a florist he bought a bouquet of roses for Madame Makaver, but he picked them up too early and had to keep them fresh in a glass of water in his wash basin. He had learned English in Palestine and had even read Oscar Wilde's *The Portrait of Dorian Gray* in the original, but here in New York he could never make himself understood. Consequently his stay in America had driven him into petty-mindedness and depression. He bumbled about, got lost, sweated, stammered, stared people in the face to make sure they were not laughing at him. On the eve of Passover the weather suddenly turned as stiflingly hot as if it were midsummer, and his suit hung on him like a dead weight. Nevertheless, at dusk he was finally ready to prepare for the Seder.

He took a hot bath in the bathroom down the hall, where someone had left a piece of soap, so he was able to lather and scrub himself. Returning to his room he made a mistake, as always, and stumbled into the room opposite whose occupant directed him to the right room with unusually little unpleasantness. Dr. Alswanger dressed and sighed. He stood in front of the mirror on the closet door and looked at himself. In Palestine it had never occurred to him that he was short; on the contrary, he had always regarded himself as of average height, But here, among the American giants, he was acutely aware not only of his smallness but of all his other physical disadvantages. He had grown not in height but in breadth, had a large head, broad shoulders, short legs. On the ship from Haifa to Marseilles, and then from Marseilles to New York, they had provided generous meals and Dr. Alswanger had put on a great deal of weight and now his dinner suit could no longer be buttoned up, his shirt collars were too tight, and even his shoes pinched his feet.

Around six o'clock Dr. Alswanger completed his toilet. He elegantly covered his shoes with spats, donned his broad-brimmed black hat, took up the bouquet of roses, which had already started to wilt, and went down in the elevator. Like himself, Boris Makaver lived on Broadway, but uptown not downtown. So while it was indeed the same street, to get there he had to take the subway, and as though one train were not bad enough, he had to change lines. Alswanger had asked directions, but everyone had given him different information: one had advised taking the BMT, another the IRT; a third suggested he go to Eighth Street, and a fourth to Fourteenth Street. Dr. Alswanger elected to walk to Fourteenth Street. He had spent time in many big cities but had never encountered such vast crowds anywhere else. People milled around in the tens of thousands, bumping into each other on the sidewalks. It all looked like one gigantic demonstration, which included many Jews. The shops displayed foodstuffs and bottles of wine labeled *Kosher for Passover;* some even boasted a license from a *Bet Din*. One restaurant had filled its window with a Passover platter, matzos, candlesticks, a Haggadah. Like himself, smartly dressed men and women carried packages and bouquets of flowers, probably also on their way to a Seder. But with them Dr. Alswanger felt none of the kinship that one Jew feels with another. They all spoke English. None of them looked Jewish.

In the subway there was a crush seldom found even in the buses of Tel Aviv. A conductor wedged him into a car like some kind of parcel, and once he was inside, a wave of other passengers broke over him with irresistible force. His roses were squashed. His fresh shirt was soaked with sweat. He rode past several stations without having the faintest idea where he was. He asked people, but they didn't hear him. The train rattled and roared, stopped and started, whistled in warning and at length as though signaling an impending catastrophe. The fans droned, the electric light glared, his ears and eyes hurt, as Dr. Alswanger stood dwarfed by a huddle of young men who pressed against him, their bodies giving off an odor as they babbled and brayed over the top of his head. He found it increasingly difficult to breathe. How long could a person survive a journey like this? Dr. Alswanger wondered. In his heightened state of tension, he had a vivid picture of the Jews who had been packed into freight cars and transported like cattle to the slaughter. Well, let me imagine that I'm one of them. How am I better off? Thank you, dear Father in heaven, for allowing me to experience even a millionth part of what they must have felt! How can we know anything of what those victims endured? In the midst of the greatest martyrdom of our history, we are sunk in banality, foolishness, greed.

Dr. Alswanger so lost himself in these meditations that he did not notice the doors open and large knots of passengers disperse. As the car emptied, he noticed a Jew reading a Yiddish newspaper. His inquiries in Yiddish of this man revealed that instead of going uptown, he was headed toward Brooklyn.

Eventually, at about half-past seven, he reached Boris Makaver's apartment building. As the elevator operator took him up to the fourteenth floor, Dr. Alswanger examined his flustered self in the mirror. Everything he was wearing was wet, creased, crumpled. His collar was dirty, his bow tie had been jerked askew, all that was left of his bouquet were a few stems and leaves that looked like battered willow branches after a beating on Hoshanah Rabbah. He wanted to throw them away, but he didn't know where.

No sooner had he rung the bell than the door opened and Boris and Frieda Makaver both came forward to receive their guest. Boris seized his hand, pressed it warmly, and held on to it, shouting out the traditional greetings: "Doctor, we've been waiting for you! *Gut yontev! Borekhabo! Sholem-aleykhem!*"

Frieda took the remains of the roses, thanked him, and told him she had read his work. She not only named the titles of his books but also cited articles he had published in a variety of journals. Here, in this apartment on the fourteenth floor, he was esteemed once more; here he was Immanuel Alswanger, the learned writer, the man of ideas that were open to challenge but that, like the man himself, had to be treated with respect.

Tears came to his eyes. Did this mean that the world still existed? That the end of everything and everyone had not yet come? And only a short while ago he had thought that he was as forgotten as a dead man.

It occurred to Dr. Alswanger that something similar might well occur in the World to Come. First he would suffer, lie in agony, endure the torments of the grave, believing that the darkness, the worms, the oblivion would go on forever. But then suddenly angels would appear to him and lead him to a place where every soul had dignity and a name, and where it received a welcome and an honor it had never known and never expected.

2

D r. Alswanger had attended Seder feasts in the homes of the wealthy before, but he had never seen a Seder like Boris Makaver's. The dining room was smothered in flowers, the long table weighed down with the gold and silver of the dinner service and the candelabrum. The Seder platter was an antique from the sixteenth century, the Goblet of Elijah had been made in Spain, the pages of the Haggadah had illuminated margins. The wine came from Baron Rothschild's cellar in Rishon Le-Tzion and, according to the label, was seventy years old. Boris had donned a white robe and a gold-embroidered skullcap, and like an Oriental monarch seated himself at the head of the table on the chair piled high with pillows, as custom demanded. Frieda sat next to him like a queen. Reytze, Boris Makaver's relative and housekeeper, was planning to leave him. Believing that Boris should have married her and not brought a German woman into the house, Reytze would not and could not share the same home as Frieda. Consequently, before she left she was determined to prepare a Seder that would never be forgotten.

Dr. Halperin declared that in all his life he had never tasted better fish. The dumplings had the flavor of Paradise. The soup spread through the veins like the elixir of life. Even the traditional sweetener of the bitter herbs was an indescribable delight, for Reytze had blended it from nuts, apples, wine, and an unknown spice that enchanted the nostrils. Matzo crumbs gathered thickly in Dr. Halperin's shaggy mustache as, grunting with pleasure, he chewed unceasingly with his yellow teeth. He threw loving glances at his sister, Frieda, thanks to whom he was now the brother-in-law of the rich Makaver, who had already promised to pay for the publication of his collected works in both German and Hebrew. Boris had also paid for a translation of Dr. Halperin's new book, *Asceticism and Spirit,* in which Halperin gathered the reflections of his old age——a new view of the history of philosophy that showed how all philosophers, from Thales to Bergson, from Husserl to Vaihinger, and including the Epicureans, had preached asceticism. In every generation, philosophy had attempted to deny life, which was why it had failed. In its striving toward an illusion of eternity, philosophy had neglected the true worth of the transitory. A big New York publishing house was about to sign a contract with Halperin, who asserted that his new book would completely overturn all accepted readings of philosophy. The name of Zadok Halperin, known until now only to a narrow circle of academics, would become world famous.

Although it was not fitting to smoke at a Seder table, Dr. Halperin, clad for the occasion in a new suit and a clean shirt, could not restrain himself. As soon as Boris turned his head, he lit a cigar. Frieda rebuked him severely for dirtying her costly tablecloth with ashes, to which her brother responded with a nasal snort: "Well now, look at that! A man can't smoke in peace. Everything is forbidden! Strictly forbidden!"

And he took a last greedy puff before Frieda removed the cigar from his hand.

Dr. Margolin, who wore an elegant tuxedo and had brought the hostess a bouquet of orchids, was fastidious about what he ate. Only now did physicians generally agree that eating too much animal fat was a chief cause of thrombosis, but Dr. Margolin had long followed his own set of unbreakable medical rules. Since he avoided eating eggs and fatty meat, he barely touched the boiled matzo dumplings and the fried matzo-meal pancakes. He meticulously removed every vestige of skin from his portion of chicken, and looked askance and aghast at Dr. Halperin, who did everything that doctors declared harmful, yet who had reached the age of sixty. The short, fat Halperin had a huge belly, chain-smoked cigars, never took any exercise, and gorged himself on all kinds of rich delicacies that raised his cholesterol level and hardened his arteries. This man spat in the face of medical science. But Halperin was descended from a long-lived family, and Margolin firmly believed in the power of genetic inheritance. All human endeavors were as nothing compared with the chromosomes. In them, in the genes, lay every human fate. They determined everything: an individual's physical strength, intelligence, personality, length of days. Margolin himself came from a family whose members did not live long, which was why he had been a hypochondriac for many years now. He had prepared himself for death while he was still in his twenties, and the fear of death never left him. The happiest moments of his life had been clouded by the question of how long they would last. His disposition had been steadily poisoned by having been forced all these years to deal professionally with sickness and death. He knew every symptom, every statistic. Peculiarly, on the average doctors lived far shorter lives than other people. All the odds were against him.

Dr. Halperin joined in the recitation of the Haggadah at the top of his voice, but during the meal he asserted that he was an atheist. Dr. Margolin did not have a high opinion of Dr. Halperin either as a philosopher or as a man, believing that Halperin had accomplished nothing in his work. At his core the man was a gross sensualist, full of ignorance behind the mask of deep learning. His sister, Frieda, was perhaps not as knowledgeable, but her tastes were more refined. Margolin regarded himself as a victim of skepticism. He understood all points of view, knew the counter to every argument, could never throw off the yoke of doubt. Moreover, having been a psychologist even before he knew of Freud or Adler, he detected personal exculpation in all philosophies, a subjective compensation for all sorts of physical and spiritual deficiencies. Margolin did not chant the Haggadah but either murmured the words or said them silently.

His lifelong preoccupation had been to psychoanalyze Jews, the Jewish religion, the Jewish character. Somewhere deep within himself Solomon Margolin agreed with the anti-Semites: in philosophy and mind-set, the Jew was a parasite. First Joseph came to Egypt, then he brought his father, his brothers, their families. Soon they established a state within a state in Goshen. From then on, the same pattern was repeated in all countries, through all generations. Moreover, even in those early days, Joseph had tried to acquire private property, to give Pharaoh the whole land of Egypt, to make all Egyptians "slaves unto Pharaoh." Fortunately, among Jews there was also a powerful anti-parasitic element which had always urged the people to create their own country. The young Jews in Palestine who were currently waging war with Britain were of this sort. Who could tell? Perhaps even a parasitic plant secretly yearns to bring forth its own green leaves. And from the biological point of view, the parasite represents a higher level of existence than its host. Didn't the whole human species feed parasitically off the world of flora and fauna?

After the Seder, Dr. Halperin began interrogating Dr. Alswanger. What did he want? What had he come for? What plans did he have for the human species? Conscious of the mockery in Halperin's tone, Alswanger nevertheless slowly explained his plan. There was a need for a fusion of science with art that would take into account "the whole person." Biology, psychology, religion, and philosophy had to merge into one applied science. Dr. Alswanger himself was not, God forbid, a Communist but a follower of Plato's *Republic*. It was high time the world was ruled by learned people instead of by politicians. The world's parliaments should be filled by wise specialists, and state commissions should comprise experts in different fields. Society should ensure that its members were scientifically governed instead of letting them blindly tap walls and come into collision with other people and their plans. The longer Dr. Alswanger spoke, the more confused he became. He advocated a sort of religious Communism and technocracy combined with psychoanalysis, Hasidism, medicine, and a host of other incompatibles. Dr. Halperin did not stop smiling under his mustache.

"What, in practical terms, do we need to do now?"

"Begin with small samples. Create the first sanatoria or laboratories."

"What should we do there? Recite the psalms?"

"One could recite the psalms. Prayer is an important therapy."

"Your ideas would be fine if we could stop time for a while, in the same way that Joshua made the sun stand still."

"Why stop time?"

"Because at the very moment that you are planning your sanatoria, Russia and America are building atomic bombs."

Boris rapped his knuckles on the table. "Gentlemen, atomic bombs are leaven, and this is the Feast of Unleavened Bread. I don't want atomic bombs at the Seder."

"Well then, open the door and let in the Prophet Elijah."

Herman had asked his uncle for permission to bring a guest with him to the Seder, and since Boris was perfectly agreeable, Herman had brought Sylvia, a big, dark young woman with a long nose, black bulging eyes, thick lips, and curly hair cut short like a man's. Boris took one look at her and wondered, What's this? A young woman or a trooper? Sylvia did not please Frieda either, since she sat next to Herman at the Seder and never stopped grinning at him, from time to time even winking. Sylvia was a Party comrade in whose mother's house Herman boarded. Since Herman knew some Russian, he would read the leading articles from *Pravda* and

Isvestiia aloud to Sylvia. Together they worked for the Party. Sylvia had been curious to see what an old-fashioned Seder looked like, and before taking her, Herman had appealed to her not to contradict or anger his uncle. Now, however, Sylvia kept on asking questions: Why were they eating matzo? What was the symbolism of the bitter herbs, the greens, the shank bone, the roasted egg, the four cups of wine? Boris took the trouble to answer her, but then the young woman challenged him: "Why celebrate freedom attained more than four thousand years ago when slavery still prevails today?"

"Where? Not in America."

"Do you know what goes on in the South?" demanded the young woman.

"No, I do not."

"Do you at least know that a *numerus clausus* is enforced in American universities? Have you ever tried to get into a swanky hotel? Do you know that they don't admit Jews there?"

"Why should I care about Jews who want to eat forbidden food? I myself never go to such Gentile hotels."

"Do you know that there are companies that refuse to employ Jewish workers?"

"So what can I do? As long as the Messiah doesn't come, we remain in exile."

"In the Soviet Union, anti-Semitism has been rooted out."

"In the Soviet Union, Jews have been rooted out."

Sylvia wanted to plunge directly into a dispute, but Herman pressed her foot under the table and stared at her in astonishment. What was the sense of arguing with these fanatics? Why waste words? But that was Sylvia's nature: she always felt obliged to support the Communist cause wherever she went—at the butcher's, in the grocery shop, in the beauty parlor where she had her hair done. Herman used to joke that if Sylvia were to reach the moon on a rocket, she would immediately lecture there on the latest resolutions of the Central Committee. Herman had long been convinced that American Communists had not the faintest notion of how to organize. Here they had been spoiled by the sham freedom the capitalists threw out as a sop to the masses; if the movement was ever called upon to engage in a genuine conspiracy, American Communists would be less prepared than their kind anywhere else in the world. They were too soft, too scrupulous, too sentimental for genuine struggle. Herman sat quietly looking into the Haggadah and later listened attentively to the argument between Halperin and Alswanger. It was interesting to observe these two intellectuals. At first glance, they seemed to share the idealistic bourgeois view that overlooked and deliberately ignored economic and political development, class struggle, historical inevitability, all objective criteria. They prattled on about human society as if it existed in a vacuum and everything depended on what a pair of totally impractical people decided. Yet there was a marked difference between the two. In his way, Halperin was more clear-headed, had his feet more firmly on the ground, and was therefore a little more progressive than Alswanger, who was entirely wrapped up in words, in spinning prose, in illusions.

Herman thought that during the current waiting period, when the revolutionary forces needed to regroup and therefore mouthed allegiance to coexistence, they ought to be reaching out to people like Halperin. In France and Italy, the Party had attracted many intellectuals. They knew how to approach them. Their propaganda was individualized, subtle, tailored to the needs of the day. Here everything was done clumsily, bombastically; the Party did not seize the initiative and was content to appeal to the same element all the time, using florid rhetoric and hackneyed slogans. For instance, when Sylvia spoke of anti-Semitism in the Soviet Union, she instantly invited exactly the answer she received. In any case, at the present time it would be better to avoid the Jewish Question—there were other issues that could be used more effectively.

Herman frowned and glanced into the Haggadah. What a ludicrous ideological fabrication! Among Christians its foundation was a Jesus who was resurrected from the dead; among Jews it was built on an abstract God, a vast code of absurd laws, a promise of a Messiah who would come riding to the rescue on an ass. Compared with this pious edifice, the Leaning Tower of Pisa stood straight, yet one dared not underestimate its strength. When one tried to demolish ruins, they sometimes collapsed inward, killing the demolishers. One had to dismantle them piecemeal, plank by plank, brick by brick. There were even times during the razing of a ruin when one was compelled to prop up a cornice temporarily. The rule was that there were no rules: that was the true meaning of dialectic. In his grasp of this principle, Comrade Stalin stood above all others. The greatest of all dangers to the Revolution lay in closing the mind, in wanting to fit the flux of time into a clichéd pattern.

13

Stanislaw Luria could not sleep. The medication the doctor had prescribed for him did not help at all. He lay in bed with the reading lamp burning on the night table because he was afraid to switch it off. Since the séance, he had developed a dread of the dark. He could not wholly believe that Sonia had revealed herself to him the other night— but then who was the figure that had emerged out of the darkness, embraced him, kissed him, spoken Polish to him? The more he thought about it, the muddier everything became. It must have been Sonia. He recognized her voice. He knew the touch of her lips. But how was it possible for Sonia to reveal herself to him when they had burned her to ashes? And if she had revealed herself there, in that dentist's apartment, why did she not sometimes come to him at home? Then again, this was something he was greatly afraid of. Whenever he so much as started to think about it, fear gripped his heart as in a vise. He sat up in bed and shouted out, "It's a fraud! A fraud!"

Ah, his nerves! They were so wound up. He lay awake through the night and trembled at every sound, however faint. The apartment was full of rustling. The furniture creaked. Although the windows were shut tight, the venetian blinds quivered and rattled. In the bathroom, the pipes whistled. The radiator throbbed and drummed. There were disturbing incidents. He put things away and they disappeared, so that he had to spend days searching for them. First his fountain pen vanished, then his reading glasses; neither his slippers nor his hat could be found. He would turn off the lamp, yet later he would find it burning, as if a hidden hand had switched on the electricity. He put a book down on the table, but when he wanted to continue reading, it wasn't there. Later he would find it under the bed or even beneath his pillow. Was it possible that Sonia's spirit was giving him signs? Or had he been possessed by some malign demon?

He would call Professor Shrage, but the professor did not answer the telephone. Luria would go over to the professor's lodgings and ring, but no one came to the door. He telephoned Mrs. Clark at her office, but she told him angrily that she categorically refused to organize séances for him. One needed a strong heart for such things, and she had warned Sonia that séances were damaging to her husband's health.

How could he have a strong heart when he was broken in every respect? Even when he had married Anna, he was already ruined physically and spiritually. Her absconding with Grein had destroyed the little that was left in him. Boris Makaver still offered to support him, but Luria refused. He owed three months' rent and expected to be evicted from the apartment at any moment. Unpaid bills for the telephone, the electricity, the gas lay everywhere. In March he had not even submitted his tax return to the IRS. Somewhere he had the initial papers toward citizenship he had taken out when he first arrived in America, but they, too, had disappeared. What would he do if he needed proof that he had come here as a legal immigrant? There were probably other documents elsewhere, but the official bureaucracy's records were as chaotic as his own. They could deport him and no one would know what had become of him. In Poland they would imprison him.

Luria was plagued by all sorts of suspicions. For example, he had not the slightest doubt that this Yasha Kotik was a Soviet spy. Perhaps he and Anna were conspiring against him. Perhaps they intended to abduct him and return him to the Bolsheviks. That was highly probable. Since he refused to divorce Anna, she had decided to kill him so that she could marry Grein. How difficult was it to abduct someone like himself? Who would stand by him? They had liquidated Americans more important than he and no one had come to their assistance. Soviet ships regularly docked in New York. Soviet spies infiltrated everywhere. Communists and fellow travelers were employed in American government offices, on all American newspapers. They held positions of authority in the State Department; they had penetrated the FBI. They were undermining America like termites. Even the so-called capitalist newspapers were full of Soviet propaganda.

Their front-page articles appeared to revile Russia, but their arts pages were controlled by Communists who disseminated Party propaganda. Who could estimate the power they wielded in the Army, the Navy, the Air Force? One thing was certain: they had more than enough power to liquidate someone as insignificant as himself.

Was there any escape? To whom should he turn? To a lawyer? To the police? To the FBI? They would say he had a persecution mania and would send him to a madhouse. So twisted were their minds that, although millions were being victimized in broad daylight, those who complained were regarded as lunatics. Only the persecutors were sane. *They* had rights. Everyone helped *them*. Uncle Sam had loaded Stalin with billions and had lent him hundreds of ships which he now refused to return. President Roosevelt himself had been infected with their propaganda.

Should he flee? Where to? Their agents were everywhere. Should he try speaking with Anna? She was obviously now one of them. Perhaps he should simply disappear somewhere in the Midwest. He would change his name, grow a gray beard, bury himself somewhere on a farm. But did he have enough strength to work? No, he didn't have the strength even to shave or bathe himself. He had stopped eating. The apartment was filthy, but he couldn't be bothered to clean it. For whom? He was cut off from society, completely isolated, like all those humanity has cast out. Someone had even stolen his address book with all its telephone numbers.

Luria went over to the window. Outside, it was spring. The sun was shining. He stared out in amazement—it looked like high summer! He decided to go out. His gold watch had to be pawned or else he would die of hunger. There was a pawnshop somewhere near here, on Third Avenue. But where was the watch? It had been lying on the night table.

The watch wasn't there! Luria sighed. Would anyone believe this? He searched for it in all the drawers, in his pockets, on the shelves. Had he been robbed? Had thieves broken in? If so, why hadn't they taken other things? Was Sonia playing games with him? Why should she want to distress him? Did she bear him a grudge because he had married Anna? Perhaps Mrs. Clark was offended and it was she who was causing all these mishaps. That woman looked like a witch. She had virtually imprisoned Professor Shrage. Naturally rationalists scoffed at such ideas, but then was Hitler a rational phenomenon? Was Stalin? Were two world wars the product of logic? The human species wallowed in swamps of absurdity, darkness, mystery, magic, yet it continually spoke about understanding. That in itself was madness. The confident clear-headedness of contemporary people was a dangerous delusion. In the Middle Ages, people were closer to the truth than now. Then at least they knew that there were sinister forces at work. They even called them by their names: Satan, Lucifer, Belial. Modern people were crazed by reason. A gang of intellectuals had brought the human species to the brink of the abyss.

Well, there was no deliverance. Who should provide it? As insane as they were, they had the power. These madmen had armed themselves with atomic bombs, with universities, newspapers, magazines. They psychoanalyzed one another. They justified all savageries, all nightmares, all satanic arts. They had names for everything: for murdering six million Jews, for liquidating millions in Russia. As soon as they gave the monster a name, it ceased to be monstrous. They needed nothing more.

2

Yes, I'll go to them, Luria promised himself. I'll go where all the Jews have gone, those who were the best of the nation. Who was left? Adulterers like Anna and Grein. If there is a World to Come, I want to see it, and if there's nothing there, then life is worthless in any case. Then a man is nothing but a microbe. Then there is certainly no reason to suffer. Are we forbidden to kill ourselves? Will God punish us? Let Him punish us! He punishes us enough as it is!

Luria found his gold watch and went off to pawn it. As he stepped outside, he realized that he had forgotten to put on his necktie. Well, too bad. The young man who sat behind the pawnshop grille turned the watch over for a long time, opened it to examine its mechanism, even used a loupe. After all that, he offered twenty-five dollars. Twenty-five dollars for a watch that in Poland before the war had cost a thousand zlotys! But Luria had no strength to wander from one pawnshop to another. "Well, so be it," he said, and the youth gave him the money together with a ticket. Luria didn't even bother to count the money. It would suffice until the end, he murmured as he walked down Lexington Avenue. Yes, it was settled. But how to do it? Hanging? Poison? No, not that. Gas took too long, it stank, and he might harm the neighbors. The best thing was to drown himself, but in such a way that caused the least suffering. At night, having drunk a half bottle of cognac beforehand, he would take the ferry to Staten Island. He would tie a heavy weight around his neck, throw himself into the sea, and sink immediately. The cognac would serve as an anesthetic, unless he could get some opium or morphine somewhere. The main thing was to be in a drugged stupor during the last moments. The whole business would probably last less than a minute. When the brain received no oxygen, one lost consciousness right away. Sleeping pills or a massive dose of chloroform would be the best. But one needed a prescription for things like that. Solomon Margolin? No, he wouldn't do it, and Luria didn't want to ask any favors of him. That doctor was no stranger to Anna and had his own unfinished business to settle. It would be perfectly all right to do the deed in the middle of the sea. But where? How? Unless he were to travel to Europe by ship. But one needed a passport and all the rest of it for that. Were there no ships to Florida or California? Perhaps one could sail to Canada? But then he had no money. There was a ship to Boston, or to Providence, he remembered. At the thought of Providence, Luria smiled. Providence—a divine dispensation that looked on impassively as six million people were tortured and made not the slightest movement to intervene.

When should he do it? Now? Luria stopped abruptly in the middle of the street. First he had to acquire a weight, otherwise he would thrash about in the water and scream for help. Where did one find a weight? Perhaps somewhere on Third Avenue. He turned back. In an antiques shop there he had once noticed an old-fashioned scale with weights. But that might be too costly. He walked along Third Avenue looking into the antiques shops. All those old objects had once belonged to someone. They were all relics of the dead. Death whistled along the streets, but the living neither knew nor cared. They were like starving wolves who devoured the carcasses of their own kind. Look—here was a skeleton for sale—they even turned death into a commodity. But they would all come to this. Death would not overlook anyone. The street was crowded with corpses-to-be.

Having already crossed Forty-second Street, Luria walked farther and farther downtown. He hadn't eaten since yesterday, but he felt no hunger. On the contrary, he still felt almost sated. He stopped at a shop full of furniture. Books lay on a table outside. What sort of books were these? What did they contain? He opened one in the middle and read: "Her mother was an ambitious woman. She wanted to provide Beatrice with a husband who could indulge her every whim and who could in some measure restore the family to its former social status.'' So, she was ambitious. Had she realized her ambition? Luria wondered. He looked at the title page—it was by a woman, a name he didn't know. Had this author achieved her own ambition? This book was selling at five cents. What about the others? *The History of Railroads in Ohio, How to Achieve Success in Love and Work.* Perhaps that one is for me. Yes indeed, how did one achieve success? The book cost ten cents, and it occurred to Luria to buy it, simply out of curiosity, to have one last look at the illusions of the human species. He took out a dime and put it down on top of another book. Apparently the shopkeeper inside was not remotely interested in his goods—one could have taken it for nothing and walked away.

At Thirty-fourth Street, Luria went into a cafeteria. I'll drink some coffee. What harm can it do? Even cattle are fed before they're slaughtered. The stomach does what it's meant to do—it digests. Therein lay the utter absurdity of it all—every organ did what it was designed to do: the stomach digested, the brain thought, and after death a whole new round of activity started. The microbes consumed everything; protons, neutrons, electrons continued their ceaseless whirling and circling. The atoms probably had no knowledge that their owner was dead or had committed suicide. And in what possible way could a human being be thought of as their owner? To them it was all one where they lodged—in men, in mice, in muck. They had their own atomic considerations, and regarded the whole concept of individuality as nothing short of ridiculous. But whose purpose did this serve? To what end did this planet revolve? How long would it continue turning on its axis and circling the sun? There had to be some sense somewhere.

Luria went up to the counter and took a cup of coffee. After some hesitation he took a cookie as well. Sitting down at a table, he opened his book at random and read: ''Everyone needs a clearly defined and achievable goal. It is astonishing the number of people who set themselves no goal at all. They drift with the tide. The years pass and they never know what they want. The story of all successful people has one common thread: very early on, each of them set a goal for himself that he wanted to achieve.'' Luria shut the book immediately. What did I want to achieve? I studied law without having any aptitude for it—why didn't I study something that really interested me? But what? I was very fond of reading explorers' stories, but I certainly wouldn't have become another Roald Amundsen or Sven Hedin. My true longing was for peace of mind: a good wife, a contented child, a soft chair, a comfortable sofa. I've been lethargic ever since childhood, almost as if I hadn't rested sufficiently in a previous incarnation. Perhaps that's why I want to make an end—so that finally I can sleep.

Luria drank his coffee and ate his cookie. This snack in the middle of the day had made him hungry, languid, weak in the legs. Someone had left a roll behind on the table and Luria picked it up and started chewing it. This wasn't stealing—they'd throw it away in any case. Yes, indeed, what should people do if they had no goal in life? All these recommendations were for the strong, not for the weak. Take this young woman who was clearing the tables. She could never become a Rockefeller, a Ford, an Edison. She'd go on cleaning these tables for a few years more, then she'd marry a janitor or someone and would soon become pregnant. She'd bear a child every year. On Saturdays she'd drag her drunken husband home from the bars and he'd curse and abuse her. The children would be a compound of their parents' limitations. And what about Communism? It was created by the strong for the strong. The weak would clean tables in every generation, even if they were to fly to Mars, even if machines were to take over all human labor.

Luria rose to go, leaving his book lying on the table. While he was standing at the cash register waiting to pay, someone nudged his elbow—it was the young woman who cleaned the tables returning his book to him. He responded, "Perhaps you might like to read it. I've finished it."

"What is it? *How to Achieve Success in Love and Work.* Oh, no thank you. I have no time to read." And she gave it back to him, the cover damp from her hand. He watched her turn again to the tables with her rag, an expression of something like regret darkening her face. She had no need of books. Books couldn't help her. It struck Luria that in a certain sense that woman did have a goal in life—it was not to have any goal but to follow wherever the occasion might lead. The real unfortunates were those like himself, incapable of clearing tables, who could not decide whether or not to define a goal for themselves. That was why he was sentenced to death. But would he at least have the strength for that?

Yes, he must find a weight or some other heavy object.

3

Not far from the Bowery, Luria found what he was seeking. On a table cluttered with all sorts of bric-a-brac lay a huge magnet in the shape of a horseshoe, with a hole on each side. Was this some part of a generator? He picked it up, and its heaviness astonished him. He asked the price, and the amazed seller looked him up and down as though asking, What use is such a magnet to you?

"Two dollars," he replied.

Luria paid him at once. Through these two holes one could thread a rope and hang the magnet around one's neck. Ashamed to be seen on the street carrying so odd an object, he bought a newspaper in which to wrap it and decided to go down to the Battery to inspect the ferry that went to Staten Island, even though he found it difficult to walk carrying something so heavy. If I do it, it'll have to be at night—a very dark night when the moon isn't shining, he decided; yet all the time he had the feeling he was playing games. He was very far from having resolved to carry out the plan. It was clear to him that such things could not be decided in advance. Moreover, everything had to be just right. The last shove had to come suddenly or it would not come at all. Well, all I've lost is two dollars. Suddenly Luria felt a schoolboy's curiosity about the magnet. While he was still in high school he had conducted experiments with a magnet just like this, scattering iron filings obtained from a locksmith over a sheet of paper placed on top of it. Oh, how distant all that seemed now! In those days, the Russians still occupied Warsaw.

He had to get home and put the magnet down, so he took the Third Avenue El. Thoughts of death accompanied him up the steps. How many of the people who had climbed these stairs over the years were now dead? Millions of pairs of feet that had trodden here were now rotting in the earth. But surely they must have left a trail behind somewhere. A bloodhound could pick up the scent from footprints even days after they had been left, so perhaps there existed some sort of power that, years later, could identify the steps on these stairs. Where did I read it? The cosmos was full of tracks. A record remained of everything. It might be that even my present thoughts will not be lost. Perhaps in heaven some kind of apparatus exists that films human beings, their thoughts, their emotions. I'll soon be dead, but somewhere or other there'll be a picture of me dragging this magnet about. But how does it help? If we accept that God is clever, does that mean He is good? There was no proof whatever of that.

Luria sat staring out the car window. How ugly New York looked from here! The buildings that could be seen were no more than heaps of brick, remarkable only for not collapsing. The apartments were all small, cramped, occupied by people who had long grown accustomed to mechanical thundering in their heads day and night. What could they hope for? After decades of work, they were discarded like so many worn-out rags. When they went to claim their unemployment insurance, the officials treated them rudely. When they got old, they begged in the streets or drifted aimlessly in nursing homes. But they lacked the courage to end it all. Even when revolutions took place, they fell victim to tyrants a thousand times worse than their former oppressors.

In one building they evidently offered music lessons—several men were blowing trumpets, someone was beating a drum, and together they looked like a group of circus clowns. In the gloom of a billiard hall, a few youths played pool on a stained table. Pawnshops, dingy eateries with benches at the counter, bars, scrap-metal dealers selling pots, pans, and other odds and ends passed below the tracks. The day had been hot, but the night promised to be rainy and cool. Ah, of all lies spring was the worst. It had all the drawbacks of autumn, Luria mused. It's always full of rain, cold, and disappointment. The train stopped every few minutes and new passengers got on. How shabby they all looked! Raw faces, rough-hewn as though with an ax, wild-eyed, outsized hands and feet. One woman heaved herself in, so fat that she could barely squeeze through the doorway. Her angry glance seemed to say: I'm not fat for fun! When she sat down, she occupied two seats. And look at the clothes. Where did these people find such garments? Their outlandish blouses and jackets the color of sulphur, with clashing stripes and checks, reminded Luria of Polish peasants and their *ciuchy,* the secondhand clothes they used to sell in Targówek. Here, in this poverty, ugliness, tastelessness seemed to have crowded together. These people had no scruples either: give them power and they would do exactly what had been done in Russia. Each of them gave Luria a single glance, and then averted his eyes. Where did they live? Where were they going? He would not have been surprised if this El was headed for Łowicz or Nizhni-Novgorod.

Luria got off and walked down Lexington Avenue. Every time he came home and the door of the apartment building was opened for him, he was astounded anew. Why were they postponing his eviction? The apartment was the only thing that seemed to bind him to life. As he opened his front door and put down the magnet, he heard the telephone ringing. Should I answer? Who could possibly still want to speak with me?

He lifted the receiver and a young woman asked, "Excuse me, sir, do you listen to the radio?"

"What? Seldom, seldom."

"May I ask what programs interest you?"

He replied that no programs of any kind interested him. He was ill. He excused himself and hung up. That's the only thing they care about, he reflected. Everything is money, money, money. The telephone itself, which a moment before had awakened a spark of hope in him, now filled him with bitterness. He did not switch on the lights but walked from room to room in the half-darkness. Dust covered everything. The air was stuffy. Clothing lay scattered across chairs, on the floor. Moths had managed to find their way in. At the sight of what had become of Anna's precious rooms, something within him crowed. He was overcome by weariness and lay down on the sofa. His stomach rumbled, there was a sharp pain across his heart, his head ached. Do I have a fever? He touched his forehead, and it felt burning hot. Well, perhaps I'll die a natural death.

He closed his eyes and lay for a long time like one possessed by an evil spirit. He was aware of a powerful rush of noise that came not from outside but from within himself. His mind seemed to be rattling along like a train that made station stops, because he could clearly hear the doors opening and closing. Through his shut eyes he saw windows, the slats of venetian blinds reflected. Oh, I'm tired, tired! he groaned. He had only one de-sire—to sleep. Dozing off, he dreamed that he was in a room crammed with pipes that even jutted out of the windows. Through these pipes one communicated with the neighbors and with the buildings opposite. Voices traveled through these pipes, water gushed out of them, foodstuffs dropped from them—beans, cereals, flour. What kind of mechanism was this? he wondered. How did it work? Had it replaced the telephone, or was it some primitive throwback to the past? Among the pipes sat a gigantic dog, as big as a horse. Luria froze in terror: a dog like that could devour a man. He opened his eyes. The darkness of night had enveloped the room. Sud-denly he became aware that someone was standing at the foot of the sofa. He was not startled. It was Sonia. She looked as she always had, but her face was luminous, radiant, encircled by a still-brilliant aureole. I must be dreaming, he told himself. Or has she entered through the pipes? She looked at him with smiles mingled with sadness, like someone who longs to speak but is dumb. He wanted to ask her something, but his Polish had deserted him. None of this lasted longer than a second. Almost immediately the figure vanished again. For a long while he stared at the dark spot where but a moment before he had seen Sonia quite clearly.

Well, so that's how it is, he remarked to himself. Now he knew with profound inner conviction that this time he had really seen Sonia and that very soon he would meet her again. He wanted to get up, but he was too weak to stand. For the first time in months he experienced a sense of complete tranquillity. He turned with his face toward the back of the sofa and dozed off once more.

14

In the middle of the night, the telephone shrilled insistently in Grein's apartment on Fifth Avenue.

"Who can possibly be calling now?" Anna demanded.

"It must be a wrong number," Grein answered sleepily. No one knew where he could be reached except Leah and Esther, neither of whom would have called at this hour. Grein waited awhile, but the ringing didn't stop. Stumbling to the telephone in the dark, he picked up the receiver.

"Hello!"

For a moment no one said anything at the other end. Then Grein heard a man's voice asking in Yiddish, "Is that Mr. Grein?"

"Yes, I'm Grein."

"Please excuse me for waking you. There's been an accident. May I speak to Anna?"

"Who are you?"

"I'm her first husband. My name is Yasha Kotik."

Grein went cold, overwhelmed by a combination of shame, anger, and revulsion. "Who gave you my telephone number?"

"Your wife, Mrs. Leah Grein."

"My wife? When?"

"Five minutes ago."

"What's happened?"

"Stanislaw Luria is dead."

Grein paused. He was suddenly terribly afraid. "When did this happen? How do you know?"

"I've been staying with him for the past two weeks. I've been in Hollywood, but nothing worked out there, so I came back to New York. We were living together—the two abandoned husbands."

"What happened?"

"He died suddenly. He woke up and complained of a pain in his chest. I wanted to give him a shot of whiskey, but it was already too late."

"Where are you calling from?"

"From his apartment."

"Have you called a doctor?"

"No. He's a corpse all right. On that subject I'm an expert."

"Call an ambulance. Contact the police."

"How can the police help him? I telephoned your wife and she gave me your number."

Grein wanted to say something more, but suddenly the lights were switched on. Anna stood there barefoot and in her nightdress.

"What's happened?" she almost shouted.

"It's for you," Grein answered hollowly, handing her the receiver. Then he quickly returned to the bedroom and shut the door. Well, I've killed him! he told himself. It's the same thing as committing a murder. Grein lay down on the bed. Through the closed door he could hear Anna gasping and sobbing. Then the door opened and in the glow that shone in from the hallway, he saw Anna's face. In those few minutes she seemed to have changed dramatically. Her hair was in disarray.

"Hertz, this oughtn't to have happened!" Anna screamed in Yiddish. "Oh my God!" And she began blubbering like a small child who'd received a slap. Grein remained lying on the bed.

"Get up! Help me!" Anna howled.

"What do you want to do?"

"I'm going to him!" Anna replied. "I've killed him! I! I!"

And she burst into a fresh fit of weeping that each moment assumed a new tone, as if a series of entirely different cries was being torn from her in succession. Grein got off the bed and Anna switched on the lights. In a few minutes her face had grown puffy and swollen. Blue rings had appeared under her eyes. Since she was unable to get into her corset on her own, Grein had to help her. Then he, too, hurried to dress, thrusting his right foot into his left shoe in the confusion. Bills and coins tumbled from his trouser pockets, his hands trembled, and every few moments he felt like vomiting.

"Take me to him!" Anna demanded.

Since the car was locked in the garage, Grein decided they should take a taxi. They hurried out into the corridor and rang for the elevator, but the night-duty operator was apparently asleep, since minutes passed and the elevator still did not come.

Anna jerked away impatiently. "Let's take the stairs!"

They hurried down nine flights. The summer night was cool. Fifth Avenue was deserted. Grein and Anna stood looking for a taxi, but five minutes went by without a sign of one. Anna grew steadily more exasperated.

"Go and get the car!"

But now it was too far to go to the garage. Fortunately a taxi suddenly appeared and both rushed to get in. Oddly, Anna had forgotten her former address and muttered and stammered until she remembered the intersection nearest the building. In the taxi Grein and Anna did not exchange a single word and sat far apart, each absorbed in individual despondency. Anna emanated anger and something akin to hatred. Apart from his churning stomach, everything in Grein was frozen. I won't go up there! I won't go up! he decided. Like a schoolboy, he was filled with the dread of seeing a corpse, and with shame before Yasha Kotik. Even the taxi driver was evidently aware of the grief and utter dejection in the back seat, for from time to time he turned to look at them, frowning and grumbling because the short trip came to only twenty-five cents. Grein refused the change from a dollar bill, but the driver didn't say thank you and drove off in late-night haste. A police car and an on-duty policeman stood in front of the building, while out of it came the elevator man Anna had ridden with when she left her home. He looked at Anna in fury and muttered something to the policeman.

"I am Mrs. Luria!" said Anna.

The policeman shrugged his shoulders. "Well, go up."

"Hertz, come with me!"

"I'll wait here."

"No, Hertz, don't leave me alone now!"

Even in the midst of all this turmoil, Grein wanted to make a favorable impression on Yasha Kotik, so he adjusted his necktie and felt his cheeks to see whether his beard had grown too heavy.

I remember her telling me he was short, Grein recollected, thinking about Kotik. At the same time Grein was horrified, filled with the icy coldness that comes from contact with death. He shuddered, and his feet seemed about to flee of their own volition. Who knows? I might yet be accused of murder! the thought flashed through Grein's mind. Even the elevator now reeked of death, polluted with the ritual impurity of a corpse, "the progenitor of impurity," as the Talmud called it, in reference to the verse Grein now recalled from the Pentateuch: "He that toucheth the dead body of any man shall be unclean." How outlandish to call a dead person "unclean"! he thought. But then they mean the body, not the soul. The conception was that the physical body alone, deprived of the immortal soul, was a lump of putrefaction. They entered the corridor in time to see another policeman emerging from Luria's apartment. He looked at Anna and called out, "The wife?"

And he let Anna and Grein in.

Yasha Kotik met them wearing pajamas and slippers. He was short, no taller than Anna, but there was a nimble litheness in his figure and bearing. Anna stared at him in astonishment—he had already dyed his formerly gray hair light brown, so that only the bags under his eyes and the creases around his mouth testified to the bad times he had known and the wretched night they were enduring.

2

"Where is he?" Anna demanded, before Kotik could open his mouth.

"There," he responded, pointing to the bedroom. Just as Anna was about to enter the room, out of it, in dressing gown and slippers, came Mrs. Katz. Looking older and more wrinkled, she glared balefully at Anna, as though trying to stab her with the hatred in her eyes. Unwillingly, Grein nodded a greeting, but Mrs. Katz made no acknowledgment. She was evidently on familiar terms with Kotik, because he asked her in Yiddish, "Well, did you manage to close his mouth?"

"I've bound it up with a cloth," Mrs. Katz replied.

She went out, slamming the door behind her. Anna entered the room where the corpse lay, and she too slammed the door behind her, clearly wanting to be alone with the dead man. Her movements were rapid, angry, full of the resentment that overcomes people when they can no longer right any wrongs. Only now did Yasha Kotik silently begin sizing Grein up with an expression of neither hatred nor contempt but, rather, of mocking curiosity mingled with the deference actors always pay to people outside their profession.

"Are you Mr. Grein?" he inquired.

"Yes, I am."

"I know how you must feel, I know. Don't ask what kind of night I've spent. In Russia, they didn't make such a fuss about these things. Dead is dead. But lately I've grown a bit unaccustomed to death. Now I see that people die in capitalist countries as well. Truly a surprise."

"Was he ill?" Grein asked.

"Forgive me for receiving you in my pajamas. Ill? Who knows whether a person is ill or well? I've already been to Hollywood, and I managed to escape from that madhouse in the nick of time. I knew my share of lunatics in Stalin's state, but that was a brand-new sort of insanity. In Hollywood, someone speaks to you and you can't understand what he's saying. Then, right in the middle of talking to you, he runs off and says, 'I'll see you later,' but that later never comes. You ask what's happened to him, but no one has any idea; it's as if the earth has swallowed him up. Everyone was very glad to see me, and everyone paid me great compliments, but after a while they all vanished and it was impossible to find them. When I asked what I should do, they all told me to wait; in Hollywood you have to learn patience. Eventually they brought me face-to-face with the Great Man himself, the one who brought me over to America, in fact, and he says, 'You're a wonderful actor, but why're you so short?' Then he asks his secretary to measure me, so she brings over a tape measure and starts taking my height as though I were being conscripted into the Czar's army. I ask, Am I tall enough? Will I do for a soldier? They speak to me half in Yiddish, half in English, mangling our mother tongue something terrible. They dragged me about like that for several weeks. Don't ask me what I came away with, because I don't know."

How can he babble on like this while a dead man's lying in the other room? Grein wondered. And in any case, why's he telling all this to me?

"Do you perhaps have a cigarette?" Kotik inquired.

"No, I'm sorry."

"Oh well, it doesn't matter. I arrived back in New York and had no idea where to go. Then I remembered Anna's second husband. I'd been here once before, on an occasion when I met Anna as well. She's probably told you herself. He made a good impression on me. Since we both had the same wife, we were related in a way. The Warsaw playboys used to call men like us 'brothers-in-law.' Now you have her, Mr. Grein, and whether you like it or not, we are also, so to say, not altogether strangers. After all, where does kinship come from? From this."

And Kotik made an obscene gesture. Immediately afterward his eyes grew large and full of grief. "Well, he's gone to his reward."

"How long have you been living here?" Grein asked, for the sake of saying something. He was suddenly afraid of the silence.

"Two weeks, but they seemed as long as two months. He poured his heart out to me. Neither of us could sleep, so we smoked cigarettes and talked. He told me everything—his whole life story. Hitler fixed him, the way he fixed all Jews. His heart wasn't here but there, in Warsaw. Some woman who talks to the dead, a witch or a weirdo, showed him his first wife in a dark mirror or something, and that confused him completely. She lives with some professor, or God knows who. I spoke frankly to him. *Panie* Luria, I said, I don't believe in superstitious nonsense like that. The dead are dead and cannot speak. Who says they can? When you make heaps of ash out of people, they certainly can't perform any actions anymore. And how did she manage to cross the ocean? We argued back and forth, and every time he always threw out the same remark: We'll soon see. We'll soon know. He wanted to drown himself. He showed me a magnet he wanted to tie around his neck so it would weigh him down. I wasted no time, I can tell you, and I hid that piece of iron so he'd never be able to find it again. But who could have guessed he was so sick? In the old days people didn't drop dead just like that—one, two, gone. They lingered on suffering for weeks or even for years. Why don't you sit down?"

"No, thank you."

"For the same money, you might as well sit. Why's Anna shut herself up? Perhaps you might take a look."

Grein went up to the door but didn't dare open it. He listened for a while, but heard no sound from within. He tensed and knocked lightly with one knuckle. Something moved inside. After some hesitation he opened the door a crack. Anna was standing next to the bed. From where he stood Grein could not see the dead man's face, only the body covered with a sheet. Anna glanced behind her, with the reproving expression of

someone interrupted in the middle of prayer. Grein withdrew, closing the
door behind him.

"What's she doing in there?"

Grein made no reply, and Kotik started twirling around in one spot,
his body making elastic, almost serpentine movements.

"Quite a bang, hey?" he observed. "That's what he wanted: to leave,
banging the door behind him. Protesting against the whole world and
throwing the world back in its own face, so to speak. He talked and talked.
He lay in one bed and I in another, and he spoke like a poet, like a prophet.
He spoke in Polish, but I understand Polish. I only have difficulty in speaking it. He blamed both society and himself. He'd taken it into his head
that he'd wronged his family. I tried to talk him out of it as much as I
could. The dead, I said, don't bear grudges. But that woman, the professor's mistress, awakened doubts in him. He believed that as soon as he
shut his eyes for good, his wife would be waiting for him."

"What did he say about me?" Grein asked, and immediately regretted
the question. Kotik made a face and his eyes seemed to say, If that's all
you want to know, then you're a fool as well. But he replied, "What does
one say in such cases? He accused. I wanted to comfort him, so I said,
'You took away my wife and someone else took her from you. It's even.'
But he argued, 'I took nothing from anyone. Everyone took from me.' He
never spoke badly of you. What's more, he had, as they say, a purpose in
life. Only a few days ago he started saying that he wanted to go to college."

"To college?"

"Yes, to take an English course. If he knew English thoroughly, he said,
he'd be able to get some sort of job. Well, I thought, that's a good sign,
because if one wants to commit suicide, one doesn't start studying English.
In the World to Come they speak only Yiddish or Hebrew. Right?"

Grein bowed his head. His stomach started cramping again. To judge
from the way Kotik prattled on, the whole thing was nothing more than
a little game for him, Grein thought with regret. His type danced on graves.
Suddenly the doorbell rang sharply. Kotik threw a questioning glance at
Grein before hurrying off to the front door with an odd hopping gait.

3

"**W**ho's there?" Kotik asked.

All that could be heard was a growl. Kotik opened the door to reveal Boris Makaver standing on the threshold in a buttoned-up overcoat and a black hat, staring into the apartment with big dark angry eyes. Grein saw him as well and jerked backward.

Kotik evidently didn't recognize Boris, because he asked, "Who are you?"

"When did this tragedy occur?" Boris shot back wrathfully.

"In the middle of the night."

"Who are you? Do you live here?" Boris demanded.

Grein had pulled back in such a way that he couldn't be seen. He heard Kotik say, "Yes, I live here. May I ask who you are?"

"I'm his father-in-law."

There was dead silence for a moment.

"You don't recognize me, hey? Now I recognize you," Kotik finally called out with a tremor in his voice.

"Who are you?"

Where can I hide? Grein wondered. He suddenly dashed into the hallway, and sidling past Kotik and Boris, he locked himself in the bathroom. Now he had only one desire—to get out of this apartment as quickly as possible. Standing at the locked bathroom door listening to what was going on in the hall, he shuddered violently and had to make a determined effort to control himself so that his teeth didn't chatter. Hiding himself here reminded him of something, but he didn't know what. He stood there like a thief interrupted in the middle of his crime, speechless and full of fear, holding his breath. He couldn't catch every word, but he heard Boris boom out, "Indeed!"

"Yes, indeed," Yasha Kotik retorted. "You've gotten younger, and I've grown old."

"I don't want to lecture you," Boris observed after a pause, "but by Jewish Law you're not permitted to be in this house. You're forbidden to be under the same roof with her."

"I didn't know that things would turn out this way and that Anna would come here."

"Get dressed and get out. She will have to sit the Seven Days of Mourning here."

"Where should I go? I have no place to stay."

"I'm not obliged to argue with you. All our misfortunes are your fault," Boris responded in his thundering voice. "But, I repeat, you're forbidden by Jewish Law to remain under the same roof with a woman you've divorced. Now you can see for yourself what becomes of mortal flesh. I'll give you a few dollars so you can rent yourself a room."

"I have to wash and get dressed. Even in Stalin's state they don't just fling you out into the street. There at least they take you to the clink."

Making no further reply, Boris moved away and Kotik knocked at the door of the bathroom. "Found yourself a hiding place?"

"I'm leaving immediately."

"Did you hear what he said? He's throwing me out of here. He's going to give me a few dollars for a room."

"I can lend you some money," Grein blurted out, shocked at his own words.

"I've got some of my own. I'm not too proud to take a handout if I need it. But I've still got enough to rent a room for a week. I even paid Luria my share of the rent, though he didn't pay any rent at all, and if he'd lived they'd've chucked him out of this apartment. Well, in the end he evicted himself."

Grein thought things over for a moment or two. "I can't stay here. Please be so kind as to tell Anna I've left."

"What? I'll tell her, if the old man lets me. He nearly burned me alive with his eyes."

Anna suddenly appeared in the hallway. Again her face—tear-stained, flushed, somewhat rumpled—bore the expression of someone who had been disturbed in the midst of prayer. This was exactly the way Grein's mother used to look as she left the women's section of the synagogue during the Days of Awe when Grein was still a child. Anna stood for a while in silence, at a loss. The bathroom door was open and the two men stood one on each side of it.

"He hid from your father in the bathroom," said Kotik with schoolboy mischievousness, wagging a finger. Anna stared at him. Evidently she had no idea what he was saying. In her glance, filled with the preoccupation of someone in the middle of a disaster who could not be bothered with trivialities, there was also a sort of maternal compassion, an adult's forgiveness of children.

"Anna, I can't stay here," Grein said.

"What? Well, go. Don't forget your hat. It's cool outside and you'll catch a chill."

"My hat's in the living room."

"I'll get it for you."

"She's devoted," Kotik remarked, both to Grein and to himself. "The old man's right. I did her wrong. But in those years I was completely unthinking. I did things and I didn't know what I was doing. I was the most famous actor in Germany. Theaters fought over me. I had two pastimes—acting, and the other thing—you know what. Well, the daughter of a Hasidic family, the child of a wealthy man, came on the scene and I ruined her. In those days I wanted to ruin everything. It was a sort of ambition with me—or madness. Call it what you like."

Anna returned with the hat. "Here's your hat. Where are you going? Home?"

"Your father said you'll have to sit the Seven Days of Mourning here," Grein half asserted, half asked.

"What? I've no idea. I only know one thing: I killed him," Anna said to herself and to no one in particular, "as surely as if I'd taken an ax and chopped off his head. If only they sent people to the electric chair for what I've done, I'd feel a lot easier."

And in Anna's eyes there appeared something like a smile—that nonsensical laughter that often erupts in the midst of the weightiest griefs.

"Anna, don't let yourself brood on such thoughts," Kotik interjected. "It's true that he blamed you, but you don't get a heart attack from that. Look how much I went through in Russia, and yet I'm still alive! These things are all predetermined. A human being is like a Hanukkah top that children spin. One top spins for a long time and another barely gets started before it falls over. A doctor in Minsk told me this analogy, and I can't forget it. As they say, he hit the nail right on the head."

"Well, Anna, I'm going. It may well be true—perhaps he didn't die from all this after all," Grein murmured.

"He did! He did! He was never so ill. But now it's too late! Too late!" Anna turned to Kotik. "It might be better for you to leave as well. Papa is terribly worked up."

"I have to get dressed—I can't go in my pajamas. I also have to pack. I didn't know it would end like this. For the last few weeks I was his friend. He confided everything to me, and now you come and drive me into the street like a dog."

"I'm not driving you. But Papa—"

"Where shall I go with my bundle? I don't know New York, I don't know where to go."

"What are you doing here anyway?" demanded Anna, in a tone suggesting she had only just realized Kotik had no right to be there at all. Her eyes seemed to swivel in her head, as though she had suddenly grasped the outlandishness of the situation, as if it were some kind of nightmare.

"I explained everything to your Mr. Grein. I've been living here for the past two weeks. I came back from Hollywood and didn't have any place to stay. I remembered that your husband lived alone in this apartment. The first time, when I met you here, he was very cordial to me and proposed that I come and stay with him. So I telephoned him."

"Were you present when he——" And Anna broke off abruptly.

"Yes. He virtually died in my arms. He woke up and said he wasn't feeling well. I went to get him a drop of whiskey—I've got a bottle of whiskey here—but when I came back, he was already dead. It hadn't been more than a minute."

"Oh my God! What did he say?"

"When? Before he died?"

Anna did not reply.

"He said he felt very bad. He started to groan and I hurried as fast as I could to help him. He loved you, Anna—he loved you very much."

Anna's face was bathed in tears. "Well, I killed him! That's how I repaid him! Take your hat." And she handed Grein his hat.

4

Grein was about to go to the door when Boris Makaver suddenly materialized before him.

"Are you here, too?" Boris almost shouted. "So why are you running away? 'Hast thou killed and also taken possession?' " he added bitingly, quoting Elijah's accusation against Ahab over Naboth's vineyard.

Grein's lips trembled. "I've taken possession of nothing."

"You killed him! You're a murderer! At least go and take a look at him! We have to bury him as well! Someone must attend to that."

Grein did not reply.

"Come in. Come with me!" Boris commanded in a voice both strong and thick with tears.

Grein let himself be led with the suffocating fear of someone who knows that a gruesome sight awaits him. Boris suddenly turned his head.

"I've told you to get out of here!" he shouted at Yasha Kotik. "You're not permitted to talk to him!" he shouted even more loudly at Anna. "At the very least, don't sin openly in my sight! Even the worst libertines refrain from that!"

"Papa!"

"Silence! Harlot!"

Boris seemed shocked by his own words. His face turned blue and his bloodshot eyes bulged even more. He grabbed Grein by the sleeve and pulled him along with the familiar tug of close acquaintances. He growled, snorted, tried to say something, then hastily flung wide the bedroom door. The corpse was covered with a sheet and Boris lifted it aside. Grein took one look and knew that he would never forget this sight until the day he died, that it would haunt him day and night. Stanislaw Luria lay with his face bound up with a cloth to keep his mouth from falling open. This was not the Luria Grein had known but someone else only vaguely resembling him, the face as yellow as ivory, the nose completely altered: instead of being short and broad, it had lengthened and taken on a Jewish curve. The old cleft in his forehead had deepened and widened, and his bushy eyebrows hid his eyes. His mouth seemed to be emitting a dull cry of distress, expressing a sorrow not of this world. An accusation lay on the thick lips and in the corners of the mouth, along with the saintly humility of a murder victim. It seemed as if the corpse were struggling to speak a last word which it could no longer utter but which Grein heard quite distinctly: "Well, they've taken care of me. Look what they've done. It's an outrage, a scandalous outrage. Why did I deserve this? 'Look, O Lord, and see!' The murderer even comes to gaze at his work." Grein went ice-cold, as if someone had clutched his ribs with frozen fingers. "This is Gehenna, Gehenna," he mumbled. His heart pounded rapidly as if the organ were itself shocked by what it saw. I'll collapse and die here, Grein thought. Instead of one funeral, she'll have two. Boris covered the corpse with the sheet again.

"According to Jewish Law, we are obliged to lift up the corpse and lay it on the ground," he said. "But in America all Jewish laws have been abrogated."

Grein was silent.

"Has a doctor been here?"

"I don't know."

"We can't bury him without a death certificate from a doctor," Boris said, speaking from experience. "They might want to conduct an autopsy on him. Be so good as to call Dr. Margolin."

"What's his telephone number?"

"He's not in his office yet. Call him at home. Wait, on second thought, I'll call him myself."

As Boris strode from the bedroom, Grein was left alone with the corpse. He did something which he himself could not explain: he again uncovered the dead man's face. As he stood and looked, his heart, which had resumed a more regular beat, began to leap and pound once more. Grein seemed to be testing how long he could endure the pain and whether he might even be able to grow accustomed to it. Hearing someone turn the doorknob, he hastily replaced the sheet. Anna came in. She stood at the door gazing both at Grein and at the shrouded figure. Only now did Grein realize that it was no longer night. The sun streamed in through the curtains, its light merging with the still-burning lamps. For a while Anna said nothing. Her eyes were filled with a pain for which there is no cure—the pain of birth and death, of sin and ignorance. Her gaze came to rest somewhere in one corner of the room, where it seemed she saw a shadowy net from which spread all suffering and misunderstanding. Then she came close to Grein.

"He did it out of spite," she said.

Grein went cold again. "Hush, Anna."

"Yes, he wanted to die. He knew I'd fall to pieces that way. I'll never be myself again. Never!" Anna spat out the last word.

Grein knew that he ought to comfort her, but he could find nothing to say. He was drained and hollow. In a strange way he envied the dead man, who lay there at rest, without any obligations, without any cares, without any pangs of conscience. No, there was no soul, none! something in Grein screamed out. We are worthless machines that wear out and are sent to scrapyards. God wanted to insult us, to spit in our faces. He wanted to display His own greatness through our smallness.

Boris came in. "I've called him. He'll be here immediately. We have to organize the funeral."

No one answered.

"Be so good, Grein—I must have a word with you."

Boris motioned for Grein to follow him into the other room and Grein complied. Kotik was no longer there. He was apparently in the bathroom.

"What's that scum doing here?" Boris demanded. "I had no idea he was still alive."

"He's in America. He's been to Hollywood. He moved in here."

"Moved in? Here?"

"Yes."

"What for? Well, better not to know too much about the likes of you two. Since everything's been turned upside down, it's best to leave it so. I want to tell you one thing: you've committed a grave sin, an outrage— you see yourself what the consequence has been. But it was preordained, in any event. I've blotted her out as a daughter, blotted her out. Never-theless, she's still my own flesh and blood. Now she's no longer a married woman and it's time for you to bethink yourself. It doesn't pay to sin against the Creator of the universe. I begged him to give her a divorce, but modern people don't want to reflect."

"Yes, yes."

"So it's like this—get a divorce and let there be an end to this scandal!"

"I'll do everything I can."

"The situation is a daily slap in the face for me!" Boris exclaimed rapidly, swallowing his words.

Grein suddenly felt a familial closeness to this old Jew, something he had never experienced until this moment. Boris was now his father-in-law. Grein had never had in-laws. Leah was an orphan. This feeling of closeness to a man who was the father of his wife, who lived in her, was entirely new for Grein. His lovers either had no fathers living or had never intro-duced them. At that moment he felt a surge of love for Boris Makaver, and great shame that he was causing him disgrace.

"Anna is my wife whatever the case," said Grein, not fully recognizing the import of what he was saying. "I love both her and you. I've always looked on you as a friend and a father."

Boris Makaver's eyes filled with tears. "What have I got besides her? Even if I were to have ten more children, she would still remain my most precious possession."

Emitting deep bass growls, Boris started coughing and wiping his face with a handkerchief. Smoothing down his beard, he said, "As long as you're not married according to the Law of Moses and Israel, my life's not worth living."

15

Anna prepared to observe the Seven Days of Mourning in her old apartment, and her father sent Reytze to look after her. Obedient to Jewish Law, Grein did not go there, but Dr. Margolin, Professor Shrage, Henrietta Clark, Dr. Halperin, Anna's cousin Herman and his girlfriend, Sylvia, and Jacob Anfang all called. Even Frieda, Anna's stepmother, came to talk with Anna and comfort her. Her neighbor Mrs. Katz offered to go shopping for her, because a mourner was forbidden to go into the street.

It was bizarre for Anna to be sitting in mourning for a husband whom she had deserted. Normally she did not believe in all these Orthodox Jewish laws, but Luria's death had awakened in her stronger guilt feelings than she had ever known. At every opportunity, she repeated her own words: she had killed him. Every time she remembered this, she wept. She was also afraid. Who knew what his soul might do? How could she be happy with Grein when for her own pleasure she had sacrificed another human being? Anna was not satisfied with merely observing the Seven Days of Mourning herself. She called up an office downtown which appointed Jews to say Kaddish and study the Talmud in the name of the dead. If there was a God, Anna did not want to wage war against Him. She had to appease Him as far as possible.

Anna dressed completely in black, as befitted a widow. She flattered Mrs. Katz—who had become a regular caller—to her face and cursed her with the deadliest curses behind her back. Reytze busied herself in the kitchen and sighed: Boris's marriage to Frieda had been a severe blow to her. She no longer felt at home in his apartment. It was true that Frieda had done everything she could to befriend Reytze and to lift her spirits, but Reytze had fallen into a depression. Reytze had loved Anna like a daughter, but Anna had set out on a dangerous course. Reytze was filled with sorrow. She had devoted her life to Boris, and now in her old age she was left completely alone, without a husband, without children, merely everyone's servant. Every day she wanted to leave Boris, but where could she go? In America, who needed an elderly woman who knew not a single word of English? At least in Anna's apartment Reytze was spared having to see her new mistress, the "German *rebbetzin*" as Reytze insisted on referring to Frieda. But how long could one sit in mourning? Everything had collapsed. Reytze was left without a refuge.

She brewed tea, boiled coffee, offered the visitors cookies, crackers, fruit. Jewish Law obliged a mourner to sit on a low stool, but Anna occupied a chair while callers sat, walked about, passed judgment on the pictures on the walls, conducting themselves as if they were at a party and not in a house of mourning.

To Reytze such behavior during the period of obligatory mourning seemed, like everything else modern people did, a complete farce. The telephone rang and Anna took the calls in the bedroom, where there was an extension. Happening to be in the hallway, Reytze heard Anna say in English, "Darling, is that you?" That was how she spoke to Grein.

After Reytze had provided everyone with refreshments, she herself came to sit in the living room. She was no stranger here. Since she was a relative of Anna's late mother, Anna used to call her *Tante*. Everyone knew her from the days in Berlin.

"Well, when will your book be published?" Dr. Margolin asked Dr. Halperin.

Halperin took the cigar from his mouth. "Who knows? In Germany when I published a book, I was the boss. Here I'm dependent on a translator. Can one really carry thoughts over from one language to another? At least half the content gets lost."

"How long will the book be?"

Dr. Halperin didn't know that either. "They want to cut. In Germany I never heard of cutting a book. If it couldn't come out in one volume, then it came out in two. Here they regard a book as a shapeless mass from which you can lop off slices. Yes, yes, this is America. But what can one do? The whole world's grown either mad or impoverished, or both at the same time."

"But books are still published in Europe."

"True, true," replied Halperin, flicking the ash from his cigar. "But these days who needs philosophy, of all things? However, my agent thinks my book will create a furor. Even the publisher is enthusiastic."

"Perhaps."

"Yes, perhaps. But this is definitely my last attempt. It's nearly time for me to go to sleep." And Dr. Halperin chuckled.

"You're as healthy as an ox," Dr. Margolin rapped out.

"Even oxen don't live forever," Halperin retorted.

Herman Makaver, who until now had been sitting in silence smoking a cigarette and listening, suddenly broke in: "Dr. Halperin, may I ask you what your book is about?"

Dr. Halperin knotted his bushy eyebrows. "Certainly you may ask, but to answer such a question is quite another matter. All I can tell you is that it's a philosophical work."

"A new system?"

"I believe it to be a new system, yes. But then I'm a biased judge. A critic could come along and say that what is new in it is not wisdom, and what is wisdom is not new."

"What, briefly, is the idea?"

"Ah, *Panie* Makaver, you're a stubborn young man. Mine is the work of a lifetime and you want it all in a nutshell. The chief idea is that what we call knowledge—empirical knowledge and even intuitive knowledge—is not the whole of knowledge. Experience is also a source of knowledge, although it is subjective and unique. In Genesis it says, 'And Adam *knew* Eve his wife,' from which we can infer that the ancients understood that sexual experience was a sort of knowledge. I go further. For me every experience is an attempt to grasp in its essence what Kant calls *das Ding an sich*. Philosophers have either neglected or marginalized experience. I start from the view that human beings learn from everything: from eating, from love, from war, from smoking a cigar—"

"Isn't this a materialistic approach?"

"Not unconditionally."

"Where can such a philosophy lead? Spinoza also knew that there was such a thing as experience."

"He knew, but he regarded it as knowledge of either the third or the fourth rank. I don't remember which exactly. Spinoza's ideal was the adequate idea. But I believe that even inadequate ideas approach the truth more closely than mathematics or logic. In one chapter I argue that to know the nature of the divine, human beings will have to be much more active and experience a great deal more than they experience today. People will have to learn how to enlarge their lives in the same way as a microscope magnifies a cell. They will have to be able to enjoy and to suffer on many more planes than formerly. In brief, a person who eats good food, drinks fine wine, smokes expensive cigars, and so on delves more deeply into the nature of the world than someone who eats bread and onions and drinks water. My teaching is the absolute opposite of asceticism.''

''In other words, the capitalists know God better than the workers.''

''If you want to carry the thought to extremes, yes. But surely that's why the workers are fighting for a better deal. The struggle for existence is the struggle for understanding.''

''So it turns out, according to you, that Rothschild was closer to God than, for example, the Chafetz Chaim?''

''Want is also an experience. The poor man who has no bread but is hungry bites into understanding with his hunger. But certainly the actual experience is worth more than the dream of it. You can say what you like, but I support the use of narcotics. Opium, morphine, hashish are not simply intoxicants but lessons in the philosophy of being in exactly the same way as alcohol and tobacco. That's why there are so many drug addicts and drunkards.''

Dr. Margolin put down his cup of coffee. ''What about murder? Isn't murder an experience?''

''Yes, a great experience. That's why wars take place. But there's no skill in having that one experience at the expense of exterminating millions of others. The price is too high. That's why hunting is a great lesson in philosophy. A person who goes hunting knows something that an impractical man who sits all day in a study house will never know.''

''*I* go hunting, not you,'' Dr. Margolin retorted.

''I envy you. But we can't all know everything. Each one learns his own lesson. Knowledge can never come only to a single individual—it grows out of the cumulative experience of the whole human species.''

Late at night everyone went his separate way. Anna did not sleep in the bedroom in which Luria had died but made up a bed for herself on the sofa in the living room. Reytze slept in the bedroom and left the door open. Anna got into bed and prepared for rest. On a table she had set out a radio, books, newspapers, magazines, as well as the telephone and a lamp. She had, as it were, surrounded herself with the defenses of civilization. She propped herself up on two pillows and leafed through a magazine. Papa's idea that she should observe the Seven Days of Mourning here had been crazy from start to finish, but since she had agreed, she had to stay until the end of the Sabbath.

At night Anna usually spoke at such length to Grein that she started to fall asleep at the telephone and the receiver dropped from her hand. In this way they tried to distract themselves from the fear they both felt. But tonight Grein had forbidden her to call. He was too exhausted from all the nights past and had to sleep. Anna called to Reytze, "Reytze, are you sleeping yet?"

"What? No."

"Can't you sleep either?"

"At my time of life . . ."

"Reytze, do you believe there's a World to Come?"

Reytze started to reply, but the telephone rang. Anna snatched up the receiver. "Hertz?"

"It's not Hertz—it's Yasha."

Anna scowled. "What is it?"

"I hope I haven't wakened you."

"No. What do you want?"

"I left a suitcase full of plays in your apartment. There's a chance that I might get work in a Yiddish theater and they need a play. So when can I come to collect the suitcase?"

"Are you really going to perform in Yiddish?"

"In my situation I'm prepared to act in Turkish. What difference does it make to me? A man looked me up—he's some kind of patron to a Yiddish theater. His name's Plotkin, Morris Plotkin. He persists in believing that if I acted on the Yiddish stage, it would draw huge crowds. But my old luck hasn't left me—the man's sprained his ankle. Other than that, I wander up and down Second Avenue. Once it used to be the Broadway of Yiddish theater, but now it's half dead. Given that I'm half dead, and it's half dead, together we'll make a perfect corpse."

"You can come and get your suitcase. I don't need your plays."

"When shall I come?"

"Whenever you like. Tomorrow."

"Ai, Anna, I didn't know that it could be so lonely in New York! Over in Russia it's bitter enough, but one's never alone and one has no opportunity to think. Here I've moved into a furnished room and it's worse than a jail. I lie on the bed and all sorts of thoughts run through my head. Bang! Crash! If you're tired, Anna, I won't pester you anymore.''

"Talk, talk, I'm not tired.''

"My whole life passes before me like a movie. Who could have foreseen that I would live in New York and all the rest of it? In Hollywood there were moments when I almost went out of my mind.''

"You were always a madman.''

"But there's such a pandemonium there that your head starts spinning. First they're going to give you a contract at seven hundred dollars a week, then they give you a fig in vinegar. First you're a big shot, then you're nobody. It's like that in Russia, too. First they're going to raise you to the highest heights, almost up to Comrade Stalin himself, and suddenly they punch you in the guts, and then you're a counter-revolutionary, a mad dog, an enemy of the proletariat. I didn't know America was also like that.''

"Hollywood isn't America.''

"What is it, then? It's the same in New York. They've already offered to make me a star on Broadway. There was supposed to be a play, with money, with all the trappings. I go to sleep happy, and the next morning it's all over. I've got an agent who's a crazy man. He keeps screaming that the whole of America will go wild over me, but in the meantime he wants to send me to play in the Jewish hotels in the Catskills. I've even given some thought to hanging myself. By an American rope.''

Anna was silent for a moment. "So what? I won't observe any days of mourning for you.''

"Who needs your mourning? As far as I'm concerned, they can chop me into pieces and throw me to the dogs. But here the dogs all have very distinguished pedigrees, so Yasha Kotik's flesh probably won't be much to their taste. Anna, may I ask you something? I'm only going on like this because I'm lonely.''

"What do you want to ask?''

"Are you at least happy with that Grein?''

"He's all I've got. But Luria's death has spoiled everything. I'll never ever be happy.''

"Silly, you'll forget. If I should go the same way, I only want one thing of you: light a memorial candle for me. Not every year. Only on the first anniversary. After that, I'll cope on my own.''

"What's happened to you? I thought you'd cheer me up.''

"Not tonight. I want to tell you something, Anna, but don't get cross:

if things turn out badly with your Mr. Grein, you can always call me. Give a whistle and I'll come running like a dog. That's what I wanted to tell you. I don't need the plays at all, but I'll come and fetch them just the same.''

2

A ll the lights were burning in Grein's apartment on Fifth Avenue: in the kitchen, in the living room, in the bedroom, in the bathroom. It was half-past twelve. Anna was spending the night in her old apartment, observing the Seven Days of Mourning. Grein couldn't sleep. Since he had seen Luria's corpse, the bone-yellowness of his skin, the altered nose, the bloodless ears, the compressed lips uttering a dumb cry, he had developed a schoolboy's fear of the dark. He switched on the radio and listened to some chitchat and commercials for restaurants and nightclubs. It was all very eerie: the lamps blazing in the middle of the night, the voices carried here over rooftops and through walls by electromagnetic waves, the new grave into which they had laid Stanislaw Luria. Jack had already married Patricia, that Gentile girl from Oregon, and they had gone off on their honeymoon; Anita had moved out of the house; and Leah was living alone in the apartment. Esther had probably married that old Morris Plotkin by now. Grein sat on the edge of the bed. What would happen if a fuse suddenly blew? In one second everything would become pitch-dark and dead silent. If only he had a candle at the ready! But why should the power suddenly fail? Grein shivered and the telephone rang. It's Anna, he told himself. She can't sleep either. Lifting the receiver, he asked, ''Anna?''

He heard scuffling and mumbling at the other end of the line, and then Esther's voice: ''It's not Anna.''

Grein's spine tingled. ''Esther, is that you?''

''Yes, me.''

For a long while both were silent. Then Grein asked, ''I suppose you know what's happened?''

''Yes, I know everything. Otherwise I'd never have called in the middle of the night. I know she's sitting the Seven Days of Mourning in her second husband's home.''

''How do you know? It wasn't reported in the newspapers.''

"I met her first husband, Yasha Kotik. He told me everything."

A sour taste filled Grein's mouth. "How did you come across him?"

"Everyone knows everything in New York. Morris Plotkin gives money to a Yiddish theater and Yasha Kotik's getting a part. It's all signed and sealed."

"Have you married him already?"

Esther did not answer immediately. "Yes, I'm married. I'm now a little wife. You can congratulate me."

Grein was aware of the same cramps in his stomach as he'd felt when he'd been told that Stanislaw Luria had died. "Well, so."

"Yes, so."

"So why are you calling me at this hour?"

"Why not? Plotkin's no sultan, and I'm not Scheherazade. No janissaries guard me. Actually, I do have a janissary—that Sam, I told you about him, Plotkin's factotum—but he doesn't keep me under surveillance."

"When did all this happen?"

"What? It happened. You can't go on talking and talking—the time comes when you have to act, whether you want to or not. I'm now Mrs. Plotkin. If you don't want to congratulate me, we'll manage without your good wishes."

Grein wanted to slam down the receiver, but he didn't. His throat felt parched. "Where are you calling from?"

"From my bedroom at home."

"Where's your husband?"

"My husband had a car accident. He's in the hospital."

"Is it serious?"

"Not serious, but he's sprained his ankle. Usually Sam drives, but this time Plotkin was driving and another car smashed into him. We were supposed to go on our honeymoon, but now they'll strap up his foot. That's my luck. I met Yasha Kotik in the hospital. That's the kind of man Plotkin is—he lies in the hospital in great pain and they all come to bother him about the Yiddish theater. It's really comical."

"Is he a Yiddish actor, then?"

"You mean Kotik? Why not? If the Gentiles don't want him, he comes to the Jews. In addition to which, Plotkin's mad about the Yiddish theater. He's friendly with all the Yiddish actors. He knows whole plays by heart. He's from the old school, from the days when Yiddish theater was a religion. I only recently found out that he was an actor himself once."

"Well, then, you move in the highest circles."

"Yes. The very highest."

Again both were silent for a long while. Then Esther said, "There's no reason we shouldn't remain friends. Plotkin knows about you. I've hidden nothing from him—I told him everything. He's old, but he has the attitudes of a younger man. He could teach many young people to understand the world."

"If he's so wise, what do you want from me?"

"Certainly not wisdom. Listen to me, Hertz. I told you before what I was going to do. I never kept any secrets, either from you or from him. I spoke to him very frankly and I told him just how things stood. He knows I've loved you all these years and that my feelings haven't changed. He wants to meet you. Don't interrupt me! I've earned the right for you to hear me out for a few minutes! You've already seen what happens when you cause people torment. They can't endure it and their hearts burst. How far was I, do you think, from coming to the same end as Luria? You won't believe it, but while I was standing with Plotkin in City Hall, I suddenly got such a pain I nearly fainted. A fist seemed to be squeezing my heart. Well, I thought, at least he'll pay for my funeral. But I recovered. How are you? What are you doing? I'm sure the whole business with her husband is giving you no pleasure."

"No."

"But what did you expect? If you go to war, the smell of gunpowder gets in your nostrils. If you're a slaughterer, you watch cattle die in pools of blood."

"I beg you, Esther."

"It's not your fault, only hers. *She* swore to be faithful to him, not you. Believe me, you've sinned more against me."

"You're still alive."

"Yes, I'm alive."

"And not alone either."

"What? Yes, you could put it like that."

The conversation again ground to a halt. They seemed to be listening each to his own silence. Then Esther burst out, "Hertz, I need to talk to you. I didn't telephone you for no reason."

"What do you need to talk to me about? We've already said everything that needs to be said."

"I've told you that we can remain friends. When all's said and done, it's you who drove me to this. If you hadn't tormented me with Boris Makaver's daughter, everything would've remained as it was."

"Esther, I bear you no grudges, but don't let's start the old quarrel all over again. You've married, and that's that. We must put an end to things."

"To our friendship as well?"

"To everything."

"Well, I can't force you. Believe me, it took me a long time before I decided to call you. I even pricked myself with a needle and vowed in my own blood that I'd never call you again. When you come, I'll show you the paper. It's perfectly legible—my blood isn't water. It's thicker than ink. Perhaps that's my misfortune—people with water in their veins can be very ruthless. You had better know, Hertz, that these are the last words I'll ever speak to you. Since you don't even want my friendship, I must surrender. More precious to me than life is my pride. Not your empty pride, which is stupid sexual ambition and male arrogance—I've thrown that away long ago, dearest—but human worth, the dignity of God's child. Since you say no, no it must be. I'm not a beggar pleading for a kind word or a caress. Since you want to break it off, let's break it off and say goodbye forever. It's not my fault that we met and our souls were irresistibly drawn together. You kept trying to break it off. You made such strenuous efforts that I often wanted to laugh and cry at the same time. With our kind of bond, when one tears away, the other feels the pain. It's like Siamese twins. But when you ripped yourself away, and ripped a chunk of me away with you as well—what could I do? I tried to heal the wound—is that so wrong?"

"Say what it is you want!"

"I want to talk to you—that's all."

"Well, talk—I'm listening."

"There are things one can't say over the telephone."

"Why not? I can hear you just as well as if you were next to me. If you don't want to run up a big telephone bill, I'll call you back."

"What? Who said anything about bills? You should be ashamed in every fiber of your being! Plotkin's a man who throws thousands around—tens of thousands—even millions. Money's no object for him, and all you can talk about is a telephone bill. Just don't hang up! Hanging up the receiver can be like hanging someone from a gallows. One's left like a dumb idiot with one's tongue dangling out. Don't get agitated if I say things I shouldn't say, or even if I spout utter nonsense. I don't have to act the sophisticate for you. I'm yours, body and soul. I don't sleep at night, that's why I'm so wound up. From the day I decided to take out a license with him, I've never shut an eye. I know you don't believe me—my doctor doesn't either. I tell him, and he says I'm imagining it. Because I take the pills he prescribes, I must obviously be sleeping—that's according to his book. But what does it say in the Yom Kippur liturgy? 'My heart knows the bitterness of my soul.' I lie there, my head's as heavy as a stone, I close my eyes, but I can't sleep—my brain turns around obsessively like a mill wheel, exactly like Titus the Wicked. You can imagine what kind of bride I made at the wedding. But at least I have one skill—I can act, and you don't have to be a great actress with Morris Plotkin. He's already an old man. All he needs is a pleasant word or a wisecrack. Our relationship's platonic—God knows what to call it. Men either abandon themselves completely to sex or else it's all spiritual for them. It's like a long intro-duction to a short book. He only wants to show off in front of others. Who knows what men like that want? He's the exact opposite of you— so much so that it makes my flesh creep. It's almost as if some joker in heaven wanted to make fun of me. Hello? Can you hear me or not?''

"Yes, I can hear you."

"Where was I? Never mind, it's all the same. Yes, I can't sleep. I can't eat either. I've lost eighteen pounds in these last few weeks. You won't recognize me when you see me, Hertz. They pay me compliments. I've grown ten years younger, they say. How can people know what others suffer? Sometimes they only realize when you're stretched out dead. I live off coffee and liquor. Yes, dearest, your Esther's become a drunk, but thank God, nobody's the wiser. How can I get drunk when I'm drunk before I touch a drop of liquor? I want you to know one thing: I haven't betrayed you—not spiritually, and not even physically. I belong to you, not because I want to, but because I have no choice. I was very angry with you, but after I did what I did, the anger vanished. I'm a rich woman now. I can't tell you in what kind of luxury he lives and all he does for me. He's smothered me in jewelry. On the very morning after the wedding, he rewrote his will. He made over huge estates to me, as if there won't be taxes for the next hundred years. Oh, Hertz, I really want to laugh. You were too stingy even to buy me a ticket to the theater, you haggled with me over every penny, and here comes a man who showers me with gold. My mind's in a complete whirl—I often think the whole thing's nothing more than a dream. I have no idea how this man made such an enormous fortune. He's one of those that money chases. Everything comes to people of its own accord—riches, poverty, honor, disgrace. One doesn't have to run after anything. What was I saying? I start speaking and

I forget. Oh yes, I was saying all that because what use is money to me now? I'm sick, Hertz, I'm sicker than you think. I've done it and I don't regret it. You've justly deserved it. But I didn't make myself better—I've only killed the rest of me. A disaster could happen at any moment. I'm not afraid of death, but I don't want to go mad. There were insane people in my family, and that's why I'm afraid.''

"You must see a doctor.''

"What doctor? I'm seeing a doctor already.''

"Not a doctor like that.''

"You mean a psychiatrist? I've been. My life was once an open book for you, but I didn't tell you everything. I kept a few secrets. Those doctors couldn't help me at all, Hertz, and you know that yourself. There's only one person who can help me now, and that's you.''

"How can I help you?''

"Don't be nasty to me—that's all. I don't want you to be my enemy. I fear your hatred more than I fear death.''

"I'm not your enemy.''

"Contempt is worse than enmity. You know that perfectly well.''

3

"Esther, it's getting very late.''

"How much later can it get? It's been late so long that it's already early. What does it matter if we don't sleep for one night? I haven't slept for more nights than I've got hairs on my head and I'm still alive. Hertz, I must see you!''

"When?''

"Now, tonight. Today. Call it what you like.''

"In the middle of the night?''

"What's wrong with the middle of the night? Why do people make such a fuss about the night? You can sleep tomorrow, or whenever. Don't pamper yourself so much!''

"Esther, you've talked for so long—let me also say something.''

"What? Say it.''

"Esther, I've done enough bad in my life. I can't go any further along that road.''

"What road? What are you babbling about?"

"Esther, I've done too many bad things. This business with Stanislaw Luria is the end. I killed him. Literally. And now Leah is very ill, as good as killed. I can't live this kind of life any longer. I must put a stop to this duplicity. As long as I have to live, I want to live honestly—if not, it's better for me to drop dead."

"What's happened? Have you become a penitent?"

"I simply can't sink any lower."

"What'll your repentance consist of? Being faithful to Boris Makaver's daughter?"

"I must be faithful to someone. I'm sick as a result of all these lies."

"I see! Well, a penitent is a penitent. If you're truly repentant, go back to your wife, who gave you the best years of her life. She's dying because of you. Boris Makaver's daughter is young and healthy, and rich into the bargain. She'll inherit everything her father owns, and I hear that her husband also left her a bundle—insurance or something. If you're feeling compassionate, have compassion on the weak, not on the strong."

"Whatever the case, we both have to control ourselves, otherwise it'll lead to such a mess that we'll never be able to crawl out of it."

"You're preaching, eh? Your mouth is moralizing, but your mind is calling to me. I wouldn't be so sick if you weren't calling to me the whole time. I hear your voice—I hear you calling to me. I sit and try to read a newspaper, and suddenly I hear your voice as clearly as I hear it over the telephone."

"Esther, you're sick."

"I may be sick, but I'm not deaf. I know you'll say I'm hallucinating or something, but I hear you all the same. And every time I hear your voice, my blood freezes and my breath stops. You probably don't know yourself that you're calling to me, for these things have to do with the unconscious. It just shows that you're yearning for me, and you don't realize it."

"I know, Esther, I know exactly."

"You yearn?"

"Yes, I yearn."

"Well, thank God you can still utter a word of truth. You long for me so much that you nearly go mad, and because of that you're also driving me mad. Hertz dearest, these things are stronger than we are. I used to think that people were masters over themselves, but it's not so. I shouldn't tell you this, but who else can I tell it to if not to you? When he touches me, I'm paralyzed with terror. I screw up my eyes and try to imagine that it's you. But that just makes it worse for me. I don't know what to do, Hertz. Every second I want to run away. But where can I run to? And I can't make a fool of this Plotkin. When all's said and done, he didn't force me. He's an innocent bit player in a terrifying drama. I want to die. I've thought about taking sleeping pills, but I couldn't do it. I'm telling you the holy truth, Hertz—I swear by the bones of my sainted parents, and I've never taken an oath like that before. I'll probably be with them soon, so I'd never desecrate their memory.''

"Esther, what shall I do?''

"Are you dressed or lying in bed?''

"I'm dressed.''

"Let's meet. If you want, you can come to me. He has a private house on Hicks Street. You're allowed to admire a house.''

"I won't set foot in his house. And certainly not now, in the middle of the night.''

"Foolish boy, he asked me to invite you. That man doesn't understand the meaning of jealousy. It often seems to me exactly the opposite—there are such men. He nags me to death about why I don't bring you. What's the matter with me? Everything around me is bent and twisted. He's not a normal person either—that's the bitter truth. He says such things that I don't believe my own ears, and it's not easy for me to repeat them. I often think the whole modern world is one huge madhouse. How else could there be a Hitler and a Stalin and all the other Satans? I once visited a lunatic asylum to see an uncle of mine, and I saw one lunatic making fun of another. All you need to do is drive over the Brooklyn Bridge and right away you're on Hicks Street.''

"This talk is futile. I won't visit you now.''

"Well, you can meet me in the street.''

"Where?''

"Where's your car?''

"In the garage.''

"I'll take a taxi and come to Manhattan. We can meet on Fifth Avenue or on Broadway, or wherever you want.''

"Everything's closed.''

"Who needs it to be open? We'll sit down somewhere and talk. If you've got the car, we can sit in the car.''

"Really, Esther, we're too old for that.''

"One of my uncles cursed me by saying that I'd never grow old. That's my bad luck exactly. Tell me where I should meet you."

"At Broadway and Forty-second Street."

"Why there? Well, so be it. I'm leaving the house now, but I don't know if I can get a taxi. Hicks Street is a bit out of the way. If I'm a little late, it won't be my fault."

"Truly, Esther—"

"I don't want to hear any more. Goodbye!"

And Esther hung up.

Grein looked at his wristwatch. It was a quarter past one. He yawned and rubbed his forehead. It occurred to him that Anna might also take it into her head to telephone. "Well, this is a fine net I'm caught in!" he said aloud, stretching out on the sofa. Only now did he realize his fatigue. He lay with his face turned to the back of the sofa, half dozing, half thinking. For a while the thread of his thoughts was broken and he very nearly fell asleep, but he soon started awake. He'd lost twenty minutes. No, not lost, just forgotten. Something had happened to him in that time. He got up and began switching off the lights, but not all of them, ensuring that he wouldn't be left in the dark. The night was warm, but he felt cool, so he carried a light overcoat over his arm. He rang for the elevator and it arrived quickly. The operator seemed astonished that anyone was going out so late, but he said nothing. Grein started walking uptown. Fifth Avenue was deserted, dark. It occurred to him that, because of daylight saving time, it would still be dark when the new workday began. The Fifth Avenue bus stopped and Grein boarded it. Inside were other passengers, young couples who had evidently been enjoying themselves in the nightclubs of Greenwich Village. They giggled, horsed around, embraced. A young woman, her mouth ceaselessly chewing gum, laid her shorn head on a youth's shoulder. She glanced at Grein with tired, smiling eyes and the unruffled, carefree indifference that comes from attaching no importance either to oneself or to others. The majority of the young men wore war-veteran badges in their lapels. Like Grein himself, they were carrying on love affairs, but in groups, with the timeless instinct of the herd that had been inherited from the caves of the primeval world. Grein looked out of the window. The display windows of the fashionable boutiques were now dim. In the darkness the mannequins laughed with secret midnight life, their daytime inanimateness nothing more than a charade. Do I feel good? Do I feel bad? Grein wondered. He could give himself no answer. Now more than usual he was conscious of the spirit of American freedom. Nobody asked anybody for explanations. No policeman demanded that people show their papers. But behind all those freedoms lurked the constraint of birth and death. At the same time that he, Grein, was traveling to a midnight rendezvous, his victim Luria was rotting in the earth. Now Luria would never return, at least not in his former shape. Even if the body was nothing more than a garment, Grein still had rent a divine garment, leaving a soul naked. Yet despite that jolting fact, Grein could still feel anger when he read in a newspaper that vandals had smashed a window or overturned a gravestone.

Grein got off at Forty-second Street and strolled toward Broadway. He walked slowly, pondering his own folly. For a time he was seized by a kind of joy, a love of destruction coupled with delight at foolhardiness, a feeling that often strikes someone who can stand outside himself and view his own conduct through a stranger's eyes, when almost as if by magic or psychic illness he has been split in two. What, for instance, would his father have said, could he have seen how his son was conducting himself and to what extent his deeds mocked his father's thought? And what about his mother? And what would Anna say if she telephoned him in the middle of the night and didn't find him at home? Well, I'm lost, he decided. Perhaps it would be better if I stopped trying to resist. I'm like Pavlov's dogs—when the bell sounds, I slaver. I'm even more stupid than Pavlov's dogs. Everyone has moments of disappointment in himself, but I'm like an automaton that's been wound up once and forever.

Broadway was as bright as if it were the middle of the day. A cafeteria was open and people who stayed up at night were eating a late snack, reading newspapers bearing tomorrow's date as though rushing to meet the future. What do the poets call it? "The bright tomorrow . . . the day that is wiser than the night." But after two billion years of growing wiser and wiser, the day was still a fool. What was it like, that first day at the beginning of Creation? It must have had great illusions, that time when "the evening and the morning were the first day." It could certainly not have imagined that after billions of years during which evenings changed to mornings there would arise a Hitler, a Stalin, an Esther, a Yasha Kotik.

Esther had not yet arrived, and Grein paced backward and forward, periodically glancing through the cafeteria window. A cook in a tall chef's hat passed by, his face lean, bags under his eyes. To Grein he looked like a priest officiating at some dead-of-the-night idol worship. A short fat man was simultaneously eating and doing a crossword puzzle with a pencil.

Suddenly Grein saw Esther. He barely recognized her. She had never been so elegant, so expensively dressed that it bordered on the vulgar. She wore a Spanish mantilla over her head, a black sleeveless gown cut deeply down the back, and long, elbow-length gloves. Grein was somewhat intimidated by all this finery. Esther had indeed lost weight. She had grown slimmer and seemingly taller. Her face was pale and had changed the way faces do when someone tears herself out of her old environment and embarks on a new and unfamiliar adventure. Esther saw him and they stood regarding each other for a while. He knew that he didn't need to say it, but he couldn't restrain himself. "Why have you dressed up like this?"

"For you, dearest, for you. Now I see it's chilly. I should've put on a wrap. Perhaps we can go inside somewhere."

"Where? Into this cafeteria?"

"What? I'll get a taxi and tell the driver to take us for a ride. It doesn't matter where. I want to talk to you privately. Here's a taxi—look, it's the same one I came in! Good. He doesn't understand any Yiddish!"

They both got into the taxi and Esther said to the driver, "Mr. Pezzana, it's fated that we should drive around all night. Take us somewhere—it doesn't matter where."

"Up Broadway?"

"Yes, why not? But don't hurry. All we want to do is talk. I'll give you a good tip."

"Okay!"

"Sit next to me. I'm cold," Esther said to Grein. "You know what? Since you're not wearing your coat, put it around me. That's right. It was blazing hot all day, so I never imagined it would turn cool. I have absolutely no imagination—that's my problem. Ah, now it's warm. Don't you like my dress?" She changed her tone. "It's the most expensive dress one can buy in New York."

"You know I don't care about expensive dresses."

"Plotkin's mad about clothes. Well, move closer. Don't be such a devout Jew. You're not such a saint. All I want is a little warmth."

16

Things went badly with Boris Makaver's ships. At first it looked as though the four partners would make millions, but now they faced a real danger that they would lose everything. They knew that fitting out ships to carry cargo would cost too much, but they found that to scrap them involved unforeseen expenses. The shipyard's charges had to be paid. The number of laborers and experts required to dismantle the ships was so great that over thirty thousand dollars in wages had to be paid out each week. But the greatest damage was caused by theft. Not only were parts stolen from all sides, but there was vandalism and sabotage as well. Those Boris and his partners had appointed to guard against theft either stole themselves or were in league with other thieves. When the partners tried to intervene, they were threatened with beatings or death. Every time Boris went to the shipyard where the vessels were moored, he came away terrified. He had absolutely no idea what they were doing with his possessions. Huge hammers pounded, cranes hoisted loads. The Gentile workers yelled like savages. Those firms that had agreed to buy up the steel, iron, electrical apparatus, and other machinery and instruments sensed that the new owners neither knew how to handle what they possessed nor understood its value, so they offered virtually nothing. Apart from the $750,000 that Boris had invested in the venture—borrowed from the bank against mortgages on his buildings—he also had to find money to pay wages. From one day to the next—and from one sleepless night to another—it became clear to him that he had made a grave error. He might lose everything; he was deeply in debt. There was no longer the slightest possibility of extricating himself from this catastrophe. How great the debts actually were he would know only later, when all the transactions were completed.

Accustomed all his life to being successful, Boris at first did not believe that he could become utterly destitute. He hoped for a miracle. He solemnly vowed to give huge sums to charity. He consulted lawyers and business advisers, seeking all manner of expedients. But, as the biblical proverb has it, neither advice nor understanding could avail. His enterprises had failed. All the worldly possessions he had accumulated over the years, and for which he had risked his life fleeing Hitler, were trickling away like wine from a leaky barrel.

At night Boris lay wide-awake. With that money he might have performed works of charity by giving interest-free loans. Perhaps he might have been able to save Jews from Hitler's hell. Now most of it had been plundered by robbers and racketeers. Quarrels had broken out among the partners: they abused, cursed, and even struck one another. As though from a conflagration, each one tried to save his own belongings, but nothing could be salvaged. Ashamed before Frieda and unwilling to distress her, Boris kept his troubles secret from his wife. But how long would he be able to cover them up? He tried to restrain himself, but against his will heavy sighs escaped over and over again, until Frieda asked, "What's troubling you, Borukh?"

"Nothing, my soul, nothing."

"Are you in some physical pain, God forbid?"

"No, perish the thought."

"Is something amiss in your business affairs?"

"Well, I wasn't born a rich man. It's all from God."

"I want you to know one thing: I don't need wealth. Heaven help me, I didn't marry you for your money."

"God forbid. It's all foreordained from on high." And Boris fell silent.

Because of the ongoing tension, the daily scramble and haste, and the acrimonious wrangling with his partners, Boris began to suffer severe headaches. The windows in his bedroom were always wide-open, the nights were still cool, but however comfortable Boris tried to make himself with only a sheet for a covering, he felt hot all the time, so that he had to take off his pajama top during the night. At rest he lay perfectly still, yet his heart pounded like a drum and he suffered serious nosebleeds. He knew what all these symptoms meant: his blood pressure had shot up. He was not only in danger of being left naked to the elements but also under imminent threat of another heart attack. As he lay in bed, he mentally recited the confession before death: "We have trespassed, we have dealt treacherously, we have robbed, we have spoken slander . . ." At each phrase he beat his breast with his fist under the sheet. I am in the gravest danger, he said to himself. The blow could come at any moment. It was obvious to him that his heart was being subjected to excessive strain, forced to pump away like the emergency motor on a sinking ship. It emitted a wide variety of strange murmurings. Its rhythm was irregular: every now and then it either missed a beat or gave a rapid double beat as though trying to recapture the lost one.

Boris listened attentively. I must be calm. I must stop worrying! he told himself. I'm dangerously weak. What'll happen to Frieda? I haven't even had time to take out insurance for her. And what'll happen to my soul? I leave nothing behind—no son to recite Kaddish for me, no one who might study the Talmud in my memory. All that'll remain is a daughter who's a harlot. I've lived without a thought to the final reckoning. How will I justify myself in the World to Come? I haven't given a tenth of my income to charity. I've been distracted from study. I've built for the Devil. How does Ecclesiastes put it? "What profit hath he that hath labored for the wind?" Yes, the psalms are right: "The fool and the brutish person perish and leave their wealth to others." What's more, I knew it all the time. I can't justify myself by saying that I didn't know the truth. I'm one of those who's acted wickedly by design, not one who has sinned unwittingly. Why did I send Anna to study in Gentile schools? While other Jews were raising devout children, I prepared my daughter to be a betrayer of Israel. Without understanding what I was doing, I drove her along the road she now follows.

Boris fell asleep and dreamed of a huge conflagration. The whole of New York was on fire. Some skyscrapers were in flames; others crashed to the ground, collapsing one on top of the other like trees during a hurricane. An earthquake had opened an abyss down the center of Broadway within which Gehenna burned and blazed. Alarm bells clanged. A piercing and unremitting wail, like the ceaseless shrieking of an ambulance, filled the city, while in the middle of the sky a monstrous volcano spewed forth flaming lava. However did a volcano get into the middle of the sky? Boris wondered. This could mean nothing but the destruction of the world. He opened his eyes and it was day. His clock showed twenty minutes past six. Knowing that summer and winter Solomon Margolin rose daily at six o'clock and took a brisk walk at exactly 6:45, Boris hurried off to his study to telephone him. "Shloymele, it's me."

Margolin paused. "What's wrong?"

"Shloymele, I don't feel well."

"Who feels well these days?"

"Shloymele, I'm sick."

"What's the matter with you, you old mule?"

"My heart's pounding like a robber's."

"You *are* a robber."

"Shloymele, this isn't a time to make jokes."

"What do you want me to do? Recite the psalms?"

"Shloymele, I can't breathe. I'm afraid this is the end, God forbid."

"You're not dropping dead yet. You'll eat a big hole in America's food supply for a long while to come."

"Shloymele, I must come over and see you."

"So early? I'm going for a walk."

"Well, for once you won't go walking. You'll follow the commandment to save a life."

"Well, come, and I'll break you on my wheel."

"Where shall I come?"

"I'll take a taxi to my office. If the door's locked, just wait for me."

"Thank you very much."

"And get a move on!"

Boris hung up the receiver. Well, he's still a good friend—a very dear friend. He went into the bathroom and took a shower. When he came out he saw Frieda wandering about in her dressing gown and slippers.

"Why have you risen so early?" he asked.

"I won't let you leave without at least a glass of tea."

Boris dressed, washed his hands, and recited the *Shema*. Frieda handed him a glass of tea and an egg cookie. She didn't look at all well herself, Boris thought. Her complexion had taken on a yellow tinge and he wanted to ask what was wrong, but he was anxious to see Dr. Margolin. Outside, the morning was clear, cool, rich with the promise of a long summer day. Boris was suddenly reminded of sour milk, spring onions, little radishes. He was ill and hungry at the same time. His intestines rumbled. That's how human beings are, he thought, they stand at the threshold of the grave, but their guts do as they have always done, every organ has its mission.

He hailed a taxi and directed the driver uptown to West End Avenue, to Dr. Margolin's office. In reality, I can't even afford the indulgence of a taxi. I am penniless, penniless—as the Talmud says, "clean of all worldly goods." Even the shirt I'm wearing is no longer mine. The taxi stopped and Boris saw Margolin waiting for him: six feet tall, clean-shaven, straight as a ruler, immaculately dressed in a light-colored suit and white shoes. He emanated a freshness entirely un-Jewish, looking like a nobleman, a Yankee, a complete Gentile. It was almost impossible to believe that this man was over sixty and had once been a yeshiva student. What had they called such looks, those mongrels? A pure-blooded Aryan. Dr. Margolin glanced at Boris Makaver with his head tilted mockingly to one side and an expression of feigned sorrow on his face.

"Well, simpleton, come in."

"I beg you, Shloymele, be serious. There's a proper time for every-thing."

"What's the matter? Has one of your moldy ships gone down?"

"Not one, but thirty. Shloymele, I'm ruined, I'm a pauper."

"Well, I'll give you alms. Come, *shmegege*."

Once inside his office, Margolin ordered, "First of all, get on the scale. That's right. Hoo! What do you eat? Stones? Lead? You're getting heavier all the time."

"I swear I haven't been overeating."

"What've you done, then? Listened to decent advice? Take off your coat. Roll up your sleeve." He took Boris's blood pressure.

"Yes, it's gone up."

"How high?"

"Too high."

"What shall I do?"

Margolin didn't reply. He regarded Boris in silence. He wanted to take a cardiogram but he needed his nurse for that. In any case the stethoscope told him everything he needed to know. He lit a cigarette.

"Do you want to die now, or do you want to live a few years longer?"

"What's wrong, then?"

"Drop your stinking business and take an extended holiday out in the country. Take your wife with you."

"Are you mad? Are you conspiring with my enemies? The onus is on me. They're tearing me to pieces. My partners—"

"Well then, go out and order your shroud."

"Shloymele, it's impossible! I can't just drop everything and run off."

"Then go to the devil, you idiot!"

Dr. Margolin spoke with brutal frankness. It was essential for Boris to free himself from his worries. Excitement could be lethal for him. Margolin was fully informed about Boris's position since Anna had called him several times. Anna herself was in constant contact with Reytze.

Now Margolin demanded, "Haven't you got a little nest egg somewhere? Haven't you put aside a few thousand dollars as a cushion?"

"I've invested absolutely everything in the ships."

"I'll lend you five thousand."

"Shloymele, I'll never be able to repay it."

"Fool, you'll still end up swimming in money. People like you make money in the grave."

And instead of writing out a prescription, Margolin sat down and wrote out a check.

2

Boris was so disturbed and preoccupied that he did not register what he had been given. He took the check Margolin handed to him for a prescription. He glanced at the piece of paper, appeared to read it, saw his name and the signature, but his mind could not comprehend what his eyes saw. He had already asked whether he could get it filled at any pharmacy when he suddenly realized that this was a check. His forehead turned red, his face wet and hot. He wanted to say something, but a lump formed in his throat.

He heard Margolin say, "*Now* I'll give you a prescription."

Boris snatched out his handkerchief and wiped his face. "Shloymele, you're a true Jew!"

"You're a true Jew yourself!"

"Shloymele, I won't take it."

Margolin immediately bristled. "Why not? Is it beneath your dignity? We've known each other for forty-eight years all told."

"Shloymele, you're a saint. You've got a Jewish heart. If I weren't too embarrassed, I'd kiss you on both cheeks. But I don't need a check. Things aren't that bad yet."

"Hasidic moron! Arrogant ox! Snob! What am I doing? I'm lending you a few dollars. You ought to be ashamed of yourself!"

"Truly, Shloymele, I don't need it."

"If you don't, you don't, but never cross my threshold again! I thought you considered me a good friend, but now I see you have only contempt. So leave here and go to hell this minute! Go on, get out! Find another doctor, you scum! But on the other hand, you're right. I really am a pig. What's five thousand dollars? In fact, if you need money, my entire bank account is at your disposal."

"Shloymele, what's the matter with you? Why are you swearing at me? I don't need any more for myself. As for my investment, let's not fool ourselves—it's a company, not a private partnership. I don't have to throw any more money away. This enterprise consumes people's dollars the way the lean cattle swallowed the fat cattle in Pharaoh's dream: 'When they had eaten them up, it could not be known that they had eaten them.' "

"Who gives a damn about your company? I wish they'd all go to hell and never come back. It's imperative that you get away to the country and cut yourself off from everything for a few weeks. There's only one cure for you now—rest. Since you've put everything you own into those filthy ships, you have no money to go anywhere. If you rest up and gather your strength, you'll soon be able to put things right. People like you don't go begging from door to door."

"Shloymele, you're a dear person, a true and good friend, but I've got too much to do in the next few weeks. I'll simply worry more there than I do here, that's the trouble. I have a thousand different commitments, and if I go away, everything will fall to pieces."

"And what'll happen if you drop dead? Will the world stop functioning? Will the earth stop turning on its axis? Primitive oaf!"

"A dead man doesn't have to pay any debts. A dead man is relieved of the obligation to observe the commandments."

"You're worse than a dead man. You're a living dog! If you don't take that check, I'll spit on you and never set eyes on your filthy mug again. You cretin! You dimwit! You bum!"

"God in heaven, have you got a mouth!"

"If I didn't fear God, I'd punch out all your teeth!"

"Enough, Shloymele, enough. Don't become a murderer. I honestly don't need a loan, but since you're carrying on in this shocking way, what can I do? With God's help, I'll repay you. All the same, I can't just run away and let everything go to rack and ruin. To do that you have to be a complete criminal. I have appointments to meet people. Even while I'm here, my telephone is ringing off the hook."

"As it says in the Torah, 'See, I have set before thee this day.' You must choose between life and death."

"What should I do, then?"

"You've still got a daughter somewhere."

"I want nothing to do with her!"

"What are you making a fuss about? She's no longer another man's wife. I'm beginning to think you're an ignoramus as well."

"Why am I an ignoramus?"

"Because what she's doing is hardly a sin. To pull out one blade of grass on the Sabbath is a thousand times more sinful."

"I know, I know. But still. My daughter. The disgrace."

"And while she lived with Luria, did she observe the laws of female purity? Who are you fooling—yourself? From the point of view of Jewish Law, the modern generation are all bastards conceived at the time of their mothers' impurity."

"Yes, true."

"So why are you beating a dead horse? Call her up and explain the situation to her. She knows everything, in any case. You were never a businessman. You head was always lost in popular reference books and other nonsense written for the layman. Anna ran your business in Berlin as much as she did here. If she'd been with you, she'd never have let you sink into all this mud. Who knows? Perhaps she can still pull you out of it."

"No one can do anything now."

"Go and hand all your rotten affairs over to her. Then get away and imagine that you're already in the World to Come and you're eating the flesh of Leviathan. But not too much of that, mind you—you also have to go on a diet. You need to lose twenty pounds. What use is this paunch to you? For whom are you fattening it up? The worms? If you have complete rest for six weeks and lose twenty pounds, your head'll become clearer as well. Meanwhile, Anna will do whatever can be done. She's young and she's got a good head on her shoulders—except when it comes to men. There she's got even poorer judgment than her father."

"Where shall I go?"

"To the seaside somewhere, but not to those Jewish hotels where they'll cram you with liver and onions and stuffed derma and all the rest of that muck. Take a bungalow somewhere."

"Truly, Shloymele, I don't know what to do."

"Get out of here, or I'll take a stick to you. Oh yes—stop puffing those cigars. At least for a few weeks."

"If I don't smoke, I get even more agitated."

"Instead of smoking a cigar, recite a chapter of the Psalms. As the Gemara says, 'If it doesn't help, at least it won't do harm.' And then sit still for a while, relax! Don't make efforts in all directions. The Master of the Universe constructed his miserable little world in such a way that no single person is irreplaceable. When I heard that Roosevelt had died, a part of my heart was ripped away. But then Truman appeared and now he steers the ship and it still sails on. It's like that with everything. We take ourselves too seriously. To Nature, we're no better than lice—that's the bitter truth."

"When a louse has debts, it also gets distressed."

"A louse doesn't incur debts. A louse is not such a fool as a man. If it gets a drop of blood, it sucks; if it doesn't, it lies completely still and waits for better days. Some creatures don't waste energy to no purpose, especially when it's not good for them. Only we humans think that the responsibility for the whole cosmos rests on our shoulders."

"I'll live, Shloymele. You talk good sense."

"It's easy to advise others. When it comes to myself, I'm worse off than you."

"What's the matter?"

"Ah, I'm not a decent human being!"

"Still with your women?"

"It's no good."

"Haven't I pleaded with you enough?"

"Of what use are your pleadings?"

"You ought to find a respectable woman and get married. How much longer will you live alone?"

"Yes, how much longer? But this is all idle talk. If you could sit patiently without a wife for twenty-three years, you're kneaded of a different dough from me. You've got sour milk in your veins, not blood. Where you get high blood pressure from is truly impossible to understand. Apparently sour milk also needs clear tubes to flow through. Your daughter, on the other hand, is certainly a warm-blooded creature, but I've had no luck with her. First she fell for that Yasha Kotik. Then she started running after Stanislaw Luria, may the earth lie lightly upon him. And now Grein. I'm telling you, Borukh, the whole question of mating is a deep mystery."

"That's what the Cabalists say."

"How would they know? How many wives did Rabbi Isaac Luria have—
or Rabbi Chaim Vital? And they never visited heaven either. You tell me.
Women come to see me and they strip themselves completely naked—
not merely physically but spiritually as well. What do you know about
these things, Borukh? If you knew what went on in my life, you'd weep
and laugh and spit."

"I don't want to know. But at the very least, take care of your health.
You're a doctor, after all."

"And how does being a doctor help me? Your sacred books speak
constantly of free will. But I'm telling you that a human being has as much
free will as a mite or a stone. I make solemn resolutions, I swear holy
vows, and immediately afterward I break every one. We're machines,
Borukh, blind automatons."

"No, there is such a thing as a soul."

"Where's the evidence for that? We've built everything on some measly
Pentateuch penned by a petty scribe. Afterward countless hacks pitched in
and added their two cents. None of it has any connection with reality."

"Then who created the world?"

"Who created God? We've deluded ourselves that everything must be
created. Everything existed from the beginning of eternity."

"Where did it come from? Where did it originate?"

"I don't know. But get one thing into your thick head: we Jews receive
no special privileges from Nature. The whole of our history is one huge
pogrom, from Egypt until now."

"If that's true, then we ought to convert, God forbid."

"And what is Jesus? Again a Jew, again the tired old story of turning
the other cheek and getting Paradise as a reward. It's the same fantasy
adapted for Gentiles. Nature seems miraculous, but it's possible we only
imagine it to be so. For a worm that slithers around trash cans, garbage is
the highest harmony, the greatest aesthetic pleasure."

"So what should we do?"

"Whatever you want."

"And if you want to kill someone?"

"You kill. Who decides that slaughtering an ox is better than slaughtering a human being?"

"Truly, Shloymele, you terrify me. How is it possible to live with such
thoughts?"

"We can. I do, don't I? The Germans slaughtered six million Jews and
they're still living. The sun shines over Germany, and German fields ripen.

At the same moment they were murdering Jews, birds sang and trees blossomed. The only justification we're given for all of this is that we'll be rewarded in the World to Come. But what'll you do when you get to the other world and you find, as Rashi observes in another context, 'There are no woods and no bears'—that it's all imaginary? Will you revile God?''

"Stop, I beg you, Shloymele, stop! This conversation is making me worse, not better.''

"Well, go home and pray. Personally, I can no longer tie on a pair of phylacteries and talk to the wall. Nobody has the faintest idea of what those 'frontlets' were that Moses commanded the Jews in the desert to tie between their eyes. They certainly weren't bits of parchment in wooden boxes held on by leather straps. As far as science is concerned, 'frontlets' are the anterior bones of the skull. Those things you call 'phylacteries' are as much biblical 'frontlets' as you're the governor of Ohio.''

"A Creator does exist—He does!''

"Let Him, but I don't love Him. If He's got something to give, let Him show His hand. If He wants to play hide-and-seek for three billion years, He's welcome. Where do you want to go? Go to Asbury Park. It's got the sea, as well as Jews with their synagogues and all the rest of their paraphernalia. Let me know where you are and I'll drive out and see you on a Sunday.''

"Are you just saying that, or will you keep your word?''

"I'll come. Is there anyone here I can talk to? I'm neither a Jew nor a Gentile, neither an American nor a European. What I say to you I can say to no one else. You're the only person in the world who calls me Shloymele, and for me that's worth a million dollars.''

3

Boris Makaver sat in the taxi that was taking him home, and his eyes were wet. No matter how many times he wiped them, they kept clouding over. The check in his breast pocket both warmed and burned him. From the warnings Solomon Margolin had given, it was clear to him that his life hung by a thread.

Will I really be able to rest? he asked himself. My head's bursting.

He knew that as soon as he entered his apartment, the telephone would start ringing and he'd have to talk and talk. His partners had quarreled so violently among themselves that it had come to blows. He was the only one who prevented these maddened beasts from ripping each other to pieces. He was the oldest of them, and the only learned man among them. But if he were to flee like a bankrupt, he would demonstrate that all his ethical instruction was not worth a penny.

He went up in the elevator. How was he to tell all this to Frieda? She had married a Croesus and would now have to live with a pauper. She might even come to regret their match. She had often told him that she had once been in love with that painter Jacob Anfang. Well, Shloymele is right: let me imagine that I've died already. At the front door Boris started fumbling for his key, but Frieda had evidently heard his footsteps and she opened the door for him, greeting him with a half-astonished smile, her face somewhat flushed. Boris went inside.

"Friedele, how are you?"

"Borukh, I must tell you something."

"I must tell you something as well."

"Come into the living room. Sit down. So."

Frieda made herself comfortable on the sofa while Boris threw himself into an armchair. Only now was he aware that his legs seemed to have been hacked off. His heart began thumping and pounding all over again. Green spots appeared before his eyes.

"Friedele, things are very bad for me!" Boris blurted out.

Frieda raised her eyebrows. "What's happened?"

"Friedele, I've lost everything!"

Frieda's face retained the amiable expression of tranquillity and mild reproof of a mother whose child confesses to her that it has lost a toy or broken a bauble. "Well, don't worry about it. With God's help, we'll find enough to live on."

"Friedele, I'm also not well. I've just come from Solomon Margolin."

"Yes, I know. I've already made the reservations, so you can have a complete break."

"But how is that possible?"

"Dr. Margolin telephoned a little while ago."

"What? Well, then you know everything."

"We'll leave today. You'll get well."

"You're a saint!" Boris Makaver's eyes filled with tears.

"Don't exaggerate. I'm your wife."

"Not all wives are alike." And Boris could say nothing more.

"Borukh, I want you to know that I'm pregnant," Frieda announced after a pause. Boris heard the words, but he did not see her face. A great joy welled up within him but he lacked the strength to exult out loud. Again and again he tried to wipe away his tears, restraining himself with immense effort from sobbing. He sat motionless and speechless while everything within him stiffened and trembled at the same time.

I hope I live at least until the circumcision, a voice within him prayed, even as he realized that the child might be a girl.

"Why are you silent?"

"Everything is from God," Boris gasped.

"Wait, I'll bring you something."

Frieda went out, returning after some time with a tisane. Boris drank it down, but it did nothing to make him feel stronger. All his energy had dissipated. As Frieda bent over him devotedly, despite all his weakness he felt something akin to masculine desire.

"Friedele, *mazel tov!*"

"You may give me a kiss!" And Frieda pressed a kiss on Boris's lips.

She went into the kitchen and busied herself there for a long time, finally returning with a cup of coffee. Boris waved it away.

"Lie down on the sofa."

"Not here. Could you perhaps make up a bed for me in my prayer-house?" As he said this, Boris was thinking, If I die, I want to lie there until the funeral.

"Lie down here!" Frieda half urged, half commanded.

As she made a movement to help him rise, someone rang the doorbell. Fear that it might be one of his partners enabled Boris to regain both his strength and his speech.

"Who's that? I can't talk to anyone now!" he called out in a clear, strong voice.

"I won't let anyone in."

Frieda went to the door while Boris sat listening intently, aware that his attentiveness restored his strength like a tonic or an injection. He was ready yet again to stir himself to anger, to dispense moral admonitions. He wiped his face, blew his nose, and roused himself from his torpor to become Boris Makaver once more. He coughed and growled like a prayer leader preparing his voice before commencing the service. Well, with God's help, we'll fight another fight! he decided. If my wife expects a child, it's a sign that heaven wants me to live. He now regretted that he had asked Frieda not to admit anyone. It would be better for him to spell out his position precisely to his partners instead of hiding away like a thief.

Frieda suddenly appeared on the threshold. "Borukh, it's your daughter!"

"Anna!" Boris remained seated, his eyes bulging.

"Yes. Dr. Margolin told her to come."

"What for?"

"Dr. Margolin is right. She's still your daughter."

"Well, let her come in. When it rains, it pours."

Boris thought that both Shloymele and Frieda were behaving foolishly. Too many surprises were not good for his heart. A verse from Proverbs suddenly occurred to him: "A good report maketh the bones fat." Aren't I fat enough already?

Anna came in wearing a light-colored suit with a flower in her lapel. Boris had not seen her since Stanislaw Luria's funeral, when she had been swathed in black, walking bowed beneath her black veil like a broken old woman. Evidently she had found comfort soon enough. Now she looked extraordinarily young, almost as if her girlhood had returned. She had either cut or restyled her hair, was slimmer, and had a glowing suntan. All the paternal affection that had awakened in Boris when he imagined she was doing penance drained from him in an instant. This was not his daughter but a shrewd New York survivor, a cat that always landed on her feet. It'll be exactly the same when I die, Boris thought. Her type dances on graves. For them death is something that happens to other people. He looked at Anna keenly and in silence.

"Hello, Papa."

"Sit down. How are you?"

"Fine, thank you."

"Anna, would you like something to eat or drink?" Frieda courteously offered.

"No, thank you."

"Well, I'll leave you in private." And Frieda went out.

"Papa, I know everything. I've spoken with Solomon Margolin. I knew about your business affairs even before."

"What's the matter? Why is he alarming everyone?" Boris demanded truculently.

"I'm not 'everyone,' " replied Anna. "You forget, Papa, that I'm still your daughter."

"A daughter who does not follow God's ways is worse than a stranger."

"Papa, let's not start those old disputes all over again. I've come to talk business."

"What business? I'm finished as a businessman. If you were waiting impatiently to build your future on an inheritance from me, you can give up hope now."

"I don't need any inheritance, Papa. I've never been impatient for it. I don't want to quarrel with you, but if you'd consulted me first, you'd never have ended up in this mess."

"What mess? I can live without money. All I need is a piece of bread and some water. The real misfortune is the one you caused me."

"Papa, I didn't come for you to preach to me. I'll soon be a woman of thirty-five. You must let me go my own way."

"What way is that? Well, if you want to cut yourself off both from this world and the World to Come, it can't be helped. I'm ill. I can't take care of anyone any longer."

"What kind of crazy ships did you get tangled up with?"

"I wanted to become a second Rockefeller."

And Boris laughed aloud. Anna also smiled.

"Truly, Papa, you're just like a child."

"Don't think you can help me."

"Whatever can be done, I'll do. I've got my own business now. I've bought a big building with furnished rooms. It's not the prettiest business, but I can't sit with folded arms."

Boris had an impulse to ask about Grein, but he didn't want to mention his name. That man, whom he had always loved like a son, had brought shame and disgrace on him, had ruined his life. Now Boris decided that it was Grein's fault that he had invested all his capital in those ships. Had it not been for Grein, he would never have undertaken any business venture without his daughter's advice. It was always like that: one misfortune brought others in its wake. When a person sinned once, he forged the first link in a whole chain of sins, evils, and afflictions. Nonetheless, Boris was curious to know what Grein was doing, whether or not he was trying to get a divorce from his wife, whether Anna was at least living in peace with him. He waited for Anna herself to broach the subject, but she sat on the edge of her chair, equable, elegant, her legs crossed, her hands in their white gloves clasping her purse, wearing the expression of a professional who has no interest in anything but business. So she's bought a building— that means Grein doesn't even provide for her, Boris concluded. So now she has become a landlady, renting rooms to all sorts of drunkards. And what was Grein himself doing? Perhaps he's already cast her aside. Anything was possible with wanton people like that. Should I tell her that if God wills it she'll have a brother or a sister? No, better not! Boris resolved. He himself hadn't yet fully absorbed the good news Frieda had given him. Everything had come too suddenly, too quickly. He kept this news for later, like an animal who hastily buries a piece of meat or a bone.

He heard Anna say, "Papa, please be good enough to show me all your papers."

4

When Anna left her father's home, she walked to the side street where she had parked her new car. In the few months since Luria's death she had changed to an extent that astonished even her. She had lost all her uncertainty, her terror, her feeling of being trapped in a dead end or an inescapable impasse. Many factors had contributed to this sense of liberation: first, she was now legally free, a beautiful young widow. Second, she had received a death benefit of ten thousand dollars, which together with the money she had realized on the war bonds and the jewelry she had sold in Miami had given her almost twenty-five thousand dollars in funds. She had bought a building, learned to drive, and picked up some idea of how to do business in America. An atavistic desire to make money had been aroused in her. There was also a third reason for her newfound self-confidence. After Yasha Kotik had returned from Hollywood empty-handed, he was on the point of becoming a Yiddish actor on Second Avenue and had even been prepared to do one-night routines in the Catskills. Then suddenly he had been cast in an important role in a Broadway theater and the New York press raved about his talent, repeatedly publishing photographs of him. Overnight Yasha Kotik shot into the public eye and Hollywood immediately changed its tune, offering him a contract to act in several movies. Once again Yasha Kotik had become a star. Since Anna had signed a three-year lease on her apartment on Lexington Avenue and Kotik needed a furnished apartment, she sublet the place to him.

And now Kotik had fallen in love with her all over again—at least so he protested. He showered her with theater tickets. He pressed gifts on her. At every opportunity he asserted that he had never stopped loving her and that she had been the reason he had struggled so hard to get to America. At every meeting with her he confessed his crimes, recounted his escapades, bewailed his woes in Russia, described in detail the prisons in which he had languished, the hospitals in which he had suffered, the bizarre people with whom he had come into contact. Here in America he had already established connections with all the leading theater people—producers, directors, dramatists, critics. Anna's name was even mentioned in the theater gossip magazines. Countless times Anna assured Grein that Kotik meant nothing to her. He aroused a revulsion in her that the years had not erased, but at the same time he awakened her curiosity and served as a stick to beat Grein with. Let Hertz know that someone else wanted her, that if he betrayed her she could pay him back in his own coin.

Anna herself could not explain how it had happened, but now she had the upper hand over Grein. Since Kotik had met Esther, Anna learned that her rival had a husband called Plotkin, an ignorant old man who met Yiddish actors in the steambaths and lavished handouts on them. As Kotik depicted her, Esther was a broken woman, middle-aged, half-mad. Anna came to the conclusion that there was no point in lying awake nights and contemplating suicide on account of someone like that. She had even stopped dreaming about Leah giving Grein a divorce. Anna had, as it were, awakened from a nightmare. She had done many foolish things in her life, but she was still an active and beautiful woman who had made herself wealthy and independent, had completed a university degree in Germany, and spoke five languages—or six, depending on whether or not Yiddish was a language. When she remembered the day she had gone to Luria to collect her things and the counterman in the drugstore had cursed at her and the elevator man had insulted her, it all seemed like an evil dream. Every afternoon she had been on the brink of insanity. She had been one step away from killing herself. Now she was elated, bursting with energy. Even the fact that Papa had as good as lost everything seemed a trivial matter. She would soon save something from it, and this time she would see to it that she also got a share.

This is America, not Europe! Anna told herself. Here one has to shake a leg and do things, not wander about with one's head in the clouds. Since the whole of America was predicated on achieving success, one had to be a success oneself.

The day itself appeared to be a success—sunny, clear, not too hot. The breeze that blew off the Hudson carried with it the scents of summer.

Outside the florist shops on Broadway stood banks of flowers selling at bargain prices. The greengrocers were laden with fruit. The ice-cream vendor in the white uniform of a ship's officer rang his little bell merrily. A water truck drove slowly by, refreshing the streets with spray. From the time Anna had bought a car and learned to drive, New York—indeed, the whole of America—had become more accessible to her. From Riverside Drive she was soon rolling through Central Park, where the trees seemed greener than in previous years, perhaps because it had rained a great deal during the spring. She stopped the car at a bridle path to watch a young man and woman riding on horseback. The smell of horse dung blended with the scent of grass, water, and gasoline. It's good to be alive, despite all the difficulties, Anna thought. America is a blessed country. Here, if you want to accomplish something, there aren't so many obstacles. Anna drove to her apartment on Fifth Avenue, because she had promised to have lunch with Grein and because she had many people to telephone, something most conveniently done from home. The chief rule was to do whatever one did as comfortably as possible. Talking had a different effect when one was sitting in a comfortable chair from when one was standing in a filthy telephone booth choking for breath; one did business one way when one had money in the bank, and another when one grasped for every penny. Even in love, one dared not be totally dependent on the person one loved, Anna reflected. If he thinks you're dying because of him and he's everything in the world to you, he walks all over you, even if he's in love with you. One must always keep a trump card in reserve.

Anna drove along Fifth Avenue, and at every red traffic light she glanced into the store windows. There was no end to the costly goods on display—clothes, jewelry, lingerie, furniture, silver—all in the latest styles. Even the dust jackets of the new books seemed to be more colorful and attractive this year than ever before. There were thousands of talented people in New York who kept devising new charms, new variations, new attractions to entice customers, in exactly the same way as flowers decked themselves out in every imaginable color to attract the bees that pollinated them. Yes, Freud was right—everything was sex, Anna philosophized. What, for example, would have been the value of my going home if Hertz wasn't waiting for me? It wouldn't even have been worthwhile to brew coffee.

She opened her front door with the key and heard Hertz speaking on the telephone. As soon as she came in, he hurriedly terminated his conversation, seeming to cut himself off in mid-speech. So he's prattling to that crazy Esther woman! Anna noted to herself. It's a sickness with him. Of course he's still sleeping with her, the pig—all his vows aren't worth a groschen! Anna was furious but she was determined not to show her rage. I'll teach him a lesson when it suits me best, she resolved. Grein came out to meet her wearing slippers, trousers, and an unbuttoned shirt. Apparently he had been in the middle of dressing when that other woman had telephoned him or he had telephoned her. Anna noticed that his golden hair had thinned out in the last few weeks, and his temples were streaked with gray. He was going bald.

"Well, how are things at your father's?"

Anna bit her lips. "I told you, without me he's no businessman. He almost lost everything. That's the harsh reality. He really looks ill."

"Did he say anything about me?"

"Not a word."

"What did he talk about?"

Anna could no longer contain herself. "What were you babbling about with that demented Brooklyn shrew? Why did you hang up the second I walked in? If you're so attached to that middle-aged hag, why are you giving me the runaround? How much longer do you think I'm going to tolerate you and your false promises? How long do you propose to go on playing this disgusting farce with me?"

Grein did not answer immediately. "I was speaking to Leah, not to her."

"What've you got to say to Leah?"

"Leah's ill. She has a breast tumor."

Grein went pale and his voice trembled. Anna was silent. She could see that he was speaking the truth.

"When did this happen?"

"Suddenly. They're operating on her tomorrow."

"That's bad," Anna said. Her words carried a double meaning, as if she were thinking, If this can happen to one of us, then we're all living on borrowed time.

She went into the bedroom, took off her suit, put on a housecoat and slippers. Just to check, she felt her own breasts. Perhaps she also had a lump. No, thank God, none. She went into the kitchen and Grein followed her.

"Where is she having the operation?"

Grein mentioned the name of the hospital.

"Well, it's not necessarily cancer. Doctors take great precautions these days."

"I don't want to anticipate the worst, but her mother died of the same thing."

In that case, he'll soon be free, the callous thought flashed through Anna's mind, and she instantly recoiled from it. "Such things are not always hereditary."

"Let's hope not."

"By the way, what did my mother die of?"

"From consumption. You know that perfectly well."

"No. I remember very little now."

Grein paused awhile. "Yasha Kotik rang."

"What did *he* want?"

"A water pipe burst in the closet. His clothes got soaked."

"What? The real-estate company's responsible for that, not me. They've probably got insurance."

"Because he's subletting, he can't file a claim."

"What? Yes, that's true."

For a time Grein said nothing. Anna busied herself with the percolator and the coffee. On the table in the dinette stood a bouquet of flowers, and she added fresh water to the vase. The sun shone in. A warm breeze blew through the open window. A solitary fly buzzed and beat against the panes. An airplane roared across the wide expanse of blue sky. The aroma of the coffee blended with the fragrance of the roses and freesias and Grein felt almost drugged by the powerful scent. With his shirt hanging out of his trousers he sat down vacantly on a chair, numb with the stillness of death. Wherever he had turned recently he had heard the same story: heart attacks, cancer, strokes. Though it seemed to him he knew few people in New York, he had enough acquaintances to be shocked at so many deaths—clients whose old age he had insured with the stocks of his mutual fund, teachers who had been his colleagues in a number of Talmud Torahs in Brownsville and the Bronx had all suddenly dropped. The news Leah had given him about her surgery had been a stunning blow. Leah had spoken bluntly: she had developed this cancer, she believed, because of the heartache and the shame he had caused her. She had even mentioned Stanislaw Luria: "First you cleared him out of the way. Now it's my turn."

17

On Monday Anna had to drive to the Jersey Shore to see her father in Asbury Park to have him sign some papers. She had worked out such a good deal with an underwriting firm that there was now a possibility of saving part of Boris Makaver's estate. In just a few days she had done wonders: she had won over the quarreling partners, engaged an eminent lawyer, and contracted with an agency whose sole business was to guard against harbor theft. In so doing Anna realized she was putting herself physically at risk, and indeed she had almost immediately been warned of "consequences," but she was determined that justice would prevail, even if it were to cost her her life. In an amazingly short time she made connections and enlisted the support of authorities from whom no one believed it possible to get a hearing. A number of ships had already been scrapped and their parts plundered, destroyed, or sold for next to nothing. But some twenty ships remained intact, and they were valued at more than the three million dollars paid for all the vessels together. Anna stopped the dismantling, paid off the laborers and engineers, and relocated to a cheap shipyard where the rent was one-third of what they had been paying. And now the same U.S. Navy that had sold the ships was interested in buying some parts back. The more Anna learned about the mistakes her father and his partners had made, the more astounded she was. These men had traded like ignorant fools; they had lost their heads. Ships were not buildings on which one took out a mortgage and counted on tenants to pay it off. Trading in ships demanded initiative, intelligence, knowledge, and presence of mind.

As always when Anna was excited and engrossed, she almost stopped eating, smoking a great deal instead, growing thinner, each day her eyes burning with obsessive fire. As her voice grew hoarse from so much talking, her mind worked with ever-increasing speed. Every moment another plan occurred to her. At times she woke in the middle of the night and telephoned one or another of the partners. She also discussed everything with Grein. Many of her schemes were so harebrained and fantastic that no practical person could believe them feasible, and after a while Anna herself laughed at them. Other of her ideas were shrewd, logical, easily implemented. The treasury of human intelligence evidently contained countless expedients for saving a business gone bad. It was amusing to hear Anna talking with authority about practices, people, and legal instruments of whose existence she had known nothing and of which even now she had no complete understanding. From her lips spoke the age-old spirit of commerce that bought and sold without knowing what, that reduced all values to prices and quantities, that measured everything exclusively in terms of profit. Her reason—like reason in general—speculated about matters it could not fully grasp, passing over the essence of things in order to direct all its energy toward a single objective. From time to time Anna threw an inquiring glance at Grein. He was more alien to her than any ships, any business dealings. Something was going on inside him that she could neither comprehend nor brush aside. He seemed entirely to have evaded her understanding, and she had no idea how to penetrate his mind or to control him. Perhaps that was why she found it so difficult to tear herself away from him. In the midst of all her strictures and complaints, she was overwhelmed by a desire to kiss him, to hear a word of praise from him.

Since Anna intended to stay overnight in Asbury Park, because she had a great deal to discuss with her father and wanted to have one good night's rest, enjoying the pure sea air, she had reserved a room for herself. It was the day that Leah was scheduled for surgery. Grein went to the hospital before the operation, meeting Jack, Anita, and Jack's wife, Patricia. Leah lay in bed surrounded by flower arrangements. In a second bed lay a woman who had undergone surgery for ulcers, and in a third a girl with her back in a cast. Every time Grein had to visit a hospital, he was deeply shaken; it resembled a factory of pain and death where everything private was laid bare and defiled. The visitors, it seemed to him, all looked about stealthily, spoke insincerely, asked questions it was hardly worthwhile answering. The healthy seemed to have lured the weak here under false pretenses, deceiving them in exactly the same way that the Nazis had the Jews when they led them into showers and choked them with gas. As if the weak understood this, they wore solemn expressions, replied reluctantly, and glanced beyond the heads of those who bent over them in a show of devotion.

Grein had been standing for some minutes in Leah's ward, but Leah appeared not to see him. Jack threw him a casual "Hello" and Anita ignored him. Leah was saying something in a low voice to Anita. She seemed to be warning, admonishing, condemning. Her face was thin, her cheeks sunken, her nose pale and sharp. To Grein it seemed that the mother was cautioning the daughter to guard against the nets spread by men, not to believe their promises. Grein had brought a bouquet of flowers, but there was nowhere for him to put it, so he laid it on the windowsill. One patient had no visitors at all and she looked at the others with envy, malice, and an expression that seemed to say: They won't fool me any longer. Now I see the whole truth. Once and for all!

In the evening, after the operation, Grein went to the hospital again, but visiting hours were over and they would not allow him in. Over the telephone they had told him that the operation had proceeded normally. Returning home, he found the apartment gloomy but not dark. Without switching on the lights, he threw himself into an armchair in the living room and sat silent and abstracted. This was the first time in months he was alone. His conscience black, he was thinking, but about what he himself didn't know. Leah, his wife, who had once been prepared to sacrifice her life for him, had received him with hatred today. Anita had avoided meeting his glance. Jack had tossed him a greeting like alms to a beggar. Even Patricia felt more at home there, among his family, than he. Before she left, Anna had parted with him coldly, giving him to understand clearly that she didn't trust him—as soon as she left, he would call Esther. He did exactly that, but no one answered the telephone.

Grein had not eaten lunch, but although it was now ten o'clock, he wasn't hungry. In the apartment he had books, a radio, a television, but he had no desire to read, to listen to music, or to watch the trivialities and inanity of television. He had developed a phobia about going into the street. Even strangers, he thought, stared at him with hostility and suspicion, ready at any moment to pick a quarrel. Although he assured himself it was all a delusion, he could not rid himself of it. For some reason, the elevator man was angry with him, and those neighbors who rode up with him viewed him askance, reluctantly, almost as if they were displeased that he lived among them. The doorman started whistling every time he appeared. Worst of all, his clients had recently turned away from him. He had stopped receiving letters and orders. Every time he called the office he got the same answer: "Nothing. No one."

Some sort of mysterious and metaphysical conspiracy was being directed against him, as if the powers that controlled the world had lost patience with him and were determined to sabotage him or to do him harm. Now he sat in the chair all alone at night and tried to take stock. Was this because of his sins? Or had some upheaval taken place in his mind? Was he falling into some psychic illness? He, Hertz Grein, was surely not the most sinful man in the world. The higher powers protected such wicked people as Stalin and his ilk. In Germany there still lived murderers who had smashed open the heads of tiny children, yet they had made careers for themselves and lived in prosperity. His nerves were simply shot. But what could he do? Take a trip somewhere? The mere thought of staying in a hotel, sharing a table with strangers, filled him with horror. He didn't want to look anyone in the eye, had not the slightest desire to spend time in the company of other people, to hear them chatter. He was jumping with impatience, aversion, regret. He would have gone away if he could find an island where he could be either completely alone or with Esther.

Did he love Esther, then? Would he be capable of helping her if she was in need? No, he didn't love her either. He lusted after her, but he detested her melodramatic performances, her prattling, her egoism. Since she had married that Morris Plotkin, his lust for her had fused with revulsion so that he wanted either to kiss her or to spit on her. Deep within himself he wanted to see her receive her retribution: to see her lose everything, get sick, die. He even dreamed that she was dead and he was standing next to her grave. On the other hand, he knew that were Esther really to die, something in him would die as well. That woman could make him happy—not permanently but for many hours. When he was with her, everything became interesting, charged, intense. Time flew by and he was not aware of its passing. He became totally engrossed, like a gambler in cards, a drunkard in liquor, a drug addict in opium. But how long could such a condition last? Spending days, even weeks, in Esther's company, he found that sooner or later a quarrel would break out between them, so bitter, so filled with hate, that he would flee as from a fire, afraid that in his rage he might commit murder.

What exactly do we fight about? Grein now asked himself. He tried to remember but could recall nothing. Their quarrels were all over vanities and trifles. Once, for example, Esther had mocked his Warsaw accent and her satirical imitation of the way he pronounced certain words had pro-voked such a fracas—how?—that he had actually slapped her. On another occasion a raging scene had broken out over some disparaging remark Grein had made about Liuba, Esther's best friend. But the words themselves had merely been a pretext, the spark that had ignited the gunpowder. Every time they were together, tempers flared, a quarrel brewed: the desire to sabotage and even to defeat each other became overwhelming. War broke out abruptly, with accusations, vituperation, curses, even blows. Every time he fled from her, it was with the feeling that he had escaped a mortal danger, a demon, a cataclysm that wanted to destroy him. More than once he'd told himself: She's my enemy! A deadly enemy!

Now Grein closed his eyes, resting his head against the back of the chair as the summer night droned outside. America was full of hotels, beaches, farms that took guests. All the pleasures the summer could offer were available to him, yet he sat in the dark apartment like a prisoner. He could visit nothing, travel nowhere, for he had no one he could escort, no one who could accompany him. Going to eat in a restaurant or a cafeteria repelled him; he even found it difficult to take food from the refrigerator to feed himself. But why? How had this happened? And how could he go on existing? Must he put an end to his life?

I've made a mistake, a great mistake, he muttered. But exactly what that mistake was, he did not know. Ought I to have stayed with Leah? Was a husband obliged to live with his wife even if he no longer loved her? Or should I have conducted myself like an Orthodox Jew, observing all the laws in the *Shulhan Arukh* despite my knowing exactly by what human processes all these laws and strictures came into being? No, I couldn't do that, and in any case, it wouldn't have helped me. It's true that I find existence tedious, but I can't serve a God who gives not one proof that He either needs my service or has any regard for human beings. Since God is determined to keep silent for all eternity, I owe Him nothing.

2

Around eleven o'clock Grein decided to go out. There was a grill on Eighth Street where he often took his meals. After all his hectic comings and goings, he now found it strange to be alone at night, walking slowly along, a man who no longer had any reason to hurry. Stanislaw Luria was dead. Leah was in the hospital following cancer surgery. Esther had another man. His children had left him. Everything had fallen apart. He strongly suspected that soon Anna would leave him. From the time Yasha Kotik had started cozying up to her, she had altered her tone toward him, and he had noticed in her the self-reliance and self-confidence of someone who had freed herself of a powerful and troublesome dependency. She even boasted to him that Kotik pursued and overwhelmed her with compliments. Other men were also trying to win her affection—even Dr. Margolin, who had given up the effort in Berlin, had again tried to establish an intimacy with her. During their first weeks in the Fifth Avenue apartment, no one had telephoned her, but lately the phone rang all the time. Among those who called were Kotik, Margolin, Korn, the house agent, Boris Makaver's partners, and random men whom Grein did not know. Anna was going uphill and he was going down. He was eating up his money and doing no business. Well, I'll just disappear, Grein told himself. I'll leave everything and run away. It was as if fate was driving him on.

Flight had become an *idée fixe* for him. He had thought about it for years, and now he even dreamed about it at night. Often it seemed to him that he had been planning it since he was a boy. Very often he had tried to calculate the minimum a person needed to get by, reading with particular interest articles about the diets of different peoples and about families forced to live on a limited budget, counting every penny. Grein often imagined that he lived alone in a dirt-cheap apartment without heating or a bath, owning nothing but a bed, a table, a few utensils, some books. His clothing consisted of a pair of inexpensive denim trousers, a sweater, a pair of stout shoes, a few shirts that he himself washed in the sink. He ate black bread, potatoes, porridge with milk, and occasionally a piece of fruit or some vegetables. Everything—food, clothing, expenses—was reduced to the essential: he went nowhere, telephoned no one, wrote no letters, visited and received nobody. He needed only two thousand calories per day, a blanket to cover himself, a piece of soap, and a library card so he could borrow books. He had settled his accounts with the world and had even learned to control his sex drive. He had saved enough to eke out an existence and be free from all care, all haste, all competition. He had enough time to devote to his studies—not ones with practical goals fueled by worldly ambition, but the leisurely studies with their own particular melodies joyously undertaken for their own sake, that Jews once pursued in their study houses.

This same fantasy repeated itself with variations. Sometimes he imagined himself in New York, on the East Side; at others on a farm in Canada or South America, where everything was cheap and life was quiet, full of timeless repose. Sometimes he planned to settle on a tropical island somewhere, like Gauguin; at others in Palestine on a kibbutz. Sometimes in this dream he would write a book: not simply another one of the countless books that one read and cast aside, but a tractate containing elements of eternity, a new philosophy bordering on religion. Walking from his home to the restaurant on Eighth Street, Grein again began ruminating on his plan. Hadn't the time come? Leah would soon die. Esther had already left him. Anna was slipping from his grasp. He possessed only some $20,000 in stock, which yielded nearly $1,000 a year in dividends. In a few years' time he might be left without a penny and be forced to seek work as a factory hand or even as an elevator operator. He was serious about his idea and had arrived at the crossroads—it was now or never.

He stopped at the display window of a bookstore and looked in. God in heaven, so many books, yet not one that could tell a person how to live! So much advice, yet not the slightest concrete help for someone at an emotional and spiritual dead end! What would happen if he was suddenly without money? What would happen if his citizenship papers got lost and he couldn't prove that he had entered the United States legally? First he would rot in prison, then they would deport him on a cargo boat to Poland, where he would probably be imprisoned once again. No learning, no religion, no poetry, no sociology would help him then. And what comfort could all the books displayed here give Leah? How could all these speculations about existentialism help her? How did the psalms put it? "The wicked walk on every side when the vilest men are exalted." They never came to the essence of things. No, I can't endure this situation any longer! something in Grein shouted. I must escape! This was evidently my destiny right from the start. But where should I run to? How do I put my plan into action?

Grein suddenly started. Somebody called his name, laughing. He turned around to see a Cadillac convertible stopping behind him and Esther giggling and pointing him out to a man sitting beside her—a stout person with milk-white hair, a sunburned face, and the rested appearance of someone newly returned from a summer resort. He wore a silk shirt and a cravat embroidered in gold thread, which was held in place by a diamond stickpin. He reminded Grein of those prosperous old men celebrating golden or diamond wedding anniversaries whose photographs often appeared on society pages. Esther was also smartly attired in a white dress and a broad-brimmed straw hat with a green band. The person in a red shirt behind the steering wheel who was trying to draw the car up parallel with the sidewalk had a smooth face and a head of thick brown hair that sprouted from low on his forehead. From the photographs Esther had shown him, Grein recognized both Morris Plotkin and Sam, the hermaphrodite.

"Well, have you inspected the books long enough?" Esther asked. "See how he spends a summer evening!"

"Then you're Mr. Grein?" Plotkin called out hoarsely, with the self-importance of the rich. "Esther speaks about ya day and night. Yeah, it's Grein all right—I recognize ya from the photos. Well, climb in—we'll take ya for a drive. The bookstore's shut anyway—ya can't buy any books now. My name's Plotkin, Morris Plotkin."

"How do you do?"

"And this is my old friend, Sam—people call him my twin brother, because he follows me around like a Siamese twin. Ya know what they are, two brothers joined at birth who can't be separated from each other!" And Plotkin laughed heartily.

"How do you do?" said Sam, in a voice neither masculine nor feminine. He didn't turn around because he was still grappling with the steering wheel, trying to straighten the car, and he appeared to find this whole encounter disagreeable. Grein tried to avoid getting into the car and started making an excuse, but the door opened and Esther grabbed him by the sleeve, dragging him in. Plotkin made room for him. Apparently stopping here was not allowed, because a policeman suddenly appeared and began rebuking Sam, making gestures as though to give him a ticket. Sam apologized and instantly began driving out of the narrow space into which he had only just laboriously maneuvered the car.

Esther started: "Isn't it strange, Morris? We were just speaking about him and here he is. Isn't it a fact that we were just talking about him?"

"Yeah, sure. It's not the first time it's happened to me. Not long ago I was walking down the street thinking about a friend I hadn't seen for thirty years—Mottele, that's his name. What's happened to Mottele? I thought. Who knows if he's still alive. Perhaps he's no longer even in America. That guy was a passionate socialist, and after Kerensky's revolution he wanted to go back to Russia and lend a hand. Just as I was thinking this, Mottele appeared in front of me as though the earth had spat him up. 'Mottele, you're here!' I said. And he answered, 'I was just thinking about ya.' "

"That's a classic case of telepathy."

"Sure. But how to explain it? Esther's told me about a certain Professor Shrage and I want to see him. If he can call up my father and get him to speak to me, I'll give him a thousand dollars for starters."

"Who? Your father or the professor?"

"Oh, you're a real card! If we needed money in the World to Come, I'd've started putting it aside long ago. But ya can't take your money with ya, that's why ya gotta spend it here. If a day passes and I haven't spent any money, I feel lousy, because if I don't spend it myself, somebody else will. Ya follow my reasoning?"

"Very clearly."

"Sam, where ya going?" Plotkin raised his voice. "Why're ya dragging us downtown?"

"We're going home."

"Home? Ya crazy or somethin'? With Mr. Grein along, we gotta celebrate—right, Esther? Turn the car around and let's go to the Zvezda, the Russian Tea Room. Ya know where that is, Mr. Grein?"

"I know, but I'm not in the mood for it now."

"Whaddaya gotta be in the mood for? It ain't the White House—only a café where they sing Russian songs and eat bliny and shashlik. If ya don't wanna eat, ya can just knock back a shot of vodka. We gotta get to know each other, Mr. Grein, because Esther's head over heels in love with ya, and anyone Esther loves is a friend of mine—right, Esther?"

Grein suddenly became aware of the smell of liquor. Plotkin, it appeared, had been drinking, and so had Esther. Sitting next to Plotkin, Esther seemed somehow a different person: livelier, worldlier, more cheerful. Even her laughter sounded different, perfectly adapted to the circumstances.

"Morrie, you're an understanding man, and that's why I love you. If you'd been twenty years younger, I'd've gone mad for you. Hertz, we're going to the Zvezda whether you like it or not!" Esther said. "I've longed for you the whole day, and it's time you and Morris became friends. When I love people, I want them to love one another as well."

"Shall I drive to the Zvezda?" asked Sam in a tone that blended anger with meekness.

"Yes, to the Zvezda!" Plotkin ordered. "I'm your boss and nobody

else! If I tell ya to go to the Zvezda, go there, and when I tell ya to go to
hell, go straight to hell! They won't whip ya in the World to Come, so
what's there to be afraid of?''

"They'll whip him, all right, they'll whip him!'' Esther chimed in.

"Why should they whip him, when he never sins?''

"He has sinful thoughts.''

"Izzat true, Sammy? What kinda thoughts d'ya have? Tell me. If there's
a dame y're after, we'll stop by her place. If she won't come willingly,
we'll take her by force. We'll just kidnap her.''

"Please, Morris, stop that nonsense!''

"Ya see how he speaks to me! I didn't realize you were so tall, Mr.
Grein. Why're ya so tall? I've grown widthwise, I'm ashamed to say. Oak
trees are like that—they grow thicker and thicker. They suck up the juices
of the earth and they grow wider instead of taller. Whaddaya say about
Esther? You were her lover for eleven years, so ya know the merchandise,
after all.''

"I have only good things to say about her.''

"What? Sure. Esther's like strong brandy. It burns ya, it sets your guts
on fire, but it warms ya. I'm not jealous—that's not my nature. I had a
brother in the old country, he used to wear my trousers and my shoes and
everything else I owned, and went off dancing with the girls. I sat at home
and played with the cat. But if I so much as touched one of his things,
straightaway he started throwing punches, may the earth lie lightly upon
him. And that's the way it still is with me. I'm always ready to share with
anyone—he doesn't have to be a brother. I'm a Jew, but I got a big Russian
heart. If someone else's satisfied, I'm happy. That's the kind of guy I am.
Hey, Sammy, get a move on. Step on the gas! Time doesn't stand still!''

3

It was summer, but the Circassian at the door of the Zvezda on Fifty-
seventh Street wore a sheepskin hat and a long Russian greatcoat with
small daggers in rows of pockets across his chest. Plotkin slapped him on
the shoulder and slipped a coin into his hand. The restaurant was crowded.
On the stage, in front of a small orchestra featuring a harmonica, a cello,
a balalaika, and a little drum, a gigantic man wearing an embroidered

Russian shirt over his trousers was singing a Russian song while a young woman accompanied him on the piano—although there was such an uproar that the singer could hardly be heard. All the waiters wore boots and Russian shirts belted at the hips. Plotkin was immediately given a table. He had told Esther he wasn't hungry, but as soon as the waiter came up, he ordered shashlik, vodka, strudel, wine—a whole feast.

Esther exclaimed, "That the man doesn't burst is a miracle from heaven! On my life, Morris, I'm beginning to think you're trying to kill yourself!"

"*Nichego,* eating is healthy! There's nothing more healthy than eating!" Plotkin retorted. He waited until the others had ordered before pursuing his argument. "All this talk about calories and losing weight isn't worth a pinch of snuff! I had a grandfather who could put away a whole side of mutton and wash it down with a quart of aquavit, and how long did he live, d'ya think? Ninety-eight years! It's possible he even stole a few extra years, the old faker. Well, and what about me? I'm no spring chicken myself. As ya see me now, Mr. Grein, I'm not far off seventy, and I'm nowhere near kicking the bucket. I got the best plot in the cemetery, everything's paid for, cash up front, but I'm not in a hurry. What's the rush? They've been warning me for over forty years that I might bite the dust any day, but I'm still raising a ruckus. The chief thing is the heart, and a doctor once told me I got the heart of a lion. As long as y're human, ya gotta eat, otherwise ya start thinking all kinds of thoughts. When a guy's hungry, he thinks he's some kinda philosopher. Take our Esther here—if she didn't fast all day, she'd stop brooding. But what can I do for her? I can't push food into someone else's stomach. Liquor's also good—there's no better remedy than a glass of brandy. Look at my Sammy—as soon as he gets up in the morning, he knocks back a glass of whiskey, and for him, that's just rinsing his mouth out."

"You're lying, Morris."

"What? Ya calling me a liar already? He can drink anyone under the table. I seen a lotta drinkers in my time, but he's in a class of his own. He can polish off a bottle of whiskey and drive like he's stone sober afterward. When I drink, I get jolly, chirpy, I can kiss the whole world, but he stays crabby. Liquor's water for him. Esther, on the other hand, likes tiny tipples—she lets everyone pour her a little. Here's the vodka. Mr. Grein, show us whatcha can do, because in my book, if ya can't drink, y're not a man, even if ya seduce a thousand women a day."

"He can drink. He can. But he's one of those who never gets drunk," Esther threw in.

"So. Good health, Mr. Grein. Another shot? Have a bite. Esther, take a little. It won't harm ya. Sam, whaddaya sitting there like a stuffed dummy for? Show whatcha can do! He's had a bad day today. Often for no rhyme or reason he gets the blues and then nothing helps. He clams up and ya can't get a word out of him, and he glares at me as if I was his worst enemy. Mr. Grein, make yourself at home with Esther, and with me, too. I don't like pretense. Since you were her man for eleven years, don't behave like a stranger to her. I had a wife and we got divorced. Four weeks after the divorce, she married someone else, and we remained the best of friends. She came with him to visit me, and we used to go out together."

"Did you know him from before?" asked Grein, for the sake of saying something.

"Sure. How else? He was my best friend, but when it comes down to things like that, there ain't such a thing as friendship. He got hungry for her, and I saw the writing on the wall. We already had three kids, but whadda they say? Love's no game. We were friends until the day he died. He brought up my kids. They called me Daddy Number One, and him Daddy Number Two. Now they got kids of their own. I'll soon be having a great-grandchild, because my eldest son's daughter goes to college already, so it probably won't be long before she finds someone who'll take pity on her. I hear you also got grown-up kids, Mr. Grein."

"Yes, a son and a daughter."

"Good. One ought to have kids. Since we take from the world, we oughta give somethin' back to it."

"What'll I give back to it?" demanded Esther. "I long for children. I always wanted to be a mother. When I was four years old, I made dolls out of rags and cuddled them to my breast. Hush, the baby is sleeping! Don't wake it! My mother, may she rest in peace, used to say: 'Oh, she'll be such a devoted mother!' But I've remained a dry gully."

A waiter in an embroidered shirt came up to the table. "*Gospodin* Plotkin, there's a telephone call for you."

"A telephone call? Here? Listen to that! Just listen!"

"Who can it be? A man? A woman?" Esther asked half-jokingly.

"That's our secret," answered the waiter shrewdly.

"A popular man isn't he?"

"Well, ya will have to excuse me."

Plotkin rose with difficulty, almost overturning the table. He winked and smiled, remarking to Grein as he left, "Just don't run off with my wife!"

And he gave him a hearty slap on the back. Sam also rose and followed his boss like a bodyguard. Grein and Esther were silent for a long time.

"Well, so—that's him," Grein observed at last.

"Yes, that's him."

"I must say, he's more sympathetic than I imagined."

"He's a big-hearted bear!" said Esther. "Until I met him, I didn't know what goodness was. He's less a Jew than a Russian, with a real Russian soul, ready to give his life away. But where did you disappear to? You were supposed to call!"

"Esther, Leah's in the hospital. She had breast surgery today."

Esther trembled. "I noticed you weren't the same."

"Esther, I can't sit here any longer. I must leave."

"Wait, you can't just leave without saying goodbye. How serious could the operation be? I waited three days for your call. I tried to call you as well, but the telephone at your place is busy all day. Who spends the whole day on the telephone there? On the few occasions it was free, *she* answered, so I gave a false name. I felt you were hiding, so I went up to Lake George. Then suddenly you're standing on Eighth Street staring into a window. Where's she gone?"

"Anna's in Asbury Park with her father, and she's staying overnight."

"They're saying in town that Boris Makaver's lost his last dime."

"Who's saying?"

"I told you before, New York's a village."

Both again lapsed into a lengthy silence.

"Who can be calling him on the telephone here?" Esther wondered aloud. "Well, I never imagined we'd all be sitting at the same table— you, me, and my husband. If anyone had suggested it to me, I'd've taken it for a cruel joke. What happened to Leah so suddenly?"

"It happened, and that's all."

"Yes, it happened and that's all. But before it happens, a person goes through a thousand hells. I don't want to distress you, Hertz, but it's your fault. You know that things like that come from grief."

"Thank you for the information."

"Before Boris Makaver's daughter forced her way in, you managed to keep your home together. I never wanted you to break up everything and come to me. I never demanded that offering. I'm not a Moloch that requires human sacrifices. But Boris Makaver's daughter came along and you immediately lost your head. First you killed Luria, and now you're killing Leah. I'm trying to save myself, but I don't know whether I'll succeed."

"At least you won't go under with him."

"I *am* going under, Hertz, I am. He's a wonderful person, but he's not for me. He drags me from pillar to post for days and nights on end. You used to complain that *I* talk too much, but that man never stops jabbering for a second. I suspect that's why he got married. Since I've been with him, I've got only one dream—to be alone for a minute. I have to discuss some important things with you."

"Esther, I can't possibly sit here any longer!"

"Why're you running away? I've been looking for you for days. If you want to quiet your conscience with the thought that I've found a purpose and a home, you're fooling yourself. Nothing will come of all this, I'm afraid."

"What do you want to do? Move back to rented rooms in Brighton Beach?"

"Hertz, he's driving me mad! He's a pleasant man, a dear man, he throws money about, but I don't have the strength for him. He keeps on inviting people to visit. He talks on two telephones at the same time. You used to say that I'm an extrovert, but you should see this one. You're a restless person yourself, but life with you was a haven of tranquillity by comparison. Around you it's quiet, but around him there's a frightful commotion all the time. I'm afraid I'll go out of my mind."

"I want you to understand one thing: I can't take any more burdens on myself."

"Who wants anything from you? I work out my life without taking you into account. If I leave him, it's not because I want to steal you away from Boris Makaver's daughter. I had an affair with you against my own will. When all's said and done, I didn't rape you."

"Esther, I'm living through the worst crisis of my life!"

"What? How can I help you? You got others into a fix and trapped yourself at the same time. I must talk to you. He wants to take me to Europe. I've even applied for a passport. He's mad about Paris. I always wanted to go to Paris myself, but the more he talks and enthuses, the more terrified I get. I have the weirdest feeling he'll destroy me. Not out of malice, God forbid, but with his unending hustle and bustle."

"Doesn't he ever get tired?"

"He even talks in his sleep. In Paris he's got a million bosom friends. He's badgered by all kinds of frauds and parasites, but if they leave him in peace for a moment, he calls them up and complains that they don't come to see him. I implore you, Hertz, don't leave me now. In the first place,

I've longed for you. How could I help it? I couldn't just blot those eleven years out of my life. And in any case, he'll linger here until four in the morning. He sits down at one table, but not an hour passes before we're moving to another. Look, he's coming back now. Tell me—when can I see you?"

"I'll call you tomorrow."

"When? I'm afraid I won't be alive much longer."

Morris Plotkin came up. "Well, what do onetime lovers speak about when the husband isn't around? Reminiscences? Sweet memories? There's guys who're jealous about the past. They marry a woman and want to pretend the past never happened. That's rubbish, nonsense! My rule is that if a woman hasn't loved, then she's a block of wood. At my time of life, ya want a woman who knows it all and can do it all. I'm like that sultan that Scheherazade told a thousand stories to. I love an interesting story, especially from someone who experienced it personally."

"He actually talks more than he listens," Esther said spitefully.

Morris Plotkin was about to respond when he suddenly clapped his fat hands together. Someone was approaching the table.

4

"Esther, just take a look!" Plotkin shouted.

Grein turned around and saw Yasha Kotik, wearing a yellow suit with red stripes and a scarlet tie with a pearl stickpin, leading a young woman by the hand. She was a slim, freshly dyed blonde with a sharp face and cunning eyes, and a smile that blended submissiveness with impudence. There was something common and disreputable about her whole getup. Although long dresses were the fashion for evening, her dress barely covered her knees, and Grein noticed that under one stocking she was wearing an ankle bracelet. Her breasts were pointed, her eyelids shaded blue, her eyes highlighted in mascara—even her eyebrows seemed artificial to Grein. She had painted her lips in such a way as to turn her mouth into two red lines. The red paint on her nails was glazed and compounded with another, unidentifiable shade. Grein hadn't seen Kotik since Luria's death, and he looked thinner, older, his face the color of putty. He seemed to be pulling his companion after him, while she kept bobbing her head like someone entering a low doorway or preparing to look beneath the hood of a camera. Their whole entrance looked stagey.

"Yasha Kotik!" Plotkin called out. "Here's a guest! *Molodets! Molodets!*"

As Grein got up, Kotik approached and clicked his heels theatrically, bowing deeply, his putty-colored face with its deep creases wreathed in derisive smiles. "*Gospodin* Plotkin! Madame! *Panie* Grein!"

He called out each name in a different tone of voice and accompanied each with a different gesture, like some master of ceremonies. He began twirling his right hand theatrically, and his whole bearing seemed to ask: What kind of ménage is this? Then, altering his tone again, he observed ingratiatingly in Polish, "A small world, isn't it? Permit me, *Panie* Grein, to introduce you to a great and famous Polish actress, *Panna* Justina Kohn."

"Not great, not famous, just an actress," said Justina Kohn self-deprecatingly. "A former actress, actually, because there's no work for me in New York."

"Please, siddown, siddown! First, we gotta siddown," Plotkin yelled. "And whaddaya speaking Polish for? This is America, not Poland. Hey, waiter! Bring two chairs. Sit! Sit! Of course one oughta get up for a lady, but it's too difficult for me. My pins aren't working too well. Here's a chair. Another one? Thanks! We're all friends here—my name's Morris Plotkin," the old man introduced himself to the couple at the adjacent table who had given up two unoccupied chairs. "I'm a friend of the whole human species without exception—white, black, Indian, Tatar. Yasha Kotik, the world's in a whirl because of ya!" Plotkin pressed on relentlessly in another tone. "Ya've conquered the American press! All New York's in an uproar about ya!"

" 'Confusion now hath made his masterpiece.' I only do a little acting. Why the mad enthusiasm? Hasn't New York ever seen any theater before? I simply got cast in a role that suits me. And the public, they clap so much that my back hurts from bowing all the time. I've just come from the theater—straight from the boards to the Zvezda to order a few *blintshkes* and a bowl of borscht."

"You're my guests, my guests!" shouted Plotkin hoarsely. "Where's the waiter? We'll drink some vodka as well. I wanted to call ya and congratulate ya for taking the town by storm, but somehow I never got around to it. Where'd ya find this beauty? She lights up the whole room! Ya don't see good-lookers like her in the States, ya know!"

Justina Kohn smiled craftily. "You're making fun of me. Not everyone can be beautiful."

"I'm not making fun. I'm no scoffer! When I say something, I mean it. This is my wife, Esther. A simple Jewish name. I think you've met Esther, Mr. Kotik."

"Yes, indeed. We met each other at the hospital."

"What? Oh yes, when I was lying there with a sprained ankle. What a ludicrous situation—get married one day and a limping bridegroom the next. But what can we do? I was hoping ya might still act in the Yiddish theater in America, but it just wasn't in the cards for us to get such a talent for Second Avenue. Broadway grabs all those who're really good—it's an old story."

"I'll still act in Yiddish. What kind of English do I know, after all? In Germany I had to play a Jew who spoke bad German, in Russia I played a Jew who spoke bad Russian, in Poland a Jew who spoke bad Polish, and now in America, inevitably, I get to play a Jew who speaks bad English. There has to be something I do badly before I can get onstage—that's my luck. Second Avenue's the only place I can play someone who doesn't speak a broken language. *Panie* Grein, I didn't know you came here."

"I didn't know that I'd be here tonight myself."

"Have you lost weight? How's Anna?"

"She's fine, thank you."

"We've spoken over the telephone, she and I. When was it? Yesterday? The day before? I'm your tenant, after all."

"Not mine, *Panie* Kotik."

"What's the difference? A pipe burst and ruined all my clothes. I go to the—what's he called here?—the super, and he says I should demand payment from you. Funny, no? So how did you all end up together here? And what's happened with Boris Makaver? Lost every penny has he?"

"I see the entire city's talking about it."

"People know. Nowadays he's your father-in-law, so to speak, but once he was mine. For him to fail in business is something truly amazing, because that man can make money from mud. Perhaps I shouldn't say it in front of everyone, but we're all friends here—Anna was already in love with you way back in Berlin. You were God knows where, yet she kept on talking about you: my teacher, my first love. I used to ask her, What are you going on about? He's probably forgotten you exist."

"I never forgot her," said Grein, astounded at his own words, stunned by the whole situation.

Esther immediately grew tense and alert. "It makes no difference now, but there was a time you used to say only one woman existed for you, and you know who I mean.''

"Mr. Plotkin just said one can't forget the past. He's quite right.''

"Are you confessing that you were in love with her all these years?''

"I'm not confessing anything, Esther. This isn't Russia, and no confessions are required.''

"Yet people do confess.''

"What's this? A jealous scene?'' asked Kotik ironically. "Over there it's quite a business, this confessing! Confessing saved my life. I quickly realized that they want only one thing there—for you to confess. Once you've confessed, they forgive you everything. I'm an expert at making a clean breast. Where's the waiter?''

"Pardon me, *Panie* Grein,'' Justina Kohn interjected. "I've heard your name mentioned somewhere, but I can't remember where. Are you perhaps a relative of the late Stanislaw Luria?''

Grein went pale. "You might perhaps call it that.''

"What's she saying? What's she saying?'' Kotik interrupted hastily.

"She's cooking a pot of trouble.''

"I may be making a mess of things. Do you know a certain Professor Shrage?''

"Yes, I do.''

"I was once in his home and I think it was there that your name was mentioned.''

"Are you acquainted with Professor Shrage?''

"A little. I know his wife, that crazy dentist.''

"She isn't his wife.''

"What? Just shows what a devious cow she is! Both screwy and sly. Now I can tell the whole story. That old bitch employed me to play the role of Sonia, poor Luria's late wife. She didn't pay me properly, either, the witch.''

"Ai-ai-ai, you didn't need to tell that! You didn't need to! You didn't need to!'' Kotik yelled out. "One doesn't give away information like that! Certain things must remain a secret—you take them with you to the grave, as the saying goes.''

"Why should it remain a secret? A cheat like that should be arrested. You yourself said that's what killed him.''

"I never said anything of the sort! Keep your mouth shut! Of course one shouldn't fool people about such things, but people fool one another all the time—oh, how they do! Life itself is one big deception. Ask me—I know. If I were to tell a thousandth part of what my own two peepers have seen, I could write a very thick book. I'll give you just one example.

"I was still in Berlin at the time, and all Germany was buzzing over me. The two most famous people in the country were Gustav Stresemann and Yasha Kotik. I got to know a German baron who was bonkers about birds. Listen to what I'm telling you. Outside Berlin he kept a small house crowded with birds, and he'd even written a book about them. He had a wife, the daughter of a Cossack general who'd fled from the Bolsheviks and become a chauffeur in Berlin. The daughter was a pushy broad, and she got her hooks into the baron. Apart from birds, my Junker loved experimenting with dogs. He cut them up while they were still alive— what do you call it?—yes, vivisection. He wanted to see how their hearts pumped blood and things like that, so he collected all kinds of devilish instruments. He castrated one dog, in the name of some cockeyed science. He boasted that during the First World War he'd singlehandedly slaughtered a dozen Frenchmen with a knife.

"And then in the middle of all this madness, Yasha Kotik arrived. What business did I have with the baron? Quite simple—I was playing hanky-panky with his Cossack honeybunch. What kind of a slut she was I can't tell you in mixed company. From the time whores took to the streets, there's never been a whore like that one. What aroused her best of all was to deceive her husband at the very moment she was looking at him. Her main problem, of course, was how to do it."

"Yes, indeed, how does one do it?" demanded Plotkin.

Esther grimaced in disgust. "Listen to me, men. I'm no saint myself, but one doesn't discuss things like this at the table."

"Where else should one discuss it? But no means no. Here's the waiter!"

Grein suddenly turned to Justina Kohn. "Did Luria believe you were his dead wife?"

"Oh yes, he believed all right. Why shouldn't he? It was pitch-dark and I seemed to appear from nowhere. I spoke to him in Polish. How could it occur to anyone that it was all staged? I'll never forget the way he moaned. Thanks to that, I met Yasha Kotik."

"I've asked you not to say too much, sugar," Kotik broke in.

"It's too late now. I've already given it all away. What was Luria to you, *Panie* Grein? Your cousin?"

"No, no relation."

"Well well, go on making your mischief!" Kotik sighed. "Even as we talk, the cat slinks out of the bag. We ought to be able to keep secrets, but what's the good of trying when the guilty one herself spills the beans? If I were to tell you half of what's happened to me, your hair'd stand on end. But Madame Plotkin is right—such conversations are not for the table. One thing I must tell you, though: the individual himself is the worst informer. He betrays himself every time. In Russia, when people were being wiped out for saying a word or thinking a thought against Stalin, people used to come to me and spill their guts. I always used to say to them: Do me a favor, uncle, and keep it to yourself, because one of us is definitely an informer. Do you think it helped? There was a doctor in Berlin who always used to say, 'People don't die—they kill themselves.'"

Morris Plotkin thumped his fist on the table. "Did he say that? It's true, it's true! But life becomes tedious. There's a saying: Whoring grows boring. You can even get tired of eating dumplings. I've wanted to call it quits more than once, but every time another pretty birdie flutters by. Listen, kids, tonight we'll all get drunk!"

5

When Grein finally left the Zvezda, it was after two in the morning. Plotkin, Kotik, Esther, Justina, and several others who had joined the group—another table had been pulled up and added on—stayed behind. Grein walked for a while not knowing whether he was going east or west. A cool breeze was blowing. Well, this is the underworld! he told himself. I'm one of its most prominent citizens. A living futility.

Having hailed a taxi and given the driver the address, Grein gradually became aware that he wasn't going where he was supposed to but in entirely the opposite direction. What's he doing? What's he doing? Grein fretted. Is he drunk? About to call out, he suddenly realized that instead of giving his new address on Fifth Avenue, he'd asked to be taken to his old address on Central Park West. He wanted to tell the driver to turn around, but he hesitated. Well, it makes no difference, Grein told himself. In any case, I'll have to go there tomorrow to collect my mail, which had been accumulating for days. Well, I won't get any sleep tonight, he decided. He laid his head back in the corner and sat quietly. So she employs actresses to impersonate the dead. One of those cheats. But for what purpose? Well, the whole world's built on deception. He recalled the argument of an anti-religious pamphlet he'd once read: that Moses had employed a crowd to make a fearsome noise and light fires behind Mount Sinai, because without those stage effects, the Jews would never have accepted the Ten Commandments.

How strange it was to return home once again to his old apartment late at night! But now everything was deserted. In the totally silent park, the yellow fires of streetlamps glowed. Grein went up in the elevator, took out his key, and opened the door, switching on the lights in the hallway. He had expected to find the mail on the floor near the threshold, because Leah had been in the hospital for some days now, but Bill, the man who distributed the building's mail, had evidently opened the door and put the letters on the commode. I'll have to give him a tip, Grein thought. He stood glancing over the letters. Nothing from any of his clients. Advertising leaflets, an invitation to a Democratic Party meeting, appeals from philanthropic societies. One letter was from Morris Gombiner in Detroit. Grein wanted to read it through, but it was too long and the handwriting too dense. Well, I'll save it for tomorrow, he mused, at the same time as he decided not to spend the night here. Anna might telephone first thing in the morning. Perhaps she'd even called tonight.

He had stretched out his hand to switch off the lights, when he suddenly tensed. He had heard a rustle, footsteps. In one second he was paralyzed with fear. Had thieves broken in or was it just a mouse? He thought he heard someone whispering. It's all my nerves! he reassured himself, standing stock-still, uncertain what to do. Should he go forward and switch on the light in the living room? If there really were burglars in here, they might kill him. He waited awhile and silence returned. Well, I imagined it. His fear evaporated and he strode into the living room and put on the lights. There, in a dressing gown and slippers, stood Anita, his daughter. She looked strangely pale. Leah's dead! was his immediate thought. He was so stunned that he seemed to lose the power of speech.

Father and daughter stared at each other. Then Grein said, "How's your mother?"

Anita did not reply immediately.

"How's your mother? What are you doing here?" he asked again.

Anita came a step closer. "You know my mother's in the hospital."

"What are you doing here? You're supposed to have moved out!"

Anita seemed to be thinking something over. "Father, I'm not alone," she said at last.

Grein reeled as if someone had given him a resounding slap in the face. In a second he understood everything.

"Who are you with? With a man?" he demanded.

Anita nodded.

"So."

He stood and looked at his daughter, experiencing something akin to what he had felt on the night he learned Stanislaw Luria had died. Outwardly he appeared quite calm, but his intestines started rumbling and churning, and his stomach seemed to distend. He was overwhelmed by something like pity for himself, for his own naïveté. Despite all his experience and distrust of women, he had still cherished the illusion that Anita was chaste. In fact, she had behaved too well, sitting in the apartment for days on end, seldom chatting on the telephone. Leah used to complain that the girl couldn't speak a coherent word to anyone. Everyone in the family had predicted that Anita would be left an old maid. Grein was the only one who believed his daughter had inherited the chastity of her grandmothers and great-grandmothers. But now here she was, standing opposite him, a girl not yet twenty years old, unceremoniously telling him that she had a man in her bedroom. He was seared by the disgrace of it, and overcome by the malicious love of destruction that accompanies such disgrace. He was as embarrassed as a schoolboy being shown lascivious acts for the first time, and equally ashamed for the other one, the unseen man in the bedroom who was listening in on all that passed between father and daughter.

Grein said, "Well, I'm going."

Abruptly he turned toward the front door, tried to open it, but couldn't. The latch had apparently jammed. He turned the handle this way and that with the helplessness of someone caught in a trap. He was flushed and had an urge to vomit.

Anita came up. "Wait, I'll open it for you."

The tone of voice she employed made it seem as if she, the daughter, had through some kind of witchcraft become the adult and he, the father, had been reduced to a clumsy boy. She moved next to him, but he turned sharply away from her lest she touch him. Afraid and disgusted, he was unwilling to look at her as she opened the door and released him as though from a cage. He wanted to ring for the elevator, but now he couldn't look anyone in the face. As he pushed open the door into the stairwell, he knocked off the metal lid of a trash can. He picked it up and tried to cover the refuse, but the lid wouldn't fit and the contents stank. For a while before descending the stairs he stood utterly confused, then started down in a very odd manner, taking one step, then standing still before taking another. I should've broken all her teeth! something within him raged. He was reminded of a verse from Leviticus: "And the daughter of any priest, if she profane herself by playing the whore, she profaneth her father." And I am descended from the priestly caste. He went down one flight and delayed for a few minutes, totally dumbfounded by the fact itself, by the circumstances under which he had found out about it, and by the pain it was causing him. But I've done exactly the same as that man! Grein reminded himself. He had no conception of what the other man looked like, but he was an enemy, a lurking foe who dishonored, trampled underfoot, sullied, destroyed. But Grein realized that he could condemn only his daughter, not the man. And in truth not even his daughter. Her behavior was all part of the limbo in which he had been floating from the time he had abandoned the strict observance of the Jewish religion.

Now he started running as though someone were chasing him, lurching down the last flight of stairs only to find himself in the basement. He could smell the stench of oil. In front of him gas meters, washing machines, a brick-red wall suddenly loomed. Shocked by the incomprehensible mistake he had made, he started to run back, located the door into the lobby, tried to open it, but couldn't. Was it locked? I'll be taken for a thief! Sweating profusely, his shirt sodden and sticky, he gave one vigorous jerk, the door opened, and he was outside almost at once. The night was cool and the street was deserted—not a solitary person, not a single automobile. Imperturbably the traffic lights went on changing from red to green, and something about the outlandishly cheerful rhythmical flashing of the signals, with no one to heed them, suggested that within each lurked a secret agent, planted before they disappeared by those who had now vanished, in order to spy on Nature. Grein stood for a while staring blankly in front of him. What should he do now? Go to the subway?

Suddenly he was overcome by something like an outraged curiosity, and he crossed over to the other side of the street. He looked up at his apartment.

The light in the living room was still burning. After a while the lights also went on in the adjacent room. His arrival in the middle of the night had evidently caused them confusion as well.

I must see him! I must see him! Grein decided. He'll have to leave there

sometime. I must get a look at him. Grein sat down on a bench. Yes, the
Gemara's rhetorical question about the frailty of women was true: "Given
temptation, what shall the daughter do except sin?" I've brought her up
with the belief that there's nothing beyond this world, that everything is
lawless, arbitrary. She had my example to follow. So what right have I to
be angry? In addition to everything else, I'm a fool. What did I expect?
They're all insolent sluts, whores. Their whole culture is harlotry. Grein
tried to console himself, but he grew more and more agitated. She had
probably lost her virginity long ago. He had raised a whore. A guardian of
whores, that's what he was. Moreover, she had been deceitful, consistently
giving the appearance of a virtuous soul—don't look at me, don't touch
me. How do young people like that regard him, the father? Obviously they
laugh at him. She had probably lain with her man in Grein's own bed.
Now Grein couldn't take his eyes off the window. Any minute he expected
to see a shadow, a figure moving up there, but all was still. Well, it's my
just reward!

For a while his mind was vacant, and he seemed to doze off. Then he
shook himself awake, raised his eyes once more, and saw the windows
were all dark again. That means they've returned to their carnality.

In his imagination he saw his daughter and that man. But she was still
only a child. Not so long ago he had taken her to Coney Island and Luna
Park and she had ridden on a carousel. Perhaps she had even started her
fornication in high school. By now she might already have had who knew
how many men. This was the generation he had raised: Jack had married
a Gentile woman, and his own daughter was a whore. Leah had wanted
to take her to a psychiatrist! Only now did Grein realize that this was the
same day on which Leah had undergone surgery. The mother was lying in
the hospital with cancer and the daughter was lying in bed with a lover.
Harlots like her were capable of fornicating on their parents' graves.

There was a bitter taste in Grein's mouth, and he shivered. Well, I've
done the same with the daughters of others. What does the Torah say?
"As I have done, so hath the Lord repaid me." What's more, I'm a
murderer as well.

He remained sitting on the bench, still staring up at the darkened windows. His thoughts seemed to ramble dreamily. What would happen if
the window opened and that man were to leap out? Would they accuse
Grein of murder? Anita might testify that her father had pushed her lover
out. The court would believe Anita, not him. And what would have happened if that man had shot Grein the moment he opened the front door?

That lecher and Anita would have fled and Grein would have lain dead and rotting in the apartment until Leah returned from the hospital. There would have been no evidence against anyone. That whoremonger would probably have shoved the revolver into Grein's hand to make it look as if he had committed suicide. And what would have happened if Grein had stabbed both the lover and his daughter, as Pinehas had slain Zimri the son of Salu and Cozbi the daughter of Zur? What kind of alibi could he have produced, unless Esther were to testify that he had spent the evening with her? But then Kotik and Plotkin and all the rest of that crowd would know the truth. The waiter would testify that Grein had left early, while the others stayed behind in the restaurant. The taxi driver would remember that he had driven him here. And what about the elevator man? No, Grein would not be able to evade punishment. Were a week or more to pass before the murders were discovered, Grein might perhaps have escaped. But where could he run to? No, he would have gone straight to the police and said, I've just killed my daughter and her seducer. In court he would say, I did not bring up my daughter in order for her to leave my home for a brothel.

Grein got up and started walking downtown. From time to time he looked behind him, almost as if he was expecting someone to follow him, run after him, or call him back. His legs staggered under him. His heart felt hollow. He grew weaker every moment. He started looking for a taxi, but no taxis were running at such a late hour. A bus drove past, but it was going uptown to Harlem. Then Grein spotted a bench, sat down, and after a while stretched himself out on it. Since it was hard, he put his handkerchief beneath his head and lay there like a bum, a drunk, one of those derelicts whom the city has spat out. He was awake but dreaming, and in his mind he seemed, like a rope maker, to be drawing out a string with knots in it. How many knots were there supposed to be? And, above all, what purpose did these knots serve? No, I'm dreaming. I'm lying on a bench next to Central Park. In an hour or two I'll be the victim of a mugging. Something in Grein laughed even as he continued pulling out the string and counting its knots without end, as if this was the eternal punishment the higher powers had imposed on him.

6

S omeone woke him and he opened his eyes to see a policeman. Bright day had dawned and cars were already rushing back and forth. For a moment he had no memory of what had happened. What am I doing here? Why am I lying on a park bench? Did I get drunk? Then he remembered.

"You're not allowed to sleep on a city bench," the policeman said, almost apologetically.

"Oh, sorry."

Grein rose and started walking. He had fallen into a deep sleep and woken with an ache in his bones. Well, look what I've come to! He sensed that the policeman was still watching him, so he wanted to disappear all the more quickly. He turned into a side street and had walked for nearly half a block when he saw a synagogue, open and lighted inside. Without thinking, he went in and saw something he had long forgotten. Since coming to America he had been to synagogue a great many times, but only on the Sabbath or the High Holy Days, not in the middle of the week. Here, however, a minyan of Jews was reciting the morning prayers before going to work. The prayer leader was swaying over the lectern. Jews in prayer shawls and phylacteries were either standing in place or walking about. One was praying without a prayer shawl—obviously an unmarried man. Grein stared and stared. He already only half recollected how phylacteries were worn—the leather straps, the rolled-back sleeves. A little old man with a gray, close-cropped head and the face of a butcher touched the ritual fringes of his shawl to the phylactery on his head and kissed them. A tall young man turned a page in his little prayer book. So all this still exists! Grein said to himself. They would have prayed together here regardless of whether I had come or not. At a loss about what to do, Grein remained standing at the door. As long as they don't ask me to pray! he hoped, but at that very moment a small man approached him to ask, "Do you want a prayer shawl and phylacteries?"

"Yes."

"A quarter," said the little man.

Grein started searching for a quarter, but having no coins he gave the man a dollar bill.

"I'll give you change later."

"It's not necessary."

"Thank you." And he unlocked a cupboard and removed a prayer shawl and phylacteries.

I really don't know how to put these on, Grein mused. Only now did he realize that he had never worn a prayer shawl on a weekday because he was already an unbeliever when he married. He took up a small prayer book and read over the laws. Yes, you put on the prayer shawl first, before the phylacteries. The one he had been given was large, not the kind worn in America but of an old-fashioned European amplitude with broad stripes and long ritual fringes. Am I permitted to put it on? the question flashed through his mind. I am impure! Nevertheless, he enfolded himself in it, then rolled up his sleeve, wound the first phylactery around his left arm, and placed the second on his forehead. No one was watching him. When he came finally to binding the leather strap around the fingers of his left hand, he was a little confused before he remembered that he had to wind it so that the strap formed the Hebrew letters denoting the word "Almighty." What am I doing? he asked himself. His night on the bench had left him somewhat dazed so that his mind was now working slowly, half asleep. He had no strength to stand, so he sat and began reading that section of the Pentateuch prescribed for the morning service which dealt with the consecration to God of the firstborn of all creatures:

And when the Lord shall bring thee into the land of the Canaanites, as He swore unto thee and to thy fathers, and shall give it thee, thou shalt set apart unto the Lord whatever is firstborn; all the firstlings of the young animals that is a male shall be the Lord's. But every firstling of an ass thou shalt redeem with a lamb, and if thou wilt not redeem it, then thou shalt break its neck.

In what way is the ass guilty? Grein asked himself. Why does it deserve to have its neck broken? How could God issue such commands? Apart from that, one thing was certain: the Jews who were praying here seduced no women, drove no people to death, sickness, madness. They had raised their children through generations in chastity and purity. If any remnant of proper Jews was to survive, it would come from the men gathered here. Whereas my family's Jewish life ends with me: I am an adulterer, a murderer, a liar. My children have totally rejected their heritage. I have broken the eternal bridle which God's immutable law places on human conduct. I belong with the Bolsheviks, the Nazis, the criminals of all nations. I embody the limbo of the underworld.

He recited a little more of the liturgy, paused, went on, and stopped again. All manner of ugly and desperate thoughts kept intruding. Perhaps he should sink even lower. Perhaps he should literally commit a murder.

He could get a revolver somewhere. He would shoot his daughter, her debaucher, Leah, and then himself. There must be some sort of thrill in packing someone else off to the next world, otherwise they wouldn't write so much about it or trumpet it so frequently over the radio and on television. Perhaps he should perpetrate some massive fraud. But who would allow themselves to be defrauded by him? Perhaps he might go somewhere where orgies were held. As long as one was falling, one should fall to the bottom of the abyss. He paused awhile and then recited: "The Lord is gracious and full of compassion . . . slow to anger, and abundant in goodness . . . The Lord is good to all, and His mercy is over all He has created."

But was this true? Grein demanded of the prayer book in his turn. Was God really good to all? Had He been good to the six million Jews in Europe? Was He good to all the oxen and pigs and chickens that people were slaughtering at this very moment? Was He good to the tens of millions of people dragging themselves through life with cancer and dying lingering deaths? Was He good to the millions of innocent people rotting in Stalin's slave-labor camps whom only death could redeem? And even assuming that their souls would all eventually rise to Paradise, was it necessary for the road there to be paved with so much suffering? Could anyone really call such a God good? And could one go on serving Him day in and day out without any certainty that He either wanted or valued such service? No, I can't do it!

He felt an urgent desire to snatch off the prayer shawl and phylacteries as quickly as possible. He stopped reciting the liturgy.

As he was glancing at the prayer book, Grein noticed that some of the other worshippers were conducting private conversations in the middle of the service. He scrutinized each member of the congregation. Who were they, these Jews who came here day by day, Sabbath after Sabbath? Why had they not turned aside from the path of their parents and grandparents even in uncongenial America? Were they immigrants? Were they born in America? Did they come from learned or simple homes? Was their coming to pray connected with some philosophy? Or was it just routine for them? But what, actually, did "routine" mean? It wasn't easy to get up at daybreak and go straight to synagogue: it demanded effort, discipline, expense. New York was not some small Polish village where everyone lived a short distance from the dusty lane in which the prayerhouse stood. Here the Gentile influence was all-pervasive. Here there were countless impediments and temptations. Here, above all, one had to have a strong character.

But these worshippers looked neither like strong-willed people nor like deep thinkers. They were simple Jews, probably small-time shop-keepers, office workers. They wore cheap American clothes—shirts of all colors, straw hats, loud ties, wristwatches with metal straps.

The congregation stood for the recitation of the Eighteen Benedictions, but Grein remained seated. Well, let Anita be a whore! he thought fiercely. She's right, too. Why not enjoy life as long as one can? That was *her* way of enjoying it. People had tortured each other long enough in the name of God! It was high time they did as they pleased. Did the wicked kill each other? So did the pious. Since God had created a world in which only the fittest survived, then combat was perhaps the highest commandment. Who had given teeth to the tiger, horns to the buffalo, poison to the serpent? Who had made the jungle? Who had infused humankind with anger, fe-rocity, hunger for power? Free will? What ethical lesson was taught by consumption, cholera, floods, famines? Why did God require five-year-old children to die from starvation? And even if He did require it, it's His concern. I won't praise Him for it!

Grein hastened to free himself of the prayer shawl and phylacteries. He was a little taken aback by the heretical thoughts which had assailed him in the synagogue, of all places. As he started to remove the phylactery on his forehead, it occurred to him that if everything he had just argued was true, then Hitler was right! This was precisely Hitler's rationale! This was the way all vicious murderers had thought throughout the ages, placing, as they did, man and man's will at the center of the universe. Does this mean I'm on their side? Do I agree with the Nazis who ordered Jews to dig their own graves? Humanism posited man as the measure of all things. So what did that say about humanism? Human beings must develop, pro-gress—not technologically but morally—or else what purpose did they serve? But then why did one individual suffer while a second enjoyed a surfeit of the best that progress could offer? Wasn't progress itself the result of countless outrages? Wasn't the French Revolution a milestone in the progress of mankind? And weren't the humanists delighted with the French Revolution and its guillotines? Who were humanism's heroes? Gen-erals, always military leaders. Wasn't Stalin, too, a product of the kind of humanism that placed man's will at the center of all human endeavor? Everything Stalin did was supposed to be for the good of humanity.

Well, I can believe neither in God nor in man. That's the bitter truth. Grein sat quite still. Nevertheless, if one had to choose between God and man, then God was preferable. Man was certainly negligible. Even if God was a murderer, He was at least a great murderer, a clever murderer, a murderer who tyrannized over billions of worlds for all eternity. Even Spinoza's conception of God as Immanent Cause was more comforting than all promises made by men.

Grein stopped and began to recite the Eighteen Benedictions. He could not simply sit here with his mouth shut; he had to play by the rules of the game. He murmured the words that had been repeated thousands of times by his father, his grandfathers, his great-grandfathers all the way back to the first century and the time of the Men of the Great Assembly. These words at least expressed the benign wish that both God and man should be good, merciful, holy. Jews had contrived to create a good God, and it was He whom they served. Let the real God be as clever a murderer as He wished—the Jews of Poland, of Spain, of Babylon, of the Holy Land had their ideal God: a God who was good to everyone and was merciful to all His creatures, a God who supported the fallen and set upright those who were bowed down, who was righteous in His ways and compassionate in His dealings, faithful to those who called upon Him in truth.

Could Grein turn away from all these tenets? Could he make peace with reality? No, he could not. This picture of God was in his blood. Just as he could not eat a rat or a bedbug, could not walk stark naked through the streets, or relieve himself in the middle of Times Square, so he could not make peace with murder, plunder, wantonness even though he himself was guilty of them all. He was like a thief disgusted by stealing, like a murderer whom killing filled with horror. He was an unbeliever who was compelled, in times of trouble or at the sight of injustice or shame, to raise his eyes to heaven and appeal to the God whose existence he denied, and this because among Jews God was a sickness, an obsession, a mania. For a Jew, the thought that God was good and just was the quintessence of life. Whether he wanted to or not, a Jew perpetually had accounts to settle with the Almighty: he praised Him or blasphemed Him, loved Him or hated Him, but he could never be free of Him. Whatever other complexes the Jew suffered from, the God complex was his ineluctable fate: he could as little escape from Him as from his skin, his blood, his marrow. Whenever a Jew imagined that he was fleeing from God, he was in reality turning blindly in circles like a donkey in a mill or a caravan lost in the desert. Actually, this was true of the whole of humankind. One could as easily free oneself of the concept of God as one could free oneself of time, space, causality. The good and the just, the true and the omnipotent had to be indwelling somewhere.

So what was the sense of fighting against one's own nature? Where had his own attempt to flee led him, Hertz Dovid Grein? Where had it led the world? I must play this game until the end. Without it I can't breathe. Without it I have no identity.

He bowed in the prescribed manner at the moment in the liturgy when the prayers proclaimed: "We ever thank Thee, who art the Lord our God and the God of our fathers. Thou art the strength of our life and our saving shield." He repeated the words slowly, seeming to turn them over in his mouth, the better to savor their taste. Then he concluded the recitation of the Eighteen Benedictions:

> My God, guard my tongue from evil, and my lips from speaking falsehood. May my soul be silent to those who insult me; be my soul lowly to all as the dust . . . Speedily defeat the counsel of all those who plan evil against me, and upset their design.

Yes, he was compelled to speak to the good God and thrash things out with Him. It made no difference whether He was there or not, whether He was truly beneficent in His inscrutably divine manner or whether He was bad, indifferent, or an Almighty devil. Since it was Thursday, the day of the week on which the liturgy prescribed the recitation of special prayers of petition, Grein began to repeat: "We have trespassed, we have dealt treacherously, we have robbed"—the confession which the observant Jew made every Monday and Thursday, on Yom Kippur, and on his deathbed.

7

When Grein left the synagogue, the sun was shining. The street was crowded with children. Garbagemen rolled trash cans toward trucks that ground up the trash. Puerto Ricans—half-naked, in multicolored shirts, with faces that told of innumerable wars, centuries of miscegenation, primeval acts of violence, limitless sorrow that generations could not efface—sat in doorways and on stoops. A cart harnessed to an old horse was laden with half-rotten tomatoes, and the vendor was yelling like one possessed. A black policeman appeared from somewhere, deftly twirling his baton. On the sidewalk, next to a trash can, lay a drunk, his face battered, unshaven, inflamed as though with plague, babbling and slavering while his eyes cried out with the pain of those who have lost all control over themselves. This derelict seemed somehow ignited from the alcohol, as if he might burst into flames at any moment like a paper lantern. Grein walked to Central Park West. Although he felt hungry, he had already decided, without any long reflection, to fast the whole day. He went straight to the building in which his family lived and rode up in the elevator. What am I doing? he asked himself in amazement. They're probably still here. But he knew they weren't. He rang the doorbell, and when no one answered, he unlocked the door and called out, "Anita!"

He was certain that no one would respond, but he heard shuffling footsteps and Anita appeared, still in her dressing gown and slippers. She looked sleepy, pale, disheveled. Grein stared at her as if at an hallucination that would not disappear.

"Is he still here?" he asked.

"No," Anita answered, as though inviting a strange man into her parents' home was a commonplace and accepted thing.

Grein was silent for a while. "I want to stay here. You've got your own place—don't come here anymore."

"No."

And Anita returned to her bedroom.

What Grein had just done was not in character for him, and he knew it. He was ruled by a powerful feeling of guilt, a meekness he had never experienced before. He was no longer Hertz Grein but a broken Jew, a sinner, a man ashamed. He went into his study and sat down. During prayers, after prayers, on his way here, he had made a resolution—to return to Leah. Esther had a husband. Anna was young and energetic. If anyone needed him, it was Leah. He should never have left her: all his punishments had come as a result of that one act.

He took stock of what he was doing. Leah was tired, ill, embittered, without a single spark of sexual desire. He had as good as sentenced himself to a life without physical love. But all the appalling things that had taken place since he had left Leah had shown plainly what he must do. He had only two roads he could follow: one into the abyss of murder, fornication, falsehood; the other to abstinence and self-restraint. For him there was no middle way.

He had known it the whole time, but it had never been so clear to him as on this morning. He had killed a man. In a moral sense he was a murderer. Stanislaw Luria would still be alive if he had not gone off to a hotel with Anna that night. It was possible that Leah, too, might not now be lying in the hospital with cancer. It was even possible that Anita would not have left home or plunged herself into this filth. In the space of a few months, he had scattered death, pain, sickness, impurity all around him. He was a murderer, a murderer! He, Hertz Grein, who had always felt such an overpowering anger at and fearful aversion to murder, was himself a murderer. He alone had sent a man to his grave. However much he might repent, however much he might torment himself, he could never repair what he had destroyed. He was like Cain, who had killed his brother Abel. Indeed, he was worse than Cain, because he had been educated on Jewish sacred books and he knew what it meant to shed blood. How did the higher powers regard him? If Stanislaw Luria's soul existed somewhere in the higher spheres, did it know and remember who had driven it out of its body? And who knew what punishments still awaited him?

He was certain that Anna was at this moment telephoning him and wondering why he was not at home. She surely suspected that he had gone off to Esther. Even his penitence involved causing sorrow to someone. But Anna would neither die nor develop cancer. He would explain everything to her in a letter. Who knows? Perhaps she would understand his position. Perhaps she might even find it a relief to be free of him. Their living together had not been all that she had hoped for. Through all the love-making and caressing, disillusionment had cried out unacknowledged. For the rest of this year he would pay the rent on her apartment. He would take responsibility for all the expenses.

He noticed the sacred volumes on his shelves and got up to take one down, choosing at random *The Path of the Upright* by Moshe Chaim Luzzatto. At the end of the edition he possessed there was a letter from Rabbi Elijah, the Gaon of Vilna, to his family, written before the Gaon went up to the Holy Land. Grein started to read slowly:

And it is known that this world is wholly vain, and that all pleasures are as nothing. And woe to them who pursue foolishness which cannot avail . . . for on the morrow one weeps on account of those things that have today awakened laughter, and time betrays. Like a scale it raises up what is light and lowers what is weighty, and this present world is like unto one who drinks salt water. The more he drinks, the thirstier he becomes. Think on the first who lived before us, and consider that their whole love, desire, and joy has now all been lost, and in recompense they receive for it many punishments. And what is the world of pleasures, when at the end it must vanish into the earth that is full of worms and maggots, and all pleasures are transformed into bitterness. For every man, even in this world, all his days are but anger and suffering.

As Grein read, the words seemed peculiarly apt to him. It was as if his father were speaking. He even saw his father's figure before him. These yellowing pages contained the eternal truth. The Gaon's letter was full of advice on how to bring up children, how to teach them the paths of righteousness. But what had he done? Arbitrarily abandoned his children to lawlessness, given them an example of debauchery, egoism, and wantonness. Why should Anita be better than he was? She had never looked into a book of ethical precepts. She had never heard a word of moral instruction from him. In the books she had read, in the plays she had seen, the heroes, the principal characters, were always murderers, adulterers. What right did he have to expect anything of her? It was all his fault. It was he who had severed himself from his roots. It was he who had driven his children to apostasy.

Someone knocked at the door, and Anita came in. "Father, I owe you an explanation."

"What can you possibly explain?"

"Father, I love him. We want to get married."

Grein was silent for a while. It seemed to him that his daughter was looking at him in a different way than previously, with more respect and intimacy, almost as though through some sixth sense she perceived what turmoil raged within him.

"Who is he?"

"He's an interesting person. But naturally you won't like him."

"What is he? A Jew?"

"No. A Christian."

"I see."

"Actually, he's not a Christian either. He's a freethinker."

"A Communist?"

"A progressive."

"Do you know that these 'progressives' have destroyed twenty million innocent people in Russia? Do you know that they've sent millions of people to slave-labor camps?"

"It's all a fabrication. It's all slander devised by the capitalist press."

"But I've talked to people who've been imprisoned in such camps. They were treated exactly as the Nazis treated the Jews."

"They're lying."

"Do you really believe that Bukharin, Kamenev, and Zinoviev were spies?"

"They were certainly traitors."

"Well, what can I do? There is nothing I can do about it."

"You don't have to do anything. I simply don't want you to think that for me love is just a game."

"I'm not talking about you. For your Communists human life is just a game. I can't describe to you the savagery they've perpetrated over the last thirty years."

"One can't make a revolution wearing silk gloves."

"How would you like it if they sent you away to dig for gold in northern Siberia, or if for no reason they threw you into prison and left you there for ten years?"

"I'm not an enemy of the working class."

"What possible bond do you have with the working class? You haven't done any work in your life. You don't even want to clean up your own room."

Anita stood there a little longer. Then she went out and slowly shut the door. Grein closed his eyes. Now, on top of it, she's become a Red! When did this happen? Well, it was all the same. They were evidently totally indifferent to the sufferings of others. They loved wickedness. They even exalted Stalin. They needed only an excuse, a justification. They were like hunters who first reared wild animals and then shot them. For such people, the chief thing was that blood should be shed. And I, Hertz Dovid the son of Reb Jacob the Scribe, have also joined the gang. I have become a killer myself and I have raised killers. Give power to Jack or Anita and they would send people to the wall with as little hesitation as the NKVD. Our grandfathers would have assigned them all to the same species—the wicked of the earth.

Grein was utterly stunned. How on earth did I fail to see this before? From the beginning, what was I thinking? Did I think a miracle would take place for my children? No. Silently and unconsciously, I helped all this along, made it possible for everything to be as it is. I have been a libertine, a voluptuary. I have fornicated and murdered, and I have raised fornicators and murderers. That's the naked truth. And in addition to that, I have dignified it with a euphemism and called it skepticism.

18

On Friday, when Grein went to visit Leah in the hospital, he told her he was returning to her and would be living in the apartment again. Leah listened and said nothing. After a while Jack and Patricia arrived. Anita did not appear. The visiting hour passed quickly and Grein left the hospital with the feeling that Leah either didn't believe him or simply didn't care. What difference did it make to her now? her eyes seemed to say. It's too late, too late. They were supposed to discharge her on Monday, but a complication had developed. The hospital was on Fifth Avenue. Grein didn't take the crosstown bus but walked home through the park.

For years his days and nights had been one long hurry. He always had to be here or there, to be accountable, report to this person, telephone that one, keep watching the clock. But all of a sudden he had acquired a great deal of free time. An entire summer Friday lay before him and he had nothing planned for it. He sat down on a bench in the park, considering what he should do. He could not drive far upstate to call on his clients while Leah still lay ill in the hospital. Moreover, not only was summer a time when business was far from people's minds, but stocks were falling in value every day. He'd already seen the morning newspaper and the headlines of the afternoon papers were mainly devoted to baseball. It was very hot in the park and the leaves on the trees looked dusty and tired. A few vagrants lay on the grass, dozing or trying to doze. Some boys were playing ball. A Friday inertia he had long forgotten had settled on the buildings along Fifth Avenue and Central Park West, almost as if, through some conjurer's trick, the whole of New York were in a state of Sabbath eve in-betweenness. Grein suddenly remembered the bustle in his parents' home on Fridays—no midday meal was eaten so that everyone would have a good appetite for the Sabbath feast that night, the floor was scrubbed, the Sabbath stew was prepared for the next day. His mother would send him, little Hertz, to the grocery store to get provisions on credit, and it had happened more than once that the unpaid shopkeeper angrily refused credit and he had come back empty-handed. He would go off to the Hasidic prayerhouse where his father worshipped, but the beadle, Reb Hirsh, was sprinkling the floor with water and sweeping it out with a broom. Even in the holy place where the Ark stood, the young Hertz could find no respite.

In the years during which his business was growing and his love affairs were multiplying, he often thought about the time when he would be able to free himself of tension. He had always known that an end had to come to the turmoil, intrigue, urgency, and rushing about. He suffered increasingly from nervous anxiety, which manifested itself in palpitations, headaches, and fatigue; he lived in constant terror of a heart attack. He had already promised himself that when he was fifty he would give up this madness, return to studying, perhaps even write a book. How long could he go on driving himself around and around in circles?

But now—not at fifty but at forty-seven—the time had come and here on the very first day he had no idea what to do with himself. Study? What should he study—Jewishness? What should his Jewishness consist of? Could he abide by the *Shulhan Arukh* with all its laws and prohibitions? Could he really pray three times a day? He had good reason to renounce the world and its vanities, but he had absolutely no footing for a religious way of life. Could he believe that God had revealed the Torah from heaven? Could he have faith that by scrupulously observing the laws of Judaism he was serving God? Was there a place for someone such as he, who believed in God but not in revelation or dogma? Could a synagogue exist for pure deists or God-seekers?

Judaism's fundamental tenet, as Grein saw it, was that people should live in such a way that they did not build their happiness on the misfortunes of others. Human beings, God's creatures, should not sin against one another and should help each other as much as possible. That was the essence of the Torah, of Christianity, of Buddhism, of all religions. Everything else could be labeled folklore. But when one removed the folklore from the religion, it was naked and almost completely negative. Little that was positive remained. One was left knowing a thousand things one was forbidden to do, but next to nothing about what one ought to do. Discipline, harmonious coexistence, contentment, and empathy all went by the wayside. What flavor did Jewishness have in the absence of beards, sidelocks, study houses, sacred books, prayer shawls and phylacteries, Sabbath and festivals? A Jewishness like that could not only fail to fill the day; it was also in danger of disintegrating at any minute because of a lack of regimen and symbolic structure. Acting as individuals rather than as a group, human beings could not serve God any more than they could defend their homeland. They could no more wage war against Satan individually than they could beat back Hitler or Stalin singlehandedly. Grein had preached the same to Luria that night when, immediately after his sermon, he had taken Anna away from her husband—as though he had deliberately set out to demonstrate that fine words are often the antithesis of fine deeds.

In the space of those seven months, much had happened. Luria had died of grief. Leah had developed cancer. Jack had married a Gentile. Anita was living with some Communist, also a Gentile. Esther had married Morris Plotkin. The punishment for Grein's sins had come swiftly and unambiguously. He had been prepared to receive even the final blow—death. It was out of fear of death, in fact, that he had now left Anna. But what, practically speaking, could he do now, this Friday? And how should he spend tomorrow—should he observe the Sabbath? Should he light Sabbath candles tonight? Should he buy food so that he would not have to handle money on the Sabbath? Should he stop eating unkosher food? And what would happen when Leah returned home? She was not religious. He could not force her to salt meat, to observe the dietary laws.

Among the ideals Grein had sketched out for the day when he would return to God was vegetarianism. How could one serve God when one butchered God's creatures? How could one expect mercy from heaven when one spilled blood every day, dragged God's creatures to the slaughterhouse, caused them terrible suffering, shortened their days and years? How could one ask compassion of God when one plucked a fish from the river and looked on while it suffocated, jerking on the hook? Grein had once visited the slaughterhouses in Chicago and had vowed to stop eating meat. He realized that even by eating milk and eggs one was killing cattle and birds: one could get milk only by destroying the calves for which the milk was intended, and the chicken farmers sooner or later sold the fowl to the butcher. Why should he not behave in the same way as millions of Hindus? One could easily exist on fruit, vegetables, bread, cereals, oil— the products of the earth. If humankind was to continue multiplying, it would come to that in any case.

Theoretically this was fine, but trying to implement it was tremendously difficult. Only today, at lunchtime, he had found himself in a quandary. He had gone into a cafeteria, but all the sandwiches, salads, and prepared dishes contained meat, fish, milk, or eggs. He couldn't even drink coffee with cream. He had eaten a plate of vegetables with bread, a bowl of prunes, and washed it all down with tea. But what could he eat for supper? And for breakfast tomorrow? Furthermore, how could he wear woolen clothes and leather shoes? They sheared the sheep only until they slaughtered them. One thing led inevitably to the other. He would have to wear only linen garments and shoes with wooden or rubber soles. What would Leah say? She was no more a vegetarian than she was religious. And what would he do when he called on his clients? No one had any confidence in a businessman who behaved like Gandhi. The women always acted as if their lives depended on his tasting their special delicacies. And what would he sleep on at night? The mattress contained horsehair, the pillows were stuffed with feathers. Whatever one touched was made of some other creature's flesh, hide, hair, bones.

Grein rose from the bench and set off for home. As he walked, he thought about God's ways. Since God hated bloodshed, why had He created a world founded on murder? Why had He created thousands of species of animals and birds and snakes that could live only by devouring other living creatures? Why the struggle for survival if violence was repugnant to His Beloved Name? And what ought America to do if the Bolsheviks attacked? Should one desist from dropping the atomic bomb because it would destroy innocent civilians? Should one passively permit the Stalinists to operate an NKVD in America and execute millions of people as they had done in Russia and were now doing in China? No, practiced literally, the teachings of Christianity were certainly inadequate to counter human wickedness. Most of those who called themselves Christians knew this; this was why, as far as they were concerned, the Sermon on the Mount was only a piece of poetry, irrelevant to daily life. But could the world live according to the spirit of Judaism? Could one keep the commandment "Thou shalt not kill" and still wage wars? Could one apply that commandment only to people and not to animals? Could one really distinguish between attacking another and defending oneself? And what about those people who had too little territory? Could they not argue that their aggression was a form of self-defense? And what would other nations do in response to this claim?

2

I'll spend this Sabbath exactly as my father would have spent it under similar circumstances! Grein decided. I have no other model but him. One cannot serve God in the abstract. One has to have a direction, a path. Let me make the attempt this Sabbath at least! What would my father have done now in my situation?

As soon as Grein had considered his father's example, he knew what to do. He had to prepare food for himself for the Sabbath, but it had to be food that did not need to be kept in a refrigerator, because when one opened a refrigerator one kindled a light. According to Jewish Law, it was forbidden to touch a refrigerator on the Sabbath. Then what kind of food could it be? Bread, fruit, nuts—I think those are permitted. I'll look it up in the *Shulhan Arukh*. Grein left the park and walked to Columbus Avenue. In an A & P he bought himself a loaf of black bread, a bottle of corn oil, a package of raisins, a pound of apricots. In a health-food store on Broadway he bought almonds and shelled peanuts. Shopping for the Sabbath while taking care that no foodstuffs came from living creatures taxed Grein. On the other hand, as in his boyhood, he was making preparations for the Sabbath. On the way home it occurred to him that his father would not have used any of Grein's household utensils, so in a shop that sold kitchenware he bought a plate, a knife, a fork. Passing a liquor store, Grein was reminded that he needed wine to make *Kiddush* on Sabbath eve, Sabbath morning, and Sabbath night at the ceremony of *Havdalah*, and finding kosher wine on the shelves, he bought a bottle. By now the parcels he was carrying were heavy, but he did not take a taxi. Where was it written that everything should be easy?

He walked along carrying his packages and the sweat poured off him. He had only just begun to follow a disciplined way of life, but already he had the satisfaction of doing something concrete. Now he was no longer alone. Thousands of Jews were, like him, preparing for the Sabbath.

The elevator man was astonished when he saw Grein carrying an armful of provisions. He knew Mrs. Grein was in the hospital and that Grein lived elsewhere. He's probably quarreled with his mistress! the Gentile mused. He stared silently at Grein, with a look that seemed to say: I know exactly what you're going through.

Now Grein began bustling around. Leah had two candlesticks and there were candles in the kitchen cupboard. Grein polished the candlesticks and inserted the candles, ready for lighting. He would leave the electric lights burning only in his study, because it was forbidden to switch electricity on or off on the Sabbath. What about the elevator? His father would not have ridden in any elevator on the Sabbath. It was true, the prohibition against riding in an electric elevator was no more than a strict legalistic interpretation of the injunction "Thou shalt not kindle fire in any of thy dwelling places," and it was certainly a very long walk, but he had to observe his Sabbath exactly the way his father would have observed it, not deviating by so much as a hairsbreadth. He would walk up and down the eleven floors. Who said that it was dangerous to walk up and down stairs? He would go slowly and rest. He did not, God forbid, have a heart condition. People of his age went mountain climbing. One could surely manage for one day, even in New York, without an elevator. What about carrying things? His father, may he rest in peace, would not have carried a pocket handkerchief on the Sabbath. He would simply tie the cloth around his neck, as his father would have done, when it would then become a permissible article of clothing.

Among the hundreds of books on Grein's shelves was an abridged *Shulhan Arukh,* and there he ascertained what he had to do next, that evening, and the next morning. He would have to bathe in honor of the Sabbath, and for the same reason, he needed to put on better-quality clothes. Before going to synagogue to welcome the Sabbath, he had to clean and sweep out the apartment. Until now Grein had avoided going into the bedroom where Anita had lain with the stranger, but he was obliged to purify her room as well, so he took out the vacuum cleaner and went over the carpets. For a long time he had not done as much physical labor as he did that Friday. For years he had tried calisthenics and devised programs to prevent his muscles from growing weak and flabby, but this Sabbath eve had given him a better workout than any gymnastic exercise he had done from a book.

He vacuumed the carpets, polished the floor, carried out the garbage. Then he took a bath. Let me imagine it's a ritual bath, as the Law requires. He dried himself and put on a clean shirt from the linen and underwear

he still kept in Leah's apartment. Then came the time for lighting the
candles. To guard against causing a fire in the building, he put the candlesticks on a metal tray. The two little flames burned sluggishly in the extreme heat, casting almost no glow. He spread a tablecloth over the table,
set out the bottle of wine, the cruet of oil, and a wineglass, made ready
the loaf of bread, the fruit, the nuts. The table suddenly became an island
of Sabbath celebration surrounded by, but separated from, the quotidian
and the commonplace. Grein stood for a while astonished. May this be
acceptable to God! He felt as if through some secret power his mother's
spirit hovered here and kept watch over everything he was doing; he almost
expected to catch a glimpse of her in a corner. Soon afterward, he went
out. Because he had already kindled and blessed the candles, he did not
use the elevator but went down on foot.

It had been twenty-five years since Grein had last experienced any sense
of the sanctity of the Sabbath, but now he felt as if the Sabbath reigned
over all the world. The neighbors observed him with curiosity, as if they
instinctively apprehended that he was different from them in some way,
and different from what he had been before. He went to worship in the
same synagogue where he had attended the morning service after discov-
ering Anita with her lover.

He found the synagogue open and illuminated with the stately brightness
of a holy place. Other Jews had also come to welcome the Sabbath, not
penitents as he was, but Jews who had never forsaken God's ways.

The congregation was a small one, not more than perhaps twenty men,
since the majority of regular worshippers were spending the summer in
the country. But the lights burned with Sabbath radiance, and the large
house of worship with all its appointments stood ready for them. This
handful of Jews all stared at Grein. On an ordinary Friday night an unknown face was a rarity. But a few recognized him from his previous visit.
Their eyes expressed the reserved welcome given to strangers at a family
gathering. Everything now went forward as it had thirty years before, a
century before, perhaps even thousands of years before. Jews recited the
Song of Songs to themselves before the cantor prepared to usher in the
Sabbath. As his voice echoed upward, the worshippers wandered about,
murmuring and gesticulating as Jews had done in synagogues and prayer-
houses when Grein had been a schoolboy: even the smells seemed the same
to him.

A young man came up to Grein to ask, ''Are you commemorating the
anniversary of a bereavement?''

"No, I'm not," Grein replied, himself uncertain about whether the answer was true or not. He could not remember the dates on which his parents had died. Perhaps an anniversary did fall today. In all these years he had never once said Kaddish for his departed parents, though both of them had spoken a great deal about it when they were alive and had begged him not to neglect this pious duty. He had taken it for granted that he need not keep his promise because the dead knew nothing. This unexpected question about memorial prayers now jolted Grein's memory and he seemed to wake from an attack of amnesia.

When *did* my father die? And my mother? In the summer? The winter? In what year? What month? What day? Why had he never thought about it? The answer was clear: he was far too preoccupied with his own affairs, his lusts, his cares, his fantasies. He had been so self-absorbed that there had been no cranny even to remember when his parents had departed this life, to honor the holy promise he had made them.

3

Grein stood repeating the liturgy, and uncertain as he was about whether God heard or wanted to hear them, or whether they had any relation to what he called the Absolute, he felt the prayers purify him. He was overcome by humility, warmth, intimacy. The words refreshed his soul. In all the worldly books on his shelves, there was not one volume in which such words as these could be found. Even when those secular words were elevated, Grein did not trust them, because he knew the identity of their authors and how they had conducted their lives. Secular poetry lacked the clarity, the faith, the correspondence between word and deed that infused the words Grein was now repeating, written by saints, hallowed through generations of faith and martyrdom:

> He with His word was a shield to our fathers, and by His bidding He will revive the dead. He is the holy God, like whom there is none. He gives rest to His people on His holy Sabbath day, for He is pleased to grant them rest. Him will we serve with reverence and awe, and to His Name we will give thanks every day . . . Our God and God of our fathers, sanctify us with Thy commandments and grant us a

share in Thy Torah, sanctify us with Thy goodness and gladden us with Thy deliverance; purify our hearts to serve Thee in truth.

After the service, people came up to Grein to wish him a blessed Sabbath. As their friendly eyes regarded him, Grein was aware that no other group would have made him welcome so soon. For the Jewish Communists he was a class enemy. For the Zionists he was a potential donor from whom to squeeze money. At the theater, in a cabaret, even at a lecture by some professor or other, he was nothing more than the anonymous purchaser of a ticket. No one would ever greet him or look at him with love on such occasions. But here he was a brother and the congregants openly exhibited their kinship with him. Among the worshippers were several elderly men, one with a lame leg, another with a tumor on his forehead. Where else would such maimed old men have any human worth? To the world at large they were so much refuse. But here, in the synagogue, they had dignity and value. Here others wished them a blessed Sabbath. Here they were called up to the reading of the Torah. Here the weakness of the body was no disgrace.

Grein left the synagogue and walked home. Again he did not use the elevator but took the stairs. He climbed up several floors and stopped to rest, several more and stopped to rest again. This walking up the stairs had taught him something: he was neither so young nor so fit as he once was. He opened his front door and saw the Sabbath candles burning on the sideboard, the wine, the *Kiddush* cup, the bread, the oil, the fruit. Now he knew exactly what to do: he would follow a regimen prepared for him through generations. He greeted the angels that accompany every Jew home from the synagogue on the Sabbath, recited the blessing over the wine, performed the prescribed ritual of washing his hands and reciting the prescribed blessing before eating, made the blessing over the loaf of bread. It was odd to go through these rituals completely alone. He was like a Jewish Robinson Crusoe. He sat at the table, reflecting that if he had conducted himself this way through all the years past, Jack would not have abandoned Judaism and become a Communist, and Anita would not have become a wanton. What had his children ever seen in him except falsehood and egoism? It was all his own fault.

After he had recited the Grace after Meals, an eerie feeling overcame him. He had not been so utterly alone for a very long time. He went into his study, wanting to take down a particular book from his shelves, but he suddenly stopped. This Sabbath he had to act as his father would have done and he knew his father would not have read a book.

On the top shelf stood another edition of the *Shulhan Arukh* which Grein opened and began browsing through. After a while he began to chant the words aloud, employing the melody they had used in his yeshiva. Everything in this sacred volume was predicated on the belief that the Torah was given directly by God and that everything a diligent scholar might discover in the future was already revealed on Mount Sinai. As soon as one doubted that God had given the Torah to Moses, this book was utterly without foundation. But however much he himself might doubt, these words steadily acquired a savor in his mouth. The yellowing pages, crumbling at the edges, spoke directly to him, Hertz Dovid Grein, demanding that he lift himself up, purify himself, become finer, better; they reminded him what he owed to himself, to God, to his family, to other people. Here the writer affected no superiority, employed no stylistic flourishes to demonstrate talent or originality. There was no barrier between the writer and him. The writer chastised and consoled him like a father. This book taught the old lesson, that at every moment human beings had to choose between good and evil, between God and Satan, between impurity and holiness. A human being was afflicted with all kinds of plagues and with the fear of death, but he had one great possession—free will. That was his weapon. That was the reason he was born.

Suddenly the telephone rang. Grein's reflex was to rush over to it, but he stopped himself: on the Sabbath his father would not have answered the telephone. Who could be calling now? he wondered. He imagined the ringing would stop soon, but the caller did not hang up quickly. Ten times the telephone shrilled before it fell silent. Grein was left with both curiosity and satisfaction that he had controlled himself. For many years he had controlled himself only on those occasions when he had been compelled to do so, through force of external circumstance. He had almost forgotten that there was such a notion as freedom of choice.

After a few minutes the telephone started ringing again, and again Grein counted ten rings before it stopped. Who could it be? Perhaps they were calling from the hospital. No. Could it be Anna? Esther? Could it be a wrong number? Once more he had to exercise the strongest effort of will not to lift the receiver. Something within him argued that talking on the telephone on the Sabbath was not a sin. Its proscription was simply an overstrict interpretation of the Law, but he had promised himself that at least on one day he would observe every injunction his father would have observed. If he were to break this promise, then his word, his resolution, had not the slightest value. Then he would be utterly lawless.

Not five minutes later the telephone rang for a third time, and went on ringing a full fourteen times. Evidently the caller suspected that someone was at home and did not want to answer. But why this persistence? It seemed as if Satan, the archenemy of free will, was putting temptation in his way in order to exult to the higher powers: "See how little his will is worth!"

After that the telephone remained silent for the rest of the evening. Grein spent so long browsing through the *Shulhan Arukh* that his eyelids started drooping. He had eaten but wasn't full as one is after a meal with meat or even milk. He now had a craving for meat, soup, eggs. He felt weak and hollow. The candles had long since burned out. It was dark in all the rooms except the study. The night was hot. Grein undressed and mechanically reached for his shoe trees before remembering that these, too, were forbidden on the Sabbath.

He went into the living room and, having put a pillow and sheet under him, lay down on the sofa, weary and somewhat empty. Would he have the strength to continue this life? Could he really follow his father's path? In a few hours a long summer's day would begin. Would he go to synagogue again? Climb up dozens of stairs again? Make *Kiddush* again? Browse through the *Shulhan Arukh* again? Everything else was a sin. And what would happen when Leah returned?

Cars rushed by outside. Every now and then a siren sounded. The apartment was neither light nor dark. A glowing sky peered in, a midnight dusk. Perhaps he should get drunk, Grein thought. All his lusts, fears, worries returned. He felt thirsty, though he recognized that this was more a symbolic than a physical thirst. Once more he started thinking about Esther, Anna, his former libertinism, and he was suddenly afraid of the monotony. The years he still had to live seemed to stretch before him like one long summer Sabbath. Suddenly he sprang up as though something had bitten him. In the bathroom, a faucet was dripping and the drumbeat of the water was like an unendurable pain. He twisted the faucet with all his strength and then shut the door tightly. Returning to his bed, he began to mumble a prayer that God would give him the strength to fulfill what he had undertaken.

19

Three guests came to spend the Sabbath with Boris Makaver, taking rooms in hotels and eating the Sabbath feast at his bungalow. The first to announce himself was Dr. Margolin, then Anna called, and finally Boris's nephew Herman phoned. Boris wasn't surprised to hear from Dr. Margolin and Anna. But for Herman it was no ordinary thing to want to come out to Asbury Park, especially for the Sabbath. As a rule, Herman avoided his uncle's parties. He had to be invited often in order to get him to come once. Boris had not even bothered to send Herman a postcard from his vacation retreat, so the young man did not have his uncle's address and had got it from Anna. Boris was astonished. Who knows? he thought. Perhaps he's heard that I'm ill and he's after some of his inheritance. However vigorously people like Herman attacked capitalism and constantly extolled labor, they chased after money and regarded work as poison.

If someone wanted to visit him Boris would not, God forbid, refuse. Although the kitchen of the bungalow was small, making it difficult to get everything ready, Frieda set to work with a will. She bought braided Sabbath loaves, baked egg cookies, and roasted several chickens. Putting away her sacred books, her manuscripts, the proofreading of her latest book that had already been set in type, she efficiently gave herself over to keeping house. As a scholar, she was well aware that even the Sages of the Talmud had done humble work in honor of the Sabbath; Rav had cleaned and cut up chickens, Rabbi Joseph had salted carp. Boris wanted to help her—Frieda was now a pregnant woman, after all—but she would not allow him to do anything. Dr. Margolin had given strict instructions that Boris should have complete rest.

In the shade of a tree in front of the bungalow, Boris lay on a lawn chair paging through some sacred books, as well as the Yiddish newspapers that were delivered to him. Only here could Boris stop to take stock. What good advice Shloymele had given him! He would certainly have dropped dead in New York from his overstrained heart, his numerous cares, the bitter quarrels with his partners. Here, in the shade of the tree, the whole sorry story of the ships did not seem to be such a tragedy. He would lose money—so what? What difference did it make? His father had been a poor man all his life—what entitled *him* to be rich? He'd been wealthy long enough! Besides, Anna had really worked wonders, saving hundreds of thousands. Everything might still turn out well. Having read through the Yiddish newspapers, Boris asked Frieda to take them away. The writers were undeniably knowledgeable, and each in his own way was very clever. But all in all, they had nothing to say, shifting this way and that, offering one hypothesis after another. One was observant and another was an unbeliever; one insisted on the centrality of the land of Israel, and another argued that the Diaspora couldn't simply be waved away; one was earnest, heavy-going and confused, and you couldn't grasp what he was after, and a second offered smart-alecky witticisms. But the sum total of it all was zero. You could go on reading the same newspapers for a hundred years and not grow a hair wiser. Every line revealed plainly that these journalists were only after money, glory, their own success.

The Beginning of Wisdom was another matter. Even before one began reading, the printed letters themselves emanated the fear of God, truth, love. The author, Rabbi Elijah ben Moshe De Vidas, lived centuries ago, but one could hear his courageous voice as if he were still alive. Every word was a comfort, a balm. Every single page indicated exactly what a man must and could do. With *The Beginning of Wisdom* Boris was not just another anonymous reader, part of a faceless mass, but an individual for whom all worlds had been specially created. Angels and seraphim attended his good deeds. He, Boris, personally could bring the Redemption closer or, God forbid, push it further away. What's more, when he died, he would not be simply material for another obituary notice, paid for with a few more dollars, but a soul expected in the Upper World, where his deeds would be weighed with mercy and, after the obligatory punishment in Gehenna, he would attain Paradise, where the secrets of the Torah would be revealed to him and he would be led to glorious kingdoms and palaces, unlike anything known in this world. The author believed in every word he preached to others. For him, every individual Jew was the sole purpose of Creation.

Boris examined the work intently, from time to time reading the words aloud. The day was hot, but a breeze blew in from the sea. Dr. Margolin had advised him to lose twenty pounds, but Frieda kept bringing refreshments out—a glass of lemon tea, a piece of fruit, a slice of white cheese. It was difficult to believe that she was a highly educated woman, a writer who had read many books and spoke many languages. She bustled about preparing for the Sabbath as his mother and grandmother had done, peace be upon them. And in her womb she carried his child.

Boris breathed in deeply, raising his eyes to heaven. While he sat here, the Master of the Universe directed the world. The sea soughed, the birds chirped, the sun moved slowly westward. From somewhere a little bird flew down and alighted on Boris's book. For a few seconds it wandered among the characters of the Rashi script in which *The Beginning of Wisdom* was printed and then flew away again. On his sleeve Boris suddenly noticed a ladybug, its tiny body finely lacquered, immobile as though frozen, showing no sign of life. How did it get on my sleeve? Boris wondered in astonishment. Did it fall from the tree? He broke off a piece of cheese and placed it next to the creature for it to eat, but it made no movement. Perhaps it's dead, Boris speculated. He nudged it gently and it rocked inertly. Well, it's probably lived out its days! Boris decided. It's done its penance. It was needed for some purpose—of that there can be no doubt. Suddenly the insect spread its little wings and flew away.

Oh, that's good! It's good! All those ships meant nothing to me, Boris assured himself. With God's help, I won't die of hunger. Above all else, I dare not waste the time that has been granted me on foolishness. I must thank the Master of the Universe for all the great mercies He has shown me. If I hadn't been a fool, I could've made dozens of Jews happy with the money I put into those ships. I could've bought a ship to the World to Come.

A limousine—a long, wide, brand-new car, a kingly conveyance—drew up and Solomon Margolin got out. Boris had never seen him so elegantly dressed, in a white suit and a Panama hat, carrying a bouquet of flowers in one hand and a package in the other. Boris jerked up abruptly, ready to rise and receive him, although Margolin gestured to him to remain seated. Boris got up anyway.

"Shloymele!" he shouted, so loudly that Frieda heard and came out.

Boris seldom kissed anyone, but this time he embraced Margolin and insisted on kissing him on both cheeks so that the doctor had to stoop down to receive the greeting.

"Shloymele, may God invigorate you as much as you have invigorated me by coming!"

"Don't raise such a racket. It's not good for your pump."

Margolin had come armed with gifts. As he gave Frieda the flowers and the package, she blushed, wiping her hands on her apron. The doctor had chosen flowers of a kind not found in these parts and had probably paid highly for them; as for the package, it was extraordinarily heavy. Frieda carried out another lawn chair for their guest, offering him lemonade and cookies, but Margolin wanted nothing to eat or to drink, remarking, "The less we put into our bodies, the better."

"What? That's what *The Beginning of Wisdom* maintains," Boris said.

"In that instance *The Beginning of Wisdom* is right."

Frieda took the flowers and the package into the bungalow, and the men fell into conversation. Boris remarked, "Shloymele, you saved my life!"

"Well, that's my business, after all."

"Shloymele, if you hadn't sent me here, I'd have perished, God forbid. You know what's written: 'He who saves one life in Israel is as if he has saved the whole world.' "

"I know, I know. I know everything that's written. I see you've got *The Beginning of Wisdom* right here."

"Shloymele, you don't know what kind of book it is! Every word is gold inlaid with diamonds! Every word should be devoutly kissed!"

"What does the rabbi say there? I only remember that for the slightest little sin he instructs fasting in penance."

"I'll tell you one thing: if people had listened to him, we'd've had a radiant world."

"They'll never listen to him. They're already preparing for a third world war."

"Who's preparing? What are you saying?"

"Comrade Stalin. Our side's also realized they've made a mistake. They shouldn't've let Stalin grab Poland, Hungary, Romania. As long as the Russians don't have the atomic bomb, we can still thumb our noses at them, but in a few years it'll be too late."

"What can we do? Start another conflagration?"

"Somebody will soon."

"I beg you, Shloymele, don't talk about such things. As it is, people don't live long. So what's the sense of killing one another? Doesn't the Angel of Death take care of enough? I'm telling you, Shloymele, the wicked are mad.''

"They rule the world."

"What kind of world? What do all these wars achieve? Why can't they straighten things out once and for all? I've just been through the newspapers. All you read about is robbery, thievery, violence.''

"That's how the world works. If you knew Darwin, you'd know that the struggle for survival is the force that created the world.''

"I've read, I've heard. It's nonsense, nonsense. The Master of the Universe hates violence. 'The Lord will abhor the bloody and deceitful man.' It's written in the psalms.''

"Then why did God arrange things so that when two stags encounter the same hind, they lock horns with each other until one of them falls? That's not a result of free will. Deer aren't wicked. They do what's in their nature to do.''

"Who knows? Perhaps animals can also be wicked. Good creatures exist, too. A lamb does no one any harm.''

"Yet wolves eat it.''

Boris reflected for a while. "What do we know? It's all a great mystery. One thing is certain: human beings must be good. Since they understand what good is, they do not dare to be bad.''

"Well, the Jews in Poland were good. So where are they now?''

"Where are they? In the radiance of Paradise! The Master of the Universe can do no wrong. The Creator of heaven and earth cannot be wicked. I could never believe that! Even if I were to arrive in the World to Come and see with my own eyes that Hitler was sitting in Paradise while the Source of All Wisdom was burning in Gehenna, perish the thought, I would still cry out with Jeremiah that 'evil cometh not from the Lord.' ''

And Boris's eyes filled with tears.

2

Not long after Solomon Margolin's arrival, Anna drove up, bringing a passenger—her cousin Herman. Like Margolin, they had made reservations in a hotel, since there was no room for them in the bungalow.

Studying the faces of his daughter and his nephew, Boris saw anxiety, abstraction, and exhaustion in both of them. Was it the summer, the heat, the dust of the great city? Boris wondered. Or had something happened to them? Anna and Herman had never been close. Anna asserted that Herman physically repelled her. Since Herman resembled his uncle, short and stocky with hands and feet too big for his body, Boris instinctively understood that Herman's looks were too Jewish for Anna—he was too much of a Makaver. Anna had more of the Landau side of the family in her, but she indelibly carried something of her father. Now she ran up to Boris, embraced and kissed him. Her face was as hot as if she were feverish as she kissed him on both cheeks, on his forehead, and then kissed his hand. All this kissing was not to Boris's liking. That was really taking affection too far, and he saw it as a sign that something was wrong. Had Hertz Grein cast her off? Boris wondered. Anna had also lost a good deal of weight, and her eyes held fear and the kind of smile that could turn to tears at any moment. Well, she's earned it! Boris told himself, even though her bearing made him ill at ease. He started coughing and clearing his throat like a prayer leader in the synagogue.

Herman was not the same either. He seemed somehow to have grown smaller and his clothes looked unkempt. He peered out from behind his pince-nez with a glance at once embittered and fearful. His thick lips expressed something like resentment or regret.

"Well, children, how was the trip?" asked Boris.

"She's a good driver," Herman answered.

"She's good at everything—that's her biggest disadvantage. If you have broad shoulders, you carry heavy burdens. If a woman can do everything, then she's forced to do it on her own."

"Oh, Papa, how clever you are! You express an entire philosophy in a single phrase."

"It's all in our sacred books."

Frieda came out, kissed Anna, and invited the new arrivals inside, anxious to offer them something to eat, but Anna responded, "I'm not hungry. If you've worked up an appetite, Herman, go in and eat."

"I'm thirsty."

And Herman went into the bungalow with Frieda. Dr. Margolin had driven off on the pretext of looking for a magazine he hadn't been able to find in the vicinity. Boris suspected that he had gone to Atlantic City and only hoped that he would not drive back once the Sabbath had begun.

After Herman had gone, Boris waved his daughter to the lawn chair that had been put out for Dr. Margolin. "My child, you look tired."

"Yes, Papa, I am tired."

"What's happened?"

Anna paused awhile. "You'll be all right, Papa—you've got me for a daughter. What I've done with your ships you'll never appreciate. A manager who did this for you and demanded a hundred thousand dollars for his work would be a bargain."

"I'll be happy to pay you."

"I didn't do it for the money. It's still not fully clear how we stand, but I've saved as much as I could. If they'd've offered me half a million dollars for your share, I wouldn't have taken it."

"Well, you've been an outstanding agent—my partners know it's all fifty-fifty between us. Now that Frieda's pregnant, I don't want to delay any longer. I want you to have what's yours. Why should you wait for your inheritance? No one can take your place here." And Boris laid his hand on his heart.

"Don't worry, Papa. I'm not after your money."

"It's more yours than mine. You seem a bit depressed, my little one. Aren't you well, God forbid?"

"I'm as strong as iron."

"Do you perhaps need to take some time off?"

"I won't rest until this whole business is finalized. I also own an apartment building, and I'll clear ten thousand in profit if I sell it now."

"Sell it and get rid of it."

"So long as it's worth something to someone else, it's worth something to me. It nets two hundred dollars a week in income."

"How much did you invest in it?"

"Seventeen and a half thousand."

"What's the mortgage?"

Anna mentioned the sum and its cost.

"Well, it's excellent interest. But you don't get that two hundred dollars for nothing. You have to work for it."

"Of course. Would I get it for nothing? You just said yourself that if one has broad shoulders one has to bear heavy burdens."

"You don't have to bear any burdens."

"Oh, I'll bear them, Papa, I'll bear them. I can see the whole of my life ahead of me. I'll become a Boris Makaver in a dress. I have no knack for anything else."

Boris closed his eyes. "What's happened?"

"Grein went back to his wife."

Boris was simultaneously pleased and irritated. He felt an inner wrenching and his eyes again filled with tears. "What's wrong?"

"She had a breast removed and he became religious."

Boris wiped his face with his handkerchief, emitting stifled sighs between rumbling coughs. "Naturally, for her cancer is a terrible misfortune, may she be granted a complete recovery—but for you it's salvation."

"I don't know what you're saying, Papa."

"It was no good."

Anna turned her head away. "Papa, you ought not to have asked me, and I ought not to have told you."

"Who's entitled to ask, if not me?"

"Papa, I'm unhappy. More unhappy than you can imagine!" And Anna snatched her handkerchief out of her purse.

For a long while father and daughter sat in silence, absorbed in their own thoughts. Then Boris remarked, "A blister must burst!"

"Papa, I beg you—you understand nothing, so don't talk about it. I'm dogged by unhappiness as if it were my destiny. I can foresee my years rushing by without happiness. Your lot will be my lot. But in old age a man can still become a father, while in ten years I'll be finished."

"You don't have to wait ten years."

"What can I do? It takes years before I start to like anyone. Right now I'm so disappointed and depressed I don't even want to look at anybody. I'll live out my years alone. In fact, I've been alone all my life."

And Anna began snuffling into her handkerchief, trying to check her sobbing. She coughed, choked, blew her nose, her eyes red and bulging, extraordinarily like her father's. Suddenly she emitted the same anguished wail that had escaped her when she had received the news of Stanislaw Luria's death. "Papa! Mother!"

And Anna could say no more. She choked, sobbed, and trembled, and the chair shook beneath her. Boris felt an unwonted heaviness.

"Daughter, you'll still live to thank God for this."

"What? I'll never thank God! What has life given me? Alone—again alone! My end will be like Mama's!" Anna finally cried out the fear she had been trying to articulate all along. At the same time, she had the chilling feeling that in uttering these words she had sealed her own fate. Boris was equally shocked, almost as if Anna had voiced a dread that had been gnawing at him as well.

"Bite your tongue! You're crushing my heart! Be silent!"

"Papa, you'll soon have other children."

"Be silent! What are you saying? No one can take your place. Khanele!"

And Boris could no longer speak for the lump that stuck in his throat and choked him. His heart did not so much beat as flutter like a fan. Not while they're here! Boris pleaded with himself and the heavenly powers. Not on the Sabbath!

In a little while Anna calmed herself, and Boris, after a spasm of coughing, cleared his throat of phlegm. He swallowed a pill he was supposed to take only at night, and it immediately made his face blotched and fiery red. Anna rapidly powdered her nose and freshened her lipstick.

"So he's really become a penitent?" Boris asked.

"He wrote me a letter eight pages long."

"What did he say?"

"He blames himself for Luria's death. He writes as if it were his fault alone. He takes responsibility for his wife's illness. He's developed a complex, or God knows what. Everything I touch immediately becomes a mess."

"My child, I don't want to cause you further grief, but no one did Luria any favors."

"Papa, I know everything. Don't think I'm so obtuse. I wake up every night thinking about it—I did even when Grein lived with me. But what could I do? Luria never stopped tormenting me. All he ever talked about was his dead wife. He kept on threatening to kill himself. He became totally helpless."

"I warned you in Morocco."

"Yes, Papa, you always warned me, but it's my luck to be drawn to whatever's no good for me."

"It's high time you did something that'll bring you great happiness."

"Even the straight becomes crooked in my hands. Well, that's enough!"

Again both were silent for a while. It seemed as though they were listening to each other's thoughts with the distaste that comes of long knowing how another thinks.

"Why's Herman come here out of the blue?"

Anna seemed to rouse herself. "I don't know, Papa. There's something mysterious about it. He searched for me all over New York before he finally found me and got your address. Something's troubling him, but he's not saying anything. During the whole trip here he didn't utter a single word. I've never seen him like this. What can he want from you? I hope it's not money.''

"What does he need money for? He's got a job.''

"Who knows? Something's happened—that's certain. I understand he wants to talk to you. I'll go in and send him out. But don't let it upset you.''

"What should I get upset about? If he weren't the last member of the family, I wouldn't think twice about him.''

"Shall I bring something out for you?''

"No, Khanele, I don't need anything. All I need is a little fatherly pleasure from your having a happy family life.''

His nephew always spoke, Boris thought, as though reading from a book. He usually spoke clearly and to the point. But this time Herman was tongue-tied, repeatedly calling Boris "Uncle" and quite uncharacteristically talking of his father, his mother, even his grandparents. Whatever's happened to him? Boris wondered in astonishment. Perhaps he's also become a penitent. Or does he need money?

Boris listened attentively as he heard Herman say, "Uncle, you mustn't think I haven't appreciated everything you've done for me. We do have entirely different ideological viewpoints, it's true, but what's the saying? Blood is thicker than water. I no longer have anyone in the world except you.''

"If it weren't for your Bolsheviks, you'd still have another uncle and an aunt and I don't know how many other family members. If it hadn't been for Stalin, there wouldn't have been a Hitler and your parents would still be alive.''

"That's your opinion, Uncle. I don't want to start a debate. It's a fact that capitalism demands wars. What caused the First World War? There weren't any Bolsheviks then.''

"Kaiser Wilhelm wasn't much better than Hitler.''

"Capitalism requires wars. But let's put that aside. Uncle, I want to speak to you about a specific matter.''

"What is it?''

Herman began coughing lightly. "Uncle, I'm going to the Soviet Union,'' he said rapidly, almost as if he could hardly utter the words.

"What? Go in health and peace. If that's what you want, I have no objection.''

But Boris's expression changed. He opened his eyes wide and gave Herman a sidelong stare, almost as though he doubted that he had heard correctly.

"Uncle, I know everything you're thinking. But the situation is such that I must go."

"If you must, you must. There you'll see the truth. But it'll be too late. It's like the World of the Dead over there—no one ever returns from it."

"People do come back, Uncle Borukh."

"Those who come back are capitalists, generals—not people like you. You'll arrive and perhaps they'll receive you with open arms at first. But two months later one of your comrades will inform on you, or they'll simply find some fault in you. I don't have to tell you what'll happen then."

Herman took off his pince-nez. "Uncle, you exaggerate."

"Well, I'm warning you. What else can I do? They've put a bullet in bigger fish than you over there."

"They don't shoot everyone. They're not insane. The press here wants to persuade the world that Russia is one huge madhouse. How on earth could they have won the war against Hitler if they were really as crazy as the capitalist press says, and if the people really hated the regime so much? It's a proven fact that they broke Hitler's back."

"With American money."

"No one can win a war with money alone."

"Well, well, what's the point of talking? It's Sabbath eve. I helped you to come to America because I wanted to save you. But if you're fool enough to want to destroy yourself, what can I do? You're not a child any longer."

Herman again took off his pince-nez. His eyes narrowed and sharpened, looking somewhere far into the distance. Grief tightened his fleshy lips. "Uncle, I'll be perfectly frank with you. I *must* go."

"Why *must* you? Who's forcing you?"

"I'm a member of the Party. We have strict discipline."

"What'll they do to you if you don't go? Pour salt on your tail?"

"It's not so simple. I don't have full American citizenship. I've only got the initial papers. When I arrived here, I had to swear an oath that I wasn't a leftist."

"Do you mean to say your own comrades will inform on you even here?"

"If one breaks discipline, one becomes an enemy."

"And if they do inform on you, so what? They won't deport you. Where can they deport you to? To Poland?"

"It's not a question of that."

"What *is* it a question of, then?"

"One can't be a member of the Party for so many years and then suddenly desert. It's also my deepest conviction. I was in Spain and I'd never have got out of there alive if it hadn't been for the Party. Through the Party I got the job I have now. I'm not going for good, only for a short while, for a year at most. The problem is that I won't be readmitted here if I leave without a permit. Getting a permit isn't easy either. But I wouldn't like to lose the chance to have American citizenship."

"Why be a citizen of a country made up of exploiters and fascists? Since the only justice in the world prevails in Stalin's state, why not stay there, in the Red paradise?"

"Don't be so sarcastic, Uncle. One can see all the defects of a country and still get used to it."

"What precisely do you want?"

"I want to marry Sylvia. Perhaps you remember her. She came to your Seder."

"I remember her very well. What's the matter? Is she also decamping to Stalin?"

"No, she's staying here."

"So what's the point of getting married and leaving her a deserted wife? I don't want to speak evil of anyone, God forbid, but today things are very different from what they used to be. In the old days, a young man would get married and then go off and spend years studying in a yeshiva or with a rabbi in whose house he lived. His wife, he could be certain, would remain pure. These days—" Boris broke off.

Herman replaced his pince-nez with what looked like a scornful smile. "That's not the problem."

"Then what exactly *is* the problem? And what do you want me to do? Perform the marriage ceremony? Give away the bride?"

Herman lowered his head. "If I'm to get married, you're my closest relative."

"Do you want to get married according to the Law of Moses and Israel?"

"Her mother wants it. It makes no difference to me."

Boris pondered for a long while. "I can't understand the sense of the whole thing—apart from your wanting to ensure that they'll readmit you to America."

"My having a wife here would help."

"I see. But first the Russians have to let you out, and they're like Pharaoh—they don't want to let our people go. The Gemara says: 'Even though he sins, he remains a Jew.' You disavow everything Jewish, but for Stalin and all the other enemies of Israel you're still a Jew and always will be. Only today I read in an article that the Jews are suffering terribly over there."

"Where did you read that? What are they doing to them?"

"What aren't they doing to them? They're even beating them up on trains. It's worse than in the days of the Czar. All Jewish officials are being dismissed. More and more Jews are being sent to Siberia."

"And you believe this?"

"Yes, I believe it. Why shouldn't I believe it? Wicked people do wicked things. The Jewish Communists themselves are unbridled in their wickedness. They inform on one another. You can be the most loyal Communist alive, but one of your comrades will suddenly turn around and accuse you of being a Trotskyite. Before you know it, they'll drag you to prison. Who'll defend you, America? The prisons over there are packed with hundreds of Americans and Britons and people of every other nationality. The Bolsheviks are afraid of no one. Now that they've won the war, they spit on the whole world."

"Uncle, you've got entirely the wrong picture."

"Would to God you were right. You're a fool, and I'm sorry for you. As long as you remain here, you're a free man. As soon as you fall into their hands, you're a slave. May they suffer as many plagues as the numbers of innocent people they've tortured and destroyed! A human life has less importance to them than the dirt under their fingernails. They killed their own generals, their own leaders—what was his name?—Bukharin and all the others. They've rocked the whole world, and now suddenly they imagine that everyone's spying on them. Someone like you has no more significance to them than a flea. They'll wipe you out, God forbid, and no one'll bat an eyelash. You know I'm speaking the truth."

"No, Uncle Borukh. If I believed you were speaking the truth, I wouldn't have anything to live for."

"Well, what can I do for you? When do you want to get married?"

"This week."

"When are you leaving?"

"In a matter of days."

"Well, if you want to kill yourself, go ahead. At least take your wife with you—she might be able to bring you a food parcel in prison."

Herman bit his lip. "She must stay here."

3

D r. Margolin had told Boris he was going to buy a magazine, but that
was a lie. If he knew the truth, Margolin said to himself in the car,
he would never have kissed me. He'd have spat in my face. He'd have
been right, too—absolutely right. Even as the thought occurred to Margolin, he took his hand off the steering wheel and wiped his sleeve across
his brow as if Boris Makaver had indeed spat on him. He said aloud, "I'm
not a human being."

What had happened was this: Lise, his wife, who in 1938 had gone off
to live with a Nazi, had come to America bringing the Margolins' daughter,
Mitzi, now a young woman of seventeen. The Nazi had been killed on the
Russian front in August 1943, and Margolin himself had helped to bring
the women to the United States, having agonized long and hard before
reaching his decision. During the weeks of sleepless nights in which he had
wrestled with himself about whether to send the affidavit or not, he had
even started taking opium. But he had finally done what he had not believed
himself capable of doing and what, if he had been told someone else had
done it, he would have regarded as an abomination and the person who
had done it as a foul scourge, an inhuman monstrosity, someone, by the
Talmud's definition, forbidden even to be encountered on the street because of conduct too corrupt to endure. He yearned for Mitzi, his own
flesh and blood, and he could not forget Lise either. The woman wrote
letters full of pleading, full of love, full of longing, according to which her
parents, who were still alive at the time, had driven her to do what she
had done. Hans, the Nazi, had himself warned her that if she did not come
to him, they would imprison Margolin in Dachau. In her letters, Lise
solemnly swore that she had never loved Hans, that he had been repellent
to her, that in the single year she had lived with him before they sent him
to the Russian front, she had not spent a single happy day. The child Mitzi
had hated him and had never stopped speaking of her father. In the school

to which they had sent her, they had known she had a Jewish father and Lise had been forced to swear that Hans was the child's biological father— "What an utterly appalling lie!"

It was not only Lise who wrote; Mitzi also inundated her father with letters. As proof that she hadn't forgotten him during all those years, she sent him the notes he'd written her when she'd gone to summer camp, the drawings he'd made for her, the photographs that had been taken of them standing together in various settings. This was to demonstrate that the daughter had never forgotten her father and had treasured everything that kept him alive for her. Like lawyers who plan the defense of those accused and employ every piece of evidence that might mitigate their punishment or disprove their guilt, so mother and daughter kept assembling material that attested to their abiding devotion to him. But Margolin knew what he knew and remembered what he remembered. The stark facts of the matter were that Lise had deserted him to live with a Hitlerite and Mitzi had attended a school where they taught her that Jews were lower than lice and where they sang the *Horst Wessel Lied*. If the Nazi had not perished on the eastern front and Hitler had been victorious, he would never have heard from either Lise or Mitzi again. Moreover, Margolin himself had been a hairsbreadth away from being stranded in Europe and being sent to be gassed or burned in Majdanek or Treblinka. For a long while neither Lise nor Mitzi had known whether he was alive.

Dozens of times he had decided not to reply, not to have any further dealings with either of them, but he had done exactly the opposite. There had been a time when he had wanted to send for his daughter alone, but Mitzi refused to come without her mother. In the end, he had sent both women an affidavit and money for their expenses as well. They had arrived in the spring. Lise had wanted to move into his apartment, but Margolin had rented an apartment for his wife and child on First Avenue, next to the East River. Lise, who had run an exclusive fashion boutique in Berlin, had found a job immediately. She spoke perfect English and knew French as well. Mitzi had entered Vassar.

It was for Boris Makaver's sake that Margolin had kept the whole thing secret. Here in New York he had no close friends, maintained no connections with people he had known in Europe—those he remembered from forty-five years before had all died out—and the majority of his few distant relatives lived outside New York. Who could have counseled him? Who would even have been interested? But Boris had known Lise, remembered Mitzi, and knew every secret. Were Boris to learn that he had taken Lise back—"the Nazi," as he venomously called her—he would wish never again to hear Margolin's name mentioned. He would recoil from his oldest friend as from a disease. It filled Margolin with a mystical terror when he considered that his action would implicitly ask Boris—and all Jews—to forget and forgive everything the Germans had done.

Yes, because of Boris Makaver—his Jewish conscience—Solomon Margolin maintained two apartments. Boris represented Margolin's parents, his grandparents, his obligation to the tormented Jewish people. Instead of being ashamed before God, he was ashamed before Boris Makaver. That Boris had made his peace with Anna had in some strange way alleviated Margolin's own guilt. Perhaps that was why he had taken so much trouble to bring them together again. But even so, he was not prepared to tell Boris the truth. In his imagination he even heard Boris denouncing him: "Unclean lump of putrid flesh! Hateful filth! Dog! You're a Nazi yourself! May your name and memory be erased!" Margolin was even afraid that Boris might have a heart attack as a result. The old man's hatred of Nazis knew no bounds. He had said countless times that he would rather perish than ever set foot on German soil again. Every time he heard that German-Jewish refugees were writing letters back to Germany or traveling there on business, he trembled with fear. That the world did not take revenge on the Germans and forgot about the six million martyrs was for him a sign that the globe was inhabited by yet another generation of the kind that had brought on the Flood. He would often observe: "Let them hurl the atomic bomb at one another, the workers of iniquity. The world deserves nothing better than to be burned to ashes."

In his conversations Boris also strongly condemned the Jews. Why were they silent? Why did they forget? Boris believed that the whole Jewish people should go into mourning. A *Bet Din* or a Sanhedrin should institute a mourning period of a hundred years: Jews should be forbidden to wear bright clothing, to play music at weddings, to drink wine; instead, they should be compelled to sit on the ground for an hour each day and recite the Book of Lamentations to memorialize the destruction of Jewry. There ought to be grief for generations to come. If we forget our own loss, how can we expect others to remember? On this subject Boris could expatiate for hours. Often he would even reproach the Master of the Universe. What did he want of Jews? What had happened in Europe was not a punishment, a test of fidelity. There was absolutely no explanation. In a case such as this, one dared not say that God was just, for that in itself was a great blasphemy.

Margolin himself had never been able to come to terms with what he had done. Who could know how many Jews that creature Hans had murdered? He had written love letters to Lise at the same time as he had smashed open the heads of Jewish children. Indeed, the fact that Lise had formerly lived with a Jew had probably aroused in him a savage murderousness toward all Jews. Margolin would never forget the afternoon he had returned home to find Lise packing her things. He asked where she was going and she had replied, "To Hans." Yes, at that time the learned Dr. Margolin had been nothing more than a Jew whose blood had been *nochmal so gut* when it flowed from the knife. Lise had sent their little daughter to learn that exterminating Jews was the highest duty of a German. That had been November 1938, the time of the great pogrom called *Kristallnacht*, when Lise had raised her arm and unashamedly cried out, "*Heil Hitler!*" Her father, that old fool, had become a Nazi, and her brother a storm trooper. If Margolin had not been smuggled into Switzerland, his own brother-in-law would probably have lugged him to a death camp. Then Lise would never have mentioned his name again.

Yes, Solomon Margolin lived with a hideous secret, a spiritual cancer. There were moments even now when he wanted to sever all his connections with Lise, with Mitzi, to flee from them as from lepers. But when Mitzi embraced him, caressed him, covered his face with kisses, he felt profoundly undecided. She was his daughter, his father's grandchild. She even resembled her grandmother Fradel. And it appeared that Lise loved him deeply. She was in America now—what did she need him for? She earned enough to support herself, she was still a beautiful woman, she could easily find a husband here. So why did she continue to cling to him? Why was she so submissive before him? Why did she look at him with such love, with such guilt? But what had been could not be erased. It was continually present and plain as day. Who said the past was dead and gone? In the spiritual sphere, everything remained—every sin, every good deed. The immortality of the soul was manifest even in this world.

Margolin had taken Lise and Mitzi with him to Asbury Park and had put them up in the same hotel in which he was staying. The semester at Vassar had ended, Mitzi was with her mother and they had not wanted to spend the weekend alone in scorching New York.

What a bizarre double game he was playing! He would eat the Sabbath meal with Boris, would recite the blessings over the wine and the bread, hear Boris sing Sabbath hymns, say the Grace after Meals, and then go back to sleep with a woman who had left him for a Nazi. But Anna was expected at her father's table, and Herman, that Communist, as well. Boris Makaver's was no pure Jewish home either. The kind of Jewishness which Boris tried to maintain was crumbling. Soon no vestige of it would remain.

Margolin suddenly jammed on his brakes. He had gone through a red light and almost knocked down a policeman. The officer turned around to stare at him. ''What's the big idea?''

And he began writing out a ticket.

4

D r. Margolin entered the lobby of the hotel and went up in the elevator astounded at himself. What could all this mean? How could I have such a weak character? It's still not too late to walk away! something within him prompted. Well, it's an irreconcilable conflict. I'll never be free of it.

Once he had been a strong person. In his youth, and even in middle age, he had often exhibited exceptional firmness of character before those who had tried to impose their will on him. He was capable of refusing large sums of money, important positions, and had always done so in the name of pride. But what was pride? Aristotle called the moral person the proud person. Margolin had once questioned whether he should convert. He could have married an exceptionally beautiful woman of the noblest German aristocracy. But however little he believed in either Moses or Jesus, he refused to change his religion. It was a denial of human worth, he told himself, and that was enough. In conversation with professors and high-ranking military officers he had often expressed dangerous opinions and had never feared reprisals. He had always been prepared to risk everything for the right to speak his own mind. So why was he so weak nowadays? Was it old age? Had he even less belief in spiritual values than formerly? Or had America reduced him to the level of everyone else? How on earth could he have taken back a wife who had abandoned him at the very moment his life was in the gravest danger and rushed to embrace the archenemy, the vilest monstrosity that humankind had produced?

"Eight!" the elevator man called out, and Margolin thought, Perhaps I should leave now and never come back. She can't force me! He said to the elevator man, "I'll go down again. I've forgotten something."

"Yes, sir."

As Margolin went down, other passengers got in on every floor, and he stared at them. They were all Jews. What kind of Jews? What connected him to them? What connected them to one another? The women had all painted the nails on their fingers and toes red. The majority dyed their hair in order to look more like Gentiles. They were more naked than clothed. They carried scandal magazines, the latest bestsellers. At night they probably amused themselves in nightclubs where they sang cheap songs and mouthed obscenities from the stage. As the elevator descended, they chattered among themselves about a boxing match due to take place that night, and about the horse races in Atlantic City. In what way were women like these more Jewish than Lise? Margolin asked himself. Wouldn't they, too, have run off with Nazis if the Nazis had been willing to take them? He stood for a while in the lobby reading the headlines of the newspapers and magazines displayed there: sex, sports, hunting animals, slander, murder. The world that he inhabited was neither Jewish nor Christian but idolatrous through and through, and the Jews were its chief servants, the most experienced idol makers in the business. What would happen if he left Lise? Whom would he replace her with? That woman over there with the throaty voice and the ankle bracelet?

He bought one of the magazines he had been glancing through. In taking it down, the news vendor knocked over a paperback entitled *Tomorrow You'll Be a Corpse*. On its cover was a picture of a nude woman with a bullet hole in her forehead from which what looked like red paint dripped.

Yes, tomorrow you'll be a corpse! That's the sum total of everything, Margolin mused wryly. Even trash like this calls the truth by its proper name.

And he entered the elevator and went up again.

He knocked, heard Lise's voice, opened the door, and went in. Lise, a dark-skinned woman of average height with black hair and brown eyes, was wandering about in a negligée in the heat. She would have looked Jewish had it not been for her Gentile snub nose. She was already past forty, but her body showed no trace of age. Even when she lived in Germany she had kept to a strict diet, did gymnastic exercises every morning, and had regular massages. Her body was the net in which she ensnared him, attracting him twenty-four hours a day. Of all the women he had

known, none had satisfied him as Lise had. She submitted to all his caprices,
yet never demanded that he lavish money or costly gifts on her in return.
In her own way she was a perfect being, a precision machine capable of
carrying out with clockwork regularity the functions for which she had
been built. During all the years he had lived with her, there had never
been the slightest malfunction, in either her household or her business
management. She planned everything down to the smallest detail. Every
time Margolin gave her a medical examination he was astounded. Everything was in perfect working order—her pulse, her blood pressure, her
blood count, her sight, her hearing, her reflexes. Her capacity to adjust to
his every mood was inscrutable. She read his thoughts, anticipated his
words, enjoyed the same food as he did. She was brilliant, Margolin had
often thought, at sexual foreplay, afterplay, at all the whispering and endearments that added excitement to making love. She heard all kinds of
stories from the women who patronized her boutique, and she knew precisely which to recount, and when, and how. She dressed tastefully and
modestly, did not paint her nails, used cosmetics discreetly, seldom wore
jewelry. In the Berlin days, when Margolin arranged soirées for his friends
and acquaintances, Lise was the perfect hostess, and he used to call her his
"woman of valor," Hebrew words she had learned to repeat with the
same perfection as she spoke English or French.

During those years in Berlin, Boris Makaver had been a frequent guest.
Lise maintained an entire service of kosher cutlery and crockery just for
him, and would order meals by telephone from a kosher restaurant. In a
drawer she kept a skullcap that she brought over to him before he sat down
to eat, and she always had a copper ewer and basin ready for him to
perform the Jewish ritual of washing the hands before meals. There was a
time when Boris had secretly been in love with this German woman who
pampered him so much, and he even maintained that she had a Jewish
soul, showering her and Mitzi with gifts. Now, of course, Lise understood
perfectly that Boris would never make peace with her, and that he was the
sole and great obstacle preventing Margolin from living in the same apartment with her. Nevertheless, she never once uttered a bad word against
him. Now she went up to Margolin, kissed him, and asked after Boris in
a tone that suggested that nothing had disrupted the friendship between
herself and that observant Jew.

"Where's Mitzi?" Margolin asked in German.

"On the beach."

Margolin started pacing back and forth. He felt hot and wanted to take a lukewarm bath. Lise knew instantly what he needed and went off to run the water for him. Then she asked him to sit down, knelt in front of him, and according to the German custom untied and took off his shoes. It immediately occurred to him that she had taken off the boots of Hans the Nazi in exactly this way when he returned from a Hitler rally or from smashing Jewish shop windows and daubing Jewish buildings with swastikas and hate slogans. As she knelt before Margolin, he had the urge simultaneously to lie with her and to strangle her.

He murmured in Hebrew, "You unclean lump of putrid flesh!"

"What does that mean?" She never spoke to him in anything but German.

"It means," he replied in English, " 'Tomorrow you'll be a corpse.' "

"Yes, of course. Sooner or later."

She undressed him, kissed him, and led him into the bathroom. He entered the tub and she knelt down again, this time soaping and scrubbing him.

"Mitzi has already found some company here," she remarked.

"Who?"

"A young man. He's living two doors away. A Mr. Berkowitz and his crippled mother."

In this way Lise was trying to bolster his confidence, assuring him that Mitzi had forgotten what she had been taught in the Nazi schools and that she made friends with Jewish youths. But Margolin knew perfectly well that Mitzi had no love for Jews. She had told him that openly. Not as tactful as her mother, Mitzi had let slip the opinion that Jewish students in America were vulgar.

Well, that's it! That's it! Margolin thought. The whole world is morally bankrupt.

20

Herman Makaver had left for Russia and only one person had heard from him. From Moscow a letter arrived for Sylvia, in which Herman supplied an address and promised to write again soon, but weeks passed and Sylvia did not receive even a hint of a message. She sent a cable, but there was no reply. She inquired about Herman at the Soviet consulate, where she was told that they knew nothing. Boris had already returned to New York, and Sylvia came to seek advice from "Uncle Boris," as she now called him. This large, dark young woman who had peppered Boris with confrontational questions at his Seder table solely to provoke an argument now stood before him and wept. She wiped her big nose with a tiny handkerchief and wailed in broken Yiddish, "I can't understand it! I can't understand it!"

"You still don't understand," Boris said angrily. "I warned him, I warned him. I begged him, I pleaded with him not to join with murderers."

"But why? What've they got against him?"

"What've they got against one another? The wicked exist only to do evil."

"But why?"

Sylvia wept, stopped, stared vaguely in the direction of the window with her enormous black eyes, and again started sobbing as she asked Boris, "But what can I do?"

"If you believe in God, recite the psalms."

"What God? Which God? What does God have to do with it? Oh, Mama!"

And Sylvia began blubbering exactly like a young woman in the old country who had been wronged.

Boris himself began blowing his nose and wiping his eyes. Herman had been the last member of his family, the youngest son of his brother Dovid Meyer. All the others had been exterminated by the Nazis. Now Herman was rotting somewhere in a Soviet prison—or had perhaps already been shot. However much Boris raged that Herman deserved to have his flesh torn from his bones and vinegar poured into the wounds, the whole affair kept him awake at night. What did they want, those destroyers, what did they want? he asked himself.

If you don't serve them, you're a fascist, and if you do, it doesn't get you anywhere either. You can never satisfy such devils. These young people know what's what, they read the newspapers, yet Communism draws them like a magnet. Communism has become their idolatry. Boris vividly recalled that he had seen terror in Herman's eyes. That young man had gone to Russia, yet he was afraid. Somewhere deep within him he had known that he was crawling into a trap, yet he crawled into it nevertheless. Where was the logic? Well, and this Sylvia—would she at least learn a lesson? Boris knew she would not. She would mourn for Herman for a few weeks or months, and then she would decide that he had probably been a secret enemy of the working class all along. Hers was the kind that hanged their own brother and then threw stones at his corpse. Their rule was that the hangman was always right.

Boris had promised Sylvia that he would see what could be done. But where could he inquire? Of whom? Once one crossed the Soviet border, one was as good as in the next world. Moreover, he had other cares. Frieda was experiencing a difficult pregnancy. She had turned yellow and she had started to swell early. Dr. Margolin assured them that everything was as it should be, but Boris was deeply concerned. His wife was no longer a young woman. This was her first child. She needed prayers offered on her behalf. His own health had improved a little during his few weeks by the sea—his blood pressure had come down and he had lost twelve pounds, but he was still far from well. The deal with the ships had been partially straightened out, but although Anna had done wonders, it wasn't easy to extricate himself from that mess. Boris had been compelled to sell a building that netted him four hundred dollars a week. Every few days his partners had a new falling out, and once more Boris had to work to keep peace among them, because if no one took responsibility, everything would collapse.

The times when Boris would rush from one cafeteria to another, meeting businessmen, smoking cigars, speaking and shouting for hours on end, had passed. He sat in his living room in a silk dressing gown with slippers on his feet while Frieda nursed him. He had stopped smoking, drank watery tea, did not eat his fill. All day long he felt a gnawing in the pit of his stomach, and often felt so weak that he imagined his soul was leaving his body. He would telephone Solomon Margolin, but the doctor only cracked jokes. "If you die of hunger, you can sue me," he would say, or "Just imagine it's Tisha b'Av."

Tisha b'Av had long since passed and the summer was rushing by with extraordinary speed. Although it seemed they had celebrated Passover only recently, the Jewish penitential month of Elul was fast approaching. Through the open living-room window the din of Broadway forced its way in, but Boris was no longer swept up in the turmoil of New York. He had lost as much energy as he had weight. Having given up smoking made him feel that every day was the Sabbath. In addition, Boris had learned that his rebbe in Williamsburg was critically ill and had little chance of recovery. Boris had seen him only a few weeks previously, when the rebbe had solemnized Herman's marriage. At that time the rebbe had looked frail but not ill. He had even discussed with Boris his desire to emigrate to the Holy Land. I don't want to be buried in America, the rebbe had said, explaining that he would wait until the political unrest in the Holy Land had quieted and then go. The Zionists were Gentiles, to be sure, but in what way was the land of Israel to blame? The land itself was holy. Now Boris was told that the rebbe had stomach cancer and that it was too late even for surgery.

God, dear God! Truly, life is worth nothing, Boris told himself. It's one step from the cradle to the grave. I'm ill myself—perhaps a great deal sicker than they tell me. Perhaps I'm already more in the next world than in this. If that's the case, why am I still making a fool of myself with business deals? And what will become of my poor innocent unborn child? God forbid, he might never know his father! Oh, it's bitter, bitter! Let me at least master a little Torah! Let me at least serve the Almighty before I leave. He went into his *cabinet* to take out a volume of the Talmud but instead telephoned the rebbe.

A young woman answered. "Hello?"

"Dvoyrele, is that you? This is Boris Makaver."

"Yes, Mr. Makaver, I recognize your voice."

"How are you? How's the rebbe?"

"So-so."

"Dvoyrele, I've heard that there's a hospital somewhere called the Mayo Clinic. People say they do wonders. The greatest doctors in America work there."

"My father doesn't even want to go into a hospital here in New York."

"But we are taught that the commandment to save a life supersedes all other commandments."

"He doesn't want to."

"What's he doing? Is he lying in bed?"

"No, he's sitting up."

"He's studying?"

"What else?"

"Dvoyrele, today I'm sending you a check for five hundred dollars," Boris said, astounded at his own words and at the large sum he had named.

Dvoyrele paused a moment. "Why so much?"

Boris's throat filled with tears. "I want them to save the rebbe."

"If only money alone would do it!" And Dvoyrele let out something like a laugh.

Boris spoke for a little longer, then replaced the receiver. He went over to his bookcase and took down *Yoma*, the tractate of the Talmud that deals with the laws governing Yom Kippur, the Day of Atonement. Well, as long as I'm alive, I can still do something. Every minute is precious! Every dollar can bring relief to someone! As long as one breathes, one still has free will! Going from his *cabinet* to his little prayerhouse he glanced at the Holy Ark, went up to the curtain that screened the Torah scrolls from common view, and began speaking to the Master of the Universe: "Father in heaven, have compassion! I feel oppressed, Father, horribly oppressed. Father in heaven, have compassion on Herman. He is unfortunately sadly deluded, but his trouble is very great. Save him, Father in heaven, protect Chaim Moshe the son of Sarah Itte that he may escape from the hands of the wicked and come to his senses. We are all deluded, alas! Bitterly deluded! Each one in his own way. We are, alas, all fools, dear Father in heaven—very great fools!"

2

G rein quickly perceived what he had known from the start: keeping a resolution wasn't easy. After that first Sabbath came others, and he broke all his promises, all the laws. He had sampled Jewishness, but nothing more. Temptations came and, as is generally true of temptations, they were unforeseen, accompanied by complications for which no human being is ever prepared. In the first place, Leah returned from the hospital a different person. Her illness, Grein's conduct, and the behavior of her children had embittered her and awakened in her something like vindictiveness. She told Grein openly that she neither believed in his penitence nor cared for it. If he was returning to her only because he wanted to make his peace with God, she did not want him in the house. During her illness, Leah herself had become even more of an unbeliever. She argued that God did not exist, and had no good words for Jews. She had been in a Jewish hospital and complained about the Jewish doctors, the nurses, the whole administration. In the Gentile hospital to which she had been admitted years before when she had broken a leg, she had been treated with far more consideration. Jews kept on yelling that they were the Chosen People, Leah complained, but they were coarse, money-grubbing, egotistical. Of what did their chosenness consist?

Grein tried to persuade Leah that the modern Jew who had cast aside all religious constraints was not a Jew, but Leah responded tartly, "There are no other kinds of Jew today. Hitler wiped out the Jews with sidelocks."

Then Leah started saying she was quite content that Jack had married Patricia. That Gentile girl had been more attentive to her than Anita, and had come to the hospital every day. Patricia was supposed to visit her parents in Oregon and had already bought a plane ticket, but when Leah had fallen ill, Patricia had canceled her vacation. She brought Leah gifts and flowers, and had behaved throughout like a devoted daughter. Anita seldom came to the hospital, and when she did she had been sour and self-absorbed, not hiding that every visit was a torture for her.

"In the hospital I saw the truth," Leah complained, "the whole bitter truth."

Grein wanted to take her to the country, but Leah didn't want to go anywhere. She returned to her antiques shop on Third Avenue, arguing that she could not depend on him. She had long since accepted the idea that she had to provide for herself, she said. However much longer she might have to live, she wanted to work and earn an income. When Grein

mentioned that he wanted to keep a kosher kitchen and observe the Sabbath, Leah responded, ''Run off to Boris Makaver's daughter. She's a great
saint.''

Grein's pleadings that she go away with him were to no avail. All
through the hot summer days she sat in her dusty shop from early morning
until evening, and again started attending auctions. Grein spent his nights
at home, but Leah paid no attention to him. He spoke to her, but she
barely answered him. Since her illness, Leah—quiet, passive Leah—had
become full of hatred and rage. She had locked herself away, as it were,
and there was no longer any access to her. Jack and Patricia had taken a
bungalow somewhere on Long Island, and Leah would ride out there on
Sundays and Mondays when she kept the shop shut. Patricia was pregnant.
Grein would soon become the grandfather of a child who would trace its
descent on one side from scribes, rabbis, observant Jews, and on the other
from generations of Gentiles. Patricia was of Irish and Scottish stock, and
had a German grandfather. Her cousins had probably been Nazis.

Grein had not told Leah what he had discovered about Anita, but their
daughter herself told her mother that she was preparing to get married.
From Leah, Grein learned more particulars about Anita's choice of husband. His name was Fritz Genzl and he was both a Communist and a
German, not American-born but an immigrant from Germany, where his
family had remained. His brothers had probably burned Jews, laughed
while Jews had dug their own graves. Difficult as it was to believe, Leah
had nothing against the marriage beyond feeling that Anita was too young,
and disapproving of the fact that Genzl was not a professional man—a
doctor, a lawyer, or an engineer—but an ordinary car mechanic in some
garage. Whether Grein himself became an observant Jew again or not, he
had snapped the chain of generations, mixed his blood with the blood of
the enemies of Israel. He, Hertz Dovid Grein, was a last twig on the Jewish
tree. Whatever might happen to Jews in general no longer had any bearing
on him. It had fallen to his lot to disrupt a heritage that derived from the
Patriarch Abraham and extended down through millennia to the present
day. In all the years before, he had never given the slightest thought to the
possibility that this might occur. He had pursued his own affairs, his own
passions, and had left his children without direction or discipline. Now it
was too late. Not only his children but also Leah, the daughter of a pious
Jewish home, was ready to abandon Judaism. Grein was silent and stunned.
He repeatedly asked himself the same questions: How did all this come
about? How could it happen so fast? The answer was clear. Jewishness was

not some kind of wild grass that grew on its own. It was a garden that one had to tend continually. When the gardener forgot them, or made himself forget, the plants withered. Even here the principle of cause and effect was in precise operation. There weren't any miracles: if one didn't teach one's children to be Jews, then they became atheists, Communists, assimilationists, converts. The biblical injunction "And you shall teach these words diligently to your children" was not simply a pious platitude. If this precept wasn't followed, moral chaos was the result.

The thought that he had neglected this principal duty had, as it were, stopped Grein's spiritual stocktaking in its tracks. He could almost hear Satan arguing with him: "It's too late, in any event. Since you cannot repair anything, everything must remain as it is. If your own faith were at least whole, there might have been some sense in becoming a penitent. But your faith is no faith. You believe in nothing except an unknown and never-revealed power. Your God is not the God of Abraham and Moses—and certainly not the God of Rabbi Judah the Prince or Rabba or Rabbi Moshe Isserles. He is no more Jewish than Gentile. There is no way in which to serve Him. This struggle with yourself is nothing more than a neurosis."

Thus spoke his Evil Inclination. The battle lines within him were drawn.

His Good Inclination would respond: "If that is true, then Hitler was justified: might makes right. So run, Hertz Grein, and shout, 'Long live Stalin! *Heil Hitler!*' Consort with all the corrupt, the murderers, the wrongdoers and liars. Share their thoughts, their fate. Stop thinking about the categories of good and evil. Live like a dog and die like a dog! 'Let us eat and drink, for tomorrow we shall die.' "

The egoist in Grein wanted both at once: to be both a Jew and a Gentile, both holy and profane, both a giver and a taker. He wanted to perform the deeds of Zimri but to receive the rewards of Pinehas. He sought a compromise that would grant him all the pleasures of worldliness and all the comforts of religion. Was there not such a formula, such a reformed faith? Wasn't there a religion that would permit him to keep both Anna and Esther and allow him to go on maneuvering as he had done all these years? The egoist in him continually searched for permission: since the Torah had allowed polygamy, why could he not keep several lovers at the same time? To be sure, Esther was now another man's wife, but since Plotkin was not jealous, why should Grein not be permitted to possess her? The prohibition contained in "Thou shalt not commit adultery" was based solely on the requirement that one should not take that which belonged to another, but if it made no difference to the other, why shouldn't one take?

But another part of Grein concluded that all these sophistries and justifications had only one purpose: to nullify all duties, to render everything lawless. Then he reminded himself yet again that he had killed a human being. His victim, Stanislaw Luria, was now lying in his grave. His blood, like the blood of Abel, cried out from the earth.

3

The day had been hot. At night a sliver of new moon in the sky affirmed that the penitential month of Elul had begun. Without jacket or shoes, Grein was lying alone on the living-room sofa when Leah came in from the kitchen.

"Hertz, I can't bear this any longer!"

Grein stared at her.

"What's the matter now?"

"I have to get away! I'm suffocating!"

"I begged you to do that all summer."

"I couldn't have gone anywhere then. I was too ill. I'm still ill, but this city's killing what little's left of me. The shop was closed for three weeks. Now I'll have to close it again. It isn't worth paying the rent."

"Sell it all and make an end of it."

"That's easy to say. I can't sell a thing. I never see a customer, and if you sell wholesale, you have to give everything away for nothing. The stock cost me more than I'll get for it."

"In that case, close the shop. You haven't invested millions."

"Hertz, I'm losing my strength. I'm afraid I'll never be able to open the shop again."

"If you can't, you can't."

"It's easy for you to say. I put my life into that shop. I got sick because of it. The dust ate me up. You'll never know what I went through there. You're responsible, of course. It would never have occurred to me to become a businesswoman if you hadn't spent all these years running around with all sorts of sluts. I used to sit at home and nearly go out of my mind; I used to lie awake at night shuddering with fever. You have no conception of what you did to me. I hoped that I'd be able to lose myself in the business, but I went from one hell into another. You promised you'd help me, but you never set foot in the shop. You were too busy with your whores. Now I can't do it anymore. I feel as if my skin is being flayed. I want to get away, but where can we go? I've become afraid of people. I can't look anyone in the face. I imagine that everyone's staring at my breasts, that everyone can see I've got only one. Oh, I want so much to shut myself away in a quiet corner where no one can see me, but where can I hide? There are people everywhere, and they start cross-examining you.''

''Perhaps we could stay on a farm somewhere.''

''What farm? It's even worse being a guest on somebody's farm. I can't possibly do without a private bathroom. I have to be able to lock myself in without anyone beating at the door.''

''We can get a room with a private bathroom in a hotel.''

''Where? In the Catskills? I don't want to go to any hotels. I can't share a table with strangers anymore.''

''Perhaps we could go to a hotel in Atlantic City. There we can eat in restaurants.''

''What? I don't like the sea. I always hated places where people pad about barefoot in the sand. I can't do battle with the waves. Now that they've cut off one of my breasts, I certainly don't want to bare myself to people and have them pointing a finger at me.''

''You don't have to go bathing.''

''I love the mountains, not the sea.''

''Let's go to Lake Placid. It's high up, and they've got hotels which don't offer meals. You can eat in a restaurant.''

''Where on earth is it, this Lake Placid? Oh, I know. You probably used to go there with your sluts. I don't like those Gentile places. I like Jewish food, not tough meat dripping with blood.''

''It's packed with Jews.''

''What sort of Jews? German refugees? I detest them! When I hear them speaking German, I want to block my ears. They examine things in the shop a thousand times, touch every stick of furniture, poke at it, run their fingers over the upholstery, always on the lookout for defects, and talk so much they give you a headache. Then they put down a deposit of five dollars and it takes forever before they pay off the rest. They bring you five dollars at a time, and each time you have to give them a receipt, and even then they drag in experts to have a look.

Where these people get so much time, I don't know, because all that coming and going and jabbering for three hours about an old sofa is worth more than the piece of furniture itself. Then they start telling you about all the valuable possessions they had in Germany and what spas they used to visit and how good and cheap everything was in the fatherland and how expensive everything is here. Hitler kicked them out, and America saved their lives by letting them in, but that doesn't stop them from criticizing America. Then suddenly one of those German bitches will come in and tell me she's consulted a decorator and she doesn't want the sofa any longer and I must return her money. Or else she tries to exchange it for something else and the whole rigmarole starts all over again. I never want to see them again, do you hear? I got cancer because of them.''

"So we won't go to Lake Placid.''

"Where should we go, then?''

"Let's go to a hotel in the Adirondacks—you can have complete privacy there.''

"Where's that? I don't want to go far from home. I have to see the doctor every week. I don't want to be far from New York. If I die, I don't want my body to be transported.''

"Truly, Leah, you're making me very anxious.''

"I don't feel well. It's not only the breast. The doctor tells me it's all been cut out and I'm completely clear, but I feel as if something's rotting inside me. Let's not fool ourselves—my time's come. You'll soon be free and you can run back to Boris Makaver's daughter.''

The telephone rang, and Grein went to the study. He had resolved to stop running, but he forgot and immediately broke into a dash. The study was dark and he wanted to switch on the light, but he couldn't remember where the switch was. He rushed to the telephone in the gloom, banging against it before he snatched it to his ear, knocking his temple sharply as he did so.

"Hello?''

"Hertz? This is Anna.''

In the murk he pulled up a chair and sat down. After the letter he had written telling her he was returning to Leah, Anna no longer called him on the telephone. He had sent her a check for the rent, but she had returned it with a curt note saying that she was quite capable of supporting herself. Now he asked, "Are you in New York?''

"Yes, I'm here.''

"How's your father?"

"Papa? He's not so well, but he's all right. His wife is in the last months of her pregnancy."

"Indeed."

"Yes, indeed. How are you? I thought you now spent your days in the study house."

"It hasn't come to that yet."

"Why not? According to your letter, there's no alternative. How's your wife?"

"Not too well."

"Hertz, I don't want to upset your life. You've decided this is your duty. You obviously know what you're doing. Perhaps you're right as well."

"You know I couldn't abandon her under these circumstances."

"Yes, you're absolutely correct."

For a while both were silent. Then Anna said, "I still regard you as a good friend."

"Besides your father, you have none greater."

"What? What is friendship? Hertz, I want to tell you something, and at the same time I know I don't need to tell you. We killed a man and we scarcely did much better to ourselves."

"I know, I know. I think about it all day long."

"You, at least, have a home, I've been left completely adrift."

4

Again both were silent. Then Anna said, "Hertz, I don't sit hoping that something bad will happen to your wife. It never even occurs to me. May she live for a hundred years. Even when you lived with me, you kept seeing that Esther. What was between us is something we must forget. I don't mean literally, but it was just an episode in our lives, something over and done with. I'll remember it to my dying day."

"Yes, yes."

"Hertz, I know you'll think I've gone mad, but I'm going back to Yasha."

Since Anna didn't say "Yasha Kotik" but only "Yasha," it took a while before Grein understood whom she meant. He wanted to laugh, but tears came to his eyes instead.

"Is that so?"

"I know what you're thinking, and what everyone will think. When Papa hears, he'll spit, and that'll be the end. He's angry with you, but for Yasha he has a terrifying loathing. I'm even more afraid of Dr. Margolin. He can't do anything to me, but contempt is like a physical force. He knows what I went through in Berlin—I've told you a little about it, too. Hertz, I know everything, but I can't be alone. I'm simply afraid to be alone. Yasha has an infinite number of faults, but I have feelings for him. He always had a profound effect on me. I see all his negative qualities clearly, but he interests me. I don't have to tell you how talented he is. He's conquered America. They're showering him with money."

"Yes, I know."

"It's good one can't spit through the telephone. If one could, you'd probably have spat on me by now."

"No, Anna. If I'm going to spit, I must spit on myself."

"You do what your conscience dictates, and I do the opposite. I had to talk to someone, and who can I talk to if not to you? I've as good as lost Papa. What I'm going to do now will finish everything. It'll be the final break. Dr. Margolin is extremely clever, but he's a hard man. He knows only one thing—logic, although in his view life has very little logic. I have a cousin, Herman, but he's gone off to the Bolsheviks and they've probably done him in by now. Many women have sisters, but I have no one. By the time my sister—or brother—grows up, I'll be either old or dead. I must talk to someone."

"Yes, Anna, you can talk to me."

"What can I tell you? I know I'm making a mistake, but I can't help myself. Three men in one life is enough. Too many. I can't start up with a fourth. I can't, and I don't want to. I'm one of those who cling to the old days. You too were part of my past, after all. I can't bury the past. I wanted to be with you because you were my first love, but since my first love has fled, I have to turn to my second. If that doesn't work out either, I'll go to Luria in the next world."

"Don't make such a tragedy of it."

"What should I make of it, then? Yasha did me more harm than any other person in the world. Now he sweet-talks me and promises me heaven on earth, but I know he'll behave exactly as he did in Berlin. The only difference is that he's older now and probably hasn't got the energy he used to have."

"Yes, I understand."

"Someone who's lived his whole life in lies and falseness doesn't suddenly become honest. Now he's howling that he's madly in love with me. He sends me so many flowers that I'm embarrassed in front of the elevator man and the building staff. My neighbors must think I'm Rockefeller's mistress. He telephones me thirty times a day. Between one act of his play and another. As soon as he leaves the stage, he rushes to the telephone. When he first started pursuing me, I cursed him. I told him I didn't want to hear his name mentioned. He's managed to team up with someone called Justina Kohn, a cheap number, supposedly an actress—or God knows what she was—in Poland. I hear you met her at the Russian Tea Room—the Zvezda or whatever they call it. She's that worthless trash Professor Shrage's crazy dentist hired to fool Luria. I don't want to speak about that—it's too painful. They ought to hang women like her—it's the least they deserve. Well, that's the type he picked for a lover. Now, apparently, he's chucked her out. But you can never know with people like Yasha. You ran back to Esther—why shouldn't he go back to Justina Kohn? I know it's filth, but I'm crawling into it. Can you understand this?"

"Yes, I understand."

"What do you understand?"

"We ourselves are filth. Filth attracts filth."

"What? Yes, perhaps you're right. But what can I do? You pick up the Gemara and persuade yourself that you're a yeshiva student again. I can't study the Gemara. All this talk about God doesn't interest me. Only yesterday I saw a movie that showed savages in Africa tearing their flesh before jumping into a fire to serve their gods, and I thought, How do we know that our God is better than theirs? We would certainly appear as ridiculous in their eyes as they appear in ours. I can't talk to the wall and convince myself that I'm speaking to someone who's listening. I envy those who can."

"I hope you love him, at least."

"What? I don't know how to answer you. When I was nine years old, I knew who I loved. Now I don't even know that. I only know that I can't be alone. I'm simply going mad, and I can't just go tap a strange man in the street on the shoulder. I must have a relationship with someone—it can even be a bad relationship, as long as it's a relationship."

"What is this? Sexual desire?"

"I don't know that either. A man knows when he wants and what he wants. Women generally know nothing. It's all emotions. What can happen, I ask myself. If it doesn't work out, it doesn't. He won't poison me, and he won't strangle me either. I can always leave him. At the same time I'm terrified to death. When I think about Papa, it's so unbearable I want to die."

"Does he want to make it official?"

"What? It's all the same to him. But that doesn't mean I could go and live with him just like that. He must commit himself to something. America isn't Germany. Here he'll have to pay alimony. Ah, I don't know myself what I'm saying. But I've had enough of free love. I'm not made for it. The few months I lived with you taught me enough."

And Anna fell silent.

"What exactly do you want from me? Advice?" Grein asked.

Anna did not answer immediately. "You'll laugh, but I can't decide anything without you. I know it's a ludicrous situation, but everything in my life is abnormal and upside down. When everything's said and done, you left me, I didn't leave you. I hoped you'd be my final refuge. You'd have been all I could've wanted if you'd come to me with your whole heart and not divided yourself among three women. In these weeks that I've been alone, I've had time to think everything over. We both left our homes on a mad impulse, without any plan, without working anything out, and the whole thing was improvised from start to finish. If your wife hadn't fallen ill, something else would've interfered. What's happening with that Esther? Are you still in contact with her?"

"No, not at all."

"Where is she?"

"I don't know that either."

"It doesn't matter—she'll look you up. You won't get rid of her so easily. What's your opinion of Yasha? Tell me frankly."

"I can't speak frankly any longer."

"You too? I thought that you, at least, had found yourself."

"No, Anna. I haven't found anything."

21

An hour before noon Yasha Kotik awoke, opening his eyes with the cunning expression of someone who has merely been pretending to be asleep the whole time. He sat up and regarded Justina Kohn, who lay in the other bed—Stanislaw Luria's bed—stark naked, only half-covered with a sheet, examining her with an expert eye. In the old days one used to be able to size up a woman in the morning, but these days even in bed they used cosmetics and all sorts of creams and ointments. Her lips were scarlet, her face thickly plastered with makeup. But her breasts betrayed her, hanging loose and slack, like two empty wineskins of the type Kotik had often seen in Central Asia. Her throat was wrinkled, and one of her sides, near her ribs, bore a surgical scar. Well, she also hadn't had it so easy! Kotik noted mentally, massaging his chin as if he wore a beard. She wanted to be a second Greta Garbo or another Marlene Dietrich. Well, I'll have to send her packing. It's getting too dangerous. He pulled open the drawer of the night table in which, before going to sleep, he'd stuffed a wad of money. I have to guard this carefully—that woman's got itchy fingers. He counted the bills and calculated awhile, his forehead wrinkling and the two creases around his mouth deepening. Dollars, hey? he said to himself. Do you know how much the world loves you? People long for you everywhere. There's nothing they won't do for you. But here you lie in my bedside drawer and you're nothing more than pieces of paper—the loot of thieving Uncle Sam.

Kotik tried to estimate how much Anna was worth. She'd invested about fifteen thousand in the building with the furnished rooms. Her car would probably bring at least two thousand. She admitted that she'd put ten thousand into stocks and that from the ship deal she'd wring at least twenty-five thousand for herself. All together, that came to fifty-two thousand. But that wasn't all. She had a good head on her shoulders. She had *smykałka*. Her building brought her two hundred dollars a week in profit, and she had other investments as well. Anna had confided everything to Kotik, given him all the details about Luria, about Grein, about the Italian youth in Casablanca. She was no longer the childlike Anna from Berlin days, the innocent girl he'd used and discarded. She was now a mature woman to whom one could talk frankly about worldly matters. She wouldn't be able to keep him on too tight a leash either, because as a businesswoman she'd be occupied all day. How could she keep tabs on him? He had to attend rehearsals and she had to manage her affairs. He'd give her a child or two so that a couple of new souls could wander about. No one lives forever, after all, and there had to be someone to leave the goodies to in the end.

"Hey, you slattern!"

Kotik grabbed hold of Justina's hair and yanked it sharply. Justina resisted awhile and then opened her eyes.

"How long are you planning to snooze?" Kotik demanded. "It's almost afternoon. In Brooklyn they're already blowing the shofar at the penitential prayers. They've exploded an atomic bomb downtown."

"*Ach, ty błaźnie!* Oh, you clown!"

Although Kotik spoke to Justina in Yiddish, she consistently answered him in Polish. She knew Yiddish perfectly well—after all, her mother had been a common market vendor for the non-kosher butchers in Warsaw—but for her, speaking Yiddish meant returning to the airless cellar and the crushing poverty in which she had grown up. Kotik could permit himself to speak Yiddish because he was a success in America and could give everyone the finger, but as soon as she uttered a word of that language, she felt as if she had never lived. Then everything seemed to have been a fleeting dream: acting in the Polish Teatr Mały, her *amours* with famous Polish actors, the reviews of her work in the Polish press, the posters with her picture.

Justina yawned. "What's the time?"

"Later than you think, my chickadee. The cock has crowed and they're doing a beautiful job slaughtering him. They've already made him into sandwiches in Glitsenshtein's kosher restaurant. Are you hungry?"

"No."

"I am. Go and make breakfast and then get out, because I've got decent people coming over."

"What people?"

"All sorts. I'm a businessman and I've got my reputation to consider. How would it look if first thing in the morning they came across a has-been broad here? They might think God knows what."

"Shut your trap."

"You know what I feel like? Eggs with onions. You know how to make onions?"

"Your breath'll stink."

"Not raw onions—fried onions. No, you wouldn't know. My mother used to make them for me when I brought some dough home. I started out in life making gaiters, and twice a year I used to give the bit of bread I earned to my mother. Here they call it 'payday.' Come into the kitchen. I'll cut up the onions myself. Is there butter in the refrigerator?"

"There's everything there."

"Can you cook at least?"

"What's the matter? Do you want to marry me?"

"I'd like to get married. Why not? But I need a missus with money. Why're you looking at me like that? The acting business is built on sand—here today and gone tomorrow. Three months ago I didn't have a penny to my name. Now they're making a fuss about me. Tomorrow some poisonous critic might crawl out from under a stone and tear me to pieces, and then everything's kaput again. All these contracts they offer aren't worth a dime. One actor here used to earn a quarter of a million dollars a year, and a few weeks ago they found him dead in the Bowery with exactly twenty-three cents in his pocket. That's how it is in America."

"And what'll you do? Marry a millionairess?"

"Why not? Since you can sell the same goods either cheap or for a fortune, why not hike up the price? At my age it's not a question of love—actually, I don't even know what love is. I'll tell you something, my sweet—I've never known anything about it. A quilter used to work in the same workshop where I was apprenticed—my blood runs cold when I think of that hellhole now—and that poor sucker was so much in love that his jabbering made me senseless. He had an ironclad memory, so he could recall every syllable his floozy bleated at him. He would sit at his machine endlessly repeating her drivel and asking, 'Yankele, what did she mean?' They used to call me Yankel in those days. Apart from being a lunkhead about women, he was a skillful artisan, and I was just a fifth wheel where work was concerned. My job was to stretch the legs of the boots by beating them with a log. Whenever the boss went out, we all used to relax a bit. Anyhow, that dummy would read volumes into anything his ladylove said, and from all his puppy-love talk I guessed that she was hot in the pants, so I managed to persuade him to send me to her to plead his case. As soon as I saw her I knew she was a worthless piece of trash, so I grabbed her by one of her braids and asked, Where and when do we get together?''

"You'll never live as long as the lies you're telling."

"It's the unvarnished truth. The whole world takes me for a liar, even when I'm telling the truth. Never mind, I don't quarrel with the world any longer. At one time I used to get angry and swear the holiest oaths, but they still never believed me. Why should I be surprised? How can crooks believe anyone else is honest? More things happen to me in one week than happen to others in a whole lifetime. It was that way when I was a kid and wore my brother's trousers, and it was that way later in Berlin when the whole place was gaga about me, and still later in Russia and in Poland, where everyone thinks the same thoughts. Now the commotion's started here. How can dunderheads believe it? Often I don't even believe it myself—it makes as much sense as a saddle on a cow. Come, let's fry the onions."

"What do you mean by commotion?"

"A real hullabaloo. People telephone, they send me invitations, they write me notes. Uptown, downtown, here, there. I've got to keep an address book so I can go on delivering greetings like the post office. I bring regards from a brother, a sister, a sister-in-law, a lover. I saw this, I heard that, I talked to your third cousin twice removed. Meanwhile, I'm keeping an eye open to see if I can get a little something for myself. What's wrong, are you jealous?''

"I've got my pride!"

"What's so special about you that you've got the nerve to claim any pride? Yasha Kotik detests pride. In Russia they sent all the proud types to the wall. In Hollywood they do the same as in Moscow. If your shirt's not tucked in, they pack you off to hell. It's exactly the same system, but what they do with revolvers over there, they do with dollars over here. They do it everywhere—in the Army, in the theater, in the universities. In Warsaw there used to be a hospital for skin diseases—the Szpital Świętego Łazarza—and whenever a new patient was admitted, the others would immediately smear him with shit and force him to eat axle grease with mustard."

"What for?"

"Sick people also want to amuse themselves. Yasha Kotik's got a highly developed sixth sense. Once I got here, I took one little peep and I understood it all in a second. I've already become a Communist—a leading light of Leninism. To survive here, you've got to be even more left-wing than there—can you believe that?"

"I've no idea what you're talking about."

"Turn Red, girlie, turn Red. It's good for business. Here reactionaries die of hunger. Stanislaw Luria told me that, may the earth lie lightly upon him. He used to argue that capitalism wants to commit suicide. Try to stop a suicide from killing himself and he'll stick a dagger in you. At the time I thought he was crazy, but he knew what he was talking about. If you see two hoods attacking each other with knives, walk past and don't say a word. You try to play peacemaker, and they'll dig you a grave. If someone's standing on a roof and wants to jump off, don't stop to argue with him even for a second, because he'll jump and land right on top of you. This isn't my idea—it's the legacy Luria left me."

2

"Do me a favor and stop talking about him," Justina said edgily.

"What're you scared of? You managed to hoodwink him into believing you were his dead wife, so now he's your dead husband. You've spent the night sleeping in his bed."

"I'm asking you to shut your mouth!"

"Look, she's all aflutter! What've you got the jitters for? If the dead could take revenge, they'd flock out of the cemeteries at night in droves and strangle the lot of us. But they can't. They can't. In Russia there was a crazy professor, such a lunatic that they even kicked him out of the NKVD; he used to say that nobody ever dies of his own accord, but that those closest to him bundle him off to the next world. One gets killed by his wife, another by his son, his daughter, his best friend. He wrote a long book to prove this, but no one wanted to publish it. One winter it was so cold in his room that he put the manuscript in the stove and made a fire from it to warm himself."

"You can believe anything about a madman."

"I want to 'throw' a party, as they say here—a party that'll cost a thousand dollars, or more if necessary. But I don't know how it's done. Do you know how to throw a party?"

"What's there to know? It's all a question of what you can pay."

"I've got money. But I want to invite Anna, and she won't come here. It's her own apartment—you follow? She lived here with Luria. Here, in this bed, she lay and thought about Yasha Kotik. Now she'll have to live with Yasha Kotik and think about Grein or someone else. Am I making myself clear?"

"What's going on? Are you preparing to marry her?"

"Why not? She was once my wife, so she already knows my ways."

"Are you serious, or are you only joking?"

"Is there any difference?"

"But you said you wanted to marry a millionairess."

"She'll be a millionairess in time. She'll have all her millions tied up and looked after and I'll never be more than a gigolo to her. Anna first has to make her millions, so she'll be busy. You know what 'busy' means, don't you? You know English?"

"Yes, I know."

"I need a busy little wife. She already owns one building, and soon she'll own a second and maybe even a third. She's still young, too. I'll give her a baby and she'll play with it. You see what I'm thinking, or not?"

"I see that you're a total scoundrel."

"Are you any better? Compared to you I'm a gentleman—I'm a refined and polished hypocrite. You, sister, would sell your own mother for three dollars."

"If you're going to start insulting me, I'm leaving immediately."

"I'm not insulting you. Where are my underpants? I had a pair of shorts somewhere. Can one rent a hall in which to throw a party?"

"You can rent anything in New York—even someone to sit out the Seven Days of Mourning for you."

"I'd much rather throw a party in my own home. After a little bash, when the guests have gone, I love nibbling at the leftovers—a bit of chopped liver with some wine or stronger stuff. And if a nice girl like you stays behind, that's even better. I hate throwing a party in a strange place and then having to go home alone like one of the guests. It's a bit lonely—you follow me?"

"Don't worry—she'll come here."

"You mean Anna? I don't think so. But on the other hand, you may be right. We'll still end up living here together. Why spend money on another apartment when one's ready and waiting for you? It'll really be juicy. At my age, everything needs to be juicy. If you help me organize the party, I'll give you a hundred dollars over and above everything you'll steal for yourself."

Justina Kohn pulled on one of her stockings. "*Panie* Kotik, you've insulted me long enough!"

Yasha Kotik picked up a shoe. "What harm have I done you? I like to speak this way—and anyway, it's only the truth. Why shouldn't you steal? In your place, I'd do the same. I'll tell you something: I need someone like you. I've done a thousand things, but I've always had a broad around that I could talk to like a comrade-in-arms. In Berlin I had a Gentile chorus girl and I kept no secrets from her—absolutely none. I could tell her more than my closest friend. She hid nothing from me either. In Russia I also had a woman like that, but of course she had to keep going to the NKVD to give her reports. Besides me, she had two other clients and I knew who they were, although they didn't know about me. She'd tell me everything about them, every detail, and we had something to laugh about. All three of us were actors, and I knew what they were up to. It didn't help me very much, though, because if there's nothing to eat, you go hungry all the same. But I managed to stay one jump ahead of them—every time they tried to trip me up, things would go haywire for them. Now, sweetie pie, you become my American sob sister. You won't regret it, I promise you. You don't have to worry about anything. Yasha Kotik is only just starting his career in the United States. I'll create a role for you, and I'll give you money out of my own pocket as well. You be my bosom friend, as they say. I need a friend, not a critic. What do you need? But don't make up any lies. Let me catch you telling one lie and it's all over."

"What lies? I owe two months' rent. I need shoes, a brassiere, a corset. I haven't got a decent dress either."

"How much'll all that cost?"

"At least three hundred dollars."

"I'll give you the three hundred dollars and don't bring it up again. I don't like endless talk about money. We'll discuss it once a month, not more. My chorus girl in Berlin never cost me a cent. Every time I tried to give her a few marks she'd scream no. She even used to buy *me* presents, that German floozy. I didn't need her gifts, but I must say it was nice to get them. Later on she used to go off for hours on end with a Nazi, but that, as they say, is another story. My Russian also got nothing. The NKVD paid her. Whereas you, sugar, love money, but don't overreach yourself. If you can act, you'll get work in the theater and earn your own living. If you're no good, you'll find another job.''

"In Warsaw I played leading roles in the Teatrzyk 'Qui Pro Quo.' ''

"So what? New York isn't Warsaw any more than Warsaw is New York. What's charming there is affectation here. The public can be persuaded to believe anything. An actor hangs in limbo. Today they praise him, tomorrow they drive him from the boards. That's why I've got no intention of marrying an actress. I need a woman for a wife, not a prima donna who sells herself for good reviews. But there are certain things one can discuss only with an intimate. At the moment, for instance, I want to organize this party.''

"There'll be a party. Why did she leave him?''

"Who's she and who's he?''

"Her lover, the blond with the bald patch.''

"You mean Grein? He went back to his wife. Apparently he's become religious, or God knows what. There are people who spend their whole lives looking for God. I knew someone like that in Russia. He was as thin as a stick, with a mop of long hair. In the middle of Stalin's inferno he became observant, and where? Right in Moscow. There was a little synagogue where old Jews gathered, and he used to sit reciting the psalms. They arrested him, of course, but then they let him out again. It's all because people are afraid of death. Are you ever afraid of death?''

"Never.''

"No, women aren't afraid of dying. It's a man's fear. I'm afraid, too, but how can God help me? Even Moses died. You shouldn't've done what you did to Luria. Deceiving a man like that is worse than killing him.''

"What did I know about him? I went to that old bitch to have my teeth fixed, and as soon as I said I was a Polish actress, she started babbling nonstop. That performance didn't kill him.''

"No, but he started to believe that his wife was waiting for him. The way he rambled on, I started believing there was something to it myself. 'Sonia,' he used to say, 'is here, I heard her voice. She kissed me on the head.' What'd she get out of it, that witch?''

"Who knows? She lives with some former professor. She fooled him as well.''

"Lots of people love to fool others—that's their life. There was a Yiddish actor in Moscow who convinced his colleagues that he had a barrel of herring. This was during the Revolution, when you couldn't get a bite of herring for love or money. As soon as they heard he had herring, everyone started sucking up to him. Even the Russians started speaking to him differently: 'Nathan Davidovitch, I'll give you a leading role. You'll become famous. I'm dying for a piece of herring.' The long and the short of it was that he had to pack his bags and flee to Kiev when the counter-revolutionaries started their war against the Bolsheviks. He was left stranded in some village or other, and it was there that Makhno's bandits did him in.''

''What good did it do him?''

''Why do I need you? Adults are worse than children. Tell me the truth—how many lovers have you had?''

''I didn't count them.''

''A hundred?''

''May you have as many kinds of cancer.''

''That's enough with the curses. I once had a girl who kept an album with a separate page for each one of her lovers and his photograph.''

''Men do things like that, not women.''

''Lots of women are like men. I once had a sweet young thing with a face like a grater. Hair grew on it and she had to shave every day.''

''You've seen everything!''

''You don't believe me? It's the truth. I'll tell you something: Yasha Kotik doesn't lie unless he's forced to. Do you believe that?''

''No.''

''So go to the devil! Take your stuff and get out! See that it's far away! *Poshla von! Idź do cholery!* Go to hell!''

3

At eight that morning, Grein opened his eyes. He didn't sleep in the bedroom with Leah but spent the night on the sofa in his study. Leah had recently got into the habit of switching on the lamp in the middle of the night when her agonized groans were at their worst. She took sleeping pills and all kinds of other medication in an attempt to ease her suffering and couldn't bear the thought of Grein sleeping in the same room. Yet even here, behind the closed door, he could hear her sighing as she puttered restlessly about. First she shut the window, then she opened it. She peered into the refrigerator in the kitchen, rummaged through the cupboard, pulled drawers open, occasionally muttering to herself as she did so. While on the other side of the wall his wife, the mother of his children, grappled with death, he lay here, a lost soul, abandoned by God and by man. It was already the penitential month of Elul, the period of preparation for the Days of Awe. Normally by this time he had already bought two seats in a synagogue for the High Holy Days, but this year he had not yet even made any reservations. Leah was adamant that she would not attend services. She refused to pray to a God that gave cancer to innocent people. Grein himself had also lost all desire to go to synagogue.

On the little table next to the sofa lay a morning newspaper and a monthly magazine published by his synagogue. As usual, the newspaper was full of murders, armed robberies, burglaries, disappearances. The political news of the day centered on a decree issued by the American military commander in Occupied Germany absolving 750,000 "minor Nazis" from all responsibility. Other pages featured reports about Frank Sinatra and Mickey Rooney, and the biography of some big-time gangster who had recently become notorious. Grein had read the newspaper until late into the night as a means of falling asleep. In its very existence, this newspaper was the embodiment and voice of worldliness. On the ashes of six million Jews, on the graves of twenty million war victims, people were once more weaving webs of crime, discrimination, intrigue, pettiness. The fresh ink, the sex pictures, the laughing hordes of alimony huntresses, and the perverted court judgments that recalled the ways of Sodom reeked of a murderous indifference to the suffering of others. Despite all the talk of peace, new wars were brewing in Korea, in Indochina, in Morocco.

However much the synagogue magazine might concern itself with rabbis, cantors, synagogue presidents, reverends, it stank the same as the daily newspaper. The organization of which it was the mouthpiece wanted only one thing—money. Its cantors wore tall hats, resembling those of priests; its rabbi looked like a football player. The women of the Ladies' Auxiliary smilingly presented some professor or other with an engraved plaque of recognition in a photograph next to an advertisement in which a mortician bragged about the attention he lavished on the dead: elegant coffins, spacious graves covered with greenery in a cemetery conveniently close to the city. Leah was a member of a Bronx congregation on Clementine Street, it flashed through Grein's mind. She'd lie in their cemetery. He was shocked at his own thought, tried to drive it from his mind, shook himself. No, she will still be cured! something in him cried out. Help her, dear God in heaven! Let there be a miracle!

His sleep teeming with nightmares, Grein kept starting awake. His legs twitched, his hands trembled. It wasn't hot but he sweated, soaking the pillowcase. In his mind's delirium he was marching in double, triple, multiple funerals. From side streets pallbearers continually emerged carrying biers laden with corpses. It was apparently nighttime, because people were holding lanterns, torches, candles. Choirs chanted monotonous dirges while death marches were played. At the burial place, Grein toiled ceaselessly, dragging dead bodies sunk in mud, ashes, blood. He was hiding from someone, crawling through caves, tunnels, openings. New York merged with, and became indistinguishable from, the Warsaw Ghetto. Nazis pursued him, and terrified, he hid in a bunker. In the stifling darkness he copulated with a female who had Esther's voice but revealed herself to be Anita, his own daughter. He began moaning and weeping: See, God, see to what depths of degradation I have sunk! He sprang up, his face dripping and his throat parched, a pain in his gullet and a blockage in his nose. As a result of his breathing through his mouth, his lips were cracked and encrusted; his head ached, there was a stabbing pain in his crotch, and he had stomach spasms. When he got up off the sofa, his legs buckled under him like those of an old man. He clutched his belly. Who knows? Perhaps I've also got cancer. The Master of the Universe certainly had more than enough cancers to pass around. The telephone rang and Grein walked unsteadily to answer it. At the other end he heard a man's voice that sounded familiar but that he could not identify.

"I hope I didn't wake you," the voice said courteously.

"No, I'm already up."

"It's Solomon Margolin speaking."

"Yes, Dr. Margolin, I recognize your voice."

"You recognize it only because I told you. How are you?"

"Well, thank you."

"Do you perhaps have time to meet me for half an hour? I need to discuss something with you."

"Yes, certainly."

"When could we meet? Have you had breakfast?"

"No, not yet."

"I have an idea. Normally people meet for lunch, but why can't we meet for breakfast? It's time we were a bit original."

Grein and Margolin agreed to meet at nine o'clock at a restaurant on

Broadway. What can he want of me? Grein wondered. He had to shave and bathe quickly. The days when Leah used to get up at seven to prepare breakfast had long since passed. Her shop on Third Avenue was shut. At night she slept with her mouth and eyes half-open, pale, wrinkled, her cheeks hollow, lost in the anxious self-absorption of the desperately ill. Every time Grein glanced at her, he was terrified anew. No one on earth could help her any longer. Only heaven could, but apparently it didn't want to. And could he now three times a day call God merciful? No, it wasn't possible.

Grein was late, so he took a taxi to the restaurant where Margolin was waiting in a white suit and Panama hat.

"You're one and a half minutes late," Margolin remarked.

In the restaurant they were given a table in an alcove. Although the summer morning shone in brightly through the window, the electric lights were burning. In this spacious, elegant room, there was no sign of sickness, suffering, death. The waitresses all seemed young and energetic. The rolls were fresh from the oven. The table linen just back from the laundry gleamed. The patrons all looked well-fed and contented. An elderly man with silver-gray hair and a rosy complexion was checking the stock-market prices in the financial pages of the morning newspaper while he ate. He had somehow managed to survive two world wars, crises of various magnitudes, economic depressions, and the countless dangers that lie in wait for everybody. His watery eyes, reflecting prudence and moderation, seemed to say: Let the fools perish. With good sense, one can navigate one's way in the world easily. One simply has to know its ins and outs. At another table, an old woman was leisurely ordering breakfast. Everything about her was artificial: the dyed blond hair on her head, the rouge on her wrinkled cheeks, the complete set of teeth in her mouth, the lacquered nails on her fingers. She chose her meal with deliberation. Since the waitress displayed some impatience at the time all this was taking, the old woman appeased her with endearments. Her husband, Grein thought, the man who had amassed an estate for her, had long been rotting in his grave. The end result of his all-consuming thirst for money, of all the wrongs he had done himself and others, was that this old woman could now fuss over whatever delicacies might strike her fancy. Her glance was filled with the craftiness and egoism of idle old age. Now she had nothing to lose in this world. Everything she consumed was clear profit. Anna would probably look exactly the same in forty years, it occurred to Grein. No, I can't go through this! I must escape! But where can I run to? Christians at least have monasteries—where can a Jew flee? Worldliness has made inroads everywhere among us—there's no getting away from it.

"I'd like to talk to you about our mutual friend," Grein heard Margolin say.

"Yes, yes."

4

"I'll come straight to the point," said Margolin, putting a dab of cottage cheese on a piece of bread. "I know everything that happened between you and Anna. Why shouldn't I? Boris Makaver, primitive anachronism that he is, is my best friend. We studied together in the yeshiva. I've known him for forty-eight years. When we hummed and swayed our way together through the talmudic debate on the Authority of Priests, you hadn't been born yet. I knew Anna when she was still a girl. You knew her even earlier, but what's the difference? I watched her grow up, I was her doctor. She came to you a whole person—a complete Anna, healthy, beautiful, mature, but what she went through before you plucked the fruit from the tree, so to speak, only I, the gardener, know. Well, I won't indulge in any lectures or sentimentality. I only want you to know one thing: that Yasha Kotik is one of the most depraved brutes I've ever encountered in my life, and you can rest assured I've known more than my share of scum. He's a psychopath. For a short while we were friendly. I love the theater, and although I don't regard him as a great talent, I appreciated his work. He comes from the vilest and meanest, from the lowest dregs of the earth, and he never knew any language but Yiddish. For someone like that to work his way up and become so famous in Germany that Alfred Kerr wrote about him was really an amazing achievement. At the time I was even prepared to teach him German, but I soon saw that he had no aptitude for anything as systematic and orderly as grammar. His entire being is predicated on mistakes. He is, you might say, one of God's typographical errors, and that's where his charm lies. He has a single merit: he can be sincere when he wants to be, and then he's a gold mine for a psychologist. He can free himself of all inhibitions and strip his soul bare, and that's very interesting.

"Unfortunately, by the time I got to know him, he was already married to Anna, and I can't begin to tell you what she suffered from that swine. Perhaps the poor woman told you some of it, but I'll bet not even a hundredth part. The essence of that creature's life, the very core of his being, is profanity. He loves making everything around him as filthy as he is himself. One evening I was strolling with him down the Kurfürstendamm at the very moment that a magnificent moon floated into the sky. You know how it is—the moon can be so gloriously bright that it eclipses all the electric lamps. It seems suddenly to swim up into the heavens, miraculously, and you're left gaping in wonder. I'm not a poet, but sometimes even a down-to-earth realist can be enraptured by such things. I pointed this out to Kotik. 'Just look at the moon!' I said. He glanced up, opened his eyes very wide, and finally said, 'Oh, if only I could piss all over it!' That was the moment I grasped what Kotik is. He wants to befoul everything: the sun, the sky, God Himself if He existed. Of course, from a scientific point of view, there's nothing unclean about urine. But we're concerned here with psychology. It's impossible to describe what he did to Anna. One could write a book about it. She was young, beautiful, innocent, the daughter of a religious family, and Kotik instantly saw an ideal opportunity for defilement. There isn't a single perversion that he didn't try to engage her in. I must tell you that if profanity can be regarded—even negatively—as a creative activity, then Kotik is indisputably a genius. In my opinion, the whole of modern art has set out along this road and is inching its way forward. In today's novels, subjects are broached and words are used that a generation ago were employed only by the underworld.''

''Modern culture *is* the underworld. I've known that for a long time now,'' Grein interjected.

''That's a separate issue. How do you define modern culture? Einstein is also part of modern culture. It's become fashionable nowadays for people to turn back to religion, and I hear you've done the same. For my part, I must tell you, I haven't the slightest inclination in that direction. I like concrete facts, not abstract speculation and indefinable notions. My father believed that God sits on the Throne of Glory and inscribes people for life or death in the Book of Life on the Days of Awe. That's true religion. But when I hear someone like Dr. Alswanger talking idiotic nonsense about God, I lose all patience. If God does exist, let Alswanger spend his time in a study house instead of drifting about with old women. They tell me he's got involved with some widow and together they're organizing who knows what kind of spiritual research. She's brought him other rich old petticoats and he's investigating spirits left, right, and center. That's not to say I'm against psychoanalysis, but it depends how it's done. Freud was a genius, but like all geniuses, he exaggerated. Adler wasn't a genius, but he understood things in their proper perspective. Jung, in my opinion, is nothing but a bore. But let's get back to Anna.

"I wasn't very enthusiastic when I heard that you'd finally got together. I don't believe that a relationship can succeed when there is an age differ- ence such as exists between the two of you. Apart from that, you've got a wife and grown children. Boris Makaver tore his hair out by the roots, but I told him that you can't dictate to love. You can't wage war against Nature, I believe. At best you can only regulate it, the way you regulate a river to prevent it from flooding a town. I'm not just Anna's doctor— I'm an old friend of hers, so I know everything that went on between you—she used to telephone me often. Love is one thing, and friendship another. Man to man, I'm telling you candidly that you behaved imprac- tically. But that's something else. I want to get to the main point. I hear you've become a penitent of sorts and that you've returned to your wife. Anna, on the other hand, is so crazy that she wants to go back to Kotik."

"Yes, that's true."

"I couldn't believe my ears when she told me. I can understand a person choosing suicide, but this is a lingering death. You have to be a complete masochist. Now she'll never get out of his clutches. In Berlin it took me years to lift her out of her depression and repair some of the psychological damage she suffered from living for only a year with that reptile. Now I've told her frankly that it'd be better if she simply cut her own throat. I'm too old to start the whole business all over again. Psychoanalysis isn't my field—I've neither the time nor the patience for it. Anyway, I've got my own problems. In short, if she wants to destroy herself, there's nothing to be done. Her father is ill as it is, and when he hears about this, it'll kill him as surely as the sun is shining now. I think it's a great pity what's happened to Boris Makaver, because in his own way he's a man of excellent understanding. That business with the ships was utter folly, but he'll get out of it one way or another. You and I were never that close, but we're acquaintances and Anna regularly spoke about you in Berlin. I don't want to pry into your soul, God forbid—I'm not Dr. Alswanger. All the same, I want to ask why you are letting everything end in such a fiasco. You don't have to answer me, but what kind of penitent are you? This restaurant isn't kosher—" Margolin suddenly broke off.

"It's got nothing to do with the dietary laws," Grein responded.

"Then what has it got to do with, if I may ask?"

"With my being the cause of Stanislaw Luria's death. I also suspect that I am to blame for my wife's illness."

"There's not the slightest evidence that cancer is caused by grief."

"I believe it is. If one doesn't want to live, one dies. At the moment I'm terrified to do anything, for fear that someone else might die. You've just said yourself that this whole business will kill Boris Makaver and destroy Anna. In short, whatever I do and wherever I turn, other people become the victims." And Grein also broke off.

"I called you precisely because I'd like to prevent further casualties."

"The best thing I can do now is to leave everyone in peace. I took stock of myself and it came to me with blinding clarity that I am a criminal, and that I am living in a chaotic netherworld. There's no fundamental difference between Yasha Kotik and me. That's the bitter truth. Anna knows it—that's why she's going back to him."

5

"Well, well, I think we're both exaggerating. If you want to beat your breast and repent, I'm probably not the right person to talk to. I have my own yardstick of things. You're not Yasha Kotik."

"You've come to speak about Anna, and I'll answer you as straightforwardly as if you were her father or her brother. During the months I lived with her, I had not only my wife but another lover. I kept swearing to Anna that I'd left the other woman, but we met each other at every opportunity. Two days after Luria's funeral, while Anna was observing the Seven Days of Mourning, I went off to a hotel with the second one, who by that time already had another husband. Did Kotik ever do anything like that?"

Margolin looked down. "Is there such a great love between you and the second one?"

"If it'd been perfect, I'd never've gone off with Anna."

"I understand, I understand it all. Anna implied as much to me. If we were both twenty years younger, I'd've asked you which one you truly love—but I'm too old for questions like that. Nothing surprises me. I don't like playing peacemaker, but I don't want Anna to get hurt."

"She's got only one choice—to find herself a solid, respectable citizen."

"People aren't so easy to find. Anyway, she's a woman with a thousand problems herself. There was a time I wasn't indifferent to her myself, and that's when I saw how much turmoil there was in her soul. I don't want to distress you, but your wife is gravely ill—perhaps sicker than you know."

"I know enough. How do you know?"

"Doctors talk. The medical world in New York is a small pond."

"However long she lives, I must stay with her."

"Yes, you're right. I don't want to pry, but in general, what do you intend to do? Go back to the study house? You don't have to answer me."

"Why not? If I only knew how. I know the sickness, but not the cure. Over the last thirty years everything I've observed in myself and in others has proved to me that the whole of modern humanity is just one mass of criminals. Whatever they do, modern people are driven to wrongdoing both in private and in public. Look at Communism, Nazism, the murders in Spain, Ethiopia, Africa, everywhere. To me, modern culture is the exact opposite of the Jewishness I've known since childhood. Christianity is even complicit with this modern culture, because Christianity is a compromise between God and the world—it's given God all the beautiful words and human beings all the ugly deeds. I might have believed that people couldn't behave any other way—after all, that's the basic principle of Darwinism— if it hadn't been for my father. His example is continually before my eyes, and the older I get, the more I'm compelled to think about him. He was also a man of flesh and blood, but he lived a holy life. He actually practiced everything the Jews and the Christians preach. Without any show, he turned the other cheek. Every time I despair about the human species in general and myself in particular, I remember him and I ask myself, How did he manage to exist? What made him what he was? He wasn't unique, by the way. I knew many Jews like that. You could find them in every town and village. Among those that Hitler exterminated there were tens of thousands of saints."

"They don't exist any longer."

"They used to exist, and that's proof that they could still exist. In the heart of the Darwinian jungle, in the middle of the slaughterhouse, lived holy people who zealously avoided hurting others in their thoughts, let alone with a word. But now many Jews have even managed to make peace with the Nazi murderers. They forget, they don't talk about it. I ignored the whole thing myself. While they were wiping out my family in Poland, torturing them with the most unspeakable brutality human wickedness could devise, I was running off to assignations, fantasizing about all sorts of sexual filth. The Jewish intellectuals in New York were feasting at banquets. What's there to say about the Gentiles? For them it was just another chapter. Former storm troopers have become churchgoers who listen to priests preach about love before going off to beer halls to boast about how many infants' heads they smashed, how many Jews they buried alive. On Tisha b'Av my father used to shed bitter tears. My mother would soak her Yiddish Bible with grief at the story of Hannah and her seven sons. But nowadays our hearts are as hard as stone. I don't accuse others, only myself. How did I become a liar, a seducer, a murderer—every evil there is? Who and what taught me? Where did I learn it? After all, my saintly parents are only a generation removed from me!''

''You know the answer perfectly well—they had faith and you do not.''

''The Christians and the Muslims also have faith, apparently.''

''They have power, and power kills all ideals.''

''Be that as it may, the same Nature that created snakes, tigers, Inquisitions, Hitlers, Stalins created faith as well. Secularists say Jews lived in a vacuum, but in Nature there's no such thing as a vacuum—and even if there were, it, too, would be part of Nature. If a single flower can bloom among millions of thorns, it's a sign that many other flowers can bloom.''

''It's possible, if the right conditions exist: in the case of the Jews, profound faith and unending exile. Remove one of those two preconditions and the whole thing collapses. When faith vanishes, Jews become assimilated, and if you give them a country of their own, they'll start slaughtering exactly as the Gentiles do. You can't manufacture artificial faith or exile.''

''Everything is made artificially. Even plowing and sowing the soil is an artificial process. I'm nearly fifty years old, and my whole life has been one long chain of suffering and wrongdoing. I always wanted to be something. They say every Jew has a Moses complex. Since I was a child, I've been preparing myself. You'll laugh, but I was thinking about these issues when I was only five years old. I saw other children torturing a cat and it made me ill—it took me months to get over it. It's impossible to describe how incensed I was when I first read about the way King David caused Saul's children to be put to death. I kept on asking questions about God. Although in my youth I gave every sign of having unusual gifts, I suddenly saw them all wasted on triviality. I expended all my energy chasing after the sort of women one didn't even need to chase. I became indifferent to others—to their tears, their sufferings, even to their lives. I knew Stanislaw Luria, and I was the Angel of Death for him.''

"He had a weak heart."

"I knew him, and I sent him to his grave. Three days later I also cheated on Anna. Those are the facts."

"We've all done things like that."

"Yes, because those are the values of our culture. Everything is murder and lies and fornication. I buy a newspaper and it's full of killing and whoring. I switch on the radio, I open a book, and there it is again—in the theater, at the movies, wherever you turn. What they call art is as much garbage as the trash they call literature. High society and gangsters live alike. The judges and the criminals sit in the same nightclubs listening to the same obscenities. People get married, and on the second night husband and wife go to see a comedy that makes fun of a cuckold. Modern culture is a knot of sadism. It has spawned Nazism and Communism and everything else that's vicious."

"What about science?"

"Science serves murderers and justifies slaughter of every kind. That's the truth."

"Yes, that's the truth, but what can we do about it? I envy you. You still burn with the fire of youth, with protest and moral indignation. I have none of that left. I'll tell you something I don't need to tell you: I live with a woman who left me for a Nazi."

Grein was silent for a while. "Is she in New York?"

"Yes, she and her daughter." And Solomon Margolin rapidly drained a glass of water.

6

"Why do you do it, if I may ask?"

"I do it because the daughter is my child, and I've grown accustomed to the woman. I'm sorry to tell you this, but in my private life I don't live up to the standards of the Jewish people. I hear your son also married a Christian."

"Yes, I've lost my children. The future of Jews no longer has anything to do with me. My grandchildren will be Gentiles. In reality, my children are Gentiles themselves, the only difference being that the majority of

Gentiles clutch at religion—as they understand it—and my children are entirely godless.''

"What can you do about it now?''

"It's all my fault. That's the education I gave them, that's the example I set them. Everything that generations of Jews built up at the risk of their lives I destroyed in a few years. You're right—it's already too late. Only now can I see how much I've ruined.''

"What, speaking practically, do you want to do? You can't force yourself to believe that the *Shulhan Arukh* and the countless commentaries it begot through the centuries were all given on Mount Sinai.''

"No, I can't do that. I wish I could. But I can remove myself from a culture that produces a Hitler and a Stalin in every generation. I do still have one belief—in free will. The whole of Judaism, the majority of the commandments and all the strict rulings that were derived from them had only one purpose—to insulate Jews from the other nations of the world. The greater the temptation to mix with them, the more the prohibitions multiplied. I want to do what I've always wanted to do, what I've always dreamed about doing. I read the newspaper in the morning and I feel as if I've drunk poison, I go to a movie and I feel as though I'm eating filth. If not actually eating it, then chewing its putrid cud. My mind thinks only about adultery and murder. It's like that all day long. At night I dream about them. I'm not using you as a confessor—I know that none of this is new to you.''

"No. That's how people are. During the First World War, I worked in a military hospital. The wounded lay there and talked about nothing but whores and killing the whole day. It goes without saying that the healthy do the same.''

"I know. The barracks where they teach people to defend their fatherland is a school of sadism. They require a young man to lay down his life for his compatriots, and in return they insult him, curse him, degrade him, trample on him. In the universities they subject every new student to all sorts of abuses. The police are in the pay of the criminals. The courts deliver verdicts which mock justice. The lawyers teach crooks how to evade the law. At this very moment Dr. Kinsey is publishing research about male sexual behavior that gives a terrifying picture of modern family life—and that's only in democratic countries. Among the so-called world improvers in Russia, such savage wickedness prevails that the mind can't grasp it. There people are liquidated by the millions. Our own Jews, the children

and grandchildren of our fathers, have become agitators, agents provocateurs, members of the GPU. Their journals pervert truth and deride the
whole of Jewish history. Today they praise someone to the skies, and
tomorrow they scream that he was a dangerous traitor. How did all this
happen? How did the Children of Israel become the Men of Sodom? How
did we become the purveyors of lies and vileness? It all comes of our
frenzied pursuit of Gentile culture. In school our children are given sex
education, and as a result they become informers, whores, liars, apostates.
The obvious conclusion is that modern pedagogy is deadly poison. As long
as Jewish children studied in their own smoke-filled elementary schools,
the cheders that the Enlightenment ridiculed so much, and their teachers
used pointers to instruct them in the Holy Tongue, they grew up honest
Jews, prepared to lay down their lives for the Sanctification of the Holy
Name.''

"What do you want to do? Bring back the cheder and the pointer?"

"For whom? I have no young children, and my grandchildren will be
Gentiles. Your grandchildren will probably be Gentiles, too. We've been
in league with our murderers. Directly and indirectly we're allies of the
Nazis. Our daughters wander the streets like harlots. Our wives sit in bars,
talk obscenities, and read pornography. They paint their faces like strum-
pets and they deck themselves out like tarts and demand that their husbands
kill themselves to keep their wives in luxury. Today's Jew wants to outdo
Esau in insolence, in debauchery, even in bloodthirstiness. That's the bitter
truth.''

"Yes, it is bitter. But what can we do? Forty years ago, when I first
read Darwin's *Origin of Species,* I knew that the earth with all its green
mountains and fertile valleys was nothing but a slaughterhouse. You want
to flee to God, but God Himself is the worst murderer. Three times a day
your father used to say, 'The Lord is good to all, and His mercy is over
all His works.' But is it true? Can you say the same and delude yourself
that it's true?''

"No, I can't. It may be that for God death and suffering are good things,
not bad. But they horrify me.''

"Where exactly do you want to withdraw to?"

"To myself. To myself! Even if I were to know for certain that God is
a murderer and a Nazi, I would still cling to my ideal of goodness. I haven't
enough courage to commit suicide, but I don't want to profit from this
murderous society or play its vicious game. I won't be able to escape with

Anna. Anna wants to profit. She has that inflated drive for pleasure that transforms the modern Jew into a caricature. I don't have my father's faith, but I can conduct myself as he did. I believe in free will.''

"What will you accomplish with it? There have been ascetics in all generations, and they never changed the world. Today there are millions of monks and nuns who live holy lives in their own way. When Hitler slaughtered millions of Jews, these same monks and nuns wept over the wounds of Jesus—and they'll go on weeping like that for thousands of years.''

"Those who isolate themselves don't do it to save the world. They do it for the sake of spiritual hygiene—or even for the sake of what you might call egoism. My father didn't want to save the world.''

"He wanted to hasten the arrival of the Messiah. He wanted to sit in Paradise and eat the flesh of Leviathan.''

"I'm not interested in either. The only reason I want to run away is that the dichotomy between thought and deed has become repugnant to me. As soon as I get up in the morning, my first thought is that I'm wallowing in dirt. I can smell its stench.''

"What'll you do? What'll you live on? I'm amazed at your naïveté.''

"It's what I always wanted. I once met a magician in a circus who told me he'd been a doctor. 'I always wanted to work in the circus,' he said, 'but my parents forced me into medicine. Now that they're dead, I can do as I please.' It's exactly the same with me. It has nothing to do with any ideal. You could say that spiritually I'm ill.''

"Pardon me for doing so, but I would say that. It's a form of schizo-phrenia. One doesn't have to be a great specialist to make that diagnosis. When you say you want to flee from society, you imagine you're being original, but I assure you that there are thousands, hundreds of thousands of cases such as yours, and they all use more or less the same arguments as you.''

"Possibly. I can't crawl out of my own skin.''

"You ought to consult a doctor. Perhaps let yourself be psychoanalyzed. But you won't do it. You'll run away for a year or two, and then that, too, will become boring. That's because there's nowhere to run to. It's all a neurosis, and every neurosis is naïve. You're right that society's cor-rupt, but this is the planet we must live on. It may get better, or it may get worse.''

"Let come what will.''

"Someone ought to have been profoundly affected by what's happened.

Considering how much Jews have suffered, we might have expected a national nervous breakdown. But Jews are a healthy people. I sometimes think they're a little too healthy.''

''You mean insensitive.''

''Call it what you like. We can't return to the old ways. What's going on in Palestine is an interesting experiment, but again they're counting on miracles. The Arabs are no better than the Nazis. Besides, the kind of Jew who is growing up there will as little resemble your father as your grandchildren will you.''

''There, at least, they don't marry outside the faith.''

''They'll grow up Hebrew Gentiles. I see you have the same illusions as Boris Makaver. Religion is bankrupt—all religions are. God has revealed Himself to no one and told no one what He wants. The Bible is a beautiful work, but it was written by human beings, not by God. The distinction between Jew and Gentile is a fabrication, a thing without substance, like Jonah's gourd. Today's Jews are no more licentious than King David was. The Polish Jews you knew were an exception—not just in the world at large but even among the Jewish people.''

''They are the only people I can respect.''

''So respect them. But there aren't any left for you to respect. Present-day Orthodoxy is as worldly as can be—too worldly by far for the genuinely Orthodox. Where will you turn? Wherever you go, you'll be disappointed. Jewishness, especially the kind of Jewishness we knew, was an attempt to ignore the world, the laws of Nature, the facts of history. It originated in the ghetto and it perished in the ghetto. In Williamsburg and in Me'ah Shearim Jews are trying to rebuild it, but they'll all be wiped out again. The fact is, you can't do it without faith, without total unquestioning belief in every letter of the *Shulhan Arukh* and the *Zohar*.''

''I detest the world—that's certain.''

''Well, there's certainly enough to detest. Do you at least believe in God? Not in revelation, but in God.''

''Yes, I believe. Something directs this world, a power that sees and knows. I even believe in a Divine Providence that cares for each individual creature.''

''Well, then you have more faith than the majority of the Orthodox. But what can you do with that faith? If God chooses to keep silent, no one can make Him speak.''

''We have to discover Him in the same way as we discovered the laws of Nature.''

"That's some job! One thing is clear: you and Anna are not meant for each other. You'll go on seeking God until you die, and to the very last minute you'll know just as little as you know now. What about Professor Shrage? He's also been looking for God his whole life, and at the end, all he's found is a crazy woman, a liar, a cheat, dishonest in every possible way."

"There must be light somewhere!"

"Where? Well, perhaps. I need a little light myself."

22

At the beginning of September a subscription gala was held in a downtown hotel for the relief of Russian war victims. In reality all the money was to go to the Communist Party of America, an arrangement known only to the organizers. The other actors with whom Yasha Kotik was performing in a new play sold him two tickets at twenty-five dollars each. Kotik was a little apprehensive about going to a leftist party: he was not yet a United States citizen and had not even received his initial papers, but he knew that to refuse was even more dangerous. They were all Reds: the actors, the producer, the director, even the well-heeled ''angels'' who had financed the production. Kotik had long been aware that in theater circles—or in any circles in which artists and intellectuals moved—one didn't dare speak ill of Stalin's regime. Having acquired a reading knowledge of English, Kotik realized that the same newspapers that published anti-Communist editorials championed Communist politics on their theater pages. The critics invariably praised what was Red and panned what was anti-Red, almost as if the whole capitalist press had come to a mutual understanding nominally to attack Soviet politics while doing everything in their power to support the Reds in America and undermine the anti-Reds. So why rock the boat for the sake of the truth? It was fine with him: if Broadway was Red and Hollywood was Red, then Yasha Kotik would be Red. He had even made the acquaintance of Communists who had influence in Washington.

Kotik invited Anna to accompany him to the reception and she accepted.

While she was personally anti-Communist, she felt one had to help the Russian people. Of greater significance, however, was her curiosity about Kotik's friends. In the taxi Kotik kissed Anna and talked about getting married. How long did they need to wait? Why couldn't they take out a license and start a new life together? Kotik swore that Anna was the only woman he had ever loved. He was now earning a great deal of money. His name was up in lights on Broadway. He had contracts with Hollywood. The critics raved about him. He was ready to settle down. He wanted to have a child, perhaps even two. How long should he procrastinate? Now was the time. Anna listened quietly to all he said, smiling and biting her lower lip.

"Maybe you're speaking the truth, but how can one believe a liar?" she said at last.

"Sometimes even a liar speaks the truth."

"I've never heard a truthful word from you."

"You're hearing it now." Then suddenly he demanded, "What shall I do? Cut out my heart so you can see for yourself?"

The reception was a huge success. There were at least a thousand people present. Kotik wandered about with Anna, greeting and introducing her to numerous distinguished people among his acquaintances. Almost everyone knew him for his Soviet films as much as for the play in which he was appearing. People he didn't know showered him with compliments and begged him to describe the achievements of theater and film in Soviet Russia and Poland. There were even some who remembered him from Berlin.

"Really, the world's a village," Kotik remarked to Anna. "I thought I'd already been forgotten as if I were dead, but everyone knows me, everyone remembers me. What kind of city is New York? Where do the Americans get such long memories?"

In Russia he had spent more than one night in a hideout, hungry, lice-ridden, covered in rags, terrified that he might be arrested, exiled, sent before a firing squad, yet they knew and praised his work in New York. They addressed him as if he were second-in-command to Stalin himself, making all kinds of disparaging remarks about America at the same time.

Oh, my little chickadees, if you only knew the truth! Kotik mused. But you haven't a clue, and you don't want to know either. You like the role of the opposition and playing at revolution. You've got money, you're free, so it suits you to be "progressive" and spit in the trough you feed from—if you didn't, you'd be reactionaries.

Two women, one tall and the other short, had planted themselves in front of Kotik and Anna and could not be budged. The short one wore a turban over her black hair and diamonds that Kotik, a jewelry expert, estimated at a glance to be worth many thousands. With a flat face and eyes resembling black olives, she spoke with the unctuous self-righteousness of a rabbi's wife. Having first praised Kotik lavishly, she moved on to explain that she was a painter. She had taken up the palette as a hobby after a nervous breakdown, she confided, but she had made such rapid progress that she was about to hold an exhibition. Her women friends were all mad about her work. Her husband, who had earlier ridiculed her efforts, had now recanted and rented a studio for her in Carnegie Hall. Famous critics were enthusiastic.

"Is your style academic or modern?" Anna asked.

"Modern, of course! Who has the patience for the old way of painting nowadays? Picasso is my god. I'm dying to meet some Soviet artists, but the damned Americans won't let anyone in. These warmongers are fanning the Cold War—they can't endure the fact that the Russian people have freed themselves from slavery."

Kotik screwed up one of his eyes. "What can we do with them? Such reactionaries, such envious swine!"

"Their end will come."

"Meanwhile, keep on painting your pictures."

"Well, I try to do what I can."

"One must protest! One must picket the White House!" Kotik urged dramatically. "One must send a message to Comrade Stalin!"

And he pinched Anna's backside.

In the great hall which was normally the scene of wedding receptions, actors and actresses performed, recited poems, sang Russian songs. A Communist writer pontificated. Since the place could not accommodate everyone present, many people wandered about the corridors. Kotik opened a door to see a bride being photographed. She stood with a chaplet around her head, in a white dress with a long train and with a bouquet of flowers in her hand. The photographer was down on one knee. As if from nowhere a rabbi with a red beard and sidelocks appeared, sweating profusely and blowing his nose into a huge handkerchief. He had apparently made a mistake about the date. Kotik murmured half to himself and half to Anna, "Things here are bad for our little Jews. They do wrong by them in

America. They give them a whiff of revolution. They'd be much better off in Birobidzhan. Well, when you're among lunatics, you also have to act insane. If everyone's walking on their hands, Yasha Kotik isn't going to be the only one standing on his feet.''

Justina Kohn materialized out of the throng, on the arm of a cross-eyed youth with an unkempt shock of hair. Kotik spotted her and tried to turn aside with Anna, but dragging her escort by the sleeve, Justina blocked his way.

"Look who's here! The great Mr. Kotik!'' And Justina flashed a smile.

"Anna, this is Justina Kohn, an actress from Poland.''

"Yes, we've met.''

Anna frowned. This young woman aroused both distaste and uneasiness in her, and Grein's notion suddenly darted into her mind: this world was an underworld.

"Do you act here in New York?''

"Where? Not everyone has Yasha Kotik's talent or his adaptability. There's no Polish theater here. The radio broadcasts Polish programs, but they're all run by a gang of anti-Semites. They offered me a part in the Yiddish theater, but I don't know any Yiddish.''

"But she knows a Sabbath pudding when she sees one,'' Kotik interjected suggestively.

"My parents spoke Yiddish, but I didn't listen and I didn't want to listen. They shouted at me if I tried to speak Yiddish. That Warsaw dialect sounds so ridiculous and comical—the way they pronounce the vowels and all those guttural diminutives. This is Dave. Dave Rosenbaum,'' Justina introduced the youth at her side.

A pox on her! She's sleeping with him, the whore, Kotik brooded. I'll slap her till the teeth rattle in her mouth. Kotik brazenly looked the youth up and down with critical disapproval. The boy was gawky and graceless— nothing but an oaf, a lout. But then how good a judge was one man of another? She probably likes him, may her guts rot!

Kotik threw Justina a crooked glance. Well, we'll meet again in Birobidzhan.

2

Two couples met at the buffet table—Jack Grein with his wife, Patricia, and Anita Grein with her German lover, Fritz Genzl. Patricia hadn't wanted to come to this reception. Since her marriage, and now that she was pregnant, she'd lost interest in this milieu and had started to be embarrassed about her former left-wing sympathies and ardent longing to be an actress. But Jack had obstinately insisted that they not lose their former contacts; all their friends and acquaintances were there. Jack worked for the federal government and had signed a statement certifying that he was not a Communist, but he didn't take it seriously. Washington demanded that one sign all sorts of documents! This was his natural environment. He wandered about with Patricia clinging to his arm—they were both blond and tall, two giants. They kept bumping into friends: Hi, Bill! Hi, Al! Hi, Pam! They smoked cigarettes, stopping at the buffet to drink soda water. Most of the young couples present had just returned from vacation, so a great many sunburned faces were in evidence. They asked each other the usual questions: Where were you on Cape Cod? This year I went to Martha's Vineyard. I went to the Cape last year. How was the ocean? Wonderful! How's the baby? Beautiful! The women all carried purses full of tickets for a variety of leftist benefits. A hunchback hobbled around with a petition, collecting signatures, his black eyes moist with the holy fervor of revolution. Every time he got a signature, he nodded his head piously and briskly dabbed the wet ink with a piece of blotting paper. Like an alms collector in the old country, he seemed to be murmuring to himself, May this deed be counted as a blessing.

Suddenly Jack saw Anita, and his face filled with laughter. Although they had grown up in the same home, Jack regarded his sister as a bashful, misanthropic, antisocial creature who had always locked herself away. Their mother had often remarked that they would have to send Anita to a psychiatrist. But here she was, on the arm of a man with a mop of yellow hair, a snub nose, and gray eyes under straw-colored eyebrows, wearing a yellow jacket, black trousers, and a red shirt. Jack had heard of this Fritz Genzl. His mother had talked about him, but Jack had never met him. When Anita recognized Jack, she seemed startled, jerked her arm out of Genzl's, and made a movement as though to turn away, but it was too late. Her escort was also taken aback.

"Anita!"

"Ah!"

"Patricia, look who's here!"

"My goodness!"

Patricia embraced and kissed Anita, while Jack offered his hand to Fritz. There was no one to introduce Genzl formally, because Anita seemed to have been struck dumb, but he immediately started speaking English with a thick German accent. He was apparently a stutterer, stopping for long pauses between one word and another, while the words themselves emerged high-pitched and shrill, as though wrenched violently from inside him. There were German tones and undertones in his voice almost never heard in America.

He looks exactly like a Nazi, Jack thought, taking an immediate dislike to him. Nevertheless, he made a courteous attempt to engage him in small talk: "It's a hot day for September, isn't it?"

"*Ja*. It is hot here. In Germany it is . . . a-a-also hot, but different. Here the air is humid! Here . . . i-i-it stinks!"

And Genzl pointed to his throat, letting out a croak as though he were being strangled.

"Would you like a Coca-Cola to drink?"

Genzl did not respond immediately. "I hate that drink. It is . . . b-b-bad for the stomach. Pure p-p-poison."

"Yet millions of people drink Coca-Cola and live to tell about it," Patricia interjected.

"*Ja!*" And Genzl threw an angry glance at her.

"Have you been in the United States long?"

"N-n-nine months and . . . t-t-two weeks."

"Did you come straight from Germany?"

"*Ja!*"

Really? Are they now letting Germans into America? Jack wondered, astonished at his own thoughts. And what did *he* do during the war? Butcher Jews? Jack was no chauvinist, and the whole rigmarole of being a Jew held no appeal for him, but this German awakened suspicions in him.

He threw Anita a searching glance as he asked Genzl, "Do you smoke?"

"A-a-absolutely not!"

The answer came truculently, aggressively, as if the mere mention of smoking revolted him. Genzl's reply effectively terminated the conversation—there was little left to say to him.

Patricia tried to save the situation. "Surely you drink beer?"

"N-n-not American beer. The beer here is . . . sh-sh-shit!"

Patricia turned to speak to Anita. "Your mother's been staying with us. She came back to New York yesterday."

"Yes, I know."

"What's happening with your job?"

"Oh, it's awful." Anita seemed to seize eagerly on the question. "I sit all day writing the same few words. They specialize in issuing subpoenas. It's something like a detective agency."

"Why did you take the job?"

"Oh, it's so difficult to get work. You need to have shorthand, and I only studied it for a few weeks. There's some new system that only takes six months to learn, but I don't believe it. Where I work, the atmosphere is dreadful. Truly unendurable."

"Have you at least rented a nice room?"

"Nice? It's a terrible room. It bakes in the sun all day. The owner's unbelievably filthy and the cleaning woman stole three pairs of my stockings."

"Is that so? Why don't you call us? Your mother was expecting you to come out and see us. You didn't even telephone."

"When was I supposed to come? On Saturday I have to do the shopping, wash my hair, do the ironing and a thousand other things. My hair gets horribly dirty from all this heat and dust. I also have to go to the dentist, because one of my fillings has fallen out. Every day there's some new catastrophe. The other day I lost the front door key and I had to go searching for a locksmith and all the rest of it. When Sunday comes around, I'm dead tired. I don't want to go anywhere or speak to anyone."

"I'm very sorry."

"Do you ever see Dad?" asked Jack.

"No."

"You must know he's gone back to Mother," Jack whispered.

"She doesn't want him back."

"Even so, it's better this way."

Jack and Patricia started saying goodbye to Anita and her German. The few minutes he had spent with them had been torture for Jack. His sister never did anything but complain, always using words like "awful," "dreadful," "terrible," "filthy." There was a perpetual air of anxiety about her. This German matched her in disposition exactly. Jack said good night, and turning away, he took Patricia's arm and in silence walked with her to the end of the corridor. He can't possibly be a Nazi, Jack mused.

Otherwise they'd never have given him a visa. He'd never have taken up with a Jewish girl or come to a party like this one. He must be a leftist. But there was something crude, obtuse, cold-blooded about him that was deeply disturbing. That's how the storm troopers were. Well, one can't condemn a whole nation. Wasn't East Germany following a progressive path? One can't draw conclusions on the basis of impressions and emotions.

"What a ridiculous fellow!" Patricia said, interrupting Jack's train of thought.

"He and Anita suit each other."

3

Among those at the reception was Sylvia, Herman Makaver's wife. Herman had disappeared in Russia without a trace and it was now clear that they had liquidated him. Sylvia didn't sleep a wink, and there were moments when she wanted to curse Communism. If the socialist fatherland could wipe out such loyal followers as Herman, then the end of the world had come. There was nothing more to hope for. But her comrades had worked hard to prevent her from losing faith. In the first place, they argued, it was not certain that Herman had been arrested. Perhaps he had been sent on a secret mission about which he could not write. He might be somewhere in China or in Korea. And then, even if they had arrested him, Sylvia ought to bear in mind that there had always been informers, black sheep, agents provocateurs who had covertly undermined the Soviet Union by denouncing its staunchest supporters. Hadn't Yezhov been engaged in such a conspiracy? Hadn't Yagoda? But sooner or later such people are exposed, and faithful Communists falsely accused were fully rehabilitated. Herman's innocence would soon become manifest, and Sylvia would yet receive many cheerful letters from him.

Among the comrades there were also those who let it be known that Herman was far from being as devoted to the cause as Sylvia had imagined. He had displayed stubbornness. Once he had taken an idea into his head, it was difficult to beat it out of him. On occasion he had criticized the American Communist Party, and had even let slip one or two opinions critical of Moscow. To this day Herman remained convinced that in 1936 the Comintern had erred in dissolving the Communist Party in Poland. That was tantamount to asserting that both the Party and Comrade Stalin had made a mistake. Ideas like that were not far from Trotskyism. Someone even suggested that Herman had harmed the Party when he had been in Spain. What exactly did Sylvia know about Herman's past? If they had in fact detained him in Russia, it was a sure sign that he was suspect. There they had everyone's record. Collectively they knew things that no single individual could ever know. The comrades argued that Sylvia should free herself of mournful thoughts and remain active and industrious. She needed the Party and the Party needed her. Where would she go if she were to give up her Party work? To the few so-called socialists of Norman Thomas's ilk? Outside the Communist Party, American political life was fascist, idiotic, uncommitted, disorderly. Progressive people had to stay in the Party if they wanted to survive politically, culturally, and even personally.

Yes, in truth, where could Sylvia go? She owed even her job to the Communist Party. To be sure, she worked for the federal government, but her boss and many of her colleagues were fellow-travelers. If she displayed the slightest opposition to the Party, she would lose her job. The American capitalists lacked the sense even to control their own institutions. Comrades pulled the strings everywhere. American capitalism lacked class-consciousness and ordinary political self-interest. It lived for the present, for the dollar. It was like a fat pig that guzzled and grunted and didn't know that tomorrow it was going to be slaughtered. When anyone tried to wake it from its slumber and point out the danger, it threw itself on such persons with the full force of its rage.

After much hesitation, Sylvia finally decided to attend the relief party.

Her arrival assured all her friends that she had overcome her doubts and depression, and that her best instincts had triumphed. They surrounded her with compliments, told her all sorts of gossip, cheered her up with jokes, anecdotes, and confidential news. No one mentioned Herman's name. They even avoided mentioning anything that might bring Herman to her mind. Only one thing failed to please the crowd: Sylvia wore her wedding ring. Her female comrades held that she ought to remove that outmoded bourgeois token, but they were confident that she would do so eventually. One couldn't live in the past. Herman was no longer here, and that was that. In New York you couldn't know what had happened to someone at the other end of the world. Communists had to devote themselves to the problems of today and tomorrow, not of yesterday.

Men hovered around her as if she were an available widow. They looked her in the face, scrutinizing her attire. Although Sylvia was not wearing mourning, she had not dressed in a way suited to such an occasion. She had on her weekday clothes, with a cigarette dangling from her hardly painted lips. Her mane of hair, cut like a man's, was more disheveled than usual, while her earnest black eyes were filled with bewilderment. Yes, they'd've behaved in exactly the same way if I'd been lost and Herman had remained behind, Sylvia thought. As soon as someone falls, he must immediately be trampled on and forgotten. Is this the Communism I've worked so hard for? I had different ideals. I once believed that only among socialists did the individual have some worth. Well, I was naïve. One can't foresee anything. Herman always said that every event has its own logic, Sylvia reminded herself. God in heaven, how many times had she protested to him that she was horrified by the purges taking place in Russia, and Herman had justified everything, demonstrated to her that a functioning Party could not bow to emotion but had to adapt itself to the dialectic of events. Yesterday's friend might be tomorrow's enemy, Herman had argued. Humanity and its development were not still water but a Heraclitean stream which leaped and switched course every moment. With every change in politics or the economy came changes in all relations. Herman had given her an example from integral and differential calculus. With every change in the value of x, the value of epsilon and all the other functions of x changed as well. Thus, for example, there was no contradiction between Molotov's claim that fascism was a good thing and Stalin's call to the world proletariat and all progressive forces to fight the Nazi beast. With Hitler's attack on the Soviet Union, all values ceased, even moral values.

Everything would've been fine if Herman had just stayed home, Sylvia told herself. They lured him into a trap. Was he still alive? Or was he rotting in a prison somewhere? And what was he thinking, locked in a Soviet jail? Could he find some justification for it? Or had his personal tragedy driven him to doubts? She would have given half her life to catch a glimpse of him, to speak a few words with him.

Nevertheless, one had to go on living. One had to survive! I can't sit and mourn till the end of my days. If I'm not going to put a bullet in my head, I must lead a normal life. In the midst of all this anxiety, Sylvia needed a man. Something within her bubbled up, boiled, throbbed. Every now and then she went hot all over. As long as she'd been with Herman, other men hadn't interested her. But now she was filled with curiosity.

The comrades' glances bored into her, their eyes roved over her bosom, her hips. What do they see in me? Men are animals, animals. Sylvia took a deep draw on her cigarette and held her breath for a while. Inwardly a great wail, a cry of protest ripped through her: Was humanity only this? Was this life? Was this Communism? But Sylvia knew not to shout. There was no one at whom to shout. There was no God, no justice, no plan, no purpose. When people started beating their heads against the wall, they were carried off to a madhouse. Adults had to be capable of smiling while trampling on the dead, of seeing injustice and keeping silent——at least until such time as society was built on fathomable laws.

23

Leah was spending Rosh Hashanah with her son and daughter-in-law on Long Island. Patricia had recently begun to show an interest in Judaism and would debate with Leah for hours on end. She would soon give birth to a child. Since its father was a Jew, Patricia concluded, the child ought also to be Jewish. Jack laughed at his wife's talk. What kind of Jew am I? he asked himself. What was the point of making a brouhaha about religion, seeing that neither he nor she was religious? But Patricia kept returning to the subject. Their neighbors were almost all Jews and there was a Jewish community center. If the child was a boy, he would have to be circumcised. Patricia pointed to other mixed marriages among their neighbors in which the parents were raising their children as Jews. A child, Patricia argued, could not be left dangling in a void. If it grew up and decided on its own to be an atheist, that was fine, but while it was small, it needed a sense of belonging. At first Leah agreed with her son, taking issue with Patricia: why make him a Jew so that he could be destroyed when another Hitler arose?

But Patricia answered, "Hitler is dead and the Jews are alive."

Soon Leah switched to Patricia's side. Jack was a leftist, virtually a Communist, but waging war against his wife and his mother was not in his nature. In any case the child hadn't even been born. Patricia, however, began gathering information. She talked things over with other mothers. She learned how to prepare for the circumcision ceremony. From a neighbor, also the wife of an engineer, she borrowed a book in English about the chief principles of Judaism and Jewish Law. Jack flipped through the book briefly and then pronounced it "junk" and "baloney." Leah found errors in it: some of its assertions did not correspond with her own knowledge of Judaism. But Patricia read it avidly and even made notes. She compiled a list of all the Jewish festivals and acquired a Jewish calendar so that she knew in advance when Rosh Hashanah would fall, as well as Yom Kippur, Sukkoth, Shmini Atzeret. She bombarded Leah with questions about doctrines and laws. Was one permitted to use electricity for cooking on the Sabbath? Could one buy in New York a wooden board for salting meat? Was one permitted to take a shower on Yom Kippur? Could one get kosher ham? Patricia was fascinated by these questions and rituals.

"Do you believe in all this nonsense?" Jack demanded.

"Well, it's interesting."

"If you're devout, why don't you go to church?"

"Well, I just want to belong wherever my children belong."

Jack pointed out to her that her views weren't very progressive and that his friends would laugh when they heard what was occupying her attention.

But Patricia argued, "Mrs. Goldman is progressive and she held a bat mitzvah for Eleanor."

Jack now perceived what every man learns sooner or later: a woman is governed not by reason but by emotions, instinct, fashion, or plain stubbornness, against which rational arguments do not avail. Patricia went off to consult the local rabbi. This rabbi had once been a small-time actor and had written a play which had been performed in a theater in Greenwich Village by a touring company to which Patricia had belonged when she was a girl. But now he was a rabbi, and Patricia told him her concerns. The rabbi gave her a cigarette, listened to everything she said, offered her a drink. He told her that dozens of Christian women married to Jewish men thought as she did. Then he said, "If you're asking me as a friend, I'd tell you to run from Judaism as from the plague. It creates too many problems. Jews aren't at home even in America. But as a rabbi I am obliged to receive you with open arms."

Patricia grew attentive. "What problems? In America everyone can worship God exactly as they choose."

"Yes, but the owner of a country club is also entitled to refuse membership to Jews."

"Well, the Quakers were also persecuted."

"Not like the Jews."

"The world is going forward, not backward."

"When it comes to Jews, there is no progress."

Patricia left dissatisfied. She decided that Reform rabbis were not to her taste. If he was a rabbi, why wasn't he wearing a beard and why didn't he cover his head? And why did he speak so informally? In New York she had seen other rabbis—men with beards and sidelocks and long black coats. They were a little old-fashioned, strange, but in their eyes there was something attractive, intriguing. In her book Patricia had read about Maimonides, the Baal Shem Tov, the Gaon of Vilna. Several rabbis had fasted for long periods in penance. A certain Rabbi Akiva had allowed his flesh to be raked with iron combs, and his soul had left his body as he pronounced the words "Hear, O Israel, the Lord is God, the Lord is One." Another, Rabbi Hananiah ben Dusa, nourished himself on only one measure of carob from Sabbath to Sabbath. These were not actors but godly men. Did such people still exist today? If they did, Patricia wanted to get to know them.

Meanwhile, she reserved two places for herself and her mother-in-law in the Reform temple in their Long Island suburb for the coming Days of Awe. She had decided to buy meat from a kosher butcher and to prepare a festive meal for Rosh Hashanah. She received pointers from all sides. The bakery was the place to get challah. One of her friends, a Mrs. Stone, presented her with two candlesticks so she could make the blessing over the candles. Leah herself began teaching Patricia the Jewish laws, as well as how to cook gefilte fish, matzo balls, meat dumplings, chicken soup, moving inevitably into explanations of the Jewish dietary laws, of the rigid imperative to separate meat from milk. It was strange that the Jewish religion was so tightly bound up with the kitchen, with food. Jack hoped that eventually Patricia would tire of all this and interest herself in other things, but Patricia's curiosity knew no bounds. She questioned Leah about the laws of female purity which were mentioned in the book. Were they also observed in America? Was there a ritual bath in New York? Did Orthodox women go there?

Leah began to laugh. "Soon you'll shave off your hair and wear a head scarf!"

"Why shave off my hair?"

Leah tried to answer her, but Patricia perceived that her mother-in-law didn't know much about these things herself. She described the laws, but she couldn't explain their rationales, their origins, their meanings. In New York Patricia visited a Jewish bookstore that carried sacred books, skullcaps, menorahs, fringed ritual garments, and dreidels for Hanukkah, and the owner sold her a Hebrew Bible and a copy of the *Shulhan Arukh,* both translated into English, as well as a history of the Jews, a daily prayer book, the special prayer books for Rosh Hashanah and Yom Kippur, and a work entitled *The Spirit of Judaism*. No, Patricia no longer needed to consult ignorant women. There existed a substantial literature in English about Judaism. If in college she had been able to understand mathematics, physics, chemistry, and the history of art, there was no reason why she should not find her bearings in the Jewish religion.

Patricia soon knew more than Jack, more than Leah, more than her Jewish neighbors. She spoke knowledgeably about the Bible, the Mishnah, the Gemara. Leah wrote Grein a long letter telling him of the pride he could take in his daughter-in-law. Patricia intended to have a discussion with her father-in-law, but she wanted to arm herself beforehand with Jewish knowledge. She could offer no satisfactory explanation, however, of what was happening within her. Had she suddenly become religious? Something was driving her on, but she didn't know what. She even woke up in the middle of the night and repeated the Jewish laws in her head.

2

On the morning of the eve of Rosh Hashanah, the telephone rang in Grein's study. Grein answered it and heard Esther's voice: "It's me. Of course you thought I was dead by now, but I'm sorry to have to tell you that I'm still wandering about this world—a soul in the World of Illusion."

"When did you get back?"

"Yesterday."

"How was Europe?"

"Europe is Europe. The same Europe, but disillusioned, impoverished, dark. You should've seen Paris—oh, how sad! Well, I'd better not say anything. In London whole streets and blocks are bombed out, yet the British seem to love the Germans. While I was there, a German prisoner-of-war married an English girl and the press went into such ecstasies that you'd think the nation had been presented with the greatest honor in the world. The few Jews left there are either totally ruined or deal on the black market. How are you?"

"Difficult to say."

"I see you're in your own home."

"Yes, that's true."

"Is your wife at home?"

"Leah's with Jack."

"How is she feeling? Are you alone in the apartment?"

"Yes, I'm alone."

"In that case I can talk to you. What's happened to you? Have you broken off with Boris Makaver's daughter?"

"I've broken off with everyone."

"Well, it's high time. You always were a misanthrope. You always wanted to run away from everyone and everything. I called you first of all because I want to wish you a good New Year—may you be set down in the Book of Life for another year of health and happiness. Believe me, I wish it for you with my whole heart. You have no greater friend in the whole world than me. I know what you're going through as clearly as if I were sitting in your heart and listening to your thoughts. An ocean separated us, but believe me, I was with you all the time. I'm not talking about my dreams—that goes without saying. As soon as I shut my eyes, you're here. Even when I'm awake. How's Leah? What do the doctors say?"

"It's too early to know."

"You won't believe me, dearest, but I'm praying for her. I don't know why. According to logic, I should be her mortal enemy, but hatred isn't in my nature, and neither is logic. Where should I get logic from? Are you going to pray tomorrow? Have you got a seat in a synagogue?"

"Yes."

"Well, pray for a good year for yourself. Don't imagine the doctors know what they're talking about—they can't tell their hands from their feet. If God grants you the years, you live. Her illness could go away. More than one doctor writes off someone else's life and dies himself, and the patient lives to laugh at him. Why is she spending the festival with Jack?"

"She wants to."

"Well, she was never a proper wife to you. If you'd had any sense, you'd've divorced her years ago. She'd've married someone on her own level and been content, and the two of us would've been as happy as a husband and wife can ever be, because I can give you what no one else can. I understand you better than you understand yourself. You've told me a thousand times that you've never been as happy with any woman as you've been with me. But people have a habit of running away from happiness and thinking up all sorts of justifications for doing so. You once said yourself that people are afraid to be happy. What's there to be afraid of? I have my own philosophy: since people strive for happiness, it's a sign they were born for it. By the way, that's your philosophy, not mine. I'm just repeating your words. Often a thought occurs to me and then I immediately realize, that's what *we* think, Hertz and I. I've been possessed by a dybbuk. If there isn't a dybbuk inside me, I can't explain what's happening to me. But where does one find dybbuks these days? Why are you keeping quiet?''

"You're talking. I don't want to interrupt you.''

"I'm talking because you're keeping quiet. For you every word's like a precious gold coin, but gold coins are utterly worthless to me. How are you, dearest? What are you doing?''

"Oh, 'I sit alone and keep silent,' as Jeremiah says.''

"What's the good of that?''

"How did you get on in Europe?''

"Like a saint in this world and an evildoer in the next. I was sick the whole time. I nearly died on the airplane going there. I got such spasms that my hands and feet started twitching. I had stomach convulsions. By a miracle there was a doctor on board who had some pills with him. In Paris he caused such an uproar—I mean Plotkin—that I can't even begin to describe it to you. Paris is full of refugees—from Poland, from Russia, from Germany, from all over the world. He's got a sea of acquaintances there. As soon as they heard that the rich Mr. Plotkin from America was coming to Paris, there was indescribable bedlam. They think, of course, that he's a second Rockefeller, a J. P. Morgan. He behaved as if Rockefeller was his valet. The franc is virtually worthless, so for a dollar they fill your shopping bags to overflowing. He changed his money on the black market and almost doubled it. In short, the experience was like an endless wedding banquet. Spongers appeared out of nowhere—freeloaders, alms collectors, writers, artists, and plain hard-luck cases arrived every minute of the day. Everyone was grabbing at his pocket, and he stuffed cash into every outstretched hand. Some came twice, three times, each time with a different litany. If that man didn't dish out ten thousand dollars, my name isn't Esther. Never mind, charity is charity. But wining and dining lewd women, shoving caviar and champagne down their throats, and racing around in taxis taking them to nightclubs and cabarets—that's another thing. It's shocking that an old man should have such an evil inclination! I don't want to sin with my words, but that man doesn't need a wife. He's already, pardon me for saying so, played out—he's impotent. He says he's sixty-six, but I'm certain he's over seventy. So what's he turning the world upside down for? But that's how he is.

"These days you can't find a beautiful woman in Paris for love or money. One is more frightful than the next. They rarely have a full set of teeth, but that doesn't stop them from laughing and making faces and primping in a way that makes you nauseous. He blew in there like a hurricane, and soon I had no one to talk to. He behaved like a drunkard, which isn't surprising, because he was hardly ever sober. He soaks up champagne like water. You can pour magnums and demijohns into that huge belly of his. How his heart stands the strain is God's own wonder. He embraces everyone, he's on familiar terms with all and sundry, he kisses every face as though the whole world were his brother or sister. They all glared at me with such hatred that I was terrified someone would stick a knife in my breast. I got completely addled and couldn't pull myself together. In the beginning he dragged me along to all these get-togethers and parties, but soon I told him I hadn't the strength. I crawled into bed and lay there in a stupor for three days. But even in bed they didn't leave me in peace, because in Paris they never telephone—they arrive uninvited! In any case, the telephones don't work. Every few hours they go dead. The plumbing doesn't work either, so you can't flush the toilet, pardon me for mentioning it. I go to take a bath and suddenly there's no hot water. We were staying in one of the biggest hotels, but in France there's no difference between the big ones and the small ones. Now especially, after the war, it's total chaos. With money, naturally, there's nothing you can't buy, but then you mustn't care how much it costs you. Have you fallen asleep or what?"

"No, Esther, I'm listening."

"Why don't you say something? I want to hear your voice!"

"What've I got to say? It's you who's just back from Europe, not me."

"What does it matter that I'm just back from Europe? I'm still the same Esther. Europe hasn't changed me."

"No, it hasn't."

3

"Don't be so sarcastic. I may not have changed, but neither have you. You can try and talk yourself into believing that you're a penitent and all the rest of it, but I don't take it seriously for a moment. You're exactly the same as you were before. My mother used to say that what you lift from the cradle you lay in the grave. One never changes. You always needed to settle accounts with God. But what about it? I've also got accounts to settle, Hertz, and so what? I cry out to Him the whole day, and He ignores me completely. You at least answer me with a grunt, but *He* remains completely silent. What's the use of crying out to him? Tomorrow's Rosh Hashanah and the Jews that Hitler didn't succeed in slaughtering and burning in the ovens will again honor Him with worshipful prayers, celebrating the awesome holiness of the day and blowing the shofar, but how do the Poles put it? *Gadaj do ściany*—go talk to the wall! I'm amazed, Hertz, that you've swallowed all this. Now's not the time.

"Only in Europe can you see the extent of the catastrophe. People wander about not knowing which way to turn. First they fled from the Germans, now they're fleeing from the Bolsheviks and from the Poles, too. There's already been a pogrom in Poland—they want to wipe out their last few Jews. There's no greater destroyer than the human species. The French suffered themselves and they don't want any foreigners. On the other hand, many of them collaborated with the Nazis. Paris is full of beggars, traitors, Nazis in disguise, and Satan alone knows what other evildoers. The Communists are in complete control. People are terrified even to mention what the Communists have done in Russia. They packed Jews into freight trucks and sent them to Siberia. People died on the road. They had to relieve themselves, excuse me for mentioning it, through the windows because there was no lavatory. One doesn't even send animals to slaughter in such conditions. People tell you about so much horror that you can't listen, because just hearing it is like suffering all the afflictions of Job. I had to keep drinking and taking pills, otherwise I'd've collapsed from the strain. So why cringe and be servile? Before whom? To help whom?"

"What's your remedy?"

"There's no remedy—none! The only way to survive is to forget. People who drink should get drunk, and people who take drugs should become addicts, and people who have stones instead of hearts in their breasts should be optimistic and talk about better times to come. We shouldn't dare to praise God—you hear what I'm saying? That in itself is the worst sin. Once I, too, used to go and pray on Rosh Hashanah and Yom Kippur. You know that perfectly well. But these days I don't want to. Let the Nazis pray to Him! They all go running to the Pope and he embraces them. Now that they've murdered all Jesus' brothers and sisters, they're kissing crucifixes again.''

"Esther my darling, we can't be in despair twenty-four hours a day.''

"Why not? I've been in despair since childhood. I've always despaired, even when I used to lie in your arms and scream with pleasure. You were also always in despair, and that's why we were a well-matched pair. As crazy and twisted as I am, I still detest illusions and hiding behind beautiful words. When they slaughter a Jew and he screams 'Hear, O Israel,' it's one thing, but a person who sits comfortably in his own home eating and drinking three times a day has no right to call out 'Hear, O Israel,' because they're slaughtering someone else, not him. It's like that with everything. They murder the father, and the son speaks about a bright tomorrow. Who will enjoy that radiant morning? Not the father.''

"Esther, you're speaking about fundamental things. But despair is useless. If all people despaired from morning to night, Hitler would now be in New York and they'd be burning Jews here as well.''

"They'll still burn them here, don't worry. Jews will never have any rest. They'll strangle them everywhere. Look what's happening in the Holy Land! Ships bring survivors from Hitler's ovens, and the British shoot at them and throw them back into concentration camps. On the other hand, when today's Jews are left in peace, they immediately start making trouble. They jump in first everywhere. What do rich Jews need Communism for? They deal on the black market and they're dangerous Reds. You should see what goes on in Paris! As a people, we're mad—stark raving mad!''

"That's what I want to run away from. Our fathers weren't like this. You know that.''

"Our fathers are no longer here. Ash is all that's left of them—a mountain of ash. Hertz, I've left Morris Plotkin!'' Esther suddenly exclaimed in a different voice. "I must tell you. Who should I tell if not you? No matter what you might do, whether you stand on your head, you're still the person closest to me, and that's the way it'll stay until I draw my last breath.''

Grein was silent for a while. "Where are you? Where are you calling from?''

"I'm still in his house on Hicks Street. He's gone to live in a hotel. I'm single again.''

"What happened?"

"Nothing happened. I might as well have been living with a wild animal or a demon. I drove him to a point where he couldn't stand it. It's possible that I'm the demon, not him. But what's the difference? He's agreed to everything. He'll settle some money on me. He's even telephoned his lawyer. I could've squeezed a fortune out of him, but I'm not so despicable. I wronged him, not he me. It's not his fault that I am what I am. In all fairness I shouldn't take a single cent from him, but in his own way he's a great gentleman, even though he can also be a great pig. Who knows what he really is?"

"True enough."

"You don't need to be afraid. I won't impose myself on you. He wants to give me the house and to have several other people live here. Instead of renting rooms in Brighton Beach, I'll rent out rooms on Hicks Street—what's the difference? I won't die of hunger. He's leaving me all the jewelry as well, and I can sell it. At the moment I'm making it on my own, but I don't think I'll make it for long. My experience with Morris Plotkin and the trip to Europe have finished me off. Until he came along, I still had a bit of self-respect, but now I've lost even that. Whenever I think about myself, I want to spit. Have you ever heard of a person wanting to spit on herself? Everyone's after me to go to a doctor, but how can a doctor help me? I'm too far gone. Everything in me has gone up in flames—all that's left is ashes and smoke. I only ask one thing of you, Hertz—as long as I draw breath, don't desert me. 'Cast me not off in time of old age,' as the psalms say! Tomorrow they'll shout that out in all the synagogues. I'm not so old yet, but I'm a wreck, shattered into tiny pieces. I must talk to someone and I can only talk to you. That's the whole problem."

"Well, Esther, talk. I've always got time for you."

"What? That's good to hear. Imagine there's a person who knows only one language—let's say Yiddish—and doesn't know a word of any other. Let's say that Yiddish is dead, and that there's only one other person left who understands it. In that case, the one who knows only Yiddish will strain every fiber to reach the single person who can understand him, and follow him to the ends of the earth. That's the relationship between you and me. I can't talk to anyone except you. Others pretend to understand me, but I get the feeling that I'm talking to blocks of wood. You never answer me directly, but I know that you hear me and understand everything. So how can I live without you? You run around trying to perform virtuous deeds, but you do the most virtuous deed when you speak a friendly word to me."

"When I do what you call a virtuous deed, I do it for my own benefit."

Esther paused awhile. A choking sob came through the receiver. "Well, it's been worth everything to hear those words. I thought you'd forgotten me completely."

"No, Esther, I can't forget you."

"You . . . you . . . savage! Love is a great thing. You're looking for God, but if God exists, He must be found in love. I want to kneel before you. I want to—what do you say?—to prostrate myself before you. Don't get frightened. I'm not mad. A person can't love God, because one can't see God and He's almighty and eternal. How can a person conduct a love affair with the sun? It's like a microbe trying to have a love affair with an elephant, but on a scale a thousand times greater. A human being can only love another human being—that's the tragedy. Morris Plotkin loves everybody, but I can love only you. You're my god. Ridiculous, isn't it, for someone my age to speak like that! But it's true all the same. With you I could even have prayed to God. We'd read together from the same prayer book."

Suddenly Esther started laughing. Just as suddenly she stopped. "Are you there?"

4

"Esther!" Grein exclaimed, astonished himself at what he was preparing to say and what direction events were taking. His voice was both wary and urgent, full of the fearful excitement of someone who decides on the spur of the moment to turn everything upside down. At the other end of the line Esther seemed to have lost the power of speech. Grein himself had the feeling that someone else was speaking out of him.

"Esther," he asked, "are you still willing to run away with me to the ends of the earth?"

The expression "to the ends of the earth" was a talisman for them, a phrase they both used countless times that had a special significance for them. It was uttered in profound earnestness as well as jokingly, about all their unfulfilled plans and promises. But Grein said it now with deadly seriousness. He could hardly stammer the few syllables and seemed to be choking on the words.

Esther grew tense and alert. An incomprehensible dread seized her. Her throat constricted. "Yes, you know that!" she said.

"When? Now?"

"At any time!"

"At this moment?"

"Yes, at this very moment!"

"Come, Esther, now's the time!"

It was a while before Esther answered. "Do you mean it seriously, or are you playing cat and mouse with me?"

"Esther, pack your things and come!" Grein commanded. "My struggle's futile. I give in. To whatever power there might be."

Esther wanted to weep, but she couldn't. "I've been living for this." And she fell silent.

"Esther, I don't want to force you into anything," he began.

"Force?! This is the happiest day of my life! If I were to die now, I'd die happy."

"You don't have to die. Pack a few things and come. Leah doesn't need me. I'll leave her everything. I'll take only the bare essentials."

"What about me? He's promised me a settlement."

"We don't need any settlement. Take what you have—we won't starve!"

He paused between one word and another, feeling himself choking. A tremor zigzagged up his spine. The receiver trembled in his hand and he clutched it tightly, stunned by his sudden decision and his having waited so long to make it. Only now did he realize how deeply he had longed to take this step, and what powerful forces had been at work in the furthermost recesses of his unconscious. He acknowledged squarely that he was ruining himself and making a mockery of everything—all his thoughts, his resolutions, the letter he had written to Anna, all he had said to Dr. Margolin. But his desire for Esther outweighed everything. Suddenly he was seized by a fear that she might have doubts. His mouth went dry.

"Esther, where are you?"

"I'm here. I'm yours, yours! You can do as you wish with me. I'm like Jephthah's daughter—you can offer me up as a sacrifice. Tell me what I must do, my master, and I'll fulfill it to the letter, because you're my priest and I'm your burnt offering."

"Stop your flowery idiocies! Pack a few dresses and some underwear and take a taxi to the corner of Fiftieth Street and Eighth Avenue. That's where the Greyhound Bus Terminal is.''

"Where will you take me?"

"I don't know where myself. What difference does it make? To the ends of the earth."

"Yes, take me. He was supposed to give me a pile of money, but I don't need his money. I've got a few hundred dollars and some jewelry. Should I bring my fur as well?''

"Yes. Winter's coming."

"When should I be there?"

"As soon as possible. Whichever of us gets there first will wait for the other. There are banks and a cafeteria there."

"I know, I know. I'm going to pack right away. What made you decide this? No, I'd better not ask."

"I love you, Esther. I can't live without you. That's the truth."

"What? Well, now that I've heard that, God's paid me in full. He doesn't owe me anything more. I'll do everything you say. I've only got one desire now—to die before you."

"You must live, not die. I need you."

"If you want me to, I'll live. My every breath belongs to you."

"We'll see each other at the bus depot." And Grein hung up.

He stood still for a long time, staring ahead of him as though he expected to see the hidden forces that had led him to this denouement. He could imagine the beings all around him, those forces which, seeing though themselves unseen, sow disorder in each individual's life. He addressed them silently. Well, now that the die's cast, you might as well reveal yourselves. But he was also afraid of them and begged that they not terrorize him with their fearsome countenances. It would be enough, a sign that they were here, he reflected, if the pen on his desk were to move of its own accord. He did not formulate his thoughts clearly. They seemed to float shapelessly within him like elusive images when one is on the verge of dreams. Listening intently, he seemed to hear the hidden forces answer him: It is not fitting that you should break down the partition that separates Here from There. Rather, do what you must do. He roused himself. Well, this is it!

Although he had made no preparations beforehand, he knew precisely what he had to do. He would leave Leah fifty thousand dollars in stocks and would take the rest—some six thousand dollars' worth—with him. Of the seventeen hundred dollars in the bank, he would take only five hundred for himself. He and Esther would rent a small apartment somewhere in the Midwest or in California and live very cheaply. He could always get a low-paying job. Neither he nor Esther had any need of luxury. He would write to Leah explaining that he couldn't help himself. This force was stronger than he was. Of what concern to him now was his accounting with God, with the People of Israel, with the rest of the Jewish burden? Let things remain as they were. Let God pardon him if He wanted to, and let Him punish him if that was His will. Grein reminded himself of the words Jews would utter in the synagogue tomorrow: "Thou hast created them and Thou knowest the evil in their hearts."

He walked to the closet where the suitcases were kept. Well, I wasn't prepared for this! he murmured. At this of all times. But he also knew that there was a kind of logic in this madness. Living with Anna had not brought the joy, the exhilaration he had expected. And by going off to spend Rosh Hashanah with her son, Leah had shown that she neither needed nor wanted him. He remembered the injunction of the Gemara: "When a man is overcome by an evil inclination, he should clothe himself in black, and go to a place where he is not known, and do what his heart desires." Yes, there were indeed temptations so great that one could not resist them. They probably had a higher origin. If the Cabalists were right, there was constant coupling in the highest spheres. Who knows? Perhaps it was not bodies but souls that longed to unite. I always yearned for her—that's the truth!

The telephone rang, but Grein did not answer it. I'm no longer here! he silently answered the caller at the other end of the line. It rang for a long time. Could it be Leah? Anna? Both of them will have to forgive me. He opened a suitcase and began packing his things. He needed a second bag because he also had to take a few books with him. He sat down at the desk and wrote a letter to Leah. He still had to go to the bank. The telephone rang again, but he had resolved to have no further dealings with anyone in New York. On this Rosh Hashanah eve a new life was beginning for him.

He took emotional stock of himself: his heart was heavy, but only because he was wronging others—Leah, and perhaps Anna. At the bottom of his Jewish being, he felt the surge of confidence of a gambler who has risked everything.

5

He took a taxi to the Greyhound Bus Terminal and saw Esther as soon as he arrived. There were very few passengers and Esther occupied the whole of the front bench. She had put two suitcases down in front of her and laid her mink coat over the armrest. Wearing a gray suit with a fur collar and the diamond earrings she had inherited from her mother, she looked magnificent—pale, European, almost as if her trip abroad had stripped her of the Americanness she had acquired over the years. As soon as she saw Grein, she rose and moved to embrace him, but first he had to pay the taxi driver.

Then he went up to her, took both her hands, and said, "Well, it has come to pass."

"I can't tell you what happened to me at the last minute," Esther began.

"What? Where are we going? Wait, I'll ask where the next bus is headed."

Grein went off and returned with two tickets. "To Pittsfield, Massachusetts."

"Where on earth is that?"

"Come, the bus is waiting."

He was amazed at himself. Was this how one took such a step? Was it all so simple? He carried Esther's luggage and his own out to the bus. Sheltered inside the terminal, the vehicle looked bigger and more elegant than it did outside. It was half-empty, its seats sheathed in white covers. The driver shoved their suitcases somewhere into the bowels of the bus, and Grein put the smaller bags on the rack above the seats. Not five minutes later, the bus departed. Esther gave Grein her hand and he embraced and held her silently like a man who has got what he wanted. He knew that Esther would very soon start chattering, but he was glad that she was quiet now. He looked out at the hazy Rosh Hashanah evening and everything within him was still, full of the acceptance of one who was doing what he had to do and knew that there was no other way. Esther squeezed his fingers in hers, and this touch from a woman whom he had known for eleven years refreshed and excited him as though they had only just begun their affair. It was strangely good to be sitting next to this half-crazy Esther, ignoring everything he knew about her. He touched his inside jacket pocket where the traveler's checks were. There's enough for at least two years, he noted to himself. After that, we'll see. Now he had the feeling that everything that had happened in the previous months had been one great preparation for this finale, the climax to which all his thoughts, passions, conflicts led. Who knows? Perhaps with her it'll be easier for me to return to God. He recalled once having been told about a person who had unwittingly swallowed a needle that traveled all through his body; he suffered innumerable illnesses, all caused by one needle. Grein's passion for Esther was just like that needle.

Grein examined every passerby, every car. He felt pity for those who were staying behind in the city, with no great love, with no adventure to turn everything upside down—that shipping clerk, for example, who was pushing a rack crammed with women's coats, or that policeman who stood twirling his club. On the sidewalk Grein saw a rabbi—not the kind found in America but one who looked as if he had just got off the ship from Europe. He was a tall, stout man with a protruding belly, wearing a satin capote, white stockings, and black shoes, with a velvet hat on his head. He had a broad black beard and thick sidelocks which hung straight down, not tightly curled, covering his ears like two hat flaps that protected one from the winter cold. Grein had long forgotten such pitch-black, shaggy sidelocks, although they were immediately familiar the moment he saw them. Next to the rabbi walked a Jewish woman wearing a traditional bonnet. She looked extraordinarily small and stunted by comparison with her gigantic husband, like a peahen next to a peacock with his tail outspread. With them was a plump girl of about twelve, with two thick braids and high lace-up boots that were not common in these parts. Grein imagined that these three were opening a new chapter in Jewish history—the rabbi was a new Abraham who had left his country, his birthplace, his father's house, and had begun again in New York, exactly at the beginning of the New Year, heeding an updated version of God's command to the Patriarch Abraham: "Get thee out of thy country, and from thy kindred, and from thy father's house, unto the land that I will show thee." Grein saw them for not more than a few seconds. Had they only just arrived in America? How could they have saved themselves from the Nazis? Had they lived in hiding somewhere? Grein was profoundly impressed by the strength they emanated, an extraordinary courage, the potency of a new nation, the lifeblood of generations to come. From the loins of this mother and her young daughter could come forth a new Nation of Israel. Theirs was an elemental faith, a blind, unquestioning belief in Jewishness that required neither proofs nor sophistries; it was as basic as flesh and sex, full of life that could never be sapped. There's no question but tomorrow the rabbi will be confidently praying at a synagogue lectern somewhere in New

York. Such people find everything they need straightaway: money, kosher food, a house of prayer, Torah.

Grein could not decide whether he loved them or not. They were as alien to him as soldiers, animals, rocks—all of which know nothing of doubt. What they were, he could never be. In all his spiritual accounting, he had overlooked the fortitude, the stubbornness, the stiff-necked pride of Jewishness. Someone like that rabbi would sacrifice his life for the sake of the least teaching of Rabbi Moshe Isserles.

"Dearest, did you see that?" Esther asked.

"The rabbi? Yes."

"If there are still such Jews left, we needn't worry that the Jewish people will disappear," Esther remarked, as though she had read Grein's thoughts.

She paused awhile, and then blurted out, "Plotkin knows everything."

"How did he find out?"

"He telephoned and I told him everything."

"What did he say?"

"He bears no ill will. He understands. He wants me to write to him and he'll take care of everything. I mean the divorce—we'll go to Reno, and I'll just have to sign some papers."

"Well, let it all turn out as it will."

Esther paused. "I spoke frankly to him: this is something we have to do. You've been as restive as a caged beast, you've been running away from me for nearly twelve years, but it was no use. Dearest, you mustn't think that I accepted it all without a fight. There was a battle raging in me as well. You'll never know what I went through. Only God knows. My misguided marriage to Plotkin nearly cost me my life. I felt as if I'd grabbed my heart and torn it out of my breast the way one tears the gizzard out of a chicken. On our estate in the old country they used to slaughter cattle, and the ritual slaughterer always ripped out the lungs and liver. He would thrust his hands into the intestines and grope about there for a long time until he could tear out the parts he needed to test the purity of the carcass. Then he would spit on them to check that they weren't still bubbling. That was the way I tore out my heart. I don't understand how I'm still alive. But I couldn't go on, I couldn't. A voice was screaming in me all day and all night, and that voice kept growing louder and louder. In Paris it screamed so loudly that I was afraid others would hear it. I used to wonder why the neighbors didn't beat on the wall. But of course it was all in my mind. On the way to Italy I said to him, 'Morris, it's not working. I can't forget Grein.' He heard me out and he understood that it couldn't be any other way. I didn't see Rome at all. I lay in bed the whole time. Still, I never expected you to change direction and say, Let's try again—I wasn't prepared for that. It's a miracle. I thought I'd either have to go into a madhouse or hang myself.''

''No, Esther, now we're together.''

''I can't believe it! I can't believe it! I still feel you're playing some kind of game with me. But what can I do? I have to play along. How ever did you come to this decision?''

Grein didn't reply, and Esther didn't pursue the question. She laid her head back on the seat and tried to sleep.

Part Three

24

oris Makaver spent Rosh Hashanah with his rebbe in Williamsburg. In
that neighborhood, a Hasidic hotel with a strictly kosher kitchen had
opened, and weeks before the High Holy Days, Boris had reserved a room
for himself and Frieda. Going to Williamsburg for Rosh Hashanah reminded
Boris of how his father, may he rest in peace, had traveled to Narczew to
visit the rebbe's father for the Days of Awe and had taken his little Borukh
with him. They had made the trip in a *kolejka,* a small train with a tiny lo-
comotive that the Hasidim used to call "the little samovar." The carriages
were packed and they had passed through towns and fields. Boris had taken
a taxi to Williamsburg, and he and his wife had ridden along the crowded
streets of New York. But what was the difference really? The heart of the
matter was that on the High Holy Days he was visiting a zaddik.

Boris packed a round fur hat, a satin capote, his prayer shawl and phylacteries (to put on during the Fast of Gedaliyah on the day after Rosh
Hashanah), the prayer books for the High Holy Days, and a few other
small things. Frieda took her holiday clothes as well as the medication and
vitamins Dr. Margolin had prescribed. She was now in the final stages of
her pregnancy and had already reserved a room at the Jewish Hospital for
the birth. According to her calculations, she still had to wait another six
weeks. Her belly was large and pointed (indicating a male child) and her
face covered with yellow blotches. Dr. Margolin had explained that it was
not easy for a woman Frieda's age to bear a child, and indeed Frieda's
pregnancy was difficult; she suffered from constipation, headaches, pains

in her loins, and cramps in her stomach. Moreover, allowing herself to be examined by a male doctor was unpleasant for the modest Frieda. She had wanted to consult a woman doctor, but Boris had no confidence in any physician other than Solomon Margolin. Every time Frieda complained that she found it embarrassing to undress in front of a man, Boris would argue, "We are commanded that the saving of a life is an obligation that takes precedence over all others. Let the sin be on me." And he pointed out to her that the most pious of rabbis' wives had consulted male doctors when they had been infirm.

Though Reytze had left Boris, she had not yet found another position and she returned for the duration of Frieda's confinement. Over Rosh Hashanah the apartment was left in her care. The taxi drove down the East Side, across the Williamsburg Bridge, and after a few minutes stopped at the hotel which, far from offering modern accommodations, resembled a Hasidic inn from the old country. Jews with beards and sidelocks, and with their heads covered, wandered about in long-fringed ritual garments. From the kitchen came the aroma of the holiday delicacies being prepared there. The Jews flocked to the ritual bath nearby. It was still warm, but the days had already grown shorter. At the hotel Boris was given a large room with two beds, a chest of drawers, and a mirror. Frieda started unpacking while Boris went off to the dining room to eat an egg cookie and drink a glass of tea. Jews immediately came over and greeted him. In the old country Hasidim who met at a station knew one another but here each one had his own rebbe. No one had heard of the rebbe Boris was visiting and the others shrugged their shoulders, their eyes seeming to ask: Why on earth have you chosen that rebbe?

Boris had neither the time nor the desire to enter into a discussion about the merits of his rebbe. His rebbe was critically ill and there was no one to succeed him, while Boris himself found it more and more difficult to be on his feet for any length of time. What was there to discuss? Having finished his snack and recited the abridged Grace after Meals, he donned his satin capote and his fur hat and went off to the rebbe on Clymer Street. Since there was no provision for a women's section at the rebbe's, the few women present had to worship in the kitchen. No one had arrived yet in the room in which the men prayed, although everything was ready—there was a Holy Ark screened by a white curtain, a prayer stand, a lectern, a few benches. Bookshelves were nailed to the walls. New candles were fitted into the six-branched candelabra, but they had not yet been lighted. In the ceiling an electric bulb burned. Under the window outside, a truck was parked and Boris drew the curtain to shut out its intrusive presence. No, America was not Ger, not even Aleksandr, but the Master of the Universe was the same everywhere, and more skill was needed to be a zaddik in America than in Poland.

A small woman with a kerchief tied over her head and wearing an oilcloth apron came in from the kitchen. "A blessed New Year to you."

"And to you, Dvoyrele! How is the rebbe?"

"What can be expected?"

"Will he be coming in soon?"

"Yes. Where's your wife gone?"

"She'll be coming shortly. I thought there would be a minyan for the afternoon service," Boris said after some hesitation.

"You'll count your blessings if there's a minyan for the evening service," Dvoyrele joked weakly.

"Well well, God will always have His minyan!"

Dvoyrele went out and Boris began pacing back and forth, reciting the prescribed passages detailing the sacrifices offered in the Temple in ancient times. Now he recalled the afternoon service on the eve of Rosh Hashanah in the days of the present rebbe's father. The prayerhouse had been packed. The beadles had placed a barrier of planks around the lectern. The prayerhouse had been full of fur hats and satin capotes, beards and sidelocks, Jewish smells and Jewish voices. When the beadle had opened the door into the rebbe's room, there had been such a surge forward that some feet were trampled on as each man struggled to greet the rebbe personally. More than once someone fainted in the crush. How odd, Boris thought. In Poland Jews were in exile, trembling before every Gentile boor and thug, yet a rebbe's court was a kingdom. Here in America Jews were free, yet on the eve of Rosh Hashanah there were not even ten men to recite the afternoon service in the prayer room of a zaddik, and under the window a truck was grinding its gears. In a year's time there might be no one here at all, because the rebbe—

Boris shook his head to dispel these disturbing thoughts. Well, even in Poland people didn't live forever. What's more, people were also not so terrified of death. He began to pray fervently, translating the Hebrew words into Yiddish as he moved through the liturgy:

Happy are they that dwell in Thy house; they will be ever praising Thee . . . Great is the Lord and greatly to be praised; and His greatness is unsearchable. One generation shall laud Thy works to another, and shall declare Thy mighty acts.

The door opened and Boris saw the rebbe—short, wide, swollen. His beard, half yellow and half gray, seemed to be growing sideways. His sidelocks had worked themselves loose from their tight curls. On his high forehead lay a flattened cap. The rebbe wore a satin robe, white stockings and slip-on shoes, a fringed ritual garment that hung down to his knees. From under his bushy eyebrows peered a pair of questioning dark eyes that seemed not to recognize anyone.

Boris interrupted his prayers: "Peace be upon you, rebbe!"

The rebbe slowly stretched out a tiny hand. "And peace be upon you, Reb Borukh Makaver!"

"How are you, rebbe? It's already time to recite the afternoon prayers."

"Where is Dvoyrele? We must light the candles."

The rebbe spoke hesitantly, like someone who had just awakened from sleep. Dvoyrele immediately appeared in the doorway.

"Why don't you light the candles in the candelabra?"

"Soon, Father—I'm going to get the matches."

Dvoyrele went out, came back, lit the candles. Then she went out again.

Boris said, "I'm afraid there won't be a minyan for afternoon prayers."

The rebbe made a dismissive gesture. "Well, then we'll pray without a minyan."

2

Although food had been prepared for them in the hotel, the rebbe invited Boris and Frieda to eat the meal celebrating the first night of Rosh Hashanah at his table. The Makavers were the rebbe and Dvoyrele's only guests. Everything was done according to custom. The table was set. Candles burned in the candlesticks. The rebbe and Boris made *Kiddush* and distributed the bread to the women. They ate fine white bread and herring, apples with honey, the head of a carp, carrots. The rebbe, however, hardly touched anything. His daughter and his guests could see that it was very difficult for him to swallow even the prescribed morsel of bread. For a long time everyone sat in silence, Boris next to the rebbe, the women at the other end of the table. Every now and then the rebbe raised his hand to his brow and ran it over his face and beard. Table hymns are not sung on Rosh Hashanah, but very softly the rebbe hummed something that was both a melody and not a melody, half a groan and half the gurgle of a child learning to speak for the first time or of an old man who had said all there was to say. Boris listened attentively to every sound, every murmur, recognizing in the rebbe's muttering snatches of long-forgotten Hasidic melodies that accompanied a variety of liturgical and festival poems of pleading and praise; the sounds spoke without words. It seemed as if the rebbe were arguing: Well, what does it matter? I've lived out my life, have I not? So then, Father in heaven, have I made things any better here? I was probably needed in this world for some purpose—but for what? Where am I going? Who am I leaving behind? What will become of Jews in years to come? How many more Hitlers—may the unthinkable never come to pass—will the Master of the Universe choose to visit upon them? And the Jews themselves are getting worse, not better. So what will have been the purpose? Dear Father in heaven, the task is so burdensome. It grows more burdensome by the moment!

Boris sat in total silence. Not a single word issued from the rebbe's lips, but Boris understood everything with perfect clarity, almost as if he had suddenly been infused with the Divine Spirit. Some time had passed and Boris had already closed his eyes to shut out everything extraneous when the rebbe's sighs and groans abruptly formed themselves into words with which he began to expound the Torah, taking as his text a central statement of the liturgy:

" 'Because of our sins we were exiled from our land.' When the soul is pure, it sees no blemish in the earthly or physical. On the higher levels of spirituality, heaven and earth are one and the same. For the truly righteous man, a stone is as valuable as a sacred book. There is no distinction between the fruit and the blessing one makes over it. Since God is One, everything is one. Our Father Abraham had no need to climb up to heaven. For him, heaven was on this earth. He even set food before the angels. For in truth, everything is spirit: the tent, the sun, the ox, the dust on men's feet. 'And the Lord appeared unto Abraham in the plain of Mamre': in the trees of this earth did the Holy One, Blessed be He, reveal Himself to Abraham. But all this can take place only as long as man is whole, as long as the flesh and the spirit are integrated within him. As soon as a man starts to fall from that level of completeness, he begins to imagine that the earth is solely physical. The wicked man sees commonness, sin, wickedness itself in everything, because he sees only his own likeness. Thus, on account of our sins, we were estranged from the earth, 'we were distanced from our land,' physical and spiritual were sundered within us, and for that reason, 'we are unable to fulfill our obligations,' man cannot do his duty. Even when he desires to do so, he cannot, because everything appears trivial, mundane, obscure. He is filled only with a constant longing to leave this earth and to fly up to heaven.

"But where is the remedy to be found? Only, as it is written, 'in the house the Lord hath chosen for thee.' Man must understand that the Holy One, Blessed be He, has chosen the earth for him, that it is the earth which is 'the great and holy house that is called by His Name.' The earth is one room in a great edifice in the palace of the Almighty. What the Master of the Universe can do above, He can surely also do below, 'because of the hand,' as it is written, 'that was stretched out at Thy holy place.' The Almighty can stretch out His hand as far as he chooses; He can reach from the Throne of Glory right down to New York or even into the grave. This is the explanation of the teaching 'As much as my soul seeketh for Thee, so also doth my body.' Often it seems as if the soul alone aspires to heaven, but it is not so: 'so also doth my body'—the thirst comes from the flesh, from matter, for the physical and the spiritual are one."

As suddenly as he had begun, the rebbe fell silent. He rested his head against the back of his chair. Boris Makaver's eyes were filled with tears through which everything appeared vague, distorted, diffused: the candles in the candlesticks, the crockery on the table, Frieda's face. Dvoyrele rose and went into the kitchen. Boris wiped his face with a handkerchief. He could see from Frieda's expression that she had grasped the meaning of the rebbe's words. Her eyes seemed wider and she blushed like a young bride.

On the second night of Rosh Hashanah Boris once more ate at the rebbe's table, and the rebbe once more expounded the Torah. It was evident that he was sinking by the hour. His voice grew even weaker, and it became ever more difficult for him to swallow. By custom, the rebbe had first claim to the honor of leading the morning prayers, but he was too weak to stand at the lectern and a chair had to be placed there for him. His voice was so soft that even at his side he could hardly be heard. It seemed as if he already found himself in another world and that the sound one heard was not a voice but an echo. Boris chanted the melodies of the liturgy along with the rebbe, and even turned the pages of his prayer book.

As Boris stood there, his whole life seemed to pass in review before him: his childhood, starting with Hebrew elementary school, the musty classrooms, his games with the other boys, Sabbaths, festivals, the oral examinations, his bar mitzvah. At the age of fourteen he had gone away to the yeshiva in Ger, where he had met Shloymele. Together they had eaten the charity meals offered in different homes on different days of the week; they had spent the nights side by side in the study house. Afterward Shloymele had started smuggling in all sorts of secular books, pamphlets, newspapers, and both of them had been spiritually tainted. Shloymele had gone off to study in Berlin and he, Borukh, had become a merchant and made a brilliant match with the daughter of a wealthy family. Then had come his wife's long illness, her death, his own years in Berlin. Still later had come Hitlerism, the flight to France, to Morocco, the desperate pursuit of a visa, the voyage to Cuba, and finally to the United States. Amid all this turmoil had come the heartache with Anna and her unsuccessful marriages. For a moment it seemed to Boris that this had all happened yesterday; then it seemed very far away, almost as if he were not a man in his sixties but an exceptionally ancient one, a second Methuselah. During his years in Berlin he had forgotten about God. He had honored the outward forms of Judaism but had never really pondered their inner significance. He had immersed himself in commerce and in the encyclopedias and empty speculations that Dr. Halperin had provided for him in such abundance. He had become a wealthy patron, a substantial man of affairs, an antiques collector, a seeker after worldly vanity. It had taken coming to New York and enduring everything he had suffered here to become more intimate with Jewishness than before, to re-establish spiritual communion with a zaddik. Only here had the Master of the Universe blessed him with another union and perhaps with a son to recite Kaddish over him. But who could know whether it was not too late? He no longer had his former strength.

Boris recited the liturgy, singing its various melodies, and was astounded. Why did this cascade of words invigorate him so? These prayers were, after all, products of this world, yet they were headier than wine, sweeter than marzipan. Like a tonic, they made the heart stronger. Every phrase was imbued with righteousness and shone with purity and clarity.

Where was Anna now? How was she spending Rosh Hashanah? Did she at least know that this was a High Holy Day? What if, God forbid, the unbelievers were right? the profane thought flashed through his mind. According to them, there was nothing: no God, no World to Come— merely atoms, electrons, blind forces. One was born and one died, to no purpose. Human beings were no better than dust. If they kill you, you're one more of the dead; if they let you live, you crawl around aimlessly.

The murderer has as much right to existence as his victim. All they desired was the rise of another Stalin or some other beast. One should waste away the few years of life allotted to one, do evil, and then die like a dog. But could this be the truth? No, it could not possibly be! Where had the sun come from, the moon, the stars, all living creatures? Nothing could come from nothing. There had to be a higher intelligence, a supreme wisdom over all Creation, and where there was wisdom there had also to be grace. The true wisdom could only be good.

The rebbe began to recite the great prayer for intercession that begins "To the God who ordereth Judgment," and with all his strength Boris Makaver cried out the responses in a voice that echoed across Clymer Street: "To Him who hath compassion on His creatures in the Day of Judgment—who purifieth those who trust in Him in Judgment!"

3

Yasha Kotik arranged to hold the party in his home on the eve of Yom Kippur. Having never heard of the "Yom Kippur Balls" which Jews had organized in America years before, he thought he was doing something original. At first Anna had not wanted to attend—because it was Yom Kippur, because it was to be held in the apartment in which she had lived with Stanislaw Luria, and because Justina Kohn, Kotik's mistress, was helping with the preparations. Anna had vowed that she would not come to his party, but Kotik persuaded her. What did Yom Kippur mean to an unbeliever? It was a night like any other. And what difference did it make where the party took place? Luria was dead, and the dead don't know what the living are doing. A dead man was the same as a dead turkey. As far as Justina Kohn was concerned, Kotik had given Anna his word that he was not having an affair with her. As long as he was on his own, he had to have someone to help him. This Justina was poor, talentless, without a soul in this land, and he could put her to use. If only Anna would marry him, he would send Justina packing. Anna knew Kotik was bluffing: he'd always been an incorrigible liar. But she had her own agenda. Kotik was earning almost a thousand dollars a week, had Hollywood contracts, and, as she knew well, was not tight-fisted. He had promised to give her all his earnings. With that money she would buy stocks or real estate in both their names so that in a few years they would jointly have accumulated a considerable estate. Now that her father had sustained a substantial loss and was about to have other children, she had to make money. All she needed was her first hundred thousand dollars. The rest would follow of its own accord. If things didn't work out with Kotik, he would have to offer her a generous settlement. New York wasn't Berlin. Here they didn't allow wives to be wronged.

Apart from these considerations, she found it easy and pleasant to be with Kotik. He knew everyone on Broadway and they all knew him. The newspapers raved about him. Like Anna herself, he loved staying up late, moving from one nightclub to another. He drank, he chattered, he told uproarious jokes. For all his cynicism, Kotik was attentive to women and knew how to indulge them, whereas, for all his worldliness, Grein remained at heart a Hasid who disliked modern life and modern people, and spoiled everything. In his own way Kotik had a positive outlook on life. Promiscuous himself, he didn't demand chasteness from a woman. He didn't turn ashen when Anna told him about her escapade in Casablanca. She had received a letter from Milan telling her that Cesare, the Italian youth she had known in Morocco, was coming to New York, and Kotik had immediately proposed taking him to dinner and a nightclub. Kotik even reproached Anna for not being freer with his friends. It was no disaster if a man kissed a woman—he wouldn't bite her head off. Kotik even declared that it wasn't a tragedy if a woman slept around a bit, as long as no serious emotional attachment was involved.

"Where have you been all these years?" he rebuked Anna. "Humanity is going forward, not backward. You can't stay tied to your mother's apron strings forever."

Pessimistic by nature, overly earnest in temperament, raised by a fanatical father, always surrounded by sorrowful, afflicted men full of antipathy toward contemporary society, Anna hoped that Kotik would open up a new world, rejuvenate her, introduce her to the modern generation of which she was part. She wasn't old—barely thirty-five, and she looked even younger. She was only just beginning to live. What was there for her to be afraid of? If Kotik wanted to have other women, let him. She would pay him back in the same coin. As long as she was comfortable with him, she'd stay with him; if it became too difficult, she'd get rid of him. Meanwhile, she'd snatch a few years of happiness. Another important factor was that Kotik wanted a child. If Anna was to have a child at all, now was the time. She didn't want to become pregnant late in life like Frieda and put her life at risk. Even now it was a little late.

One thing did trouble Anna—her father. When Papa heard that she was going back to Yasha Kotik, he would go berserk. But what could he do other than curse her and renounce her as his daughter? He'd already done that when she'd gone off with Grein. At least she'd have a rabbi marry her to Kotik. Jewish Law would not label her child a bastard. She would provide her father with what he had always wanted—a grandchild, or "profit," as he called it.

She had heard from Kotik—whom Morris Plotkin had telephoned about it—that Grein had left Leah for Esther, whom he had evidently never stopped loving. Anna realized that theirs was one of those insane love affairs that couldn't be ended. All the time Grein had professed his love for Anna, he had been fooling both her and himself. Their romance had been a lie from beginning to end, not on her part, but on his. He had dragged her into a scandal, had killed poor Luria, and had destroyed his wife and family—all for nothing. How long he would stay with that half-crazy harridan from Brooklyn no one could predict, but one thing was clear: he was finished. He would lose everything: his family, his health, what money he had. The life would be crushed out of him, as often happened when people wove a tangled web only to find that the more they struggled to free themselves, the more tightly they became enmeshed. In her way, Anna still loved him, not the man himself but her memories of him, with something like the love one preserves for a person already in the grave. Some nights she would wake and think of Grein, turning over all she had experienced with him, from the first lesson he had given her when she had been a child to their reunion in New York, their telephone conversations, the evenings in her father's home, their running off together to spend that first night in the dingy hotel on Broadway, the trip to Miami, their moving into the Brodskys' apartment on Fifth Avenue, Luria's death, her sitting out the Seven Days of Mourning, the whole roller-coaster ride right up to the day she had received a letter from him telling her that he was returning to his wife. From start to finish, the affair had lasted not more than eight months, although it seemed like years to Anna. Every day had brought changes, different moods, new complications and dangers. Their days together had been one long crisis: the encounter with Mrs. Katz in the lobby of the hotel in Miami Beach, their meeting the Gombiners in the cafeteria on Lincoln Road, living with that vulgarian Florence Gombiner, their plans to settle in Miami Beach, and then Grein's unhappiness with Anna and his abrupt flight back to New York just after a hurricane.

While it was happening, it had all seemed more or less logical. But when Anna looked back on it, it was like a nightmare or the deranged vision of a person who lived in fantasies and illusions. She had gone off with a man who had given up neither his wife nor his mistress. She had wanted to start new life with him, but the whole time he had wanted only to go back to his old love. As soon as she had walked out the door, he had rushed to the telephone. He had left her alone in a strange apartment to run off to a woman who deserved to be confined in a madhouse, offering her explanations and excuses that a child of ten would never have accepted. He had even made a rendezvous with that Esther woman while Anna had been observing the Seven Days of Mourning. Leah's operation and his seeming penitence were the tragicomic finale. Would anyone have believed all this if it were described in a book? How could one make others understand such a bizarre chain of events?

But Anna was far from being out of her predicament. It was only the beginning of a new chapter. Papa was sick. Frieda might need a cesarean— so Dr. Margolin had said. Anna was returning to a man whose destructive faults and dangerous madness she knew only too well. She was sticking her head into the tiger's mouth, fully aware that she would never be able to pull it out again.

In the middle of the night, Anna started laughing in bed. Her fate amused her.

4

Justina had cautioned Kotik against inviting too many people to his party, but Kotik had asked all his acquaintances, even insisting that they bring their closest friends. At this party Kotik planned to announce that he was going to marry Anna. He now had a great deal of money and was eager to erase the memory of the bad times he had suffered. He did not keep his money in a bank but walked about with his pockets full of paychecks and cash. He had disliked and distrusted banks from the time he had lived through the terrible inflation in Germany. In Russia, of course, he had no money and there were no banks in which to deposit it. Uncle

Sam's banks were absolutely reliable, but Kotik was intensely averse to forms like bankbooks and checkbooks. Besides, he had to be careful about depositing money in a bank if he wanted to evade taxes. He had many suits, and he kept his cash and paychecks in the inside breast pockets of each. He was fond of reaching into his back pocket and pulling out fifty- and one-hundred-dollar bills. He even had a five-hundred-dollar bill hidden somewhere. Anna warned him that he would either lose the money or be robbed, but Kotik answered, "*Nichego*. I've got an angel who watches over me. If it wasn't for that angel, I'd've been pushing up daisies long ago."

The party was supposed to be a buffet supper at which the guests helped themselves, and Kotik had instructed Justina to spare no expense. From a liquor store he had ordered whole cases of whiskey, cognac, gin, vodka, and champagne. Having decided not to do the cooking herself but to order all the food from a caterer, Justina kept needing more and more money, which Kotik kept giving her, even as he laughed to himself. In the old country people used to marry off their daughters for sums like those. He knew that the slut was stealing, but what could he do about it? There would soon be a new lady of the house and then he would fling the trollop out.

Until now, Yasha Kotik had never been much of a drinker, but recently he had taken to liquor with avidity. Wherever you went in New York you were immediately offered a drink. Some people got drunk easily, but he never did. Anyway, when he was slightly tipsy, his work went better. The moment he appeared on stage, there was immediate laughter. A comedian could do as he pleased. Drinking liquor made him jolly and called forth hidden artistic powers. Truth to tell, he was always emotionally drunk in any case; somehow he had been born drunk. He spoke to people without knowing who they were. He babbled all kinds of wild foolishness. But what difference did it make? America was a free country. He often got lost in New York, like a greenhorn, but there were plenty of taxis to take him wherever he wanted to go. He had to ensure only one thing: that every time he stepped on the boards, the public laughed, and thank God, they did. Between acts, famous Americans came backstage, shook his hand, and sang his praises. He responded with whatever came into his head— sometimes graciously, sometimes churlishly. He could even be insulting, and it made no difference—they laughed all the same.

His method consisted of "telling the truth"—and the truth was always comical, frighteningly funny. Most people were ashamed to tell the truth, but Kotik had long ago abandoned all sense of shame. He loved pornographic pictures, for example, and didn't hide the fact; his pockets were crammed with them. A woman would give him her telephone number and he would write it down on one of these lewd cards. If she became embarrassed and protested, he would apologize, give her a suggestive wink, start shaking a leg and behaving like a dog in heat. He spoke only his own argot, half Yiddish, half English, with bits of Russian, Polish, and German, and words that he made up himself.

He was an extraordinarily lucky man, and everyone knew it. He ate all kinds of fat and sweets, yet never gained an ounce. He stayed up night after night, drank, fornicated, yet every time he went to the doctor he received a clean bill of health. The critics could not find enough words to laud him, the public was wildly enthusiastic, the directors fell over themselves to flatter him. He seldom answered mail, though the postman laid whole piles of letters at his door every day. But one couldn't just keep on taking. One had to give something in return. This party had to become the talk of New York.

In the midst of the pandemonium Kotik was making his own calculations. To have an actress for a mistress was one thing, but to marry someone like Justina Kohn was out of the question. He wanted no competition in his own home. He didn't want a woman who waited for press reviews and bitched at the critics. He liked classy women and certainly didn't want to have a child by a whore. Moreover, Anna was practical. From his money she would make more. Her father might have lost a huge sum, but he'd still leave his daughter a handsome inheritance. It was true, the old man loathed Kotik as if he were a cockroach, but if he gave the crabby old bigot a grandchild, he'd come around. Generally speaking, the old forgave the young, just as the poor forgave the rich and the betrayed their betrayers. Now even the Jews would forgive the Germans if they threw them some sop. They had forgiven Stalin everything. That bastard spat in their faces and they thought it was raining. Well, it was getting late. Kotik got out of bed. That night he had slept alone——a new experience for him. At four that morning he had crawled into bed exhausted, and now it was 11:15.

There were still three days before the party, but the apartment was already in chaos. Justina had prepared the buffet table. Wines and brandies were already set out. Someone was due to come and clean the windows. Justina had engaged two black women to help with the work, and they were expected at noon. Well, I'd better hide the dough somewhere, otherwise they'll turn the place upside down looking for it. Kotik wandered about stark naked; he never slept in pajamas. He opened his clothes closet, rummaged through all his breast pockets and trouser pockets, and amassed a substantial bundle of money and checks. Today I must get a safety-deposit box in a bank. He stopped at a window and looked out for a while, musing about sex. He had had all kinds of women in his life—blondes, brunettes, redheads, gray-haired ones; he had even had a fling with a Chinese woman, but strange to say he had never had a black woman. The opportunity had simply never presented itself. Well, that was something to try. If Justina had hired only one, not two, he'd have had a chance. Never mind, there were more where these two came from.

The telephone rang and Kotik answered it. "Hello?"

"Are you up?"

"Yes, Anna. Come over right away."

Anna started telling him something about Solomon Margolin, and he heard her out. She had been to see him and he had confided to her that Lise was in New York and that he was back living with her. Did Kotik remember Lise?

Kotik gave a long whistle. "How could I forget? The woman with the fashion boutique on the Kurfürstendamm."

"Yes. You have a perfect memory."

"But she went off with a Nazi."

"The Nazi died in Russia."

Kotik whistled again. "Well, so he's taken her back, has he?"

"Yes. He lives with her."

"And he preached morality to me, the swine!"

"Yasha, I've invited them to the party."

"What? Will they come?"

"It's quite possible. A woman needs a social circle. She can't always be alone. Papa knows nothing about the whole thing. If he were to find out about it, he'd have nothing more to do with Dr. Margolin. You know Papa's views on such things. I must tell you that when I heard it, I was shocked myself. But since I'm taking you back, nothing amazes me any longer. If someone told me that a woman was going to marry her hangman, I'd believe that, too."

"I'm not a hangman or a Nazi. Have you seen her?"

"Lise? No. But he says she hasn't changed at all."

"Well, let them come. Couldn't he find some woman other than that Nazi? May his filthy guts rot, the pig."

5

All the time Kotik was preparing his party, he had a nagging fear that God would punish him, and a premonition that the night would be a disaster. He regretted that he had chosen the eve of Yom Kippur, but it was too late to change the date. Kotik was astounded: where did this fear come from? Was he getting old?

Kotik was not spending Yom Kippur eve at home but in a hotel room. He had to perform onstage that evening, and he couldn't endure all the bustle in his apartment. Perhaps his aversion stemmed from the time he was still a boy living with his parents in a single room, when Sabbath eves or the eves of festivals had always been a torment. Kotik lay on his bed in the hotel room smoking cigarettes, downing an occasional swig from a bottle of whiskey, and taking a sort of spiritual account of himself. Like most artists, Kotik was religious, even superstitious. He had his own reckoning to make with God, with the higher powers, with the demons. However sinful he was, he had his limits. Sleeping with women was one thing, but destroying a human life was another. In Russia he had guarded against the greatest of all temptations—to inform on people. He had gone to the NKVD only when he suspected they were testing him. In money matters he was clean. He had never stolen. On the contrary, he had always been robbed and cheated himself. His sins had almost all been sins of the flesh, but in this arena Kotik was of the opinion that there was no morality involved. What did God care who lived with whom? And how did it hurt God if an actor traipsed across the stage holding Jews up to ridicule? Didn't actors of other nations make fun of their own brothers? How else was humor possible? Deep inside, Kotik regarded himself as an honorable man. If he did something that went against his convictions, he always tried to redeem himself by giving charity. He had walked through the streets distributing alms. He listened to the grateful thanks of the poor and was certain that God heard what they said and kept a ledger of Yasha Kotik's good deeds.

He did not believe in observing the Sabbath, fasting on Yom Kippur, or eating matzo. In Berlin he had seen Reform rabbis breaking all the Jewish laws. Here in America, rabbis came to see him backstage on Friday nights or during matinees on Saturday, so why should he be more observant than they were? But this party that he was organizing for Yom Kippur eve troubled him. Where was the sense of it? Whom would he be spiting? One could never know. This time it might just occur to God to punish him.

The audience that night was small—half the house was empty. From the stage Kotik could see the vacant seats and felt out of sorts. For the first time in his career, he didn't set the mood onstage and the audience sensed it instantly. The applause was perfunctory. Kotik started delivering his lines, but no one laughed. Getting irritated, he began improvising and trotted out the well-worn comic routines that never failed to provoke hysterical laughter. But this audience preserved a dead and mystical silence. Aha, the punishment is beginning, Kotik warned himself. He was hot and in moments his shirt was sopping with sweat. He started making vulgar gestures and speaking Yiddish directly to the audience—a guaranteed method of getting a laugh—but this was evidently not an audience, only a gang of enemies who had come to gloat over his fiasco. Kotik realized that he had exhausted his whole bag of tricks and would have to struggle through this performance as one struggles through an illness, an operation, a misfortune. By the third act some scattered laughter could be heard, but only from one or two women. The other actors shrugged their shoulders. One of them muttered to Kotik, ''This is how God's punishing you!'' And Kotik nodded in assent.

Broadway was a village, Kotik knew that the news would spread quickly. The gossip columnists had their informers everywhere. Things like this could not be hidden. To go to his party after such a flop—the first in his whole life—and play the role of the grand host was a bitter pill. Kotik now had only one desire—to be alone. But all the members of the acting company had been invited, and they were to go straight from the theater to his home. There was only one way out—for him to get so plastered that he wouldn't give a damn about anything. He had no liquor in his dressing room, however, so he was forced to remain sober at the worst moment of his life. He was sweating profusely, his hands shook, his throat was dry, and he couldn't look the other actors in the face. He no longer even cracked jokes. His tone was serious, his voice changed. Well, this is the end, Kotik decided. What do they call it? The beginning of the end. He'd always known such a day would come. During all the years of his success, failure had been skulking in the shadows. It had been waiting for its chance. Kotik had sensed its presence many times, almost as if an unseen enemy accompanied him everywhere—silent, malevolent, alert, ever prepared to use its strength. Many times Kotik had driven it away angrily, flailing his arms, raising his voice, but it had never vanished completely, merely stepped aside like a mad dog. Moreover, it was not only onstage that the archfiend waited in ambush for him; it also threatened impotence in his sex life. It accompanied him from the stage to his bed.

Now it had achieved what it had always wanted. It no longer kept its distance but had entered him like a dybbuk. It had driven him out and taken his place. How could one make others understand? Kotik asked himself. Only the one who is possessed can understand it. Earlier he had been hot, but now he felt cold.

One of the actors remarked, "Don't despair, Kotik, it happens to us all."

"Yes," Kotik answered, not recognizing his own voice, almost as if the Other were speaking out of his mouth. Kotik was aghast, and he knew that the others were shaken.

In the car, sitting with his fellow actors and actresses, Kotik didn't utter a word. He had nothing to say. The words which lay on his tongue were awkward, and foolish into the bargain. He smoked but could not taste the tobacco. The whole time he felt the need to clear his throat, to cough, to spit up phlegm. He was ashamed to go to his own party, like a small-town bridegroom embarrassed at his wedding. Now he was afraid of Anna, of Justina, of Margolin, of everyone. His silence evidently affected his companions. It was as quiet in the car as if they were on their way to a funeral.

I must snap out of it! I can't let the night turn into a total disaster! Kotik tried to steady himself. If I'm an actor, now's the time for me to show that I can play a role. But he put all his hopes in liquor. I'll drink so much, he promised himself, that the Other will drown.

But even while he was still in the corridor, Kotik had a painful encounter. As soon as he walked out of the elevator, his neighbor Mrs. Katz— the same busybody whom Anna and Grein had encountered in Miami Beach—opened her door. Mrs. Katz attended services on the Days of Awe and was a member of a synagogue. She even had a tiny mezuzah on her doorpost. Throwing a poisonous glance at Kotik and his companions, she said in Yiddish, "A blessed festival to you!"

Instead of answering with a witticism or some small talk as he would normally have done, Kotik kept silent. He stared at her intently, with distaste and distress.

Mrs. Katz pulled a face. "Don't you recognize me?"

"Yes, I recognize you," Kotik responded, but in a voice and tone not his own.

6

In the invitation, which he had composed himself—full of suggestive jokes and sly innuendos—Kotik had indicated that he had a performance on the night of the party, but that this should not prevent his guests from coming early: two beautiful women would stand in for him and ensure that the company felt at home. When Kotik and his fellow performers entered the apartment, the party was already in full swing. The crowd greeted him with shouts, applause, and pleasantries. In full view of everyone, Anna embraced and kissed him. Here they had evidently not yet heard what had happened to him in the theater, so Kotik briefly regained his confidence, but when Anna asked how the performance had gone and how much the audience had laughed, Kotik frowned and replied, "The laughing's over!"

Anna tensed. "What happened?"

"For the Gentiles it's also Yom Kippur."

"Well, don't take it to heart. They'll still laugh and laugh."

"For all I care, they can cry for the same money."

Kotik went over to the drinks table, poured himself a full glass of whiskey, and downed it. Having nibbled a cracker, he drained a glass of cognac. His head became fuzzy at once, but the liquor did nothing to lighten his mood. He took yet another drink.

Anna came up to him. "Why are you drinking so much? Are you trying to drown your sorrows?"

It irked him that she had her eye on him and knew what was bothering him. He wanted to cut her off with a sharp retort, but he didn't say anything at all. Instead, he turned away from her and started weaving his way among his guests. They surrounded him, waiting for him to crack jokes, but he didn't speak; he muttered something and made a gesture of excuse to prevent them from detaining him. He knew that the other actors were reporting tonight's flop to the entire room. He opened the door of the bedroom and saw Justina standing in the dark passionately kissing some man with crinkly hair whom Kotik did not know and certainly had not invited. He felt the color drain from his face. So this is what she does! Justina tore herself away from her beau and, coming rapidly over to him, opened her mouth to say something, but Kotik slammed the door in her face. Enough! I'll fling her out! He was looking for a spot where he could be alone, but people were milling everywhere in groups and in pairs. Since he felt depressed, everyone else looked cheerful and talkative. They drank,

smoked, ate, shrieked. Having evidently grasped that he was in no mood
to be entertaining, they contrived to avoid him. He returned to the drinks
table, but Anna was standing there, playing the perfect hostess and mixing
cocktails for the guests.

When Kotik approached, her face brightened and she remarked,
"You're not going to get drunk, are you?"

"What d'you want? Lemme get a drink," he said, half-pleadingly and
half in anger. He poured himself a glass of vodka and started sipping it,
but he was aware that with every sip he was growing more and more
aggressive. Don't make an ugly scene! he warned himself.

He was eager to cart a bottle away with him, but Anna was watching
from the corner of her eye. Look at that! You can't hide anything! Kotik
was horrified. What kind of actor am I if I can't even conceal my rage?
He took a mouthful of vodka, but he didn't swallow it right away; instead
he rolled the liquid from cheek to cheek like someone trying to deaden a
toothache with alcohol. He wanted to eat some of the many delicacies lying
around—crackers with chopped liver, knishes, butter cookies with herring
marinated in wine, salt crackers with anchovies and egg—but he couldn't
decide what to take. This hesitation dumbfounded him. Was it really worth
pondering such a trivial thing so deeply? Did it make any difference what
he ate? But he still couldn't decide what to take. Am I going mad? he asked
himself. He gathered his strength and with a trembling hand picked up
something that at least he loved to eat: a cracker with Roquefort cheese.

Anna said, "That's too rich for you. Take something else." And she
handed him a plate of crackers with herring roe.

Well, everyone can see I'm finished, Kotik said to himself. I'm wandering aimlessly around like the village idiot. What'll happen now? If I'd
only saved enough money. But I've got nothing.

He suddenly remembered the bundle of bills and checks he had removed
from his pockets before the party. He had intended to put them in a safe-
deposit box, but hadn't done so. Did I hide them somewhere? That slut's
probably lifted them by now! Where did I put them—everything I own!
There was close to five thousand dollars! He started looking around him.
Could I have put them in a drawer? But which one? And none of the
drawers are locked. He wanted to start searching but was ashamed to do
so in front of his guests. Moreover, that in itself might lead to a robbery
if the cash was still there. Where's my head, my memory? Those hired
women have been puttering about all day! I've got nothing, nothing! I can
start begging from door to door tomorrow! He was overcome by hatred

for Justina Kohn. She's a thief! There isn't a worse piece of trash in the whole world! He now regretted ever having been involved with her and had a sudden urge to beat her up, to throw her out bodily in front of everyone. Or perhaps I should report this to the police.

Suddenly he heard Anna calling him. Solomon Margolin had arrived, accompanied by his German woman. Kotik saw them as if through a haze. A hush fell over the gathering. Margolin didn't look like someone who normally went to actors' parties: dressed in a tuxedo, he was the only formally attired guest, looking extremely tall, erect, stiff, immaculate. Lise, the German, wore a long black evening gown cut very low. Anna had told Kotik that Lise hadn't changed, but this was not the Lise he had known in Berlin; this was a middle-aged woman. Kotik went over to receive his guests. He knew he ought to speak German to Lise, but he had forgotten the little he had known. Instead, he bowed, gave Lise his hand, and called out loudly, *"Heil Hitler!"*

As soon as he had uttered these words, Kotik knew he had made a ghastly mistake, but the phrase seemed to have tumbled out involuntarily, almost as if a dybbuk were bellowing from within him. He was seized by a dread of his own coarseness. Anna stifled a scream. The whole crowd fell silent. Solomon Margolin turned white, then red, then white again. Lise hastily snatched back her hand. Kotik wanted to apologize, but neither did he know what to say nor could he remember any German. His face paled. "Ah, I'm drunk," he began mumbling in Yiddish. "I'm completely drunk!"

"Yes, so it seems!" Margolin snapped.

Anna started chattering away to Lise and Margolin, desperately trying to make amends to them, to distract them, and erase the insult. She called over other guests and introduced them to the doctor and his wife. Kotik stood around wordlessly for a while; then he turned away, rushed over to the liquor table, grabbed a bottle, and made his way to the bedroom, stumbling over his own feet. Fiery circles spun before his eyes. Well, I'm kaput! Kaput! he muttered to himself. He wanted to open the door of the bedroom, but someone had apparently propped a heavy chair against it from the inside. Could it be Justina?

Kotik pounded on the door. "Open up, you whore!"

He heard whispering and realized that it wasn't Justina inside but one of the other guests. Mumbling something, he went off to the bathroom, locked himself in, and began drinking from the bottle with the frenzied haste of a chronic drunk, like the derelicts one saw drinking in subway lavatories. As he drank, his head seemed to fill with lead and his legs buckled under him. He recognized that he had never drunk as much as he was drinking now. He wasn't getting drunk—he was committing suicide.

7

Kotik sat on the toilet seat for a long time. His head drooped because he couldn't hold it upright. He had not succeeded in driving away his angst, but the liquor he had poured over it had dampened it. His mind was empty and full at the same time. Something inside him shriveled up in pain, but something in there laughed as well. Well, nothing matters to me any longer! he said to himself. Now they can steal, rob, cheat me as they like! I don't need the critics to praise me anymore! Something inside him babbled away as in a dream. Now he was two Yasha Kotiks: one sober and one drunk, and the sober one comforted the other. What am I afraid of? If I could sleep in the streets of Moscow, I can survive doing the same in New York. People like me are afraid of nothing! He tried to get up and go back to the bedroom because he had to lie down, but his legs wouldn't carry him. The floor swayed beneath him like a ship in a storm. My, that's some drink you've had! said the sober part of him to the drunk part. You certainly put it away! A pretty picture you'll make for your guests. Saying *"Heil Hitler!"* to that Lise woman was insanity. He made a strenuous effort and got up. Clutching the walls, he shuffled his way to the bedroom door, but it was still barred. Suddenly he was overwhelmed by anger. What was this? A brothel? He fell against the door and with the full weight of his body pushed aside the chair that blocked it from within. In the half-darkness he saw a couple start up out of the bed. The man hastily adjusted his clothing. The woman shrieked. The man began to curse Kotik, half in English, half in Yiddish, but although the voice was familiar, Kotik didn't recognize whose it was.

"This isn't a whorehouse!" he snapped.

The couple left the room, and Kotik fell on the bed. He lay there, powerless to move, with the relief of a sick person who has barely managed to drag himself to a resting place. Oh, I never knew that lying down could be such a pleasure! the sober part of him observed. As he lay there, the bed seemed to rock. Well, tonight was my last night on the stage. From now on, I'll be a drunk. I'll drink myself to death—if I'm able to get anything to drink.

For a long time his mind was a blank. He started to doze off with open eyes. He seemed to have become one with the bed, the walls, with the noise that drifted in from the other rooms. Repeatedly someone would open the door, pause in confusion, then close it again. These were guests trying to come in to make love. Pigs, pigs! Kotik said to himself. Can't wait until they can get to a hotel! The door opened again, but this time it was shut from inside, not outside. A woman's form emerged through the darkness. It was Anna. She stood erect and unmoving. Then she said, "Yasha, what's troubling you?"

He wanted to answer her, but he couldn't utter a single word. "Yasha, what's happened?" she asked again.

Kotik's lips started trembling helplessly. "Leave me alone!"

"Yasha, you can't just abandon everyone and lie here! It's a shame and a disgrace!"

He wanted to justify himself, but one needed a great many words for that. Consequently all he could say was: "*Shuddup!*"

"Blind drunk, are you?"

He made no reply. He had only one desire—for her to get out of there as quickly as possible.

"What happened at the theater? Did you go onstage drunk?"

That would've been a better idea, the sober Yasha thought. The drunk Kotik simply croaked: "Go!"

"Yasha, you're killing yourself!" Anna began. "You say you love me, but is this the way you show it? Everyone's laughing behind our backs. I'm ashamed to show my face."

"Go home!"

"All right, I'll go. Only remember, this is the last time I'll ever speak to you again. I barely managed to persuade the Margolins to come here, and how did you receive them? I didn't know you were such a drunk. Well, I ought to have known. You taught me a good lesson the first time around."

"Go! Get out!"

"Well, good night. Don't ever dare to call me again. Now I'm cured! Cured! Even madness has a limit. You're ruining yourself, but that's your tragedy!" And Anna went out and shut the door.

Let her go to hell! the sober Yasha said. I don't need her! I don't need her! I don't want to make people laugh anymore. How long must I go on being a clown? There's nothing to laugh about. One ought to cry instead. It's better to be a bum on the Bowery. I'll collect relief checks from Uncle Sam. Many times I've wanted to run off the stage. One can't be a comedian forever. Enough! I'm breaking all my contracts. Yasha Kotik is bankrupt! He closed his eyes and lay half asleep, half awake. He heard talking, but, like a child eavesdropping on adults, he couldn't distinguish the words. He seemed to sink into himself. The door kept opening. People came in to look at him, to speak to him, but he had cut off all contact between himself and the outside world. His intestines rumbled and sloshed. Strong vapors rose from his stomach to his brain and his mind grew ever fuzzier as he hesitated, powerless, in the darkness. Who knows? Perhaps this is the end already. Perhaps I've drunk myself to death. And he answered himself: Well, so what? It's better this way!

He had apparently fallen asleep. He opened his eyes and everything was quiet. For a long time he could remember nothing. Then he recalled that there had been a party. The blind had been lowered over the window, but around the edges dawn was already seeping in. Kotik was aware of a dull pain in his head, a heaviness in all his limbs, but the few hours of sleep had sobered him up—not completely, but for a while. He was like a dangerously ill person who wakes in the middle of his sickness and for a time reasons as clearly as a healthy man. Well, all was lost—the theater, Anna. What would his guests think? They would make a laughingstock of him. But think back: what horrible disaster had actually taken place? In what louse-infested book of laws was it written that Yasha Kotik was not permitted to get drunk or even to fail once in a blue moon? At that moment Kotik remembered that it was Yom Kippur. He lay still as though paralyzed. Yes, this was the punishment! God was beginning to show His might. All through his life, Kotik had been secretly afraid of Him and His vengeance. He had been aware of how God lowered at him from heaven and postponed, deferred, held back the day of retribution. A schoolboy explanation hovered on his tongue: God is slow to anger and full of loving-kindness.

25

After Rosh Hashanah Grein and Esther left Pittsfield, Massachusetts, for a small town in New Hampshire where they made the acquaintance of a Mrs. Smythe. She and her present husband—the fourth—lived in the valley outside town with his daughter and son-in-law and had a farm on a nearby mountainside. But stepmother and stepdaughter were continually at loggerheads, so Mrs. Smythe had opened a small real-estate business. Of French extraction, Mrs. Smythe was one of those American women who, however much they drift from one small town to the next, put up with boorish husbands, and do all kinds of heavy labor, nevertheless read newspapers and books, play bridge, and have the intelligence and energy of big-city women. Grein had come to her seeking a room, and she soon got to talking with him. As is often the case with taciturn and solitary people, Grein was able to strike up acquaintanceships more quickly than any extrovert. Seeing in her face that this woman had an instinctive understanding of human predicaments, he almost immediately confided to her that he was looking for a place where he and his companion could lock themselves away or be alone together. Mrs. Smythe nodded at once and remarked, "I've also been looking for such a place for many years. That's why I went off to a farm on a mountain."

She and Esther liked each other immediately, and Mrs. Smythe soon had a proposal. In Maine, not far from Bethel, there was a farm for sale: not the sort from which one could make money—"Certainly not someone like yourself, Mr. Grein"—but ideal for people who wanted to get away.

Comprising seventy acres of land, this farm had an old house, all sorts of workshops, barns, and outbuildings, not to mention orchards and a well. Coal- or wood-burning stoves supplied heat in the winter, and there was space for a garden and enough grassland to keep a few cows. A tenant farmer could easily be found for the lot behind the main house. The farm's chief merit was its beauty, and while the place would cost twenty-five hundred dollars, they would need to make only a thousand-dollar down payment on it. What could he lose? If he and his friend liked the idea, she would drive them out there in her car, since the place was only an hour and a half away.

Grein agreed at once, and during the drive Mrs. Smythe recounted the history of the farm. It had belonged to an elderly bachelor, a recluse who had lived there with only an Indian servant—who worked like a slave, virtually supporting his employer who, during his last years, had been ill and bedridden. The Indian cultivated the garden and the orchard, milked the cows, tended the fowl, and in addition rubbed turpentine into the old man's hair, gave him massages, bathed and groomed him. Everyone had expected the childless owner to bequeath the farm to the Indian, but he had died without a will, so the farm had passed to his niece, the wife of a physician, and the Indian had disappeared without a trace. Everything on the farm had been left as it had been—the furniture, the books, the crockery and cutlery—so one could move in immediately. Mrs. Lockyer, the doctor's wife, had sold the cows, but since the barn was still standing, Grein could buy a young cow and rear its calves, an activity that demanded no work at all. If it was true what he said—that he needed only potatoes with milk and a book—he would have it all without the slightest effort.

Mrs. Smythe talked fast and drove fast. It was already the beginning of October, but the day was as warm as if it were the middle of July. Meadows and farms reminiscent of Poland stretched out on both sides of the road, while the country smells brought to mind the manure ever-present in Polish villages. Even the cloud formations were European. Here and there in front of the houses stood piles of chopped wood ready for the winter, while geese and ducks swam in shallow ponds. God in heaven! In all the years Grein had struggled in New York, he had forgotten the unspoiled world of nature God had created. Even when he had taken summer vacations in the country, he had always stayed in hotels. Here, in this spacious state of Maine, an old, familiar small-town atmosphere had been preserved intact. Here one could forget about civilization and its complications. In the autumn morning the farm looked like the Garden of Eden. To be sure, the house was old, the furniture brittle and warped, the carpets worn and faded, the floorboards cracked and broken in places, but what did he and Esther need luxury for? The library immediately commanded his attention. It was obvious that the elderly recluse had been a serious reader and a devout Christian, for his shelves were crowded with scientific works, now mostly outdated, and a great many books about religion. The ground was hard and full of rocks, but all kinds of wildflowers grew in it, and the orchard was strewn with small apples that had fallen from the trees. Flocks of birds still chirped and whistled, and Mrs. Smythe reported that deer and other animals often strayed here. Grein would have to keep a rifle.

When she saw the farm, Esther began laughing and dancing, crying out with joy: "Dear Lord! I've dreamed about this all my life!"

Grein himself could hardly believe that he could possess all this for two and a half thousand dollars, but he remembered having read about such bargains. Ground that yielded no profit had no value on the market. Mrs. Smythe apparently had a twinge of conscience, because she added: "Well, folks, I won't deceive you. In winter a farm like this can seem desolate. When it snows, you're alone in the wilderness. But there's electricity and you can reinstall the telephone. You need a car, of course. The next town is thirty-five miles away."

"I can't understand why you didn't bring your car," Esther said to Grein.

"I left it for Leah."

"You can buy a secondhand car," Mrs. Smythe interjected. "For two hundred dollars you can even have mine. If you take care of it, you can still get a good five years out of it."

Everything was settled in a single day. Mrs. Smythe drove Grein and Esther over to the owner, Mrs. Lockyer, and Grein gave her a check for a thousand dollars. Title to the farm and everything on it was transferred to Grein on the understanding that he was to pay off the remaining fifteen hundred dollars over ten years. Grein also bought Mrs. Smythe's Ford, so that she had to borrow a car from Mrs. Lockyer.

He and Esther sat chatting with the two countrywomen until the day passed and dusk came on. Then at a grocery store Grein bought bread, cheese, apples, oranges, and many cans of vegetables, soups, and fruit juices, returning to the farm with the feeling of someone who has taken a major step, yet doesn't believe himself that he has.

2

The twilight glimmered far longer here than it did in New York. As the windows grew steadily bluer, the stillness outside thrummed and vibrated. A solitary fly buzzed against a windowpane. They had not yet switched on the electric lights, and although Grein had bought candles at the shop, he was in no hurry to light them. Esther lay on the sofa, Grein sat in an old armchair. The sun had already set, but the dusk still lingered, a smoldering red and purple. The farmhouse stood near a road, but hours went by without the sound of a passing car. Esther was unusually quiet, while Grein mused to himself. He was struck forcefully by a verse from Psalms: "Here will I dwell, for I have desired it." This is it, he murmured. This is where I'll stay! There must be an end to my wandering.

It was two days before Yom Kippur. He had packed a small Bible in his suitcase—where did all our prayers come from, if not from here? He had fasted every year, and this year would be no exception. If God heard the prayers of people at all, He would hear them from this isolated spot. Among the books left by the former owner, Grein found *The Life of Saint Teresa,* and now he read it. How similar all religious people were! Everything was the same: the feeling of guilt, the humility before God, the dread of sin, the capacity to see God in every object, every thought. But how could he compare himself to this woman? She merely spoke of sins, but he had actively committed them. Even settling up here was what the Catholics called being in a state of "mortal sin," since he was living with another man's wife. But when a man falls victim to a passion from which he cannot free himself, isn't this in itself a godly thing? There evidently existed a limit to human freedom of choice.

He was ready to live out his days here with Esther. But Esther's moods changed from moment to moment. Did she have regrets? Grein was prepared for that, too. If Esther were to leave him, he would live without her. He had no desire to go anywhere else. He had failed in his relationships with people, and that meant that he had to be alone. Apparently there existed souls for which being alone was the greatest good. Again he remembered Jeremiah's lament: "He sitteth alone and keepeth silence because he hath borne it upon him." Solitude was his destiny, his fate. Abruptly there was a rustling outside as if someone were walking, but silence soon descended again. A half-moon rose in the sky and the first stars appeared. He had fled from New York, but the cosmos had accompanied him here. He glanced at Esther, swathed in shadows on the old sofa. Although he could not see her eyes, he sensed they were smiling.

"Esther, this is our own cloister," he said.

"Yes, you always said that you envied monks."

"Why shouldn't there be a cloister for a monk and a nun together?"

"Yes, there can be everything."

He wondered at Esther's laconic answers. Usually she spoke in long monologues. What had taken place had stunned both of them. It was a bizarre tangle: eloping on impulse and at the last moment, stumbling to New Hampshire, settling into this half ruin, far away from people and lacking all communication with the outside world. He had read about similar cases in books—about couples who had settled in Alaska, in the jungles of South America, or in the forests of British Columbia. But they were Gentiles, not Jews—people who loved hunting and fishing and who had inherited the pioneering spirit from generations of their forebears. Jewish businessmen did not abandon their families and sources of income to wander off into the jungle. And indeed, for both of them—for Esther as much as for Grein—a deserted farm in Maine was the equivalent of a hut in the primeval jungles of Brazil.

One thing was clear—he wouldn't be able to sit around here without an occupation of some kind. He'd have to work. Work was the only justification for leading this kind of life. But what could he do? Become a farmer? Find some hobby? Get busy on the book he had once wanted to write? No, a book was now an even remoter possibility than ever. He had nothing to say to humankind. His experience was an exclusively private matter. No one could learn anything from him. In reality, every philosopher had created his philosophy solely for himself. The principle of individuality was so strong that the thoughts that suited one person suited no one else. Nietzsche's philosophy was crafted solely for Nietzsche, as Schopenhauer's was for Schopenhauer and Spinoza's for Spinoza. When the same thought occurred to two people, it became two separate thoughts. How had Leibniz put it? Monads lacked windows. How could one being possibly see into another? True knowledge was available only to God, the being that Leibniz called the monad of all monads.

Night fell. Esther lit the candles and started bustling about—supper had to be prepared. In the bedroom was a pillow, a blanket, and some yellowing linen. The dust had to be swept out, the rooms aired, provision made for two people to subsist. How dimly the candles glimmered in these old rooms! It was difficult to believe that candlelight had once been the general form of household illumination. In this faint gleam everything looked mystical, insubstantial, isolated in immemorial seclusion. Esther's shadow fell across the walls, the ceiling. A cricket chirped, not a field cricket but the familiar domestic variety they often heard behind the stove in the old country. Grein still sat, seeming to listen to the silence within himself. Something inside him was thinking without words. This particular evening became intertwined with the many evenings he had spent as a child with his parents on Smocza Street in Warsaw. The cricket was singing the same tune now as it had then, a haunting refrain one could neither articulate nor describe. One could only listen, and what one heard was an assurance that everything was in its place: God, Providence, punishment for sin, reward for virtue, death, resurrection, transmigration of souls, spirits, and—presiding over everything—a divine eternity. To Grein it seemed as if the cricket was saying, Don't be so troubled, there is a role for you. You are a part of the plan, a part of the history of the cosmos. An Eye exists that looks down on you and sees all your misfortune, all your sorrow, all your confusion. Grein remembered the evening prayers and the recitation of the *Shema*, and he had an urge to pray. He started to murmur an entreaty for Leah.

26

The night following the end of Yom Kippur, Yasha Kotik went onstage certain that this was the last time he would ever do so. He had promised himself that if the public did not laugh at this performance, he would act no more. But the audience roared with laughter as they always had. During the day he had discovered the money and checks he had stuffed in a drawer the day before. God, it appeared, had no imminent plans to liquidate Yasha Kotik; He had simply given him a warning.

Anna came to the theater, having forgiven him everything: his foul mood, his getting drunk, and his insult to Solomon Margolin's German wife. She and Kotik agreed to go to City Hall the very next day and take out a marriage license. Anna had decided to keep this arrangement from her father as long as possible, for fear the news would cause him another heart attack. After the performance, instead of going to the apartment on Fifth Avenue that Grein had rented for her from the Brodskys, Anna went back with Kotik to her former home on Lexington Avenue, from which Justina Kohn had been permanently expelled. Anna had seen to it that everything was cleared away after the party. All that remained was a table crowded with full and half-full bottles of liquor and a pile of unopened parcels—gifts from the guests. Although the two servants had spent the whole day cleaning up, there were still cigarette ashes in odd places, and someone had burned a hole in the sofa. During the same twenty-four hours, Kotik had acquired dark blue circles under his eyes and the creases around his mouth had deepened, but Anna had made arrangements for him to go on vacation and rest. Luria was dead, and Grein was as good as dead. Her father had a wife who was preparing to go into labor any day.

Yasha Kotik was now her only support. Anna had made up her mind to have no sexual relations with him until they were legally married, but after all, he had once been her husband. She undressed and lay down in the same bed she had occupied when she had been Mrs. Luria. Alongside in a second bed lay Kotik, too exhausted to come to her. They switched off the night-light and lay in their separate beds like an old married couple. Kotik briefly muttered something, then fell into a deep sleep in which, as he always had, he breathed in a way unlike anyone else. He would inhale with a snort and remain silent for a long time, snuffle again, and then fall silent once more, almost as if he were experimenting with the activity of sleeping. Covering herself with the blanket, Anna was aware that she ought to feel agitated, but she was overcome by a rare sense of indifference. Now she was no longer afraid of anything. Regrets? Let Grein have regrets. Even the possibility that Papa might have another coronary and die did not seem so terrible to her now. He was no longer a young man and had already lived his life and, in any case, what could she do? She was not in control even of her own life. Some destiny was being worked out for her. Apparently there existed powers that amuse themselves by playing games with human beings and making fools of them.

Anna fell asleep and dreamed about Stanislaw Luria. He appeared on a narrow street somewhere, wearing a fur coat and huge galoshes. His face was yellow, and around his ears hung tufts that looked like sidelocks made of straw. What could this be? Anna wondered. Has he become observant in the other world? He approached her and said, *"Mazel tov!"* At the same time he laughed, revealing a toothless, decaying mouth from which issued an unearthly stench.

Anna trembled and started awake. The overpowering fetor lingered for a while in her nostrils. It was only a dream, nothing more, she consoled herself. Over there one didn't wear straw sidelocks and one didn't congratulate one's own widow. Although she had plenty of covers, she felt cold. She listened for a sound from Kotik, but could not hear him breathing. Perhaps he had died, it occurred to her, and immediately she became aware that all her thoughts were revolving around death. But why? She was still a young woman.

Mentally she started speaking to Grein, as though certain that she would reach him telepathically. Well, are you happy now? she asked him. Now that you've got your Esther. Why did you ever leave her if you love her

so much? What are you doing now? Are you sleeping? Are you awake?
You know I bear you no grudge. You turned my life upside down, but it
was upside down in any case. I don't even have any regrets. One never
seems to have any regrets about love. I don't even regret what I did with
Cesare. I regret nothing and expect nothing. All I want is a little rest.

Kotik suddenly stirred. "Aren't you sleeping?"

"I've just woken up."

"I've been dreaming about your husband," Kotik called out after some
hesitation.

Anna tensed and grew alert. "What did you dream?"

"I don't know. I can't remember. He congratulated me, and wanted
to hit me."

Anna's skull seemed to tighten. "Congratulated?"

"Yes, he said *'Mazel tov!'* "

She said nothing more and Kotik went back to sleep, but Anna did not
shut her eyes for the rest of the night. The blackness steadily lightened
into gray, and a while later the sun came up, turning the room blood-red
and reminding Anna of that other early morning when she had vowed to
her father that she would stay with Luria. How long ago had that been?
Less than a year. No more than ten months. But now it seemed amazingly
far away. At that time, if someone had foretold that in ten months she
would be in the same bedroom with Yasha Kotik lying in the next bed,
she would not have believed it. If that was possible, it might even be that
there was indeed a World to Come and that Luria was genuinely congrat-
ulating her. Everything was possible: the most impossible things were
possible.

Although it was only the beginning of October, it was cold outside and
Anna felt chilly under the blanket. Keeping one eye shut, she watched
Kotik with the other. His face seemed to be dripping with blood, and he
was frowning strangely, as though straining to see something in his sleep.
A crooked furrow slashed his forehead, and the corners of his eyes were
creased with wrinkles. Overnight his beard had sprouted, and white
patches were visible here and there. For some reason he reminded Anna
of a murder victim. This was probably the way the Jews Hitler had destroyed had looked. Into her mind flashed a report she had read in a Yiddish
newspaper describing the great number of Jews whom the Romanian Nazis
had driven into a slaughterhouse and butchered there. Yes, such savagery
had been perpetrated in this world, and whatever the future might bring,

the record of these events would remain in perpetuity. No power could ever erase the appalling disgrace—not even God.

Anna turned over and covered her face with the sheet. She had to sleep! What was left for her but a snatch of sleep?

2

Since the superintendent of Boris Makaver's building would not permit a sukkah booth to be erected on the roof, and Boris did not have a balcony, he decided to spend the eight days of the Feast of Tabernacles with the rebbe. In his tiny courtyard the rebbe had a ramshackle sukkah knocked together from planks, one of its walls formed from rusty pieces of corrugated iron and its doorway hung with a sheet. But what difference did it make? The booth was made according to the specifications of the Law. Dvoyrele, the rebbe's daughter, had draped the interior with a blanket and a floral shawl, and had hung bunches of grapes on the red fir branches of the open sukkah roof.

The first night of the festival was chilly and it even looked as though it might rain, but after evening prayers the sky cleared. Dvoyrele covered the table with a cloth and recited the blessing before she lit the candles in new glass candlesticks—the silver ones had been lost to the Nazis. The rebbe made the blessing over the wine using a small glass which shook so violently in his hand that the wine spilled. From a neighboring courtyard a radio blared, while somewhere else a dog barked. In a hoarse voice the rebbe intoned the invocation: "Blessed art Thou, O Lord our God, who has chosen and exalted us above all nations, and hast sanctified us with Thy commandments."

Boris's great black eyes filled with tears. Solomon Margolin had examined the X-rays of the rebbe's intestines and had given the sick old man not more than three months to live, perhaps even less. From the medical point of view, the rebbe was all but a corpse. But, then, wasn't everyone a potential corpse? Boris mused. How long would he continue to wander about in this world himself? But before he left, he would become a father once more. Frieda's belly grew higher and more pointed almost by the hour. Now, exactly like Dvoyrele, she recited the blessing over the candles in the sukkah and stood in the doorway waiting for Boris to complete the inauguration of the festival by reciting the blessing over the wine himself.

The rebbe ate virtually nothing, merely chewed for a long time with his toothless gums at his morsel of challah, tasted a sliver of fish and half a spoon of chicken soup, and constantly trembled as though quaking with the fear of heaven. It was obvious to Boris that the man was already in the higher worlds; he seemed to embody the cry of the psalms: "All my bones shall say, Lord, who is like unto Thee?" Every one of his limbs seemed to quiver with a different palpitation. His head shook from side to side as if he were saying, I had not expected this. Every now and then his shoulders shrugged as though he were asking, Where can one hide from so great a holiness? His hands twitched as though they were repeatedly attempting to latch on to something but did not dare to do so. His eyes, in which severity was mixed with dread, glanced around surreptitiously, as though the rebbe were mortally afraid of the forms that surrounded him. Undoubtedly they are all here, Boris reflected, the shades of the Seven Faithful Shepherds traditionally invited to be present in the sukkah during the Feast of Tabernacles—Abraham, Isaac, Jacob, Joseph, Moses, Aaron, and David. The rebbe could probably see them. They were revealing the secrets of the Torah to him. So great a trembling comes not from the body but from the soul.

"Rebbe, have a little more soup," Boris entreated.

The rebbe made no reply.

"It's cleared up a little," Boris remarked, glancing through the fir branches.

The rebbe tried to look up at the sky, but he could not raise his head. Involuntarily his body kept sinking downward and he was compelled to expend what little strength he had in the effort to remain upright. His eyelids drooped and he struggled to keep his eyes open. He spoke so softly that Boris had to strain to hear what he said.

"How is Khanele?" he asked suddenly.

For a moment Boris froze. "Who knows? I have no idea nowadays."

"What happened to the other man?" the rebbe asked in a clear voice, almost that of a healthy person.

Boris frowned. "Ah, Rebbe, besides being offenders against Israel, such people are completely insane."

"In what way?"

Boris began recounting Anna's entire affair with Grein, hesitating over every sentence, but the rebbe made a gesture indicating that he wanted to hear it all. Boris knew that on the eve of Rosh Hashanah Grein had left his wife and eloped with Esther, and he mentioned this as well.

The rebbe clutched his beard. "Where did he run off to?"

"Only the Devil knows about his own!"

"Tut!" interjected the rebbe, indicating that there was no need to curse.

"What's the sense of it? Running from one to another like a farmyard rooster."

The rebbe threw Boris a sidelong glance, signifying that he did not approve of these words either.

"What does such madness produce?" Boris demanded, raising his voice slightly.

"Passion exists," the rebbe managed to say.

"Even passion must make some sense."

"Well . . ."

Boris waited for the rebbe to say something more about it, but the sick old man did not refer to the matter again. He fell silent and his head shook more and more vigorously, as if in denial, as if the story Boris had recounted had intensified his fear of God, as if he were saying: If one can bind oneself so closely to a creature of flesh and blood, how much more closely ought one to bind oneself to the Creator of the universe. Boris opened a prayer book. Where was Anna on this holy day? Where was she wandering, poor child? Did she yearn for Grein? Or had she already found someone else? He remembered Yasha Kotik. That mongrel had led her astray. Had it not been for him, she would have been the mother of children by now and her head would not have been filled with all this folly. In Berlin he should never have permitted her to marry that depraved scum, may his memory be erased! But what else could he have done? She had threatened to commit suicide. People in such situations are capable of anything.

As Dvoyrele brought in meat and vegetables with sweet carrots, Boris glanced at her. She too had once had a husband who had perished at the hands of the Nazis. She had been a widow for years, and it seemed never to have occurred to her to marry again. She had sacrificed herself for her father. She was a granddaughter of the holy Reb Yechezkel, the Zhiritsover rebbe. Saints had coupled with righteous women so that now she could carry plates into the sukkah. Boris was overwhelmed by a feeling of love and compassion for Dvoyrele. How was it possible that I didn't think of courting her myself? Boris asked himself. It never entered my head. If something is not destined to happen, one doesn't give it a thought.

"Why haven't you eaten the meat?" Dvoyrele asked her father.

"The chicken was enough for me."

"Beef gives you more strength," Dvoyrele said, half in earnest, half in jest. Her smile was a blend of resignation and refined mockery, while her eyes said, By now it's all the same to me. I'm only saying so in order not to keep silent all the time.

3

In the middle of October, Zadok Halperin's book appeared in print. As soon as he received the first copy, he locked himself in his room with it. He leafed through it with trembling fingers, then he started to read, smoking, snorting, and grunting as he did so. His whiskers quivered. He knotted his bushy eyebrows. The longer he read, the more clearly he perceived the catastrophe that had struck his life's work. Without his knowledge, the publisher had cut whole chunks out of it, and cut them in the very place where the work's central thought had been expressed. Although Halperin himself had proofread the whole book twice, many errors had slipped through—not simply typographical errors but also inaccurate quotations and a variety of glaring lapses which would provoke the ridicule of the learned. Only now did he realize the translation was bad and often untrue to his meaning. This was not the work of a scholar but a heap of garbage. Every now and then Halperin cried out, "It's chaos! Chaos!"

He was cold, yet he was sweating and felt a hollow sinking feeling around his heart. Instead of producing a book that would revolutionize philosophy, he had served up a batch of unconnected fragments badly translated and riddled with errors. Even the cover was cheap, like that of a sensational novel, and in the short biographical sketch that appeared on it they had added six years to his age and presented him as an old man of seventy-six.

For a brief while Halperin had a desperate desire to pick up the telephone and curse out the publisher as an incompetent. But what would cursing accomplish? The damage could not be repaired. This was like cutting someone's throat—however much the victim might writhe and wheeze for air, there was no getting around his being murdered.

Well, it's a mercy on me, a mercy, Halperin told himself. This is New York, not Bern or Zurich. You can't make a silk purse out of a sow's ear. All I'll get for my swearing is heartache and indignity. After all, what does Ecclesiastes say? "What profit hath he that hath labored for the wind."

Halperin seized the book and flung it across the room. It fell open to the floor, face downward, and lay in a corner, a stack of paper and ink, a collection of molecules and atoms that pursued their own existence without the vaguest notion that they were supposed to represent a radically new philosophical system. Halperin wanted to be rid of this monstrosity, but how? Should he fling it out the window? Should he throw it into the trash can? One of the neighbors might fish it out. Slowly he lowered his head, and everything within him silently grieved. He suddenly perceived his mistake, where his life and thought had gone wrong. He had premised everything on this world, on people, on human fallibility. What did his philosophy amount to but a justification of hedonism, a belief that human beings could, if they chose, reach the truth through luck, through crowding the greatest variety of experiences into the shortest possible time, through taking advantage of the manifold opportunities offered by their intelligence, their five senses, their relationships with their fellow beings? How often Professor Shrage had argued with him, protesting in the words of the psalms: "Place not thy confidence in man"? But in what, then, *could* one place one's confidence? In the gods those same human beings had invented for themselves? In that case, one could have no confidence at all. Then the world belonged to Hitlers and Stalins, not to thinkers and philosophers. The best he might have hoped for was to make a name for himself in the history of philosophy, a name known to other bookish people. The world would have remained exactly the same.

Dr. Halperin lit a cigar, but as soon as he had taken the first puff he broke into a fit of coughing. The smoke was as bitter as gall and tore at his windpipe, leaving him wheezing and gasping. Grabbing the cigar, he carried it into the bathroom, where he flushed it down the toilet. If only one could do that with all of human culture! he thought. If only there existed toilets into which one could fling whole civilizations! Well, Nature takes care of it in any case. She wipes everything out, erases everything, turns everything into mud and slime. What's more, she does it slowly, by degrees. She has plenty of time. And what about that cigar? Where is it now? It's lying somewhere in the sewer. It'll never be a cigar again. In

fact, it was never really, wholly, independently a cigar either—it derived
its identity exclusively from its place in the existence around it.

Zadok Halperin bent down. He had a sudden urge to vomit. Sour fluid
rushed up from his stomach and filled his mouth. There was no possibility
of correcting anything now, not even the date of his birth. Anyway, what
difference did it make to anyone how old he was? He existed for no one.
Frieda was pregnant: she'd soon give birth and bring a new human creature
into the world. With his ships Boris Makaver had crawled into a morass
from which had he barely extricated himself. Solomon Margolin had always
despised him. Professor Shrage was senile. "Well, it's time I died," Halperin announced loudly. I've had enough of the whole stinking mess. Something'll probably soon come my way—a heart attack or a fatal disease. If
Shrage is right and there is a World to Come and all the rest of it, then
I'd better have a look at that rubbish. And if it doesn't exist, then it's
simply time to wave goodbye.

The telephone rang, but Halperin didn't want to answer it. Who could
be calling and what could they possibly want? "I'm not at home!" he
shouted into the air. The copy of his book lying crumpled in the corner
now caused him physical pain, pressing his heart, constricting his throat,
pinching his belly, yet it also filled him with laughter. Well, that was my
last card. I played it and lost. Fate didn't want Zadok Halperin to achieve
fame and glory before he died. Had he deserved this comedown, then?
What good had he done for others? And if he had done good, would anyone
have owed him anything?

Now Halperin vividly recalled the Hitler massacres, the Stalinist purges
and liquidations. Before his eyes, human beasts had subjected some twenty
million people to unimaginably sadistic tortures and feral carnage while he,
Zadok Halperin, had been possessed by only one desire: to achieve worldly
honor, to read his praises in the newspapers and the journals, to be re-
spected as an intellectual giant. Well, the powers that governed this
world—or blind chance—had determined otherwise: he had no more right
to personal distinction than any of those others.

The telephone stopped ringing, and fully dressed, Halperin lay down
on his bed. He remembered once reading about Africans and Hindus who
make up their minds to die, and merciful death comes to them right away.
Could this be true? Could a human being die simply because he willed it?
If that were possible, then he wanted the end to come just like that.

He closed his eyes and listened attentively. Yes, come, death, come, he
urged in his thoughts. If you're a thing of substance, show your ugly mug!

The telephone rang once again. Who in living hell could possibly be calling? What more do they want of me? He rose and grabbed the receiver. "Hello!"

It was his publisher. "Dr. Halperin, I've got good news for you!"

Halperin made no reply.

"Can you hear me?"

"What's your news?"

The publisher babbled brightly on about some professor or other who hadn't slept the whole night because he had been so absorbed by Halperin's book. He was writing an enthusiastic review for a distinguished journal, the name of which the publisher cited with quivering awe. The publisher himself was arranging for a major book club to distribute Dr. Halperin's book in tens of thousands of copies. The negotiations were as good as finalized. All that was needed was a go-ahead from the club's chief executive.

Dr. Halperin heard, but the words brought him no joy. Instead, he snapped tersely, "The chief executive will refuse!"

27

Professor Shrage lay ill in bed. He had caught a chill and could not shake it off. He had diarrhea, his throat was inflamed, sharp pains stabbed him in the groin and behind his knees, and an abscess was ripening in his ear. He had asked Mrs. Clark to call a doctor, but she had ignored him.

How low can a person sink? she asked herself indignantly. Evidently he's lost all faith in the higher powers.

After she had recovered from her own crushing despair when Edwin passed over, she had repudiated doctors, and with the power of will and prayer had reconstructed organs and glands for herself, had filled her arteries with fresh blood and her bones with new marrow. Since everything was spirit, how could a physician who dealt exclusively with matter be of any possible assistance? Mrs. Clark had preferred to telephone a friend of hers, a certain Mrs. Bailey, to ask her to pray for the professor. Shortly afterward Mrs. Bailey called back to say that although she had prayed, she had the disturbing feeling that her orisons had met with resistance. The sick man himself had obstructed them. Moreover, Mrs. Bailey intimated that the professor had fulfilled his mission here on earth and that the Masters needed him Above. Although she did not say this explicitly, but veiled her meaning in all sorts of theosophical phrases, Mrs. Clark understood and trembled with fear. She knew that Mrs. Bailey was not speaking lightly. She had Contacts. She played a major role in the Hierarchy herself. The professor had to cross the threshold between Here and There.

Deeply as Mrs. Clark believed that no such thing as death existed, and that what the common herd called death was nothing more than an illusion—a crossing from one level to another, from one sphere of activity to a second—she was nevertheless overpowered by dread. Not only was the professor unprepared for this Crossing, but she was unwilling for it to take place now. He, poor man, had recently sunk into doubt. His faith had evaporated. He had let slip words better suited to a materialist. Besides, she had grown accustomed to him. For all his caprices and moods, it was good to come home in the evening, after standing the whole day at her dentist's chair, and find him there. However much he had yielded to skepticism, he was still Professor David Shrage. More than once she had seen an aureole around his head. Shafts of light radiated from his eyes. Inanimate objects seemed to come to life in his presence. During the periods when he temporarily forgot his doubts and ignored the parasites that had little by little devoured him, he was filled with heavenly goodness and harmony. Now, if he were to cross over to a Higher Sphere, who could know whether he would communicate with her? He might very well return to his first wife, that Edzhe for whom he had never stopped longing. She would be left to spend her last years alone.

Mrs. Clark could not free herself from the duties of her practice. Patients had made appointments weeks in advance. Furthermore, she had financial obligations, debts. She supported a number of institutions and had arranged for her sculptures to be cast in bronze, an enormously costly undertaking. But leaving the professor alone or, perish the thought, taking him to a hospital was out of the question. Consequently Mrs. Clark had engaged a nurse recommended by Mrs. Bailey, a widow by the name of Mrs. Wolinsky. Mrs. Wolinsky, however, complained that the sick man would eat nothing and would not even permit her to make his bed. As soon as she opened the door of his room, he gestured to her to close it again and leave him in peace. Mrs. Wolinsky further complained that she couldn't sit alone all day. Cold drafts blew through the apartment. The paintings and sculptures rattled. The air was full of rustling, creaking, and soft sighing that came from the ceiling, from the corners, from the bathroom. Mrs. Wolinsky was not very well herself and such an atmosphere made her worse.

Mrs. Clark knew that Mrs. Wolinsky was telling the truth. For the last few months the professor had been most obstinate, persistently and increasingly willful. At home after work she spoke to him, but he did not respond. She would bring him a glass of tea, some groats, a slice of toast, but he refused to touch any of it. She offered to give him massages, but he declined those as well. He lay in bed with his beard uncombed, his brow flushed with fever, his cheeks sunken. He had mislaid his false teeth somewhere, and however much Mrs. Clark searched and rummaged, she could not find them; she had a strong suspicion that he had flushed them down the toilet. Without his teeth, his face had grown strangely small and shrunken, almost like the shriveled heads on view in museums and pan-opticons. His eyebrows had grown wild, covering his eyes like those of a hedgehog as he lay totally self-absorbed, unwilling to share a word, a smile, even a thought. The telepathic contact she had enjoyed with him in earlier days had completely broken down.

In the evenings Mrs. Clark sat in the living room and tried automatic writing, automatic painting, automatic piano playing. On her right she laid out a sheet of paper and a pencil, on her left a drawing pad with a box of pastels, and she wrote with one hand and drew with the other, while she kept her eyes tightly shut in order to induce a trance. Tall figures emerged on the drawing pad, heads in pointed caps, bodies in long robes, thronging one after the other, a band of jesters or otherworldly clowns with out-stretched arms and splayed feet. The females had disheveled hair, enor-mously wide hips, breasts which hung down to their navels; the men possessed exaggerated limbs, Mephistophelean beards, twisted goats' horns. The pencil on the right wrote half-sentences containing unknown names and words in a language that combined English, Yiddish, and German. A certain Mr. Ghoreyaux tried to establish contact with her, but who he was and what he wanted remained an enigma. After a while Mrs. Clark dropped her hands, but instead of falling into a trance, she simply dozed off and sat dreaming that she was extracting a tooth from the mouth of a Russian Orthodox priest, but it was such a long tooth that it couldn't be a human one. Was this patient a priest or an elephant? Mrs. Clark wondered in her dream. And what function did a tooth like that serve in a human mouth? Unless it was made of rubber? But then what use was it? It surely had to serve some biological purpose! She twitched and started awake, feeling very cold. The clock showed fifteen minutes after twelve.

Henrietta went off to look in on the professor. "How do you feel?"

The professor moved his jaws as though he were chewing. "Not well."

2

Mrs. Clark had gone to her office. Mrs. Wolinsky, the nurse, was puttering about in the kitchen, preparing a little broth for the professor. Winter had come early. Snow had fallen in the middle of November, a wet snow that melted as soon as it fell. A late-autumnal gloom pervaded the bedroom. For a short while snowflakes clung to the outside windowpanes, but soon melted and disappeared. The building was already being heated, but although the radiator rumbled and hissed, the air in the apartment remained cold. The professor lay in his bed wearing a dressing gown and a pair of thick woolen socks because he could not get his feet warm. All night he had coughed and gasped for breath. Though he had dozed off, he had soon awakened again. With all the force he could muster in his sleep, he had hoped—placed an order with the higher powers—for dreams that might reveal something, but his visions had teemed with all kinds of foolishness. He had bought an umbrella, but as soon as he opened it, it became a chair. He found himself in the subway. What was the sense of carrying a chair onto a train? He decided to leave it behind on the platform and boarded the train, but the train did not move. Through the window he saw a conductor go up to the chair and start cleaning it with a feather duster. The professor was astonished: was this part of a conductor's duties, to dust chairs that passengers left behind? The professor opened his eyes. What was the meaning of such dreams? What would Freud have said about the one he had just had? It was senseless—nothing more. Random combinations of disconnected images and ideas. What did the Poles call it? *Marzenie ściętej głowy*—"the dream of a severed head." Did this mean that Nature had room for purposeless things? If so, then everything might be purposeless.

The professor lay in his bed begging for a revelation, for a gleam from the other side of the curtain, a sign that there was something beyond physicality, but he was granted nothing but bodily aches and empty imaginings. How shocking if the materialists were right! Well, mercifully the end was coming. If there was nothing in the world beyond, then there was nothing. One would at least have peace in the grave. But how was it possible that nothing existed beyond the earthly? Was it conceivable that the cosmos was the result of pure chance? What possible relevance could chance have in regard to the operation of the universe? How could it be supposed even for a moment that the powers which had brought forth a Plato, a Newton, a Pascal could themselves be deaf and blind? If a patch of earth could give life to a rose, and the womb of a woman could bear a Dostoevsky, how could millions, billions, trillions of worlds be nothing more than insensible matter? One thing, however, was surely possible: that human beings remained just as limited later as they were earlier. They had puny bodies and tiny souls. The bodies rotted and the souls burst like soap bubbles.

Whatever the case, the final knowledge was all much closer than it had ever been. If there was something to see, then, God willing, he would see it, and if there was nothing, then he, too, would become nothing. The professor addressed his own soul: Have patience, soul. You are not alone. Thousands like you are on the verge of leaving their bodies. "Many have drunk, and many shall drink." Since you have been able to wait this long, wait a little longer. A doctor? She is right: one doesn't need a doctor. Pains? Edzhe suffered far greater pains in Majdanek or Auschwitz.

The professor glanced at the window, watching the snowflakes fall slowly and steadily. Every now and then a crystal rebelled against the law of gravity and started moving upward, but not for long. The inexorable law was more powerful than a scintilla of frozen water. In this world there was no possibility of rising in rebellion. If falling had been decreed, objects were obliged to fall; if hexagonal shapes had been ordained, then snowflakes had to be hexagons; if one was ordered to die, then life was obliged to leave one's body. Everything was obviously predetermined. At bottom the fatalists were right, but human beings were made in such a way that they were unable to accept fatalism. Continually being pushed, they had to preserve the illusion that they were walking of their own free will. That was how fate wanted it.

The professor closed his eyes and saw Edzhe. She was standing next to the bed, Edzhe as she was in former days, but now bright and radiant in gold and green. Her hair glowed like the rays of light that lingered on the horizon immediately after the sun had set. She smiled and stretched out her arms to him, beaming with delight, emanating a contentment and certitude not of this world. Am I asleep? the professor asked himself. No, I'm awake. With considerable effort he opened his eyes. The vision faded, but not all at once. For a while a bright, bare outline hovered in the air, as if a painting had dissolved into a wall, leaving only its frame behind. Soon everything grew gray and gloomy once more. But the professor retained a feeling of refreshment, a lightness of heart, a tang on his gums like the aftertaste of citron. No, it wasn't that.

An hallucination? the professor asked himself. He took his pulse to establish whether or not he was feverish. Yes, the beat was fast, perhaps a hundred times a minute. He shut his eyes again: perhaps the vision would return. But no. He saw only a rosy darkness flecked with gray. Soon he dozed off, and found himself yet again in the subway, where he was once more battling the umbrella that had transformed itself into a chair. Even as he dreamed, the professor criticized his own reverie. What was this? A symphony with variations? Is this the leitmotiv of my life? Couldn't I come up with anything better than this absurdity?

Suddenly he found himself in a small village. He urgently needed to use the toilet, but the way there led through heavy mud, so he was forced to trudge through the swamp with dirt up to his ankles. All of it was filth, the residue of years of uncleanliness. Dear Lord, I'm sinking under the stench! What a dreadful end—to be drowned in ordure! He entered the outhouse, which had no door. About to sit down, he discovered that someone else was already seated there, and he was overcome with mortification. He wanted to flee, but found himself hemmed in by excrement. How on earth did I end up here? he was asking himself when he woke with a start, to find that his forehead was wet with perspiration and that he in fact had a pressing need to relieve himself. Inching his way slowly out of bed, he thrust his shaky feet into his cold slippers and started walking, but the floor jerked up from under him and he fell heavily.

Mrs. Wolinsky heard the thud and came rushing. She helped the professor rise. He wanted to ask her to lead him to the bathroom, but he had lost the power of speech. Moving his lips like a mute, he dumbly wondered, Were these the final agonies of death?

3

The warm days had passed, and on the farm where Grein and Esther had secluded themselves the cold had set in and it was raining. Grein had gathered enough wood to light a fire in the grate, but it heated them only when they sat right next to the hearth. Their faces were warm, but icy chills ran down their backs. They had decided to spend the winter here, but now Esther began insisting that this was impossible. What would they do during the endless frozen months? They would go out of their minds. She had bought a radio, Grein had ordered books from Boston, and a telephone, electricity, and a refrigerator had all been installed. Apart from the thousand-dollar down payment, Grein had already spent a further two thousand dollars on the house and expenses, but Esther never stopped complaining. Although Grein reminded her that she had always spoken of going off with him to live on an island, Esther retorted, "I meant an island with palm trees, not a miserable place out in the sticks like this."

First she covered him with kisses, then she pelted him with reproaches. Why did he have to be different from all other people? Why couldn't they have taken an apartment in New York, or at least in Boston? Why did they have to gather dust here among the skunks and snakes that nested in the grass? There was no question of her becoming a country bumpkin in middle age. She needed heating, the chance to get out, to go to the movies, to a theater, to a party. She had to have people around her. However much they might be in love, they couldn't cling to each other twenty-four hours a day. One needed a social circle, otherwise one could go mad.

Grein turned pale. "Where can I find you a social circle? I don't have one myself."

"You can find one. There's everything in a big city."

He tried to read, to write. He drew up a work schedule for himself: for one hour he read philosophy, for another hour he studied physics, for another mathematics. This winter he wanted to immerse himself in those disciplines he had neglected during the years he had been a teacher in a Talmud Torah or an agent for the mutual fund. He even tried to study with Esther, but she lost patience almost immediately. She also suffered from headaches. Above all, she could not relax. First she lay down, then she got up; she turned on the radio and turned it off again; she sat down to write a letter, she went off to the kitchen to busy herself with house-work. Grein watched with chagrin how, consciously and unconsciously, she sabotaged all his plans. The meals she prepared were either overcooked or undercooked. She broke the dishes. She peeled potatoes and cut her finger. When she gave him a plate of groats or a glass of tea, she always contrived to bang it down in such a way that it spilled over a book or a manuscript. One day she complained that she had a fever and hysterically snatched up the thermometer. Next she announced dramatically that her heart was beating too slowly and that she was on the verge of dying. She grew afraid of going outside even during the day, and he had to stand listening for her returning footsteps every time she went to relieve herself. On one occasion when she'd gone outside to empty the slop pail, Grein heard an ear-splitting scream. A deer had wandered up to the house. On another occasion a stray dog found its way there. Grein tried to make friends with it and coax it into the house, but under no circumstances would the mongrel come indoors, barking and growling and behaving like a wild beast. An overwrought Esther swore frenziedly that the creature was mad or possessed by a dybbuk.

The days were wet, foggy, dark. The car that Grein had bought from Mrs. Symthe kept on breaking down so that it became dangerous to take it over the muddy roads that led to the village. In any case, there was nothing to do there. The movies were almost all about gangsters or cowboys and Indians. The local farmers were deeply suspicious of this Jewish couple from New York who had so uncharacteristically come to spend the winter on a deserted farm. Someone warned Esther that there were criminals in the vicinity and that her husband ought to keep a rifle, a danger she instantly magnified: "They murder out here as well. That'll be our bitter end."

Night fell early. Rain poured down, wind howled. A menacing darkness glared in through the windows. Esther smoked incessantly, lighting one cigarette after another. She kept cognac in the wardrobe and continually poured herself glassfuls, sometimes even taking a swig straight from the bottle. At the beginning she had undertaken to clean their living quarters thoroughly, to change the furniture, to hang new curtains, but nothing came of these good intentions. Overcome by inertia, she soon stopped even preparing meals, so that either they ate out of cans or Grein fried some eggs in a pan. Dust and garbage gathered on the floor, but she couldn't be bothered to sweep it out. Because she was terrified to go to the outhouse at night, she began using an old-fashioned chamber pot that had been lying around for years. During the day she wandered about undressed, uncombed, unwashed. But worst of all was that she had suddenly become frigid; the insatiable passion for Grein that had consumed her all these years had abruptly vanished, and she no longer desired any of his caresses. She had become exactly like Leah.

When Grein asked what had happened to her, she replied, "I've entered a tunnel. I can't see anything but shadows."

"Let's leave here."

"Yes, let's go—but where? Unless to Miami." And after a pause she added, "This farm was madness. Right from the start. Sell it, if you can. Whatever you get for it will be money earned for nothing."

Grein made no reply. It was no longer a question of money. He had invested a great many hopes in this farm, believing that with Esther he could be happy under any circumstances. He had drawn up for himself a meticulous schedule of when to study and even of what to write. Now everything had collapsed. Now he longed for Leah, for his children, for Anna, and for New York.

Something started gathering momentum within him, and he knew exactly what it was: material for a major quarrel.

28

A year had passed, and a birthday party was to be held at Boris Mak-aver's home. In truth, Boris himself had neither the patience nor the strength for parties and, in any case, celebrating birthdays was not a Jewish custom. What was there to celebrate in having been born? The Gemara says: "It has been resolved and concluded that it is better not to be born," and Ecclesiastes observes: "Wherefore I praised the dead." Nevertheless, Frieda stubbornly insisted that they should invite guests to celebrate their child's first birthday. There was no one to invite, however. Professor Shrage was already in the other world. Herman had been liquidated in Stalin's Russia. Anna was drifting around Hollywood with that charlatan Yasha Kotik. Grein had disappeared; rumor had it that he had gone to the Holy Land, settled somewhere in Me'ah Shearim, and become a penitent.

Of all the old company, the only ones left were Zadok Halperin and Solomon Margolin. Halperin had not only survived his book's mortifying failure but remained exactly the same as he had always been. Now as before he ate a great deal, smoked thick cigars, and continually articulated radical paradoxes, the only evident change being that his whiskers had turned from black to dirty white. Boris continued to support him, and he was now busy writing yet another book. This time he was in contact with a publisher in Switzerland who would gladly produce the volume—all Halperin had to do was pay the costs of paper and printing, because the German book market had shrunk dramatically and Switzerland itself did not have suffi-cient readers to support philosophical works.

Lise's presence in New York was now common knowledge, and an angry rift had existed for months between Margolin and Boris. As Margolin had feared, Boris had denounced his oldest friend as putrid and impure flesh, called him an apostate, spat in his face, and blotted him out of his life. But when Frieda developed a cyst in one breast after her confinement and needed surgery, Boris would not permit his wife to do anything before she consulted Dr. Margolin, to whom Boris then sent a check, which Margolin instantly returned. In reality Boris still owed the doctor five thousand dollars, but however successfully he had managed to wriggle out of bankruptcy after the debacle with the ships, he was still unable to take any money out of his business. Matters came to a head when a meeting was arranged between the two of them at which Margolin was able to assure Boris that Lise would convert to Judaism—not for appearances but from inner conviction—going regularly to the ritual bath and doing every-thing required of a convert by Jewish Law. And indeed she did. Lise went to the ritual bath and added the name Sarah to her own name, as custom demanded of all women who converted to Judaism. Boris could not really ask for more, even though he knew quite well that all this was really done not for its own sake but to appease him, and that the modern American rabbi who officiated ought never to have admitted a person like Lise into the Jewish faith. But then how could he demand proper Jewish observance from a German woman when he had raised a corrupt daughter? The terrible forewarning of the Mishnah had been fulfilled in his own days: "The face of the generation is as the face of a dog. Almost all were guilty."

In addition to Halperin and Margolin with his wife, Boris had invited Dr. Alswanger, his business partners with their wives, as well as an em-issary from the newly founded, independent State of Israel, a man by the name of Ben Zemach. For her part, Frieda had invited a rabbi she had known in Germany who had survived and re-established his congregation in New York, ministering to refugees and their families who had been members of his synagogue. Boris was opposed to this rabbi, because his synagogue was a Reform temple, but the man had been a close friend of Dr. Tamar, Frieda's first husband, and she insisted he should come. Boris yielded, since he had no intention of quarreling with the wife who in his old age had borne him a son and had nearly paid for it with her life.

Nevertheless, it pained him that this was not a party like those of earlier days. Strangely, although Grein had done him a great wrong and had reduced Anna to her present deplorable situation, Boris missed him more than any of the others. He went so far as to make excuses for Grein. He had loved Anna and Anna had loved him. They had, as it were, been born for each other. Instead of having disowned Anna as his daughter and reviled her with curses and anathemas, he would have done better to help Grein dissolve his marriage. He ought to have tried offering Luria a sum of money to divorce Anna. He ought to have approached the whole matter with a willingness to help instead of with the full weight of Jewish Law. Perhaps Luria might still be alive today if Boris had been ready with money and gentle words, had tried to reason through the situation with him like a father and a good friend. It seemed to Boris that if the same thing were to happen now, he would know better. He would devise a plan, be reasonable, treat everything in a systematic way. Ah yes, one is always wise after the event, when the mistakes have been made and one can no longer correct them. What was the old saying? *Mądry Polak po szkodzie,* "A Pole wises up after the damage is done."

When Boris lay awake at nights, he always thought of Grein and all the things he had done: his running away with Anna, his return to his wife, only to go off to a farm somewhere with that Esther a short while later, and finally disappearing and becoming a resident of Me'ah Shearim. None of this was inconsequential. Ordinary people didn't do such things. Boris had always believed Grein to be of a higher sort—what was it called?—a personality. Of course he had made mistakes, but he was paying for them. Boris would have given much to see Grein, talk to him, hear what he had to say—it was no trivial matter to become a *real* penitent. There could be no doubt about that. Shloymele had given Boris a detailed account of his debate with Grein, the things Grein had said, his contention that the modern world was the underworld. Those were words Boris could not forget. They went to the heart of the matter. Every day, ten times a day, Boris was compelled to remind himself of that assessment. In his view one had truly to be a genius to be able, in such simple words, to characterize modern man and all his doings and desires.

2

Frieda Makaver had spent some time searching for Jacob Anfang, the painter with whom she had once been in love, but was unable to find him. He had moved out of the studio in Greenwich Village. One afternoon, as Frieda entered the elevator of the Public Library on Forty-second Street and Fifth Avenue, she unexpectedly encountered Anfang there. He seemed shorter and had aged: the curls at his temples had already turned gray and his luminous eyes were set deeply in networks of fine wrinkles. He was wearing a camel-hair coat and a black silk scarf loosely knotted, in the way of artists, around his throat. He blushed when he caught sight of her, and stammered as, in the European manner, he bowed and greeted her.

Frieda, too, turned red and lost her tongue for a moment. Then she said, "Are you also going to the second floor?"

"No, to the third."

"Do you perhaps have a little time to spare?"

"Yes, certainly. For you, always."

"Perhaps we might drink tea together somewhere."

"Certainly! With the greatest of pleasure."

They chose a restaurant on Fifth Avenue. As Anfang took off his broad-brimmed hat and overcoat, Frieda noticed that the bald patch in the middle of his head had grown as broad and round as a plate. He was wearing a shabby, ill-fitting black suit.

"I've been looking everywhere for you," Frieda remarked.

"You've been looking for me? I thought you were about to have a child." Anfang spoke disconnectedly and hesitantly.

Frieda's eyes glowed. "I am the mother of a son!"

"Really? Congratulations. Well, you've done well, very well. Since God wants the human species to exist, someone must see to it. After all, God Himself can't wash diapers."

"Oh, the way you put things! God can do everything."

"Of course He can. But He has come up with a skillful division of labor, just like the American industrialists—Ford, for example."

"What a comparison! How are you? I looked for you in your old apartment, but you'd moved out."

"I didn't move out, exactly—they threw me out. They were right, actually. People must pay rent."

"When did that happen? Where are you living now? Why didn't you let us hear from you?"

"I live in a furnished room on Seventieth Street, not far from the Hudson."

"Then you're a neighbor of ours."

"What? It never occurred to me."

"Have you given up painting?"

"Yes, I have."

Frieda made a movement as though she was swallowing something. "What do you do, if I may ask?"

"Ah, I do nothing. I have an acquaintance who arranged some lessons for me. Two women have decided to become painters and I'm their professor. Whether they'll learn anything is another matter."

"Is that all you do?"

"Yes, that's all. I've taught myself to need very little. The landlady is a pleasant woman, and she's good to me. She lets me keep a bottle of milk in her refrigerator, and she cooks rice or kasha for me. I've done portraits of her and her children. Well, that's all."

"That's not a serious way to live."

"Why not? I don't go hungry and I sleep in a bed. What more does a person need?"

"Many people need a great deal more."

"Not me. What's become of Anna?"

Frieda began recounting everything that had befallen Anna. From time to time her upper lip trembled, her throat constricted, and she had to cough slightly to speak. The waiter brought her tea, but she let it get cold. She suddenly remembered that early morning when she had gone to Jacob Anfang to propose marriage and how he had refused her. How could I possibly have done such a thing? she asked herself. I'm usually so shy! She turned hot all over and her body shook exactly as if she were sailing on the ocean. It cost her a strenuous effort to utter the words, as if Anna's tragedy had somehow been her own shame and disgrace. When Frieda started talking about Grein and what had happened to him, Anfang's eyes narrowed slightly with an expression at once tender and abstracted, almost as though he was embarrassed by what Frieda was telling him.

"Yes, each of us seeks his own way out," he observed.

"You are a religious person yourself," Frieda half stated, half questioned.

"Yes, but I followed another way."

"May I ask what way that is?"

Anfang hesitated a moment. Something like derision flashed in his eyes. "If I were to tell you, you'd flee from me. Or perhaps even worse."

"Why should I flee? Each of us is accountable to himself."

"I have abandoned Judaism. I am no longer a Jew," Anfang rapped out; his expression grew stern and his eyes were full of distress. Frieda felt as though her brain were rattling in her skull like a nut inside its shell. She turned cold. Sitting rigid and helpless in her chair, she was seized by stomach cramps. She had no idea what to say. "Why, exactly?" she finally managed to ask.

"You're shocked, aren't you?" Anfang demanded. "I was reading, and the New Testament attracted me. There I found an answer to all my questions."

"What does it say that cannot be found in our own sacred books?"

"I don't know. But at least there is no brutality, and no animal sacrifice."

Frieda's eyes filled with tears. "Perhaps not, but the Nazis exterminated six million Jews and the Christians were silent. The murderers carried out the slaughter and the priests looked on."

"Those were not true Christians."

"Who exactly are the true Christians?"

"We Jews."

"Why should we call ourselves Christians? God isn't three persons and has no son."

"It's all symbolism."

"The Inquisition was no symbol."

Anfang did not answer. Frieda looked at him. Through her tears his face seemed blurred, distorted, shapeless. He smiled weirdly. Frieda wiped her eyes. God in heaven, have compassion upon him, she prayed to herself. This poor man is in great anguish.

3

It was still a secret, but Esther had married Dr. Alswanger. She had fled from Grein, leaving him alone on the farm in Maine. After a terrible fight at the beginning of December, Esther had packed both her suitcases and, dragging them out into the road, had stopped a passing car on its way to Bethel, and from there caught the Greyhound bus to New York, arriving back in the city the day after Morris Plotkin's funeral. His end had come suddenly but not unexpectedly. For dinner he had eaten a whole duck roasted for him by his bosom friend Sam, and in the middle of the night he had suffered a fatal heart attack. Strangely, although Plotkin had talked for years about his various wills, he had died without one. His children tried to grab the whole inheritance for themselves, but Esther hired a lawyer who, it turned out, was in cahoots with the other claimants, because he persuaded Esther to "settle" for a pittance—a Pyrrhic victory, because it emerged that Plotkin was nowhere near as rich as he had always boasted. He had even left substantial debts behind. At just this wretched moment, Dr. Alswanger reappeared on Esther's horizon, proposed to her, and she accepted immediately in terms more forthright than gracious: "Pardon me, Doctor, but I'm so desperate that I'd even marry a cat." This was an insult, but Dr. Alswanger was quite accustomed to swallowing insults. Besides, the arrangement was mutually convenient. Apart from his needing a wife, by marrying Esther he could acquire American citizenship, an important consideration, since he could no longer return to Israel, where his enemies were waiting "to tear him to pieces," as he put it.

As a believer, Dr. Alswanger was not satisfied with a civil ceremony and arranged for a proper Jewish wedding to be performed by a rabbi. He took Esther away to Lakewood for a week, during which it rained the whole time, so Esther spent every day lying in bed, speaking without stop about Grein. She poured out her endless complaints to Alswanger, invariably using the formal mode of address to the man who was now her husband.

"I'm his sworn enemy, do you hear? I never knew that love could turn to hatred."

"Passion *is* hatred," Alswanger growled.

"No question. You're a very wise man. Ah, if I'd only known that twelve years ago, I'd never have fallen into his clutches!"

"We can put everything right. We can still be happy together."

"No doubt about it. Speak wise words to me! I love wisdom."

"Surely it's time we addressed each other familiarly?"

"Of course it is. But I don't find it comes naturally."

Because Alswanger had nothing to do, and the few other guests in the hotel were all old women, he suggested to Esther that they undertake a "soul expedition," which was Alswanger's unique method of psychoanalysis. He urged her to speak fully and frankly while he sat with a writing pad and a fountain pen and made notes. She told him everything, holding nothing back: her girlhood lusts, her sins as a wife, her problems with her first husband, the ingenuous fumbler she had divorced, and the imbroglio with Grein. As Esther laughed and wept, she admitted to such outlandish acts that Alswanger did not believe they could possibly be true. It was unimaginable that any single individual could have experienced the number and variety of sins and follies she confessed to, but Alswanger knew there are no lies in the human soul. Is there any real difference between a deed and a desire? Since human beings are part of nature, every one of their words and thoughts is part of the cosmos. One has merely to differentiate between the essential and the trivial, between the dream and its interpretation. Dr. Alswanger did not agree with Freud or Adler or Jung. Of course, each of them had approached the truth, but they had only scratched the surface. Each had exaggerated, emphasizing the literal meaning of words as he heard them and consequently confounding disparate things. Certainly sex was important, but sex wasn't everything. Certainly people wanted to succeed and to dominate others, but this was a symptom, not a cause. Certainly the individual belonged to a collective, the species, but this wasn't the whole picture either. Alswanger compared Freud, Adler, and Jung to Copernicus, Galileo, and Kepler. Each of them had discovered a small piece of the truth about solar systems, but only Newton had joined the fragments into a scientific whole.

Dr. Alswanger's theory was that all forces contending in the human soul represented a struggle between slavery and freedom. He had applied the ancient Jewish concepts of the Good and Evil Inclinations to analytical psychology. The Evil Inclination was causality—bare, elementary nature, the formlessness and void which lurked behind all physical laws and which had a purpose somewhere, though one that was not perceptible. Like two parallel lines, causality and teleology—the design and purpose of nature— met, but only in infinity. The human soul, however, sought to avoid by all possible means the long road to this meeting. It wanted to evade causality and discover a miraculous shortcut. Because human beings could not be free in every area, they struggled in a multiplicity of ways to find their own forms of freedom, and Alswanger believed that by examining these struggles, one could assess the human personality and find a solution to all human fears and anxieties. The crux of the matter was how much and in what way each human being was prepared to suffer for the privilege of free will, and how far each one's understanding enabled him to distinguish between freedom and slavery. The wicked man was a fool because he neither knew what freedom was nor was willing to fight for it. He was also psychically ill, because insanity was nothing more than the complete abrogation of freedom. The neurotic was the person who neither could make peace with slavery nor had the strength to win freedom for himself. He always found himself in between, in a no-man's-land, and was consequently assaulted by both lines of fire.

Esther's talk, her bizarre assertions, her digressions and fantasies, all confirmed Alswanger's theory. From her tormented being screamed the God-fearing conscience of generations of rabbis, rebbes, holy Jews, in conflict with the sexual desire of generations of Jewish daughters who had chastity forcibly imposed upon them instead of being patiently taught its wholesome advantages. Alswanger believed that much of the unhappiness of modern people in general and modern Jews in particular stemmed from society's having kept women spiritually enslaved and given them no opportunity to think or to be in the front lines of the fight against evil. Women were wronged both by nature and by society. Jews had even robbed women of the right to study the Torah and deprived them of the obligation to perform numerous commandments, so that they had become the bearers of assimilation, itself a particularly ugly form of slavery. There was only one solution: to give the Torah back to women, to make them equal partners in the Covenant at Sinai. As far as the Gentiles were concerned, their salvation lay in accepting Judaism, because every religion other than Judaism was a compromise between freedom and slavery, not an open and unyielding war against Satan.

4

In the middle of her party, Frieda called Dr. Margolin aside. "I'd very much like you to take a look at the child," she asked.

"Isn't he sleeping?"

"Just a look."

"What's the matter? You're taking him to a pediatrician, aren't you?"

"Yes, but there's something I can't understand. A one-year-old child should surely start trying to speak by now. It seems very strange that he hasn't."

"Oh, mothers, mothers!" Margolin replied testily. "All they do is flutter and fuss. Later, when the little bastards grow up, they pack their parents into old-age homes."

"Oh, the things you say! Not all children are like that. 'Honor thy father and mother' is one of the Ten Commandments."

"If only people observed the Ten Commandments!" rejoined Margolin. "We keep on coming up with new ideas, new bases for ethics, all kinds of new ideologies, and on a stone our Teacher Moses scratched out Ten Commandments that are as relevant and necessary today as they were four thousand years ago. If people only observed the Ten Commandments, we wouldn't need any police, any armies, any atomic bombs, any of our abhorrent social controls. But the human species would rather read ten thousand books written by idiotic professors than uphold the ancient and eternal truths."

"True. True. You've never spoken more justly."

"What's the good of words? As soon as I see a beautiful woman, I forget them all. Come, let's take a look at your little bridegroom."

Walking ahead, Frieda led Margolin into the nursery, the same room that had once belonged to Anna. The portrait that Jacob Anfang had painted of her still hung there. Frieda switched on the light. The child lay in a nickel-plated bed, the very best that money could buy. A dazzling whiteness gleamed from the little pillow and the coverlet.

Margolin shook his head. "We never had such comforts. In our homes the cradle hung from a rope and infants used to lie in their own feces, pardon my mentioning it."

"Well, we grew up in spite of it."

"Those who lived grew up. In my family, five children went to sleep and never woke up again. My poor mother kept on getting pregnant, and the beadle of Gehenna carried them all away to the cemetery. Wait, I'll have a look."

Margolin moved closer, taking a monocle out of his waistcoat pocket and screwing it into his left eye as he did so. For a long time he stood by the little bed without moving a muscle, totally absorbed in medical contemplation. The longer he stood there, the more serious he grew. He began to harbor a suspicion, although he had not the slightest evidence on which to base it except that Frieda was an older woman when she had conceived. This child looked perfectly healthy, but over the little face lay a dullness and foolishness difficult to identify or to define. The infant's lips were too thick, and Margolin didn't like the smile that hovered over them. The child seemed to be sunk in the abnormal complacency of those whose mental development is arrested. Its eyelids were heavy and slanted. A mongoloid baby! something inside Margolin screamed out. His heart contracted as though squeezed by an inner fist. He wanted to say something but didn't.

"What's the matter with the child?" he asked instead.

"Nothing. But something . . . Other children his age are livelier, more active."

"You're just imagining things."

"No, I'm not."

"There are no certain means of establishing the intelligence of infants this age. We have to wait."

"Dr. Margolin, this child isn't normal!" Frieda cried out.

Margolin's eye twitched and his monocle fell out. As he deftly caught it in midair, a shudder ran down his spine. "Maternal hypochondria! There are children that don't speak a word until they're four, and when they do start prattling, you can't shut them up. He'll grow up to be a second Boris Makaver, but without any of his father's faults."

"Dr. Margolin, to whom should I go? Perhaps something can be done," Frieda asked in a husky, trembling voice.

"I don't know. It's not my field. But I can make inquiries. I'm one hundred percent convinced that it's all your imagination. Jewish mothers brood too much. Do you want him to be an Aristotle so soon?"

"I beg you, Dr. Margolin, don't joke. I may not be a doctor, but I'm not blind."

"If you say a word about this to your husband, it'll kill him, God forbid," Margolin warned.

"I won't say anything. But I want to know the truth, at least."

"I'll speak to a specialist at my hospital."

"When?"

"Soon—tomorrow."

"Thank you. I ought never to have had a child at my age! Everything's turned so dark now!"

"It'll soon be bright again. You're just talking yourself into things."

"No. How long can one hide it from Borukh? He dotes on the child. I've never seen anything like it before."

Solomon Margolin lowered his head and stood there bowed, grieving as though this tragedy had befallen him personally. I never knew I was so deeply attached to Boris Makaver, he thought. The child did not yet have enough symptoms by which to judge, but Margolin comprehended that the highly educated Frieda Makaver knew what she was talking about. He had seen her reading serious studies about children. By now she probably knew no less than a doctor and had in addition the opportunity to observe the child daily. In the short time they had been standing there, Frieda's appearance had changed. She seemed suddenly to have aged—dark rings appeared under her eyes and she turned ashen. Margolin even noticed a few hairs sprouting from her chin. He moved closer to her.

"Madame, you know the Gemara, and therefore you know that 'where there is both certainty and doubt, one should cling to the certainty.' The child is most likely normal, but the least suspicion to the contrary could kill your husband. Your first duty must be to him."

"What? Yes. *I* probably deserved no better than this, but why *him*?"

Epilogue

A letter from Hertz Dovid Grein to Morris Gombiner

My dear Moshe, Thank you for your letter. You are the only person to whom I write from here. I've severed my connections with everyone, even with my children. You ask me for my reasons and want to know all the details. The reason is very simple. I became totally convinced that everything I believed to be of secondary importance was in fact central. I always used to ask my father, peace be upon him, questions inspired by doubt. Where in the Torah is it written that Jewish men are not permitted to shave their beards? Where is it written that Jews are forbidden to wear a short jacket and a derby? On one occasion, I remember, my father answered me tersely: It's not written anywhere, but if you put on a modern jacket today, tomorrow you'll sin with a married woman. At that time I didn't understand his words, but they were prophetic. One cannot keep the Ten Commandments while one lives in a society that breaks them. A soldier must wear a uniform and live in a barracks. Whoever wants to serve God must wear God's insignia, and must separate himself from those who serve only themselves. The beard, the sidelocks, the girdle worn during prayers, the fringed ritual undergarment—all these are the uniform of the Jew, the outward signs that he belongs to God's world, not to the underworld.

Yes, the underworld. I counted up all my days and all my deeds, and I perceived with blinding clarity that I had been living in a criminal underworld and behaving like a creature of that underworld. As soon as my friend was out of sight, I immediately started having illicit relations with his wife. No solemn resolutions I made were of any use. I now believe that even our saints would have been no better if they had lived among the wicked. What we call European culture or American culture is actually the culture of the underworld. It is built on the principle of instant gratification. For all its flowery language, this culture acknowledges only one power: might. I lived in sin with women to whom I was not married, derided people, drove others to sickness, suffering, death. Yes, I was a murderer, too. I didn't do my killing all at once, but little by little. My children both married Gentiles. My daughter chose a German whose brothers were probably Nazis who ordered Jews to dig their own graves. It is only a short step from shaving off your sidelocks and putting on a necktie to breaking God's laws and mingling your seed with the seed of Amalek. This is not true just in my case. The modern Jew is, and must be, an assimilationist. His road leads to conversion.

I am now in Israel, and for some time I have been able to observe the enlightened Jews here. They give the appearance of having fled from assimilation, but in reality they have brought it with them. They speak Hebrew, but they imitate the Gentiles at every turn. The country is infested with their Gentile books, their Gentile plays are performed to popular acclaim. Indeed, the Jews here are deeply distressed that they cannot imitate the Gentiles even more closely than they do already. In regard to family life, I had better say nothing. The Israelis call themselves Jews, but in what way are they Jews? Hebrew—or a language that was virtually Hebrew—was also spoken in Moab and other countries neighboring Canaan. For a while I perused the Israelis' newspapers, read their books, went to see their plays. All of them are filled with idolatry, adultery, and bloodshed, not to mention slander, gossip, obscenity, mockery, and idle talk.

One day I went to Me'ah Shearim and there I saw that there are still Jews. They wear garments that bear witness from afar that they are God's servants. When one puts on a capote, a fringed ritual undergarment, a prayer girdle, when one grows one's beard and sidelocks, when one studies the Gemara (yes, really and truly the Gemara), one doesn't read secular books, or go to profane theaters, or have assignations with women. To be sure, one could still be a swindler or a bankrupt. There are no ironclad guarantees. But one cannot be a Jew if one does not belong to God's army and does not wear God's stamp upon oneself. It is unimportant what that stamp looks like. It may be that in other times observant Jews wore different kinds of distinctive clothing. The essential thing, however, is that it must be a clear sign. The argument that ''a Jew without a beard is better than a beard without a Jew'' is worthless wordplay. There is no such thing as a Jew without a beard and sidelocks, without a fringed ritual undergarment and a Gemara. If one turns one step away from the old Jewishness, one finds oneself in the midst of idolaters and murderers, and one rears children who marry Nazis. (Children are the best test. They are the touchstone!) There is not, and there cannot be, any compromise or middle way or reform. All the restrictions and prohibitions of Jewish Law are essential, as necessary as isolating and protecting people from deadly rays or from the plague. One cannot wear Gentile clothing, take pleasure in their literature, be entertained in their theaters, eat in their restaurants, and then observe the Ten Commandments. It's impossible! That's why Tolstoy finally put on a peasant blouse. That piece of clothing was his attempt to separate himself from the corrupt world. It was useless, because the Russian peasant wasn't the kind of being Tolstoy imagined. I'm certain that if Tolstoy had lived longer, he would have turned to Judaism—that is, to the prayer shawl and phylacteries and fringed ritual undergarments and the dietary laws. There is not, and cannot be, any other kind of Jewishness.

Of course, you wouldn't recognize me if you saw me. Now I look like my father, may he rest in peace. You won't believe it, but I have a gray beard. I am still very far from *being* like my father, though. My mind's been poisoned from living for so many years the way I did. I sit with the Gemara before me and my head is full of all manner of abominations. I've remained (99 percent of me) a wild beast, a man of the underworld. But I've bound the beast with the leather straps of my phylacteries and the threads of my ritual fringes. Even a tiger cannot bite when he is bound and reined in. That is Jewishness.

You ask me about faith. What shall I say to you? Whoever has read the modern Bible critics, archaeologists, historians, and all the rest of them can never again be whole in his faith. Faith exists on an extremely high level, and one can reach it only after much suffering and many good deeds. At the very moment that I wind the leather strap of my phylacteries around my arm and I kiss the boxes which enclose the sacred words, it occurs to me that the Torah is a work of the imagination and that Moses did not stand on Mount Sinai—in short, that as Rashi famously observed about the biblical story of Elisha: ''There are no woods and no bears,'' that it's all a fabrication. But then I tell myself that since my phylacteries bind the tiger within me, I have no choice but to put them on. One essential of faith I have never lost: belief in the existence and the unity of the Creator. I am also close to belief in the existence of a Divine Providence that cares for each individual. What difference does it make who gave us the Torah? The Torah is the only effective teaching we have about how to bridle the human beast. No one has better tamed that beast than the Jew—I mean the true Jew, the Jew of the Scriptures, of the Gemara, of the *Shulhan Arukh,* of the books of ethical instruction. The Christians have a handful of monks and nuns. We created an entire nation that served God. We were once a holy nation. Thank God, a remnant of that nation has remained.

The same God that created the tiger also created the rope and planted in the human tiger the desire to bind himself. The first people to bind the beast in themselves and to teach other people how to bind it were the Chosen People. As long as the other nations continue going to church in the morning and hunting in the afternoon, they will remain unbridled beasts and will go on producing Hitlers and other monstrosities. That is now as clear as day to me.

Well, that's about all. For the time being, I live off my savings, but I need so little that I have enough for years. Of course, one is obliged to give a tenth of one's income to charity, and it is even better to give a fifth. Without such giving one cannot be a Jew. I hardly need to tell you that every day is a struggle for me. Very often I think that I should shave off my beard, abandon everything, and flee back to the jungle. Every day is full of temptations. Boredom torments me the most. As modern people see it, we live a totally stagnant life here. It often becomes so difficult that I want to kill myself. But every day also has minutes and sometimes hours of exaltation. I take great pleasure in prayer, and I am beginning to savor the true taste of a page of the Gemara once more.

About the possibility of your coming here—why not? But I warn you in advance that if you do not return completely to Jewishness, I will have nothing to do with you. Believe me, this is not because I am a fanatic. In my situation, I have to protect myself. One loose knot and the wild beast springs free again.

No, I don't want you to send people my regards. Apart from Leah, peace be upon her, I no longer have anyone. In my heart I am bound to my family and even to my good friends, but I must remain isolated. The whole point of Jewishness is isolation, after all. As Proverbs observes: "Happy is the man who does not walk in the way with them." The emphasis is on the phrase "does not." There can be no connection between a bound animal and an animal that roams free.

Stay well, and may the Almighty help you.

DOVID